ASCENSION SYMPTOMS

By

Dino Peyton

Table of Contents

Dedication

I dedicate this book to the black LGBTQIA+ community that I've been happily a part of my entire life and hope that when any of you read this book, you feel the connection between us that many non-progressive individuals of the world would like to destroy. I hope that these stories will act as a guiding light that brings us together in these difficult times. I love all of you.

Acknowledgement

I want to thank everyone in the black LGBTQIA+ community for showing me how to thrive in this life that is like the EXTRA difficult version of a game. Everything that has held us back and made us feel as if we were less than, has forged us into diamonds.

About the Author

As a gay black man in my thirties, I am glad that I've found myself in the chaos that this life brings. Growing up in a world where we're taught to hide who we are and conform to what the hetero sexual community deems as straight, I hated that there wasn't any real representation of our community in Supernatural, Fantasy, Horror television shows, movies, books and comics until now. I currently live in Columbus, Ohio and have used a popular meme to fuel my short stories of the paranormal happenings in my state.

Ascension Symptoms

Our *Darker* parts

"I'm almost eighteen. I can stay out if I want, Grandma." I looked my old-bitch of a grandmother in the face as she crossed her arms. I could see the familiar expression that she made while thinking about how much she regretted the day that my parents dropped me off ten years ago. "Go to your room and ask God for forgiveness." "I'll do that when you ask him to forgive the times you used to beat me." She picked her bible up and slung it at me, but this time I caught it and threw it back. It hit her in the mouth, and she cried as she left the room. Old bitch! Now that she can't take her anger out on me, her only other option was to cry. I walked into the kitchen and made myself a sandwich that I paired with a bag of my favorite chips. By the time I was done, the old head had made her way up to her room with whimpers of pain as I walked into the front room and picked up the clunky remote. I pressed the on button for the cable box and then turned on the television with another button. I couldn't choose between my favorite black family movie, where the nice grandmother invites the family over for dinner, or the comedy about the professor who changes his identity with a serum, so I watched them both. I fell asleep halfway through the second movie and entered into a nightmare. My legs changed from human to snakes as I ran through a dark forest with dark green scaly monster hands on my extended belly. My shoulder burned as balls of fire and beams of light whizzed by to reduce everything to ash. The pain in my shoulder intensified as I picked up speed, and all of my surroundings became a blur. I opened my eyes to the rising sun of a Wednesday morning with my back itching from sleeping on this ugly ass couch. I went upstairs and took a shower, and got ready for school as my old bitch of a grandmother made breakfast for herself. Seeing her limp around the kitchen was all the sustenance that I needed this morning. "Bye Maw-Maw. Love you!" I grabbed my book bag and remembered that there were two months left of the school year. Soon I won't have to see these fake people with their rules of who fits into whatever category that they chose for me. The teachers give us outdated lesson plans from the seventies and not the new books that the kids at the highschool down the street get. Since I got accepted into Ohio State University, I can also say goodbye to my grandmother and hello to college women. I worked my ass off last summer and plan to do the same all of this summer to add to my savings. When I add that to the money I made from selling my grandmother's pills, I'll be good for a while. "Good morning, trouble." "Good morning, Mr. King." I waved at my wealthy neighbor, who we see four times a year. He was nice in a dad kind of way, but for someone with a bunch of children, none of them ever came to visit. I thought he was gay for the longest time because he was always with men instead of his hot wife, who hated me as much as my grandmother. Her high yellow ass acted like being dark-skinned was a crime. "Would you like a ride to school?" He looked like he was about to go for a jog and not a morning drive, but he pulled the car keys out and pressed the button to turn the alarm off. "Yes, I hate catching the bus." "I can't believe how much you've grown into a young lady in a short amount of time." "Yeah, time flies when you're going through puberty." I really hope this niggah meant that I was turning into a well-rounded young lady instead of a well-rounded young lady. It would be all bad for him if he tried something. "I respect your grandmother for sending you to public school. We homeschooled our kids." "Was that expensive?" "No, not at all. If you want my honest opinion, it worked wonders for them. They didn't have to compete with other kids or worry about what they wore in comparison to someone else. It just hasn't caught on yet, but it will."

Of course, it would be for rich people who send their kids to boarding school or have the means to pay a tutor. "Is this your last year?" "Yup, and I can't wait to move into my dorm at Ohio State University." Just thinking about it made me hopeful for all of the goodness that awaited. With my full ride and saving money, I'll stay in a dorm for the first year but get an apartment for the sophomore year. From that moment on, I'll be on the path to becoming a chef/ boxer. "What will you major in?" "I want to own my own restaurant, so food science and culinary arts." "That's smart. We don't have enough restaurants in Columbus with diverse menus." As we made our way to the school, my stomach started to rumble, and he pulled out three twenty-dollar bills and handed them to me. "Here, Honey." "Oh, no, I can't accept that. My grandmother would freak out." "Then don't tell her." He placed it in my hand, and a small bolt of blue static electricity jumped from his hand to mine. "Ouch! I'll take it as hush money from that assault sparky." He laughed as I got out of the car, and I had to hold back my shiver as I noticed him looking at my butt. "Thanks for the money." He nodded and reached over to shut the door while getting one last look at my ass as I walked to the school. I picked up the scent of spicy cinnamon and knew that the bitch of the school was back. Whenever I smelled that perfume, I knew that China Parsons was back from her trip to jamaica. She had to be somewhere nearby because that lingering smell was fresh. "Oh look, it's the teenage train wreck." "Oh, look, it's the only black girl in the world whose skin will crack because her mama is white." Her friends gasped as I kept walking and made my way inside the old building. I've hated that materialistic bitch since the first day that we met at church, and her mother invited me over for dinner. Little did I know that she felt sorry for me and had her daughter watch me just in case I stole something. I pushed the old memories to the back of my mind as I reached the office. East-Hill High school has been around since the civil rights movement and was made specifically for black people. Now it's a run-down school without air conditioning and piss-poor teachers whose favorite phrase was I get paid even if you fail. Speaking of which, I was about to pass the teacher I hated the most. Vivian Roberts. I helped this bitch when she slipped and fell last year, and she acted like it was the worst thing in the world for me to touch her. Ugh! White people. "Mrs. Phillips, it's good to see you here on time." "I know it must be hard to have to deal with that funky breath of yours, but a simple good morning will do." Luckily Principal Raymond wasn't around to hear that, or I'd have another two days of attention. "I heard that Idna Phillips." Ughhh, I hated my name. This is the mid-nineties, and I have a name of a woman from the sixties. "Saturday detention." I turned on my heel while rolling my eyes at the head-honcho of the school. "So I have to leave the house on the weekend to venture out into the world as a woman all by myself because of your abuse of power." "Lovely, I'll see you next Saturday as well." I turned around and kept walking to my first-period English literature class as she followed behind me. Once I reached the door, I turned on my heels and gave her the fakest smile that I could before walking into the crowded classroom. Our teacher was nowhere to be seen, and my follower took a seat in the chair as the class quieted down. "Mrs. Brownstone has a family emergency, so I'll be overseeing the class until the substitute arrives." I took my seat next to the only person who was worthy of my presence, Misty. She hated the teachers as much as I did, and for some reason, they gave her respect. "Grand rising." Her unorthodox greeting turned the heads of several students, and she shot them mean-mugs as I leaned over and touched her shoulder. Always hilarious. "Grand rising, Mistycia." We spent the next forty minutes as a free period, where Misty and I talked about our plans for the weekend. "She's a buster and doesn't have a life, so she has to suck mine away." My left ear started to ring as I turned my head to the right and reached up in time to stop a paper ball from hitting me. Everything happened so fast that I barely noticed who threw it. "Mr. Chapman, Saturday detention." Seriously! I have to see that ugly face on Saturday? The bell rang, and I said goodbye to my only friend as I made my way to Spanish class. "Good morning, students." "Good morning Mrs. Alvarez." We all spoke at the same time as the school's favorite and most attractive teacher walked in smelling like lavender with her long curly hair falling down her back. Time always flew by whenever I was conjugating verbs and practicing how to form complete sentences. The best forty minutes of my life ended as the bell rang, and I made my way to my second favorite class, Physical education. Which should actually be called "Let them play with outdated sports gear on old-ass mats and no way to shower afterwards." With my heightened stamina, my body can remain active for longer periods of time before I perspire like everyone else. The real problems were the smelly kids that I have to share this school with. Our showers supposedly didn't work, but I overheard a cheerleader telling a volleyball player to just shower here before the game because her water was off at home. That, plus the funny way that the staff treats my fellow members of the LGBTQ community, makes me want to burn this place to the ground. I'd had enough during my sophomore year when I was accused of stealing the teacher's car keys and suspended for a week because they found them in my locker. Misty did a tarot pull and told me that it was Davina Scott, but I was too late to do anything because she died over the summer in a car accident from stealing cars from the airport. That was another birthday-Xmas gift that made my year. After a couple of rounds of volleyball, I moved on to basketball, but the principal came in and pulled me out of the class. "There's been an accident." A smile crept over my face as I realized it had to have happened to Granny good-bitch. "Did she fall and break a hip?" "Yes, and when she fell, she snapped her neck and died." My whole world stopped as the thought of finally being rid of her washed over me. "Do I have to go to the hospital to identify the body?" My back itched as footsteps approached us from behind, and I turned around to see two white female officers walking towards us. "Idna Phillips, You are under arrest for the murder of Yancy Edgerton. You have the right to remain silent…" She read me the rest of my Miranda rights, but all I could process was how I was once again taking the blame for something that I didn't do, and now my plan of making it in life will be ruined. Thankfully we were close to the entrance, so they walked me to the entrance/exit, and I turned to see Principal Raymonds walk to the office with a smile on her face. They walked me to the car, and I had to sit through them arguing about the best Horror movie ever made. "I think the one where the demons come out of the television is a great one if you ask me." Officer Wells in the passenger seat, turned around and gave me a look that would have killed me if magic was real. A chill ran down my spine as she turned around, and they continued their discussion like I didn't exist. Every woman that I find attractive turns out to be a snobby bitch. "I get that you're just doing your jobs, but I didn't do it." "You should really shut your mouth, Little girl. You do not have a lawyer present, and we are not detectives." Damn, I take it back. Officer Laymens in the driver's seat is an ugly bitch. After a thirty-minute drive, I was strip-searched, processed into the system, and given a room that was supposed to be temporary, according to Officer wells. Three hours passed, and a tall, dark-skinned hottie walked into the room. "Hello, I'm Iris King, your lawyer." King! As in one of Zacharia King's children? "My father sent me over. I'm sorry about your grandmother." "I appreciate it. She will be greatly missed." The cops were always up to no good, so I decided to show as much sympathy as I could. I haven't seen a judge yet, and as a young black woman, I know that he/she will take one look at me and think *Thug*. That's what wealthy white people do. They fill the jails with my people while widening the gap between the classes. My grandmother has money because she married rich, and now that I think about it, I wondered if it was mine now. "I didn't do it. I swear. I got ready for school and left like normal after she made breakfast for us." Iris nodded and reached over to give my hand a squeeze. *Mmmm, if only I was a couple of years older.* "I know. The mortician ruled it an accidental death because she took her pills too close together and fell due to drowsiness." "Thank goodness. I would never hurt her. She was the only family that I-." For dramatic effect, I laid my head on the table as she continued to rub my hand. Her warm touch, plus the fact that I've been exonerated, made real tears fall as I looked up and the officers from before walked in. Their white faces were now red because I was telling the truth from the beginning, and now once again, the white people are wrong. "My ancestors are rejoicing in my freedom granted by people who can actually do their jobs correctly." They released me from the handcuffs, and Iris gave me a ride home. "That was fun. But can I ask a question?" "Yes, as your official lawyer, I can answer any question that you have." "Great, Did my grandmother have a will?" "You're going to ignore the fact that you were racially discriminated against." "White people can get away with anything. If God doesn't do anything about it, why should I care, I'm free and rich, right?" Iris nodded and smiled as we turned onto my street. As a child, I used to imagine what the house would look like under my control, and now I feel like this was the universe's way of saying, "Here, this is for your troubles." Iris let out a beautiful laugh, and I found myself staring at her too long, so I looked out the window as we pulled into my driveway. "Can I get emancipated?" "Yes, If you were a teenager."

She placed the car in park, and I turned to look at her and waited for all of this to be some kind of dream or something. "Huh?" "Your grandmother didn't know how old you were, so she enrolled you a year after you moved in with her." "I knew it. I remember the day that she slapped my tooth loose when I told her that she had made a mistake." I got out of the car and realized that I'd shared too much as Iris got out with a startled look on her face. "She used to beat you?" My hot lawyer pulled her bag out of the back seat as I nodded and walked up the steps. Three hours ago, I thought that I would never see this place again. Now I own all of this. "Your grandmother's lawyer stopped by my office and brought over the will that is not from her but your parents." Once again, I found myself staring at her with a blank expression on my face, but this time it was because she spoke of the people that left me with the old-bitch. "Your parents left you ten million dollars, and your grandmother left you fifteen million and this house." My mouth hit the floor as I cried happy tears. "There is one stipulation with your grandmother's money." I knew the other shoe would drop sooner or later. "You have to spend two months at a juvenile wellness center as a mentor." Say what? Kids? Oh, hell no! "Where?" "In Athens, Ohio." "Uhh, more white people." Iris and I laughed, and I made the decision mentally to do what I had to do to get the money. My eyes drifted to the spot where my grandmother kicked me in the ribs when I was eleven for accidentally dropping my PB&J sandwich on her rug. Now it was a place for her special china plates, and I'm going to use those bitches for target practice in a week. "Okay, I'll do it." She slid the paperwork over to me and got up to leave. "I'll come by in the morning to get this." The tall, beautiful woman walked out with a smile on her face, and now that I'm an adult, I got one last look at her ass before she shut the door. I should be broken up, but the old bitch had to go. I'll never forget the look on her face when I started to fight back. Kids should feel safe in any home that they're in and not have to contend with adults who have anger issues and think blowing up is the right way to react. All it did was make me explode in anger the same way that she did. Now the old-bitch is dead, and I'm partially disappointed that I wasn't the one who found the body. Since Misty didn't believe in house phones, I'd have to wait to see her when I decided to go back to school. I ran up to my room and pulled the shoe box out of the bed. Nine thousand dollars, in all cash that ranged from one hundred to fifty dollar bills. "Pizza!" I ordered a large half cheese-half pepperoni with a two-liter of my favorite cola. Maw-Maw hated it when I ordered pizza, and I had to wait for her to go out of town with the church. Now I can cook whatever I want whenever I want. An hour passed by quickly as the pizza delivery driver rang the doorbell. "Coming, give me a second." I grabbed my kitchen knife and went to the door to see a gorgeous light brown-skinned beauty holding my food. "Hello." "Hi, I'm Sambrina. It'll be thirty-five-eighty-six." I placed the knife in my back pocket while handing her the two fifties. "Keep the change." "This is too much. I can't take this." "No prob! I plan on ordering from your job a lot. Thank you." "Are you sure?" "No, I'm Idna, but you can call me by my middle namepm Tia." She smiled from ear to ear as she handed me the food and bowed a little but quickly realized it looked stupid, so she walked away. "Goodnight Tia." I shut the door and locked it before walking over to the front room that I made more to my liking. "Tomorrow, I'm going to the mall and treating myself to a shopping spree. Shoes, clothes, video games, and groceries. I also need to clear out old-head stuff along with the matronly design out of here. It was depressing, and I needed to get past all of this old energy. "Mmmm, Cheese!" The last time I had pizza was when the school threw us a party and surprised us with a cold pizza party. My anger was like wildfire as I made them warm it up by making a protest. In the end, it tasted way better, and even the staff agreed after everyone had their fill. "What to watch?" I turned the television on and used the menu guide to search for another movie. It felt good for everything to finally be going my way. "Oh, shit! I just remembered that an adult show came on the expensive channels, and now that I'm an adult, I can watch whatever I want." I clicked on the show about four black girls' best friends and watched three episodes in a row when someone rang my doorbell. I grabbed my smaller knife and walked into the foyer as the annoying sound echoed through the house again. Before I could get to it, Misty walked in and hugged me. "Girl! I thought they had you." "Me too, but the old bitch died by her own hand." "Huh?" "Yeah, she took a pill that made her drowsy at the wrong time." Misty moved out of the embrace and closed the door with her leg as I sheathed my knife."Damn, that's crazy as fuck." We walked into the front room, but the second I turned around to offer her some pizza, I screamed. She was extremely tall with extra arms and a large eye on her forehead. "Your awakening is my gift to you." She reached out with all of her hands and placed them on my neck as a tear slid down her cheek. "Let the quickening begin!" She tightened her grip until it was unbearable and snapped my neck. My ears rang, and it was all that I could hear while falling to the floor. I awoke on the couch with my back on fire and my legs feeling as if I had run three miles. The time on the cable box showed that it was eleven eleven, and the burning sensation spread from my back to the rest of my body as I got up and walked outside to get some fresh air. A large full moon pulled my attention to the night sky, and the cool ground helped alleviate the intense heat that I was feeling. I stood still with the cool evening air blowing around me as my skin absorbed the moonlight. Misty told me about sun and moon gazing last summer, and I try to do it once every month to ground myself. With all that I've been through in the past ten years, I had to find some type of balance for my unbridled rage. I breathed in and out while a cool spring breeze made my thick curls move with the wind. The elemental combinations helped regulate whatever it was that I was going through, but my shoulder blades and legs felt as if I had started a workout routine without stretching first. I allowed several minutes to pass before going back into the house and cleaning up my mess. After I was done, I went upstairs to get in my own bed, but as I bent over to get in, an intense pain formed in my lower back and caused me to cry out. It felt as if my back was splitting open, and as I landed on my bed, I could hear the sound of my backbones popping. Several things happened at once as I tried to roll over, but the heaviness in my back prevented me from moving. I was able to turn my head, and when I looked back at the double row of brown bird wings protruding out of my back, I screamed. The top of my head throbbed as two golden ram horns grew from the sides of my head, and the tips of my toenails tingled, and it crawled up my legs as they split into several snake tails. Some of them had the rattlesnake end, and others were normal but thicker. My hands changed from human to brown scales, with my nails extending into long black claws. The part of this nightmare transformation was the lower wings on my back to glow with golden sparkling energy and become the upper portion of two different types of monster snakes. They looked up at me and bowed their heads as the left one, with a head like a cobra, breathed fire while the one on the right, that resembled an anaconda, exhaled a cloud of cold mist. All of this has to be my way of processing the death of my grandmother and the weed I smoked when I went to get slushies with Misty yesterday afternoon. She said it was some good stuff from a farmer friend of hers named Zephyr, and now that I thought about this from that point of view, all of this made sense. I was abused by the mountain troll for all of my life, and now that I'm free, I have to move forward. "This is a dream." My voice was that of a monster as it bounced off of the walls of my room, and I felt the familiar sense of drowsiness kick in. I blinked several times as my eyelids grew heavier, and everything went black. The last thing I remember feeling from the dream was my entire body breaking out in gooseflesh and then waking up to the sun on my face. I was still tired, but my body was back to normal. My bones snapped and popped as I stretched out to my full length and looked over to the pile of money on my nightstand. "Ding-dong, the bitch is dead. Ba-ba-bo, this bitch is dead. Bing-Bing-Bong, the bitch is gone." I continued to sing and dance for the rest of the morning while getting ready for the day, and then I remembered that I hadn't signed the paperwork, so I read through it and signed my name to the old money that was now mine. Another hour passed, and I used the skills that I learned from home economics to make myself something to eat for breakfast. It felt good to eat my food in peace and use the dishwasher without an old tree towering over me to make sure that I didn't break it. Once I was done and drying my hands, the doorbell rang, and I made the short distance to the door to let Iris in. She was dressed in a beautiful suit that accentuated her perfect figure, with her dark hair pulled up into a bun. "Good morning." "Good morning to you as well. Here you go." She pulled them out and nodded as she looked through all of them. "Okay, We're all set. I'll call you and have a car come to get you. Have a bag packed for summer/ fall clothes because the facility is air-conditioned." "Will do." I put my thumbs up and walked her to the door with a smile on my face that I knew wasn't right for someone who's guardian just died in this very house. A chill ran down my spine as I remembered what Misty said about ghosts and unfinished business. "Are you okay?" "Yes, I was just thinking about what I should say to her church." "Oh, Yeah. Just be careful. You know how our religious brothers and sisters can be." Her pessimistic view brought a smile to my face as she waved goodbye, and the sunlight caught her at the perfect angle. In the distance, I could see a thick rainbow above her head, and it only added to her beauty. "Have a good day and remember, you don't have to go back to school right away. I filed the paperwork of your age, and the school board has allotted you three weeks off for the loss of a loved one." "Ha! Okay!" I hoped no one was around to hear that because it would have conflicted with what I had to show to the world about the death of my old-head guardian. "Try not to let it get to you. Remember, she's in a better place." Iris made sure to say that on my behalf, and for that, it made me happy to have a trustworthy female lawyer on my side. I nodded as she hopped in her two-door sports car and pulled out of my driveway. "Alright, Tia. Let's get this day started." Since it was still early, I decided to clear out the things from the old heads room and put them in the basement so that I could move my own things into my new room before I went shopping. Passing by my room brought up the memories of the dream that I had and made gooseflesh crawl up my exposed forearms. That was the weirdest nightmare that I'd ever had, except when I was six, where I was in a cave, and a monster with five glowing eyes stared at me from the darkness. When I told my grandmother, she called the leaders of the congregation of gullible colored folk, and they came over to pray the demons away. Their songs and scriptures still make me laugh to this day. All of that God is good bullshit did help me feel better after I realized how stupid her generation was by waiting for a Male savior to help them out of life's problems. If there was a powerful being who was both judge and executioner, then it wouldn't be a male. Women have countless advantages when it comes to true strength, physical endurance, intelligence, and overall worldly coexistence with nature. I stuffed all of her things in nineteen garbage bags that I then carried down to the basement. The normally open space was full of her shit, and I couldn't have been more proud of myself for not being one of those young ladies who pretended that manual labor was for men. As I moved stuff around to maximize the space, the doorbell rang, and I sprinted up the steps to the hallway and then to the door. I realized as I twisted the doorknob that I wasn't out of breath, but the sight of Heather King took my breath away. "Greetings, Idna. I'm so sorry for your loss. I brought this over for you." All I could do was blink for a couple of seconds, but I managed to pull myself together enough to move to the side and invite her in. "Good morning Mrs. King." My face got the memo late as she walked in, and I couldn't stop smiling. She turned around and handed me the container of great-smelling food. Is everyone in this family as attractive as they're talented? My right palm tingled as we made our way into the front room. Thank goodness, I was done cleaning up. Now my front room was better suited to accommodate guests without feeling like the divine oppressor is looking over you. "Achu-Achu-Achu-Achu-Achu!!" I ran to the half bathroom to get a roll of toilet paper and wet a towel from all the mucus that came out of her while I silently laughed. It took me half a minute to collect myself as the hair on my arms stood on end, but when I stepped out into the hallway, she was clean and held a peacock-colored handkerchief in her hands. What the fuck? How was it physically possible that she was completely dry? I saw the thick clear bodily fluid come out of her nose like a wet fart. "This season is a nightmare for my allergies." That was almost as weird as the dream that I had this morning. "Are you sure you're okay?" "Yes, That just happens sometimes when our bodies build up a tolerance to the medicine. You'll see what I mean in a couple of years. I'm going to go take a shower. I suddenly feel like I did manual labor. My number is on the card inside the container of cookies. Call me if you need something, Honey." "Yes. Ma'am." "Keep the door locked. You live alone as a black woman in America." I did as she suggested once she closed the door, but hearing her say that didn't make me feel good at all. Her house was twice the size of mine, and she had a husband with a body that would make the supposed Greek gods jealous. As I spoke the words, the sky rumbled with thunder, and hearing it made me frown because it was a sunny day with clear skies. "Sorry Big man, Didn't mean to take thy name in vain O'Lord of Ego's!" More thunder erupted in the sky as I broke out in the stupid little dance that my old-head-ass grandmother used to do when she felt the Holy Ghost. With my finger in the air, it felt like I was controlling the thunder as I looked down to the ground and moved my feet. "Let me stop." Now that my life is finally moving in a better direction, I should let go of my hate towards organized religions and the people that follow them. It's not their fault that they've been indoctrinated into a brainwashed mentality of faith without questioning what you're following or their narrowmindedness in thinking that certain religions were brought to other parts of the world by acts of kindness. People died for false rulers who made it law to follow their faith or be tortured to death. As a black woman, I knew that we have had it worst than anyone who has ever walked the face of the earth. My only real question is, why? What did we do that was so bad that we had to be raped, beaten, and made to be a piece of property where we were bargained off by our fathers. Learning African American history and then seeing how much of it is still in the culture that we made from the ground up gives me the burning desire to crush all who stand in the way of what I feel is right for us as women. My stomach rumbled, and I looked over to the container of food that was full of four separate dishes in plasticware. Opening it made my mouth water as I smelled the brownies and cookies first because they were on top. I took a glance at the note that was in the shape of a peacock feather and then put it aside to pull out a dish with noodles that were covered in meat sauce with cheese on top. The large oval-shaped pasta reminded me of seashells, and I didn't wait until I warmed it up to taste one. From the cheese to the sauce, I was in love and wanted another. That high-yellow bitch can cook. Her hair was thick enough to qualify her to be fully black, but that body was on the thin side, and if I had to guess, Iris inherited a lot of her genetics from her father's side of the family. After eating five in a row, I closed the top and opened the cookies to read the card. The small rectangular piece of paper was covered in a peacock's feather design with her name and number in white letters. "Cool." I placed it in the house key bowl and took the food to the kitchen. Just because I'm an adult doesn't mean that I had to be a slob. This was a very nice four-bedroom house, and I plan to keep it that way. Once I get my license and buy a car, I'll be a full-fledged adult. Since I was dressed and ready to go, I went to the wall phone and called a taxi-cab that said I had to wait thirty minutes for them to arrive. "Okay, See you then." "Have a nice trip, Darling." The elderly lady had a nice voice that was unlike the hag that raised me and I wanted to know if she had grandchildren that she loved, but she hung up before saying anything else. I ran up to my room and changed my clothes, and grabbed more money. As time passed, the cab driver honked his horn. Now I was fine as fuck with a pocket full of cash. On the way out, I picked up my keys and made a mental note to buy a knife and mace. I walked outside to see a short black stud with nose piercings and tattoos. "Hello, Are you Tia?" "Yes. I'm going to the mall downtown." "Okay." She opened the door for me and tried to make conversation, but I was so distracted by the dream that I had I couldn't truly focus on anything else. "I'm sorry, I didn't hear that. My grandmother died yesterday, and it's hard to get my mind right." "Oh dear, I'm so sorry for your loss." She reached back to place her hand on my knee, but my hands moved like lightning, and we held hands for a couple of minutes. "Um, Honey. I'm not a lipstick lesbian, but you're going to need to buy some lotion while you're at the mall." I almost screamed at the sight of my monster hand and pulled it back into my lap as she looked forward with a bewildered look on her face. For the rest of the trip, she didn't say anything and dropped me off on the south side of the mall. All the stores that I needed were at this entrance anyway. The cute barista at the slushy shop might be there, so that made all of this extra special. I walked through the swinging doors and had to pretend not to be stunned when I saw Gabrielle Vontrel. She was the perfect mix of black and Mexican with her curves and curls. "Hey, Phillips. Make sure to stop buying when you're done shopping." "Ochay!" No! What is wrong with me? She laughed while tending to the customer that walked up, and I made my way into my favorite shoe store Step-Sista. "Hello, do you need help with anything?" Damn, Hoe! I just walked up on this bitch. Can a girl make a choice for herself without you trying to make a dollar right now? She froze and blinked several times as she looked closer at me. "What?" "N-Nothing. I thought I saw your eyes change into snake eyes. I must still be high as fuck from last night." She shook her head, and I ignored her as a pair of Vixen-X9s caught my eye. Their gold/white trim made me want to try them on, but I hated sharing things like that, so I picked up a black pair and then turned to look at the spaced-out cashier. "Hey, can I get these in nine and a half?" She nodded and walked to the back as more people walked in, and I noticed that one of them looked familiar. "Oh shit, I thought you were in jail for murder?" William Belt, one of the cool white kids who smokes a lot of weed, walked over with a smile on his face. His blonde hair was pulled back into a ponytail, and he looked down at me with his bright blue eyes. "I was, but for once, the system worked for a sista, and they did their job. My grandmother passed away after falling down the steps and hitting her head from taking the wrong medicine. After I dabbed him up, his friend, who used to stare at me in math class, walked up with his fist out. "Damn, girl, It's like that?" I rolled my eyes as Phil Smithstone smacked his teeth and pretended to be hurt. "I don't get down with weird ass nigga's. You used to stare me down with those green eyes of yours and thought that I was into light skin dudes. Nah!" Truthfully I'm bisexual, but at this point in my life, I want women. Men have too many heads and not enough lips. "I-I have your sh-shoes." What the fuck was up with her? First, she's pushy. Now she's timid. "D-Do you n-need to try them on-n-n?" "Frances, are you on that shit again?" She turned to glare at Phillip as he and his group laughed. My total was almost four hundred dollars, so I allowed her to keep the change as a tip and made my way to Mel-body. A store that was made by a black woman for black women. Normally finding clothes that are made for our size was hard, but thanks to this store, I have a bra and pantie set that fit perfectly. I turned to see Melissa Thompson, a former junior church member who my grandmother asked to come over so that I wouldn't hang out by myself. "Idna, Hey. I heard about your grandmother. My condolences." "Thank you. I'm trying to keep my spirits high. God works in mysterious ways. He called her home." She nodded and held her hand up to the sky. "Amen. She will be missed." Not really. "It must be hard to stay in the house all by yourself. If you need a friend to come over until they put you in foster care, I'll bring the bible babies with me." The what? Girl no! You bitches are a tragedy waiting to happen. "I appreciate the offer, but I'll need some time to grieve alone." She placed her old lady-like hands on my shoulder and nodded as I sucked my breath in through my nose. "I'll get going. If you need us, call, okay." "Okay." Her little group of church hoes left, and I gave my shoes to the cashier so that I could shop around the store. With the two hundred dollars I found in my right pocket, I was now at eight hundred dollars. That's the perfect amount of money to buy several outfits and new underwear. I loved how the employees of this store allowed me to shop in peace as I spent thirty minutes picking out five hundred dollars worth of clothes. "Did you enjoy your experience here today?" "I did. Thank you for asking…Stacy." I walked out of the store with the biggest smile on my face and had to catch myself just in case someone I knew saw me. I looked over at Wet-spot to see if Gabby was busy, and my smile returned because she was free to talk and waved me over. "Looks like you're having a good day." "It'll be even better if you can give me your number and a strawberry-Kiwi blast?" Her eyebrows shot upwards as she turned around to make my drink. After a minute passed, she returned with my drink and her number on a receipt. "That'll be twelve dollars." I handed her a fifty-dollar bill, and she smiled just like the pizza delivery girl. "I'll call you later." "Please do." "Hey, do you have a cell phone that I can use to call a cab?" "No, My parents won't allow me to get one until I'm eighteen. But if you wait ten minutes until I'm off, I'll give you a ride." "Okay." I took a seat and spent the time looking at my new clothes. "Are you ready?" "Yup." She grabbed a couple of my bags, and we walked to the indoor parking garage. "My car is right there." She pressed the button on her key ring to pop the trunk of a brand-new all-black sedan. "Here, I'll put these in. It's open." I hopped in the passenger seat of the vanilla-honey-smelling car, and she got in seconds later with a smile on her face. "So! Where to?" "Vinewood Avenue." "Ohhh, Fancy." She started the car, and we made our way through downtown traffic while making small talk. I found out that she was the same age as me, wanted to take a gap year before college and is one hundred percent a lesbian. Perfect! "I have a confession. Every Christmas, my friends and I would drive down your street to see the decorations. Your house was always my favorite." A frown made my lips poke out as she pulled into my driveway. "How do you know which house is mine?" "Oh, Gosh. That made me sound like a stalker. No, Nothing like that. I saw you helping your grandmother last year." That proves that perception is only half of every story or situation. It was supposed to be a joyous occasion, but the old bitch got angry and called me a bitch because I accidentally stepped on one of her light bulbs. I told her that there was no way in hell that I'm supposed to respect her more than she respects me and crushed several other lights as I stormed off. Gabby parked the car as I realized I've been in this situation four times in a row as of late. Getting a ride from someone when I needed it. Mr. King, Iris, the taxi and now Gabby. She popped the trunk, and we grabbed my stuff as Iris pulled into her parent's driveway. "Hello, Free woman." "Hello, lawyer, that does her job. Good afternoon to you." We made our way into the house, and Gabby placed my clothes on the couch as she moved her fingers from me to the window that pointed at the King's house. "What did she mean by that?" "My grandmother passed away recently, and they locked me up with no real evidence thinking that I did it. She choked on her pills and fell to her death. I didn't even have time to mourn her properly without being taken down to the station while at school by white officers." Her eyes grew big as she took in all of what I said. Technically I did kill her because the medicine that she took was a muscle relaxer of a higher dosage instead of her usual pill. "That's awful." She scooted closer to me and hugged me with her big breasts pressing against my shoulders. "Do you want to watch some television?" I handed her the remote and got up to get us some refreshments. "Ohh, do I smell kettle corn?" "Yup! It's my favorite. Do you want lemonade or strawberry lemonade?" "Strawberry." We chose to watch a movie about a witch who was cursed by a goddess to exist in the form of a man to learn humility, but she turned out to be a serial killer. There were so many jump scares that I almost spilled my juice several times. Once the movie was off, she put her hand on my knee and looked me in the eyes. "Can I use your phone? I need to call my cousin to see if she took out the chicken like our mother asked this morning." "Yeah, it's in the kitchen on the wall." I helped myself to more popcorn as she switched her big booty cheeks into the kitchen. "I'll be right back." "Okay." "Don't you mean, Ochay?" I had to add almost choking on my food to the list of embarrassing things as I coughed up bits of popcorn. Once my throat was clear, a weird ringing in my left ear formed, and she returned with a smile on her face. "My cousin asked if she could borrow some money, and I said yes. I also told her where I was so that she could come pick it up. Is that cool?" Seems like you already made your mind up! "I'll run the money out and come right back in." I nodded but felt myself becoming more annoyed as the seconds turned into minutes. What woman in this day and age invites anonymous people over to another woman's house? Especially one that she knows lives alone. I can fight my way out of almost every situation, but not one where I get jumped or shot. Twenty minutes went by, and someone honked their horn outside. "I'll be right back." "Okay, I'll search for another pay-per-view movie." I took another glance at her ass and decided to forgive her this one time. It's not like it was the middle of the night, and she allowed a home invasion to happen. Gooseflesh crawled up my arm as she returned with a preteen behind her. "Can Tischa use your restroom?" "Sure, It's right through there to the right." "Thank you." The young girl went to the restroom while my date and I flipped through the selection of movies. "How about that one?" "Yeah, I heard that it was supposed to be based on true events." I pressed the pay button, and three minutes later, her little cousin came out of the bathroom. "Mom said that she'll have dinner ready by six." "Tell Mom to stop by the grocery store and pick up some ice cream." Watching the interactions between people that lived together always piqued my interest in the way that they either hate each other or have a communal understanding of respect. Both of them spoke about their parents like there was genuine love there and not mutual resentment. "Bye." Gabby walked her to the door and returned with another smile on her face. "Sorry about that. Those of us who come from working-class families have to help our parents out financially sometimes." "As wealthy as my grandmother was, she never gave me an allowance. I had to make all of my own money by getting a job." Her dark brown eyebrows knitted together as she reached out and placed a hand on my shoulder. "She must have wanted you to not have to rely on anyone." Or something? I changed the subject to college aspirations, and time flew by as it was now the afternoon. "I'm hungry. Would you like to go out to eat?" "How about I cook you something?" "I'd love that. I'll help." "Can you start by grabbing your keys?" She looked at me with a puzzled expression as I grabbed mine and stood up. "We need to go to the grocery store." "Oh! I thought you were trying to make a joke, and I was mentally kicking myself for not understanding what you were implying." Gabby let out a small giggle as we walked outside to her car. "It's such a nice day. Thank you for this." I winked at my caramel-colored date and took in a breath of fresh air through my nose. "I love the spring air. It reminds me of newness and necessary growth." We sang along to the music on the radio while stuck in traffic for the entire ride until she turned on Allen's road and pulled into the parking lot. It had a large amount of cars for a late afternoon, but I just wanted to get in and out as soon as possible. "Is this still a date, or are we now onto a second date because we've changed locations?" "This is definitely date 2.0." I grabbed a cart, and the both of us spent a large portion of the afternoon in the grocery store having fun. She was very charming and super funny for a woman who wants to be a mortician. Now that I have everything that I need to make lasagna from scratch, I plan on making it with a salad and homemade garlic bread. "Damn, Girl. You just bought up the mall and the grocery store on the same day. Should I be worried about this being a condition caused by grief?" "Oh hell No! Look here, Mrs. Hottiness. You are not my therapist. I am fine. My grandmother was old, and it was something that I prepared myself for a long time ago. Okay!" I snapped my fingers as she popped her trunk, and we started to put the groceries in. "Right! I'm just saying that it wouldn't be right for me to come into your life when you have lost someone important." I snorted while putting the last bag on my side, and she touched my shoulder again. "This is me being serious, Idna." "I know, and I appreciate you being here for me. But right now, we can spend time having fun in celebration of the lives that we do have." "Yeah, You're right." We got in the car, and the trip home was just as fun as the way there, with less traffic and the replay of the hottest song out right now. "That's my jam. I swear I could dance to it all night long." "I'm going to have to take you up on that while dinner is in the oven." We pulled into my driveway, and the feeling of this being mine gave me a chill as I got out of her car. I am an adult. This is my life. I guess granny good-bitch did teach me something worthwhile after all, Independence. We brought the groceries in, and I learned another thing about my beautiful new friend. She was another one of those women who hated manual labor. I could hear her heavy breaths falling like it was a bad thing to put effort into carrying heavy loads and walking a couple of steps. "Phew, Alright, I need a check." "Look at the universe working its way out. The tip." She feigned a laugh as I put the stuff away, and a chill crawled down my back. The weird sensations have been happening since the first weird dream, and it kind of annoyed me that I couldn't reach out to Misty. For one, I had a dream about her, and now I'm experiencing a weird tingling sensation that is accompanied by goosebumps. She'd be able to divine the answer in the special way that she does. "What should I do first?" That was a good question. I've only ever made this once and would rather her show up later after it was all cooked. I also wanted to clean myself up with a classy dress that I bought. Gabby narrowed her eyes and looked to the floor and then back up at me. "How about I go home and let you do this so that it could be our third date? I want to change into this dress that I've been saving for a special occasion." My body froze mid-shelving, and I turned around to face her with what I hoped was a normal smile while slowly nodding my head. I was just thinking that, and BOOM! Yeah! Tomorrow I'm going back to school just to see Misty. "I'll be back in two hours." "Make it three and a half." Gabby nodded and blew me a kiss. "Seven-thirty it is. Until then." I snapped out of my daze to put on the fake mask that allows me to gain the upper hand in any situation and grabbed the kiss out of the air, and put it up against my breasts. She fell against the doorway and pretended to swoon as she laughed. The creepy mind stuff will have to wait for later. Now I have to remember what I'm supposed to do first. I continued to put the groceries away and played back last week's home economics class about lasagna in my mind's-eye. I locked the door while remembering to brown the meat in chopped onions and garlic. Then I pour pasta sauce and let it simmer until the water is gone. Next, I boil the noodles in a pot of salted water while I make the bread from scratch. The last part is easy with all of the food that I was forced to help the old head make for the church. "Damn, Another thing she taught me about existing." Time flew by as I executed everything with the ease of a traditionally trained Chef. With everything prepped to bake, I spent another hour cleaning up and getting myself ready for my third date. The black dress was something that a teenage girl shouldn't wear, but now that I've been told about my real age, I've been on a whole new level mentally. With my hair up in a bun, I put on the earrings that I bought and added the necklace that I just now noticed was a dragon claw holding a shimmering moonstone. It was out of a bag of jewelry that Misty gifted me for my birthday last year. With one last twirl, I stopped to look at myself in the mirror and gasped as this was the first time that I'd done something like this. I walked to the kitchen with my high heels making a lot of noise and turned the gas oven to three-seventy-five. Ten minutes passed, and the oven dinged as I turned around to put the lasagna in. "I think thirty-five minutes should be good enough." When I made this at school, the electric oven took forever and, in my honest opinion, took away from the taste. This one will not only be better in every way imaginable, but it will also put my neighbors cooking to shame. My stomach rumbled, and I reached for the cookies that she made. All of her desserts will pair nicely with the ice cream that I bought. If she was smart, she'd come back with an extra change of clothes. Then I'll really be able to ascend to true womanhood. The hairs on the back of my neck stood on end as someone rang the doorbell. "Coming!" I really had to stop saying that. I am not some housewife whose number one job was to get the door.

I am a new-age woman who knows her worth and has plans to shatter the glass ceiling by being my authentic self. The feeling on the back of my neck returned, and when I opened the door, my mouth fell open. Iris was in a multicolored sequin gown that left her right shoulder exposed. Her breasts looked as amazing as her makeup, and the shoes had to be double-digit expensive. She smiled with her mouth but frowned with her eyes as she looked me up and down. "Girl!!! Are you coming with us to the fundraiser?" Wow, another one of life's weird coincidences. "No, I have a date coming over soon." "Well, okay. I was just coming over to see how you were, but I see you're fine. Call me if you need anything, okay." "Will do." Gabby returned as she turned to leave and stopped to let her pull out of the driveway but turned her head to the left and then right when she parked. "Is everything okay?" She nodded and got out of the car as a cool breeze blew by us. "Damn, Girl. How does that saying go? Heaven's lost angel." Gabby laughed so hard that she snorted and bent down to pick up a bouquet of flowers. "For me?" "Yes, I feel like a freeloader, so I decided to spend my tip on these." Seeing them, plus her smile, felt good. With the privacy of my front yard, there wouldn't be anyone around to see me hug or kiss her. Before I could do anything, she reached out and pulled me into a hug while placing a kiss on my cheek. "You look amazing, by the way." "Thank you." We walked inside, and I placed the flowers in water as she used the restroom. We had another ten minutes to wait until the lasagna was done, so I placed the garlic bread in the secondary oven below it as Gabby walked in and breathed in the delicious aroma. "Wow, It smells great. I see that Mrs. Norris's home economics classes were put to good use." "It's the only one that does. I don't see myself as a math teacher or a HIStorian." My beautiful date and I laughed at the emphasis on my wordplay. "Right, I still remember the look on Principal Raymond's face when you told her about how our true origins were erased by the very patriarchy that made the world the way it is now. She knew that you were right and was stuck on stupid." I burst into uncontrollable laughter as Gabby's smile was both awkward and humorous. It took me a full minute to gather myself, and I still didn't know why I laughed so hard. "I'm sorry. I don't know where that came from." "It's fine. I would be a mess, too, if my last remaining relative died." Her choice of words deflated my happiness balloon, and I had to bite back my sharp tongue because I actually liked her. The only response available was to shrug my shoulders and change the subject. "Do you want some wine?" "Girl, yes. I was scared to ask because of you only recently finding out about your real age." "We're still under the age of twenty-one, but it's my house, and I've been hiding this from my grandmother for a year. Can you get the cups from that cabinet next to your head?" I walked over to the pantry and went to my hiding spot behind the boxes of devil food cake that my grandmother refused to touch or go near to pull out my bottle of chardonnay. "I've been ready to open you and drink your sweet-sweet nectar like Dracula did to Mina from the moment I bought you with that fake ID that granny threw out the next day." "Huh?" I turned around and felt a wave of embarrassment wash over me as Gabby stood in the open doorway. "I used to have this obsession with the myth of vampires, and this is the first time that I'm drinking alcohol." "Oh, I feel honored." "It's not your first time, is it?" She smiled as she shook her head no, and we walked out of the pantry with smiles on our faces. I was still embarrassed, but I could see that this night will be one to remember. "Oh, It just occurred to me that I might not have a wine opener." "I have one on my key ring." She sauntered off to get it and returned with a black multi-use tool. Once our cus were filled, I put mine up against hers while looking her in the eyes. "To new relationships."

"To new lives." I liked her better, so I clinked my glass against hers and then took a large sip. At first, the warm liquid fizzed in my mouth, but once I swallowed it, the taste was worth the wait. My attractive date thought so as well, with her head nod and lip-smacking. I love black women. "This is one of the best nights of my life. Thank you, Gabby." "I should be thanking you. It's a good night for me as well. I haven't done this in a while." We talked until the oven dinged, and I took out the food. "Wow." "I know, right? We'll let these cool down. Do you smoke?" Gabby gasped while putting her left hand over her exposed cleavage. "Like a chimney. I'll take our glasses into the front room while you take care of this." I nodded as a chill crawled up my spine, and she hummed while walking into the other room. After turning off the ovens, I closed the pantry door and made sure that everything was locked up from the kitchen to the bathroom. I almost freaked out when I used the downstairs restroom and saw that the window was unlocked. Normally I use my own bathroom, but I must have opened it when I was cleaning earlier and forgot to lock it. "What shall we do while we wait for the food?" My legs knew the answer before my heart did as I walked over to sit next to her and press my lips against hers. It was the perfect mix of soft and sweet affection that made both of us wanting more. Time stood still for me as we continued to make out like we would never see each other again. My mouth couldn't get enough, but she pulled back and cleared her throat. "Excuse me for a moment." I drank a nice portion of my wine before she came back, and another round of goosebumps crawled over my back. Now is not the time to be thinking about Misty, but I need her. "Oh, well, let me catch up." Gabby finished all of her wine in one gulp and did the same but almost choked because my wine was a little drier than the previous cup that I had. "Next time, I'll add ice or fruit?" "Yeah, then we could have a BBQ out back." My eyes grew big at the thought of her wanting to spend time with me, and I lost myself to my emotions. Our make-out session continued, but this time, we slipped our hands under each other's dress and used our fingers to pleasure each other until both of us cried out while we reached our orgasms. That was the first time that I allowed someone to touch me other than myself, and it felt good to lose my V-card to a gorgeous young woman who came on my fingers. "Damn, We didn't even get to the weed." Yeah, but it was worth it. I wanted to get up, but I felt my body becoming extremely sluggish. "I don't feel so good." The energy of my climax was beginning to wane and was being replaced by a sudden need for sleep. "About time!" Gabby clapped her hands before getting up and unlocking the front door. Now I couldn't move, but my five senses remained as the sound of heavy footfall over the hardwood floors entered my home. Gabby walked in with three men who were the size of football players and had sinister looks on their faces. Tears formed in my eyes as I watched someone that I thought I trusted point upstairs and then at me. "I'm done with her. She's all yours." Hearing those words brought on more tears but a burning sensation that spread all over my body quickly formed. It brought back my mobility, but I felt my skin tingle as it changed into scales, and my dress tore while the monster body parts grew out of my body. Half of them were frozen in terror, and the others ran to the door, but it locked as an unseen force snatched them back into the front room. I glared at my date, who took my virginity moments ago like it meant nothing and also brought danger into my home. "It was you who unlocked the bathroom window." My monster voice echoed around the confines of my home and brought all of the invaders together like metal to magnets. "What have I done to you to deserve this?" Gold and black energy swirled around her leg and snatched her over to where I stood. "P-please don't eat me." That was not my plan, but now that she mentioned it, they did smell good in a raw meat kind of way. It reminded me of the meat part of the charcuterie board that my grandmother's wealthy friends would bring over. Four of my tails reached out and wrapped themselves around two of the closest men as they yelled and screamed. My entire body tingled as it doubled in size, and I tossed the two men into my mouth like they were chips and chewed them. The sound of their screams echoed inside my mouth as I used my large teeth to grind them together. While chewing them, I remembered to chew them twenty times before swallowing. "Mmm, just enough room for one more." The last man yelled and tried to hold onto Gabby, but my tail snapped his neck as it retracted to toss him into my open mouth. I took my time with this one and made sure to show my date just how much I enjoyed the meal that she brought to me. "Get up!" She looked at me with a confused look on her face and remained on the floor. "Do I have to repeat myself, Bitch?" My bouquet of tails brought me closer to her as the weird energy from before swirled around my body. She slowly got up and looked down at the floor as I licked the side of her face. "Make me a plate. I'm still hungry!" Gabby turned around to walk to the kitchen, and I followed closely behind her as she whimpered. All the utensils that she needed flew out of their spots and smacked her in various parts of her body. "Pick it up!" My date bent over while whimpering to pick them up with shaking hands. Once she was right-side up, I aggressively walked us over to the counter and stood behind her as she made my plate. She started with the salad, and I reached out with my monster hand to force her to cut the lasagna first. Tears fell down her face, but I didn't give a shit. This was not a dream, and my transformation was very real. There was no other explanation for all of this. My grandmother was right. I'm a demon. Gabby went for the salad again, but I snapped the wrist of her free hand and made her go for the bread with her other hand. "P-Please, I'm sorry. I-I won't tell anyone." I squeezed her hand tighter while pointing at the salad, and she nodded as more tears came out of her eyes. "I really don't know why you're crying. I'm the one who was drugged and coerced into sex. Oh! Let's not forget the fact that you were going to let them rape me." My voice echoed around the room once more, and I was starting to love the power behind it. "Join me in the dining room after you make your plate!" I turned around and walked into the dining room as my body changed back into my human form, but I still had the two snake demon heads at my side. "Are you two hungry?" Hearing the sound of my now normal voice felt weird, and as they nodded their heads, it only added to this new supernatural turn of events. Apparently, I'm a demon, Damn. I really hate when the old head is right. A ringing formed in my ears, and I picked up the sound of Gabby trying to escape through the back door. She pulled with all of her energy until the doorknob broke off, but it still didn't open. Next, she moved onto the window, but my patience had already worn off, so I thought about her sitting across from me with her plate of food in front of her. A small cloud of my energy formed in the chair across from me before it took the form of her holding a plate of food. "There, now we can eat." More tears streamed down her face as she whimpered and put her plate on the table. I wiggled my fingers at her silverware and made them fly out of the room as she went to reach for them. "Use your hands, Bitch!" My eyes stung as I glared at her, and she trembled as she did as I commanded. This definitely was not how I planned this night to go, but once again, I'm happy with the outcome. For some unknown reason, I now have the power to execute all of my plans and end anyone who gets in my way. A smile curved my lips as I ate my food while looking at Gabby. "You don't even know." She took one look at my eyes and cried some more. "You don't even know." I repeated. Even though I still had the taste of her friends on my tongue, the food that I made was just as delicious. My whimpering guest finished off her food and tried to get up, but I froze her to the spot With a thought. Ohh, I'm getting good at this. "Sit down." She did as I commanded once more ,but her eyes were closed with tears coming out of them, and the sight of her crying was starting to really annoy me. "Look at me." She heeded my command and this time I could see with perfect clarity that my eyes glowed with golden-yellow light. "Bitch, You will not ruin my meal. Eat-Eat!" I yelled the command that was new to me but felt familiar in a way as my Monster snake companions lunged forward and snapped her up like two rabbits sharing a carrot. They broke her in half, and each devoured theirs in a separate way. The one on the left grew longer as its body swallowed her whole, while the one on the right chomped her up like a swamp gator. "Was she tasty?" Both of them visibly smiled as I rubbed their heads, and they licked their lips. I continued to eat and hoped I wasn't going to have to shit for three as the sound of footsteps appeared out of nowhere, and Misty walked into the dining room. "You look good. I'm proud of you." She rolled her shoulders as the dark skin of her hands turned blue and extra arms sprouted from her back. Misty's body glowed with a rainbow of whirling colors before she grew to a scary height, and several eyes formed on her forehead. "Holly shit! You're the monster that I saw in my dreams as a child." She shook her head no as a mirror appeared next to her and showed my semi-demonic form change into the monster that I was before sitting down to eat. A bouquet of snake tails from the waist down and four large brown demon-bird wings with my two little cuties coming out of my side and golden horns on the sides of my head. Misty tapped the mirror, and it vanished into nothing as she stepped forward with her arms outstretched. "Now I can hug you without being scared of activating your divinity." I frowned as she pulled me into her multi-armed embrace and turned my head to the side. "Huh? Misty, I'm a demon, Not a goddess." She took a deep breath while tightening her hold on me. "Girl, You are the goddess of monsters." My snakes wrapped around her at the exact moment that my upper arms did, and I cried because it was the first time that someone hugged me of their own volition. "Wait! Haven't we hugged before?" "Yes, but think about the last time we hugged." I did and remembered it was when school let out for Christmas break. She took me to get a Christmas tree for our house and hugged me in between several trees with an abundance of animals around us. During spring break, she stopped by, and we hugged the tree outside before she went on a vacation with her family. "Damn, you're right." "I don't want to sound weird, but you're an important player in this game of order and chaos chess that I have going in this universe." I pulled away with a frown as a hiss escaped my mouth. "Not like that." Misty took a deep breath, and in the blink of an eye, we were sitting in the front room on my couch. She was still in her goddess form, and I was still a monster, but to me, it felt a little more normal than eating a girl that I've had a crush on since the moment I laid eyes on her. "Awww, Honey, I'm sorry about that. I knew if I didn't step in, you would've been killed as a mortal and then made to reincarnate all over again. No one knows who you are except for me and Gaia." "Misty, Who am I?" She crossed her arms, and I did the same as my snakes crossed themselves, and the two of us moved our necks like we had an attitude. "Hmph!" "Hmph!" It was a thing that we did when we first met where we imitated the uppity black girls who grew up rich with expensive mindsets and car services. Misty held her hands out, and two wine glasses appeared on the table in front of us. "To make an extremely long story short. Your first life was as the celestial deity named Tiamat. She was a dragon goddess who I allowed to exist here in this universe to get away from her abusive family. After living as a dragon goddess, she transcended to another form and became the mother of monsters that the Greeks called Echidna." I burst into laughter at how on the nose all of this was from my experiences to my name. Of course, I'm an ancient monster deity who befriended the coolest person in existence. "So you're a goddess too?" "Best friend, I made all of this." "Everything?" Misty nodded and took a deep breath before telling me her life story. An hour passed, and my best friend told me the story of how she created the infinite universe that we live in before having to escape to it because of family drama. That explained a lot, but to know that my roll dog is the most powerful being in all of existence gave me an extra sense of confidence moving forward in life. "I had a dream that I was running as a monster while pregnant. Was that an Echidna dream?" "Very good, It was indeed." "What about the dream where you killed me, and I turned into a monster after waking up under a full moon?" "Yup! I woke up in the astral realm so that we could have some privacy for what I'm about to tell you." I furrowed my eyebrows as I looked around the room at the streaks of blood from dragging them across the floor and the parts of Gabby's friend's that fell out of my mouth. "All of this is a part of your inner world. Like your Olympian neighbors who live across the street. The kings are the Royal family of "Greek" deities." I didn't understand her use of air quotes, but I did remember doing a book report on female goddesses in the eighth grade. Hera was the reigning queen, and she had two sisters and three brothers who supposedly made the world the birthplace of misogynistic egos that it is today. "Close, That type of thinking started with Goddesses like my mother and then spread to their male consorts." "Hold up, shut the front door!" That was something that I hadn't expected to hear. I also noticed that my friend could read my mind. "You can too." "Is that one of those basic powers that you were referring to?" "Yes, also, my name is Aura." A chill crawled all over my body as she spoke her name out loud, and I was forced to shiver. "I need your help to break some supernatural creatures out of a siphon-holding facility." "A what?" "Siphoning-holding facility, where deities suck the power out of less powerful beings, and most of the time they're children." I could feel my mouth tingle as my teeth elongated at the same time that my nails did. "You have to calm down, or you'll affect the deities across the street like you did with the quick release from jail that was followed by your inheritance, then the constant sneezing and thunderclaps." Aura waved her hand, and five white glowing spheres appeared in front of the television. "They are my gifts to you. For your ascension." Each of them changed into all the people who died in this house but with animal body parts. "From this moment on, the five of you are her property and do whatever she says in the hope of reincarnating out of her divine grasp." My grandmother frowned as her knees bent, and she bowed to the will of her divine command that was filled with power. "I should also tell you that I manipulated the time inside of this house to move at a slower rate until you are well-trained in your powers." A smile creeped over my face as I looked from Aura to my grandmother and then the rest of the kneeling group. "All of you are excused to exist in your animal forms but as miniature beasts." My breath came out as a golden haze that swirled around them into what I desired. This was fun and a power that I will most definitely be revisiting later. "I can do whatever I want to them?" "Whatever your monstrous heart desires." "Oh, I see what you did there with the telepathy again." We laughed and talked about everything that we could, as the frozen beams of moonlight outside made everything look like a fairytale. "How do you feel?" "Honestly, I feel great. Even though you just told me that I'm basically your secret spy into the juvenile center for wellness, I'm good. More people to eat." "I'm talking about emotionally. How do you feel?" "I'm looking back on the DRUGGING AND RAPE ATTEMPT with twenty-twenty hindsight. It had to happen that way so that I can be all that I am at this very moment." Aura smiled, and her glow brightened just a little as she pulled me into a warm side hug. "I need to ask a couple more questions, though." "Ask me Anything!" "I remember reading that my previous monster life had a husband. Do I have to get married to an evil monster?" She pulled back with a laugh that must have been really funny because she continued to laugh really hard for a whole minute. "You need to see this." The television came on and showed me a light-skinned boy with green eyes and an afro having fun on the playground. His body was surrounded by indigo energy with flecks of red in it as it swirled around him. "Just wait." A cardinal flew past the boy, and he jumped off the jungle gym to follow it into a spot at the bottom of a plastic barrel slide. In the blink of an eye, the bird turned into a lighter-skinned boy with bright green eyes and ghost-like bird wings. "Is that other kid a god?" "Yes, He's the west wind, Zephyr." The boy with the cute little wings looked from left to right as the other boy tapped him on the shoulder. "It's rude to ignore your future husband." "Sorry, Jay. I thought I heard someone say my name." "And I thought you were a buster. Bloop!" The boy with the afro flicked the winged boy with the low fade on his shoulder and ran in the opposite direction as he began to chase him. Jay's surrounding energy changed from the outline of a boy to a tall monster with bat wings and snakes for arms. "He has a part to play in this as well. My revenge on those who have abused the power of divinity will hit a crucial point in creation's awakening when he awakens himself." The image faded, and I had a newfound respect for my best friend. "Well, that answers that. I guess that I should check that off of the list of supernatural questions." "How about we practice some of your powers on the servants?" "Ohhh, girl, yes!" I was so excited that I didn't know what to do first. Should I break my grandmother's ribs or make Gabby eat her uncle? Whoa! How did I know that they were related? "It's an inner knowing that comes with being aware. Claircognizance is how you know things that you wouldn't normally know. Over time you'll develop more powers that are just as surprising and even more that are kind of involuntary. Like Clairalience and Clairgustance, both are linked to your physical body. Others will make themselves known after you gain better control of the first two." "Can I appear and disappear wherever I want to?" "Yup, Think about somewhere that you want to go inside the house and allow the energy to transport you there." Aura vanished in a puff of smoke to reappear on the couch across from me in a cloud of sparkling dust. I imagined myself standing behind the couch, and in the blink of an eye, I stood in the spot that I thought about, but my feet were submerged into the hardwood floor. "I'm stuck." The old flooring broke apart like cheap linoleum as I pulled my feet out and walked around to the other side. "It gets easier the more you practice. How about you try moving things with your mind?" I held my hands out and thought about my grandmother's goat face. The air shifted as she flew into the room backwards with her hoofed feet kicking the air. I slammed her into the wall before making her body bounce off of the ground. "Telekinesis, Check!" With a flick of my fingers, she changed back into a goat and flew back into the other room. "Double check!" I really wanted to try using the elements, so I called Gabby and her uncle into the room so that my snakes could use their powers on them. "Shall I burn him, Mistress?" "You can talk?" "Now that you have fed us, we can do many things, Mistress." Both of them showed me how they had just as much control of their element as I had with my divine energy, except for two things. Both of them had a way to transport us somewhere, but neither of them could move things with their minds. Apparently, that was a common power amongst attachment deities and the two of them are basically made from my energy. I looked at it as if we had a combined array of abilities that I couldn't wait to use on the help. "Elemental Tele-transportation." "Check!" We shared a laugh as one of my servants tried to walk up the steps, but I turned him into a pile of glowing dust with a glance. The pile swirled and took the form of the first man that I ate, whose name I didn't know. Now that I looked around the room, I realized that I should name my new friends and give the servants their names as well. "Get in here!" The sound of farm animals filled the house as the five of them ran into the room. "Thank you all for gathering here on this glorious occasion. Cobra head, Your name is Arigawna, and You'll be called Baselina." They opened their mouths and allowed their elements to clash as their features changed. Each of them had an extra eye on their forehead, but Lina had a crown of horns, and Ari had an extra row of teeth in her mouth. "If I name them, will they change?" Aura shook her head no and took a sip of her wine that wasn't in her hand a second ago. "How do you do that?" "My mother invented the saying "to be seen and not heard", but in my case, it was "Get out and don't come back until I'm able to say that I'm a supreme mother." "Your mother was like my grandmother?" "Yes, That's what pulled us together." "When you said that you had powerful parents who emancipated you when you were younger, I thought you meant rich people. Not the first family of creation." "Just think of us as the family elders. Like you with all the divine monsters in this universe." "Right, I'm a queen." "You're physically something else, though." "Once again, I'm confused. Lay it on me, Sista." I narrowed my gaze on my hand and made my glass of wine vanish from the table to my hand, but the wine didn't make the trip as it pooled onto the coffee table. "Damn it!" "You'll get it. Trust me. I used to have problems with shapeshifting and duplication. Now I've made all of this and have a family that I want you to meet someday. My grandchildren call me Mama-grand." "You be baking cookies in a bonnet and gown?" I laughed so hard that gold lightning bolts shot out of my mouth. "That's new!" I clasped my hand over my mouth as more energy formed and crawled across my arm to the rest of my body. "Lightning check!" All of this made me feel like I was Cinderella, and she was my fairy godmother. As we spent a large portion of the time practicing my powers on the help and then learning how to fly after, Aura made the room bigger. She told me that wings weren't her thing, but to help me get more acclimated with mine, she turned her backhands into crow wings, and we whizzed around the house, picking off the help like birds of prey. Twenty-four hours literally flew by as I gained more confidence while turning corners with my shoulders and allowing the wings to do a lot of the work. It felt like I was learning how to hunt with muscle memory kicking my brain into overdrive. I was now able to transport myself around the house with the help of my side snakes. Together we could allow the elements to take us where we wanted to be or move as a mist of three different temperatures around the house. After I asked a hundred questions about how slavery happened and how women went from being the most powerful to the most abused being on the planet. Aura also told me about how humans used to be an all-powerful race of beings with powers that rivaled the first divine beings and how those same beings turned them against each other. "So the part of me that is human is also Divine?" She nodded and sent a blast of telekinetic energy at me as I moved through the wall as hot air. "Yup, I would like to say more, but that's a story for another time and place." My body normalized as I landed on Gabby's back and pushed her face down to the floor. The sound of her nose breaking mixed with the sound of everyone else trying to escape made me laugh so loud the windows shook. "Oops!" I jumped off of Gabby and pointed at the windows so that they wouldn't shatter as Aura landed next to me. Seeing her true form was a true treat, but she shifted into her human form with long black locs and that beautiful dark- chocolate skin tone. Oh shit! I have a crush on my best friend. I can't! She's the mother of existence. Aura turned her head towards me and smiled as embarrassment creeped over my body. "You're getting better at hiding your thoughts and emotions. I sensed something about chocolate in my mind's eye." Hey now! What-What! "How much time do we have left on my little pocket home dimension thing?" "Two more weeks, and I'll have to leave to handle another one of my family projects." "May I ask what it is?" She shook her head no and looked at me with glowing eyes. "There is so much to tell, so I'll say this. I have a lot of moving parts to the mass awakening that I have planned. My next stop is in a dimension that exists parallel to this one." She must not be able to speak more on the subject, and I fully understand her now as a person who wants to keep my divinity a secret. "If I open the door and one of them gets out, will someone see them?" Changing the subject was becoming something that I'm getting really good at. It made me wonder if it was another thing that I was the goddess of. Deflection. "Their only power is to change into their animal form, but other than that, no one will see them as anything other than that because they've died and are bound to you." I noticed a couple of training sessions back that Gabby and the others were secretly talking about an escape plan like they weren't in a house with a Monster-Goddess and a Four-armed, Multi-eyed Deity. "You should also know

that this home is rightfully yours, and it is linked to your awakening."
My eyebrows furrowed from confusion. "Look at it this way, you
have a house with the ability to do whatever you want. If you desire
for it to turn into a monster cave, it will. If you want more rooms, they
will appear." I poked my lips out and looked Aura in the eyes. "Why
would I need more rooms?" "After you save the kids, they won't have
anywhere to go. Can they stay with you?" Hell no! This is not a foster
home for supernatural misfits! "Did you hear me?" "Nope!" "I don't
know. Being a guardian or parent isn't something that I think I want
to do." "Tia, It's tied to your divine role as the mother of monsters. I
can't take them to where I live because they're not of my physical
density. Please think about it. My only other option is making a pocket
dimension for them to live in and giving them to my daughter." Aura
exhaled as she placed her hand on my shoulder. "I've put a lot on her
plate by asking her to do the unthinkable. Right now, I'm asking you
to do the opposite. These kids need someone who is strong and
powerful." My ears rang from her words, and the more I thought about
it, I actually liked the idea of other people smacking the help around.
Like a little dragon taking Gammy-Goat by the legs and flying with
her through the air as she screamed or bleated. A smile curved my lips
at the idea of Gabby and the gang at the mercy of cute fairies with
monstrous appetites. I started to laugh as more scenarios played
through my head, and Aura removed her hand. "Okay! Let's do this!"
"I literally made a monster." "You did! ROAR!" The help scurried
out of the way as my roar moved around the house and carried my
intent for the necessary rooms. "Nine rooms. Wow! I'm glad I won't
have to share bathrooms with everyone. Wait! Will some of them
have to use the restroom outside?" "Girl, No! They're just as sentient
as you. Although some of them aren't able to take human form, so
they might remain in beast form but be seen as everyday animals like

them." "I hope this isn't going to turn into a house full of girls. I'll go crazy if our periods link up." "Oh, That reminds me." Aura clapped her hands, and a dark brown metal box with a large golden T on it appeared in my lap. "You made this from your own scales when you were Echidna and gave it to me as a gift. I made half of the stuff in there, and the rest are things that you made in your past life." It opened, and I looked down into a large room with shelves of weird-smelling items. Most of them glowed with various colors of light, while the others were surrounded with shadow energy. "Put your hand in and think of forgetful water." I did as she asked, and a glass bottle flew into my palm. It was the size of a perfume bottle but had mineral water inside that held specks of orange, yellow and green glowing bits in it. "It's enchanted to grant you the ability to cast amnesia on other deities. You have to let them know who you are and then allow them to take in some of your power so that you can use that as a way to make them forget." "It won't work on me?" "Nope, You're going to be the carrier of the forgetful magic. Use the steam that the twins make to spread it around the building, and then it will transport everyone here." "Do I drink it now?" "Yes, that way, it will be in your system prior to entering the building. There's an anti-transportation spell on the land that won't let you leave until they forget about all of you. The downside will be that they become slightly stronger, but they'll think that they ate all of the divine beasts and go on with their lives. Once you see that their house is up for sale, buy it and give it to me." That house was way more expensive than mine, and my millions had to be preserved for my new life of supernatural luxury. When I make them forget, I'll have to make them put it on the market at a lower rate. "Not knowing what is going on in your head is cool and all, but I loved our tele-empathic connection. Now we're like normal friends." "Not to put your business out on the front street, but aren't you way more powerful than me?" "Now that you've awakened to who you were in a past life, it makes your mind unable to read without you being fully aware. I'd basically be opening your head up like a baked potato." My eyes grew big from her analogy, and I had to change the subject fast before she said something else creepy. "What happened to the rest of the divine monsters?" "In your first life as Tiamat or the next one when you're Echidna?" "Both, I guess." Before she could answer, my forehead pulsed with energy, and I could see the events in my mind's eye. From my perspective, a large black and gold serpent dragon moved through the galaxy and destroyed solar systems as it moved on to use the excess energy to make life abundant in other worlds. Once it stopped, the dragon looked at me with golden eyes like mine, and I was sucked towards it at superspeed. In the blink of an eye, I was now in the dragon's body while it moved past planets until a swarm of multicolored lights flew at me. I opened my mouth and released a bright gold blast that decimated a large portion of them, but they returned fire with energy attacks that felt like razors piercing my skin. In another blink of an eye, I was now fighting in my monster form against Heather, who was in the formal attire of a goddess. Her boobs jiggled as she sent white-hot energy at me, and I let it collide with a golden blast from my eyes. The power gained momentum, and in the blink of an eye, I was standing on my balcony, looking down on a little girl with a fox tail riding a weird horse. It had small butterfly wings with a snake head that looked right at me. "Do you want to play Goddess?" "No, you go ahead." Its little wings glowed as they moved and carried them into the sky, and someone touched me on the shoulder. I turned to my right to see a woman that was my height with big brown eyes and rich brown skin. She leaned in for a kiss, and the vision ended as I blinked it away to look around my front room. "Whoa!" "Congrats, you just experienced your first waking vision." Aura got up and held her hands out to me. "Now that I've taught you everything that you need to know, I have to move on." I gasped and put my hands to my lips as my eyes grew big. "You're going to die?" My best friend looked at me with a smile while shaking her head no and shifting her weight to her left hip. "No, I try not to stay in this dimension for too long, or my enemies will start to sense my divine workings." I got up and hugged her as tears formed in my eyes. Our time together always went by so fast because we were having fun. "If you want to reach me, you'll have to go through the dream realm." "With all that you've taught me, you say that like it's something that's normal." She pulled away from our hug and held my arms while looking me in the eye with a serious look on her face. "Tia, this is your new normal." Her physical outline glowed with blue-white energy, and my best friend winked at me as she faded away.

That is still the coolest thing that I've ever seen. I picked up the potion that she made and put it up to my mouth. I expected it to taste awful, but it reminded me of peach and citrus-flavored syrup for slushies and snow cones. "Had to make sure that it was tasty so that when they ask what that smell is, you can say it's a slushie, and no one can sense the lie." Her voice echoed in my head as the memory of our hug made me wrap my arms around myself. At that moment, everything that I've been through played through my mind, and I now realized all of this led up to me remembering that I am divine judgment incarnate. All the time of the moonlight pocket dimension passed and made my ears pop as they receded into the sky. For the first time in three weeks, I walked over to the door and opened it with normal hands. The evening breeze billowed by me as I stepped outside with my servants waiting in miniature animal forms in the doorway. "It feels so good out tonight." I waved them outside, and the men turned into small dogs as Gabby and the old head turned into cats. "Ha! That's hilarious." The sound of heels hitting the pavement pulled my attention to the wrap-around driveway as Iris and her mother walked over to me. "Hey, We wanted to come to check on you, but your lights were out. Did you just get home?" Iris hugged me, and her mother bent down to pet one of the girls, but she ran off into the yard's overgrowth. "Aww, who were those little cuties?" "A friend had a couple of friends who needed me to watch their pets while they were out of town." Thinking of that reminded me to cast a spell on Gabby's cousin, who would probably go to the po-po about her missing family members. "Did you hear me, Idna?" The sound of my first name made me turn my head to Mrs. King, who placed her hand on my shoulder. "It's good to know that you're taking this well." "Thank you, Heather." I placed my hand on hers as some of the animals ran back into the house, and Iris pointed at the full moon. "I love nights like this. It's like anything can happen." "It is indeed a night of wonders." Ten minutes passed, and the remaining animals slowly walked into the house as a breeze blew by us. "I filed the paperwork, and you should receive a call from the bank sometime next week. I also contacted your school, and they have agreed to allow you to take all of your final exams at home with your principal as the administrator of the tests." "I'm down." "Great, I'll make it happen." They pulled me into a side hug before leaving, and I made my way into the house. Closing the door manually felt weird for something that I've done my entire life. With everything back to its normal size, I felt like I just came back from vacation. "Oh, Right. The little cousin that used my bathroom." I walked into the small downstairs bathroom and summoned the box that Aura gave me. She said that I had to think of what my problem was, and then the perfect solution would come to my hand. "I have a loose end to a home invasion problem." My ears picked up the sound of bird wings flapping at an extremely fast rate as a black hummingbird landed on my finger. It opened its beak, and a long tongue came out with an eyeball on the tip. Before my ascension, I would have screamed, but now this was just another one of those things that's normal to me. "You seek aid in dealing with loose ends, Mistress?" It had the voice of a grown man, and the storm cloud gray eyes looked me up and down while moving closer. "There is a young mortal who used this restroom before her family came back that night to rob me. I don't want her going to the police and filing a missing persons report." The bird's beak opened wide as the eyeball tongue retracted back into it. "Take me to the family who invited the person into the house." The box vanished as I closed it and exited the bathroom to search for Gabby. "Wait! What am I doing? Betrayal-Bunny!" The air around me shifted as it pulled my first love into the room as a rabbit. The bird flew over to her side, and she changed from animal to human while the hummingbird used its tongue to lick her exposed body. "I have her scent." It flew to the back window as I opened it with my mind and sent the rabbit away with another thought. An hour later, the small bird returned to my bedroom window, and it opened to let him in. I smelled smoke on his feathers as he flew past me and landed on my bedroom television. "It is done." The screen came on to show the news covering a house fire. Its headline said one survivor of a house explosion who is in critical condition. "I didn't want the kid hurt." "She will suffer small burns, and I placed a hex on her that prevents her from speaking about coming to this side of town. She unlocked the bathroom window." "That little bitch!" "Mistress, May I have some ice cream?" "First, tell me what your name is?" The eyeball looked at me, and the skin of the tongue made it blink a couple of times as the seconds passed. "You don't have one do you?" "No, I came to life when you called for me." Wow, I just assumed that it was some demon that Aura had made and placed in the box as a gift. "How about I call you Ivan?" "I love it, Mistress. Can I try vanilla?" I pointed to the small table next to the armchair in my room and made it appear with the lid off. "Enjoy yourself, Ivan." I turned and walked to the bathroom as the house turned on the shower for me. "Thank you." If the furniture started to talk, I'd have to make a supernatural kid's show about how to eat bad guys. I let my clothes dissolve into nothing as I stepped into the shower and used my magic to clean myself for an hour and a half. The mystical upgrades to my home allowed me to do things that made it feel like my own personal hotel. Once I returned to my bedroom and Ivan was gone, but the box was sitting on the table with its lid open. The urge to jump inside while being completely naked overpowered me, but my commonsense summoned a comfortable bra and panties before making silk pajamas appear last. My wings unfurled from slits on my shoulder blades and carried me over the large cavern of stone shelves. "Ivan-" "Yes." The sound of his wings was louder than the last time that I heard him as he zipped to my side and was now slightly more human-like. His brown skin and afro made him look like a normal black person, but the cyclops' eye and small buzzing wings made him look like an abstract fairytale creature. "Are you busy?" "I am not." "Can you give me a tour of this place?" He bowed and turned towards an aisle of plant people who moved like they were at a dance party. "These are flora spirits from different parts of the planet." He moved in closer to whisper in my ear as they stopped dancing and turned to look at us. "If they invite you to a dance party, say no." The smallest plant crawled over and handed me a leaf with writing on it. "Do you want to dance? No, Thank you." I used my pointer finger-claw to puncture the box for no and handed it to the little plant, who made another one from its face. "Come back so that we can make an element contract." I looked at Ivan, who nodded his head yes, and then back to the cute little plant person. "Okay, I'll even bring friends." "Come on, mistress." Ivan showed me seven more aisles that were filled with crystals, weapons, elemental spirits who were bound to inanimate objects, and glass jars filled with various parts of legendary beasts. The last aisle was full of spells in books, rolled-up scrolls, and frozen animals with plaques on them that said their name above the crime that they committed. "Those are familiars like the ones in your house." "What are you?" "Come on. My kind are over here." His little wings moved faster as they carried him to guide us to the longest aisle in this magical place. The shelves were made of thicker and darker stone that held various body parts of monsters with plaques that held their information on them. Ivan floated over to the empty one and took a seat on the shelf. His plaque said that he was made from a Bird-god's fifth eye. "You made me into this, Mistress. I am forever grateful." He bowed again and turned back into an eyeball. The next shelf had a bat-dragon pelt that looked up at me as I walked over to it. "A sky goddess's pelt." It dissolved into a brown cloud that fell to the ground and swirled like a hurricane at my feet before moving upwards and clinging to my clothes. Lightning formed around my lower arms as the surface of my clothes moved like clouds. "Okay, I'm definitely taking you with me." I pulled it off me and moved on to the next shelf as it floated next to me like a small tornado. "Oh, cool." A silver clam shell with blue scales on its surface hovered on the shelf in front of me. "Hello." The insignia glowed bright, and it flipped over as the top shell opened up to show me a black pearl. "Hey, Mistress. I heard that you inherited this dimension and couldn't be happier. I'm also sensing new wealth has entered your life." It was the voice of another male supernatural creature, and to be honest, it made me feel good. If I was surrounded by a bunch of females, I wouldn't be able to think straight. "Like you said, It's an inheritance of currency in the mortal realm." Silver light moved across the surface of the pearl, and he changed into a thin, dark-skinned man with even darker eyes. The shell became a business suit as he adjusted the inner shoulders of his blazer. He looked really nice, and although I'm at a part in my life where

I know that I want to be with a woman, and this clam-god would be a perfect date to show off to the world. "I'm Shelly." It was hard not to laugh as he extended his large hand. "I'm Idna, but call me Tia." "Oh, No! You are the mistress of the realm." He bowed as Ivan did, and I turned to the shelf behind me. A large pale tooth sat on a shelf above a plaque that said it belonged to a tiger goddess. I reached out to pick it up, and the moment that my skin made contact, the surface sparkled like it was covered in orange glitter. It floated off of the shelf and turned into a woman with all of my features but hazel green eyes. She pulled me into a hug as the little tornado moved out of the way, and Shelly looked to the ground. "I knew that it would work. Thank you, Goddess. From this moment forward, I am your loyal bodyguard." I tried not to look down at her big breasts as she moved while hugging me, but my eyes caught a glimpse of her partially smashed nipple and almost lost it. "Here." I placed the same amount of clothes on her that I had on, but the top changed into a t-shirt with a tiger claw on it. "I've watched the mortal world from the spiritual realm for millions of years. I couldn't wait to be called back into the world of the living." "Do you have a name?" "I had a name, but since this is a new life, I want a new one." "How about T-T?" She smiled and nodded as her fangs showed through her lips. The only shelf left on this side was a clear crystal bowl with normal-looking dirt in it. "The soul of a forest spirit." I expected it to come to life as I reached for it, but nothing happened until I had a vision of dumping it out into the backyard. "I know what to do with this. Let's go." Since everyone could fly, I grabbed Ivan, and we made our way up to the ceiling exit into my bedroom. "Shelly, T-T, Rooms will appear for you out there. Tornado, we need to come up with a name. Come here." It moved over to me, and I couldn't decide if I wanted it to be another divine helper or make it into an animal. The neighbors might think that I'm crazy if I pop up with another animal, and if I was being honest with myself, knowing that more people are coming to live here makes it kind of stupid. "I have an idea." I walked to the window and crawled down to the backyard as the tornado followed. "That is a garage. It's where mortals allow their transportation vehicles to live." It flew under the door, and the sound of metal being bent filled the air until the doors opened to show a brand new dark brown S.U.V. "Perfect!" I walked to the back of the yard where my grandmother used to have a garden and poured the dirt out onto the ground. It glowed with green energy as it fell into the ground and then moved upwards to take the form of a small bush. "Good evening, Mistress. I am Keierratavrit. I'll be your groundskeeper." Her voice reminded me of the nice guidance counselor who was young and full of life. "Can I call you, Keierra?" "You can call me whatever you want, Goddess." "Keierra, it is. I'll just sit this right here. The bush glowed as the ground beneath my feet pulsed with energy, and it merged with the house's magic. Whirling green energy moved around the bowl as it turned into a small fountain."Cool!" I decided that I had enough magic for the night, so I went upstairs and pulled Ivan out of my pocket for one last bit of supernatural delegation. "I need you to keep an eye on the five previously mortal spirits." "As you command, Mistress." It glowed with my gold energy and then flew out of the room while I made myself comfortable on my large bed. Once I started to feel myself becoming sleepy, I stretched one last time and drifted off into whatever lucid dream that waited for me in the fifth dimension. The first thing I felt before opening my eyes was a strong gust of wind that pushed against me as I looked down on a large island that floated in a dimension with purple-indigo energy in the background as far as the eye could see. Ari and Lina were at my side as my wings carried me to the beautiful island. Aura appeared next to me as I landed in front of a normal-looking house. "Come here. I am so proud of you." She pulled me into a hug, and my wings folded into the weird space of my shoulder blades that closes completely once they're all the way in. "I don't have a lot of time, but waking you up has tipped the scales of power, and the kings are suspicious of you." Her lower hands gently pulled the twins to her face so that she could smell their breaths as they licked her chin and cheeks like a dog. "Good, the spell has been activated." "Do they know that I'm a goddess?" "No." My best friend squinted as she looked at my aura and then pulled my head closer to look at the spot where my horns come out. "I'm looking for seal marks." She continued to search for another minute before backing up with a smile on her face. "Did I pass the test?" "You passed mine. When you change, there aren't any residual signs of it, and in doing so, you've also connected to me on the level of the four bodies. Our friendship is the heart. We think a lot alike, we're both beautiful goddesses of gorgeous melanated color and now that I've initiated your awakening, you finished it with flying colors." "All I did was fall asleep." Aura shook her head as she placed her hands on my shoulders. "No, You gave those monster pieces a place in your home, and your anger towards the beasts of betrayal has calmed down without even realizing it. Before you take your test, take a deep breath and allow the information to come to you. Take all of the awakened with you when you go to the wellness center." Her tone made it seem like she was about to say goodbye, and when she pulled me into another hug, I knew then that it was coming. "Before you say goodbye, I have another question." "Girl, you can ask me anything. Your body has changed, not our connection." "It has changed in the way that it brought us closer together. My life was a mess, and you're always there with a broom and dustpan. Thank you, Mist-I mean, Aura." Her divine laughter echoed around the open space around us as she gave me one last squeeze. "You didn't ask your question." I took a deep breath before asking the question about the vision that I had, where an extremely attractive young woman stood next to me on a balcony. "You have to allow some visions to happen on their own. If you think too much about them, it will impair your judgment. Just let it be." Time slowed down as she spoke the last part of her sentence, and I was snatched backwards until I awoke in my bed with a gasp. My breathing normalized, but I could feel my teeth and eyes tingle as they changed to human. Note to self: Practice dream astral projection more. I got out of bed and spent two hours getting ready for the day in my new bathroom. The helpful hint about using my mind power was something that I was grateful for as all the information that I sat through since ninth grade was at the forefront of my mind. "Grand rising, friends." Ivan, T-T, Shelly, and Keierra sat at the kitchen table while the help served them breakfast. "Grand rising Mistress." The sound of them speaking in unison was another way of the universe letting me know that everything was alright in the world. Well, my world. Darius was limping while wearing a diaper, and Dwaylon had bloody bandages wrapped around his waist as he slowly washed the dishes. The look on their tormented faces was enough for me to join my new family and enjoy the plate that was waiting for me. "Mmm, Bacon, Eggs, Toast, and jam. Oh yes, It is a great morning indeed." "Mistress, I think that it would be smart for us to call you Tia when the mortal gets her to administer your test." They nodded and changed from monster-like to full human, but Keierra went back to being a bowl of dirt. "Also, we made these." Each of them made wallets appear with all of the information that they would need in them." Since T-T spoke first, she handed me hers, and I looked over everything in it. "Welcome to the house, Cousin!" I tried my best to imitate a country accent like the one my real cousins have who live in Alabama. "I reckon Imma have better time visitin' than a fox in a hen house!" Yeah, I've found my soul family. "Sorry to burst your fun bubble, Mistress, but I saw a squirrel trying to get into the yard last night." "Is that not a normal thing?" "It was a divine servant of your neighbor's daughter, who is a nature goddess." Damn it! This must be what Aura was warning me about. Fuck! "He couldn't get in because I sent a female to distract him." I held my hand up to the pile of talking soil but quickly pulled it back after looking at the breakfast food covered in dirt. "Good job, Key." She gasped, and her dark black color gleamed with a speck of green energy. "Is that a Nigga-Name?" "Whoa! Whoa! Time out." I made a T with my hands and then looked at the moving pile of dirt. "I'm sorry, Mistress. Did I say something wrong?" "Let me ask you this. Where are you from exactly?" "Here. I came into existence right before this land mass was severed from the sunken part and the place that is now called Africa. The people who I looked over have settled into a land that they call Nigeria." I calmed down and was glad for her response. The last thing I needed was a racist earth spirit. "Key, It's called a Nick-Name." We ate breakfast as I schooled them on what happened to people of color on the planet and the slang that they would hear that was a result of our people making something from having nothing. T-T was the only one that wasn't mad, but I could see that this was a sore subject for her. She was a deity who died during a great war and was always on the side of humanity's ancestors. "So we don't attack the first white person that we see. Okay?" "Okay, Mistress." All of them spoke except for Key, and I had to engage in a stare down as the pile of dirt remained silent for an entire minute. "Fine! But if I sense a racist on the property, I'm going to maim them." "No! I can't have any slip-ups. After they've moved on to another place, you can break the ankles of whoever the nearest racist is." "As you command, Mistress." She changed back into her human form that was like mine, and I now realized that I would have to tell Principal Raymonds about how we're related. "Shelly, you're a family friend who knew my grandmother from church." "Yes, Mistress." "Ivan, T-T, you two are my cousin's on my dad's side. Key, You're a family friend who needed a place to stay." "Yes, Mistress." I noticed that the help was done and decided that they deserved a break, so I held my hands out as my energy brought them all to my side. I glared at Gabby first and changed her into a rabbit that ran away as quickly as it could. "T-T, did you cut the bacon?" Dwaylon started whimpering as she squeezed his bloody stomach wound. "Yes, Mistress. I hope you enjoyed it." "I did, can you cut up some meat for dinner? For some reason, I have been craving a glazed ham." since she was done with her food, she nodded and dragged him to the basement. I turned Evan, the one I tend to ignore, into a small bull statue that I moved to the kitchen counter with my mind and turned my attention to the remaining farm animals. "I think we need more eggs." Darius's stomach rumbled as his body changed into a female chicken, and he ran out of the room before he laid a bunch of eggs. Good, he's learning. My last little pet was the bitch who stole Christmas ten years in a row. The self-righteous abuser who kicked me in the ribs when I was a kid. The woman who said I was too young for pads because that would make me do unholy things. I looked from her to my new family, who were done with their food. "May I have a word with billy goats gruff over here?" My team got up to leave, and I stared at her for ten whole minutes before nodding my head at the plates. "Y-yes, Mistress." She gathered them all and took them to the sink as I followed behind her like she used to do to me. "Did you always hate me?" Silence. "Did you hear me?" I placed a monster claw on her shoulder and gave it a little squeeze as she ran them through the water. Yeah, the dishwasher is for me to use. "I-I wasn't ready to be a parent the first time and the second time was not something I wanted either." Her voice broke as she cried while scrapping the leftovers in the trash. "Yeah, Yeah. Where was that sincerity when I needed it? If you didn't want kids, then why were you out there being fast?" If I took this long to answer her, she would follow it up with an attack or hair-pulling, so I decided to give her a taste of her own medicine by grabbing her by the back of the throat and lifting her off of the ground. "I-I hated being born p-p-poor. The only way to secure a good life was to get pregnant and marry rich." She managed to catch herself but almost slipped on the floor as she regained her balance. "Did you love my mother?" "N-No, I hated having kids. I didn't want to give birth to the child that would give birth to Mother Gaia's beast of judgment." My eyes stung as they changed, and I let out a growl. "What?" "I come from a line of earth pr-priestesses who were in service to the Goddess. When she asked me to take custody of you, I said yes but resented my lineage for the divine connection." "You knew what I was, and still, you didn't show me an ounce of love." "I didn't want to be in service to a Goddess who allowed men to conquer us. That's why I turned to the Christian faith and it allowed me to find a husband. Those stupid visions that she continues to show me weren't as reliable as money. You were never hungry and had a roof over your head. No one touched you in a sexual kind of way, and despite going to that school, you're very smart. I-I think I did a good job, even though it was pushed onto me."

She must have figured that the worst that I could do was hurt her or kill her because the last part of her statement made it sound as if I should be grateful for my abuse. "That's the woman that I remember right there. The one who slapped me for asking about Jesus. The woman told her friends that it was unfortunate that I was as dark-skinned as I am. The woman that told me I wouldn't make it in the world as a shadow person." Her hands shook as I removed mine and walked back to my seat. "Hurry up. I'll be taking my tests in an hour." The old goat cleaned as fast as she could, and I noticed that she moved fast for an elderly woman. Her death and servitude-rebirth must have given her a boost in stamina. Note to self: See what we can do about making her feel like an old person. The sound of the doorbell made me look at the clock because I wasn't expecting my tormentor of four years to arrive yet. "I'll get it." Shelly called out. As I turned the corner, a chill crawled over my skin, and I made eye contact with Mrs King and then her husband. Story time. "What a lovely surprise, Thank you for coming over." "We came to see how you're doing, but we see that you have more guests. When did they get here?" Damn, Nosey! She scratched her nose as Mr. King handed me a bouquet of flowers. "I'll take those." Key walked out of the other room with a vase that was halfway filled with water and waved to my guests. "They arrived earlier this morning." "Hello, I'm Key, a family friend." I pointed to my clam-god accountant as he stepped behind them to shut the door. "You've already met my accountant Shelly." He waved as T-T and Ivan came down the steps. "We're her cousins. On her dad's side." Damn it, I hope that didn't sound rehearsed. "Hello, I'm Heather, and this is my husband, Zach. We stopped by to check on you. Do you need anything?" "She's in good hands." T-T leaned up against me, and for the first time in my life, I realized that her statement was true. I do have a group of people who have my back, front, and sides. Key even has the ground we stand on, so yeah, I'm good. "That's good. We all miss your grandmother very much, and I know that she is looking down on us from heaven." "Meow!" We looked up the steps to see my grandmother in her cat form, and I bit back the urge to laugh as she hissed. Mr. King placed his arms on his wife's shoulders as she walked away. "You got a feisty one there." "Yeah, her owner decided to leave them with me permanently, so I'll have to retrain her." Everyone laughed, and the Kings looked at us with slightly amused faces from our obvious inside joke. "We'll be going. You know what to do if you need us." They left, and all of us walked into the front room and talked while we waited for the time to pass. I learned that each of my new family members came from abusive homes like me and have always yearned for trustworthy companionship. T-T was the daughter of the lion Goddess Sehkmet who made the deserts of the world, and Shelly had a mother who sold him to a sea dragon for an immortality potion after she unknowingly gave her's to Shelly when he was an infant godling.

Key was a disgraced nature spirit who didn't want to marry a mortal chief that her mother arranged for her and was exiled from being the patron deity of her people. Ivan was plucked out of his owner's face during a fierce battle, and no one cared to pick him up except for Aura. The doorbell made us all look to the hallway, and I decided that I should be the one to greet my principal. "Grand rising, Mrs. Raymonds." "You can just say good morning, Idna." "You are not in the halls of the school, and you're most definitely not scolding a child. Save the negativity for next year's freshman." Her familiar frown turned into a weird smile as she stepped into the house. "Follow me." I took her into the front room and introduced her to the gang before rushing her into the kitchen. "You have two and a half hours. You may begin." Even though I knew the answer to every question, I made it appear as if I was having a difficult time on most of the tests until the very end. She never gave me the benefit of the doubt, and I'm sure that she thought that I was going to spend the rest of my life in prison. "I'm done." Principal Raymonds arched an eyebrow at me as she turned her head from the newspaper that she was reading. "With a full ten minutes to spare. I hope for your sake that I don't have to fail you and see you again next year." She took the test and began to grade it with a look of satisfaction as I purposely got the first one wrong. "Uh-Huh!" She continued to grade my tests while the look on her face changed, and I waited for her to finish in complete silence. "Congratulations, Mrs. Phillips. You passed." I grabbed the tests to see what grade she gave me on them and did a little dance from the two B+s and three A-s. "I brought your cap and gown just in case. Walk with me out to the car." My dancing continued as I called over T-T and Shelly, who joined in without question. "Hey-I passed. I'm walking to that diploma-Hey!" A chill crawled over my arms to let me know that an enemy was moving closer as Iris walked up the driveway. "What are we celebrating?" "I passed!" She screamed, and we jumped up and down like normal friends until T-T joined us to pull me away. "Yes, our girl did it." "You're the family that my parents were talking about." "Yes. I'm Shelly, a long time family friend, and this is T-T, her cousin." "Greetings to you. Isn't it a beautiful day?" "It is." Iris smiled, but I could see the gears working in her brain as she looked at the rest of the house guests that came outside. "That's my other cousin Ivan, and this is key, another family friend." "Hello." "Welcome to our home." Iris frowned as she shook Ivan's hand. "You all live here?" "Yes, we heard about our little cousin staying here in Maw-Maw's house, and we came to a decision to be here for our little cousin now that we are adults." "You all couldn't have come at a better time. We could use all the help we can muster for the kids at the wellness center. Do any of you want to join her in volunteering?" All of them nodded their heads yes without hesitation and looked at me as I smiled. "Perfect! I'll arrange a suitable mode of transportation for all of you." "No need, We have a ride." I reached into my left pocket and pretended to press a button on a keychain as Miranda honked her horn in the garage. Yeah, these are my people. "What's the address?" She pulled a card out of her pocket, and Ivan took it and placed it in his front pocket. "We will see you in a week." "I look forward to it." My little group walked into the house and waited for the door to shut and shared a look that brought the seriousness back to our situation. In a week's time, the other shoe would drop. My team and I spent seven days on our plan of action, and now that I had a seasoned strategist on my side, I felt another surge of confidence. I decided that Ivan should stay behind to watch over the help, and he agreed with a smile on his face. We made clothes to wear and brought extra things that we thought would come in handy as we filled Miranda's trunk. Miranda Drove us to the wellness center in half the amount of time with her magic until we reached a road that led into a forest. After riding through forest wildlife, we passed through an open silver gate. Shelly placed his hands on the wheel, and our little group took in the scenery so that we knew all the exits of the estate. Key pressed her forehead to the window and looked at the forest floor. "I'm not sensing any magic on the flora." T-T moved to the other window and exhaled before speaking. "I am, It's coming from beneath the building." I agreed with T-T. There was a weird residual power emanating from the ground. It reminded me of how I felt before my life started to change for the better, and I met my new friend group. "The exact number eludes my mind, but I can sense ancient creatures down there." "Good job, T-T. From this moment on, we will have to use our powers sparingly." Everyone nodded as

Miranda moved her windshield wipers, and we pulled up to the grand entrance. The kings walked out of the door with extra family members who were equally as attractive. "Everyone, this is my stepson and daughter, Artemis and Apollo. This is our Son Hermes. He's adopted." Damn, was all of that necessary? She could have just said these are our kids. "I'll send someone to get your things and park the car." Key stepped forward and grabbed the unnecessary car keys from Shelly. "No need, I'll park her and bring in our things. Where is the garage?" Artemis stepped forward and pointed as she walked to the passenger side. "How about I show you the way while they get a tour?" We spent an hour of my life that I would never get back walking around the facility and then thirty more minutes to give us key cards. Our wealthy hosts had an important meeting to attend, so they left us at the administration desk to finish the paperwork. Ten minutes later, Key joined us with her own card and a weird smile on her face. "This place is sick!" She moved her eyebrows as the desk attendant came by to take us to our rooms. "Hello, I'm Dina. Mrs. King has an entire wing reserved for the five of you. Follow me!" We walked to the west side of the building, where our bags waited for us in our rooms. "How did they know whose bag was whose?" "The kings are good at stuff like that. Mr. King has the hearing of a superhero, and Mrs. King always knows the right call to make. Apollo knows which medicine works well for our guest, and his sister keeps the wildlife at bay with her knowledge of flora and fauna." The five of us shared another look from our inside joke and passed by a room that made the hairs on the back of my neck stand up. "What's in here?" "Nothing at the moment." The door was all black with a keypad above its knob. "This way." We made a left and walked down a long hallway of empty rooms until we made a right to where our rooms were. "We use these rooms for the staff, and each of them has a phone. Lights out at nine, and please don't wander the hallway or the grounds after sunset. It's dangerous. Any questions?" "Yes, what are the meal schedules?" We came up with a plan to eat less and then pull food from a portal that's connected to my house. "Breakfast is seven to eight-thirty. Lunch is from noon to one-fifteen, and dinner is from six to seven." "Cool, what's for lunch?" "Show up at twelve to see." All of us shared another look that said we'd be eating out of the bag, and I realized that she didn't tell us what we would be doing first. "Hey, excuse me. Dina" "Yes." She flinched after turning around, and I thought for a second she saw my true form. "Are you okay?" "Y-yes. I thought I saw something behind you." "Were you going to ask me something?" "Should we go to the guests and start to help them while we wait for lunch?" "No, wait in your rooms until lunch. There's a community room down that hallway with everything that you all would need to entertain yourselves." Dina walked away while placing one hand over her forehead and the other against the wall as she braced herself to walk away slowly. "Her brain waves indicate that she was recently frightened." T-T narrowed her eyes as she watched Dina walk away, and the rest of us headed to the common room. It had a large TV with a large shelf next to it that was full of videotapes. Another shelf was filled with board games and playing cards. "This makes me feel like we're guests instead of volunteers." "I agree." "Yeah." "Let's play with these colorful cards." Everyone turned to look at Key, who held up the deck of cards. "What? It's not like we're in immediate danger. Come one." She was right If they planned to attack us, we had the upper hand with our numbers and how well-prepared we were. "Who's up for a game of gold-wish?" "You mean goldfish, right?" "Nope!" After an hour of playing a game that was very similar to Goldfish but with weird rules and then the intercom called us to lunch. "If they feed us some nasty white people food, I'm going to go back there and make my own food." I said as everyone laughed. We passed empty rooms that made the hair on my arms stand up, and I made a mental note to figure out why this place held a strong static charge. "Whoa!" We stepped into a large cafeteria that was way too big for twelve kids and ten staff members that lived here. The food smelled amazing, but the look on the guest's faces said that they were in constant pain. "Hello." "They can't speak." The attendant sitting at the table pointed to his throat, and I looked closer at their throats to see thin scars on the girls and thicker scars on the boys. "I'm sorry." If Aura had sprung all of this on me at once, I would have went the fuck off just by seeing the little kids in pain. None of them touched their food, even though it smelled amazing. "What can I get you?" The kitchen hand picked up some tongs, and I chose fried shrimp, garlic mashed potatoes, and pan-fried broccoli. "Where shall we eat?" "How about by the window." Even though we just arrived, It felt like we were at boarding school during spring after all the other students went home. The moment we sat down, T-T leaned in while chewing on a chicken tender. "Is this normal?" "For a place that's supposed to make them better, No. But the food is good, right?" Everyone nodded as they dug into their food, and we tried not to talk about supernatural stuff for forty minutes. I was pleasantly surprised by the food, but we were monsters, and I wanted to eat more junk food that my body burns through. We didn't say anything the entire walk and closed the door as we piled into my room. "I'm not sensing anyone watching us." Key placed her palms against the walls while she closed her eyes and turned her head in different directions. "Did anyone sense anything from the kids?" "Yes, but hold on, someone is coming." A minute passed, and we heard the footfalls of three people moving to our wing. "Open the door." Shelly opened it, and the sound grew louder as they turned down our hallway, and we pretended to do separate things. "Yeah, I was telling her that her man did not want her, but she has these weird trust issues, Girl." I touched Key's knee as she poked out her lips and moved her head. "Okay! Her Nanny messed her up big time. My Mama's cousin's best friend's sister's uncle's doctor's mother said she saw them at the ice cream spot on twentieth and Fox." The King adult-children walked in, and we turned to look at them. "Hello, welcome to our home." Apollo's smile was so gorgeous that I almost had a hard time deciding who was more attractive, Him or his sister. "How was your meal?" Iris stepped out from behind her tall sister and pulled me into a hug. "It was interesting. Why didn't you tell me that this wellness retreat was for children who are mute?" "Because that would be a lie. They're not mute." My team and I shared a look, and I backed up from Iris with a frown on my face. "I saw their throat scars, and that was the quietest meal that I've ever had." "Of course you did. You're a newly awakened Goddess." My lawyer's eyes glowed with rainbow colors as her siblings summoned light to their hands. "I guess the cat's out of the bag!" T-T made claws, and my team powered up as they lunged forward to attack us. Iris hit me in the chest with a stream of rainbows, and I fell back against the wall. "It's on bitch!" My monster voice came out as a shockwave that sent her flying through the doorway. Out of my peripheral vision, I could see Shelly and T-T going up against Artemis, and Key pulling Apollo into a puddle of quicksand. "Tell me, Iris. Were you really my friend?" She floated upwards as her laughter echoed around the hallway. "Hell No! After we absorb your power, we'll sign your money over to us, and I won't give you a second thought." "I'm going to enjoy eating you." My teeth elongated as I stepped forward, but a flash of white light appeared on my left and took the form of Heather King holding the pizza delivery girl, Sambrina. "Stand down, or I'll kill her." I gave the signal to my friends, and they vanished from where they stood to reappear as a charm bracelet on my wrist. "I did what you asked. Let her go, Hera!" She lifted Sambrina into the air, and her eyes glowed as she sucked out her soul. "No!" The second that I moved my legs, I was overcome by a sudden sense of tiredness that made me fall to the side, and everything went black, like when Aura killed me in that dream. I blinked my eyes open to look around a room that was not at all what I expected. I was still in my human form, but now I wore clothes like the guests, and my cornrows were taken out as I moved my thick hair out of my face. I still wore the charm bracelet, but my wrist was sore as if they tried to take it off by force. "Good, You're awake." Mr. King appeared out of thin air and stood next to me with a weird smile on his face. "I'm forbidden from touching you. You're safe." "I highly doubt that." "I promise." He took a seat at the edge of the bed and smiled while crossing his arms. "How did you do it?" "What?" He exhaled an annoyed smile as he looked to the floor. He vanished without saying another word, and I waited for a long time for someone to show up, but no one did. After an entire day went by, I tried to summon my team, but no one responded. I even called out to Miranda, but it resulted in her appearing as another charm on my bracelet, and our bags appeared next to me on the bed. Three days went by, and I had to survive off of junk food until Iris appeared in the room without an entrance. Not even the twins dragon heads could make a portal for us to walk through or transport us out of here with enveloping magic. "Hey, Bestie!" Iris teased. "Hey, Bitch what's up?" I answered. Since her mother went back on her word, I decided to fight divine fire with divine fire from now on. She floated off of the ground with her hair moving as if she was underwater. "You haven't even asked how we incapacitated you." "Ha! You mean the food that we ate for lunch. I'm a new goddess. Not stupid." "Oh, really. You thought that you killed that old bitch, but I did. You thought that your life was going your way, but that was me. I fast-tracked all of that shit!" I narrowed my eyes at her as I got up off of the bed. "You killed her?" "Yup! I pushed her down the steps with a thought." I lunged at her, but she glowed and vanished into nothing as I roared in anger. "You want some company? Here girl!" Her voice echoed around the room, and the blank wall across from me melted as it opened into a hallway. "Whatever you can do, I can do better!" My monster body parts came out as I got up and walked down the newly formed hallway and froze when I saw a community room full of monsters. Everyone turned to look at me as I normalized to my human form. All of them had a visible glowing number eight on their bodies that made the air smell like static electricity. "Cool, A new friend." A female demon that was my height with orange eyes and sharp teeth walked up to me with her hand out. "Hi, I'm Lakshemi, but you can call me Mimi." She had one brown bat wing and long black claws like mine. "I'm Tia." Everyone gasped and got up out of their chairs to walk over to me with looks of astonishment on their hybrid faces. "Like the supreme Goddess of Monsters, Tiamat?" A small Japanese girl with a fox tail tugged on my hand with her little claws as she bounced up and down. "Calm down, Fefe. She just got here." "Welcome to life as a battery for the immortals. I'm Fin, a chimera-pegasus." "I'm Bri." "I'm Anna." "I'm Michele. We're Cerberus." A young brown skinned girl about my age stepped forward Her eyes changed from honey-brown to blue and then green while the personalities announced themselves. "I'm Ray, and this is Jakir. We're the reincarnation of Janus." He motioned to the empty space next to him, and I waved as the next person stepped forward. She was drop-dead gorgeous in her frozen tundra kimono and long silver hair. "I'm winter, an Ice demon." Her cold aura reminded me of Lina as she moved back to let a young dark-skinned man with fire-bird wings step forward. "I'm Firestone." He didn't say what he was, and I just guessed that he was some kind of phoenix. The remaining three didn't say anything as everyone waited for me to speak. A faceless ghost, a shadow on the wall, and a pretty little girl dressed in boy clothes. "Fefe got it right, I am the reincarnation of the goddess Tiamat, and I'm here to save you." Half of them looked genuinely surprised and happy, while the others shot me looks of disbelief. "No one is more powerful than the overseers. The quicker you realize that, the better." Firestone turned and walked away as the creatures who didn't speak joined him. "Are you hungry?" I held my hand out to my room, and my bag flew into my palms. "Nope, I got that covered. I refuse to eat any more of their tainted food." After Mimi pulled me over to the other side of the room, I sat and told them about my plan and showed them my charm bracelet that currently housed my friends. Firestone snorted and crossed his arms. "Prove it." I can't. For some supernatural reason, my powers aren't working correctly." "Did you eat her food twice?" I nodded at Mimi to answer her question and realized that it was the baked dish and the cookie that I had with the ice cream. "Beware Greeks with gifts. That's how they abducted all of us." Three days passed, and I expected the King family to make an appearance or use their powerful voices to fill the room, but nothing happened. My powers were still being blocked by something, and the more time I spent here, the more I felt like I was a caged animal. I wanted to spread my wings, and not being able to summon the twins was like having missing limb syndrome. The only good thing about this was that I found out that the kings are part of a large group of deities from all of the pantheons who suck the power out of lesser divine beings to continue their reigns of tyranny. Having half of my power with minimal physical affection made me feel like I'd been demoted to an assistant. My stomach burned like I was being stabbed over my belly button, and I lifted up my shirt to see a small golden eight forming on my dark skin, I gasped. "What is this?" "Just breathe, it will be over in a second." Mimi placed her hand on my shoulder as the pain subsided, and I now had a tattoo like theirs. I felt a sudden wave of exhaustion wash over me as I tried to get up but fell back onto my bed. It reminded me of the time that I took a sleeping pill a year ago and slept for half of a day. "Can we have some more of your snacks?" Fefe's question made me smile as I drifted off into the dream realm. My consciousness floated through the darkness before I snapped my eyes open to see the team that I thought abandoned me. "She's awake!" I turned my head to the left to see T-T sitting on the bed next to me. My clothes clung to me as static electricity crawled over my body. "Miranda. I missed you too." My new family and friends filled the room with looks of concern as I slowly sat up. "You've been asleep for nine days." Key reached over and hugged me, and I could see that their appearance had changed the morale of the other divine monsters by the smiles on their faces. Firestone's lips moved but his words were inaudible. "I didn't hear that Say it again!" The Phoenix demigod mumbled something that sounded like you were right, but I needed to hear it again. "Huh, The forest creatures outside didn't hear you. Can you repeat that?" He exhaled a hot breath that raised the temperature of the room. "I'm sorry I doubted you, Great mother of monsters." He pretended to bow to the floor, but Shelly stepped forward and sat on the bed. "Our connection to you was interrupted by the queen goddess's spell. We didn't know that it'd make us revert back to inanimate forms." Miranda made more static roll across my body, and it was hard not to laugh out loud from the way that it tickled. "We have all of our powers but can't teleport out of here." Damn it! "How do you feel?" I didn't know how to answer that. I felt like my head was being hit repeatedly with a hammer, and my stomach still stung from the unwanted tattoo. "Like I'm hungover, and this is killing me." I lifted up my shirt and looked at a healing scab. "That was not like that yesterday." The new monsters talked amongst themselves as my team looked from them to me. "It's a good thing, right?" "They'll be pissed about it. But they won't come in here." "Mr. King and Iris visited me here before they opened the wall into a hallway." "Yeah, right! None of us has seen them for a hundred years." I leaned forward as my monster features formed on my face. "They've had all of you here for a century?" My blood boiled at the thought of them being trapped here as living batteries for those parasites. Three of them were children, and the most beautiful one of all was missing a wing. Yeah! I'm going to fuck Iris up first! The stinging sensation on my stomach faded as my horns and wings grew out of my body, and all of my energy returned. How could I forget that it was my own rage that fueled my very existence? Every member of my team bowed as I got up to stand, and the rest of the monster followed suit. "There is no way in hell that I'd let them continue hurting all of you." Lina and Ari moved out of my sides, and I rubbed their chins. "We've missed you, Goddess!" The sound of their combined voices was music to my ears. I held my hands out to the captured monsters, and my energy enveloped their bodies as it changed them. Mimi let out a loud roar as her wing grew back, and the others let out similar sounds while the glowing eights vanished. I didn't know how powerful they were or if they'd be able to put up a fight against the overseer, but I figured that at least they could have a fighting chance like this. "Key, Shelly, Miranda. Once I make way for us to escape, get to the kids upstairs and take them home." "Yes, Mistress." "What about us?" Firestone and the others stepped forward with smiles on their faces from the newly revived powers. "You all are with me. We're about to fuck this place up. Let's go!" I sent a blast of energy at the ceiling and made dust rain down on us before leaping upwards through the large hole with everyone following behind me. The tunnel I made led upwards through a thick stone floor to the basement of the facility. I exited the hole first with T-T right behind me as we landed on the cool stone floor. "You know what to do." Miranda peeled off of my clothes and joined my rescue team as they left through the exit first. I looked behind me one last time before flying through the exit in search of the divine thorns in my paw. "Up there!" I smelled Iris and Artemis before they appeared and tackled her as she tried to hit me with a rainbow blast of energy. "Not today, Hoe!" The two of us fought for dominance as we tumbled, and my support began to fight other deities who teleported into the hallway. T-T let loose an onslaught of attacks on two opponents, and the minor distraction almost cost me a wing as Iris directed hot rainbows out of her eyes. I dove to the side and used telekinesis to pin her against the wall with her laser vision pointing downwards. "You can't hold me forever, Monster!" She was right, but I had a plan. The twins extended themselves over to where she was and combined their elements to make forgetful steam that rendered her unconscious. "Nighty-Night!" I turned and allowed the steam to fill the small space of the hallway but focused on making it transport the captured monsters while working its magic on the evil deities. "Damn, Mistress. They're out cold." I simply nodded as Shelly came around the corner with a sad look on his face. "They've eaten all the children and are on their way here." Just as he finished his sentence, Hera and Zeus appeared in a burst of light. "I told you, she is Her!" Hera spat. Ari and Lina kept spewing their mist that moved on its own to the vents. "Yes, My queen. As always, you were right." "Go get the others." White lightning moved across the King of the gods body as he tried to teleport but fell to the floor, and I was left alone to face my ancient enemy. "I know that you were something special from the moment that you came to my house to sell those atrocious candy bars. I wanted to suck your soul out like I did that little friend of yours, but the idea escaped my mind every time." Hera smacked her teeth and summoned more of her peacock-colored energy to her palms. "It's sad that you were able to procreate and even worse that you let the world treat women of color the way that they do. You have failed as a queen, and once I've defeated you, you will forget about all of us and sell your house for less than market value." Before she could throw her multi-colored energy balls that were bigger than the ones that belong to her weak husband. I fell backwards and allowed my body to turn into the mist that I was spreading around the facility. "Not gonna happen. I've been to every single place on this planet. You can't hide from me, bitch!" "I'm not trying to." I solidified behind her and punched her in the side with all of my strength. She gasped and sucked in a lot of the mist as she fell to the floor. "I don't sense anyone else here, Mistress. The others have teleported home." T-T walked over to my side, and I held my hands out to instruct the mist to spread to every corner of the facility. "Let's get out of here." The mist moved upwards and transported us to my front room, which was now full of newcomers. "Is everyone okay?" My team nodded as I looked around the room and noticed that the Shadow was gone. "Where's the shadow?" "It left the second that you reinvigorated our powers. Thank you, by the way." Mimi answered. "I think she deserves more than a thank you." Aura walked out of the wall to my left, and I ran to hug her like it was the first day of school. "I missed you, friend." "I missed you too." "You're definitely not mortal." Firestone walked over and pulled her hand to his lips. "That is no way to talk to someone's grandmother." "Mmm, let me know if you need help chewing your food." "Boy, get out of here." "We can't, we don't have rooms yet." Fefe held her fluffy tail in her hands as she moved closer and smiled at Aura. "I like your hair." "Aww, I like your tail. It's so pretty." Aura replied. "Ivan, Can you come here?" He walked in with a handful of wooden animals that he placed on the side table before hugging me. "I'm happy that you've returned safe and sound, Mistress." "Me too, Thank you for looking after the help. Were they good?" I asked, while patting his back. He let out a laugh as he picked up the wooden goat. "She gave me attitude for a couple of days, but in the end, I showed her who was in charge. I see we have new arrivals." "Yes, please show them to their rooms." "As you command, Mistress." He walked out of the room and took our new friends with him as I turned to face Aura. "How do you feel?" "Like I should have killed all of them." "Trust me. I know how you feel. They're technically my in-laws." My eyes glowed as our eyes met. "Wait, What?" "It's a long story." I definitely wanted to know more about that, but my mind wouldn't drop the experience that I just went through. "Did you know that it was going to go down like that?" Aura held her hand up and shook it like a tambourine as she squinted. "In a parallel dimension, you ate all of them and then gave the monsters that you saved their divine power. Typhon wakes up way too early while in school and eats his racist teachers." "Oh! That's all?" She slapped my shoulder as the wooden animals made sounds. With a glance of my eyes, they glowed and changed back into their normal hybrid forms. "Thank you, Mistress." "Bring us refreshments." Gabby nodded as her team went to do as I commanded. "I have one more surprise for you. Come here." My best friend took me by the hand, and we walked over to the large window that faced the King's residence. "Express how you feel." Aura pointed at the house, and the windows exploded one by one. "You try." I closed my eyes and took a deep breath as I imagined a house fire. "Damn, Girl!" The smell of burning housing materials filled my nose before I opened my eyes to see everything engulfed in yellow flames. "I'll let you know when it's officially ours." "I have so many plans for that house. Thank you, bestie!" We remained in our side hug as we watched the house continue to burn, and the new guests filled the house with noise. Ten minutes went by until the fire department showed up to try and put it out, but I kept stoking the flames until every single thing was reduced to ash. The sound of Fefe telling Gabby that she had to play with her or she'd eat her made us laugh as the fire continued to incinerate everything. "I'd say what a fitting end, but you and I both know that this is only the beginning." Aura let out a laugh while leaning her head against mine. "You ain't neva lied." I said, as the firefighters finally managed to put out the flames.

<u>W</u>icked Betrayal

I shuffled the deck of cards I received from my mentor for my sixteenth birthday sixteen years ago and spread them out in front of me as my client anxiously waited in her seat. "Reba, choose three cards." The image of two swans landing in a lake entered my mind as she did what I asked and then changed to procreating seahorses. After she was done I chose nine cards that I placed underneath hers. "Are you ready to hear what the universe has to say?" "Yes, lay it on me." I flipped over the cards that she chose and gasped as the mental message that I just saw made sense. "The Queen of Cups represents your heart being open for new love. The Empress also signifies your calling in love because of that. This King of cups may be a male but I'm sensing it to be a female lover coming in to offer you love." "Yes, I'm a lesbian." I flipped over the first three cards that I pulled and smiled as this was turning out to be a love reading that was foretelling energies of a match sent by the goddesses. "The Emperor is the divine match for the Empress, and the knight of swords coupled with the chariot is a sign that your true love is being divinely guided because she knows who she wants." I flipped over the next three cards and this time she gasped like she knew their meaning. "I had a dream last night where I was riding a horse with a torch in my hands and stopped in front of a woman who was holding a bag of coins." I thought about it for a second before letting my guides feed my intuition with more information. "Your desires will pair well with the money that she has, but this knight of cups is signifying that you need to be patient because this love will come to you." I flipped over the last three and stared at it with wide eyes as I looked down on the Queen and King of Pentacles with the Lovers. "The both of you are destined to meet each other. Do you go to a park that's near a lake or pond?" Reba smiled as tears gathered in her eyes and nodded. "Yes, I live down the street from a park that I'm always scared to go to because of people and their dogs." I saw the image of a bright sunny day in my mind's eye with three trees being significant to the message. "Today is the thirty-first of April, so on the third of may, go to that park around mid-morning and where the color red to attract your true love." I reached out to pick up the cards as she whipped away her tears, and a stronger vision came over me. Reba was walking alongside her future love in the park when a big dog came out of nowhere. The owner called the dog's name, but I didn't hear it because it wasn't vital to the message. I did hear the sound of a whistle and a taser crackling with electricity. "Do you own a taser?" "No, should I get one? Oh my God, will we get robbed?" "No, dogs don't like the sound of them, so buy one and get a dog whistle as well. You'll need it." "Okay, Thank you for everything, Vanna." "You're welcome. Just heed my warnings." Since she was my last appointment of the day, I closed up my shop and walked to my car as the winds of change blew in my direction. The image of a calendar changing to April of next year entered my mind and I took it as a sign that there would be major changes happening to the world next year. "Hey, Madam Seer, can you tell me what the Lottery numbers are? Or is that not what your pagan demon Goddess has in store for me?" He laughed as I turned around to see Doctor Manuello putting his bag into his luxury car. This man was the type that relied on science instead of faith and one of the people who started the petition to get me and my "Devil worship" out of the strip mall. "No, but I can tell you how good your Mama's pussy tastes." I smacked lips together as if I was savoring a flavor and watched his smile fade while I got into my car as he called me a dyke while giving me the finger. "If only he knew that my Goddess was very real. The religion that he was indoctrinated into was forced on our ancestors during slavery hundreds of years ago. It was one of the things that I truly hated about this world. On the way home, I stopped at the grocery store to get myself vegetables for dinner. When I reached for the portobello mushrooms, my ears began to ring as a thick-bodied woman walked by, and I saw her name written on a caution sign. "Excuse me, is your name Devon?" Her nostrils flared as she looked me up and down while stepping backwards. Right! Sometimes I forget that Covid gave people situational complexes about their personal boundaries. "Yeah, Why?" "I'm a Medium who channels spirits, and they have a message for you." She rolled her eyes as I saw an image flash in my mind of an elderly woman who wore a nurse's name tag with the name Ernestine on it. "Ernestine has a message for you." "Oh, Hell no! I rebuke you, demon." The ringing in my ears intensified as I saw the sign of a popular club in neon lights, and then I saw someone pouring something into an alcoholic drink before handing it to her. I took a deep breath so that I could give her the message that her grandmother wanted me to relay and actively ignore her rude behavior about my gift. "You're going to go to a club and receive a drink from a stranger. DON'T DRINK IT!" She made a cross with her fingers while reciting some nonsense from the bible. All I could do was shake my head and hope that the message got through because her grandmother's spirit pulled away as she practically ran out of the produce section. "Whelp, I tried!" I grabbed all of the ingredients that I needed for dinner and hoped that I wouldn't have another experience like the one I just had. Once I was home, I started dinner while pulling out my phone to call my mother since I hadn't heard from her in almost a month. She didn't answer, so I decided to call my father, who sent me straight to voicemail and then sent a text message saying that he would call me after he was done with work. I waited for him to return my call, but after two hours of waiting, I decided to drop it and get in the shower to wash away all of the day's energy. Being the black sheep of my family was something that I was used to, with them all having the ability to cast mystical energy and me being a high priestess of the goddess Hecate. You would think that I would be treated like the prize that I was, but they view me as an embarrassment on our long line of powerful Sorceresses and Sorcerers. The only family that treated me like I was a person were my grandparents, who left me enough money to be able to follow my passions and not have to worry about how I was going to pay bills. My mother resented me even more after that because they gave each of them a million dollars while I had ten million in a trust. After my shower, I poured myself a glass of wine and decided to see if I had any new followers on social media before going to bed. There were several messages from the people who watched my collective reading videos, but I had the same amount of followers as yesterday. I decided to scroll up and nearly screamed out loud when I saw that my family was in Brazil for my twin sibling's birthday. "They told me that we'd celebrate their thirty-fifth birthday next week at my family home." Tears fell down my face as I scrolled up to see all of my family there and that they had been in Brazil for two weeks. If I brought this up, my parents would just blow me off or act as if I was causing a scene by speaking up about my feelings. My ears rang as I felt a hand over my shoulder and saw the image of my grandmother smiling at me in my mind. "Thank you, G-Maw! I love you too." Seeing that really brought down my mood, but I knew that this was something that was common in the black community. Everyone who was born in the fifties and sixties were given a broom to sweep everything under the rug that they didn't want to talk about. As an eighties baby, I always spoke up about what was bothering me but lost a lot of friends along the way of self-discovery and self-worth. Once I fell asleep, I had a dream where my grandparents walked into my shop with gifts in their hands that they presented to me while tears flowed down their faces. I received a purple snake from my Grandmother that turned into a scepter when I grabbed it, and my Grandfather placed an Amethyst crown on my head. "We are so proud of you. Just by being you, you've healed our family line. Don't let them get to you. Remember that we are always here with you." The dream changed to show me standing in front of my mentor Ms. Donna on my sixteenth birthday when she gave me my first Deck of Tarot cards and a box of crystals that I still have to this day. Her head split into three separate heads as she winked at me her rainbow aura that only I could see flowed around her body to the point that it became a tornado of whirling colors. "You've got me, and I'm always here for you." I woke up to the light of a rising sun on my face a full minute before my alarm went off. "Yea-yeah-yeah. Don't be mad that I beat you." I didn't have any appointments, so I decided to use the day to do walk-up readings with the people I came in contact with. After a well-needed meditation where I spoke my daily affirmations out loud, I took a shower and got ready for the day. "I'm going to wear this little number with these little cuties right here. Oh! I hope I meet a gal with good energy that can handle my spirit." I saw a small flash of light in my right eye peripheral vision that I took as my guide's way of confirming that as a yes. It gave me an added sense of giddiness that I took with me to the diner down the street, where I ordered a veggie omelet with hash browns and herbal tea. I tipped the server with fifty dollars because she always treated me nicely before leaving to allow my intuition to guide me to my first walk-up. When I walked outside, both of my ears began to ring as I passed by a tall, gorgeous dark skinned woman with big breasts and long curly hair. "Hello! Can I talk to you for a minute?" "Oh honey, I'm not joining whatever religion you're with if the god is male." That made me smile and giggle as she stepped closer, and I checked my watch to see that the time was nine-thirty-six. Cool! "I'm actually a medium. Would you be up for a reading?" She looked me up in the eyes while extending her hand as she stepped closer with a smile on her face. "Yes, and I'm Erin, B.T.W." "Oh, right! I'm Vanna." A second passed before I realized that I was staring at her too long, and she furrowed her eyebrows at me before clearing her throat. Seeing her smile pulled me out of my daze as the spirits around her showed me a broken heart coming together. "I see love coming into your life. If you don't mind me asking, are you single?" "Oh, so this is how you get numbers?" "No, I'm being serious. Our spirits are showing me two halves of a heart coming together to form one heart." "I am single. Give me something else." The image of a hospital and stethoscopes flashed in my mind. "It doesn't really work like that, but I am also getting a sense that you're new at your job. You're a Doctor." "Yes. I'm the only woman of color and the youngest doctor in my pediatric ward." "Let's see what else the spirits want me to convey." I took a deep breath as the image of her pulling me by the hand at night entered my mind. "Would you like to have dinner sometime?" That made her arch her eyebrows as the wind blew like it did yesterday, and she slowly nodded her head. "I would love to. But I have a confession to make first." The ringing in my ears calmed down as she looked to the ground and then back up at me. "You gave a woman a reading last month who was a friend of mine. She told me that you were a lesbian who was single, and I've known about you for quite some time." That explains why my ears were ringing louder than usual. It was times like this that I really questioned how my abilities worked for me when it came to things like this. I'm a powerful seer who didn't see this coming at all. "Put your number in my phone, please." I did as she asked, and we shook hands before I hopped in my car and waited for a message from spirit as to where I was going to go next. After driving for twenty minutes, I found myself at a hair salon where I got my hair done by a woman named Mellisa who needed to hear a message of an apology from her father, who used to abuse her. From there, I bumped into a Mexican named Hector, whose late uncle warned him about buying weed in a bad area and getting robbed. I hit the freeway and stopped at a gas station where I gave the woman at the pump next to me reading about not having sex with the man that she had been on three dates with because he was HIV positive. "Thank you, I have been on the fence about letting him go in raw, and now I'm glad to hear that my intuition was on point." "Tatiana, Allow me to tell you something that was told to me when I was in college. Always listen to your intuition." A woman pulled up to the pump on the opposite side of mine, and when I saw her son in the back, I felt the urge to do another reading. "Hi, Is your name Ashely?" "Are you going to serve me with papers?" I bit back the urge to laugh as I shook my head no and extended my hand for her to shake. "My name is Vanna, and I'm a Spiritual Medium. Can I give you a reading?" "Yes, I'm always open to hearing good news." "Then don't shoot the messenger." I took a deep breath and allowed the message to come through as I saw peanuts in my mind's eye while feeling a minor irritation in my throat. "Right off the back, I can see someone choking after eating nuts. Does your son have a peanut allergy?" "Not that I know of." I saw the image of children and a pinata that confirmed my suspicion about this being for her son. "Have you been invited to a child's birthday party?" "Oh my God, That's where we're headed now." "Okay, that's what it is. Keep a watchful eye out for what he eats. I'm really seeing something about peanuts." "I will, thank you!" As she walked to the car, she stopped and turned on her heels to face me with a concerned look on her face. "My sister is throwing a carnival-themed party. Do you think it has something to do with caramel popcorn and peanuts?" "Your question made the right side of my throat itch. Yes, that's it." "Thank you, Ms. Vanna." "Your welcome, Ashley." After I left the gas station, I received a text message from Erin that said she was happy that we met, and I pulled into a fast food restaurant so that I could reply. We ended up in an hour-long texting conversation where I found out a lot more about her, and we made plans to have dinner later that night. I went inside the restaurant to order a large fry with a sweet iced tea and felt the pull of spirit towards a man sitting with his family. "Hello, my name is Vanna. I'm a spiritual medium, and a Mother is coming through with a message about a car. I see a car riding down the street with a trail of fluid behind it." The wife gasped and slapped her husband's arms as they locked gazes. "I told you that I had a dream about the brakes going out on the car, Mikey." As she spoke, I felt a sudden urge to yell like I was in danger, and so I put my hand on the table and looked him in the eyes before speaking. "This feeling rarely happens when I channel spiritual messages, so I need you to be very careful when driving home. I'm sensing that it would be dangerous to take the freeway." "That's it! I'm calling my sister Linda to come and get us." After his wife started to make a scene, I decided to get away from this energy. Spirit didn't give me any other signs, so I went shopping for new clothes to wear on my date since my hair was already done. "Hello, if there's anything that you need help with, just let me know." "I will thank you." Once I had four pairs of shoes, three outfits, five dresses, and four new pairs of sunglasses, I handed over my bank card to pay the thousand dollar total. "Would you like to donate to one of our three charities?" One of them was for LGBTQIA+ kids, while the other two were for kids on the spectrum of Autism, and the other was for the future leaders of tomorrow. "I'll donate a hundred dollars to these two and a thousand for my little rainbow squad." "Oh, Wow! Thank you." Growing up, I didn't have anyone to talk to about liking girls, and I made myself a promise that I'd help people in any way that I could. "Here you go, Have a nice day." When she handed me my card, I received a vision of her being held at gunpoint as the sunset outside. "What time do you close?" "Nine o'clock. Did you want to come back for these?" "Uh, No! Close at seven." She frowned and laughed as another customer came up to the counter. "Just because you spent a thousand dollars and donated another thousand doesn't give you the right to tell me when to close." I took a deep breath as my spirit guides showed me images of her life that I could use to get her to believe what I was about to say. "When you were six, you stubbed your toe on a coffee table and said a curse word that resulted in your mother whooping you. You lost your virginity in college with a guy named Billy. You first wanted to be a health inspector but realized that you had a gift for clothes." Her frown turned into a wide-eyed stare as she put down the other customer's clothes and leaned against the counter. "H-How do you know that?" "I'm clairvoyant! Now listen to me. Close at seven. Not Nine!" "Why?" "Because if you are in this store by yourself, you'll be the victim of a robbery." "You should listen to her. She's a powerful seer and helped my brother get over the loss of his boyfriend, who passed away last year from covid." I turned to face the woman who I never saw before and smiled as she did the head nod that was universal to all black people. "He was a client of yours." I saw the image of Timothy Derlings in my mind as I looked her in the eyes. "You're Timothy's sister?" "Yup!" "How's he doing?" "Very well, thanks to you." I left the boutique with a smile on my face as I headed to my car and felt her spirits give me a pat on the back. Normally I allow people to use their own discernment when it comes to my readings, but sometimes it is better to give them a strong nudge for their safety. The rest of the day flew by super fast as I went home to try on the clothes that I bought and then do a collective reading that carried on for an hour. Erin called me at eight o'clock to say that she was on her way to pick me up, and that made me slightly nervous because it'd been a while since I went on a date. My abilities always show me what the person's true intentions are, and my last three girlfriends were nothing like they claimed to be. A drug addict who planned to steal my wallet, another who wanted to have a threesome with her male cousin, and the most recent was a rich girl whose parents covered up a hit-and-run murder. I pushed all of that nonsense to the back of my mind as I finished getting ready for my date with Erin. When she called to say that she was outside, I did the silliest thing that I could to calm my nerves before walking outside to see her standing next to the passenger side door. "Good evening, beautiful." "Back at you, Gorgeous." We hugged, and I inhaled her sweet aroma as she rubbed my lower back and giggled. "You smell amazing." "So do you. Is that from Armia's collection?" "Wow, It is! Your gifts are always on point." To be truthful, all of my senses were stronger during the spring. It was like my inner divine feminine energy was waking up with the planet every year around this time. After Erin let me go, she turned around and opened the door for me. "Oh, Are those manners?" "Yeah, I save them for special instances such as this." The drive to the restaurant was full of good moments where we learned more about each other by playing twenty questions and truth, or truth, as she called it. "So we come from funny-acting families that treat us like outcasts. We're the youngest child, and we're self-made. Talk about a perfect match. Are your parents still together?" "Yup, they even teamed up on ignoring me ninety percent of the time. What about your parents?" "Mr and Mrs Orthodontist are still together and have a family practice that my siblings work at as well. I'm the only Doctor that works at a hospital." Wow, that's like me being the only seer in a family of magic casters. I couldn't teleport or shapeshift or even change the weather with a spell. But if you need to know what spirits are around you, I'm your gal. When we walked up to the restaurant while holding hands, my ears began to ring, just like in my vision, and the rest of the night went as smoothly as my day did. I just hoped that the clothing boutique owner would heed my warning and close early. The last thing that I wanted to see was her on the morning news or, worse, dead. Our date went by as quick as my day did and I found myself reflecting on my walk-ups. "Are you okay?" "Yup, I did a bunch of walk-ups today, and it drains my energy reserves." "See, it's women like you who would make great superheroines." "Nah, I would hate to save an elderly man who was misogynistic or a catholic priest who abused kids. I'd let them die." She laughed as we pulled out of the parking lot, and we had the most intellectual talk about theology, where I had to hold back my knowledge of the supernatural world. That was something that I would tell her after we got married, like my favorite tv witch. The last thing I needed was for her to know that I come from a family of beings who live long lives and can cast mystical energy to manipulate an outcome. When she pulled up to my house she put the car in park before leaning forward to open the glove box. I thought she wanted to kiss so I leaned forward with my lips puckered as she laughed and told me to hold on for a second. "This is for you. Open it first and then we'll see if you still want to kiss me." When I unwrapped the gift I gasped at the sight of a purple crystal rose that was made of raw amethyst. "Oh my Goddess, it's beautiful." She leaned forward at the same time that I did and pressed her soft lips against mine as time stood still around us. Our kiss lasted longer than I thought it should for a first date but I couldn't get enough of her. It was like she was someone that I had a past love life with and my lips knew the exact way that we should kiss. "Damn." She said, pulling away. "Thank you for tonight. I needed something to get my mind off of things." "Likewise, I had a patient die yesterday and it broke my heart to have to tell her mother that she didn't make it." Hearing that made me want to invite her inside to have a drink but I needed there to be a reason for a second date. "When would be a good time for a second date?" The smile returned to her face as she looked me in the eyes. "I'm free tomorrow. How about I make dinner for us?" "Sounds good to me. Your place or mine?" "Mine, I've been neglecting my kitchen and I think she is feeling some kind of way about it." I laughed so hard that I snorted twice and it caused her to laugh with me until I closed my gift box and got out of the car. "I'll text you my address when I get home." "Okay, I'll bring the wine." "See you then, Vanna. Good night." "Good night, Erin." After she left I did a little dance as I walked into my home and searched for the perfect place to put my new gift. Since it was for me I didn't want to put it on my altar so I placed it on my nightstand that didn't have a lot of things on it. Once I meditated and put it on my selenite slab I took a shower before falling asleep while watching nature documentaries. I had a recurring dream of my family standing in a circle while talking and laughing as they ignored me. Everytime I tried to get closer to them they moved out of reach to the point of sprinting away. I continued to follow them through the house until they separated and I was now walking into my mothers home office. "Mom, why wasn't I invited to Brazil?" "Because you're an embarrassment to this family. I should have smothered you when I felt your absence of mana." I blinked and my mentor Ms. Donna appeared next to her and grabbed my mother by her hair. "How dare you treat your child like that. Apologize, NOW!" Her voice echoed around us as my mother tried to run but Ms. Donna yanked her back into her seat. "What did I say, Bitch!" "I-I'm sorry." Even though she apologized I could tell that she didn't mean it and it still hurt me to hear her say that. "Begone!"

My mother vanished in a puff of smoke as the room changed and we were standing in my front room. "Remember what I told you. Blood doesn't make you family. Trust does." She pulled me into a hug as I cried and woke up at three-thirty-three in the morning. "Thank you spirit. I am grateful for you always being here with me." My mentor passed away in her sleep five years ago but I always felt that she was always by my side. I meditated as my ears rang and fell back asleep to have dreams of me and Erin on three more dates. The first was of the date that would happen later tonight. The second was of us going to the movies and the third was when we'd share a cheese pizza at my place where it would lead to sex afterwards. I woke up to the sound of my alarm going off at seven and started my day by making myself breakfast before I sent a good morning text message to Erin. She replied with a smiling emoji and a rising sun thirty minutes later after I got out of the shower. Seeing her message made me giddy like a schoolgirl for our date later so I had to calm my nerves before shaving my legs. I didn't inherit my family's ability of healing fast like my siblings or the power to use arcane knowledge to heal. That reminded me of the dream that I had so I called my mother and was surprised when she answered. "Yeah!" "Good morning mom, How are you?" "How many times do I have to tell you to call me by my name?" Yep! That's the bitch I know and was unfortunately born from. "My apologies, Vira. I hope you slept well." "I didn't. What do you want?" "Why didn't you tell me that all of you were going to Brazil?" "They don't like your kind down there and we didn't want to have to put off another family vacation because you chose to be gay." I bit back the urge to call her a bitch like I did when I went off to college so I took a deep breath and decided to tell her about what's been going on in my life as of late. "Work has been going well. I've helped so many people and I've even met someone new." "Okay, did you come to rub it in my face?" "Well that's all that I wanted, I love-." She hung up before I could finish my sentence and I went to my room filled with crystals to meditate. "I am not my family. I am not my mothers anger. She is a being of her own free will. I'm living in my power and will not let her anger invade the good that the spirits have brought into my life." After I spoke my daily affirmations out loud several times I picked up my sound bowl and used it to clear out the excess energy of my aura. "Thank you spirits, ancestors, Goddesses, gods, Mothers, fathers and sexless energy that has been with me since birth." The image of Ms. Donna holding my mother by her hair entered my mind while I was getting dressed and I laughed so hard that I could barely stand. That elevated my mood as I went to the grocery store to buy the wine for my date later. I bought two bottles of white and one red with the intent to keep one of the bottles for myself when my family gets on my nerves again. I bumped into three people who had the same spirit attached to them that turned out to be their father. Each of them were half black and half something else but when they learned that they were siblings I could sense that this was the beginning of a beautiful relationship. It made me want a stronger bond with my own siblings but I knew that it would be like force feeding children food that they didn't want. The last time we were together was for my graduation party that my grandparents forced everyone to attend. After I got everything that I needed I went to check out and felt another spirit nudging me to speak to the cashier. It was a mother who died of a heart attack while her daughter was out at a club and she didn't find her body until the next morning. "Hello, How are you today?" "I'm good, Cindy. How about you?" "I'm doing okay. Did you find everything that you needed?" Her mother kept tickling my ears and it made me giggle as I put all of my stuff on the conveyor belt. "I'm a spiritual medium, would you be open to a reading?" "Yes, I had a dream about my mother last night and she's been on my mind all day." "I'm picking up on that. She keeps tickling me. Is that something that she did with you?" Tears formed in her eyes as she rang me up and I heard the name Boo-bear. "Did she call you her little Boo-Bear?" "Yes, Whenever she would wake me up for school, she'd tickle my feet and say It's time to get up Boo-bear." "I'm also sensing that she passed in her sleep and you didn't find out about it until the next morning." "Yes. I shouldn't have gone out that night. If I knew that that would be the last time I'd see her I wouldn't have gone out with my friends." Her mother showed me the image of forgiveness and trying to hold water in her hands as Cindy whipped away her tears. "Don't beat yourself up for things that were out of your control. Your mother is telling me that you have to let that go. It was going to happen whether you were there or not and beating yourself up isn't going to help you heal. Your mother keeps saying that she is proud of you for going back to school and for honoring her by naming your daughter after her." "Oh my god, I just had a baby and she has the same color eyes as my mother." "She's saying thank you for being the light of her life but I'm also seeing a father holding a toddler. Are you close with your father?" She shook her head no and I realized that the mother wanted her to reach out to her father. "She wants you to build a connection with your dad." More tears fell as she finished ringing me up and nodded yes. "I sent my dad an email earlier this morning, asking if he wanted to meet his granddaughter but he hasn't replied yet." "He will. He thinks about you all the time and wants to be in your life just as much as you want to be in his." I felt her mother's spirit pull back as I handed her my card and then watched as her mother hugged her over her shoulders. Cindy shivered as she put in a discount for me and then took my card to finish my transaction. "Thank you. I really needed to hear that." "You're welcome. Take care of yourself, Honey." I spent the rest of the day being excited about my date later and when the time came around for me to leave a weird cold chill crawled over my body. It vanished just as fast as it arrived and I spent the entire drive to Erin's house thinking about what it was. She stood outside of her two story home with a bouquet of real assorted flowers in a clear crystal vase and a huge smile on her face. "Hey, Gorgeous." "Good evening Beautiful." "I love this dress on you." "Thank you. Your catsuit is hugging all of the right places." Her body was the right size of thick and tall with her big breasts sitting nicely. "This is for you." "And these are for you." She walked me inside of her beautiful home that smelled like vanilla mixed with cooked vegetables. "Are you hungry?" My stomach grumbled as she finished her sentence and we looked at each other as she walked me to the front room "I am, Are you coming for my job?" "As long as you don't start practicing medicine I won't have to. Come on, I already have our plate made in the dining room." She pulled my chair out and grabbed the wine opener as I felt the weird feeling crawl over my body again. "Are you okay?" "Yeah, It's been one of those days that started off on the wrong foot." "Aww, I'm sorry to hear that. Do you want to talk about it?" "No, talking about those people will bring down the mood. Tell me about your day." Erin told me about how she lost another patient and one of her nurses has gone missing after going on a date with a butcher that she'd been dating for a couple of months. The energy of the conversation gave me the chills and I kept seeing a large feast laid out in front of me with a human skeleton on the table. It gave me the creeps because I knew what kind of world we lived in so I went to the bathroom to shake off the feeling by splashing water on my face. "Are you sure you're okay?" "Yeah, I'm good." "Is it okay if I hug you?" I loved how she asked before touching me because it showed how much she valued someone's personal space. "I am a hugger. Come here." The weird feeling intensified but I didn't see anything from spirit so I remained in her arms and it turned into us slow dancing the night away. Before I left we took several pictures that she posted to social media after I added her as a friend. I drove home on cloud nine as I thought about how good it felt to be with someone who was on my level mentally. Most of the time I felt like an outcast in the lesbain community because I wasn't able to hook up with every lip out there so it made me hesitant about meeting new women. Once I made it home I uploaded my own pictures to my personal page and put the flowers on the table in my front room so that they could catch the sunlight as it rises. The weird feeling followed me home so I decided to take a shower and go to sleep. I had another dream about my family being distant but this time my grandparents appeared and pulled me into a hug before the dream changed to show me walking towards large doors that had a pentagram in between outward facing Crescent moons. The doors opened to show me a large entry room that was filled with beings of all kinds going about their business. Some were animal hybrids while others had elemental auras like my family members. Everyone waved as I passed by and flashed me smiles like I was well acquainted with them. "Hello, High priestess." The sound of my late mentor's voice made me turn around but I woke up before I laid eyes on my late mentor who taught me everything I know. "Seriously! Ugh!!" Trying to figure out what that place meant stayed on my mind for the rest of the day as I tried to not get angry from being so close to seeing my mentor face to face. The last thing she said to me was that she was proud of who I've become and how I haven't allowed my family's wrongful treatment of me to darken my heart. Hearing from her niece that she died in her sleep solidified that I'd lost the only person in the world that had cared about me. I meditated and said my daily affirmations before making something to eat while watching the news. The screen changed to show a breaking news story coming on and I turned it up as the reporter stood outside of the club that I had a vision of. "I'm standing outside of The Lovers lounge, where Devon Rogerson says she accepted a drink from a man last night that was laced and he followed her to her car where he then raped her." I realized that I can't save everyone but when it comes to black women I tried a little bit harder because of how the most horrible things happen to us. It was times like this that I was grateful for my heightened awareness and discernment. Seeing that in bold letters made me think of the time that I was vacationing in greece and knew that this attractive girl was trying to come back to my hotel room so that she could let in her male friends who had plans to rape me. After I came back to America I reached out to Ms. Donna for more intense training that made me into the powerhouse that I am today. Ding! I looked down at a text message from Erin saying good morning and it brought back my happiness as I turned off the muted television to reply with sun emoji. We communicated that way for a half of an hour before she had to get back to work and I looked over my schedule to see how many appointments I had today. A group of three siblings at ten, a man named Eric Billings at eleven-thirty and a woman named Helen at one. "Alright supreme seer, let's get this day started. We've got people to connect with loved ones on the other side." Being a Cancer sun and Aquarius moon rising gave me all of the extra power that I needed to put emotions into my words. It took me a little longer than usual to get dressed because I couldn't decide on what heels I would wear with my new clothes, but after my guides helped me I was ready to go. The drive was full of idiots who couldn't use a turn signal to save their life and when I pulled into the parking lot I almost got into a car accident with Doctor Manuello. "I guess you're used to flying brooms, huh?" I smacked my lips together really loud as he walked by and looked up to the sky before looking at him. "Is your moms favorite fruit pineapples?" "Look here bitch! My mother died thirty years ago. Watch your mouth or I'll have to do something about it." "What about your oath?" He stepped forward and I made the hand symbol for protection just to scare him but I watched small orbs of blue light swirl around his head as he jerked forward as if something hit him. "W-what have you done to me?" I saw the image of an elderly latina in my mind smacking him upside the head and realized that his mother intervened on my behalf. "It was Juanita who did it." "How do you know my mothers name?" She showed me the image of her holding a wooden spoon and tapping her foot repeatedly as he turned around to leave before pulling away. "Next time I'm going to get the spoon." Hearing that made him sprint to his practice and give me a laugh while I made my way to my shop. That was the first time that a spirit affected someone on the physical plane and I patted myself on the back because I was leveling up as a spirit medium. When three people walked in at ten for my first appointment I was ready for them with a big smile on my face. "Good morning. How are you three doing today?" "Good." They answered in unison and followed me to the room that I use for large parties. Right off the back I felt really hot as the image of a house on fire entered my mind. "I have to introduce myself, I'm Vanna, a spiritual medium and I channel the spirits of deceased loved ones." "I'm Thomas, these are my twin siblings Hailey and Jacob." The image of burned bones entered my mind as I shook their hands. "I'm feeling flames burn down a house. Has someone you know died in a house fire?" "Our parents died in a house fire seven years ago." "They're telling me that you three blame yourselves for the fire." Hailey gasped and looked at Jacob who leaned forward and put his head in his hands. Thomas took a deep breath before putting his hand up like he was a student. "We put our money together and bought them that house after my father retired from the post office." The next thing that I saw was a mother holding three babies with a medal around her neck and a huge smile on her face. "Your mother is stepping up with a smile on her face. She's showing me three babies that she's very proud of. I keep hearing they did it." "We created an app that translates documents once you've scanned them for people who migrate from other countries, in honor of our grandmother who was haitian." "She's patting you three on the back. She is also saying that you have to forgive yourselves. There was no way that any of you would have known about the fire." Their spirits pulled back and I took that as a sign that they've said all that needed to be said but another spirit came forth with angel wings. "Your parents have stepped back and an angel is standing behind all of you." They shared a look that said that it meant something serious as a chill ran over my body. "We are the descendants of a fallen angel that chose to die with her mortal husband." For the first time in my life, I was at a loss for words as its wings enveloped them, and I saw the light glowing on separate parts of their bodies. "Jacob, you have a strong aura. Thomas, you get vivid glimpses of the future while awake, and Hailey, you have the power to heal." Each of them nodded as the angel stepped back into the spirit realm. "As someone who is a part of the real supernatural world, I have to say that was even a surprise for me." "Yeah, you smell like magic." I frowned because that was the first time that I heard that in all of my thirty-three years of living on the supreme goddesses' green earth. "What kind of magic?" "You have a weird eye on your forehead." "Yeah, as a diviner, I can see what was, what is, and what will be." "No, it's something else." They spoke in unison before getting up to let me shake each of their hands. After they left, I went to my restroom to see what they were talking about and didn't see anything on my forehead. When the time came for me to have my next appointment, I was surprised to see that it was someone that I knew from another friend. "Eric Billings, How are you?" I instantly regretted it when I saw the spirit hovering behind him with a hospital gown on. "Not good. Kerian died last month, and I can't shake the feeling that he has something to tell me." His assumptions were spot on with how visible his deceased lover was. He kept holding up six fingers and then made the sign for making it rain in the club on a stripper. "Are you expecting some kind of payout from someone?" "No, But Kerian did play the lottery often." My right hand began to itch as the spirit showed me the sign of a wallet stuffed with money. "You might want to check that ticket. I'm seeing a wad of cash." He nodded in agreement before pulling out his own wallet and using his phone to scan the ticket. "Oh, Shit! He won!!" "No, You won." When he hugged me, I could see Kerian join our hug before he pulled back into the spirit realm with a smile on his face. "He also wants you to know that he is now at peace, and he loves you." That was the first time in a while that I saw a spirit that was more like a ghost that couldn't pass on, but now that I've been leveling up, it only makes sense. I had some time to kill before my next appointment, so I treated myself to a taco salad bowl with chicken.

The universe gave me a little surprise when I sensed my next appointment looking at me, and Helen walked up to my table with the same exact food-order as mine. "Helen, Good afternoon." "Hey, what a weird coincidence." "Yes, Would you like to join me?" "I would love to." When she sat down, I heard a toddler laughing, but I knew that at her age, she couldn't have kids. "I've been having dreams of holding a baby girl with my son's eyes." My ears began to ring as the cashier came out to wipe down the tables. I saw a gathering of blue orbs fly around her waist right before she bent over the table. "Hey, excuse me, Destiny." "Is everything alright?" "The food is perfect. I have a question. Did you just have a baby?" She looked at Helen and then back at me with a confused expression before nodding her head yes. "I did. Her name is Havana. Would you like to see a picture of her?" "No offense, dear, but we're discussing something important. Can you come back in five minutes?" "I think this has something to do with your son, Vincent." "Wait! Vince was your son?" "Yeah." She dropped the rag and pulled her phone out of her pocket. "This is his daughter." Helen gasped as she took the phone with one hand while putting her free hand over her mouth. "This is the little baby from my dreams." I loved the way the universe worked in our favor when we least expected it. "I-I'm a grandmother?" "Yes, she's with the sitter right now, but I would love for you to meet her." "I would love that too." "I get off at four, and it normally takes me an hour to get to the sitter's house and then home on the bus." "No-No, I'll come back to pick you up and take you to get this little bundle of cuteness." "Thank you, I appreciate it." "It's what grandmothers are for. We also have to discuss Vincent's trust that I'm going to give to you." Destiny blinked repeatedly as she bent down to pick the rag up off of the floor. "What, so he wasn't lying about being rich?" "No honey, I'm not rich. I'm wealthy. It's like comparing night and day." "Can I walk out of my job?" "Is one hundred and forty million dollars enough to do so?" "I'll be right back." Destiny turned around and walked back to the kitchen while we enjoyed our food. "I would have never come to this side of town had it not been for my appointment with you. Thank you, Vanna." "I would love to take the credit for this, but his spirit has been guiding the three of us together." Helen looked up to the ceiling and put her hands together. "Thank you, Vince." Telling her that he was behind her would have deflated the moment, so I dug into my food as Destiny returned with her purse and a meal of her own. "I have to eat this here, or my little bottomless pit will ask for a bite every five seconds." The three of us laughed, and it made me think of how it would be if I had my own child or children someday. I would love to teach them how to use our family gifts even if they turned out to be able to cast mystical energy or use divination like me. "That was delicious. Thank you, Destiny." "Girl! Thank you. I can now go to college without having to worry about how I'm going to make ends meet and move out of the run-down apartment that I'm in." "The house across the street from mine is a part of my son's trust." I saw the spirit of Vincent standing in between his mother and Destiny before he stepped backwards into the spirit realm while mouthing the words thank you. "You're welcome." "Huh?" "Your son just thanked me." "Is he still here?" "Sort of. He is always with you, but he is also on the spiritual plane and at peace." After I hugged both of them, I went back to my shop to do a collective reading with tarot cards and finished when I received a surprise visit from Erin, who walked in with flowers. "I was thinking about you, so I said "Go see that beautiful seer", I hope this isn't too much?" "Nope, It's just enough. Thank you." She smelled amazing, and after we talked for an hour, we made plans to have a date later this evening. "I'll call you later." "I'll be waiting." The weird feeling returned, but I shook it off as she left and returned to my recording room to do a love reading since my future lover made my heart flutter. Time flew by as two weeks passed, and I grew closer to Erin after we had sex on our fifth date. My family was even more distant than usual, but now that I had a girlfriend, none of that mattered. When my sister Nika liked one of my pictures, I called her to have lunch and catch up, and she surprisingly said yes. "Hello, sis, How are you?" "Good, You?" I went to hug her, but she didn't get up or put any energy into the side hug. Typical. "I'm doing great. My business is doing even better, and as you can see, I meet someone new." "Yeah, that's all good. We need to talk about you being with a person who isn't from a magical family." "How is that any of your business?" "We have our ways of knowing stuff without communicating with ghosts." "Spirits, Nika!" "Whatever, Vanna." "So let me get this right. None of you casters care to reach out or even check on me, and now you think you can come into my life and tell me who to be with! Girl, Bye!" I got up to leave and noticed that there were a lot of spirits attached to my sister. All of them were of the recently deceased with an energy around them of dying horribly. "Why do you have traumatized spirits around you?" "I understand that you're the bridge between the living and dead, but you're not my mother. Don't question me, little sister." I left before I said or did something that would drive an even larger wedge between us. We never had the typical sister relationship where I could go to her about my problems because she was a sorceress and I was a seer. But to hear her say that they wanted me to be with someone from a magical family was absurd. We live in a world where I help people who don't even know that the supernatural one exists right under their noses. The second I got home, I screamed so loud that I summoned a bunch of blue orbs that whirled around my body for the remainder of the day and didn't go back to the spirit realm until I meditated twice. I tried to call Erin, but her phone was off, so I sent a text message instead. She replied ten minutes later by saying that she was swamped at work and would call me back later. I didn't want to add to what she was dealing with, so I asked her to come by later to talk. Ten minutes later, she called me and asked if I was going to break up with her, but I reassured her that it was about family drama. With the bad vibes that my sister gave me still lingering around my aura, I decided not to do any readings and clean up before my girlfriend came over. The hours went by, and I waited for her to call or text to say that she was on her way, but she never did. Out of nowhere, the weird feeling returned, but this time, I saw more spirit orbs everywhere I looked. "What are you trying to tell me about spirits?" They whirled over the flowers that I got from Erin and then took me into my bedroom to show me the crystal flower that she gave me. I put it in my lap to meditate on what they were trying to show me, and after sitting on my bed for an hour, I didn't get anything. The spirit orbs still floated around the flower, but I found it frustrating not to receive any messages. "Fuck!" If she was ignoring me, I would slash her tires and mail ransom letters to her house. "But what if she's in danger?" My ears rang as I saw the orbs move rapidly on the ceiling, and I took that as a sign. I called her cell phone as I drove to her house, but it went to voicemail. When I pulled into her driveway, I saw that her lights were off, so I asked the spirits for a sign of whether or not she was home. After seeing a large red X in my mind's eye, I left and drove across town to the hospital to ask if she'd left yet. "Hi, can I help you?" "Yes, I'm looking for Doctor Johnson. Has she left already?" The nurse frowned and looked at the woman sitting next to her, who shrugged her shoulders. "There isn't anyone by that name here. Are you sure that you're at the right hospital?" "Yes, She's a pediatrician who works in the children's ward. I sent her flowers two days ago." "We don't have any doctors here by that name. Let me ask around. Maybe she might have been a consultant." "No! I know she works here." "Erin!" I made my way down the hall to the pediatric ward as the nurses followed me, but I didn't give a shit. There was no way that Ms. beautiful girlfriend lied about being a doctor, and I know for a fact that she worked here because I saw her work badge the night that we had sex for the first time. "Ma'am, you can't go back there." I kept walking until I reached the part of the hospital where they had all of the pediatrician's pictures on the wall over a rainbow, and I searched to no avail. My heart started to race in my chest as the male security guard came up to escort me out. "You don't have to be so rough." "Get your black ass out of here Nigger!" He tossed me to the ground with enough force that I scraped my hands while trying to break my fall. "Filthy monkey!" I turned around to face him and narrowed my gaze on his as he looked at me with a smug expression. "You'll regret that." He turned around to walk away, and I watched him hold his stomach before he groaned and shit on himself. It was a bittersweet moment as he tried to run into the building with shit coming out of the bottom of his pants legs. "I guess that's what happens when you think you're the shit!" After I got up, I noticed that my hands weren't bleeding at all and were perfectly healed. "Okay, That's new!" The smell of vanilla entered my nose, and I remembered that I was searching for my girlfriend. On my drive home, I decided to use the crystal flowers to find her family in the morning, and I would have to ask my family for help as a last resort. Later that night, I had a dream that I was on a date with Erin, but she didn't have a mouth. She kept pulling me into hugs where she would nuzzle my neck with her nose, and I would hear her voice speaking telepathically to me about how happy I made her. I wanted to say make instead of made because she was still alive, but she kept shaking her head no. When I woke up, I felt like I was saying goodbye to her, and it made me feel a weird sense of grief that I realized was like the sensation that came over me when I met Erin. I pulled cards for the energy that I was feeling and gasped as I looked at the two cups, the seven of swords, Death, and the magician. Every time I tried to pull extra cards for clarification, I would feel the spirits tell me no and then show me the crystal flower that Erin gave me. "Okay, show me where her family lives." I held the flower close to my chest as I remembered how good she made me feel, and the image of a senior living center that I've been to numerous times entered my mind. It was followed by the names Terri and Marcella Johnson but ended there, so I got dressed while thinking of what I would say to them. Once I got to the facility, I was taken to their room but warned that Terri had dementia and wouldn't remember his family at all. "Here we are." "Thank you, Rhonda." After she pressed the doorbell, I waited five minutes until a woman that looked like an older version of Erin answered. "Hello, I'm a friend of your daughter Erin. Can I talk to you?" "You must have confused me with someone else. I don't have a daughter." "She-

she remembers. Let her in, honey!" She turned around to talk to her husband, who I heard walking towards the door. "Quite down, Terri. For the last time! We don't have a daughter. The child that we had died at birth thirty-five years ago." "Let her in, Please." "Come in, please." She stepped aside as I walked through the doorway, and I watched as she helped her husband, who was on oxygen, get back to his chair. "You remember my sweet girl. Everyone else forgot. But I remember." "Terri, we don't have a daughter." "Y-you kicked her out after she told us about her sexuality, and I'll never forgive you for driving a wedge between me and my sweet girl. She was a healer." "He gets like this sometimes. Are you thirsty, honey?" "Yes, can I have something to drink?" "Sure darling, is lemonade good?" "I would love that. Thank you." After she left to get me something to drink, Terri pulled out an envelope and handed it to me. "Don't open it here." He whispered to me as he held my hands together with tears in his eyes. "They don't want us to remember her, but I do. My mind wasn't fully intact for their spell to work." Hearing him say that made my heart race as I thought about my run-in with my sister yesterday and kicked myself for not thinking that they had something to do with all of this. I knew that they didn't like me, but hexing my girlfriend was a new low, even for them. My grandmother's number one rule about magic was not to cast spells on each other. I shoved the envelope into my purse before his wife returned with my drink and downed all of it in one sitting before leaving. "Thank you for stopping by, but please don't return if you're going to come in with that nonsense." "Yes, Ma'am." Once I got to my car, I opened the envelope and sobbed as I looked at a baby picture with a lock of her hair in a bag attached to it. "Thank you, spirits. Ancestors, guides, goddesses, gods, and grandparents." My tears continued to flow as I drove home and pulled out all of the things that I would need to do a spirit summoning. This was the only spell that I could cast to call out to spirits, but it would require me to go into a trance that would put me into a partially induced coma for half the day. I placed the crystal flower next to me while putting the items that Erin's father gave me in a pouch that I tied around my neck. I mixed Valerian root with lavender, passion flower in my chamomile tea and drank all of it as I thought about our first date. "I call to the earth, sun, clouds, and sea. I summon the spirit of Erin Johnson to commune with me." After saying the spell several times, I felt the effects of the tea coming over me, and I laid back while thinking about how she made me feel on our first date as I drifted into the astral realm. I floated through absolute darkness until I felt someone touch my shoulder and turned around to see Ms. Donna. "Hello, my little seer." "Oh my Goddess, I've missed you so much." I hugged her like I would never see her again as tears formed in my eyes. "We have so many things to tell you." "We?" "Hey, Gorgeous." The sound of Erin's voice echoed around us as she appeared out of nowhere with a smile on her face. "No-No-No-No-No! You can't be dead. I just talked to you yesterday. NO!" She pulled me into a hug as I cried into her shoulder. The strange feeling that I was picking up on was from her untimely death. "I'm sorry for leaving you before I could tell you how happy you made me. I love you, Vanna." "H-How?" She pulled back and looked me in the eyes as she wiped away my tears with the pads of her thumbs. "Here, let me show you." The darkness around us receded to show my siblings Cedric and Syrena knocking on her front door before she answered it. "Hello, Can I help you?" "Yes, We're Vanna's siblings. I'm Cedric, and this is Syrena. We want to surprise her with a party." Erin frowned as she crossed her arms while looking at my brother and then my sister. "We haven't had the best relationship with her, and our mother wants us to fix it by showing her how much we support her new relationship." Erin wasn't buying it and pulled her phone out to probably call me. "How about I call her and see if this is okay first?" "No! Then that would ruin the surprise." As my brother spoke, I watched my sister wiggling her fingers at her sides as yellow sparks of light flowed off of her fingers. Whatever spell she was casting crept up Erin's legs and made her stumble backwards as

Cedric waved his hands upwards to cast an illusion. "I'll grab her things, Rena; you get her body." "With pleasure." My pulse started to race as I watched them pull her into the house. The scene changed to show Erin's unconscious body being tied to a table as my parents walked a circle around her while chanting some kind of spell where they spoke the name of our supreme Goddess, Hecate, several times. She opened her eyes and looked around the room in terror right before Nika slit her throat with a ceremonial blade. It was the worst thing that I'd ever seen, but I was thankful for her showing it to me because now I'm going to kill my family. "It has to be done." Ms. Donna stepped around to face me and put her hands on my forehead. "We are always with you, my dear. Call on us when you are in need." Her voice grew louder as other people stepped forward, and I recognized them as the loved ones of my recent readings. I felt a sense of gratitude flow off of them before the dream ended, and I woke up to the light of an afternoon sun peeking through my blinds. Everything that they put me through slammed into me as I cried for the love of my life who was killed because of me. She was an innocent woman who died because of their jealousy, and now I have to end the lives of the people that I'm supposed to be able to run to when I need help. After half an hour passed, I gathered my thoughts and drove to my family home to confront the people who I had a blood connection with but no real love whatsoever. My parents never hugged me, ever. When I got my period, I had to ask the guidance counselor for help because my mother was too busy to care. For the major holidays, I never received a gift until Ms. Donna gave me the crystals and tarot cards for my sixteenth birthday while my siblings got shopping sprees and cars for theirs. I could still remember the look on my mother's face when I told her that I could sense spirits and asked if she could help me develop my gifts. "Do I ask you to help cast spells? Oh, that's right, you can't. Get out of my face, little girl!" She slapped me so hard that I skinned my knee and had a busted lip as everyone else laughed. I had to watch for years as they learned to fly, manipulate the elements, transport themselves to another place with a thought, and to move things with the energy that they exuded out of their hands. When I graduated from high school, Ms. Donna was the only person to show up, and I would have had to catch the bus home if she didn't come. My painful trip down memory lane put me on autopilot as I drove to the house in no time at all and was now pulling into the driveway as the gate opened. My forehead throbbed as I laid eyes on all of their cars parked in a circle around the fountain that I used to sit on to scry when I was a little girl. I parked behind my sister's expensive yellow two-door sports car and dragged my key across it as I walked towards the front door. Bitch! Blue orbs of light floated in front of me before opening the door. I allowed them to guide me to the basement, where I sensed a lot of spiritual activity and walked in on my family chanting a spell over a teenager's dead body. "What the fuck are you doing?" Their chanting stopped as the teenager's soul flowed out of her body and separated to flow into each of them. A small spec of it hovered over me as they turned to look at me with glowing eyes. My eldest brother Martin smiled as he floated upwards with a blue aura around his body. "Oh look, if it isn't our family disappointment." Nika smacked her teeth as she glared at me with an evil glint in her bright green eyes. "How is it that we can sense everyone else's mana but hers?" "It's because she's chosen by our ancestors to be the head of the family." My mother summoned her staff in a flash of bright pink light and sent a wave of energy at me that sent my body flying backwards. I hit the wall as all of my breath left my lungs. "Get up. You got this!" The sound of My mentors voice echoed around the room, and this time everyone else heard it as she appeared next to me with her hand out. When I touched her hand, I felt a searing pain on my forehead that spread through my body as I floated off the ground. "I knew it!" "You didn't know shit, Bitch!" In the blink of an eye, Ms. Donna became younger, with a large vertical eye on her forehead and a rainbow aura that moved with powerful energy. "Who the fuck told your dumbass to kill in my name?" Before my mother could respond, my entire family was turned to stone with the snapping of my mentor's fingers. Everything was happening so fast that I didn't know what was happening or how she was able to be in a corporeal form. "I kind of lied to you. I'm sorry." "W-what's happening?" The pain began to recede as I hovered next to my mentor, who was now just as young and beautiful as I was. "I'm the Goddess Hecate." My mouth fell open as she stepped back, and her head split into three and two extra arms grew out of her back. How did I not know that she was the Goddess who created the first woman of color on the planet, Lilith, my ancestor? She looked at me with a smile as a mirror formed in her hands, and she handed it to me. "Take a good look at yourself." When I held it up to my face, I gasped at the sight of an eye like the one that she had but smaller and with less energy exuding from it. "I chose you when you were in your mother's stomach to be the new leader of your family. Their ability to cast magic is strong, but your precognitive abilities are stronger." I looked down at the energy that swirled around me and then at my petrified family. "You have abilities that they wish they had, just believe in yourself. I'll be waiting for you." She kissed my cheek before vanishing and unpetrifying my family. "I'm calling an emergency family meeting." "Ha! Little girl, you are not my matriarch. I'm yours." All of them joined together to send a combined energy blast at me, but I clapped my hands together and sent the energy back at them. My mother slammed her staff into the ground to make a barrier, but the attack shattered it and her barrier as the rest of my family dove out of the way. I could see them running towards the exit, so I focused on making the doors remain closed. Yeah, this was definitely an upgrade. "You think you're hot shit, don't you, little girl?" "I'm shocked at your language, young lady!" I responded. Electricity crawled up my mother's body and made her scream out in pain as her body began to give off smoke until she fell to the ground. "L-Look, we did what she told us to do. We didn't want to hurt Erin." Hearing Nika say her name made me think of the time when she told my mother about a neighbor

I hooked up with, and I imagined her tongue swelling up in her throat as she looked at me with pleading eyes while gasping for air. My brothers tried to form a spell to attack me, but I made their elbows bend backward and sent their spell at Syrena, who cried out in pain. Whatever it was that they had planned for me caused her to burst into flames that reduced her to ashes in seconds. "Looks like it's just you and me, Daddy." "Vanna, I've always loved you. It's just that your mom knew of your destiny. She's been jealous of the power that you hold. Let's get out of here now that all of the bad ones are gone." "Really, because I can't remember the last time that you told me you loved me, and I thought you said that you'd call me back?" "I-I was going to-to bu-but-." I cut off his words by turning him into a plant and used my power to turn my mother into a cat and my sibling into a goldfish as their magic returned to the earth." It was like a huge weight had been lifted off of my chest, but I missed my girlfriend. I wished that I could see where her spirit was and give her one last hug before she moved onto another plane. The door that my siblings were trying to escape through opened to reveal the place that I had a dream about with animal body parts and elemental auras. I sent my family to my home with a glance before floating forward through the doorway. The first person that I saw was Erin, who stood with her arms open and a huge smile on her face. "Thank you for getting revenge." I tried to respond, but all that I could do was cry as everyone around us clapped like I just won the Superbowl. It felt so good to hold her in my arms and take in her vanilla scent as she squeezed me tighter. "I'm sorry that my family drama spilled over into your life, baby." "It was all a part of the plan. Come on. We have some things to talk about." She took me to a large door that I saw in my dreams, and it opened as we approached to show the supreme Goddess sitting on a throne. I didn't know if I should kneel or float up to hug her as the beings who were sitting around her turned to face us. "Welcome to limbo." "It is an honor, my goddess. Thank you for all of your help and for guiding me throughout my life." "The honor was all mine."

She now had one head but still had the large eye on her forehead and the extra arms coming out of her back. "Erin, I believe you have something that you want to say to her." My dead girlfriend took a deep breath and squeezed my shoulder as she turned me to face her. "I know that we just found each other again, but I've asked the Mother Goddess to allow me to reincarnate." "No, I thought we were going to be together?" She shook her head as tears fell from her eyes, and I joined her in crying as my own fell down my face. "What we had helped me heal. I was going to originally die in a car accident, but when you came into my life, it altered my destiny." I looked up to the goddess, who nodded with a sad look on her face. "The day that I met you was the best day of my life because I felt my energy change when you asked me out. I didn't have anyone who truly cared for me. My father was starting to come around, but it wasn't going to be until after I died. In a way, it was a good thing that your family cast the forgetting spell on everyone who knew me." I couldn't believe what I was hearing. That was horrible, and it broke my heart to have to see her father be the only person who remembered her. "But what about us?" "What we had was something that healed us both. I promise that I'll be just as perceptive as you when we meet in my next life. I love you, Vanna." She leaned forward and pressed her lips against mine as our tears combined. How could I say goodbye to someone who I just learned to love? How could the universe be this cruel? "Don't look at it like that. I promise we will meet again, gorgeous." "Yeah, by then, I'll have saggy breasts and be in a diaper." She shook her no as Hecate floated towards us with a smile and glowing tears coming out of her eyes. "Now that you're awakened, you won't age past this point." "We need a favor from you, though?" "What could I possibly do for an all-powerful goddess and a spirit who was about to transition?" "I need your blessing to pass on. You were the only person to really see me for who I was. Just think about me whenever you feel alone and remember the good times that we shared." I pulled her into a hug as her body began to become translucent. "I love you, Erin." "I love you too, High priestess, Vanna." Erin vanished in my arms, and Hecate pulled me into a hug as I sobbed uncontrollably. Telling her that it was okay to move on was different from actually seeing her transition into another life. After I gained control of my emotions, I took a deep breath and looked up into her glowing eyes. "What was that you wanted me to do, Mother Goddess?" "How do you feel about time travel?" "Am I going to the future?" "No, I'm going to send you back in time to seven years ago. I need your power of precognition." "Aren't you the goddess of divination?" "Yes, but if I use my power, the enemy that I'm facing will know what I know. He won't be able to sense anything from you because you don't have the type of power that he can sense." Hearing that brought up the legend of her opposing giant with the ability to cancel out her magic, and I now understood what she was asking of me. "You've been there for me when no one else wanted to. I'll do whatever you need me to do, My Goddess." "Perfect! Just stay inside Limbo, or the time deities will rat us out to the others that I'm working against." The air next to me shifted as a whirling vortex of multicolored energy formed and opened to show the room that we were in. "I've already communicated with my past self, who is waiting for you with everything that you'll need to perform your task. Here, put this in your pocket." She handed me a black tourmaline crystal that hummed as it entered my palm, and It was like I received a lifetime of knowledge in the blink of an eye. I knew how to use my new powers just as well as I knew how to use the ones that I already had. It was like we had spent thirty years together in the split second that passed when she handed me the crystal. "Whao! What was that?" "It's my special gift to you. Just remember what you were taught! Knowing too much about the future is very dangerous." "Yes, mother goddess. Your will is my command." I walked to the portal with an added sense of self-worth that made me feel like an entirely new person. The Goddess was full of surprises, and I was here for all of them. There was a beautiful woman waiting for me in the exact spot that I'd be standing in, in seven years, with a beaming smile on her face. "Hello, I'm Onira. Allow me to show you to the room that you'll be using." I still couldn't believe the power that I now have after dealing with my family's wicked betrayal. The past few weeks have brought me closer to my destiny with each step that I took, and now that I've accepted the role of High priestess, I'm ready for whatever the universe throws at me.

INNER CRAVINGS

"Hey, Boss Lady, I'm done counting the registers, and I'm getting ready to head out. Do you want to go grab a drink or two Or three?" Rebecca flashed me her usual smile as she batted her eyelashes. Flattered by her invitation, I returned the smile by looking up from my computer and shaking my head. "No, thank you. I still have some work to do. You go and enjoy yourself." "Try not to stay out too long. The lady killer is still on the loose." My outward concern made Rebecca's frown turn into a defeated smile as she stood in the doorway. "I'm not making any promises." She closed the door without saying another word, and I went back to finishing my work. I've always known that Rebecca had a little crush on me, but as her boss, I had to draw a line in the sand. I like women who aren't fresh out of college and sex-crazed. Banishing the thought, I continued with my inventory projections. After an hour and a half of number crunching and typing, I was completely done with my work and checked my watch, which displayed the time as eleven thirty. "Yes!, O-F-F!" I closed my books, put them in the filing cabinet, and logged off of my laptop. Once it was powered down, I grabbed my purse and headed for the door with the intent to not think about this place for five days. As much as I loved it when the grocery store was busy with customers, I loved it even more when it was closed, and the dead silence was all that you could hear. Exiting the large swinging doors, I walked my normal path past the meat section to the snack and cracker aisle to grab a big box of my friend Zephyr's organic garlic wheat crackers and remove the bag from the box. "It's not stealing if I own it." I tossed the empty box into a trash can behind register five and walked through the sliding doors. I locked the doors and set the alarm with the app on my phone and then used another app to start my car. The cool summer breeze was perfect in the way that it wasn't too hot or too cold as a gentle breeze blew past and gave me a sign that it was going to be a good mini-vacation filled with non-work activities of all kinds. I threw my purse into the passenger and made my way out of the empty parking lot. The usually busy street was just as empty as the parking lot because of the missing women whose faces were everywhere, and no one wanted to be next. *Well, except me.* It was calming in the way that it was eerily silent, and the shadows moved with the wind. Riding past my favorite butchery, *Natalie's cut.* I could see my secret crush, Natalie, standing in front of her old school car with the hood up and her cell phone flashlight pointed at the engine. Natalie was the type of masculine-lesbian woman who made the hairs on the back of my neck stand on end and my valley wet just by looking at her. The heiress-butcher talked about that car all summer, and it was a little saddening to see it out of commission. I turned into the parking lot and pulled up to butch-butcher in distress. "Hey, neighbor, do you need some help?" Natalie looked up with a pearly white smile beaming in my direction and nodded yes. "I think I need to replace the starter, and right now, I don't have the patience. Do you think I can get a ride home?" I nodded and waved her over. She closed the hood, retrieved her bag from the back seat, and hopped in with her men's cologne infiltrating my nostrils. "What side of town do you live on?" "On the far-east side. I'm currently staying at my parent's in Dandy meadows until the renovations on my loft are finished." I used every minute of the thirty that passed to find out all that I could from my passenger and learned that we both love horror movies and food and are both single. We pulled onto a long street that was nothing but trees as far as I could see on either side and a large black gate that surrounded a huge mansion at the end. The large black metal gate opened, and I pulled onto the long dark orange brick driveway that curved around a fountain the same size as my car. "Pull around back to the guest house." Perfect! Following the pathway to the back, I stopped in front of a nice-sized guest house that was just as beautiful as the mansion behind us. The area behind the guest house was just as gorgeous, with lush green grass and trees with flower beds below them sporadically placed throughout the wide area. It was large enough for both her building and my grocery store's parking lot to fit alongside each other. "And here I thought my family had a large mansion. This is BIG as fuck!" Being born into a powerful family, I was used to seeing huge mansions accompanied by exquisite taste in decor and landscaping. The only difference was that most of my family preferred towering penthouse apartments that looked down upon everyone. "This is one of five mansions across the globe. My parents own three in the U.S, one in Brazil, and another in Ukraine." The Orange brick theme covered almost everything, along with pale gray stone and ornately crafted lighting. If marriage was something that I wanted, this would be the perfect place for a wedding proposal and the wedding itself. I turned around and followed Natalie to the door and stepped through the threshold into a cozy front room with stairs that led up and down on my left with an open doorway that led to a large bedroom. A small open kitchen was nestled in the back of the house, and it was every bit of the chef's kitchen that I imagined for my delectable little butcher beauty to own. I also noticed that she was in a small smart house with dark screens built into everything from doors to appliances and walls. Her wide front room was perfectly suited for entertaining at least fifteen guests in its circular design and huge furniture. "This is a nice setup you have here. It feels cozy." I took a seat on the large gray couch as Natalie walked to the kitchen. "Thank you. When I turned fifteen, my parents gave it to me after I told them about my sexuality. I guess they expected me to be the typical rich kid and bring home random girls every night." She opened the cabinets and pulled out two shot glasses. "Is brandy ok?" I nodded, as she held up the expensive alcohol bottle. "I'm kind of over wine for a lifetime. As kids, my parents gave it to us every night with dinner." It was common for certain families to have specific customs that they forced onto their children at an early age. My mother's side of the family loved hunting, So naturally, I understood the feeling all too well. Natalie took a seat next to me, put the shot glasses on the wooden table, and poured us a shot. She then picked it up and handed it to me with a smile on her face. "Thank you for helping me." She held up the glass to me and picked up hers. Taking the glass, I looked her in the eyes for good luck and spoke the words that I'd always wanted to say to her. "To new friendships that should have happened a long time ago." We knocked the shots back and shivered as she poured us another. Taking a deep breath, she picked the glass up and put it to her mouth once again, letting the alcohol hit her tongue and throat. "Oh Damn, I love a girl that can handle her liquor. Would you like another?" My high metabolism ran parallel to my tolerance for alcohol, and right now, I could drink all night with this woman who exudes pure sexiness. After pouring another shot she scratched her head and looked in the opposite direction, before holding up our shots for us to drink. We knocked them back but this time, I didn't shiver. "Excuse me for a sec." Natalie got up and jogged up the steps into the bedroom and disappeared into a room I guessed was an En-suite bathroom and closed the door behind her. I pressed the on button on the remote and turned on the huge TV that displayed the news. That showed images of the missing women. I was getting tired of seeing this shit, to be truthfully honest. If they wanted to find the missing women, they could. I've always known for a fact that the wealthy have more power than they let the public know about. "Colbert Wilkerson is a local car salesman whose mother says he hasn't been home in two weeks. The Columbus police department has released the following statement: Our officers are using all of their best resources to aid in the search for five missing Ohioans." "Oh, we definitely have to find something else to watch." Natalie said as she walked down the steps, picked up the remote, and changed it to the animal channel. "Now, this is more my speed. I love watching animals hunt each other." She placed the remote back down on the table and picked up the bottle of brandy to pour them another shot. "You know all about my family and their slaughterhouse empire. Tell me about your family and where you're from." I could feel my cheeks blush as I made eye contact with my gorgeous host. "Where do I start? I'm the first-born daughter of a culinary, farming force of nature who built her own line of food from the ground up by herself. I had the best schooling, especially when she discovered my affinity for the culinary arts at a young age. My father died when I was younger. So I've only ever known her side of the family. I was born on one of her many private islands, but I consider myself American." "You said last year that your mother's company is a major supplier of the food you sell. Is your mom Madam cuisine?" The fact that she remembered a small bit of info that we discussed almost six months ago made me want to pull her panties off and taste-test her inner thigh meat. "Yes, my mother is the very one and same." "Wow, it would seem as if we have so much in common." Natalie picked up our shot glasses and held mine up so that I could grab it. I emptied my glass once more, and My sexy host grabbed the glass out of my hand and took it to the sink. As she walked back over to our spot, I heard the sound of clicking metal and turned to see her pointing a gun in my face. My heart began to speed up in my chest as I looked up into a sexy facial expression of a killer. If I moved or tried to fight, Natalie would shoot me without a second thought, so My only course of action would be to do as she asked. Stepping sideways, my gun-wielding host put her palm on a glass screen that opened up the wall upon reading her handprint. She motioned with the gun towards the entrance, and I made sure to retain hold of my false frown as I walked to the door that had a stairway leading down into an underground room. She pressed the gun to my back and pushed me forwards as we made our way down. A large human-sized cage stood in front of me that took up most of the space. Inside was a bed, TV, and a small bathroom on the other side with a toilet, sink, and shower. She nudged my shoulder with the tip of the gun as the doors opened. "Get in and make yourself at home." I would prefer for her to play with my lower hole and not make a new one, so I walked in and took a seat on the bed. A normal person would be terrified in this sort of situation, but not me. This was the excitement that I craved. The thrill of what she might do to me. "I would say that

I'm sorry about all of this, but that would be a lie." To be truthfully honest, there wasn't anything that she could do that my mother's family hasn't done already, and now it was time to lean into this a little more. "It would seem as if we will be spending a lot of time together, so what now?" I kicked off my shoes and made myself more comfortable as I shed the false sense of fear that she thought she had over me. The shocked expression on Natalie's face almost made me laugh out loud. It managed to temporarily render her unable to speak as she blinked away her confusion, and the familiar sinister smile returned. "I'm not going to lie to you. In four days, me and my family are going to eat you." She leaned forward and bit her lip. "Damn, I should have fucked you before all of this or at least got a good taste of that kitty." A chill ran down my spine as the image of her between my legs flashed through my mind. "Ohh, that sounds like it would be orgasmic. But if we are going to do anything, you should know that her name is…." I put my legs in the air and slapped my favorite female body part. "Madam Dracaena, the devourer. She is as vast as she is wet." My response made Natalie rub her nipples with her left hand, slide her right into her pants, and lick her lips. She sucked her breath in as her breathing intensified. She stopped and left without saying another word, and the smell of her vagina trailing behind her. This definitely wasn't what I had planned when I gave Ms. Magic Fingers a ride home. My head and back prickled as gooseflesh formed and spread all over my body. I contemplated whether or not I should masturbate and decided that they were probably watching me, so I'll save the lip show for Natty and decided to get some rest. I awoke on Tuesday to her mother, Vickie, feeding me vegetables and telling me about her organic skincare line that she was running on the side while being a chairwoman for their family business. After lunch, I managed to get her to speak about someone other than herself and ask about my tasty treat with breasts and two pairs of lips. "Yes, Honey. She has told us all about you. But I have to say. Your mother will be a bit of a problem should she come looking for you. Our people have already infiltrated her house and businesses. "Um, Okay. I didn't ask all of that, Icky!" I clapped my hands as she took my tray, turned onto my side, and rubbed my full belly. "Don't skimp out on the salt and roasted garlic next time. You're wealthy, not dead." I used my free hand to change the channel and search for cooking competition shows. After searching for what felt like forever, I chose to watch my favorite chef named Tatiana, who traveled the world to try different foods. I did something similar when I was younger, and it gave me a better sense of what was good to sell to customers like myself who craved rich organic ingredients. Hours passed, and Vicky returned with a tray of roasted vegetables and alkaline water. "Eat-Eat!" "You sure are happy for someone who's going to die." "How can one be scared when my in-laws are treating me like the goddess that I am." Vicky laughed and took a seat in the armchair behind her. "So, like I was saying last time." She made herself comfortable as she continued her extended bragging about her business that apparently no one else carried about and time passed as I ate my food while she droned on about nothing. "That was good. I knew you could do it." Once she was gone I returned to watching my show in the hopes to forget about all the stupid bullshit I had to waste forty minutes on and fell asleep three hours later. Wednesday morning her father Bernard came in with a tray of fruit and water with fruit in it. "Hello beautiful. It's time to eat my scrumptious brown skinned morsel." I sat up and walked to the door as he pushed the tray through the slot. "Can I ask you a question?" "Yes, I don't believe in lying." I guess he must have meant besides being in a family who practices ritualistic cannibalism and abductions. "Has Natty asked about me?" He laughed as he sat in the armchair "Yeah, she keeps trying to come down here." He smacked his teeth and shook his head from left to right as he pulled out a candy bar from his pocket. "You don't think that we would make a cute couple?" "Dear, we're going to eat you." "Is that a no?" Bernard exhaled as he continued to eat his candy bar and watched me like I was an alien in a lab as he chewed. "Were you dropped on your head as a baby or something?" "No, I sustained a head injury as a kid when I flew too close to the sun." He rolled his eyes as I picked up a banana and tossed it through the slot like a frisbee pro. "I don't put things like that in my mouth. Chop it up next time." He stared at me wide eyes as anger changed his fatherly facial features into a man that wanted to slap the teeth out of my mouth. Twenty minutes passed as he watched me eat in silence and I returned his glare with an over exaggerated reaction to finishing my food. "All Done. Yay!!" He took the tray and left me alone to finish enjoying my vacation with free food. Bernard didn't return until the late afternoon with two trays that he handed to me and left without saying anything. "Aww, Still mad daddy!" I yelled out trying my hardest to sound british. He slammed the door and I spent the rest of the evening devouring the fruit. I cleaned up in the very small bathroom and decided to watch a horror movie about a witch that turns people into food ingredients for her cooking show. "You better run. She's right behind you!" By the end of the movie I was sleepy and called it a night. On Thursday Natalie's Uncle Thomas and Aunt Patricia brought in spicy curry rice and a meatless pasta alfredo that smelled like garlic. "Before you ask, No. We will not be answering any of your questions." "Did Natty ask about me?" They ignored me as they passed the food through the slot and I carried the trays to my bed. "You can't fight true love. She'll be mine by the weekend. Mmmm!" The curry was spicy just like my ex-girlfriend who was from India used to make. It was missing meat just like the alfredo but I ate it all in ten minutes and passed the trays through the door. "Berny was right, there is something wrong with her." "You feed me at weird times and say I'm weird. Wow!" They left me to eat my late breakfast that consisted of dinner-foods all by myself. I was now invested in a drama that turned into a thriller as a wealthy venture capitalist couple were having affairs with younger people, only to find out that they're each other's children that they gave up for adoption twenty years ago. I decided to feed the thriller buzz that I was on with another movie about a female cop who died and found out that his mother is a Japanese death goddess. "Okay! Woman of Death was a great movie." My in-laws returned with a late dinner and passed a tray of fried food through the slot. I gasped and took the food to my bed and thanked the goddess for this meal. It was fried onions, pickles and veggie egg rolls. Each of them came with its own sauce and I couldn't help but to cry as I smiled at them. "Thank you. I know I've been a brat but it's because I know you can do better. Even if your people aren't known for using seasonings." Aunt Patricia smacked her teeth and stepped forward but Thomas stopped her and walked them to the steps. "Night Unc and Auntie." I turned back to my show as the main character went through a power up and summoned a scythe. "Oh, shit. Now we're cooking." I picked up the fried pickles and dipped them in the ranch first. "Okay. Let me see what you're giving with the egg rolls." I dipped it in the orange sauce and ate most of it in one bit. "Mmmm." It was so good that I had to slap my pussy a couple times. If they were watching I planned to give them the best show of their life before the end. On Friday Natalie's cousin Beatrice brought in a normal breakfast with bacon, eggs and waffles that were to die for. "I'm not like my family so you can ask whatever you want." I turned the tray to face her and paused the Falcon documentary that I was watching. "Has my baby boo asked about me?" She nodded and smiled as she sipped her tea. "She's been dying to eat you for years but our parents wanted ukrainian meat so you got off lucky." "You think so, Bebe?" She glared at me with furrowed eyebrows and took another sip from her mug. "Last time I ate arm meat and now that I'm looking at you I want to taste those thighs." I flung the food at the door and a lot of it hit her as she tried to move out of the way. "Bitch! don't play. Natty is the only one that I have eyes for." She left and I walked over to the door and ate what I could as she slammed the door behind her. Thankfully the floor was good so the five second rule was extended to six minutes as I finished all of the fried food and passed the tray through the slot. "Thank you! Same time tomorrow hun!" I took a shower and continued the show that was interrupted by basic hair bitch-Bebe. Saturday morning went by and I was surprised to see Natty coming down the steps with a basket of food in plastic bags and bottled waters. "I heard that you asked about me." I licked my lips as she passed the packaged food through the slot. "I did and I can't believe you let me meet your family." I opened the meat and cheese as she sat in the new armchair. "Ally, you're going to die." "Uh-huh!" I opened the crackers and stacked them on top of eachother and chomped on them like I was a bird. "I'll believe it when I see it." She leaned back in her chair and exhaled an annoyed sigh. "Before the biblical flood the children of mother earth were different than they are now. Humankind sustained themselves on a raw fruit and vegetable diet that allowed them to live for hundreds of years. My ancestor Nalkidol, was the head farmer and saw that their crops wouldn't yield a great harvest so he prayed to the divine spirit for help. After days of praying with no response my ancestor was visited by the angel Zalmira at sundown." She was sexy when she spoke about topics that she was well versed in and it made a smile curve my lips when she stopped speaking and stared at me. "Sexy and well spoken, please go on." She licked her lips and continued her story as I ate the meat and crackers with cheese. "From what my parents have told me, Nalkidol walked with the angel for three days and three nights where she taught him how to hunt and prepare meat before being brought back home at dusk." She opened her bottle of water and took a long drink of it and then finished. "As the head of his house, Nalkidol taught his entire family how to hunt and prepare the meat for consumption. The higher power didn't like that because it wasn't sanctioned by them so they sent the flood that wiped out most of the planet's population." I held my hand and she stopped talking as I went to use the bathroom. "Sorry babe, please continue." "My ancestor along with his family and most of their village fled to a mountain that would shelter them from the flood. Nalkidol used that as an opportunity to trap the small group of people in a room that he and the great angel built. His wife Mirataltha, was the town's healer and used her knowledge of plants to keep them in a susceptible state that helped them pick them off one by one until the torrential downpour was done. After the storm ended they took the boat that the angel helped him build and sailed across the raised ocean to America." I looked her in the eyes as I tossed the empty bag onto the ground and opened the next round of snacks. "Wow, well I guess that explains why your family owns the leading empire of slaughtering houses and butcher shops." Natty blushed and looked away with an adorable smile on her face that made all the hair on the back of my neck stand up at the thought of Natalie munching on a special part of me. I shrugged off the insane sexual urge as she got up and left without saying goodbye. "We'll have to work on your manners babe." I yelled out and continued to eat and think about the story she just told me about her family's ancestry. I spent the next five hours thinking about how cute she looked in her outfit and how she finally graced me with her presence. Once I turned off the light and turned over to go to sleep, I heard the door open and someone come down the stairs. "Bae!" I yelled as she stepped into the moonlight and pressed her palm against the dark screen. UNAUTHORIZED ACCESS! "What the fuck?" Natalie placed her hand on the screen and tried again with the same results. The screen changed from the palm print reader to show her mother in her lavish bathroom putting on make-up. "Hey sweetie, your father and I have restricted your access to the meat. We don't want a repeat of Lucile now do we?" Her mother spoke in the same loving tone that mine did and then the screen went black. Natalie exhaled a hard breath through her nose and punched the wall next to her. "I'm sorry for all of this, I really didn't want to sacrifice you, but a girl has got to eat." She left and returned a couple of hours later and came back down the stairs with a gun in a holster on her hip and handcuffs in her left hand. Hopefully her parents have changed their minds, because right now I could use a good orgasm. "Put your wrist through the slot." I did as she asked and allowed her to place them on my wrists. "Ooh kinky, I like where this is going freak nasty- Natty." Natalie placed her palm on the screen and the door slid to the side to open. She motioned towards the stairs with her head and I stepped out of the most comfortable room I've ever slept in. "I'm going to miss the food and that bed. Too bad we didn't get to do anything on it." It was strange to walk out of the small guest house that I hadn't seen in days and into the evening air that tickled my skin. My car was parked in the same place that I left it and I could imagine her shooting me in the back if I made a run for it. Natalie walked beside me while putting her hand on my lower back and guided me up the steps through an immaculate patio to the double doors that opened as they stepped closer. "Oh shit! And I get fancy door service." Natalie let out a small laugh and I turned to look at her beautiful smile. "There's that smile that makes me wet like a waterfall." She grabbed my arms as we walked through the kitchen that was almost as good as my mothers. Natalie pushed open the door and we entered a hallway filled with paintings that had to be worth billions of dollars. "Aww, more mayo people. Mmm, delicious." I rubbed my stomach as she pushed open the doors and we walked into a dining room with a large U-shaped table in the center. All of her family sat at the table and stopped talking as I walked in. My father in-law stood up and clapped his hands together. "How lovely of you to join us my dear, I hope you are still stuffed from lunch?" "I still have room for more." The whole family laughed including Natalie who took her seat next to her cousin. "You are as funny as you are beautiful, It's almost a shame that we'll be the last ones to see it." Vickie grabbed her wine glass and took a sip like her comeback made me cry or something. Bernard grabbed his glass and used his spoon to get everyone's attention. "We are gathered here to feast on what the divine has brought forth. Let's begin." "Bernie, I couldn't agree with you more." The windows locked as the doors shut and I freed myself from the cuffs by reducing them to dust. My in-laws tried to get up but I held them in their seats with a wave of my hands. "I'm sure you all have questions so let me cut straight to the point. As you are all aware, we live in a world filled with creatures that are both mortal and immortal. Your family refers to the angel that blessed your ancestor as Zalmira. I call her mother." A collective gasp filled the air as I swept my gaze over the family that wanted to eat me and rolled my shoulders to unfurl my large wings. It was so difficult to not tell all of you what I was Monday night." With a thought I pulled Beatrice out of her chair and to the palm of my hand. Her pulsed race as I pulled her closer to my face and inhaled the scent of her skin. "Mmm, Your family tastes the best." A tingle crawled down my spine as I sensed my mother's presence teleporting to the space to my left. "Hello mother, welcome to the party." My mother, who was one of the first born and all powerful angels, was dressed in a long gray gown that left room for her wings in the back. "Hello, little-wing." I let Bebe fall to the floor and pulled the best mother in the world into a hug as she wrapped me in her arms and wings like she used to when I was a child. "I see you've found another one of your fathers branch of descendants." I nodded and licked my lips as my mother and I inhaled Bebe's scent. "This one and those two are mine and I want you to have the others." "Aww, Honey. Thank you." My mother clapped her hands and Natalie's father and uncle disappeared in a column of silver light. "It's been a while since we last got to share a meal." "Before we do that Mom, this is my Meal-girlfriend. Natalie." I pointed to the most beautiful and hopefully tasty women in the room and sent them to the special place where I keep my special food. I picked up my cousin-in-law and walked with Bebe in my hands before slamming her on the table. "Is this seat taken?" My mother asked Patricia as she took the seat next to her and bit into her exposed forearm. I pulled Bebe's hands to my lips and nibbled on her fingers as she screamed through her closed mouth. "Oops, mine is going into shock." My mother placed her hand on Aunt Patty to put her into a coma but she managed to break free from the hold and run for her life. "You know I don't do fast food." Gravity lifted her off the ground and snatched her backwards into the air to land on the table with a thud. "Sleep!" She took another bite from her well dressed dinner and I ate off a huge chunk of Bebe's hand as she passed out from the pain. "Do you plan on making her your wife-meat?" It was still early but I've loved her from the day that I'd first seen come into my store. "Yes, but I'll probably eat some of her toes and one of her hands first." My mother nodded with a smile on her face as she ate the entire hand in one bite and did a small dance at how good it was. "I taught you well, daughter." I grabbed the glass of wine and swallowed the food in my mouth before taking a sip of white wine. "So how are things in your nest?" she asked. "Things are great. The newbies are assimilating well and our numbers are twice as strong." I replied. "Good. Have you heard from your aunt?" That managed to raise my eyebrows as I chomped on Bebe's other hand and shook my head no. "I've been thinking about her lately and I'm sure it's a sign that she has some things in the works that are about to happen." That could be good or bad given the nature of the individuals involved. We ate their entire bodies within forty minutes and made plans to have another family dinner sometime next week. "I love you little wings and remember what I taught you." She pulled away from me and extended her wings as she dissolved into specks of silver dust with her hands going to her lips to blow me a kiss. I snapped my fingers and put all of Nattys clothes in my car and sent them home as I started a fire in the basement. My wings glowed with the same silvery cosmic energy as my mothers before I made the fire burn brighter and flew through the ceiling and teleported to my front room. "Honey, I'm home." I flapped my wings and made the small journey to my rooms without doors in the lower part of my home to see my soon to be wife-meat. The lights came on as I flew down the wide hallways and landed in front of my holding rooms. Their see through plexiglass doors reflected my nephilim form as I walked to the end of the hallway and looked from left to right. "Hey, baby. Did you miss me?" I made sure to place them across from each other so that Natalie could watch me eat her mother in a couple of days. "Ally, I-I'm so s-sorry. Please forgive me. We didn't know." I rolled my eyes at my new wife-meat as she sobbed and her mother laid unconscious behind us. "Uh-huh! Sure sweety." My body passed through plexiglass and I kept going until I had her up against the wall with tears streaming down her eyes as she took in shaky breaths. "You were right, a girl does have to eat." I moved at super speed and snatched her hand up to my mouth. Natty tugged at my grip but her human strength was no match for mine as I ate off her pinky and ring finger. "Mmmm, so good." I teleported to the cage that her mother was in and picked her up off the ground by her throat. "I just have to do this." I slapped the old bitch so hard that she came awake before hitting the floor and coughed up blood as she sobbed. "It's okay Vickie. This is a safe place." She continued to sob as Natty lost a lot of blood and fell to the ground. "P-Please. Let my Mother go and I'll stay. Please Ally!" I always loved it when my food thought that they had any say over who and how I eat. "By the removal of your ring finger, I now pronounce us Angel and wife-meat." Natty screamed as the gaping wound was cauterized with white flames and fell to the floor like her mother who was now in the corner cowering like a puppy. "Thank you for satiating my Inner cravings, Natty." I blew her kiss that knocked her out and teleported to my bathroom to clean up and roll up some weed I got from my fellow feathered long time divine friend, Zephyr.

V.v-Vs-H.O.G.S

"Well-Well-Well, What do we have here?" "Y-You got the wrong guy, I didn't rape those girls!" "Kill him, ***Dream***! "Yes, Vortex!" I reached into the deepest part of my mind and pulled out the thickest and longest dildo that I could make to shove up his ass. "No-No-No, please! I didn't do it!" His lies turned into screams as I focused on making the dildo slither up his ass like a snake and then turn into molten lava once it was all the way in. "Ahhh!-Argh!-Argh!" His body convulsed as he began to cook from the inside, and his hot blood dripped down to the floor. "Liar-Liar inside on fire!" I turned on my heel and ran out of the abandoned warehouse to join my teammates. The second I rounded the corner, a boulder flew in my direction, and I used my power to turn it into sand that I rode into battle. Below me, Shade used her shadow hair to bind Eve, but she turned into the air that permeated her grasp. "Tag, you're it!" I pulled a hair bonnet from my head and threw it in her direction as I passed by. "Bigger!" I yelled in my mind as it enveloped her entire body. "Yeah, how about NO!!!!" The heroine Muse hit me with a sonar blast that sent me flying into the overgrown forest behind the warehouse. "Caw!!" I turned my body into a murder of crows and allowed the forest to hide us in its shadows. The only way to properly surprise this bitch was to stay out of her geokinetic range. "Nightmare! Get your cowardly/sexy ass out here!" The Heroine Stone called out to me from the edge of the forest. This is what I hate about women like her. They give nice and kind lesbians a bad name by being overtly sexual. Eve was right. Shapeshifting was fun but creepy. I had a circular view of Stone as she entered the forest, and I receded with every step she took. "Okay, how about this: you come down, and once you're defeated, and we find out your identity, you'll go to jail, and I'll bribe them for several conjugal visits. I got the perfect strap on." Oh! That's it! I pulled my remaining pieces together and launched two rockets from my palms. "Then how about LAUNCH for dinner!" Prrr-BOOM! The impact shattered her pieces, but unfortunately, she'd reform in a couple of minutes, so I had to make an exit from the forest. I imagined myself taking to the air with wingless flight and instantly took to the sky. "Steady! Now!" I hated flying like this, but it was the only option left in my bag of tricks. "Don't vomit! Steady, Steady!!" I could feel my stomach becoming more upset as the trees disappeared, and I began to spin out of control. Before I could hit the ground, my body was wrapped in darkness that I recognized as Shade's long tresses. The second she dropped me to the ground, I threw up everything I had in my stomach and rolled over onto my back. "Dream, with the authority of the H.O.G.S, you are under arrest!" I snorted as she reached for the amethyst handcuffs and turned the dirt into a stampede of boars. "See ya!" I didn't bother to turn around as a boar opened its back, and I jumped inside as it became a monster truck.

"Unhand the senator, *__Fix__*!" I couldn't help but roll my eyes as my chair sprouted spider legs, and I crawled up the exterior wall of the warehouse. "Sure, I'll do that, and he'll be prosecuted in a court of law." I feigned, dropping him and then scooping him up as he screamed before he hit the ground, but my nanobot-crab pincer snapped his leg in two, and he fell to his death anyways. "You know more than anyone that you have to be careful with your words, Chatty!" "Can you help me?" She looked over my shoulder to the wall, and it began to pull me in like quicksand. "Don't struggle. Just let it take you into its suffocating embrace." My entire body became relaxed as her words washed over me, and I stopped struggling. *Impact imminent!* The sound of my AI pulled me out of the trance and allowed my nanobots to send out a shockwave that freed me from the wall and landed on top of the senator's body. "Oops, he's daisies!" I laughed out loud as my chair used its crab legs to scurry across the ground, with Chatty chasing after me. "Mio, raise sonar shield output by forty percent!" *"Increasing output!"* I continued running until I was far enough away from the widespread battle royal and released a stream of laughing gas and made propellers that helped spread it to the others. My opponent hit the ground, and I took to the sky and saw a Large monster truck trample over trees in the distance. *"Mother, my Indicators detect Dream several kilometers away!"* I turned and headed in that direction to support my teammate as a bat flew next to me out of the darkness. "Everything, get in." I opened a small hole for her, and she flew inside and landed in the seat next to me. "Are you ever going to tell me why my scanners can't sense your presence?" "A good magician never gives up her tricks, madam techno." I laughed at the mention of my undercover guardian name from two years ago. I had the time of my life infiltrating the H.O.G.S and bringing down their building with an explosion that took out the whole block. "Where are the others?" I asked. She shrugged her shoulders, and we began to separate just in case we were being followed. The both of us remained silent on the way home, but I broke the silence as I parked our transport vehicle. "Good job as always, Fix." Eve turned into a dog and ran off to her room, and I did the same to shower and allow my nanites to recharge. As I entered the living room, my nose picked up the smell of rain, and I turned to see my older sister glaring at me with her arms crossed. She floated off of the ground with lighting swirling around her. "How could you allow yourself to fall for her suggestion?" "Hello to you, too, sis. You did great out there, by the way." My sarcasm didn't help her mood as she smacked her teeth and vanished in a tornado that sent the small coffee table at me. Before it hit me, the table turned into a swarm of blue butterflies that swirled around my body and then turned back into a table. "I've always wondered if she had perpetual bitch syndrome?" Dream stepped into the room with her hands out as the table solidified. We shared a laugh as I took a seat on the couch. "Thanks, Crystal." "I know what it's like when family isn't supportive." Dream stepped further into the room and made two mugs of lavender tea appear on the table as Eve sauntered in, and our mouths hit the floor from how amazing she looked in her green_dress. "Oh, let me guess, this is date number six?" "Actually, seven. Last night was a trans woman, and tonight is a bisexual male model." "Make sure you use protection. You know how men like to trap us." Eve smiled as she waved and became an owl that flew out the window.

"Good morning, Nareka." "Good, Mrs. ***Dark***. I have your coffee waiting on your desk." I smiled at my light skin assistant even though I hated the sight of her chubby face. Her only redeeming quality was that she's amazing at her job. "Also, Amber Mells canceled, and I bumped Donna Miltons up to her spot." Perfect! I woke up this morning wanting an early lunch anyway. "Thank you! If the dog groomers call, tell them I'm not paying for that shit they tried to pull with Fenrir's fur last week. Make them wait another week and then put the check in the mail." "Yes, Ma'am." I stopped and turned on my heel and gave her the fakest smile that I could muster. "Once the appointment is done you can have the rest of the day off with pay. But make sure you set up the transaction before you leave." She nodded, and I could see the wheels turning in her head. For the last six months, I've been working her high-yellow hands to the bone with preparations for my fall collection. With summer almost over and Fashion Week around the corner, I plan to lean into my supervillain alter ego, *Attire*. The vixens should be thanking me for making them look so good and have uniforms that not only help them use their powers but also take the brunt of an attack. I put my bag down and took a sip of my coffee as I looked over the designs for Donna's dress and her nephew's suits for the wedding they would attend next week. I spent the greater part of the morning marking up all the changes that she wanted and added a cute little hat for the baby. "Ma'am, Donna is here!" "Thank you. Send them in." My shirt adjusted itself to an uncomfortable angle as they walked in, and my pants gave me a wedgie that was almost hard to hide. Okay, I understand this woman is dangerous! I extended my hand as my clothes normalized, and Donna flashed me a smile that was just as fake as mine."Good morning." "Good morning, Ms. Miltons. Can we offer you something to drink?" "Yes, sparkling water." I looked at Nareka, and she nodded and silently left the room to fulfill her order. "How are you?" Donna took a deep breath and whistled so loud it hurt my ears and caused me to become disoriented. I threw my hands up and made the surrounding fabrics into a barrier as she continued to whistle a dangerous song. I didn't have time for a comeback, so I made the curtains into a hand that punched her in the chest and sent her flying into the wall. Donna Miltons *was* Muse, and now I have the pleasure of ending her once and for all. "Oh-Oh-Oh-Oh-oh, yeah-yeah!!" Her breath came out as balls of sound, and I twisted into the air and made my barrier into a suit of armor with insect wings. "This is not the time to work on your scales, song pigeon." I flung my hands out and sent sharp bowties in her direction as she flew in a spiral upwards to my dome ceiling with her voice echoing around her body. We exchanged blow for blow as I destroyed my office, and each of us contributed to the holes in the walls. I made sure to keep the armor and wings as she continued to use the ceiling to reverberate her voice. That's it! I had to get this thin bodied bitch outside. Just as I finished the thought, she clapped and began another song that generated more energy for her to direct my way. "Sorry, pigeon! We're going to have to take this karaoke adventure to another venue." I jumped out of the window with her loud ass voice shooting by me as I moved from side to side.

"So you're **_Muse_**, huh?" I purposely ignored her question as we flew over a pond, and geese flew in between. "Attire, Vixen of last year's looks, I place you under arrest with the authority of the H.O.G.S. Surrender immediately!" The uppity bitch dove out of the way as my sentence became tangible and would have knocked her ass down had it not been for her wings turning into a beetle shell that absorbed the attack. "I hope you realize that you've outed yourself as well, Muse." She kicked off her shoes, and they turned into piranhas that chomped on my sound barrier. "No-No-No! This isn't how this is going to go-o-o!" I managed to knock them off, but they twisted in the air and joined together to form a large shark. "Looks like this siren is out of her element!" Attire yelled as she ascended high into the sky. I made my barrier twice as strong and was confident at this moment as a gust of wind lifted me higher. "I'm good at music because it's my passion, and today is a good day because I don't have to wear her atrocious fashion." I made sure to push from my diaphragm as I sang with all of my heart. I was missing an audition for a voice-over job, and this bitch just had to come up on Clair's radar. The shark moved at impossible speeds as it caught up to me and bit down on my barrier. I could see its sharp teeth made of multicolored fabric that would have looked nice as a suit for my baby nephew. It continued to chomp down on my barrier as I continued to reinforce the spherical barrier. I could see Attire making a run for it out of the corner of my eyes, so I hummed the words to my favorite song and allowed the reverberations to strengthen my barrier and expand inside the shark. *"There are days where life feels like the wild wild west, and even though I persevere and try my best, I can't help but shy away from my next test!"* My song made the shark explode, and I used the remaining echoes to propel my body forward and pursue Attire. ***"You can try to escape, but best believe you'll fail because I'm always on your tail."*** I sent another blast of melodies in her direction and managed to hit her in the back and disrupt her beetle shield, but She turned the shell into another pair of wings that gave her a boost of speed. *"I'm a musical genius of my time and use the words to catch up to her in time."* My ears began to ring, and I knew that I was reaching my limit, so I took a deep breath and expelled all of my breath as a whistle that flew faster than a bullet and pierced her right leg. "Ahh! You bitch!" she twisted in the air and removed her pants. "Give in, Attire. Land, or I'll have to use lethal force." I yelled out. "What the fuck do you call this?" She made her socks turn into leggings that stopped the bleeding as I caught up to her and blew her a kiss. "Mwah!!!" My voice expanded into the small space between us before she could react and hit her in the ribs. Attire went limb as her body began to fall, and I scooped her thick body up in my long arms. For a bitch that fought with everything she had, she smelled amazing. "Mmm, what is that? Cucumber and cherries?" I kissed her exposed side-boob as I turned us around and headed towards the H.O.G.S headquarters. "Oh, your breasts are soft."

"Are you _Mya_?" "Yes, are you Natalie?" I looked up into the most beautiful pair of green eyes that I've ever seen in my entire life and was instantly satisfied that I agreed to a blind date. "Sorry for being late." "No, no worries. I just got here myself." My partial lie managed to return the smile to her gorgeous face as we shook hands, and she took a seat across from me. "I love your top!" "Thanks, I absolutely adore those earrings. Are those hamsa hands?" "Yes, I work as a Medium and Cartomancer." "Oh, cool, so if I ask for a reading, you'd be able to tell me if we're going on a second date?" I laughed out loud as the waitress walked up with her tablet. "Hello ladies, welcome to Yancy's. I'm Sandria. What can I get you?" "Water with key lime!" We spoke in unison and then looked at each other with the same expressions on our faces. "Okay!" "I already know what I want if you're okay with ordering?" With that simple question, she just checked off four boxes on my list and helped to ease my original anxiety from earlier. "Yes, I'll have the salmon and asparagus." She smiled and nodded as she held two fingers up. "Coming up!" "So, we were talking about you doing a reading for me. I'll pay." I laughed at the irony of this situation. Yes, I can sense the future energies of her life, but my attraction to her would make my power unreliable. "Had you asked me that as a client, I would be able to do one, but now that we're vibing, it makes it difficult to properly discern the future." "You know what? I get that. I work at my family's funeral home, and seeing people I've known as neighbors or classmates is hard. I have to take the day off." Another box checked. "So we both work with the dead." Our laughter drew the attention of the tables around us, and for once in my life, I didn't mind the uncomfortability. It took thirty minutes of twenty questions for us to find out that we have a lot in common. We're loners who actually live alone and are working in careers that are fulfilling. "My family lives in Los Angeles, and I came here ten years ago to start my own business." "Me too. Well, I moved from Miamii five years ago and started our second funeral home in Cleveland and then here in Columbus." Sandria approached our table with the bill, and I reached for it at the same time as Natalie. "Oh! It's my treat." "You sure?" I responded as I let go and smiled from ear to ear. "Yes, my woman's intuition is telling me that there will be another one of these happening in our near future." My mouth hurt from smiling and laughing at her jokes, but I continued through it anyway. This woman is fine as fuck and just as hilarious. She's smart and with the perfect sense of wit that made me wet. "Most definitely, here, take my number." Natalie held her phone up to mine, and they vibrated from the exchange. "I get off early tomorrow. Would you like to come over for dinner?" Natalie arched an eyebrow in my direction and made sure to put a physical emphasis on her exposed cleavage. "Only if we collaborate on the food? "What do you have in mind?" "I know how to make the best-jerked chicken and plantains." "Oh, then it's on. I make the best oxtails and Sultana rice in the city." I got up to hug her, but she stepped back and held her hands up. "I recently came in contact with someone who got over the flu. I'd hate to be Asymptomatic." My ears began to ring as I remembered we shook hands earlier. "That's cool. Have a good afternoon, Natalie." "You as well."

"So you think he *is* cheating?" "I don't know. He has been hanging out with his boys a lot, and I have to admit that I thought he was a little gay." "Girl, no! Don't do that to yourself. And don't do that to the male gays. Not every man is gay just because he has a lot of friends. Didn't you say he was the new head of the fraternity?" "Yes, they have meetings all the damn time, and it's annoying as fuck." "Language! There are young ladies present." "Sorry, **_Marcella_**." I removed the gown as my guest looked at her hair in the mirror. "I need to apologize for having my reservations about you rocking a fade and having the skills to do....This!" She twirled and then gave me a playful wink as she waved goodbye. "Tina. Aye! Don't come back here in a couple of days talking about your edges." "I straightened up my station as the next guest walked in and took a seat in the opposite station. I turned to see the most famous woman in Columbus, the meteorologist who saves us women of color and thick hair from weather damage. "Hello, Marcella. I have waited a long time for this." "I appreciate you putting your trust in me. Now, what do you want me to do? A Bob? Or maybe some goddess twists with rust-orange here and here." My scalp tingled as I touched her shoulders and out the corner of my eye I could see My shadow-hair reflection moving erratically in the mirror. Thank goodness it was something that only I could see but unfortunately for her it means she's evil. "I was thinking we would play this as an eye for an eye." She sucked her breath in and I barely had time to shake loose my shadow mane and sling it in her direction. She did a backflip and floated off the ground as the air collected around her arms. "Nice try **_Shade_**!" I dove out of the way of her tornado fist as they whizzed past me and shattered the mirror. It was hard to breathe as the air continued to grow thin. "We never attacked any of you Hogs first, it's always the Vixens who are the victims and have to retaliate." She directed lightning from her eyes in my direction and I twisted my hair and absorbed it into my darkness-void. "Bitch! I don't know what you're talking about. You hoes think your destructive justice is the solution for everything and never think of the consequences. And now my girl is missing and I need my dress for tomorrow's ribbon cutting. Like.I.Said! You captain savior-hoes fuck everything up!" She held her hands up and the sky rumbled with her anger and changed into the Vixen Vortex and then turned into a cyclone that sucked everything into it. I willed my hair to hold on to the chair as Vortex pulled at my body with her cyclone of devastation. I whipped half of my hair to the sink and ripped it off the wall and threw it as hard as I could into the eye of the vortex. That managed to halt her arial-vacuum long enough for me to dive into the shadowy-darkness of the partially open cabinet door. She let out a loud laugh as her voice echoed around the room. "I guess you really can say, Bye felicia!" I froze in my tracks at the mention of my girlfriend's name. "Bitch! I will fuck you up over mine!" I responded. "That remains to be unseen and can be avoided if you just come with me willingly." I let go without a second thought as her voice was the last thing I heard before falling asleep from the thin air. "That's a good little dyke!"

"I got one order of fried tacos and a lime spritzer!" "Here, that's my order!!" "Thank you!" "Hello!, what can I get you!" "This is my first time ordering here. What do you recommend?" "How about the sizzlin sampler?" "Sounds good!" "Give us fifteen minutes and that'll be right up." "Okay, I'll be waiting in my car." "A food truck, really *Lynn?*" "Don't judge Veronica, we all can't have mothers who own hospitals and for your information *Platter of pentacles* is doing great." "Yeah!" clone-A shouted. "Yeah!" Clone-B added. "Alright twin sisters, let's get back to work. Are you ordering or coming to tell me how bad my food is for the human body?" I looked down on our super team leader Wise, who thinks she is the smartest doctor in the world. "No! I need *Mini's* help. Muse has Attire in holding and there was an accident at Marcella's shop. They say it was an electrical fire." I turned to my clones and gave them the head nod to lock up after they served the last order. "Alright, Let's go!" I took off the apron and hairnet and joined Veronica who had a car waiting for us. "To the loft, Hammon!" We made the short distance to the building she owned and then to the secret entrance in the basement that led to the H.O.G.S Headquarters that we refer to as the Hall. I changed into my uniform and walked down the spiral staircase to the holding cells as clones one and two returned to me through the nothingness. A cold chill ran down my back as their memories fused with mine. "Good, Almost everyone is here." Stone, Chatty, Muse and Clair waited for us as we descended the last steps and I could see that the Vixen Attire was completely naked. "Oh, you lesbains are here for the show huh?" "I definitely am!" Stone answered and she shared a hi-five with Muse. "Ladies, can we focus!" "Tell us where your hideout is." "No!" "Whelp we tried your way, let me have a couple of moments alone with her. She'll Talk." Stone stepped forward and I made a clone appear in front of her. "Move it Dwarf!" "How can you call yourself a heroine and act like a frat-boy?" She stepped forward and Clair placed a hand on Stone's shoulder." "In and out, In and out." Stone stepped back to her position and mouthed the words sorry as I leaned on the wall behind me. Everytime this bitch gets shattered near a forest she acts weird for a couple of days. Clair started to undress and our captive started to breathe differently because she knew what was up. Our girl is the strongest telepath in Columbus and once we know where their HQ is, we can finally be done with these irrational vigilantes. "Stay still." Clair waved her hands in front of Attire and she froze as she placed her hands over her heart and forehead. Both of them gasped as Clair's eye's glowed blue. "1165 Queenstone Rd." We waited for Clair to erase the last twenty four hours from her mind and then get dressed so that we could make our way to the biggest fight of our super-lives. "Mini, Call back your clones, we're going to need all of you for this." "Already done, Wise. My truck is closed. Thanks, I'll miss the dinner rush." She held up her forearm and typed on her holographic keyboard. "Fourteen thousand dollars will be sent to your personal bank account and you don't have to report it to the IRS. Anything under fifteen is a gift." "I always loved it when my second boss treated me as a student. Okay, so what's the plan?"

"***Reaper***, they're here and they have Attire!" Eve flew into the room as a wasp and spoke telepathically to us as we finished getting ready for the fight. "I told you they'd find your base of operations." Shade taunted us from the antigravity cube that floated around the room. "Yeah-Yeah hairdresser!" "Bitch I'm a beautician, there's a difference." I turned away from the unnecessary argument and walked through the wall to meet them head on with Eve who took the form of a hummingbird. "I'll take Mini and you go after Clair." I really didn't want to but I had to put my feelings to the side and pretend that I hate her. "Do you think that you can handle this?" I nodded as the rest of our team joined us and Vortex appeared in the middle of us and deposited Shade on the ground. "Hand over Attire and leave!" Vortex yelled. Stone lunged forward without warning and I altered my tangibility as she landed on me. "That's it!" Eve turned into a bulldozer and shoved Stone backwards. I used the opportunity to take on Wise instead of Clair. "I've had worse opponents." I used all the combat knowledge that I had to put up a good fight against her martial art skills. We matched each other blow for blow until she swept my feet from under me and went to stomp me but I touched her boot and made it decay. Wise hissed as my palm made contact with her flesh and she did a backflip just as I was about to grab her other foot. "Let's dance!" Clair yelled as she came in with spin kicks and I had to deactivate my power as my hands made contact with the bottom of her boots. She continued to fight me and I couldn't help but to notice who good she smelled or the way her costume hugged her thick hips. Women like her are the reason I love and adore black women. "Uh-Uh! I'm taken." Clair landed a blow to my chest that made me stumble backwards and for a second I thought she knew who I was. It's a good thing the eyes of my mask are white or she'd recognize my eye color.

Lying to her was wrong but our date was the most organic fun that I've had in a long time. Being surrounded by dead people makes one prone to being a loner. I dove into the ground as she sent another round of kicks in my direction but tumbled into a flip as I fell into the ground completely. "Get back here Ghost! We aren't finished." I watched as she spun around and ran off in the opposite direction to help Chatty with Vortex. Mmm-mm-mmm! I had the perfect view from this angle as her ass jumped up and down. The sound of several footfalls running in my direction pulled my attention to the dwarf size clones that made up the non-binary guardian, Mini. "Get out of there and face us like a woman coward!" Okay, now this is more like it. I don't have to hold my punches or become distracted by this little person's bland body frame. "Sure thing, but once I'm done we're going to help you defeat the wicked witch and my team can get back to the yellow brick road." They didn't think my jokes were funny as they each produced a different weapon and lunged at me. I touched the first one's small dagger and it turned to dust as I kicked her in the chest and grabbed the next one by her helmet while activating my intangibility and dove into the ground. I dragged her with me through the ground and jumped out while leaving her in there. "Two against one this hardly seems fair for all of you munchkins." She split apart into a kindergarten small army, and I ran at them with the intent to win.

"***Stone***, watch out!" I dove to the side and erected a wall of trees as Dream sent four rockets in my direction. "Damn, I really thought you were that stupid." Her rockets continued on to who knows where because that's what they do. Create a bunch of collateral damage and blame it on us. "No, it's just your basic bitch instinct that prevents you from washing up correctly!" I slammed my arms into the ground and sent a double attack that was part fissure and Mountain manifestation that pulled her into it and closed. Her screams were silenced, and I moved on to the most mysterious super of all, *Eve*. She somehow has extremely heightened senses, and she can become anything she wants.

I was always scared that she would turn into my tampon and kill me from my favorite female external organ. "Here, kitty-kitty!" She turned into a panther with large bat wings and leaped into the sky. "Bad Kitty!" I punched my fist into the air and sent nets made of vines into the air after her. "Aye, y'all, this bitch thinks she's on safari or something!" The vixens laughed at Eve's usual banter she spews when fighting an opponent. I continued my attack even though she dodged them all like a real griffin beast while twisting into my nets and broke them with her wings. A chill ran down my spine as my mossy hair picked up a static charge coming towards us from the left. Yeah! I sense it, too, but it's male. I froze as the person who was running at superspeed punched Muse in the throat. **Roarrr!!!** I paid dearly for my moment of pause as Eve slashed my throat open, and I didn't have time to do anything as she bit into my shoulder. Fuck! I just reformed my body and doing so out in this season has its drawbacks. STONE!! My team continued to fight, and as I lay on the ground with my red blood sprouting flowers while pooling around me. "I could see a small body of wind and another of water helping Vortex free Fix from Clair's charm. I let my team down again, and this time, I might be out for a whole season instead of a couple of days. I'd miss out on so much pussy!! FUCK!! "I'll never give it up!!" My body dissolved, and I seeped into the ground, and all of the sound disappeared. This was my favorite part about having an elemental power. The earth is everywhere, but its drawback was that the sound returned in full force once I stood up and my teammates made way for me to gain proper footing. I blinked as Shade broke out of her prison cube and used her hair like a helicopter to put distance between us but also land on the little speedster boy and flying with him upwards. "Damn it! Stone is going berserk again." It felt like I was drunk as fuck and couldn't stand up straight, but as my mind reformed, I gained control, and my emotion slammed into me, and I wanted to fuck anyone up, who got in my way. "Fi-Fy-Foe-Fum, I smell the pads of black women." The time for games was over, and I grabbed the Vixen-Everything out of the air and slammed her into the ground. She burst open like a ketchup packet and then turned into a pile of worms that borrowed into the ground. In my overly emotional state, I laughed and cried at the same time as I smacked my fists over the surface of the ground and sent a bunch of small fissures into the ground. "Stone!! There are more alley cats in the world." Wise yelled my safe word, but it was now useless because my mind was gone and replaced with *Mountain-Woman*."

"**_Wise_**?" My team looked to me as I synthesized a molecular compound to help render my teammate with the lowest I.Q unconscious. "Give me a second, I'm calibrating the genome.!" I activated my antigravity field and flew into the air as the spray was done, and I placed it in rings that I shot at Stone. "Shade, get her arms. Muse, Chatty, and Clair render her unconscious. Shade and Mini tail the Vixens!" I held my arms out and flew after the little boy who was traveling at super speed through the city. "Maximize boost output by fourteen percent!" **Vzzrrzzzz!!!** My scanners showed that he was headed to Brushing Estates. I didn't need to go any further, so I watched as vixens leader, Vortex appeared, and he jumped in, and they disappeared. Kelly Fanning, Columbus's number one meteorologist turned media mogul. "I love being right all the time!" **_Bip-Bip_**! "Wise! We have Stone under control and are en route to the hall!" "Great job, Muse!" "It was all thanks to your leadership, WiseOne." Muse replied. I faked a laugh and ended the communication. There was no one who could say that I'm a bad leader or that I'm not charitable. Lil fatties food truck does make money, but she tries my patience with the blatant use of power. How the fuck do you allow yourself to become popular and gain the attention of the local news while not having proper names picked out? "Wise to mini" **_Bip-Bip_**! "I lost them. Vortex showed up, and they disappeared." "Got it! Head back to the hall with the others." "Copy! Oh, and thanks, the money just hit my account." I held back the urge to disrespectfully say Duh! Bitch! So, I decided that ending the call was a better option. "Output increase!" *Vrzzzz*!!! The ground became a blur as I moved at dangerous speeds to our base of operations. I slowed down as I flew into the downtown area and allowed myself to be photographed by the cameras on the side of the *Intuitive-Insight* Media buildings as I turned the corner. Knowing what I now know about Kelly being Vortex, it made sense why I had the urge to give Bethany Randers the seed money to start the second-greatest media company in Columbus, Ohio. I always make great decisions when it comes to business. Owning a hospital gave me the anonymity that is necessary to make my scientific creations. My real estate business is booming, and now I have the upper hand on the top Vixen, Vortex. Below me, the crystal dome opened as I descended to the ground. "We have a huge problem. Vortex has a son with powers." Everyone gasped except for Clair and Stone, who held an Ice pack to the side of her head. "How is that possible?" Muse floated out of her chair as her voice echoed around the large room. "My brother doesn't have any powers, and we're twins." Chatty reached up and pulled Muse back into her seat as I projected a graph that showed the earth's vibrations from the mid-sixties to the present. "As you can see, sixty-six years ago, our mother earth gave off a vibration that accelerated the first heroines to the call of protecting the weak, and now, in twenty-twenty-six, we have our firstborn male to a Villain. I don't need to remind you of the Martin mannings incident, do I?" They shivered at the mention of our male enemy, who stole our eggs and made a body that had a fraction of our powers. Now, my nemesis has three more members of her team that she's filled with her vigilante justice of revenge and murder. A fucking weatherwoman!

Once again, our know-it-all leader is giving us another lecture on what she knows as if we're her students. I looked over to Shade, who bit back her urge to laugh. "***Chatty***, Do you have something to add?" "No, Professor, I just forgot to do my homework." Everyone laughed except for Wise as she deactivated her helmet and floated over to stand in front of me. "Chatty, you're on reconnaissance." **Blip**! I looked down at the address that she sent me and smacked my teeth. "Now, you know I don't like *that* neighborhood." She slammed her fists on the table and looked me in the eyes. "Good, maybe it will give you time to work on your new comedy routine." She pointed to the doors, and I left as fast as my two legs could carry me. "I don't know who the fuck she is talking to?" I said, to the ducks at my feet. Quack! "Right! You know, she took a stroll past her little girlfriend's media building and gave her more viewers and money. Her panties told me that she hadn't had sex in five months. Ha! No wonder she's such a bitch." Quack-Quack! I turned my head as two squirrels came running across the ground from our left. "Yeah, they're fake as fuck, but they hear all the hot gossip." Quack! "Okay, see you next week! Tell your mate and ducklings I said hello!" I waited for the ducks to be out of earshot before I turned to the squirrels, who jumped up on the park bench and waited for me to pull the can of mixed nuts from my bag. "Hey, friends! Before they could respond, a large owl swooped down, grabbed them by the torso, and then flew off into the sky. "Get back here!" I poured all of my energy into my power, but the owl continued onwards as all the people and animals in the park came from all over to surround me. "Humans!! Go back to what you were doing a second ago, and animals help me stop that bird!" I ran to the part of the park where the wasp nest was and took a deep breath before speaking. "Help me save my friends from that owl!" Truthfully, I could care less about the circle of life, but I needed those two squirrels to continue being my look-outs. Being able to speak to anything is fun until it wants to eat you or refuses to respond. "Excuse me, Mr. Pine tree, can you help me?" It proved my point by shaking its branches side to side. "Fuck you too, then!!" I ran by it and gave it the middle finger as a swarm of bees caught up to the owl, and it dropped the squirrels from a dangerous height. The owl turned into a bald eagle that sent the bees flying with its large wingspan. "Everything!" "Mouth of the South. Hello," her telepathic voice entered my head as she dove to the ground and turned into a ferret that ran off into the heavily wooded area. I kept going until I reached the spot where the squirrels fell and froze at the sight of their mangled bodies. "Damn it!" Now, I have to find and train two more forest critters to be my informants and not run into traffic or let the person they're watching know that they're watching them. I extended my left arm and summoned the male cardinal from the tree across from me. "I need you to keep an eye out for any strange things. If you do that, I will supply you with these." I stomped my foot on the ground, and worms crawled to the surface. My new friend hopped off my arm and onto the ground to pluck a worm out of the dirt and fly off. I wasn't sure if that was a yes or no, but I know one thing about speaking to hungry animals is that they remember who feeds them.

I dropped the worm the second I was out of that mouthy bitches line of sight as I entered a large hole in the tree. Below me, I could hear Chatty on the phone with her bitchy boss talking about me as she walked by. "I'm one hundred percent sure it was ***Everything***. She watched me as an Owl and then scooped up my informants, and she killed them and then turned into a ferret before disappearing into the forest." There was silence for a moment before she smacked her teeth. "Of course, I met a cardinal, and they're good at tracking people, so it's only a matter of time before it reports back." I flew off in the opposite direction, andmade my way through the trees and landed on the back window of the biggest house. "Mom! Your creepy friend is here!" The twelve-year-old aerokinetic unlocked the window, and I flew inside as a thick tornado appeared and took the form of our self-proclaimed team leader, Vortex. "Well!" I took my time answering her as I changed into my fourth favorite human form. "I don't know why you're such a bitch all the time. You're married, wealthy, and have three super-powered kids. Oh! And your little quick-footed son is the first of his kind in this generation. Like I said, no reason whatsoever to be a bitch." "Windy, go join your sister in the playroom." The little girl flew down the hall as her mother turned towards me with her arms crossed. "You were right. She was having squirrels and raccoons watching you. They also know about your son. Good job with that, by the way." "Eve, I know your deepest secret. I suggest that you show me the respect that I deserve." "If you truly felt that way, then you'd be bowing down to me, right, daughter?" "You are not my mother, Eve. You're our ancestor. There's a difference." "If that's all that you found out, you can go, Mom!" Instead of leaving, I walked into the kitchen and made myself a big-ass sandwich and paired it with a club soda and wavy BBQ chips. "My mom doesn't like it when we eat her favorite chips." Said the little speedster. "People have been touching my stuff since the beginning of time. I'm sure the richest woman in Ohio will be fine." The little boy zipped out of the room as I turned on the seventy-inch television. The news came on, and because it was my host's competitor, I turned it up. "Yes, I'm here with Carmen Willis, a witness who saw the fight between our protectors and the Vixens. Now Carmen, Tell us what it was that you've seen." "I saw a boy run with the speed of the Quickstress and help those villains go against the Hogs." I snorted at the mention of our rivals and their ridiculous group name. "A boy? Carmen, boys don't have the gene to manifest powers, and if they did, we'd know something. Little boys are overtly aggressive and destructive. They would have caused irreparable damage to the city." "That part!" I yelled out loud and grabbed my soda to open it. I spilled some of it on the couch and changed the channel. I already knew what happened and the major secret that Vortex tried to hide from the world, so I changed the channel to my favorite show in the world, Discords Daughter. A demigoddess who goes to earth at the request of her mother, Eris, to prepare it for her arrival so that she can kick off the apocalypse. I turned it up as the show's theme song came on, and I did my little chair dance. "How about those apples?"

"Fix, get over here now!" "Sure thing, **_Vortex_**, I'm just sitting here with my hands in my-." I ended the call before my obnoxious little sister said something disgusting. Vwommm!! A baby blue portal opened to my left as she walked into the basement I reserved for meetings. "You rang, evil old mistress." "I'm not in the mood for your mouth. I already have an attitude. Don't make it worse." "Wow, and here I thought you said you'd never be like our mother." A lightning bolt formed at my feet and traveled up my legs, and disappeared as I turned my head in her direction. "I'm nothing like her. She only had time for those who needed help while we were being abused by her boyfriend. I emancipated you from my guardianship and gave you access to all of your money. Please tell me how I've behaved in a manner that reminds you of that arrogant bitch with super speed that was our mother. Huh? I can't hear you, Trischell." "Yeah-yeah, Kelly. I get your point." "Good, we need an advantage, and you're the only one that can make something to combat anything Wise can come up with. Do you have time travel technology yet?" My question brought a large smile to my arrogant sister's face as she held her hand up to her techno-crown, and it projected the designs for a belt. "I'll have this done in twenty-four hours." She opened another portal and left while humming a little song. I knew she'd get it done even though I've been on her back non-stop about performing better. My body began to float upwards as I turned into air and moved through the floor up to my bedroom, where my husband waited. "I'm getting my clothes off, honey!" Thomas flopped onto the bed and removed his pajamas. "No, honey. I have something to do. Have that dick ready in an hour." He made the captain's salute and grabbed the remote as I flew out of the window. I made my way to the poor side of town, where a certain superhero's family member works at a pizza shop. *Michello's eatery.* My body passed into the ventilation system, and I allowed the uncomfortable temperature change to happen as the air carried me to the oven. The sounds of the food service workers having an inappropriate conversation about the new hire and her big breasts entered my incorporeal ears. "Guys, why do you think it's okay to say that about women? Those are our melanated mothers, sisters, cousins, aunties, and friends." The other guys started laughing even harder and I used the emanating heat to see what they were doing. A commercial for my new TV show came on, and they all ran away from the kitchen to get a closer look. "This is a Goddess. She gives us the news we need, not what she thinks we want. She is highly intelligent, kind, a great mother, and partially self-made." "Bro! How can someone be partially self-made?" "She didn't know that her mother had a secret inheritance, and when she turned eighteen, she put her own money into making our city a better place to live." Aww! I have a secret admirer. "Did anyone hear that?" Oh shit! In one swift move, I jumped out of the oven and placed the kind teenager in a bubble of air as I caused the building to explode around us. "You're coming with me, little telepath."

"You're _**Vortex**_!" "And you have telepathy." I hoovered over the pit I held my new little boyfriend in as he looked up in terror. "Chatty will come and find me. She always knows where I am." He pulled at the chains as if he had super strength and gave up after several attempts. "Are you done?" He didn't answer so I responded with my thoughts. "When did you get your powers?" "I can't talk on an empty stomach." I made a sideways-moving vortex appear and turned it into a platter of food and drinks. "Let's see if you can eat and talk at the same time." He froze and glared up at me before grabbing a bottle of water. He took a sip and slowly reached for a sandwich. "I received my powers during puberty, and Chatty helped me learn how to use them and keep it a secret from my family." "Did you experience any side effects from having powers and being born male?" "I experienced a lot of migraines, and the thoughts that I heard almost drove me insane. Your son will probably experience athletes' feet or minor numbing as he gets older." I allowed myself to grow as large as I could and call forth lightning as I encompassed the room outside of the pit. "Don't read my Mind!" I hated having my privacy infringed upon, and even more so when it was a man who did it. The sound of him choking brought me out of my anger, and I receded out of the pit. "Have better manners tomorrow, or your sister will become an only child." My body dissolved as I floated backwards and reappeared in my bedroom. "Fuck. Of course, you're asleep." This man better be lucky. I respect him as the father of my children and the best-looking trophy husband with a good dick, or he'd end up like the pizza shop boys. I turned and flew out the window and made my way across town to my boyfriend Artaevious's house. As I flew closer, I could hear him having a deep conversation with a younger female from Texas. My sensitive hearing picked that up before I flew into his yard and smelled the food that they were cooking together. She must be the reason he hasn't returned my phone calls or text messages. From this angle, her pale, light skin appeared greasy. Typical Light Skin privilege! She comes out of the house looking like that, and men fall at her feet. I made myself into thin air and moved into the wall as she breathed me in, and I Possessed her body. Once I gained control of her mind, I had to stifle a laugh as his real sex was made apparent by the uncomfortable tugging sensation in my crotch. I don't discriminate when it comes to possession, but this tranny bitch is going to die for lying to my man. More of her memories went through my head, and I could see that the two of them came up with a plan to extort millions of dollars from me with the video she has of us on a flash drive in her purse. "Did you hear me bae?" "No, you were saying something about killing that weather bitch?" He smiled and closed the gap between us. "I think she has the place bugged." He placed his fingers to his lips and looked around. "She's like Mrs. Claus." He moved to whisper in my ear and then placed a kiss on my neck. "Enough about that old bitch. Are you going to give me some of that or what?" With a thought, I solidified into my human form and made the tranny-bitch pop like a water balloon as her innards sent him flying backwards into the wall. "Is it still drag if a real woman becomes a woman impersonator?"

"_**Chatty**_, are you okay?" The room stopped spinning as I was finally able to catch my breath. I hated my delayed reaction to my empathy bond with my twin. By now, he could be dead, and I wouldn't know for twenty more minutes. The exact amount of time between our births. "It's Cj. Vortex has him, and she's questioning him about-." "About what?" Wise narrowed her eyes and then rolled them as she realized the truth that I'd hidden from her all these years. She shook her head and pressed a button on her wrist. "Let's go get your brother." I touched the lips on my necklace, and it sent out the small nanobots that make up my costume. Across from me, Shade flicked her hair loose, and the baby hairs traveled down her body to form her literal super suit. "I always love seeing you do that. It's so cool." "Thanks, but keep your eyes to yourself. I got a girl! And the sun sees all." Dang! You try to kiss her while drunk one time, and she never lets it go." Stone clapped me on the back as she walked by and gave me the usual once-over look that she gave me and then followed behind Shade to stare at her big booty. I shivered as I waited for her to walk a greater distance ahead of me. She was a weirdo and gave masculine lesbians a bad name. Muse flew by, and I turned and made my way to the teleporter as its particles formed around me. "Alright, everyone, take up the star formation. Chatty, concentrate on your brother." *Vwamgggggg*!!!! In the blink of an eye, we were transported to a neighborhood that I was familiar with. St. Vincent Street, The neighborhood where I spent a lot of my teen years babysitting the spoiled rich children and walking their smelly dogs. A sudden tugging sensation formed in my chest, and my heart glowed within my chest as I turned towards the largest house. "He's over there!" I ran forward and picked up the a scooter that was laying on the ground. "Can you fly me up the street to that house?" It vibrated as it came alive and floated out of my hands. I hopped on as the rest of my team followed me in the air and on the ground. "Incoming!" Muse stopped as a Large funnel cloud formed around us, and stone erected a mountain dome around them as Wise and Muse extended their force field and barrier to the rest of us. "You're going down, Kelly!" Vortex was good at surprise transportations, but Wise is better at dampening her temporal relocation energy that she generates. I continued on my path as she Vanished and took a deep breath once I flew over her driveway.

"Open a tunnel all the way to my brother!!" I pushed forwards as everything in my path made a tunnel that led me through a front room, then a basement, and finally ending as I entered into a large room with a pit in the center. My heart glowed brighter as I landed the bike near the opening and yelled down. "Thinker, Are you okay?" "I'm alright, hey! I thought you said we weren't supposed to say that name out loud until the world knows about male supers?" "We're not, but now that you've experienced Vortex's villainy, I think Wise will change her mind. Hop on." I descended down into the pit, and My brother did as I asked. "I didn't know you could do this." "Only when I'm pissed. No one abducts my little brother. "Take us up and to the fight, please." The scooter turned and took us upwards with the force of an airplane as the tunnel closed, and everything turned back to the way it was.

I watched as My sister's home reassembled and my nieces and nephew moved to help save their father, who fell into the closing walls. "Auntie **_Fix_**, help." I flew into the opening and pulled my brother-in-law out, but my bad timing cost him his feet as the wall solidified. And he yelled out from the pain of losing both of his feet. "I'm sorry, brother." I dropped him on the couch and flew out of the windows as the kids gathered around their father. Outside, Attire fought Shade and Mini with a peacoat that she turned into a rocket launcher. Next to them, Reaper and Muse fought, and I nearly laughed at the sight of the love birds going at it. Clair can sense what was, what is, and what will be. But her precognitive abilities are useless when it comes to matters of the heart. Eve and Dream were tag-teaming Stone while Bitchy big sis took on my nemesis Wise. Chatty flew away with her brother, and I started to chase after them but decided against it. Whatever Happened before was between Vortex and them. Right now, I have a score to settle with the second-smartest Woman on the planet. **_Incoming vibration!_** My plasma shield grew stronger as Muse dropped down out of the sky and hit me with a blast from her flute. "Do you ever give your lips a rest? Frrrzzzzzrr!! I sent an ion blast in her direction that coiled around her sonic blast, and hit her in the chest. "Muse!" Stone yelled as her body flew backwards. She chased after the song pigeon, and I turned and sent a plasma blast at Wise. I could see that Vortex was getting tired after making several portals at once and used the last one to send herself home. "Genius Lesbian Vs. Genius Lesbian." She turned on me with a look of pure satisfaction as she absorbed the blast with her left hand and sent it back to me with her right. I blocked it, and we spent the next four minutes playing lacrosse with the energy and trying to prove who was the smartest. "Did you copy that particle canon from my original plans, or are you still going with the lie that you made it yourself?" I yelled "You just couldn't wrap your oblong titties around the fact that I'm smarter and younger than you?" She sent a wave of green energy at me as I twisted through the air and continued upwards until I was high above the city. "You should have been a track star with all the running that you do." Wise replied and sent another blast in my direction, but I blocked it with a photon shield that sent the residual energy in opposite directions. I remember the day I asked her to announce my newly created nanobots into the medical field to help fight cancer cells in children, and she fired me for thinking of ways to not make money. Now, five years later, she is the leader of an idiot team of superheroes. "Get out of your head and get back into the fight, novice!" I dropped out of the way as she sent another wave of energy in my direction. "It was because of me being in my head that you're able to manipulate the nanobots the way that you do, thief!" Wise cackled like a witch as I returned fire with actual fire, and she turned to fly away with her energy stream trailing after her. Below me, I could see Stone hugging an unconscious Muse as I passed over them and sent out a couple of zero-energy orbs that surrounded Wise and prevented her nanite suit from working and rendering her unable to move. "They say you should never meet your mentors, but no one ever says anything about falling in love and then having the one you'd give everything to steal it and discard you as if you didn't matter."

"***Muse***, Muse! Can you hear me?" I couldn't move or open my eyes as the lightning bolt paralyzed me, and the loud footfalls of my secret girlfriend grew closer to where I landed. "You're okay. Oh thank goodness you're okay." I could feel the stinging sensation slowly return to my chest as she placed something warm on me, and I was able to open my eyes. I blinked away my blurry vision and looked down to see Stone's crystal heart on my chest. She lay motionless next to me as it healed my wound, and I was now able to move again. Vines grew out of her chest and pulled the heart back inside. She awoke with a gasp and placed her left hand on my leg. "I think we should remove the open part of our relationship." Stone nodded as tears fell down her face and her chest closed. "I do, too. I've been thinking a lot about us, and I think we should tell the others." Tears fell from my eyes as I leaned in and pressed my lips to hers. It felt good to be on the same page for once and for her to actually absorb what I'm saying. "Once this is over, we should go on a real date. Outside of our homes." "Yeah, my neighbors are tired of replacing their windows." I got up and dusted myself off. "Stone! Do you have Muse?" "Yes, we're headed back now." Once i was done Stone pulled me onto her lap. "Thank you for being patient with me, Donna." "It's you who's been patient with me. I thought that we were done for real after you saw me with the dentist." "Oh, that's because she gave me a root canal with her vagina." We exchanged the same look as I leaned in and kissed her lips. "Let's go, I'm completely healed." I held my hand out to help my girlfriend up as Dream chased after Mini over our heads. She made her hands large, and I jumped in them right before she flung me into the air. "Ooooooo-Oooo-eee-ooo!" My voice came out as an echoing force of power as I allowed the momentum to mix with the sound reverberations. I continued to sing and gathered the energy into my lungs, and sent it out just as Fix tried to run off with Wise. It hit her in the back, and she dropped our leader to the ground. "Got it!" Stone yelled as she made fists out of the dirt and caught Wise right before she hit the ground. Next to them, Reaper fought Clair with martial arts as she flipped and kicked with everything that she had. That's my girl! Out of all of us, she hated fighting but hated people who abuse their power even more. "Muse! Three o'clock!" I turned just as Dream flew at me in the form of a pterodactyl and snapped at me with her smelly beak. I could understand a bird or bat, but an ancient reptile?? It was my assumption that she could only change into things that she'd seen. When the fuck did she see dinosaurs? "Wouldn't you like to know?" She head-butted my sound barrier and instead of knocking me back I absorbed it and then used it to bind her in a spherical field of sound. She changed into an elephant and then a rhino and then a whale, but I focused on the energy and harnessed the sound of my beating heart to strengthen my barrier around her. "Let me out, Let me out!" Her voice came out like a monster as she took the form of a gorilla and beat against the interior and then changed into a little girl dressed in a jumper with a pink T-shirt and pigtails. "Don't hurt me mommy!"

"Fuck!" Eve chose the form of Donna's daughter who died from a brain tumor two years ago. "Muse! It's not really her!" I threw my arms out and sent two shrubs at Eve who flew away as Muse fell to the ground with tears in her eyes. "***Stone***!" I focused on where she would land and made the grass sprout upwards and slow her fall. "Thanks!" Wise touched her watch and made more nanobots cover her as I made the grass lean over and deposited her on the ground. Our leader gets on my nerves but she is still my boss and the person who signs my paychecks. "Stone! Watchout!" I dove into the ground as Eve sent rockets in my direction but instead of staying close to the surface I moved deeper into the ground. I refused to be a hindrance on my team this time so my best move would be to stay in the ground and wait for her to land or a team member of mine to line the shot up. In the Darkness I could see small multicolored specks of light that notified me about my team's call and where they wanted me to strike. I imagined myself as three sets of hands and grasped five big breasted bodies that wiggled in my grasp. Reaper, Attire, Eve, Fix and Dream were now rendered powerless with the W-3KN5 cuffs Wise placed on their wrist. And it was all thanks to me! "You can let go now!" "Oh right, my bad!" I released them and their bodies hit the ground with a thud as their cuffs negated their powers. "I told you, everyone and everything has a weakness." With Everything being my nemesis, I made sure to smile when they walked her into the pocket dimension we use to transport villains to Omni-Max prison. "Don't worry Mini, as your archnemesis, I'll save room for you when I'm asserting my dominance in the yard." She looked right past me as she walked by and it ate me up for her to act like what we had was nothing. Like I was nothing. "Stone! You and Muse search for Vortex. Mini go with them, please!" The dimensional door collapsed as she walked in and the three of us were left to feel like the odd women out once again. "Muse." "Yes, Stone!" "How long have we been a part of this team?" "Uh, since the beginning, I believe." "Remind me again about why we aren't allowed in the interrogation room?" "Because the three of us don't have degrees." "You have a P.H.D." "In music. Apparently that's not enough to be able to question someone." I exhaled and tried to calm myself as my songstress let the fact that our leader treats us like idiots because Mini and I didn't go to college and Muse is only good for entertaining us during our yearly celebrations. "Mini, How do you feel about this?" "I don't. As long as her money is in the account. Nothing else matters. Both of you were there when my first clone died and yeah Clair and Chatty showed me they truly cared that day, but Wise is a crazy person. Have you ever wondered how she knows about our powers?" Muse and I exchanged a puzzled look before looking back at Mini as she called her clones into her body. "I heard this from the lips of an ex boyfriend of Chatty's who frequents my truck. He said that Wise extracts their power and assimilates them to her nanos. "She was telling us about the earth's natural energy earlier." "But why would Chatty tell an average Joe, something like that? And why did he think it was okay to say it out loud?” “Yeah, and how many people has he told that too?”

“Was I on a date with ***Reaper*** or Natalie?” “Both, I’ve loved you since the first day you hit me with your spin kick and punch combo.” Clair A.K.A Maya rolled her eyes as I told her the absolute truth. Three years ago I helped Fix castrate a priest who molested children and when they came to the rescue, we fought with hand to hand combat. She’s the only woman on the planet that my powers don’t work on. Well besides Eve. Vortex evaporates and Stone crumbles at my touch. “I’m serious, I can still remember the Honey-lavender perfume you wore.” “Yeah, Okay Natalie-Reaper or lying bitch with tits I don’t give a shit about what you say. You sat at that table while I told you about my weakness. Do you know how hard it is to meet someone and feel an instant connection?” Clair stormed out of the room and Chatty shut the door as Wise stepped closer with her right wrist raised. “Where is your team leader and your fashion assistant?” We’ve been instructed to shrug but I never really took orders from the vaginal vortex with no walls. “Chatty, you’re up!” Ms.Big Mouth USA walked up and looked me in the eyes. “Where are your teammates?” I blinked repeatedly and put my hands up to my head and pretended to stumble. “She-she’s buried next to your Mother.” My team and hers burst into laughter as she glared at me with her cold dead gaze. “Make all the jokes you want, it’s only a matter of time before that tongue of yours loosens up.” “Only for my girlfriend.” “Oh, That’s done. She doesn’t play when it comes to trust or her powers. You fucked up both times.” They left and I looked across the walkway to my team who held the same grim expressions on their faces. Well, except Eve. “Why are you smiling?” “I’m sorry to have to be the one to say this but, we needed a way in and had to make it look like we actually got caught.” “What?” Dream banged on her hard-light door as tears streamed down her face. She hated being the last to know things even more than I did. “Is this true, Fix?” “It is. We need to know why black women have been going missing and what the senators were lying about." "What? They laundered money, imported drugs and contributed to human traffic-." It all made sense now. Vortex made an off hand comment about the wealthy turning a blind eye to crime so long as it keeps their pockets fed and Wise A.K.A Veronica has the biggest purse in the state and next to her was Kelly Fanning or Vaginal-Vortex as I call her, with half the wealth. "How long have you known Eve?" "Just like my name, I know Everything." It was my turn to roll my eyes as she turned into a polar bear and slammed her shoulder against the barrier. "Can you please explain?" "Yes, please tell me the reason as to why you deserve death, for using us like pawns." Dream pulled a bucket of Ice cream from her head and a spoon from her palms as Eve changed into a human form that I've never seen before. She was absolutely breathtaking with long thick hair and rich dark skin that glistened in the light of her cell. "Well it all started when I first opened my eyes and my sister Nibara floated by me with a strong gravitational pull and stole four of my moons. I tried to tell our mother but she ignored me." I smacked my teeth and crossed my arms as she smiled at my obvious irritation. "Can you be real?" I replied. "I AM, being real. Everything I'm about to tell you is the truth. So listen up Daughter."

"**_Dream_**, Can you help me with this one?" I looked over to the bitch that's been in my head like she was my therapist for the past year, asking for permission. "You know me better than I do, So sure, why not?" I closed my eyes and sat in the lotus position and displayed Eve's memories on the barrier of my cell. "Before beings with feet walked the surface of the celestial bodies, we existed as living planetary beings. "I am Talmeteth. The planet of Creation. My sister Nibara is the planet of Insight. Billions of years ago we fought over who would be the center of the universe and in doing so we destroyed half of our solar system. Our four armed, blue mother goddess didn't like that so she Fixed everything and tasked me and Nibara with helping the souls of the planets we destroyed ascend to a higher consciousness. My punishment was to always remember what we did and Nibara's was to sense what was, what is and what will be." "Clair, is Nibara?" Reaper yelled from across the room and banged her hands on the barrier. "Yes!" Eve and I spoke in unison. "Is that why you're evil?" "Yes, I've been bored out of my mind waiting on Nibara to remember herself. In every life we've looked at Mother Aura's punishment as a curse but it was actually all of the power that we needed to keep ourselves busy. I could become anything I touched and it gave me the knowledge of anyone whose laid hands on it. Clair had the knowledge of the universe at her fingertips but it was only accessible during Mother Aura's divine timing. All of the black women on this planet who have mysteriously manifested super powers are also celestial reincarnations." This all made sense and explained a lot of the solar system dreams that I've had. "I used to have dreams about a dark skinned woman with blue arms holding me and humming. I could never see her face but I knew that it was of a black woman." Eve scoffed and gave me a no duh stare. "She is the mother of all of us and the original divine female being of color." I understood that part but how did Eve and Clair get here on earth. "After Mother Aura re-made the universe she placed us on her heart, Earth and we awoke in what your people call the garden of Eden. She called in the spirits of those planets and both of us gave birth to them as the first women of the earth. Later on our daughters created the penis bearers and from there the insanity started. Little boys are so needy and whiny. Mom i'm hungry, Mom there's a tiger in the yard. Blah-Blah-Blah!" "So you and Clair birthed everyone on the planet like queen ants?" "No, like bed bugs. We ate food and made women, who we raised into strong leaders and then moved on to another part of the world. To do it all over again. And just to be clear, Those bible names are bullshit. I've been called Isis, Gweneverie, Chaos, Yang, Liar. Eve just means the beginning. To tell the truth Nibara is older than me, that's why she knows what she knows." "Why are you telling us this now, and why haven't you done something about Wise and her experiments?" "What fun would that be? I find great pleasure in watching Nibara slowly crawl into having fully autonomy over her intuition. When we were in the garden she spoke the divine mothers name and from there it's been the best rollercoaster ride I've ever been on." The doors down the hall opened and Wise walked in with her arm raised. "Let's go Dream, let's finally see where you pull things from."

"***Wise*** to the team, I'll be conducting experiments for the next twenty four hours. If there is an emergency you'll have to take care of it yourselves." I ended the communication and pressed my wrist to activate the brain scanners. "I've always been slightly jealous of you, Dream." "Is it because I look good with short hair and not like some fourteen year old boy! Or the fact that my breasts are the same size?" I laughed at her obvious attempt to rile me up and rolled my eyes as her head went into the machine. "Activate." "You have to tell your machines what to do. Ha! Fiz was right, you are not on her level." "I know what you're doing, nightmare child." "Don't call me that." "Why not, your mother called you that didn't she?" "You don't know what you're talking about." "Oh but I do. Your mother was the super heroine Mindscape, who went insane and you were placed in foster care. A couple of homes and years down the line you come into your powers when the eldest daughter of your foster family began molesting you. When no one believed you, your powers made them see the truth. But it was too late. You killed everyone in the house by manifesting a pride of lionesses who ate them alive." Dream's brain activity showed that I hit a nerve and she was experiencing a memory. ***Deet! Deet!*** "Oh good, you're done!" "What did you do?" "Nothing yet. Drones!" "Oh, and I'm jealous of you because you can imagine what you want and bring it into the world without any help from anyone else." My robotic assistants carried her to her cell and brought in Reaper who fought against her W-3KNS cuffs. "I've made those to counteract your powers of decay, but did you know that you can resurrect the dead?" I pressed a button on my wrist and a drone brought forth a dead mouse on a tray. I paced my fingers on the part of the onyx cuff that was closest to her pointer finger. "Here you go. It's just like your family business." She rolled her eyes and touched the tip of her finger to the mouse's tail. Nothing happened at first but the mouse started to move and came awake. "What the fuck? I've touched a bunch of dead bodies and that's never happened before." "You didn't know what you were before now." "You speak as if you've always known. Aren't you pissed?" "No, I've always known that black women are special, no matter if you're straight-Gay-Bi or whatever. I just hate you poor bitches and your food stamps and wic bullshit." "Bitch! People on government assistance actually need that help. We all can't have wealthy daddies who shuck and jive for the white men who used to own everything." "It kept food on the table and poverty out of our lives." The mouse started to tremble and shake uncontrollably as it coughed up blood and then killed over. "Yes!" I expected the mouse to die because it didn't have an emotional attachment to her. **Bon**! **Bon!** "Fuck! Your powers are going to be just as difficult as Eve's I see." My nanobots were unable to replicate the gene that's tied to her power and now I'll have to wait until the full moon to extract her powers. "Drones!" They moved from their spot on the wall but I held my hand up to halt them. "Oops, Almost forgot!" I touched the cuffs and reactivated it as the drones moved forward to pick her up and carry her out of the room. "What's that saying about loose lips?" I laughed out loud as they left the room and I made my way to the super computer Fix built eight years ago.

"Muse to **_Mini_**, we've come up with zilch. We're heading home, you should do the same." A smile curved my lips as I powered down and called my clones into my body. "Thank you, Muse." I made my way across town to my apartment but before I could get there I swarm of wasps prevented me from stepping forward. "Fuck me!" The moment we apprehend the more dangerous Villains, the lesser known villains come out of the woodworks. I looked around to see if anyone was watching before crouching behind a thick tree and activating my suit. "You always want to fight, but we're here to talk." In front of me the wasps turned into a hand and pointed to the roof of my condo. I ran inside and made my way to the roof as Mysticana, Fruit-Bomb and Brightness stepped forward with Wasp taking her human form. "Tell me why I shouldn't contact my team and haul the four of you into Oni-max prison?" "Because you don't have clearance to get in and they don't want you there." Brightness answered as her Sun aura faded. "Join us, we have the means to pay you and respect you as our leader." My laugh came out as a snort and then I cackled as her words played through my mind. I've never liked the idea of villains doing what they want but as a woman born to Cuban parents who migrated here twenty-six years ago, I understand just how wrong this world is and how it treats people of color. Especially women who are a part of the LGBTQIA+ community. "Why would I become evil? All I want to do is make money and I am a miniature army?" They exchanged the same look and smiled as they looked back at me. "Let me show you something." Mysticana held up her staff and made a whirlpool of rainbow energy. In its center it showed Wise fighting a three-eyed giant and a chimera beast with four heads. "Wise has replicated all of the powers she's come across, even yours. The image changed to show Wise using all of our powers against us as the Vixens fought alongside the hogs. The last image showed the destruction of the planet as a result and then ended as she removed her staff from the ground. "You know we hate you as much as every other Villain squad but we need to work together." They were right and to be honest it was sad that it took the Villains to help realize this. "Okay, I obviously can't tell all of my team, so what do you suggest?" "I sense that Attire, Fix and Vortex are already hip to what she has planned. Eve, Clair and Dream are the only ones who are strong enough to go up against her powers. "Clair? How?" Mysticana used her Staff to show me what Everything showed her and I had to steele my emotions so that I wouldn't burst into a small army. "Wait! So we're celestial bodies made into flesh? All because of sibling rivalry and an Overprotective Mother goddess named Aura?" "We know what is coming and we're going to gather as much help as we can to stop it." They left me on the rooftop to contemplate what to do next. I made six clones appear and we shared a silent understanding of what needs to be done. "Got it!"

"What about me?" Eve smiled and looked me up and down before taking a seat on the bed. "How does that saying go? Anything you can do, I can do better!" Here she goes again with her cryptic bullshit. "No *Attire*, it's an actual answer. "Clair" and I like to surround ourselves with women whose powers manifest in multiple ways. You think your only power is to control what is considered clothing, It's not. Your mind decides what it wants to wear the moment you wake up. Your mind works in the same way that Dream's does, when it comes to the manipulation of molecules. "Yeah, okay!" She didn't know what she was talking about. My power started when I was twelve and my mother sent me to school in thrift store clothes and mix-matched shoes. The kids called me ugly attire from that point on all the way to when we walked across the stage to get our diplomas and graduate high school. "Yes, and do you remember the week you worked as an intern for Melinda Voshay?" I hated the way that she intruded on my deeper thoughts and talked about them as if we were on her talk show but she had a point. That was the week my power changed from controlling the clothes that I touched, to any article of clothing in close proximity and enchanting the cloth like it was alive. *The money! I'm going to miss the money!* "You're not going to die, no one is. We'll gang up against this bitch if we have to." Eve was ever the optimist and if what she said was true then all I have to do is accept that the barrier is my shirt. "Yes!" I closed my eyes and thought about my favorite fairy tale story. The empress's new garments. My entire body tingled as the image of a skin tight multicolored suit came into my mind and I extended it out to my friends. "That's it. Keep doing it!" I could feel my body lift off of the ground as the energy clung to my body and I opened my eyes. Everyone was dressed in different material that was suited for their bodies and I used the remaining to make a suit for our queen of teleportation, Vortex. "So you think yourselves my equal, huh?" Blue veins of energy formed on the walls and spread to the floors and made glowing circles below us.

Vrrnnrr! Damn, It! Alright! Remember, what we see is real but we're just in a pocket dimension, Are you good, **_Reaper?_**" I shook my head no as Fix put her hand to the wall and pulled the nanobots onto her arm as we teleported to a forest with a glowing door in the sky. ROAR!!! We exchanged the same look as more wildlife called out to us. "I guess there's no better time than now, to acclimate our suits to our powers." Eve turned into a giant bat and flew off into the forest with Fix flying after her. Dream floated over and gave me a hug and laid her head against mine. "My air sickness is gone." She punched her fist into the air and flew after our other team mates. "Are you okay?" "No, the love of my life hates me and I don't know if we're reincarnated sisters or if she's my ancestor. What do I do Dream?" I floated down to the ground where my friend stood with tears falling down her exposed face. "Thank goodness we're "Captured." or my make-up would be a mess. I laughed with my friend but I could sense that she was hurting even more deep down. Her heart belonged to Clair and it took her two years to work up the courage to allow Eve to set them up. "How about we take our anger out on some freakshow experiments and then find a way to get your girl?"

"So you trapped them in the weird zone with those beasts?" "Yes **_Shade_**, I'm not taking any chances with them hoes." "Oh! Now you use AAVE, girl bye. How about next time you help them instead of allowing them to become villains. You should have allowed them to join us when they asked." "You don't know them like I do." **_Bing_**! Yes Mini!" "Hey, do you want to have cake and Ice cream on the roof?" Wise rolled her eyes and looked from me to the console before pressing the button. "No, but Shade said that she's on her way up there." If looks could kill she'd be a pile of bloody nanos and I'd take her thumb and transfer some money to my account for the damage that was done to my shop. That shop has been in my family for one hundred years and now it's a pile of rubble thanks to Wise and Vortex's feud. "Okay, we plan on smoking and I know how you don't want that on camera so shut them off. "I did that the moment you said cake, eww!" Wise responded. I turned around and left as Wise disconnected the sound and took the elevator to the roof. "That bitch is so fake, I'm glad she said no." "Me too!" My heart skipped a beat as I turned around and looked into the face of my beautiful girlfriend who I haven't seen in a month and a half. She was still in her costume with her bright aura flowing around her as she landed next to me. "Brightness, when did you get back?" "I never left. I had to lie to you because we knew that Wise was up to something." To my left a staff appeared and twirled into a portal that Mini and Mysticana stepped out of. "Shade, please follow me." My hair tugged at my scalp and pointed at the portal as Mini walked back in. My girlfriend grabbed my hand as we walked into the portal with the other MIni behind me as it closed and the swirling walls turned into a long hallway. My hair sensed several hundred people in the room ahead of us before the sound of them talking all at once entered my ears. Below us was a room filled with male and female supers and even more with those who are non-binary. It was a room of melanated supers of all colors. "What is this?" Brightness rubbed my shoulders and turned me towards the stage. "We are called the Melanted Guardians of power. Baby, I want you to join us. Mini has already said yes." "Baby, you know I'll follow after that sunshine valley of yours until the world ends. But Professor Psycho already has a list of our strengths and weaknesses." "Yes, but she is also in the middle of a divine battle that's about to take place." "A divine battle?" "Yes, between Eve and Clair. They do this every few million years and it could destroy or change the world. No one knows but them." "Here, this will help." Mysticana touched Brightness with her staff and I instantly knew what was happening and why. The moment her energy left my body my hair tugged at the portal and a chill ran up my spine. "We have to get back." "Say less." Mysticana held her staff into the sky and a thick fog formed at our feet. "Prepare yourselves. The fight is Here!!" My body was pulled downwards and we fell out of a cloud in the sky with a large multi-headed beast battling a ten foot tall metallic blue and silver Wise. "How cliche', She just had to inject herself didn't she?" Mini and Brightness landed next to me along with several male supers. "Hi, I'm Cards, this is Sky-fire, Arsenal, Spoken-Word, Giant, Limb and Gray-matter. We are a huge fan of yours Shade.

"Now I'm as strong as you, _**Everything**_, or should I call you Aunty.?" Wise sent a blast of lighting in my direction but my dear horns absorbed the energy and I slashed my claws down her torso. "Bitch, you are not my daughter! Mine are the Vixens your ancestor is Clair, stupid!" My wolf head bit into her shoulder as my dragon head breathed fire on her face. "You call me stupid but you don't realize that this is the strongest metal on earth. It is heat resistant." She was right, it is the strongest and it's also her weakness. She's allowed herself to depend on the nanos that she stole from Fix. "Your trash, Everything." "Your birth mother is trash, she should have rolled over on top of you when you were an infant. I Picked you up and placed you in your crib, dumb-ass." My bird head used its beak to jab at her neck but the nanos absorbed the attack just like the rest. Where is Clair, when you need her? This is her fight too. She generated a chest blast that knocked me backwards and into a lake with those smelly ass geese scampering out of the way. "Uhh! Bitch I hate this water!" I pulled all of my heads together and changed into my favorite monster form. I grew to match Wise in size as a Dragon with a praying mantis head, scorpion tale and four bird wings. It's been a while since I wore my true dark brown skin tone on my scales with my green feathered wings buffering the air around us. "Whoa!" I reached down and helped several of the supers and almost dropped them when I saw that a few of them were male. "About time! I was waiting for our sons to catch up!" They jumped out of my hand and went into action as a swarm of human sized drones flew out of Wise's stomach. "Okay, bitch we get it. You're a gal that can do it all." I clapped my wings together as a large portion of them flew in my direction but all it did was make them into a smaller army of mini-drones. I searched the ground for the one person that I can't sense with my powers and couldn't find her anywhere so I looked for Reaper. Instantly I smelled blood and flew to the southern end of the block where my teammate held a dead Clair in her hands while crying. *Always with the dramatics.* "I tried, It didn't work, I tried Eve. Why didn't it work?" I took on my first human-like form as I landed and allowed certain parts of my dragon form to remain as I pulled my friend into a hug. "You have it in you. You're just not motivated enough." Reaper narrowed her gaze on me and took a deep breath before speaking. "I realize that you're my 'Ancestor', but its like I fucking said! The woman that I love the most in all of existence is dead. I've tried to bring her back numerous times. Nothing has worked!" "Close your eyes and tell her how you feel with your heart." Reaper did as I asked and several minutes went by until Clair came awake with a gasp and stood up. She glared up at Wise who was being assaulted by every super person in the city. Clair raised her left palm to the sky while facing her right to the ground as purple energy gathered around her body. "I am she who brings forth knowledge!" Her body began to grow in size as a third eye formed on her forehead and another set of arms grew from her shoulders. She now matched Wise in being a giant and I jumped into the sky and became a monster once more and spewed fire at the Nanobot-giantess. Clair held up her hands and sent a blast of purple energy at Wise that she followed up with an optic blast from her eyes. *About Time, Sis!*

"I was never Mya St.Clair or the super heroine named ***Clair***. I am She who was born from the true mother. She, who is the wielder of All Knowledge. The giver of insight. She of the Astral body." I projected my voice out to everyone to hear as I sent a wave of energy at Wise and managed to knock her backwards. "Reaper, I forgive you and can't wait for our dinner date tomorrow." I added, and I leaped into the air and launched myself at Wise. "You are not my mother! I could never have descended for something like you!" "Is that why I'm winning?" I poured my energy into the nanos and allowed it to spread into all of them. "Ha! You're giving me your power, How stupid." "Short sighted as always." I laughed and stepped back as her Nanobots exploded like popcorn all over her body. "I'm giving everyone back what you stole and the extra will go to where it's needed." She didn't have time to speak as her entire body simultaneously exploded and the energy flowed into the city. I reached out to grab her falling body but it teleported to her secondary lab beneath the prison. "She never gives up." Eve landed next to me and for the first time in ten years I didn't want to punch her. This is my sister, my actual sister. "I love you too, Sis." "Looks like this isn't over." "It won't be until she is cut off from the earth frequency." In my mind I could see Wise being wrapped in white glowing fabric. "Attire!" We said in unison and she appeared in front of us in a ribbon of colors. "Talk about a glow up!" "You didn't know you could do that?" She answered Eve's question by shaking her head no but never taking her eyes off of me. "Is this a truce or worldly domination?" "I haven't decided. But if the latter should happen just know that you're good. I still need to look gorgeous if I'm going to rule." The ground trembled and I sensed that it was the earth herself disagreeing with my joke. "No one is supposed to rule. We're supposed to live in harmony but it can't be achieved right away or we wouldn't learn anything. But this right here." I used all of my hands to point in every direction. "This is me living in my queen of wands energy and turning the wheel to a new age." As I finished my words Wise appeared in her spaceship and released another wave of robots that attacked with the same stolen powers. I held my hands out and focused on the energy returning and nothing happened. "She must have finally analyzed my power." Eve leaped forward and flew into the air to spew her multicolored fire as the drones landed. I made myself smaller and pulled my girlfriend into my arms. "I love you. Reaper." "I love you too, Seer." I could see that the male supers were enjoying their extra boost of power and that it was always supposed to be this way. If We encouraged it they would have had a safe place to train. And not have to hide their powers from the world. Reaper kissed my cheek and jumped into the sky like a ghost with her eerie glow trailing behind her. My palms glowed and I took to the sky after my girl and took out a squad of drones with a shockwave clap. Oh yeah, this is going to be fun! The energy from my hands crawled over my body and spilled out from my eyes as a ringing sensation formed. In my mind I could see a bat, jaguar, eel and Komodo dragon sitting at a table and then it changed to a tall dark skinned man with blue eyes smoking a blunt on a couch. I blinked and put it in the back of my mind as I leaped into battle.

The 8th Daughter

"Mom!" "Shh-Shh, I know, baby. It'll be over soon." I had to lay in bed on my stomach as the pain in my back spread from my shoulder blades to the crack of my ass. Similar pain formed in my feet, and the skin of my face burned as my mother placed her cool hands on my shoulder. "Just breathe, baby. Try to stretch as much as you can." I did as she asked, but that only made the pain worse, and I cried out in pain. All of it began to recede, but certain parts of my body remained sore. Something rough brushed across my lower leg, and my shoulder blades felt extremely heavy. "See, now that wasn't so bad, now was it?" I was able to move as the pain was gone, and when I put my hand up to my head, I gasped at the large, rough protrusions I now felt. "Congratulations, Vamora, you've successfully survived the change." My mother helped me to my feet, and I almost tripped over my hooves and dragon tail. "By the goddess, look at her." My grandparents walked into my room, and our wings took up a lot of the space. "I told your father that you'd change a week early, but he said it wouldn't happen until the next full moon." I stretched my wasp wings and messaged the sore area of my upper skull. I stepped over to the standing mirror and took in my new demonic form. Goat horns and hooves, Wasp wings, and a dragon's tail. Yellow and white flames replaced my breath as it came out of my nose and mouth. "Oh! She has the day spark!" My grandfather yelled. Two years ago, I was told about my demonic heritage and began to prepare, but I didn't think it would hurt like it did. The new appendages sprouting from my back were heavy despite their appearance. I haven't applied to any colleges and planned to take a gap year after high school to travel the world. Now, I had to acclimate to the supernatural world and my powers. "How do you feel?" My mother asked. Truthfully, I felt perfectly fine; the pain was gone, and it was like I could do one hundred laps around the estate. "I feel great. But I'm extremely hungry." My stomach rumbled, and my grandmother pointed at me, and my clothes changed into casual pants and a dress shirt. They led me through the balcony doors and jumped off of the ledge. "Trust your wings. They will not let you fall." My mother stretched her butterfly wings and floated upwards. "Come on, my little firebug." Next to her, my grandfather hoovered with his beetle wings buzzing and a smile on his face as he held his hands out to me. In the distance, I could hear a crow as I closed my eyes, focused on my wings, and lifted off the ground. At first, it was uncomfortable, but as I rose higher, I felt the cold air twisted around my body. "That's it, baby." I spent the next twenty minutes soaring through the night sky and then came back home to land next to my mother. "Your father is on his way, and he sends his love. Now, I need you to stand here." She guided me to the altar and stood behind me as my grandparents took positions on my right and left. My grandmother cleared her throat and held her arms out to my mother. "I, the worker of the winds, brought you into this world." My grandfather did the same and cleared his throat. "I, whose voice is of the forest animals, brought you into this world." My mother held her hand out to them and then pointed them at me. "I, the wielder of strength, brought you into this world." Translucent energy swirled next to my mother, and my father appeared with his arms out. "I, The Traveler of Realms, brought you into this world." A tingling sensation formed in my throat, and everything around me became blurry as I lifted off the ground. I descended, and my entire body tingled as I changed back into my human form. Time flew by as we spent the rest of the night eating amazing food and opening presents. I opened a present from my grandparents, and it was a longsword with a golden blade and a black tourmaline grip. A raw clear quartz crystal was placed at the bottom at the sword's pommel. It glowed with yellow light and receded into the palm of my right hand. "This is why we said no about the tattoo." It traveled from my palm to my shoulder and then turned into the sword. The color was the perfect contrast against my beige skin. "Now, open ours." My mother pointed to a large box that wasn't there a second ago. I took the top off, and the smell of something living hit me as yellow eyes looked back at me. "A female basilisk." I yelled. I reached out for her, and she slithered into my hands. "Very good, yes, she is a princess like you." I turned to my parents, and they nodded along with my grandparents. "There are more gifts in that box." I allowed my new friend to move up to my neck as we looked at the other three items I barely noticed. A brass doorknob, a jewelry box made of redwood, and a demon goat horn like mine. "The horn is a catalyst for good luck. The jewelry box is filled with trinkets from our ancestors. Wearing them will summon their soul and allow you to use one of their powers." My mother held her hand out, and the doorknob flew into her palm. "This was made by your shadow the day you were born." She placed it on the ground, and a door appeared. My father took my hand as it opened, and we descended the stairs into a luxury home that was unlike anything I'd ever seen. "We had the same expression on our faces when we saw this for the first time." I blinked as the knowledge of every room and what was in it came to mind. "Have a seat, honey. We need to finish telling you about our true demon ancestry." A demon rat ran into the room, and my basilisk chased after it and into the other room. "I'm going to name her Huntress." "Ohh, that's good. I was going to suggest Fangora, but Huntress sounds better." My grandmother extended her fangs as she spoke and retracted them to make her point. "Mom, you're the matriarch." My mother cleared her throat and cut her eyes from me to her. "Right." She responded. "As you know, honey, we told you that we're demons. But what we didn't say was that our demon ancestors were made by a supreme being. Her name was Aura, A creation goddess. She made the mistake of insulting her mother, and she was banished to the earthly plane. Before she was captured, she devoured three of her siblings' divinity." She stopped and took a deep breath before continuing. "The sister she devoured was what we call straight like us, and the other two were queer like You. So technically you're a demon-goddess." Had I not grown demon body parts or walked through a magic door, I wouldn't have believed her and laughed at everything she just said. I wasn't raised in a religious home, and every time I asked a question about religion, my parents would scoff and say that it was the blind leading the blind. In the fifth grade, I made a catholic friend, and my parents packed us up and moved from New York to Columbus, Ohio. "Do you have any questions?" My father asked. "Yes. Why am I being told about this now? Instead of when we had our previous demon talk." They exchanged looks, and a silent understanding was reached by the four of them. "We had to wait for your divine counterpart to awaken. Her family reached out to us a week ago." "Her?" They nodded. My forehead throbbed, and for several seconds, I could see the image of a blue moon in my mind's eye. "She is the moon, and you're the sun." That last part hit me like a ton of bricks as it bounced around my mind. "The remaining divine family have sent beasts and demons from other divine creations after us since the beginning of our existence. This is why we are only born under the sign of Capricorn, the scapegoat. The sun and moon were both in Capricorn at the time of her fall from divinity. It was Aura's way of turning a curse into a blessing. They can't track us until we're of age, and tonight is the last night that you remain off of their radar." That made a lot of sense. I've always had a tendency to second-guess myself and not endeavor to do more. Being raised in a wealthy family gave me a sense that I always had a backup plan because of my trust fund. Now, all of that money meant nothing. I'm a Demon Goddess created by a supreme being who wants revenge on her family of deities I've never met. Got it! "How do you know all of this?" I asked. "Some demonic families have multiple offspring, but your grandmother and I are of an only-daughter line." "And I was cut off by my family because of it. They thought something was wrong with your mother's blood." That made a lot of sense, with my father being white and my mother and grandparents being black. My light skin was in the middle, and now that I thought about it, I was a light-skinned demon like the bitch down the street called me. I let out a loud laugh as I thought about the uppity bitch up the street and everyone turned to look at me. Their surprised expression let me know that I didn't laugh on the inside like I thought I did. "Last year, Kamika Hawkens called me a light-skinned demon before she went to college." "I ate her." My mother held her hand to her stomach and rubbed it. "Nobody calls my baby names. And besides, her family were demon hunters." That made sense. I could still hear the sound of her mother's scream when she first laid eyes on me. "Can we get back on track?" My grandmother pointed at herself, and her eyes glowed red. We all nodded as my basilisk came back into the room with a lump in her stomach. She crawled up into my lap and went to sleep as I stroked her head. "There is a Demon god who rivals your power. His name is Tirogolly. No one knows where he came from or how he became so powerful, but he knew about the two of you being born before we did." "He tried to pay me a billion dollars for you, and when I said no, he attacked us. Your father severed his left arm, and he has wanted all of us dead since. The great Titaness Hecate placed a blessing of the unseen around us until your eighteenth Birthday. It ends at sunrise, and there will be all types of beings coming at us. By now, the sword has bestowed you with its fighting spirit, and your body will protect you as best as it can, but when we say fly, you need to leave as fast as you can." The last part made my stomach lurch, and I almost jumped up from the couch and ran with Huntress in my arms to the exit. "The good news is that she sent her son to help us. He'll be your second bodyguard." She pointed at my sleeping birthday gift, and my ears popped. "Did someone say, Darren?" The hair on my arms stood up as a tornado appeared across from us and took the form of a teenager about my age. He was tall with light brown skin and hazel-green eyes. His large bat wings stretched out in the large open space, and his spaded tail slashed the air with a hello. Red lightning formed and disappeared all over his body. "Cool, you're a sun demigoddess. My younger brother is a fire demigod. Hey bro! I think this more of your speed!!" A green and blue ball of fire appeared next to him and took the form of a preteen with features similar to his.

"This is my younger brother Torin. You got this, bro!" They bumped fists, and Darren turned into a bat and flew out of the window. "Is it weird to have a bodyguard that's a kid?" He took a seat next to me and reached out to pet Huntress, and his hand changed into a dragon's claw. She came awake and nuzzled his claw. "So what's next?"

"Did you find her?" "N-No, master, she is still hidden. But the bringer of daylight is awake, and she has the wings of a wasp. They live in Ohio." Cawrr! "Go! Wait in the forest for a sign of her awakening." I pointed to the door, and my minion turned into a swarm of ravenous butterflies, and they flew out of my throne room. The last thing I need is for those bitches to find each other and awaken to their true power. I've been the ruler of day and night since the beginning of time, and I won't allow these split tails to rule. One arrogant mistake by the goddess was what brought us into existence and caused us to be hunted ever since. I unfurled my wings and teleported myself to the caverns below my mountain home. "How dare you hold me here, WORM!" I laughed my grandmother, as she sent a blast of energy at the barrier that I trapped her in. "Try all you want, grandmother. It's no use. That is what's left of my mother's power. Once I have the rest of it, you'll be the lesser being." She crossed her dark blue arms and rolled her cosmic eyes. "I am the one who birthed the first existence. You can't hold me here forever, abomination." The ground trembled as she threw her arms out and banged against the barrier. "I can because that energy is just as divine as you, granny. Now, Where have you hidden the rest of your family?" She laughed and turned into a whirling cloud of cosmic energy. Once she took that form, she wouldn't say anything else, and I'd have to wait until the next full moon when she has to take a physical form. "So be it, Maw-Maw!" With a thought, I transported myself to Columbus, Ohio, and took the form of a six-year-old boy with small crow wings. I turned my legs into a horse's and grew a scorpion tail just for fun. My body floated above the air space, and I allowed myself to fall to the ground. Umph! I snapped my left wing and right leg for double the sympathy.

Caw!! "Help!" The sound of wings flapping filled the air as I pretended to be unconscious. Pain was something I was used to with an ex-goddess as a mother. After a thousand years of abuse, I was finally able to eat her third eye and take most of her powers for myself, but she managed to send the rest of it to my sisters, who have now passed it on to the newly awakened demon-Godesses. And now I'm here pretending to be helpless for a power meal. "Oh, my daylight!" An elderly woman spoke. I felt the presence of a powerful demigod along with the family, and I almost licked my lips at the spicy smell of his power. "Please help me." I allowed my mind to slip into the astral realm as my body healed, and their gasps of concern was the last thing I could hear. I don't know how much time passed before I awakened on a couch with several beings sitting around me. "Are you okay, cutie pie?" one of them asked. "I-I think s-so, where am I?" I looked around the room to the six supernatural beings that surrounded me. "Your little wings are so cute." The green-eyed demigod pulled my wing, and I had to force myself not to wince at his strength. It felt like a pinched nerve, and I could see he wasn't using all of his strength. "I'm Vamora. These are my parents, Mira and Thomas, and my grandparents, Elandra and Marcov." "What's your name?" "Memphis. I'm from the clan of crow-hoofs." I made sure to cry a little and pout my lips for an added sense of helplessness. "You said you needed help." I jumped up from the couch, flew into the air, and pretended to be terrified for my life. "My family was captured by a demon with the power of a God. I think his servants called him Til-no, Tiity-grove." They laughed for several seconds before Vamora touched my shoulder. "Tirogollv, cutie pie." "He-he said if I didn't lure you to him, he would eat me." The oldest-looking demon flew up and wrapped her arms around me. "I don't have anywhere to live." "You can stay here with us." she said. My stomach rumbled on its own, and they guided me to a kitchen full of food. "Eat up." Vamora cut a piece of cake and handed it to me. At first, I didn't really know what to do with it, but as the smell lingered in my nostrils, I couldn't resist the urge to lick the icing. The taste of it made my tongue tingle, and I picked the fork up and dug in. Mother created me before such things were invented, and when they were, I didn't see a need for them. My number one goal was to spread the demon seed across the globe. In my hands, I held the literal interpretation of my assured victory. A piece of cake.

"So an ax, a spider bodyguard that crawled into my pocket and went to sleep and a jewelry box full of enchanted hand-me-downs. Oh! And a Horn." My mother and two fathers nodded while my baby brother played with his spit bubbles. "Can we get a grenade and rocket launcher for our birthday?" The twins asked. Mia reached for my spider while Michelle picked up the horn. "Uh, no. You will get conventional weapons like the rest of us." My father responded. I've waited for this day for fifteen years and I can't believe I'm now an adult demon with bat wings, goat horns, hoofs and a leopard's tail. The change was exhilarating and the blasts of blue moonlight that I'm able to generate from my eyes made me feel like a demon-superhero. "I know we're adopted but I can't wait for our sixteenth birthday. I want a rocket launcher." "And I really want that grenade." My parents laughed at their adopted children. Ten years ago the Alpha of the werewolves and The vampire queen gave the twins to my parents to raise, after they went into hiding. My youngest brother was the reincarnation of Cthulhu and he was supposed to be a wrathful deity of chaos but his little spit bubbles said otherwise. My maternal side of demons can only produce one offspring that is either male or female and today I was told that I'm not just a demon, but also a moon goddess. Hopefully my other half is a thick lesbian with big breast. A chill ran over my body and the image of the sun flashed in my mind. The sun's warmth made me feel good inside, like a well needed hug. My sisters sniffed the air and ran over to the windows. "We have company." Outside the window a swarm of ravenous bumblebees approached. "What's the number one rule of demon fighting?" My mother asked all of us to inspire our inner demons to come out. Since

I was still in my demon form I waited for my parents to change and my sisters to shift into hybrid wolf-bats. Baby Lu did his own thing with his bat wings like mine and mouth tentacles and spit bubbles that did whatever he wanted them to do. The second the swarm entered my mothers barrier they grew larger and we flew outside to meet them head on. My mother made a sword of ice and my father threw six bottles of his strongest potions at them. They exploded and made the smoke screen that we needed to form our attack. I could see perfectly fine through the haze and my family made me proud. Several bugs headed towards me and I held my hand out and my ax appeared instantly. "Ax and you shall receive." I yelled. The silver blade of my ax glowed bright blue as my shadow crept up my body and formed a protective shield. If this is what I could do without trying, I can't wait to see what I do when I'm properly trained. Out of the corner of my eye something gleamed in the daylight right before a sharp pain caused me to fall to the ground. My ax turned into my tattoo as I closed my eyes and all the air around me pulled upwards. *Nighmena!!* The sound of my mothers voice was the last thing that I heard before finally losing consciousness. "Hey! Wake up!" I came awake fighting the air and I could hear the blurry people backing up. "We mean you no harm." I blinked away the dryness as my eyes focused on the most beautiful woman I've ever seen. "I'm Vamora and this is my family. We came to help." Her words and beauty temporarily stunned me but the second I saw her Insect wings I jumped into the air and looked for the nearest exit. I managed to get to a spiral staircase that went upwards and took me outside. With my body still tired I didn't get far and quickly lost altitude and crashed into a tree branch that tore my wing. My body hit the ground and I got up to run but the pain in my wing made it difficult to move. The beautiful Vamora held her hand out to me and I reluctantly accepted it as she helped me back into the house. "I'm sorry that we scared you." She placed a hand on my shoulder and gave it a little squeeze. "I need to find my family." She sat next to me on the couch and I pointed at our family portrait. Just the sight of their smiling faces made me cry or roar out of anger. Since birth my parents have been getting me ready for the arrival of the demon-god Tirogollv. Not having powers to train with was hard but my parents were right about our demonic instincts. I know how to summon and direct moon energy out of my eyes but my ability to believe in myself was shattered into a millions pieces now that my family have been abducted by Tirogollv's minions. Aachu! The little demon sitting across from me sneezed and looked to the floor and grabbed a tissue from the end table. "Excuse me. Where is the bathroom?" "The middle door down that hallway." I pointed to the hallway behind us and as he walked away I caught a glimpse of his shadow. Its eyes were white but the second I looked into them the shadow shrunk and took the form of the little boy that walked down the hall. "Psst, hey!" The other kid with the shiny glow around him waved as he spoke telepathically. "His name is Memphis and he mysteriously showed up last night, be on guard around him." I never experienced the sensation of hearing with my mind and it was kind of refreshing to know that I wasn't the only one to see that. "I'm Torin, a demigod, by the way." he nodded and stood up from the couch. "I'm here as an unofficial bodyguard, the direction of all of this is up to the two of you. By the way." He spoke as if he knew things that I didn't and even though the supernatural world is nothing new to me, I could feel an intense power come off of this divine teenager. The demon world was vast, but the realm of the divine was literally infinite. "Do any of you know where his domain is?" Everyone shook their head no except for Torin who nodded yes. "The both of you have only been full Goddesses for less than twenty-four hours and you haven't actually tapped into your magic yet." He walked over to the large space we use to have small dance parties and held his hands out to me and Vomora. We got up and stood next to him and faced her family as the little crow demon walked in with a snowglobe in his hands and took his seat. "Wh- what's going on? Is he here?" Tears streamed down his face as he tried to stuff his toy in his pocket. Torin cut me a look that displayed exactly what I was thinking. "You two need to make physical contact." He looked down at our hands and I reached out as she did. My hands were just as clammy as hers and we had a mutual feeling of awkwardness. Torin teleported to the seat cushion next to the crow-wing and pulled him into a side hug and leaned his head on his. "Big brother T won't let anything bad happen, I promise." he pulled out a large bag of candied fruit and handed it to him. "My favorite, thanks!" The little demon stuffed his mouth and chewed as we all laughed at the adorable look on his face. "Um!" I held up our conjoined hands and Torin smiled. "That part was a partial truth, you don't really need to hold hands. Just stand next to each other and ingest the same food." Now I was really embarrassed and starting to get pissed off. I don't have time for games when my family is still missing. I let go of Vamora's hand and walked out of the room with a growl. I speed walked to my room and as I stepped through the doorway the temperature changed from warm to hot. My feet kept moving and I froze at the sight of all the guests from downstairs spread out in my room. Torin held his fingers up to his lips and shut the door with a wave of his other hand. Once the door closed the temperature in the room dropped back to warm and my ears popped as I looked around the room to their concerned faces. "He thinks we're down there but obviously we're not. I'm sorry for all the confusion." He reached into his pocket and handed me the little demon's snow globe. I gawked at it with raised eyebrows as he placed it in my hands. "Take a look inside." I held it up to my face and looked at the normal house with a family of five. "What the fuck?" As I looked closer my heart began to race. The twins were holding snowballs while my three parents and Lu made a snowman. "How do we get them out of there?" My question was directed to my new demigod friend who lifted a huge weight off of my shoulders with well intended trickery. "This is half of his magic and the other half belongs to a minor deity." His eyes changed from human to dragon and he sniffed the air and then exhaled blue and green flames. "This keeps getting better and better." Torin rolled his shoulders and unfurled his dragon-phoenix wings. "I didn't expect this last little bit of info, so I'll take care of that and once I give you the sign, use your sight to focus on your family and call out to them telepathically. Oh! You're unperceivable until you take the position you're in downstairs and blink." He jumped upwards and vanished in a whirl of flames. I looked at the snowglobe of my family who appeared to be having the time of their lives. Everyone had smiles on their faces and that was really all that I needed to physically relax. The new variables were unexpected but I'm a bat wing and we're good at adaptation. My original plan was to take his head like I practiced since twelve but Vamora and I have to come up with a plan together. Since this is all about us. "Thank you." My eyes stopped glowing as I looked at her and she blushed. "I'm just an innocent bystander like you, Torin is the miracle worker. His little con was funny to watch." Vamora responded. "Right, I wasn't holding your hand. It was fake..?" She nodded and pointed to my television. It came on and showed all of us downstairs in our original positions. Torin's reflection looked over at us and smiled before turning back to us. "Ok are we ready?" Vamora asked. I felt something moving in my hair and my spider demon crawled out and down my shoulder to my arms and then on the snowglobe. "Well hello sleepy head." She waved and crawled over it's surface and held out her front legs in a way that looked like she was taking its measurements. Vamora walked over to me and her serpent bracelet came alive. Immediately they started to communicate with hisses and hand movements about the snowglobe. "Is this normal?" I asked. "Your guess is as good as mine." She replied. Our pet's conversation ended with the snake touching the tail of her hip to her little feet. It was so cute I almost forgot about our current situation. I still had some questions about what we're supposed to do. "I originally planned to take him down with the help of my family and now that includes you. So what's the plan? Do we continue to play pretend until Torin comes back or do we stuff him full of so much food that he is unable to move." "Sounds like a plan." Vamora's mother rubbed her stomach and she shared an inside joke with my counterpart. "Are you a vegetarian?" "Nope, I devoured a large pizza all by myself two weeks ago." I've seen my father eat a neighbor who was a pedophile when I was six and I always wanted to try and eat something alive and whole. "Ready?" Her family looked to the t.v and vanished as they mimicked their positions. "Wait!" I pulled Vamora close and planted my lips against hers. They were as soft as pillows and she reciprocated the act by pulling our bodies together. My C-cup breast bounced against her D-cup and it took the tugging of our pets to pull us out of our passionate kissing. "Whoa." "Right!" her nipples showed through her gray top and she caught me looking and softly flicked a finger over my left nipple. "We'll pick this back up later." I nodded in agreement as we took our positions and blinked. I took a deep breath and looked around the room and when I got to Vamora she blew me a kiss that made me blush. Memphis giggled and jumped out of his seat. "Ohh, I think she likes you." "Well that's good because I like her back. We're even getting married." I don't know where that last part came from but it managed to stir a real reaction out of her. "Oh, really?" Vamora's mother pulled out her cell phone and typed in some notes as she inspected me from head to toe. "I Have an eye for fashion and know exactly what to do with that gorgeous waistline." My breath caught in my throat at the thought of actually entertaining this further. It wasn't unusual for demons to marry upon first meeting or even having arranged marriages. With us being Demon-Goddesses it kind of already feels like this was going to happen. Even if she was Bisexual, I would be at her side. I'd just have to wait until I was alone to deal with how wet her double-D breasts made me. I looked away and thought about the task at hand as Torin blinked and I couldn't tell if that was the sign or not. He looked at his watch and cleared his throat. "I had a friend that was coming to help but I guess he isn't ready yet." I relaxed a little and took a seat on my favorite loveseat. This emotional roller coaster is becoming tedious and tiring.

"Memphis, I'm telling you, you have to try this, it's so good." Torin handed me another plate of vegetables and fried chicken tenders. "Can I try some of that sauce you put on yours?" Torin snapped his fingers and a bottle of sriracha sauce appeared and drizzled the red sauce over my chicken. "You let us know if we are stuffing you full of too much food." Ms. Mira rubbed my back and placed a scoop of baked mac and cheese on my plate. "We don't have any kids around here, so get used to the extra servings." Thomas refilled my juice and I couldn't help but to laugh. No one ever treated me this way and it was almost sad that I had plans of eating everyone in this room and then the ones in the snowglobe. "So we can pretend to have a party for another hour or so, but we have to formulate a plan against what's his name." Nighmena put her arms together and sat on the arm of the chair across from me. "He's way too powerful and a thousand steps ahead of us." She didn't know how right she was and the thought of it made me almost choke on a fry. I'm known as the endless pit and I have just enough room for them once the sun and moon align with saturn. Then their powers would be too much for them to control and I'll have the upper hand. "Call me if something comes up." Torin stepped backwards into a portal made of heat waves. Now I was able to execute the next phase of my plan. "Nighmena, are you going to stay with us?" She blushed and looked over to Vamora. "I have a better Idea." She pulled a doorknob from her pocket and attached it to the wall behind the couch. Once the door appeared, She walked in and the rest of us followed as I kept eating from my massive plate. "Just to be safe we'll lock ourselves in here until we can formulate a real plan." Little ms. Wasp-wings removed the doorknob and put it in her pocket. A smile crept over my face and I quickly finished my food and placed my platter on the large table in front of us. "There are plenty of rooms up those stairs and the basement is full of all kinds of treasures. The kitchen is back there if you want more to eat." She directed that last part to me and grabbed Nighmena's hand and they headed upstairs. I was now left alone with the parents who were easy prey that needed to be distracted.. "Can we play hide and seek?" Thomas laughed and arced an eyebrow at my question. "You just ate a lot of food. Don't you want to sit down and watch a movie or something?" *Fuck!* "Oh, right. My type of demon's get their powers at birth but the drawback is an insatiable hunger and a high metabolism." That managed to persuade them to my request and I allowed them to close their eyes as I got up and ran to the stairs and went down instead of up. I took the stairs two at a time and turned into a crow once I was out of their eyesight. My wings took me a great length from the stairs as I passed twenty large rooms. Once I reached the room at the end of the hallway I turned the corner and ended up in another long hallway. I turned around and the same hallway had rooms that went on and on. This was far enough so I chose the room with the smallest door and entered into darkness.

"Sorry, I'm not really used to all of this." Nighmena stunned me as she smiled and I put my hand to my sore lip that she accidentally bit down on. "It's cool. I guess as demons we need to get used to our bodies changing when we are aroused." Our fangs clashed against each other and I was the one who was on the bottom. "This is kind of weird though, with my family in my pocket." She nodded and we both laid on our backs and looked up to the beautifully painted ceiling. "So you've known about all of this since childhood?" "Yeah. I was almost abducted when I was six. My parents ate the couple who were trafficking kids and we moved here a month later." She gasped and joined our hands together. "I'm sorry that happened to you. It must have been terrifying." She laughed and gave me a kiss on the cheek. "Not really, I just remember being sad that my parents were crying and covered in blood. Any other kid would have pissed their pants at the sight of ravenous demons, but I just jumped in my dad's arms and asked what was wrong." We shared a laugh that made my sides hurt and I used it as a chance to cuddle. Time flew by as we talked and ended up falling asleep in each other's arms. "Vamora!" The sound of her voice jolted me awake and I gasped at the sight of us on the moon and the large sun off in the distance. Her bed vanished as we stood up and took a couple steps forward. "Whoa!" The ground at Nighmena's feet glowed blue and pulled her downwards faster than I could move. Just as I was about to dig into the ground with my claws my body was yanked backwards into the sun. I remained perfectly still as the warmth that surrounded me seeped into my physical being. The only comparison was like coming into a toasty room after being out in the cold weather of winter. *We are her! She is us!* I spoke the words and heard the voice of my counterpart in my head as an image of an immaculate floating palace entered my mind. It became reality as I blinked and felt my body moving at super speed and landing in the entryway. The large marble doors opened and I stretched out my four arms and floated forward. An indoor forest greeted me with beasts of the elements of all kinds making noises as I moved past them. I moved into another long hallway with statues on one side and portraits on the other that led to similar doors like the ones I just floated through. With this being a weird memory I allowed it to proceed and I held out all of my arms and pushed against the double doors that wouldn't budge. It took everything I had to shove them open and rip them off the hinges. With a wave of my hands I repaired the doors as I stepped into the room. I looked up to the seventeen sitting deities and the tallest multicolored queen-Mother stood with her six arms crossed. "We called you here to see how far you've come in your training." She spoke, with her voice echoing around the room. "Is that why you prevented me from entering, Mother?" The god sitting next to her was almost as tall and embodied a living forest, stood and placed a hand on the queen-mother's shoulder. "Show us what you've learned, daughter." The two of them sat back on their thrones as I extended my lower arms and cupped my lower hands like a bowl. I positioned my upper hands over the lower and yellow light formed in the space between. At first it was formless but as the seconds passed it took the form of a sun and several plants with their own moons. She pointed to a planet that looked like earth with three moons and very large trees all over its surface and the perspective zoomed in to show the changing of seasons. "As the solar and lunar cycles change the beings that inhabit these spherical realms will exist for a specific amount of time and die and then be reborn somewhere else." Everyone gasped as they watched things die and wither away. "ENOUGH!" The mother goddess sent out a shock wave that scattered my planetary solar system in all directions and I could feel tears form in my eyes. "MOTHER!" My scream made the palace tremble as she glared at me with her three eyes of swirling cosmic energy. "For your insolence you are banished from this realm. I don't ever want to see your face again! Take her out of here!" The mother goddess pointed at me and half of my siblings jumped off of their thrones and attacked me. I sent a blast out of my palms that sent them flying and then turned and flew out of the doors. Everything became a blur for a couple of seconds as I traveled at super speed through space and landed on what I understood to be earth. I reached down and ripped off my lower set of arms and flung them in separate directions. My legs bent down and I sat in the lotus position as my body began to turn into a mountain. The surrounding forest spread all over me and the clouds above worked with the sea to conceal my entire form. I blinked and was now crawling my way out of the dirt in the center of a large cavern. At my feet was a flower bed of exotic colors and it moved up my body and turned into a form fitting bodysuit. The image changed again and I was now watching from above as two snarling beasts tore each other apart. It was a gory sight to see as they fell to the ground and stopped moving. I reached into my stomach and pulled out a glowing orb that I dropped into the pit below me. Once it hit the ground it became a glowing slime that devoured the blood and body parts. As the light began to dim I reached down and scooped half of it out and placed it in a crystal bowl. The rest divided itself into three small blobs that crawled out of the pit and turned into three toddlers with horns, hooves, tails and wings. The girls had bug and bat wings like me and my new girlfriend and the boy had crow wings like Memphis. I snapped my fingers and we were teleported to a kitchen and the babies were now sitting in high chairs. The crystal bowl appeared with a matching spoon that I used to feed them the rest of the glowing slime. I blinked and my surroundings changed once again as I now sat in a very comfortable chair as the babies spewed a swarm of demon beasts from their mouths. The bats and bugs flew in opposite directions and the birds stayed near their host by forming a massive flock in the sky. I blinked again and the little boy was covered in blood and standing over his sister's dead bodies. He held a spear with an all black tip that he rammed into my lower abdomen and twisted it before pulling it out. With a shaky hand I reached out towards him as his eyes glowed but he stepped back with a laugh. "You should have chosen me to be your successor, Mother." His body twisted and his scorpion tail moved like lightning as it struck me in the forehead and pulled out my third eye. He then used his tail to sling the eye into his mouth and chewed with his pointy teeth. My hands reached into my chest and pulled out my heart before snapping it in two and I threw them to the left and right, as I did my lower arms in the previous vision. The last thing I saw was Tirogolly growing a third eye and a hideous smile on his face before I woke up with a gasp next to Nighmena. "That kid was Memphis." She made fist as she got up off the bed. "And that answers the question of how he became so powerful. He's our ancestral uncle." That didn't sound right even with all that I've been through in the past twenty-four hours. Especially since it meant that the sexy demon-goddess next to me was my sister in a past life. Thinking of that gave me an idea about ancestors so I held out my hands and made my jewelry box appear. "Isn't magic the best thing ever?" I asked. Nighmena gasped and cupped a hand around her large breast. "I was just thinking that." That deserved a kiss but before I could lean in the gems on the top of the box glowed yellow. Two fireflies made of emeralds crawled from under the lid and flew to my ears. Both of them clung to my earlobe with a small pinch and turned into earrings. I could hear my parents and grandparents speaking about a game of hide and seek that Memphis started and they used to keep him busy. "They're playing hide and seek, want to join?" Nighmena looked me in the eyes and laughed so hard she snorted as she held her finger up. "W-Wait. Wait. Your family is keeping our archnemesis busy with a children's game?" The both of us laughed as we unfurled our wings and flew into the hallway. I allowed the earrings to guide me to my family who were at the foot of the basement stairs. "He's down there." My new accessories glowed and the first letters of everyone's name appeared below their ears. "Oh, Your great aunt Tamia's telepathic earrings. These are communication marks." With us already being paired we decided to split up and we went further down the hallway that was like a maze. The first six rooms we passed were full of statues and portraits to the goddess Aura and Our previous incarnations. "Huh, so that's where my selfie obsession comes from." Nighmena smiled as she fought the urge to laugh. We approached a room without a door and I could hear running water. "Oh my goddess! This room is beautiful!" My voice echoed around the wide room with a large fountain in the center and I twirled in the air as we entered. The fountain was made of black and white marble with swirls of blue and yellow all around it. The edge was surprisingly comfortable and warm as we turned to each other and held hands. "Oh my dearest, I shall never be the same after tasting the delicacy that are your lips." Nighmena feigned a swoon and gasped. "My word Mrs. Doorknob, I shall also be forever changed by the bouncing of your breast against mine." She pulled me into a kiss and broke away as her spider crawled out of her pocket and dragged the snowglobe in a net of webs. Huntress slithered out and joined her and they dumped it into the fountain. The second it was completely submerged the water shimmered and the smell of sea water filled the room. "Look!" She yelled. Six forms swam to the surface and as they emerged I recognized them as her family from the pictures on the walls at her house. I reached in with two hands and pulled out twin teenagers and Nighmena pulled out her parents. The littlest form stayed in the water as it churned into a whirlpool. He popped up and made spit bubbles that evaporated the water into a storm cloud that trailed behind him. "Bye-bye Water!" he clapped his little hand and his cute little bat wings lifted him into the air. "His first words!" Her mother and father said in unison. He floated into their arms and they all hugged. "Get over here first girlfriend." The twins giggled as I wrapped my arms around them and squeezed. We remained that way for almost a minute until Nighmena filled them in on what we were doing and I informed my parents of the good news. I made communication marks for her family and her parents teamed up and we decided to take the twins with us. "Let's finally end this bullshit." Vamora entwined her fingers in mine as we walked down the hallway with the twins crawling on the walls. "If we see something tasty can we eat it?" They asked in unison. "Oh, if we find something that explodes, can we keep it?" "Seeing as this is probably life or death, Yes!" Nighmena smiled as she looked me in the eyes. They did a little dance as they climbed and we came across a room with no light. Both of them sniffed the air and slowly crawled over to the doorway. From the look on their faces I could tell that it was the room he was in and I became giddy with anticipation. My family came around the corner just in time and joined us as the doorway closed. Several seconds passed and all we could see was darkness and out of nowhere moonlight became partially visible from above. It appeared that we stepped out of darkness and into a forest of large trees and creatures of all kinds making noise in the distance.

I watched in the form of a raven in a tree as the family that invited me into their home, walked by below me and looked ahead at the double full moons in the sky. "How far do you think his cute little wings carried him." Ms. Mira asked. A chill ran down my spine from hearing her words. For them it was still the same day that I did all of those horrible things but for me four hundred years have passed, where I've reincarnated as multiple lower level demon animals and have had several beastly mothers raise me. It was rough and the elements weren't kind to us at all but we survived. My mothers fed me and showed me the love and attention that only a true mother could. I'd have to apologize for hunting their families, causing pain to countless demons and imprisoning half the team down there in a snowglobe. But it was worth it for me to be able to be who I am in this moment. I vaguely remember the taste of that food and now that I see them I can't wait to smooth all of this over and join my family. I turned into the shadows and slowly followed behind them. "Darkness." The littlest child spoke. "Yes, this is night time. Can you say night-night?" I never knew their names and at the time didn't really care too. All I cared for was the consumption of power. Now that most of my old powers have seeped into this weird realm, I am happy with what I have and want to finally make peace with what I've done. "Darkness-Darkness-Darkness." The baby shouted and pointed in my direction and I became one with a shadow of the nearest trees. Thankfully they ignored the baby and kept walking forward and I made sure to stay a good distance away while I followed them. The baby stopped yelling darkness and they extended their wings and took to the air. At first it was hard to follow but once I caught up to them on the tree tops, our trip ended with us standing in front of a field of flowers that bloomed in the moonlight. There were no shadows so I stayed on the treetops as they stepped forward and walked through the flowers. Behind me I could hear the demon fauna start to make noise again now that the biggest threat has left the forest. A part of me wanted to stay in the shadows but with them being powerful demons, I know they'll slash first and ask questions later. "What are we going to do once we find him?" The elderly female demon asked. "How about we form a truce?" I froze and moved closer as Nighmena spoke. "He gently placed my family in a pocket dimension where they said it was like a vacation. I got them and my girl with all of you as an extended family. We'll invite him to dinner if he is in a place of compliance." I slowly climbed down the trees and changed into my real form. My pig-hooves formed first and my round body was next as my crow wings stretched in the open space around me. They were the only part of my old life to remain and the powers I have are less than half of what I used to own. Hopefully if I explain all of this they'll see me as no longer being a threat. "Piggy!" The little baby yelled and imitated our native sounds. "Oh my goodness he said his second word." Nighmena rubbed his back and moved her head to where I stood at the edge of the forest. "Who are you?" Vamora asked. Her voice made the air around us warmer. "My name is Ogar, but in a past life you knew me as Tirogollv." They gasped and everyone except for the demon holding the baby took a fighting stance. "Hold on, there's something different about him." I stepped closer and the baby held out his hands. "Piggy!" He made spit bubbles as he looked at me with his tongue out. For a moment it felt like he was hungry but as he clapped his hand a pacifier appeared in his mouth. That baby was no regular demon. "I was trapped here for centuries and it gave me time to think about all that I did to your kind and I gave my physical form and powers over to this place." Nighmena's eyes glowed blue like the moon above and she squinted as she took in my entire form. "My sight is telling me that he speaks the truth." All of them looked to her as small glowing marks flashed on their necks and they had a silent conversation amongst themselves. The baby didn't take his eyes off me as he continued to make spit bubbles and rub his hands together. "Okay, How about you join us for dinner and we can talk about making the world a butter-I mean, better place for our kind." Vamora said, crossing her arms. "Thank you, I know it's more than my soul deserves." A lot of them scoffed and made comments that I couldn't hear as they joined hands and made a circle around me. "Only we can come or go from here, so stay still." A bright yellow light formed around us and in the blink of an eye we were standing in her Kitchen. Their neck markings glowed again and then vanished as half of them left the kitchen. The two demon-goddesses remained with the baby that they put in a high chair and the twins started to get pots and pans from the cabinets. "Here, try this, it's my mom's special fruit and nut spread." Vamora stirred a glass jar and scooped out a large spoon full of the most delicious concoction. I allowed her to feed me and the moment it hit my tongue I let out a little squeal at how good it was. The rest of the family returned and we spent the next hour eating and talking. The adults opened wine and even poured some for me and I was so full and tipsy I couldn't move. I feared that they wouldn't accept me and take the revenge that's owed to them but they surprised me and welcomed me into their home. By the end of the night most of them made their way to their rooms and I was alone with Nighemena and Vamora. "We want you to stay in one of the rooms here." I squealed and tried to get up off the pillow but my stomach was too full to move so I tried my wings and it caused my sides to hurt from the effort. "Thank you. But I'll probably have to sleep here tonight." They laughed with me as each of them took the sides of the pillow and flew with me through the air. "Isn't there a phrase about crazy things happening when pigs fly?" I chuckled as a cold chill ran down my spine. We landed in my room that was tailored specifically for me. "See you in the morning." They flew out of the room while holding hands and I could sense where their night was headed. Who would have known that good things happen to those who didn't originally deserve them.

"How did the talk go?" Vamora took a seat next to me on our bed and draped her arm over my shoulder. I took that as a chance to rub her thick thighs as she leaned against me. "It went well, but that's the last time I let them do that. They tore that room up with their super powered fight. I know they just wanted to play with the pig but the room gave Mia a gauntlet and Michelle a staff. Now that they've used them I didn't feel right to take them away. My parents aren't happy." To tell the truth there wasn't anything that I could really do about the rooms and what they're capable of. They were endless and operated on their own except when it came to Me and my bae. After breakfast we went to one room that was a movie theater and another that was an amusement park. Our parents took the baby to the forest room to hunt and we took the twins to a training room. It produced your desired weapon and then made a scenario where you could be properly trained with it. I didn't know that it would lead to them destroying everything in the room. "The good side is they have those weapons that will keep them busy and dinner is taken care of." She rubbed her thumb against mine and it made me feel better. Now that I'm a full fledged Goddess of the moon, they no longer have to worry about our previous and they can focus on raising the next rulers of the vampire and wolf clans in secret. Little Lu was still a wild card and I knew they really wanted him to do his own thing. "You're right, I should be happy that we're getting married next year and my mom's friend Ally has agreed to add my honey-glaze to her shelves." I pulled her into a hug/kiss and our tongues clashed against each other as her breast pressed against mine. She moaned into my mouth and I fought the urge to dive my hands into the front of her pants. We still have a lot to do and we've already wasted three hours this morning licking and fingering each other until our toes curled. "Okay-okay! Mwah-No" I got up off the bed as My sun Goddess fiancé reached under my skirt. "Right. We still have to actually prep-and cook dinner like we said and didn't our parents agree to help?" That managed to make her blush as she stood up and straightened her clothes. "Eww, I almost forgot about my grandmother's ability to sniff out sexual energies." We shivered and she pulled me towards the door and we flew down into the hallway. With everything that happened yesterday, I still felt like all of this was a fever dream. I got the powers I was promised, victory over my enemy and the girl of my dreams. My mother was already in our large kitchen preparing greens, and when we landed in the door way she looked up with a half smile. "I'm sorry I snapped." She put down the greens and moved at super-speed to pull me into a hug that I returned. "From this moment forward I promise to run all gifts of weaponry by you." I placed a kiss on her cheek and looked at the large pile of Collard greens. "How about I help you?" "Thank you. Kelly and Robert said they'd be down here in a few so we have a lot of help for our feast. V, can you grate the cheese and sprinkle it on top of the macaroni and cheese next to it?" As usual my mother was back as the culinary General. "Yes ma'am." We spent the rest of the morning prepping the food and by noon we had everything ready and waiting in the cooler for dinner. "Since we're going all out for dinner I think we should wait a little bit longer to eat. We have a tradition in my family where we starve ourselves before a big feast." Vamora gasped and touched her breast. "My family has something similar where we eat three meals a day." She made her eyes wide as she pretended to be shocked. I slapped her thigh as she giggled from her joke. "We do the same thing for the holidays. Oh shit!" It just occurred to me that all of that stuff could be real or fake. "What?" Nighmena unfurled her wings and looked left to right. "I'm sorry, I just realized that the holiday icons might be real. For instance, old man-winter is out there somewhere." She laughed and nodded. "Yeah, His name is Boreas, he is the south wind. Eros/cupid disobeyed his grandfather and delivered the letter that brought forth valentines day. We're the demons that started the Friday the thirteenth curse. Well it was actually Aura who did it, the stars were in that formation when she fell." That was news to me because I thought that it had something to do with the new jersey devil myth. "It does, that's where Tirogollv incarnated through a human." I froze as she just looked at me in confusion. "What, you were right, bae." "Yes, and I also didn't say that outloud." My heartbeat picked up in my chest and I pressed my lips against hers. We stayed that way for several minutes and simply enjoyed each other's taste. When our lips pulled apart I opened my eyes and sucked my breath in at the darkness that surrounded us. My girlfriend gasped as she opened her eyes and locked our hands together. ***No need to fear me, for I am YOU!*** Ribbons of light formed in front of us and took the shape of a very tall four armed goddess with three eyes. She was dressed in an all gray gown that accentuated her voluptuous figure. Her rich dark brown skin was the same color as mine, except the skin past her elbows glowed with blue and yellow energy. Her long flowing purple and black hair fell behind her and sparkled with the same cosmic energy of her arms. *"I allowed the way my mother treated me to make me like her, Full of discontent and vengeance. Seeing you two come together has healed apart of me that I forgot existed and I ask that you grant me one more favor."* Aura waited for us to look at each other in agreement before she spoke again. *"Over the years my family came after me and instead of destroying them I siphoned most of their power and used some of the excess energy to turn them into inanimate objects. They're in room four thousand and two."* "Oh that's next to the *fountain room."* I interrupted and she nodded with a smile. *"Yes, once you free them the water will transport them to their divine realms."* Her body began to shrink as she stepped forward with her arms outstretched. In the blink of an eye she had us wrapped up in a hug that spread a soothing warmth over my body. Aura remained slightly taller than us and as she leaned down her head split in two and she kissed our foreheads. The second our skin touched a pulse of energy made my body tingle and I knew exactly where the room was. I knew where all the rooms were and everything in them. "Whoa!" Vamora touched my shoulder and we were back in the kitchen with no one around to tell us if what we just experienced was in our minds our another dimension type of situation."Mom, we'll be right back." I took Vamora by the hand and teleported us to the room the great Goddess told us about. We awakened a house plant that was a piece of the king of the Gods first and then an umbrella that was a goddess of darkness. We came across a deck of tarot cards that was a god of divination and then a pencil that was a goddess of writing. After we finished they told us that the goddess of wrath wanted to remain as the gauntlet and the martial arts goddess also stayed as the staff. We spoke for an hour and told them what we could about the world we live in. "I'll see to your mother, the rest of you try to safely find your place in the new existence." The tree god bowed and vanished in a whirl of glowing leaves. The remaining deities took on human forms and teleported in similar ways that were tied to their divine attributes. "Shall we go make some magic in the kitchen?" I asked as I wrapped my arm around my girl's waist. "Mena, you can't nibble on my box in the kitchen, we have to get dinner ready." I laughed out loud at her sex joke as I squeezed her waist. She knew what I meant but I Loved her sense of humor. With our large family spread out all over the mountain palace we went back to the kitchen and turned on the appliances that we needed to make dinner. I pulled out my juice injectors and the turkey baster as the oven chimed to let us know that it was ready. Time passed by quickly as we talked about our childhoods and the meat and sides were ready to eat. By the time our family came downstairs we had everything ready in the dining room that was made to seat all of us. "This looks good, I'm so proud of you two." My mother took a seat next to her soon-to-be co-mother in law and as the twins walked in still holding their new gifts with Kelly and baby Lu behind them. "Piggy, Mmmm." He bounced up and down as he slammed his hands on the high chair. "Yep, Mmm, Ham. Can you say Ham?" Kelly asked. "Ham." he repeated. My dad stood next to Vamora's dads and they held the cutting knives out to us. "We literally wouldn't be here today if it wasn't for you two." My dad said. "You should slice the first piece of demon ham." Thomas added. I didn't waste any time and neither did my girl as we grabbed the knives and cut with culinary precision. We chopped enough meat for everyone and I kissed Vamora on the lips before looking around the room at our large family. "I'm glad we invited him to dinner."

Creature-Comforts

"Who am I?" For the third time today, I asked a question that not even I knew. The guard ignored me as she shoved my food in through the slot and left without saying another word, just like she had every day that I woke up in this windowless room several years ago. I had a large television and my own bathroom, but it didn't help answer my question as to why I am here. The only thing I knew was that I'm a female in my mid-twenties who loves to watch other women get naked. How could I not know who I am but have a full awareness of what I'm attracted to? I took the tray of fruit to my bed and made sure not to sit on my wings as I sat down. They already ached from all of the flying that I've been doing around my room, and If I moved wrong, it would cause another back spasm. Knock-Knock! This was perfect. The person in the room next to mine was awake, and I could finally have a stimulating conversation with her even though we'd never seen each other's faces. I knocked on the wall and waited for her to speak to me through the wall. "Good morning, Vera!" "Good morning, R-5682. Are you enjoying your meal?" "Yes, I love the new additions to my diet. Thank you for speaking to Dr. Phyllis." "No problem. Us girls have to stick together, and I can't have you going without your meals." Even though I had never seen her face, I knew that she was one of the only people who cared enough about me to ask about how I was doing. "Did you sleep well?" "Yes, I still haven't had any dreams or regained any of my memories, though." "Give it time. I'm sure you'll get them sooner or later." I grabbed the remote to turn off the television so that she could tell me about her day. "What's new?" "Nothing much. I'm still hungry and feel like I could eat a whole horse without chewing. But other than that, I feel good, especially now that I get to talk to you." I never understood how she could eat twice as much as me and still be hungry. The guards feed her four times a day, and I hear the sound of her crunching on her meals. That has to be delicious with the way that she eats loudly.

"Have you heard anything about Toni?" "Nope, She came over to my room for dinner, and I haven't seen her since." That was still weird to me. I asked Dr. Phyllis if I could leave my room to go next door and visit Vera, but she said that Toni was ahead of me on the visitation list. Toni occupied the room on my left, and the three of us had juicy conversations that made me want to meet both of them face-to-face even more. Toni spoke to me about trying to escape, but after Vera invited her over, that was the last time we heard from her. I've never been outside of this room like she was, so it was hard for me to try and think of an escape plan. Toni told me that they were lying to us and that there was a strange reason as to why Vera wasn't allowed out of her room, but in my honest opinion, I thought that it was great. I hated not knowing who I was or how I got here, but I had all of the food and television that a girl could want.

"You got quiet on me. Are you okay?"

"Sorry, I got caught up in my thoughts. Did you ask me something?"

Another part of my amnesia was my short-term memory. "I asked if you've thought about me and touched yourself." I choked on the strawberry and had to pound on my chest to help it go down. "Are you Okay?" She asked. "Y-Yes, I just choked." Once I was in the clear, I gulped down half of the bottled water. "Good, I've thought about how you taste while touching myself and found that I love it." I've always found it slightly creepy that she chooses to use the word "it" when speaking about me and her being together. "I Feel like I made this awkward. Let's change the topic of the conversation." "I agree." Several minutes passed until I heard her big body moving around over there, and I decided to bring up the cooking show that I watched yesterday. "I finished all of the episodes of Kitchen Magic, and you were right. It just made me hungrier." "Yeah, Me too. I had to ask Dr. Phyllis about getting me another meal at midnight." "Were you dancing while eating?" "Uh-Yeah. I was dancing. That's what all of that noise was. It was so good that I jumped for joy several times." "Yeah, I heard. At first, I thought that you were in danger, but when I heard you say, "Mmmm, So good. I knew that you were eating something." "Yeah, It had a little bit of fight to it as it went down." There she goes again with her weird words that sent chills up my spine. We spent the rest of the day talking about the things that we loved eating, and she told me that she'd talk to Dr. Phyllis about getting me some more of that maple syrup that I drank like water. I fell asleep while watching a baking competition and was once again drifting through darkness until I was awakened by Vera dance-eating at midnight. Personally speaking, it gave me the creeps at how much noise she made while chewing. Whatever it was that she chomped on must have been crunchy as fuck, because all I heard was snapping and popping for an hour until I fell back asleep. I woke up six hours later to the sound of the guards talking outside my door. "Th-there's nothing left. She even ate the bones." "Shhh, the roach might hear you." I didn't know what any of that meant, but it didn't sound good at all, and I hoped that they were talking about someone other than Vera. They walked further down the hall as I got up to use the bathroom and shower with what I heard at the forefront of my mind. When she said that she could eat an entire animal, she probably meant it, but how? I could barely fit my mouth around a mango. After my shower, I walked over to the wall and knocked on it to say good morning to my friend. She knocked back as I heard her moving around over there. "I hope I didn't wake you up." "You did, but it's cool. I'm sure I've disturbed you enough times to give you a free pass. How did you sleep?" "Good for someone who can't dream. What about you?" "After I had a midnight snack, I slept like a baby." That sent another cold chill down my spine as I thought about all of the noise that she made. "I'm going to get my day started. I'll come back to the wall in an hour." "Okay, TTYL." I froze as I spoke an acronym that I had never said before and realized that it must have been a part of my memories from my life before I woke up in this room two years ago. Thank goodness for Dr. Phyllis and her extensive knowledge of everything except why I was here in the first place. She also had a gift for evading that question whenever I asked her about getting out of the room. "Breakfast time, R-5682!"

The guard slid my tray of food through the door, and I almost tripped as I got up to run to the tray of pancakes, eggs, sausage, and potatoes." "Thanks, Harold." He ignored me as he always did and took Vera her food. She must have been just as happy to see from all of the noise that she made. "Oh shit! Ahhh! Help! She's got my arm!" I heard him scream as his body was slammed against the slot and was followed by the sound of bones breaking. It almost made me lose my appetite as I heard his arm separate from his body, and he hit the floor while screaming out in pain. "Harry! Shit! We have a code Ninety-two-forty-seven! I'm requesting help at the beast's cell." I never heard them call Vera that, but it made sense in the way that she ate like a wild animal. It made me wonder what her condition was. After I devoured all of my food, I walked over to the wall and pounded on it to check on Vera. "Are you alright over there?" "Yes, I got revenge on the guard who assaulted me four years ago," I remember her telling me about the guard who threw her tray into the room and hit her in the mouth and how she swore to make him pay for it. She suffered a swollen mouth that prevented her from talking for a week.

I didn't think she'd rip his arm off when he least expected it. When I got up to look out of the slot, my eyes burned from the excessive use of cleaning chemicals. What I did see was a wet floor sign and a cleaning cart being pushed down the hall. Damn, Vera really did a number on that guy. I waited two hours for the smell to dissipate until I looked out of the peephole to see if they put another guard on his post. "Jeremy, are you out there?" Silence. I went back to my bed to watch television and allowed more time to pass until I knocked on the wall to check on Vera. "Girl, I am stuffed. I can barely move." "You ate his arm?" "Yup! That'll teach him not to be abusive." For the first time since I met her, I was at a loss for words. We made an agreement never to talk about our creature's conditions so I didn't know what she was or how she managed to tear his arm off. "How did you do that?" I could hear her laughing as she slapped her hand against the wall before she answered. "I just pulled, and it popped off." "Just like that?" "Yep! It was like pulling chicken apart." There she goes again with her weird terminology. "I know we agreed never to talk about this, but I have to ask. What's your creature condition?" "I don't want to talk about that right now. Once I tell you, you'll never look at me the same." "Okay, well, as long as you don't try to eat me, we're good." "I can't make any promises." She laughed like it was the funniest thing in the world, and I tried not to let mine show that I was really scared. Toni was a Fly hybrid, like how I was a cockroach, and the person who stayed in Toni's room before her was a ladybug hybrid named Vicky. The weirdest part about all of this was that Dr. Phylliss treated us like we were normal, even though I knew that we weren't. When I watch Television, I see shows talking about how things like us should be in a lab that runs tests on us, but it doesn't answer any of my questions as to how we came to be. The girls and I are something out of a horror movie with our creature parts. Vera knocked on the wall three hours later when they gave me dinner, and I could see the guard almost drop the tray as she ran away, screaming while Vera laughed. It was hard not to laugh as I heard her continue to yell all the way down the hall. An hour after I finished my food, there was a knock on the door before Dr. Phylliss walked in. "Good evening, Rochelle." She was the only one who called me that because I didn't know my real name. "Good evening, Dr. Phylliss. How are you?" "Considering your wing-mate has mauled someone, and now I have more paperwork to file. I'm okay. How are you feeling?" "Also good for someone who still hasn't regained her memories and is part insect." "Any headaches?" "Nope!" "Nausea or fatigue?" "Neither one." "What about lapses in time?" I shook my head no because if I did, there'd be no way of knowing. I spend all day watching television and talking to Vera. "I have a question for you." "Go ahead, ask me anything." "What's Vera's other half?" "Except that. Patient doctor confidentiality prevents me from speaking about anyone else's creature parts." Damn, I really wanted to know what she was. She took my blood and hair before leaving me to wonder about what she really was. I heard her go next door as my ears began to ring while Vera's door opened, and I hoped that this wasn't going to be the last time that I saw the kind Doctor. I listened as they talked like old college friends and laughed at whatever joke was said. Truthfully, it was kind of weird, but at least Dr. Phylliss would live to see another day. Since Vera was well-fed, I got a full night's sleep and woke up the next morning to a male guard pushing my food through the slot. "Hey, what's your name?" "Christopher, what's yours?" "I don't know, but you can call me Rochelle." "Nice to meet you, Rochelle." "Likewise." I waited for him to move away from the slot so that I could see what he looked like, and I was pleasantly surprised when he walked down the hall and turned around to wink. He was a white man with scruffy red hair of medium build with pretty blue eyes. As someone who considered herself to be pansexual, I'd definitely give him some. Oh shit! Am I a virgin? Have I been with women or men? Damn! Do I have a husband and kids out there wondering where I've gone or a thick-bodied girlfriend who hounds the local police station about me being a missing woman? This was the part I hated about having amnesia, the constant questions as to who I am and why I'm here. I took the food to my bed and devoured it while watching a show about a medium that channeled messages to people from deceased loved ones. It always amazed me how normal humans would be okay with that, but if they saw me crawling on the ceiling or flying around, they'd freak out and get the bug spray. Knock-Knock! "Good morning, Rochelle." "Good morning, Vera. Did you sleep well?" "I did, how about you?" "Yes, Thank you for allowing me to get a full night's sleep." "You're welcome. If they keep feeding me limbs, We'll both get all of the rest that we truly need." She laughed, and I pretended to laugh as I continued to eat my deluxe breakfast while binge-watching the rest of the medium show for a couple of hours. She went on to do readings for celebrities, and when I saw an R&B singer ask about her sister, I froze when she pulled out a picture of a woman who looked like me. I stood up and stepped closer to the Television as they showed more pictures and felt a weird sensation form on my forehead. She was a Woman named Sapphire Collins who vanished while on a cruise five years ago. The medium told her that she couldn't sense her spirit, so that meant she was still alive or not ready to speak to the living. After the Medium pulled back her energy, the strange sensation faded, and I turned off the television before going over to knock on the wall. "Vera! I think I just found out who I am!" I heard something heavy hit the ground before she replied. "R-Really, W-what did you find out?" It didn't really sound as if she was happy for me, but I was too excited to let her ruin it. "I think I'm the cousin of a famous celebrity." She remained silent for a couple of minutes until I heard her move closer to the wall. "I'm happy for you." It didn't really sound like she was, and to be honest, I was starting to feel as if she had prior knowledge about all of this. "Do you think I should ask Dr. Phyllis to look into this?" As I asked the question, it dawned on me that they could have abducted me and done this to me. My body broke out in a weird itching sensation as I continued to think about what I just discovered about myself. "Are you okay?" Vera's question pulled me out of my mind-maze, and I took a deep breath as I prepared myself to lie to her. "Yeah, Maybe It was just a woman that looked a lot like me." "Maybe, Hey. I'm going to take a nap and meditate. You should try to do it as well." That was a good suggestion since I had a lot on my mind, so I went to my bed and laid back while remembering the order of chakra colors."Red, Orange, Yellow, Green, Blue, Indigo, Purple, Indigo, Blue, Green, Yellow, Orange, Red." I repeated the color sequence six more times until I opened my eyes to what had to have been a memory. I was walking through the hall of a cruise ship while looking for room two-twelve. "Hey,

Sapphire." I turned around to see the most beautiful brown-skinned woman I'd ever seen, with long curly hair and the body of a goddess. "Hey, Ozeria. Looks like we're neighbors." My eyes shot open to see Dr. Phyllis sitting next to me while applying a bandage to my abdomen. "Hey there. You gave us quite a scare when you passed out." I looked her in the eyes as she smiled like that actually happened. Yeah, Something weird was definitely going on here. "Did I hurt myself when I fell?" "Yes." "How?" "You were holding the tray when you fell to the ground and landed on the edge of it." My "Injury" didn't feel like a simple cut. It felt like I had some type of surgery instead. "Dr. Phyllis, How did I get here?" She twisted in her seat to pack up her supplies and took a deep breath like I was annoying her before turning around to look at me. "You were in a chemical plant accident that fused your cells with that of an insect, Just like all of our other patients." I narrowed my gaze on her and noticed that my forehead felt weirder than normal. "Thank you for answering my question. Can I be alone, please?" She nodded, and I waited for her to leave to slowly walk to the bathroom to see what was on my forehead. "What the fuck?" I now had two long antennae in a place that wasn't there before I started to meditate. The area was sore, and as I looked at the rest of me, I noticed that my wings were larger and the hands to my lower arms were now insect pinchers. Doctor Phyllis's answer made me wonder if she did this to me as some sort of science experiment. That medium show had to have been correct. I felt it deep down in my hybrid soul. Seeing the picture of Sapphire Collins brought up something to the surface. I've been here for four years and have never had one single dream, but after I take Vera's advice on meditating, I have a dream memory of a cruise. I wanted to talk to my vicious neighbor about this since she was my closest friend, but a part of me was starting to think that she had something to do with all of this. Dr. Phyllis wasn't the least bit phased by Vera's revenge, and whenever she went to visit her, my ears rang before she stepped into the room. I needed to find out more, but since I couldn't leave this room, I didn't know how to form a proper plan. Knock-Knock! "Dr. P said you passed out. Are you okay?"

"I don't know. She said that I cut myself on the feeding tray, but I don't even remember walking with it in my hands, and now I have extra insect parts. I think my condition is getting worse."

"I can't begin to try and understand how you're feeling, but I can be here for you whenever you want to talk."

"Right! We just have a wall in between us, and the fact that I've never seen what she looks like. Thank you, Vera. I appreciate your kind words."

"No problem. Are you hungry?" Wow, Didn't take long for her to switch back to food. But I was surprisingly hungry, and lunch wasn't for another hour and a half. "Yes, I feel like I haven't eaten in days." I walked over to the service button and pressed the one for food. It took them an hour to bring me my food, but when the guard slid two trays through the slot, I jumped for joy at the sight of everything, and it made my wound burn. "Thank you. Christopher." "You're welcome, Rochelle." I ate the first tray's food so fast that I couldn't remember chewing, so I made sure to slow down on the next round of food. When I picked up the hotdogs, the weird sensation from earlier formed on my forehead as I saw a memory playing in my mind's eyes. I was walking down a busy street in New York while eating a hotdog, and a group of people was moving in each direction. The taste of mustard and ketchup lingered on my tongue as I chewed the real food in my mouth. Knock-Knock! Damn it, Vera! "How's the food?" "Delicious, but I'm sure it's not as good as an arm, though." She laughed as I heard her move around, and I turned on the television to watch something that was filmed in New York so that it could help with my memory. I found a show about a white woman looking for love in the big city and watched three seasons that were useless in helping me recover my memories. Once I was done, I slid the tray across the floor with my food just in case I "Slipped" again and decided to meditate to see if it would help. Red, Orange, Yellow, Green, Blue, Indigo, Purple, Indigo, Blue, Green, Yellow, Orange, Red. I allowed my mind to show me whatever it wanted to since it was the reason why I had amnesia. This time, my entire body relaxed as I floated through the darkness for what felt like an eternity until I was standing in the doorway to a large room. "Come in, Rochelle." I looked up to see a gorgeous, naked woman floating down from the ceiling like a wingless angel. "Do I know you?" She laughed as she landed in front of me. "Of course, I know who you are. It's me, Vera." I frowned and stepped back as she tried to pull me closer. "This is a dream, I'm dreaming." "No, I think it's time I tell you the truth about me." She pointed to the area over her shoulder and made living room furniture appear while a sheer white silk robe appeared on her body. "Don't get dressed on my account." "Okay, I won't." She snapped her fingers and made the robe vanish as we walked over to the couch. "What is this place?" "The dream realm. I connected us so that we can meet face to face." "Is this really a face-to-face meeting if I don't know what type of hybrid you are?" She shook her head as a smile curved her lips, exposing her black fangs that I didn't notice before. "I am not a human-animal hybrid like you and the others. I'm a trapped demigoddess." Vera tossed her hair over her shoulder while parting her legs to show me the part of her that I imagined myself nibbling on whenever I masturbated. It had the perfect amount of hair and wasn't too big or too small. It was just right. "Are you a goddess like Athena or Artemis?" I remembered them from a television show about a mortal who had to judge a beauty contest between her and her sisters. She rolled as she smacked her teeth, and her brown eyes turned all black. "Why does everyone automatically go to them? There are millions of other goddesses to reference!" The room shook like an earthquake as she slammed her hand on the arm of the couch. "Sorry. I don't know much about true divinity, just like I don't know who I really am." Vera took a deep breath as the tremors stopped, and her eyes turned back to normal. "No, I should be the one apologizing. I forgot about that for a second. I'm sorry." "I guess it's cool. Besides, what can I say to an all-powerful goddess when she's pissed off?" "Well, for starters, I'm trapped in this building that Dr. Phyllis owns." "Why mean how?" "She has my heart in a magic box that she uses to control me. I'm waiting for the right time to strike and get the fuck out of here." "Is that why she has me in a room that I can't get out of?" "Sort of. She uses all of you in her experiments for the world's governments. They want to make super-powered soldiers to fight in their armies." "What do they want with me? I'm a woman?" Vera shook her head as she placed her soft hand on my shoulder. "Honey, Everything starts with us. We have the power of natural creation." She moved her other hand to my stomach, and I realized what she meant by that. "Did they harvest my eggs?" "They've been harvesting all of your eggs." Now, it made sense as to why the room next to me was a revolving door of newbies, but how could I go up against a mad scientist? "That's where I come in. I'm going to teach you how to use your powers." "Did you just read my mind?" "We're in your mind, and yes. I told you, I'm a goddess." She got down on the floor and then on all fours as her body began to glow with white energy that was almost unbearable to watch. "This is my real form." It faded to show me a large brown tiger with a lion's mane and red stripes. She had a mouth full of shiny black teeth that made the hair on the back of my neck stand up as she walked over to me. "This is my true form. Now You try." "I'm not a goddess. I'm a human who is part insect." "No, They used some of my blood to bind the insects to your DNA, and you have some of my powers. Shapeshifting is one of them. Now try." I got up and took a deep breath while imagining myself as a cockroach, and my skin broke out in gooseflesh as I shrunk down to the floor. It felt weird at first to be this small, but after I spread my wings and took to the air, I slowly got the hang of being in this tiny form. "There you go, Beautiful!" I wasn't sure how much time had passed since I took this form, but it felt good to have some semblance of control in my life. Vera watched me from the couch as she clapped her hands, and her breasts bounced. "I have to end our connection because it's almost daylight outside." I shifted back into my hybrid form as the walls started to shimmer, and ran up to her to kiss her luscious lips. "I need you to find my heart and open the door to the cage that she has it in. I'll be able to get us out of here." I woke up to the sound of the guard sliding more food into my room. The time on the television screen saver said that it was seven o'clock in the evening. Damn! I ended up falling asleep for seven hours. I looked at the food as Vera pounded on the wall. "Remember, Rochelle." "Right. Let me just get a bite of those nachos, and I'll be on my way." She pounded harder as I ate half of the Nachos and then turned into a cockroach before heading to the food slot. Once I crawled out, I made my way to the end of the hall where everyone always came from and then crawled up the elevator shaft to the next floor. Each room had a different kind of animal that varied from livestock to wolves and large cats. All of them were under some kind of sedation that kept them asleep. I searched the floor for half an hour and moved on to the next one that was for the staff, and then the next was where I saw the setting sun for the first time in four years. It was so beautiful that I almost shifted back into my hybrid form as Dr. Phyllis walked by. I watched as she pressed her hand against a scanner that opened a bookshelf into a large room. I flew into the air as she stepped in, and the door started to close behind her. At first, I thought that it was going to smash me, but I was the right size to fit through. She stepped up a door with a large rock inside of a glass case with weird letters on it. "Show me more of your secrets." Dr. Phyllis held her palms over the as the rock glowed white and closed her eyes. My body tingled as she began to float up off of the ground. Her little trance lasted for five minutes until she landed on the floor while trying to regulate her breathing. "Fine! Be a little bitch then!" Dr. Phyllis walked over to the door, and it opened as she pressed the face of her watch. "Kelly, Add six vector points to the fusion generator and tell Dean to look at the genomes of the upper-level beasts. "Copy!" She continued out of the room and went to what appeared to be a bathroom for a rich person. I wanted to watch her undress, but I promised Vera to unlock her heart, so I shifted into my hybrid form and stepped closer to the dais. The rock was the size of a watermelon and made my ears ring as I put my hands up to open the cage.

I tried to lift it up, but the second my hands touched the case, an alarm went off, and I changed into a cockroach as the door opened. "Henry, I need assistance in my room." "Right away, Doctor." I stayed in my hiding spot as two armed security stepped into the small room with their weapons out. "Are you okay, Ma'am?" "Ma'am? I don't look a day over forty, Black don't crack white boy. Get Sarah up here and tell her to install cameras." "Yes, Doctor." I crawled out of the doorway as they walked out of the room and attached myself to the muscular guard who spoke to good old Doctor Phyllis. "Damn, did you see her breasts?" "Bro, What about her thighs?" They bumped fists as the elevator stopped on their floor and hopped off of the guard to crawl through the elevator shaft to my cell block. Instead of going to my room, I crawled over to Vera's slot, but an invisible barrier prevented me from stepping into the extremely dark room. "I'm not feeling good. Allow me to enter your dreams." The sound of her voice entered my mind as the elevator dinged, and the guards came out with one of the sleeping hybrids from the floor above us. I crawled into my room and changed back into my form as they walked past my room to Vera's. "Hey, Guys." "Hey, Rochelle." Great! Now, everyone is calling me that. What happened to R-5682? I turned around to eat my cold food that wasn't as good as it would have been twenty minutes ago and wondered how they were going to get that beast into Vera's room. No sooner had I thought of the question my ears rang as her door opened and I heard the sleeping beasts make a noise as Vera must have bit into it. "Hurry up and say the word, Mike." My ears rang again and the door to her room closed before they walked past me while breathing hard. "Did you see her fangs, My god or should I say Goddess?" "Fuck that! I was scared that she'd jump down from the ceiling on us. I love pussy, but not monster pussy." That was a weird way to talk about her and to be honest I was a little scared of her as well after she showed me her beast form. I just wondered what the word was that they used to keep her at bay and prevent her from maiming them like she did the other guard a couple of days ago. I chewed on my food as the sound of her crunching on the bones entered my ears.

Damn! A girl could eat! I waited for my ferocious friend to get done eating and knocked on the wall to see what was up but she didn't answer after two tries. "Okay, Dream world it is." I laid back on my bed and focused on the chakra colors as I connected to her in the dream world. "Vera!" "In here sexy!" I stepped into the room that was now like a normal bedroom and she was sitting on her bed in a long flowing gown and a crown on her head. She looked like an actual goddess with her long curly hair flowing down her back and a bright smile on her face. "You did an amazing job." "Did I?" "Yes, You managed to get up to the upper level without being seen. Now I can show you how to astral project and how to use your enhanced strength." All of that sounds nice but I need to know why she blocked me from seeing her in the waking world. "Whenever the good doctor uses my heart to further her aspirations, she drains my power and I could have eaten you, while in a ferocious state." "Is that why you tore off the guard's arm?" "No, I plotted my revenge on that man from the day he hurt me and laughed about it. Come on, let's start your training." She took me by the hand into a room that appeared and once again an unnatural amount of time passed as she taught me how to use super strength and how to project my consciousness outwards. It was strange to me because I thought I was in a dream but Vera reassured me that the fifth dimension isn't tied to the same amount of physics as the conscious realm. By the time that my training was almost over I could lift a car over my head with ease and astral project without losing my focus. "Thank you, Rochelle." "No thank you. I would have stayed her in my Stockholm syndrome life forever if you hadn't told me about myself." She leaned forward and pressed her lips against mine as the walls started to shimmer. Vera tasted like watermelon and kiwis but when I pulled back to get one last look at her, my eyes grew wide as I looked into the mouth of a Tarantula. "What's wrong?" Her voice echoed around the room and I opened my eyes to my own room. I put the last part of the dream in the back of my mind as I looked around the room. The screen-saver on the television showed the time as five in the morning. My body felt well rested but now I can see in the dark and had extra wings on my back. Whatever Vera awakened in me has made me feel more powerful. Since it was midnight I decided to astral project myself out of the room and moved like a ghost upwards to the next floor. I wanted to see one of the other hybrids up close so I walked into the nearest room where a Hen-Woman slept in her nest. She looked so peaceful for a creature that could be fed to Vera at any moment. When I stepped closer my body was sucked into her dream where she was with a group of girls who were holding up their shots in a hotel room. "Kappa-Alpha-Psi!!!" They clinked their glasses and knocked the shots back before one of the other girls turned on some music. In the blink of an eye all of the girls started to drop to the floor as a group of men walked into the room. The woman who was part Chicken screamed but one of the men knocked her out cold as the others picked up their woman and walked to the door. In the blink of an eye I was standing outside of her body as she jerked while making noises in her sleep. Seeing that solidified my suspicions about how I got here and who I really am. Now this was personal. I floated upwards through thick concrete floors until I was standing at the foot of a sleeping Doctor Phyllis's bed. Seeing her sleep peacefully made me angrier about all of this rise but I knew I had to see what she was dreaming about and learn how to open the cage. I stepped into her dream and watched as she walked into a cave with a bunch of armed men behind her. The inside was dark but my eyes saw the cobwebs and overgrown vines hanging from the ceiling perfectly as they continued on their path. "Do you have the word ready?" Dr. Phyllis looked over her shoulder at one of the men who held up an old scroll in his hand. "Yes, Doctor. I have her true name ready." "Good, Make sure you don't look her in the eyes. She's one of Anansi's most dangerous children." I wasn't well versed in ancient deities and didn't know who that was but hearing it made me want to ask Vera more questions about her origins. They reached a large cavern with more overgrowth and cobwebs that made my non-corporeal skin crawl. "Well look what the rat dragged in, delicious little morsels. Mmmm." I recognized the voice immediately as belonging to Vera but it had a monstrous echo behind it that made me want to close my eyes. "I've come to make a pact with you, Oh great goddess of fortune." The sound of her laughter filled the cavern as the walls shook and the armed men pulled out their guns. "There won't be any need for those, little meat's." The men yelled out as they looked up at a semi-invisible creature that floated downwards to land in front of us. All I could see was her large glowing eyes before she turned the men to stone statues. Doctor Phyllis Grabbed the scroll out of the statue's hand next to her and opened it as she backed up against the wall. "Veratavagalnataziragor, I command you to sleep!" The ground shook as something heavy hit the ground and all of the armed men changed back. "Hurry up and extract her heart." "Y-yes, Doctor." Dr. Phyllis handed the scroll back to the man she took it from and pulled her flip phone out of her pocket. "It's done, get the team ready to build the facility on the island." The dream ended and I was now standing next to her bed as she tossed in her sleep with a smile on her face. Was that Vera's real name that they used to keep her at bay? I walked through the bookshelf into the room where she held her heart and looked for a way to get it out. After walking a circle around it several times I learned that it would have to be smashed and I'd have to return in my physical form to do it. Now I had a smile on my face from having a way to get out of her and free my goddess girlfriend from her prison. I woke up and knocked on the wall to see if Vera was awake but after three tries I could tell that she was still asleep. "Dream realm it is." I focused on the chakra colors until I entered the astral realm that Vera made for us. "Vera!" "In here my delicious." My powerful goddess was in the back of the room on a couch while dressed like a woman of the modern era with multi-colored cornrows, a halter top, tight jeans and no shoes on her perfectly manicured feet. "Damn Girl!"

"What? this old thing?" She pulled me into a hug that made my heart race as our breasts touched. "I didn't find a way to open the cage. Sorry." "No worries, I guess we have to take more extreme measures next time. Come here." She led me to a room in the back and motioned with her head for me to get on it. "I have never tried this thing called spooning. Can I cuddle with you?" "I'm not sure if I've done it either but I would be more than happy to be the small spoon." A frown curved my lips as I thought about where that came from and how I knew what a small spoon was. But as I got on the bed a cold chill crawled up my spine like I was forgetting something. The smell of her skin made me feel more comfortable and reminded me of what I saw in Dr. Phyllis's dream. "Who's Anansi?" "W-where did you hear that name?" "I stepped into the doctor's dream and saw the day that she used your full name to bind you." Vera didn't say anything as her breaths fell on my neck. "He's an African God of trickery, storytelling and forest creatures. He also helped some of the enslaved melanated people of America find freedom. He was killed by the other deities for doing so." Damn it! "I'm sorry for bringing up something that's a hard topic to talk about." "I appreciate you saying that, but I should have told you the truth about everything. With you having amnesia I didn't want your head filled with my origins before you found out about yours." Aww, she's as sweet as she is beautiful. "Thank you for considering my feelings." I turned over and kissed her with everything that I had and when we were done we laid in each other's arms while time passed. "When I wake up I'm going to change into an insect and go up to her room and smash the cage with my bare hands." Vera kissed my lips as the walls started to shimmer. "I love you, Sapphire." Before I could respond I opened my eyes to my dark room and stretched before turning on the electronics to see the time. It was seven thirty so I figured that the guard would be coming down with my food any minute now. Ten minutes passed and they brought me my food that smelled so good that I didn't want to leave it to get cold. You have a mission to fulfill, Sapphire! I waited for my ears to ring before turning into a roach and waiting for the guards to pass by my room so that I could attach myself to him. The one that stood next to us checked our names off of a list on his as the elevator doors opened and he pushed the cart in. "Phew! That bitch gives me the creeps." "Is that anyway to talk about a goddess?" "She ain't my goddess." "Dude, You're black. Her father helped create our ancestors. Show her some respect." "Dude! My lord and savior is Jesus Christ, not some vicious beast that ripped the arm off of our co-worker. Why do you think she was trapped on this island in the first place? Her own parents didn't want her." Talk about being disrespectful. If things were different I would have bit him on the ass or ear, but I have a girlfriend to free. I stayed on him until the elevator dinged and flew off of him as they exited the small space. Being this small was so fun because I was able to fit into the tiniest spot. I made my way up to the next floor and crawled through the open spaces as the elevator came up behind me. Below me two of the female guards made out before getting on the elevator and seeing it gave me an extra push to complete my mission. I made my way to Dr. Phyllis's room while crawling on the ceiling and when she walked out of the bathroom with her breasts out I almost dropped from the ceiling onto her jiggly cleavage. Damn, her white coat betrays her voluptuous body. She applied cocoa butter to her body as I crawled behind the bookshelf and changed into my hybrid form while landing on the floor. I put my hands together before using them to smash the crystal cage with all of my strength. The alarm came on as Dr. Phyllis came in with her breasts bouncing up and down. "What have you done?"

The stone glowed white and vanished into thin air as the naked doctor backed up against the wall with her hands to her mouth. "Helped free my girlfriend." She began to shake as she fell to the floor while staring at me with wide eyes. "Y-you have n-no Idea of wh-what you've d-done." "Yes, I do." "N-no, you've free-." Her words were cut off by her entire body exploding like a ketchup packet and splattering me with her entrails. "Sorry, I couldn't allow her to spew more lies." Vera appeared in the same form that I saw in the dreams but her eyes were glowing white as small tendrils of lightning flowed around her body. With a wave of her hand she cleaned the blood off of me and moved at super speed to place a kiss on my lips. Time stood still as we allowed our tongues to dance against each other like crashing waves in the sea. "You taste amazing." "Moving forward, can you not use words like that when referring to me? It kind of creeps me out." She laughed and showed me her dark fangs as her eyes normalized to their usual brown color. "You got it. Come on, I want to show you something." I blinked and we were standing outside on a balcony that looked out onto a rising sun. "Oh my Goddess!" "You're welcome, Baby." We pulled each other into a side hug and watched the sunlight crawl across the landscape until it reached us. My melanated skin prickled as it absorbed the sun's rays and Vera stood behind me while we swayed back and forth. I could stay like this forever but I knew that there would come a time where I'd have to search for my family. "The mind is the second most powerful organ in the body. Memories are tricky. We'd have to work for a month to delve deep into your mind." "I love how you can just read my thoughts." "It's more like I read your heart and mind together. I can teach you if you want?" "Yeah, I also need to learn how to shift into a full human form for when I go to my family." "Anything you want is yours, just ask." Below us a stampede of hybrids exited a side door and ran into the forest while carrying some of the guards with them. "Are they going to be okay?" "Who cares? They deserve whatever is coming for them." True, every person here who's a hybris is that way because they were abducted. We walked into our new bedroom and Vera clapped her hands to change it to our liking as her power rippled across the room. "Okay, That's cool!" "Oh, Baby you ain't seen nothing yet." She pushed me back onto the bed as my clothes disappeared and got to work on using her tongue to open up my lady parts until I yelled out a half of an hour later while reaching my climax and squirting on her face. I found it hard to catch my breath as my toes stopped curling. "Y-You want me to do you?" "Nope, I fingered myself before we left." I opened one eye as she laughed from her joke and cuddled up next to me. I laid in her arms for a couple of hours until our stomachs began to loudly rumble from eating itself. "I'm going to make you something to eat but I have to go hunt my food. I'll be back." She kissed my lips before vanishing in a burst of white light that made a large plate of breakfast burritos appear in its place. "I swear I love that Goddess." It smelled so good that I forgot to chew as I devoured it and drank the glass of lime-water on the nightstand. After she returned we watched television for half of the day and then she cuddled up behind me until we fell asleep. Vera helped guide me through my memories that wanted to resurface but it didn't give me any way to reach out to my family. I awoke at midnight to see a full moon hanging in the sky and spread my wings to clear my head. The other hybrid beasts had managed to eat the staff that they took out to the forest. Seeing what they did to some of them gave me the creeps and sense I was three times as strong so I was good in the self defense department. Flying with the cool breeze blowing against my skin gave me an added sense of freedom as I looped through the air while heading back to my mountain home. Vera was still asleep so I took a shower before going back to bed. It took me a while to get back to sleep but when I did I was pleasantly surprised by the dream of my old life. I was sitting at an award show next to my cousin as she won the award for album of the year. She pointed at me with her free hand and I pointed back as everyone clapped. "I want to dedicate this to my twin-cousin. Our mothers were identical twins and after my mother passed away I was taken in by my aunt who told me to call her "Mom". I was almost through with the music industry because it's full of colorists and misogynists, but my sister told me to push through and she has always had my back like I'm going to always have hers. I love you Sapphire." I opened my eyes to an empty room with a rising sun in the distance. "Good morning sleepy head." Vera appeared in a flash of white light next to me with a bouquet of exotic flowers in her hands. "These are for you." They smelled amazing but the dream that I had made me want to do back flips through the air. "I had a dream-memory about my cousin." A weird smile curved her lips as she pulled me into a hug and pressed her lips against mine. "That's good. Our guided meditations have been working." I nodded as tears fell down my cheeks, but Vera wiped them away with her thumbs. "For the first time since I woke up here, I feel like I'm actually on the right track." "Just don't forget about me when you're out there with the mortals." I frowned as it dawned on me that we never really talked about our life after leaving this large island. "Aren't you going to come with me?" She was taken back by my response as I was by hers and took a deep breath before answering. "I haven't been off of this island for over a billion years. What would be out there for me?" "Me!" It was her turn to cry and for me to wipe away her tears as she looked me in the eyes. "Besides, I'm going to need help explaining everything to my family about what happened to me." "But is there a place in the world for a previously imprisoned goddess?" "We'll make one." Vera nodded but I could see that she wasn't completely sold on leaving this island and I knew deep down that it would be wrong to force her if she wasn't ready. Two months went by as the dream memories showed me more about my life and family. I was a psychiatrist that specializes in children and didn't have any of my own but I helped raise my cousin's children from birth. The last memory that I saw of my family was at a BBQ where we were celebrating another win for my cousin. I gave a very emotional speech that ended with me inviting her to stay with me in New York for fashion week and that must have been the last memory that I had before being abducted. Vera became emotionally distant and hunted in the forest so much that she ate three-fourths of the other hybrids. Whenever she came to lay in bed with me a cold chill ran down my spine as she rubbed my shoulder before we cuddled. A day after I had my last dream Vera blind folded and walked me into the forest to show me a surprise that she made for me. "Keep going, we're almost there." I hated not knowing where she was taking me but since she was the most powerful being on the island I felt safer with her guiding me to our destination. "Have a seat here." I sat on a hard rock as a cool breeze blew by and I felt her wrap a soft blanket around me until it became uncomfortable. "I can't move my arms." "You're not supposed to, Delicious." The blind fold vanished from my face and I screamed as I looked at a giant tarantula with eight white glowing eyes. "This is why I never showed you what I really look like." Vera's voice echoed in my head and as she backed up onto the large tree behind her. This must have been what Dr. Phyllis was trying to warn me about? "This is why I made myself invisible to you whenever you had a chance to see me and why I didn't want you to come into my prison cell." Her black fangs dripped with venom as the mid-morning sun made her brown hair glow as I took in her full size. "Why would you lie to me?" Her laughter made the wind blow as the surrounding creatures vacated the area out of fear for their lives. "Honey, do you think the farmer tells the cows that they're going to be turned into burgers?" Tears fell from my face as I tried to use the super strength that she taught me how to use with no luck and then I tried to shapeshift to find out that I couldn't do that either. "Are you done, Delicious?" "Why do you keep calling me that?" "Oh, Right!" She rubbed her front paws together and made a web of light appear that showed Dr. Phyllis in one of the rooms in the basement. In front of her were several cylinder tubes of insect eggs that floated in green liquid that she harvested from me and as she moved to the side I could see clones of myself in the other cylinders. That explains why the doctor always took blood and hair samples from me. "I've eaten all seven of your clones, but I've only had sex with you." I continued to cry as she made the image vanish and laughed like she did when she maimed the security guard. "I am sorry for lying to you though. My father wasn't killed by the other divine beings, I ate him like a baked potato. Mmm-Mmm-Mmm. I can still taste his blood on my fangs and hear him scream as I ripped out his heart." Of course I freed a psychopathic monster from her prison that I thought was the one. "Don't feel bad. Dr. Phyllis thought I was the one as well. Had you not been there when my heart returned she'd be in my stomach as well. But hey, you have to crack some eggs to make an omelet."

A Future With My tsaP

I awoke to a blinding light in an unfamiliar room with no clothes on and in a body that was similar to mine but muscular. "Hello!" I turned to my left and looked into the eyes of a very attractive white man dressed in a white t-shirt and boxer briefs. "Why am I naked?" His raised eyebrows made his face even more attractive as his lips spread into a smile. "I'm Va'al, and you're in my domain." I looked around the room that only had the chair he was sitting in and the bed that I was currently on. "That doesn't answer my question, Va'al." His smile faded as he got up off of the bed and touched his palm to the wall. "Devin, You're not in your time period anymore." The wall changed from stone to glass as it spread around the room and gave me a beautiful view of the forest down below. It was like having a clear view of weird animals in a nature reserve, but the only difference was the three moons in the background. Va'al placed his warm hand on my shoulder, and clothes like his appeared on my body. "How'd you do that?" He laughed as he looked down into my eyes and moved his hand from my shoulder to the nape of my neck. "It was an accident that brought you here." Gooseflesh broke out over my skin, and I could see images flash in my mind of Va'al attaching a large red crystal to what appeared to be an antenna. His body was sickly thin, and he had a lot of bald patches on his head. Behind him, a raging thunderstorm moved in and sent lightning bolts to the ground as it moved. A light blinked on his wrist watch just as lightning struck the crystal, and the energy made it glow bright as it shattered into a red glistening dust cloud. As he fell to the ground, I could see his body change into to vision of male beauty that it was now and the cloud of red energy change into my new form. He removed his hand, and I looked up into his blue eyes that glistened with tears, and without knowing why, I floated upwards and placed my lips against his. How did I know how to do that? Va'al returned the kiss with all the passion in the world as he allowed me to place my arms over his shoulders, and he hugged my lower back. "Mmmm." I moaned into his mouth, and we remained that way for a while as our erections rubbed against each other. "I've missed you, Mizzly." The sound of his voice echoing around my mind made me pull back and look into his blue eyes. "Huh?" He blushed and looked to the ground as a chill went down my spine. "Sorry, it's a pet name I made for you." Another chill ran down my spine as he kissed my forehead and took me by the hand, and in the blink of an eye, we were in what appeared to be a futuristic cafeteria. Small drone-like machines hovered around us like bees while scanning our brains and then flying into the open doorway of the kitchen. "Devin, You're fifty million years in the past." He said, dispelling the silence. "Is this Earth before all the craziness?" I asked, partially confused. He shook his head no and pressed his thighs against mine. The second they touched, I could see a spaceship leaving the earth and traveling through the cosmos until it found a planet that resembled Earth. Once the ship landed, people of all colors and body sizes flew out of the ship like superheroes and began making the planet their home. The cycle of suns and moons changed, and they managed to build a large beautiful city of the same stone that surrounded us now. He pulled his thigh off of mine, and the image faded as the drones brought back our food. "There is so much that I want to tell you, but I don't want to overwhelm you with a massive download." Hearing him say massive while we were this close to each other made my booty tingle as I stole a peak at his now normal size penis. This has to be a dream of some sort. I probably ate a bad batch of Marky's shrooms, and they put me in a coma as a result. "You're not dead, Devin." Of course, he can read minds. He's shown me visions and teleported us to another part of this place. My ears began to ring as I was suddenly aware of the clothes he made from nothing. "Time travel, A literal transformation, and psychic abilities. Am I getting that right, so far?" "Yes, brown eyes." His familiarity was both sexy and eerie at the same time. I wanted to get on his lap and let him do whatever he wanted to me, but I also want to run and find a way back home. "Why?" Va'al asked. He took a bite of the weirdly shaped fruit and looked me in the eyes as he sent his thoughts to me. "Your ancestor was Miz-lay-angoti. An elder who left this world and traveled back to Earth to help end the interplanetary war between Venus and Mars that Earth was in the middle of. Before leaving, your ancestor gave my ancestor the ruby that you saw from the vision as a marriage gift. After many cycles passed and she didn't return, My ancestor mated with another and brought my family into being." Apparently, my ancestor must have done the same, but that would mean that he and I descend from lesbians. "Cool, is that why I feel an intense attraction to you?" Va'al blushed and nodded yes as I picked up an orange banana and inspected it before peeling it open. "Alien ancestors and advanced technology. Wow!" Another chill ran down my spine as I put the banana to my lips and took a bite. Its flavor was like banana sherbert with its rich, creamy texture. "Can I get back to my time?" "I don't know." Another chill, and this time, my forehead pulsed as he looked away and grabbed a banana. My fingers worked on their own as I dropped the banana and picked up yellow cherries instead. Their usual taste was enhanced by a honey-like flavor that paired with the banana's aftertaste. After an hour of talking, Va'al showed me how to use my mind to move small objects. "I'm not one hundred percent convinced that this isn't a dream, but here goes." I Leaped into the air and Imagined myself staying afloat like he suggested and levitated upwards as he followed behind me. When I did it earlier, it happened on its own. But this felt like I was more in control. first, I was timid and scared that I would fall, but my blue-eyed friend helped me find my flow of gravity. "There you go, Mizzly!" Va'al yelled out that name again as he chased after me, and we ended up flying out the window. It was like I was a child again and made a new friend on the playground who just wanted to have fun. Another chill ran down my spine and made me stop as he crashed into me. "Are you okay?" *Don't tell him.* The sound of a child's voice in my head made me turn around in his arms and search the empty space of the sky.

"Y-yes. I thought I heard something." His concerned expression made my heartbeat speed up as we broke apart, and I shrugged off whatever it was that I sensed. "Let's do another lap over the lair and then practice another ability." Va'al nodded and blew me a kiss as he started the race without warning. "Cheater!" I yelled. Time literally flew by as we spent two and a half hours playing tag, and then he gave me a tour of his nature reserve full of prehistoric beasts. The creepiest part were the penguin-like sea birds with their weird-looking teeth. "I think they're cute." "The babies are, but the parents." I shivered, and he placed his arms around my waist to teleport us to another part of the planet. We floated over a pit of snakes that formed a withering ball of scaly skin that smelled awful. "Are they having a snake orgy?" He nodded as he laughed and moved us to another destination in the blink of an eye. We floated over a ravine where sabertooth tigers fought below and landed at the edge as they killed each other. "Shouldn't we do something?" "If I always intervened, they'd never know how to take care of themselves." "You'll let them wipe each other out?" In the blink of an eye we were back at our home and standing next to a glowing wall. He waved his hand over the wall, and it glowed as it opened to show blood, semen, and eggs. "Our drones harvested their genetic materials a couple of cycles ago." There was something about all of this that made me feel uneasy as I turned in a circle, and more slots opened. "I have everything under control." Va'al moved from where he was to my side and placed a kiss on my cheek as the slots closed, and he then teleported us to the hallway outside of our rooms. "Now that you know the basics of telekinesis, I want to show you one last thing before I retire to my room for the rest of the day." He backed up, and his eyes glowed bright orange as he shapeshifted into a weird penguin and then a blonde gorilla. "It takes some focus, but try to change into one of the beasts that you saw earlier." Va'al turned and leaped into his room with the doors closing behind him as I contemplated which animal to turn into. After a couple of hours, the sunset, and I was unable to take the form of the snakes. I decided to lay down and reflect on the day before I fell asleep. I felt my body falling as I entered the very vivid dream world with my legs running at full speed and people running behind me. "In here." I stopped and allowed everyone to run past me as something metallic chased after us. Once everyone had passed me, I held my hands out and made a wall of pulsing rainbow colors appear to block the doorway. I turned and looked into the face of a naked blonde woman with eyes like Va'al's and pulled her into a passionate kiss before she backed away and ran through the door. The dream ended, and I opened my eyes to the light of the rising sun in the east. My ears picked up the sound of the animals rousing, and I took that as a sign to start the morning by trying to shapeshift into a snake or the spider that made the beautiful webs in the tree outside my window. By mid-morning, I was still unable to transform, and my sexy blonde host came in and decided that we should try something else. "Hold your hands up and face your palms to each other." "Like this." Va'al moved closer and used his big hands to move my hands closer together. "Imagine fire forming in the middle of your hands." He let go, and I pictured a red flame igniting in my hands. Instantly, it formed, and its warmth spread onto my hands. As a child, I used to have an unhealthy attraction to fire and almost burned the house down by igniting my bed. This was something that I would have to be careful with. "Okay, Fire. Check." I concentrated on it moving off of my hands and formed it into a ball that I changed into Ice and then a clump of dirt. "Here, put it in this." He clapped his hands and made a crystal sphere form around it. "I believe the people of your time period call it a biodome." My eyebrows shot upwards as he called it into his hand. "How do you know about my time period?" As I asked my question, it occurred to me that he already knew my name and where I was from. "We're psychically linked. In time, you'll know things about me in the same way that I know things about you. Now let's circle back to transformation." He clapped his hands and made his arms change into bird wings as large blonde feathers sprouted from the pale fuzz. Va'al stretched them out to their full wingspan and flapped them to lift off of the ground. "Now you try!" He flew around the large room as I tried to imagine my arms turning into bird wings like his. An hour passed, and nothing happened as he stood across from me with a confused look on his face. ***Bon!*** He flinched from the loud sound and looked down to the floor behind me as the sound continued. "What's that?" "A particle emergency. I'll be back." He vanished in a flash of orange light, and I was once again left alone to practice my new abilities. As time went on, I was able to gain better control over the elements and the power of flight by the use of gravity manipulation. Four hours later, I learned how to teleport by using the elements and make my body grow to almost ten feet and shrink down to the size of a fly. I zipped around the room and changed back into my normal size when it occurred to me that I knew of other psychic powers. The power of astral projection popped into my head, and I lay on the bed and focused on my breathing. A throbbing sensation formed on my forehead as I remained perfectly still and felt my consciousness peel off of my body like velcro. It was the most peculiar feeling to have my sense of touch muted and my sight enhanced to the point it made the colors dance. Mastering the ability to fly gave me a better advantage to maneuver about in this form as I passed into the hallway and found myself torn between going into Va'al's room or exploring the place where he goes to conduct his experiments. After a couple of seconds, I chose his room and passed through the doors into the room that was exactly like mine. My tall, muscular instructor was nowhere to be seen and I moved through the wall into his bathroom. It was similar to mine, but I had a weird sense that it was a female bathroom because of the energy that it gave off. The sound of small feet hitting the ground pulled my attention back to the bedroom, and I passed through the wall as a little body ran into the hallway. I followed after the little form, and it led me down a spiral staircase that hit a dead end. Now that I had a better look at the kid, it looked like me as a three-year-old with wild curly hair and an animal diaper with a matching t-shirt. He ran into the wall while clapping his hands as I chased after him but bounced off of the wall. I pressed my hands against it and pressed with all that I had with no luck after a full minute of pushing. A small tingling sensation formed on my feet, and I was pulled back into my body and awoke to see Va'al giving me a foot rub. "My apologies. I have a lot of maintenance to do here." Another chill ran down my back as I looked him in the eyes, and he smiled as he made himself comfortable. "I've mastered another power." He moved closer and placed my foot on his lap as I told him about the things that I told about the things that I've created, and the power that I discovered. "Be careful, that's a dangerous power." ***Don't tell him!*** I heeded my inner child's warning and told him about my teleportation ability instead of my astral projection. "Still no luck with shapeshifting?" he asked. "No, I keep trying, but nothing happens." He let out an annoyed sigh and let go of my feet. "How hard is it really!" I was too stunned by his outburst to speak as he got up and flew out of the room. *What just happened?* We were having a great moment, and he flipped personalities on me. I spent the rest of the afternoon thinking about what I did wrong and replaying the events on repeat in my mind. With the sun setting behind me, I decided to go outside for a fly to clear the racing thoughts I had about how dangerous of a situation that I was in. As an orphan with no family or friends, there wouldn't be anyone to miss me from that time period. I'm currently between partners and the last time I was with a man. He almost killed himself while trying to keep our situation a secret. My girlfriend, after he cheated on me with anyone with a bigger dick, as she quoted it and managed to contract aids and be left with several children. As I put the past in the back of my mind, I passed over the dark sea and made my way to the small island that wasn't inhabited by anything except flora. Its large trees acted as a barrier that surrounded a beautiful field of pink flowers that only bloomed during a full moon. Va'al was right, there were things that he knew that we now shared. I landed on the large pale stone and lay flat on my back as the moon shined down on me. "Hello, ladies." As a child, I remembered that I always named things, and when I saw the moon last night, I couldn't resist the urge to name the full pink moon Luna and the red crescent moon Lumen, but Lu for short. Seeing the stars without the city lights was something that I would have paid for, and would have loved to take my blonde-haired muscle god here. My forehead prickled as Va'al appeared next to me with a basket of food. "I'm sorry, Devin." He waved his hands and made the food appear on a blanket in the space between us. "I feel bad about pulling you here, and the guiltily too much sometimes." That made sense, but why did I have a sneaking suspicion that he was keeping something from me? "It's okay. Emotions are a part of having a heart." I leaned in and kissed his forehead as he poured water into our cups.

"Va'al."

"Yes, Devin."

"Why do you want me to master transformation so badly?" He didn't answer as he took a sip from the cup and leaned back onto his elbows. "Va'al."

"I heard you, Devin. I just want to make sure I have all of the things I need to say in order before answering your question." That didn't help me any, as he remained quiet for a full minute before answering. "I want to make sure that you know all that I can teach you before sending you back to your time period." The way that he said it made it seem like he wasn't going with me. "You're coming with me, right?" My question helped change his seriousness to softer energy as he looked over at me and smiled. "I thought that you'd go back, and I'd stay here." "Alone!" My words came out louder than I expected and caused the air around us to pick up as my heartbeat increased. "I'm sorry. I thought you'd come back with me." "But we're barely a thing. I can't ask you to do that for me." His protests almost made me think that he didn't want to leave this palace, but there was no way that I would ever leave him here. Even if we lived for a million years, I wouldn't be able to live knowing that he was here with only animals to keep him company. "The place where I come from was established on lies, murder, rape and theft." He nibbled on some food as I talked and looked at me with a half smile that said my convincing was working. "We'd have to make a social security number for you to have official paperwork, and other than the occasional odd look from us being an interracial couple, we'd be good." His eyebrows knitted together as he finished the food in his mouth and rubbed the back of my neck. "Is it not a normal thing for us to copulate?" That was a loaded question, and right now, I didn't want to ruin my speech by saying anything that would make him not want to come with me to my time period, but I had to be truthful. "It is, but there are people who don't like black and white people together and even more who don't want to see men together." "I'm not following." He responded. I nibbled on my food and took a sip of the crisp water before answering. "A lot has happened between the people of color and the people without." "I'm sensing that there is more to the story." I nodded and laid on my back as a shooting star flew by over our heads. "People who are attracted to the opposite sex have the world thinking that people like us are abominations and should be killed or locked away." "What? We are their ancestors. Without us, they wouldn't exist." His eyes glowed bright orange as he levitated off of the large boulder and hovered over me. "Maybe this is why I have an uneasy feeling about going to your time period." It made sense. Shit. I didn't even want to go back. It was extremely peaceful here, and I didn't have to work for a living or deal with idiots who allowed their childhood traumas to guide their egos. We spent the rest of the night on the rock after he turned it into a bed for us to sleep on underneath the moonlight and cuddled as the breeze moved over us. My dreams came at me with full force as I found myself having the same dream as I had before. I allowed my body to move like it did before and make the barrier of light before kissing the beautiful blonde woman. Instead of waking up, I walked into another room and saw a voluptuous, dark-skinned woman using technology to look at a DNA strand. She wore an all-white bodysuit with her dark hair tied into a thick bun at the top of her head. My dream body moved forward to her workstation and froze when she looked up at me with the same blue eyes as my blonde companion, Va'al. Her gorgeous looks paired well with her eyes, and the fact that she was some kind of scientist only added to her overall beauty. She threw out her hand, and a wave of translucent energy sent me flying backwards until I awoke in my room with the sun rising to my left. My skin crawled as the image of Va'al smiling at me entered my mind before he appeared next to me.

"Grand rising brown eyes." He got on the bed and pulled me into his arms. "Devin, I think I'm ready." I could feel his erection pressing against my lower thighs as he leaned in and passionately kissed my lips. "Wait." I pushed him off of me and looked into his disappointed face. "Have you had sex before?" He didn't even consider my question as he leaned in for another kiss, and I teleported out of his embrace to the area next to my bed. "I'm serious. To have anal sex, you need lube." Va'al rolled his blue eyes and teleported out of the room without saying another word. Once again, this highly attractive and powerful man left me feeling confused about all of this. Am I a captive? Is he even going to let me leave? After an hour of waiting for him to come back, I decided to relieve myself by masturbating and cleaning up with a towel that I manifested out of thin air. "Whew!" It helped a little, but I was still perplexed as to what to do about my blue-eyed psychic instructor. If it was a perfect world, we'd be bouncing on each other's thighs, but now I don't even know if he wants me. I didn't see a trash can, so I made one to throw the towel in and made myself breakfast. "Fuck! I didn't even get to tell him about my dream." The hours flew by as I practiced my manifestation powers and made myself a room filled with books that were copied from every library that I'd ever been to. I wanted to make a television and movies but decided against it since I could do that at any time. In five hours, I used my advanced reading skills to finish forty books on astrology, meditation, healing my inner child, and a book of short stories that made me cry and laugh at the craziness the characters experienced. Once I was done, I decided to pay my angry, blue-eyed lair-mate a visit and made my way to his room. "Va'al, can we talk?" No reply. Knock! Knock! "Va'al." A full minute passed, and there was still no response, so I pressed my hand up against the door to sense his presence and felt the familiar energy of his particles assembling from teleporting into the room. "One second!" He ran up to the door and opened it with a huge smile on his face. "We need to talk." "Please, come in." I stepped into his room and immediately sensed that there was something different about his energy. It was like I could sense his happiness and a new energy emanating from his solar plexus. "You wanted to talk?" "What is going on? You're hot one day and cold the next." "I don't know what you're talking about, Devin." Va'al's confused facial expression almost made me get up and yell, but in a way, I could sense that he was being truthful. "You don't remember telling me that you were ready for sex." "Oh, that. I'm good." The roller coaster ride that this man has been taking me on is about to end NOW. "Listen, Bruh! I'm not playing games with you. What the fuck is going on? No! As a matter of fact, when can I leave?" I could feel my eyes glowing as they started to sting, and all the colors in the room became twice as vibrant. "You know what? Fuck this!" I turned to get off of the bed and felt my entire body vibrate as I changed into a swarm of red ladybugs and passed through the wall into the hallway and then my room. This blue-eyed bundle of blonde hair and muscles is playing a game with me, and the only way to tell the truth is through me. I took my human form and sat on my bed in the lotus position. Instead of dreaming, my mind entered a weird space made of red clouds as far as the eye could see. Gold light formed in the clouds like thunder and made small tenderals of lighting appear and then disappear as it traveled in all directions. **"Go beyond the barrier."** I froze at the sound of my extremely loud voice that repeated the words over and over. **"Go beyond the barrier. Go beyond the barrier."** The voice intensified until it was all that I could hear. "Okay!" I yelled out loud as the clouds vanished, and I was in my astral form at the bottom of the staircase. Since I couldn't push through the wall, I decided to try something new and imagine myself on the other side. I transported myself there in an instant but almost screamed when I saw the rows of floating bodies inside of raw, clear quartz crystals. I floated upwards and gasped with my nonexistent lungs as I took in the magnitude of the crystalized people maze. It was the scariest thing that I'd ever seen in my entire life. Was I just another body for him to add here? I moved through the thick floor and actually screamed as I stared in horror at four larger-than-normal parts of a human body in crystal containers of different shapes. The largest was a rectangular crystal with a ten-foot-tall blue skeleton inside, and next to it was a large red heart in a cube made of a thicker crystal. An orb the size of a disco ball housed three blue eyes like Va'al's, and above it was a large black brain in a pyramid. As terrified as I was, I moved through the floor and found myself face to face with the woman from my dreams. She smiled and stepped to the side to reveal my naked body lying on a huge bed. "You should get in. I have a lot to tell you." I returned to my body and opened my eyes as she shapeshifted into a naked white Va'al. He/she floated up off of the ground and landed on top of me. "Is this better?" Truthfully, I could go either way, and I kind of liked the dark-skinned beauty with the thighs of a goddess. Va'al laughed and changed back but remained naked as her exposed vagina rested against my sleeping penis. "How about now?" "Why are you doing this?" She rolled her blue eyes and rubbed herself against me as my erection formed. "I refuse to be the last of my line." She reached down and slid me inside of her, and I moaned and grabbed her hips to help push myself in more. "Then why didn't you say that?" I moved my pelvis as she ignored my question and allowed her full weight to slide me in deeper. "Fuck!" She nodded and laced our hands together as the sound of our connected bodies matched our moans of pleasure. "I want the baby juice." I laughed out loud as we continued to move that way for ten minutes until I flipped her onto her back and slammed against her with everything that I had. Time stood still as we reached our climax together, and I filled her up as she squirted on my balls. Our breathing was the only thing we could do besides stare into each other's eyes and wait for my throbbing shaft to decrease. I slowly removed myself and rolled over onto my back as she laughed and cried at the same time. "Thank you, Devin." "Fuck all of that, Va'al. If that's your real name. Why didn't you tell me about all of this?" "I don't know much about your time period, but I do know that saying 'hey, I need them babies' isn't a way to open the conversation." Her breast jiggled as she breathed and made my erection return as she laughed and rolled over onto her stomach. "I'm ready whenever you are." I rolled over on top of her and allowed her juices to guide me inside as we moaned at the same time. My hips rolled as I moved in and out, causing us to suck our breaths in with every stroke. "Am I hurting you?" I removed most of myself from her but left the tip in as I used my hands to hold myself up. "No, put it back." She moved her hips upwards, and I lost balance as I slammed into her and almost came as she made herself tighter around my shaft. Time stood still once more as I stopped moving and filled her up. "I told you, I want to have children." Before I could remove myself, she flipped us over and sat up to bounce up and down on my erection. It was almost unbearable, but I could feel her sucking up my semen like a wet vacuum. Once she was done, a part of her inner vagina released the head of my penis as she got up, and I wondered how I didn't notice it before. It was like lips within lips. "Is your name actually Va'al?" "Yes, Well. It's Va'alaymityrewsdert." She placed her hand on the wall, and a translucent screen appeared in the middle of the room with our bodies on it." I recognised the glowing row of colors as our chakras, and from what I understood from the screen, we were perfectly matched except for one thing. In the middle of her forehead was a large blue third eye that exuded black and orange energy. "It's our mind-eye." "Do I have one?" "Yes, but you haven't opened it yet." She popped over to my side and pressed her forehead against mine. It felt as if my head was being pulled open, and then it vanished as she stepped back. Red and purple energy flowed around my body and lifted me off the wet bed. I allowed my body to acclimate to the new flow of energy that I now realized was at the tip of my fingertips the entire time. With a thought, I cleaned the bed and dressed us in underwear. Va'al took off her bra and tossed it to the side as her computer flashed with a notification about her abdomen.

"I had to wait to see what your full powers were before trying to procreate with you."

"You mean steal my seed."

"You say steal. I say help me form a line of creation." It was weird for her to talk as if she was a woman from my time period and not an ancient alien Queen. "I need to show you what really happened." She turned to look at me, and all of our eyes connected as she took me into her memories. I watched as a planet was destroyed by a collision of asteroids from either side, and then it shrank out of view as the ship that I was in left the solar system at hyper speed. My reflection showed me that I was a child no older than eight or nine as I turned around and looked into the faces of sad melanated people of all shapes and sizes, with their natural hair flickering with energy. It reminded me of the cloud dream that I had in the way that the colors changed as I walked by. They bowed as I made my way to a throne, and a ruby crystal was placed in my hands once I was seated. The vision changed to show me as a young adult and overseeing the construction of a city. Day and night changed, and the city became a large metropolis of stone with glowing lines of energy that pulled in solar and lunar light to power the city. The image changed again to show several spaceships entering the air space above the palace and attacking the city. A smaller ship appeared and removed a large clear quartz crystal from the ground as the energy in the spires faded. Metallic rings floated around the city and killed people by extracting energy from their pineal glands before returning to the ship. It was like watching two horror movies in one with aliens and sentient technology that took over the world. The image shifted, and I was now walking through the room with all the sleeping people, with tears streaming down my face. "I really didn't mean to deceive you." Our connection ended but left me with the knowledge of why all of this happened and what Va'al actually wants. A family. She was alone. A first woman who wants to hold her own child and raise them into adulthood as well as help the people in the room two floors up. "Your aunt wanted your throne and killed all of your family. No child should have had to go through that, Ever!" I pulled her into a hug and kissed the side of her cheek as she cried into my lower neck. Having a family of my own was something that I thought about often but never actually put effort into. "Am I a king or royal consort?" Her laughter filled the room as she leaned back, and wiped her eyes. "I believe your people refer to it as friends with benefits." It was my turn to laugh as she playfully pushed my shoulder like a woman of my time period. Va'al got up and held her hand out to me. "As first King, would you do me the honor of helping me rebuild the city?" I placed my hand in hers, and she transported us to the energy center, and we got to work on cleaning up the overgrown vegetation. The day turned into night and then day again until we were completely done. I held my hands out and lowered the crystal that we created into the conduction slot as Va'al attached the gold and silver cords we designed to the power ring. "In three-two-one!" Our combined efforts helped the power regulate itself and then travel throughout the city in seconds. "The atmosphere barrier is maintaining the resonation output, and the particle coils are holding the conduction, My queen." "Perfect! Begin the synergy distribution." I placed my hand on the crystal console, and it glowed as it activated the awakening sequences for the crystalized people. As the solar and lunar energy went into the bodies to awaken them, they disintegrated into nothing before I could stop it. "No!" Va'al fell to her knees and cried as all of them turned into a pile of dust. "I'm sorry." She shook her head and got up off of the ground. "We knew that this would be a possibility. At least now they can go into the reincarnation cycle to be with their descendants." "Come here, baby." I pulled my wife into a hug and kissed the side of her neck as the feeling of failure emanated from her body. "We tried our best, and now we have to focus on the little ones growing in your belly. "You know they're not actually in my stomach. They're in my-." I cut her words off with a kiss to her lips, and she moaned into my mouth as I picked her up and placed her on the deactivated console. "Sorry to interrupt!" We turned to see a tall, dark-skinned woman with blue forearms and glowing blue eyes dressed in a flowing gown made of all-black fabric. Va'al gasped as she placed her hand on my back and moved us into a bowing position. "This is the mother of the people of hue. The last of the first deities, you honor is with your presence, great Goddess, Aura." I didn't know whether to stay on the ground or speak as I realized we couldn't sense her presence. "Daughter, Son. Please rise. We have much to discuss." She clapped her hands, and in the blink of an eye, we were sitting in our living room area that we created but never had a chance to use.

"As you know, daughter, the children of Earth are scattered throughout the galaxy, and because of that, they've evolved in various ways to adapt to the planet they inhabit. By this time tomorrow, a spaceship will come out of the sky and land over there. They'll need your help to fix their ship and return home." The goddess closed her eyes and took a deep breath before she finished speaking. "What you view as failure was actually supposed to happen. The souls of your people passed on a long time ago." Va'al looked away as tears streamed down her face, and she nodded in agreement. "I know, Great Mother. I was just hoping that I could give them a second chance at life." "You did. Their essence has moved on thanks to you, and now their crystalized particles can be of use to you and others." Va'al and I shared a look of confusion from what she suggested. "I don't understand." The mother goddess sat back in her seat and smiled as the information flowed into our minds. I locked eyes with Va'al and smiled as we understood what she wanted us to do. "Consider it done-." As we turned back, we saw the goddess vanish without saying goodbye and smiled as a new sense of life washed over us. "A queen, a king, and a goddess walk into a bar." My wife laughed as we held our hands out and made large clear quartz containers and then used portals to fill them with dust. After an hour and a half of portal-making, we were done and decided to make love on the couch. "Is it me, or are we getting better at this?" "It's just you, Devin." My big-breasted demigoddess kissed my lips and got off of the couch with her thighs jiggling. "Mmm." Just the sight of it made me hard again, and she turned around and laughed as she watched me grow. "This is the last time we have to finish preparing the rooms for them to sleep in until they can leave." Va'al teleported from where she was to my lap and sat down on my erection. "Ahhhh!" Was all that I could say as she bounced up and down in the reverse cowgirl position until I filled her once more with my warm seed, and we moaned in unison as she slowed her movement. It felt great to be with someone who wasn't obsessed with hours of sex and allowed us to focus on the act of sex. Va'al's inner lips gave my sensitive head a squeeze before she released me and got up. "Are you hungry?" I asked as I cleaned the bed and put clothes on us. "Yes, you may fill your queen's upper orifice." With a thought, I made food appear, and we spent the night talking about our books and discussing names to give our children until we fell asleep. "Grand rising, Husband." Grand rising, Wife." I placed a kiss on her cheek as the sun rose in the sky behind us. We allowed our intuition to guide us as we finished the room by the late morning, and a spaceship fell into our atmosphere at the exact time the goddess said. It looked like a metallic ant with light energy wings as it broke through the clouds and plummeted towards the ground. We teleported to the space where it was going to be and held our hands out to use gravity to stop its descent as the wings vanished. "Place it on the beach!" Va'al yelled. I nodded, and we lowered it onto the pale sand as its exterior cooled. After a couple of minutes, the doors opened, and several green women levitated out of the ship. Va'al gasped and clutched my arm at the sight of their extra eyes, arms, and breasts. She licked her lips as the tallest of the green women floated forward and bowed. "I am Inora, and we need your help." Va'al placed her hands over her third eye and bowed as she looked up with a smile. "The great goddess has tasked us with giving you the help that you need." A collective gasp filled the air as they made small hand gestures and fell to the ground to praise Aura. "May her loving embrace hold all of you in her arms." They repeated Va'al's chant and got up as we took them to the city that was perfect for their thick bodies. Over time, I noticed that they were like black women of earth with their thick hair and curves. The universe was definitely full of surprises with an entire race of beings that were only female. Black women are truly divine in every aspect, and I couldn't be happier to be born from one and to have one as the love of my life. It gave me a greater sense of pride to have a daughter in the near future. A couple of months went by, and the adult Aurans who arrived on the planet gave birth with the help of Va'al. and then we sent them on their way two months after repairing their ship. "Baby, you just made your first royal alliance." I kissed her on the cheek as they left our atmosphere and rubbed her extended belly as she wrapped her arm around my waist. "Inora will make a great first empress. I just hope she passes on the idea of helping others in need to her people." Va'al shivered as she rubbed my back, and we turned our attention to finalizing the time portal. "Are you sure we shouldn't wait until after their birth to travel to your time?" I thought back to the dream that I had about the future this morning and sent it to her in hopes of elevating her apprehension. "Why didn't you show me that before?" "I was recently taught by the most beautiful woman in existence how to withhold information until the time is right." She gave my butt a light squeeze and then walked over to the device we built to take the entire planet with us to the future. "Tell me again where we'll end up once this is done."

A smile curved my lips as she placed her hand on the crystal console. "Our home will be placed in a pocket dimension that'll be transported through time to my apartment and take the shape of a biodome." I could sense that it helped a little, but she was still unsure about living in a time where she could be a semi-normal woman and not a queen. "I've already set up your identity and enough money for us to make a bunch of businesses with employees for you to boss around." She snorted and looked up at me as the device turned on. "Oh no, we're focusing on the babies first." "Yes! My queen." I placed my hand on the crystal as the energy gained momentum and grabbed her hand as we traveled through space and time.

House of Voracity

"How could you do this to me?" "You have until nightfall to get your shit and get the fuck out of here, Verona." "What did I do?" "You don't meet the house standards." My mouth fell open as they turned around and left me to pack my things alone. I built this house from the ground up. I've won every category at the balls that I've entered and brought so much money to this house that I should be the family accountant instead of Trent. Ten years ago, I was the first gay-child of Mother Mo and Father John, but it would seem that none of that matters now. I don't know what happened that night that they went camping when I had the flu a week ago, but it didn't give them a reason to kick me out without an explanation. I heard the front door shut and ran to the window to see all of them hop in Father-John's van and wait for it to pull out of the driveway before going into their rooms to get their social security numbers. Somebody is going to pay me for this. Thanks to my Hyperthymesia, I only needed to look at them once, and I was happy that I never told them about it. Once all of their numbers were committed to memory, I finished putting my things in trash bags. I called a taxi and had him take me to my cousin Olivia's house on the northside of Columbus, Ohio. "Right here is good." "Sure thing, ma'am." Yes, I'm giving fish without trying. I passed him a fifty-dollar bill and pulled all of my stuff out of the trunk as my cousin came outside with all of her kids. "Hey, Cuz!" "Hey, I had Ernest clean out the basement, and we put the bed down there." "Thanks again for this." "Family has to stick together." She pulled me into a side hug as her nine-year-old twins stared at me from behind her. The small infant in her arms opened his cute little hands as he tried to wave, but his shyness got the best of him. "Um, Are you a girl or a boy?" "Boy, don't ask him that! Oops, I mean her." My cousin was just as bad as the rest of the straight people who conformed to hetero-normative thinking. "It's okay, Cuz. I'm a boy who likes girl clothes." His twin sister gasped and jumped up and down as she tugged on my jacket. "Ohh, Can I paint your nails?" I wanted to say hell no because I get them professionally done at Mia's nail salon, but I figured that I had to play nice since this was their house. "Yes, Let me get all of my stuff situated, and we can have a nail party." "Come on, kids." My cousin snapped her fingers to coral her kids. After I took my stuff into the basement, I unpacked it and took a shower in the small bathroom before getting out the nail polish. "Let's see, should we go with hot-pink or cerulean?" "I like the pretty blue one." "Nadia! Get away from that door and give your cousin some privacy." "Yes, Ma'am." "It's okay. I was getting ready to come up anyway!" I grabbed the cerulean nail polish and jogged up the steps to the front room as the sound of keys in the front door made all our heads turn to see who it was. "Daddy!" Oh great! The nigga that has a problem with gay people. It's a good thing that I'm not in drag at the moment, or he'd say I'm trying to convert the kids. Like that was remotely possible. "Good afternoon, Ernest." Instead of his usual hate-filled gaze, he smiled at me and held his hand out for me to shake it. "Good afternoon Vernon-- I, I mean Verona. Welcome to our home." His handsome smile must have been what helped him land my hot cousin. Because Damn! He walked over to his family and pulled them into a hug before placing a kiss on his wife's lips. "I'm going to go shower." "Okay, Dinner will be done in half an hour." After my cousin turned to go back to the kitchen, he walked past me and winked as he went up the stairs. Weird. "Are you ready to paint my nails?" "Yup, I have my work station all set up." "Work station, Young lady, you're eight. What do you know about work?" "I go with mommy to the nail salon all the time, and I've seen them do nails a million different ways." I couldn't help but laugh as I took a seat on the lumpy couch. The little girl had all of the things you would need to do nails but for a kid. Cute. Her brother kept looking at me, and I could sense that he was contemplating asking me a question. "Can I help you, little boy?" "I was going to ask the same thing." I let out another laugh as he took a seat next to me and turned on the television. The nerve of these kids.

They're too smart for their own good. Once my niece was done painting my nails, her mother called them into the other room for dinner and told me to wait a second so that she could make her husband's plate. I forget how hetero-normative families operate. "Baby! Is Dinner done?" "Yes, I'm making your plate right now!" Ernest came down the steps in gray sweats with his print showing the other reason why my cousin was head over heels in love with him. He slowly walked past me and watched my eyes to see if I'd look down, but there was no way that I was going to fall for that. I need this place to work out, or I would have to go live in a shelter. "Verona, You can make your plate now." "Coming." For the first time in forever, I ate dinner as a family and made sure not to look at Ernest too long as he spoke, but he kept smiling at me with those dark and sexy lips of his. This man had to be down-low or curious because he smiled when he looked at me. He was also a smart man with the way that he kissed his wife and made her feel like she was the reason that he was smiling. Damn it! Not again! I made a mental note to sleep with my taser under my pillow or keep it under the bed just in case. Since I was a house guest, I did the dishes and cleaned up the kitchen, but Ernest insisted on helping me while she helped the kids get into the bath. Every time he walked behind me, he rubbed himself on my butt and whispered the words Damn in my ear like he was about to cum. "Do fat asses run in the family?" He whispered into my ears but stayed pressed up against me, and as I tried to move him away, he just moved his hips and pressed harder. "Dude, you have to stop! My cousin loves you, and this isn't right." "She cheated on me with her best friend Aiesha last year at her bachelorette party. I want my lick back, or should I say cheeks. We don't have to tell anyone. It can be our little secret, come on." I used all of my weight to push him off of me as my cousin called out to him from upstairs. "Be right up." He winked at me while grabbing his junk and using his tongue to pretend like it was a penis head in his mouth before turning around to go into the front room. Yikes! This nigga is crazy as fuck! I went to my room and spent the rest of the night on my phone, looking at dating profiles until I fell asleep. In the morning, I was woken up by the sounds of heavy footfalls above my head as Ernest left work, and then Olivia got the kids ready for school. After getting dressed, I applied for six credit cards in my ex-house mates name and then filled out several applications at local hair salons so that I could have somewhere to be other than here. Since I had eight years of experience and a long resume of salons that I worked at, I knew that I'd land a job in no time. I also created three fake social media accounts to troll the chosen family that apparently changed the house name from House of fierceness to the House of Voracity. "Okay, but you all won't win any of the categories without the fiercest member of the house now in exile. What a bunch of idiots." I threw the phone on the bed and grabbed my bag of goodies so that I could do a bump. "Good Morning, Verona!" Oh shit! She opened the door as I put the bump back in the bag and came down the steps. "Damn, Cuz. Your face is beat!" "I may be a mother of three, but I still can serve looks on a good day." "Okrrt!" "I came down here to ask you if you wanted to go with me to the hair salon down the street?" Talk about manifestations. "Yep! I'm already dressed and ready to go." My cousin made a weird face as she shook her head no. "I told her that you were a female impersonator, and she's expecting to see Verona, not Vernon." "Oh, so I'll be serving fish today?" "If you want them coins, you will." "Say no more. I'll be ready in twenty minutes." She smacked her teeth as she crossed her arms. "Uhh -no! We have an hour until we need to meet her. Pull the best look you have out of all of that and meet me upstairs in forty minutes." She snapped her fingers three times as she got up to leave. Sometimes, adult straight people were just as confusing as children. One minute, it's "we can't understand," and the next, they're emulating our hand gestures and using our slang. I can't with these people. It took me half an hour to get ready for this impromptu interview, but after I was done I slapped my ass because of how good I looked. "Honey! You're a pretty bitch.

Mmm, I'd fuck you!" "It's giving real fish." My cousin wagged her finger as I stepped into the front room, and we did a little dance at how good the both of us looked. "You ready?" "Let's get to these coins, Honey!" We made our way outside, and I felt a cold chill crawl up my spine as a raven flew past us to land on the tree next to her car. It was beautiful but creepy at the same time, and it watched us like we were on its breakfast menu. "That's a big ass bird. Let's go before it decides to shit on my car." "Yeah, It's eyes are creepy as fuck!" We hopped in and made our way downtown to Tresses by Trischa. Since it was a Thursday, I expected the salon to be packed before the weekend, but she only had two people waiting in the lobby and one person getting micro-braids done in the chair next to her. "Trisch, this is my cousin, Verona." I extended my hand, and she bypassed it to pull me into a hug. Oh, we're touching. Yuck! "Welcome to my home away from home. Shall we get started?" "Yes, I brought my resume and my certification." "Okay, follow me. Liv, Mari will take care of you." "Thank you." "Uh, I should be thanking you. Cindy hasn't shown up to work in a month, and I need someone to fill her spot like yesterday." "Then I'm your girl!" We walked to the office that was tucked away in the back and commenced the interviewing process, which lasted for half an hour. She was pleased with my skills and references, which were partial truths. "I'm ready to hire you on the spot." I laughed at the irony of being ready to make money right now. "I'm ready to work today!" She twisted around in her chair and pulled out some paperwork from her filing cabinet before handing it to me to fill out. It took me another twenty minutes to finish them, and after I was done, she walked me out to where Olivia was waiting for me in the lobby with a new hairstyle of long wavy tresses. "All set?" "Hell yeah, she is. You can start tomorrow at nine o'clock." "I'll be here at eight." My right palm began to itch as I extended my hand for her to shake, and a gorgeous brown-skinned woman stepped through the door. "Ally! Girl! Where have you been?" "I have a new woman in my life, and she has taken up a lot of my time." "I know that's right.

Those cob-webs needed to be cleared out like a.s.a.p." All of us laughed, and when Ally looked at me, it felt like I was standing in front of a lioness. I don't know why I felt like that, but it almost made me step back instead of extending my hand for her to shake as Trischa was about to introduce us to her. "This is our new hire, Verona, and her cousin Olivia." "Honey, Your giving angel who fell out of heaven-realness." Her eyes grew big, and her mouth fell open as she looked me up and down. "Uh, Thanks, I'm part angel on my Mama's side." All of us laughed, but she just smiled as we waved goodbye. "I don't think she found that funny." "Me either. I hope I didn't offend a client before my first day." "I hope not. You need that money to pay me rent." "Girl, You tried it!" We hopped back into her SUV, and she treated me to brunch at Guy's Anytime eatery, which will make you anything you want, but their prices were high as fuck. "Talk about black-owned business price inflation." "Right, I guess it's a good thing Ernest gave me some spending money." "Not spending money. Cousin, You gave him three adorable kids. It's the least that he can do besides getting up and going to work every day." "You ain't never lied." Out of the corner of my eye, I could see a tall waiter walk towards us, and I cursed under my breath as I realized that it was an old trick of mine. "Looks like you survived that car accident." Fuck! "Hey, Lucas. I'm sorry. You met me at a bad time in my life, and I didn't want to drag you into my mess. I should have told you the truth." "Uh-huh! I better get a good tip after the seafood that you gave me." "Huh!" "You gave me crabs, Vernon." "Nigga, I ain't never had and std in my life. Boy-bye!" "Yeah-Yeah, what can I get you?" "How about a new waiter." "Good luck with that. I'm the only one assigned to this section. So what can I get you?" My cousin and I shared a look that said that we didn't know whether or not to eat here or take the chance that he'd do something to our food. "I'll take a strawberry lemonade and the chicken and waffles." "I'll have the same and sweety! You should know that you can get crabs from a toilet seat." My cousin added. He rolled his eyes as he took our menus and walked off without saying another word. "If he does something to our food, I'll use our family hoodoo and curse him. All I need is his full name." "You have great-granny's book of root workings." "Yup! Granny passed it down to me in her will." "I'm going to need to take a look at it when we get back to the house." She narrowed her gaze on me like she used to do when we were kids before taking a sip of her water. "She made me promise that none of the men in our family could see or use it, but since you're a special case, I'll make an exception." This was the first time that I heard someone speak about it, and I really wanted to know more on the subject of our magical ancestry, but I knew that all of the women in our family held it tighter than a church lady with her pearls at a gay pride parade. We talked about our childhood memories until Lucas brought out our food, and Liv handed him sixty dollars that she hexed just in case he did something to it. Damn, first I gave him crabs, and now he might go blind if he tampered with our food. "Thank you. It doesn't make up for Ms. Sexy ghosting me and leaving me with an itchy crotch, but It'll do." We waited for him to be out of earshot until we laughed and continued to have a great morning, where we talked about what had happened to us up until now. Olivia told me about her best friend's wild bachelorette party and how she had the best sex of her life. "Sounds like you like seafood, too." "I do love me some clams, but it was a one-time thing, and Ernest has enough dick for a lifetime. I know you saw it with the gray sweats that he had on yesterday." "I tried not to look, but my inner gay made me glance at it. Sorry." "It's okay. I know where he sleeps at night, and I don't think he's one of those men who's into stuff like that." *Girl, if only you knew.* "Yeah, me too." I hated lying to my cousin, but I knew that if I told her that, she would side with the man who gives her the life that she is living now, and as the father of her kids, she'd pick him over me every time. That's just how straight people are. "Excuse me!" All beautiful women dressed in a floral print flowing dress and a scarf wrapped around her head walked over to our table. "Hello, I'm Vanna, a medium/ tarot reader. There are spirits around you that want to give you a message. It's free." "Okay! I'm in." She grabbed her meal and placed it in the spot between me and Liv before pulling out her deck of tarot cards.

We continued to eat as she shuffled the cards and then spread them out on the table. "Choose three cards, please." I carefully chose the cards that spoke to my spirit, and she nodded as she turned them over. "Ten of swords. I see that you've recently gone through some kind of betrayal from people you thought were your family." "Yes, I was kicked out of a home that I lived at for almost a decade." Vanna nodded and leaned in closer to the card. "It was for your own safety. I'm sensing danger in that house." She picked up the next card and smiled as she looked at me and then Olivia. "The ten of pentacles, I'm sensing that your blood family has stepped up to offer you help in a living situation and in money." "Yes, My cousin Olivia has given me a place to stay, and a friend of hers just hired me as a hairstylist." Oh, shit! This woman is the real deal. Olivia and I shared a look as she turned around and narrowed her gaze at Lucas. "He didn't do anything to your food, so you might want to undo that hex on the money, or it could come back to bite you in the ass." Olivia's eyes grew large as she made a hand gesture with her left hand and then took a sip from her drink. "The last card is Death; it signifies the end of something, but I'm seeing this being done by your own hands. It could be a good or bad thing, and it depends on the choice that you make. Do me a favor. Choose another card." I did as she asked and handed it to her, but it only added to her look of confusion. "The moon, what the fuck!" Her tone was slightly alarming, and as she gathered the cards together, she gave me a serious look that scared me a little. "Sis, You're going to find out something scary. Be warned that all actions have consequences." I didn't like the sound of that, but as a black-gay-cross dresser in Ohio, I faced scary things on a daily basis. "Whelp, that's all the messages I have for today. Please take this as a warning and be careful with who you surround yourself with." Vanna grabbed her meal and took it back to the table as we ate in silence for a full minute. "Talk about a buzz kill." "Right! But she is right, though. The cards never lie.They just foretell of energies that will affect our future by the choices we make."

We finished our food, and I left a fifty-dollar tip for Lucas before we left to head home. On the way, Ernest called Olivia on her cell phone and told her that his parents wanted to see the kids this weekend and that he said that it was okay because he paid for her to attend a retreat in California while the kids were away. All of this was too good to be true, and I prayed to whoever was up in heaven that he wasn't trying to use this as an excuse to have sex with me. When she asked him what he'd do with a wife and child-free weekend, he said that he and his boys had planned to watch the game without the interruption of their family. Yeah right! "Okay, baby. I'm excited and can't wait. I love you." "I love you too." He hung up, and I felt a knot form in my stomach from what could happen this weekend. "I have to go grocery shopping. Do you want to come, or should I drop you off at home?" "Since we're down the street, can you drop me off at home?" "Sure thing, Cuz." After she left, I pulled out my burner phone and walked to the park that was down the street before I called the police to report a girl who was being held hostage in the basement of my old home. I checked two things off of my revenge list before I destroyed the phone, buried it in the ground, and headed home to enact the next phase of my revenge plan. I screen-shot a bunch of pictures from porn sites and added them to the dating profile that I planned to use against my ex-brother Xavier, who was even more of a man-whore than I was. Within minutes he responded with a dick picture that made my mouth drop and water with the number of veins he had on it. Damn, that's a big dick! I had every intention of masturbating to the picture, but Olivia sent a text that said she was on her way home and would need help with groceries, so I tucked my dick back into my pants as blue balls set in. After she got home, I helped her haul in four hundred dollars worth of food and made sure to tell her that this was one hundred dollars worth of work. "Miss me with that. Oh, And don't think I forgot that you know how to cook. I'm going to need you to make some of your famous snack foods for Ernest and his friends this weekend." *Great! A house full of DL niggas who want to bust a nut in a butt.* "Sure, I can make a couple of dips and twists." "Huh?" I laughed, but she didn't get the Vogue reference, so I explained it to her by showing her my moves that have won several competitions. "Oh, I see you. Knick-knack-Kitty-Cat-Meow!!!" she snapped her fingers and made a circle three times as she leaned back on her bar stool. "You catch on fast, Madam, of the big breasts." We spent the rest of the day getting dinner ready, and I made sure to stay away from Ernest when he got home. I found a bunch of expired food in the basement that I put in a box and made another mental note to mail to my old house on my way to work tomorrow. I woke up in the morning to the sound of someone creeping down the steps and turned over to see my cousin's shady husband with his dick out. "Come on, just the tip." He whispered as he came all the way down and walked over to the bed. "Get the fuck out of here, Nigga!" "Aight-Aight!" He tucked it back into his pants and left for work. Now that I was awake, I took a shower and almost slipped in the shower when I saw a big ass spider hanging from the ceiling. I tried to hit it with my shower shoe, but it moved like a professional acrobat and jumped out of the way as it ran into the opening under the wall. For the rest of the morning, I kept replaying how it moved in my mind, and I kept shuddering from thinking about what would have happened if it landed on me. After I shook off the feeling of almost dying this morning, I grabbed the box of old food and had my cousin stop by the post office before dropping me off at work. "Have a good day." "I will. Have fun at your spa retreat." It felt good to walk into a job for the first time in three years and even better when Trischa had my station already set up for me with new equipment. The only thing that I had to do was stock it with the hair care products that I wanted to use. "Is it okay for me to come in here as a boy, or do you want all of this in the shop every day?" "I prefer this, but it's not my place to force you to be what I want on a daily basis. You choose what you want to present as; just don't come in here looking worse than the clients." "Oh, You don't have to worry about that. Even as a boy, I'm pretty." "Good, Because you have two clients waiting for you." Cool! The hours went by fast as I gave the first one a blow-out, and the second one wanted her locs retwisted. My hands hurt from not being used to this, but at least I made good money and told them to spread the word about my skills. By lunchtime, I had two more clients come in who wanted cornrows with beads on the ends. "Hey, Verona, you don't have any clients. You can go ahead and have lunch if you want." "Yes, Ma'am. I just need to restock my area before I go to the burger place across the street." I made my way to the back, grabbed all the products that I needed, and felt something crawl on my foot. As a New York Native, I knew what it was and wasn't as creeped out as I was from the spider this morning, but when the rodent started to crawl up my boot, I kicked it into the shelf and headed to the front. "Trisch, can I talk to you in your office?" "Yeah. Is everything okay?" I hoped she wasn't going to freak out or get offended by what I was about to tell her. "I just kicked a rat into the shelf back there." "Damn it, I thought that we got rid of the last one. It must have had a baby. Show me." I took her to the back, and sure enough, the damn thing was gone, and I didn't see a hole in the wall for it to get in through. I felt stupid, but I knew that I hadn't imagined it." "I'll put out some traps. Thank you for telling me." I made my way out and headed to the restaurant across the busy street and enjoyed my hour-long break until I saw another dude that I used to mess with come in with his hetero family. He kept looking at me as his family enjoyed their meal, and I could sense that he was scared that I was going out in front of his family. As if! I left and went back to work to see that everyone was cleaning up their stations and getting ready to close early so Trisch's husband, who was an exterminator, could come back later and put out traps. Even though I was only getting paid for half a day's work, It still felt good to have an actual job that didn't care if I was a man dressed in womens clothing. My skills with hair speak for themselves, and hopefully, I'll have enough money saved to get me a car in a month. Now that I had an entire afternoon to myself, I decided to use the extra money I saved to go on a little shopping spree. I bought three thermometers that I planned to mail to the house of Voracity after I came up with a safe way to break them. On my way home, Ernest drove by me and stopped in front of me as I tried to cross the street. "Get in!" "I'm good. The house is three blocks away." "Yeah, but how are you going to get in the house without a key?" He flashed the spare that Olivia must have given him, and I tried not to smile, but his handsome face made it hard. "Aight, just don't try anything, or I'm telling your cousin." He put the car in park and opened the trunk for me to put my stuff in. "Do you need some help?" "Nah, I'm good." I tried to be funny by getting in the back, but he kept that door locked and opened the passenger side door while shaking his head. "Nice try, big booty." He didn't say much the entire ride home, but he kept looking over at me until we pulled into the driveway, and I thanked the gods for my cousin being in the driveway. "Damn it!" He daid under his breath. She waved as she closed the trunk of her car, but he smacked his teeth while getting out to see her off. Olivia looked at me with a half smile and crossed her arms as I went to get my stuff out of the trunk. "Did you get fired on your first day?" "You tried it! There was a rat in the back store room, and T gave us the rest of the day off so that her husband could come in to exterminate it. Mrs. Nosey." "Young lady, that is no way to talk to your mother." We gave Ernest the same look that said that his joke wasn't funny, but he just shrugged while pulling his wife into a side hug. "What?" "Not helping, honey." "Yeah, Ernie. Not helping." I grabbed my stuff and took it into the house but remembered that he had my key, so I had to wait for him to give her one last kiss before she pulled out of the driveway. "The kids are gone, and now it's just the two of us. Mmm-Mmm-Mmm, what shall I do with you?" I rolled my eyes as he stepped past me to let me in the house but brushed his shoulder against mine. Great! I went straight to my room and shut the door as he went upstairs to shower after shooting me a lust-filled look. Even though he was probably a DL-top, he had an ass that was just as fat as mine. Damn. I placed all of my stuff in the plastic drawers and did a bump before he came down with his usual shenanigans. "Hey, are you trying to smoke?" "No, thank you." "Come one, I'm not going to bite." *Yeah, you're trying to just put in the tip.* "Come on, man, what do you want from me?" He sighed as he came down while only wearing boxer briefs and a blunt in his hand. "I'm trying to show you that I'm into you, but you're tripping big time." "Bruh! You're my favorite cousin's husband. I can't fuck this up. I don't have anywhere else to go." "Yeah, but if she wasn't your cousin and if you weren't living here, would you let me hit?" I shook my head and smiled as he passed me the blunt. "I knew it! So come on. Let me at least get some head. Think about it as rent." No, this nigga did not just say that! "I am not putting my mouth where my cousin's clam has been." "Aight! Then don't ask for any of the pizza that I ordered." I inhaled the weed and had to admit that it was some good stuff. Normally, I save smoking weed for when I want to relax, but this man had me on edge with all of his sexual advancements, and right now, I needed to let it work its magic. As time went on, he kept scooting closer until he was sitting so close that I could smell his shea butter lotion and see the veins in his erect penis. "Come on, I'll be gentle." "With what, your hand. Nigga no!" "Dude, I know you want some of this, and besides, your cousin and I haven't had sex in six months. After our youngest was born, she has been too tired to do anything freaky." "So you thought, okay, let me slide up in her cousin who does drag." He shook his head yes, and I laughed at the look that he gave me only because it was cute. "Aight! Nigga, whip it out." He did as I asked, and I looked him in the eyes as I put my mouth on it and spent half an hour showing him why I'm the throat goat of Columbus, Ohio. Mr. DL came into my mouth after yelling so loud and grabbing the sides of my head as he pumped his seed down my throat. "Shit, why did you make me wait so long for that?" I went to the bathroom to spit out his semen, and when I returned, he was lying on his stomach with no underwear on. Oh! "I'll let you top me if you let me go next." I nodded as I undressed and pulled out two condoms before putting mine on. He handed me a bottle of lube that my cousin must not have known about, and I went to town on his ass until my eyes rolled into the back of my head. This was definitely not his first time, and by the way he was throwing it back, I knew that he loved being topped as much as I did. "Can you bounce up and down on me?" Once again, I nodded and was thankful for the fact that I douche on a daily basis. "Sit back while I show you the third best part of me." Ernest laid back as I positioned myself over his thighs and allowed his erect penis to slide inside of me. It didn't take long for him to cry out again as he came inside the condom, but when he kissed me on the mouth, I was too stunned to move. "I promise this will be our little secret." "Yeah, It better be, or I'm going to burn this house down with you in it." I slowly got up as he pulled himself out of me and farted out his semen as he did mine. The good part was that he allowed me to shower first, but I felt bad for helping him cheat on the cousin who opened up her home to me. How could I repay her by *opening* up to her husband like that? Ernest ordered the pizza, and we ate it like what we just did was normal and spent the rest of the night smoking his good weed while chasing it with a bottle of tequila. That turned out to be an even bigger mistake because we flip-flopped all over the house until we both could move, and I went to my room to sleep. The next morning this nigga surprised me with breakfast that was just as good as his ass. "You know I'm not gay, right?" "Okay, That was out of left field, but yeah. Having sex with a man doesn't make you gay. You're just attracted to me sometimes." "I'm Just making sure that you know what this is and don't catch feelings." "Nigga! You've been trying to get some of this for a while now. I think it's *you* who has to worry about feelings. I've had sex with so many men that I've lost count of their faces, dicks and asses." That brought a surprisingly cute look to his face as he continued to eat while battling whether or not he wanted to know more about that part of my life. "Bruh! Go ahead and ask whatever question it is that you want to ask." "Is my dick the biggest that has fucked you?" "Yes, but there are many of them who come close, and if it wasn't for them, I would have had trouble taking all of that. What about you?" "It almost brought some tears to my eyes, but yeah, you're pretty big." He leaned forward and kissed my lips, and this time, I pulled back as he tried to shove his tongue into my mouth. "That type of kissing is reserved for the nigga that I'm with. Not Nigga's who are married." "Uh-huh! We'll see about that." A part of me felt bad about enjoying having sex with that man, and even worse now that I can see him starting to actually enjoy being with me like that. "Oh shit! Did you see that?" "See what?" Ernest got up off of the bed and walked to the laundry room while looking at the ground. "It was a big ass rat watching us from the doorway." "What?" I lifted my feet up and prayed that I wasn't being stalked by a rodent. "Did you bring that thing home with you or something?" "That's not funny." "There's some rat traps over there." "Uh, I'm not putting them out." "Then you better make room for your roommate." He laughed as he walked past me, and I slapped his booty while he walked up the steps. "If you're following me, I will kill you!" The damn thing ran out of the laundry room, and I lost it as I ran up the steps with it following behind me. "Ernie, It's behind me, get the broom." He laughed so hard that he was clutching his sides, but I kept going and ran out of the house as it continued to follow behind me. "Y-Yeah, that's it. Get that thing out of here." I hopped on the back of his car and watched as the rat ran down the street.

"Thank goodness." I said getting down. "Is your secret admirer gone?" he said with a smirk on his handsome face.

"Yeah, Apparently, it had somewhere else to go." I replied.

I ran into the house before it decided to come back, and we talked about it all day when we weren't taking turns fucking each other. By late afternoon, both of us had rat traps placed around the house in areas that the children couldn't get to. The rest of the day went by superfast as I stayed in my room and called my ex-house mother from a private number seven times in a row. "Hello! Who is this?" I just breathed into the phone as she continued to ask questions, but I just breathed harder until I hung up. After I had all the fun that could be had, I decided to spend the rest of the day watching television with Ernest, and we ended up falling asleep on the couch. Sunday morning, I got a call from Trischa about a client who wanted her locs retwisted, but I had to go to her house. I agreed simply because I had to get out of the house and spend another hour getting ready. By eleven o'clock, we were on our way to the rich people's side of town with a car full of hair care products. We pulled into the driveway of the client's mansion, and my mouth fell open because it was the biggest house that I'd ever seen. "I know, right? When I did her hair six months ago, I had the same reaction." "Home-girl got the real coins, Huh?" "Her name is Adina, and her husband is a judge, and she owns the hair care line that we're using." "Yessss, I'm going to need to be her friend. Like yesterday." "Ha! Be careful. Rich people only care about optics."

The lady of the house came out as we parked, and I couldn't believe how beautiful she was, but her hair was trash. It looked like she hadn't had a re-twist in a year, and her clothes were not that of a rich woman. *Ohh, Girl-no! Not the house coat with slippers.* "Hello, welcome to my home." Trischa got out to hug her as I grabbed the stuff from the back. "Thank you for having us." "You have a lovely home." I almost laughed at how dumb she looked and realized that she was a light-skinned woman who had probably rested on being pretty most of her life. Those of us who were dark-skinned had to work harder and receive half of the results. "Yes, Ms. Ma'am. You are fierce, honey!" Of course, she knew gay phrases. "I try- I try." She walked us into the house, where two other women were waiting in robes. "Ladies, the hair goddesses are here. Who's ready to be slayed." *Girl no!* One of them eyed me suspiciously as I put the box down and extended my hand for her to shake it. She looked at it before taking a sip of her drink as the other one got up and took my hand in hers. "You have to excuse my cousin. She's a forty-year-old mean girl." "Bitch! Don't insult me in front of the help." Trischa and I shared a look that said we needed this money and got to work on unpacking our supplies. The rude one didn't want me to do her hair, so I did the nice ones, and the locs of the house owner, while the boss lady took care of madam-wrinkled face. We finished doing their hair and make-up by three o'clock, and my face ached as much as my hands from all of the fake smiling I had to do. Once we packed all of our things back into the car, Adina pulled Trischa to the side, and they had a heated conversation that ended with her saying that she won't stand by while the oppressed spew the white man's oppression. Adina pulled her by the arm as she tried to storm off and handed her two envelopes. "What was that about?" "The bitch with an attitude knows that you're a man. She told Adina that she didn't want to be touched by an abomination and instead of having my back, she decided to help inflate that bitch's ego even more by telling me not to bring you back."

"Wow! We helped them look like their black didn't crack, and this is how they repay us."

"Yeah, I just hope that she doesn't try anything funny with the product, or I'll sue."

"I'll be right there in court with a neck brace and a busted lip." I added. That managed to make her laugh, and she passed me one of the envelopes as we pulled out of the long driveway. "Five thousand dollars!" "She knows that if I complain, it will be a lawsuit, and with her husband about to run for re-election, they need everyone to think that they stand for all communities." "I wouldn't have cared if she said I had aids and chlamydia. This is a good amount of money for a full day's work." "As a straight black woman, I recognize that it was your kind who was standing next to us when we marched for equal rights and not stuck-up hoes who used being light-skinned to their advantage. Not that all light-skinned women think as she does, but I mean, damn. How do we expect white people to treat us right if we don't treat each other right? You know?" Wow, truer words have never been spoken, and I can't believe that a straight woman had my back when it was turned. "Thanks, Boss-lady. I really appreciate you sticking up for me." "I appreciate you keeping your cool. The last time I came out here with the woman who had your chair before you, she tried to steal the lady's watch because she felt as if she wouldn't miss it." Damn, why didn't I think of that? We stopped by the bank so that I could deposit the money into my account through the ATM and then a fast food restaurant before she dropped me off at home. "Alright, I'll see you Monday morning." "Yes, bright and early." She allowed me to keep the extra stuff, and I vowed to use it on my family because it was made for our hair texture. Now that my bank account was out of the negative, I had an extra pep in my step, and since Ernest was still out with his friends, I went into the house to eat my food in peace. An hour later, he came home but was too drunk to do anything besides fall asleep on the couch. Thank the gods. I went to my room and opened the dating app to troll Xavier, who sent me six messages asking if I wanted to meet up. After contemplating what I should do, I finally decided to send him the address of a worn-down apartment building on the west side. An hour later, he sent me several messages asking me to come outside, but I turned my phone off and went to sleep. In the morning, Ernest made us breakfast again, and we watched the news about a drug dealer being mauled by an alligator that was still on the loose. A chill ran down my spine as I thought about how much of a coincidence it was that I sent Xavier to that exact spot. "Who the fuck is housing that type of wild animal?" "Your guess is as good as mine." I did the dishes while Ernest rolled a blunt and put it up to my lips because my hands were wet. By lunchtime, we had sex twice because the first time was interrupted by a call from Olivia saying that she was on her way home and she'd stop by his parents to get the kids. "Aight, Babe, I miss you too." He hung up the phone with a sad expression on his face that confirmed my suspicions about him being in a loveless marriage. "Dude, I know you're not catching feelings." "I'm not. I just wished we had another day of fun in the buns before they returned." Noooo!! This was what I feared would happen. I've heard stories of men who act like him and end up killing their families to get out of being tied to them. "This was just fun. Nothing serious. Besides, you're married to my cousin." He nodded in agreement, but I could see by the look on his face that he wasn't on the same page as I was. I went to my room and spent the rest of the morning giving myself my own personal spa day with the extra products from yesterday's job. Everything was going well until I spotted the spider from the bathroom crawling out of the bathroom towards me. "Come on, you little shit!" I grabbed the bug spray that I bought and used almost all of it on the creature and then stomped it to death as I yelled out in victory. "Yeah, Itsy-bitsy found out who was the strongest of all!" "Are you okay down there?" "Yes, I finally killed that big ass spider that has been stalking me." "Good for you." *Yeah, he was still mad that his family was returning home.* I made sure to stay away from him until Olivia came back with the kids, and I told her about my fun little excursion that ended with me experiencing a hate crime from a rich, toxic female. "Well, at least you got paid." "Yup, and this is my first month's rent." I handed her the five hundred dollars that I was saving as just-in-case money, and she did a little dance as she put it in her bra. *Eww! Titty money.* The rest of the day flew by as I watched Ernest pretend like he missed his family while shooting me pouty-lipped glances whenever Olivia left the room. Once they went to sleep, I watched a couple of scary movies that I wished I hadn't and called it a night around ten. That night, I had a bunch of scary dreams where I was being chased by an Alligator while swimming at night in a smelly lake. After I woke up to use the restroom, I fell asleep and had another nightmare where I was being chased by a wolf and a mountain lion under a full moon. Never had I ever had a dream as real as that. It felt like I was really running for my life, and when I tripped over a log, I understood how the white girls in the horror movies ended up dead. The sound of Ernest getting ready for work snapped me out of it, but I hated that I was covered in sweat. Since he always woke up hours before the rest of the house, I took a shower and got myself ready for the day. "Hey, cuz. Can you help me with my edges?" Olivia yelled down the steps as I closed out the dating app to grab the baby hair brush. "Coming, give me a second." I did a bump and made sure that there wasn't any residue on my nose before going upstairs to do my magic. "You rang!" "Okay! It's giving the bride of Frankenstein with that streak, honey." I looked around to see if the kids were near us and did a twerk as I walked up to her. "Aight! Sit back and let me do what I do, Boo." I helped her lay her edges correctly but almost dropped the comb when she told me that Ernest was the reason that her hair was tousled from the morning sex. Not that I was jealous or anything. I just felt bad that she was getting my sloppy seconds. After she took the kids to daycare and school, she dropped me off at work, and I worked my magic on the first two clients until the next one came in with an attitude. She knew me from the ball scene, but I couldn't remember who she was to save my life. "Can someone who hasn't been a sex worker do my hair?" She said, trying to be funny. "Yeah, I don't style synthetic." "Bitch! Who the fuck are you talking to?" She tried to swing, but I moved out of the way and had to remember that she was a real girl. "Hey! Hey! We ain't doing that." Trisha took her by the arm and threw her out of the store, and told her not to come back or she'd beat her ass. It felt really good to have someone like that in my corner for once in my life. "If she comes back, I give you permission to handle her." "Say less." I took an early break and walked to the Chinese restaurant called A Taste of Kimiko. The food was so good that I didn't want to return to work, but after I got a call from the boss lady saying that I had a client waiting for me in the lobby. The thought of making more money gave me a heightened sense of happiness until I saw that it was Kayla, my ex-House sister who was transgender. "Hey, long time no see." "Hello, What can I do for you today?" She made a face and smacked her teeth as she got up to hug me, but I stepped back. "Sorry, ma'am, I have a strict no-touching rule after Covid." Out of all of my ex-family, she was the one that I was closest to, and it hurt when she sided with the others when they kicked me out. "I'll take a blowout." "Okay, Follow me." I did her hair while making small talk like we didn't know each other, and when she told me that Trent was dead, I almost cried into her hair. "My condolences to you and your family. The lady at the front will process your payment. Excuse me." I ran to the back as tears fell down my face from hearing the sad news. How could she just say it so casually, like he was someone we were acquainted with? I was still pissed at them for how they treated me and had full intentions of continuing my plans, but I never wanted to see any of them dead. The world has had it out for my people for as long as I can remember. Once I dried my tears, I took care of the next three clients while trying not to let the loss of a brother show on my face. "Are you okay?" Trischa came over and put her hand on my shoulder as we closed up the shop, and I could no longer hold it in as I cried uncontrollably. "No, M-my brother was killed yesterday." "I'm sorry for your loss. Do you want to take a personal day?" I shook my head no because it wouldn't help anything for me to miss money. "I'll be alright. I just need to go home and clear my head." "Okay, Can I give you a ride home?" "Yes, I would love that. Thank you." We rode home in silence, and she asked me if I wanted the day off again, but I said no before thanking her for the ride. "Have a good night, boss lady." "You too, honey. See you in the morning." After I told my cousin about the death of my house brother, she told the kids to keep away because I needed some time alone, and I spent the rest of the evening in my room until dinner was done. With Trent's death being at the forefront of my mind, I decided to give my revenge a rest for a couple of days and went to bed without saying anything to my family. I had a weird lucid dream where I was stomping on Trent's neck repeatedly until he died, and I woke up in the middle of the night in a cold sweat. It took me an hour to get back to sleep, and when I did, I had a recurring dream about being chased by the two snarling beasts from the night before under a full moon. When I woke up, I got ready for work, but Ernest came downstairs and gave me a hug as I cried once more. My body moved on autopilot throughout the entire day, and when it came time to leave, Trischa told me that I could have the day off. I declined her offer once more, but this time, she made me use the bereavement time. After she dropped me off at home, the next two weeks went by so fast that I was pleasantly surprised when the direct deposit hit my account. Since I was still grieving the loss of Trent, I decided not to use the credit cards and threw them in the trash. I had to lie to my cousin and say that they were junk mail, or she'd get suspicious. As a journalism major, she was good at finding out things with little to no leads. I treated the family to dinner at our favorite restaurant up the street, but Ernest decided not to go, so Olivia and I took the kids, and we had a good time. It kind of made me want to have a family of my own someday until the twins decided to have a food fight with the kids across from us. In my opinion, we were kicked out because we were black, and if I was alone, I would have caused an even bigger scene. "Kids, Next time someone calls you the N-word, tell me, and I'll deal with it. Now, we can't ever go back to the restaurant." "Yes, Ma'am." The youngest baby clapped his hands and made spit bubbles as he tried to say what his older siblings said. Once we made it home, I went straight to my room so that Ernest wouldn't look my way with his sad puppy dog brown eyes. Later that night, I had another crazy dream, but instead of being chased by vicious four-legged quadrupeds, I was inside a cabin full of the sound of hissing snakes coming from everywhere.

My heart raced in my chest as I tried to find an exit. The door wouldn't open, and as I turned around to run towards the window, a giant snake bit me on the thigh three times. Its fangs retracted, and the anaconda turned into my ex-house sister, Milly. "That was for Trent." I woke up in another cold sweat to see Ernest creeping down the steps with a concerned look on his face. "I heard you talking in your sleep and came down to check on you. Are you alright?" "It was just a nightmare. Thank you for asking." He nodded and took a deep breath as he stepped closer to the bed. "I miss us." Before I could respond, he left without saying another word. *I knew I shouldn't have ever had sex with that man.* The morning flew by, and I left for work with the memory of my dream at the forefront of my mind. Was it a result of being hounded by actual animals in real life, or was it because of my sex with Ernest that made me feel a weird sense of guilt? By the time the work day was over, I took the bus to the car lot on the other side of town and put a downpayment on my four-door black sedan. It felt so good to drive off of the lot while blasting nineties music on the radio. The money that I put down on the car made it so that I only had three thousand dollars left on it before it was mine. Thank the sky daddy for buy-here pay-here's. I drove home and tried not to go over the speed limit since I was a new driver with car insurance that wasn't an hour old yet. When I pulled up to the house, all of my stuff was sitting on the curb next to the trash, and Olivia was on the porch with a gun in her hand. Oh shit! I couldn't even enjoy being a new driver without something coming along and ruining my happiness. "You faggot ass bitch! How could you?" "Liv, I-." "No! Shut the fuck up and get the fuck off of my lawn before I put one of these in your ass like you put THAT in my husband's ass." She used the gun to point at my dick, and I quickly turned around to put my stuff in my new car. I noticed that there was one of the credit cards that I ordered on top of my stuff with the other mail that was in Trent's name. Perfect! The only bad part about all of this was that I would have to sleep in my car until I found somewhere to live, but the good part was that I wouldn't have to see Ernest anymore. On my way to get something to eat I saw a Motel with a Vacancy sign in the window and reserved a room for the night. I checked for bodily fluid stains and bed bugs before I laid on the bed to go to sleep. "This is my life!" I just had to have sex with him. "Fucking psycho." I went to sleep and had a dream where Olivia was talking to a crow that was perched on her hand. They were standing on her porch and as it spoke I recognized the voice as Kayla's. When I tried to step closer the mountain lion walked from the open doorway with the wolf following right behind it. I tried to turn around and run but my legs were bound together by the snake from my nightmare a couple of nights ago. It wound itself up my body until it was looking me in the eyes. The rat was crawling up the snake's back with a sinister look in its eyes and as I tried to move I fell backwards onto the ground. A bright full moon hung in the sky as they began to eat me alive and I cried out in pain until I woke up in another cold sweat. "Are you okay baby?" I turned over to see Ernie with a bleeding bullet hole in between his eyes. He leaned in to kiss me but I jumped back and screamed until I woke up on the floor of the motel room. I grabbed my phone to see that it was seven o'clock and mentally prepared myself for work. After my shower in the tub that was probably as much of a cum-dump as a prostitute on parsons avenue, I stopped by the donut shop before going into work.

"Good morning everyone!"

"Hey, Good morning. Your first client is going to be a half of an hour late."

"Cool, I want to scarf down two of those glazed twists while looking for a place to stay."

"What happened with your cousin?" I took a deep breath and came up with a lie on the spot so that I wouldn't lose my job too. "I think I overstayed my welcome. My cousin caught her son playing in my make-up." "There is an apartment upstairs that I normally use for when I don't want to go home that you can stay in." I just love how the universe is always working in my favor. She took a glazed donut out of the box as I set them down and went to her office to get the key. "Come on, The entrance is around the back." I almost choked on my donut when I saw how big the front room and bedroom was. It had a bathroom that was twice as big as the one in the basement of the house but this one had a tub-shower combo that gave it an old world kind of feel. "How much do you want me to pay in rent?" "Nothing, Save your money for you and fill that fridge up with groceries so that I can eat at your place once a week." "Deal." With everything going my way I was in a happy mood all day. After we closed I headed to the post office to change my address and then to the supermarket to get a bunch of food that set me back three hundred dollars. With it being all electric I had to wait until the morning to switch it over into my name. "Finally, I'm where I need to be in life and I did it all on my own. Well sort of." I made Cabbage and sausage for dinner while using one of my burner phones to report a fire at the House of Voracity's residence. I finished off my night with a bottle of Chardonnay and the weed that Ernie gave me in a bong. I had another weird dream about the animals that were chasing me but this time the medium Vanna pulled me into the cabin. "They mean you harm. Stay away from them. Stop trying to get your revenge." "Why? I deserve to get them back for how they treated me." She shook her head no and placed her hand on my shoulder like a friend who was telling me about myself. "They kicked you out to save your life, but your actions have dire consequences." I awoke to my alarm clock at seven thirty with the dream still on my mind and made myself a big breakfast before walking the short distance to the salon downstairs. I took it as a sign to lay off my ex-family and focus on making my life better. Olivia was my first client but she kept the conversation towards me short and left without saying another word. I thanked the sky daddy for her not telling Trischa about how our relationship really ended. A couple of my old drag queen friends stopped by to get their hair done for the ball later tonight and invited me to come hang out. I told them that I would only because I wanted to show up to show out. Once they left Trischa walked over with the other hairstylist and weird smiles on their faces. "Is it something that straight people can come to?" I was caught off guard by her question but I could see that they really wanted to support me. "Yes, we are accepting of all and everyone is welcome." That made them all giggle like school girls and we spent the rest of the day talking about what to do and what to wear. After I gave them the rundown on what to expect they were even more excited to attend the ball. "So if someone asks me if I'm real-fish, It's a good thing to say yes?" my chair neighbor asked. "Correct." I answered. "Ohhh, I'm so excited. We'll meet you here around eight." "Uh-no! That's too early. Meet me here at nine. The ball starts at eight and no one who's worth seeing will be there until nine." I walked around back to my apartment with a bunch of ideas going through my mind about what to wear. My hair was technically already done but I wanted to put on my lace front that I just made and match it with my cat suit that made my penis-tucking comfortable. Three hours passed by and now that I was beat for the goddesses, I did a bump and took a shot before the girls arrived. "Bitch!!!! You look fierce!" I yelled at my boss. Trischa was every bit a true glamazon and the others looked just as good. "Is there any other way to look?"

"Come in, I poured us some shots to take before we go."

"Ohhhh, Shot-shot-shot-shot-shot-shot-shot-shot!"

"Ayeeee! Shot o'clock!" We piled into my car and made our way to the south side of Columbus. The parking lot was packed so it took us twenty minutes to find a spot somewhere else that wouldn't get my car towed. We had to walk five minutes in the dark to the building but it was worth it because there was nothing worse than trying to get out of that parking lot after the ball was over. Once we got inside we watched my friends who invited me perform some old songs and then I had to sit through a couple of vogue battles before they changed the category to butch-queen realness. Father John walked by me without saying a word as he strutted his stuff while trying to look handsome with his wrinkled face and faux-wolf fur. The theme of the ball was kind of corny with its animal shifter theme. Everyone else wore similar animal theme costumes that were just as atrocious and I laughed at the sight of how much their style has suffered without me. "Those are the people that kicked me out. Right there." Mother Mo, turned her head as I spoke about them like she could hear me over the loud music and monotonous talking. She flashed me a smile but I nodded as the commentator got on the mic to start the next category. Once it was over they handed out awards to people who made the ballroom scene what it was. Guy won most of the awards and I was given the legend award even though I was only in my mid-thirties. I just wished that they didn't bring up the fact that I was kicked out of the house that won the top trophy of the night. *Maybe the universe was telling me that this was the closing of that part of my life.* Before we left I got the number of one of the sexiest men alive and we made plans to go on a date tomorrow. "Verona! Wait up!" I turned around to see my ex-family walking up to me with smiles on their faces. "We just wanted to say thank you, for helping us get to top-house status." Mother Mo pulled me into a hug as the rest of them made it a family hug that I really didn't want, but I decided to be nice for a change. "Even though you opened your home to me and then closed it as well, I wouldn't be who I am without you. Thank you." I answered. "Maybe we could have dinner sometime." Father John, suggested. "Maybe." I replied.

Before they could say anything else I turned around and continued with my group of hotties to my car. "Oh my god!" "What?" I froze as I saw the huge scratch on the side of my car and the word fuck you on the hood. Those shady bitches! Did they do this?" Trisch asked. "I don't know, but I'm definitely mailing a box of broken thermometers to their house." We hopped in my car and I drove home while they spoke about how fucked up it was that they did this to my car. My mind raced with ideas about what else I could do to them and I came up with a plan to mail them bed bugs after I order more credit cards in their names. Thankfully I still have the card that was in Trents name and I'm going to use that to pay for a new paint job. After we got home the girls left me to my thoughts as I headed up stairs to put my plan in motion. Once I went to sleep, I had the same usual dream about being chased by vicious animals and Vanna standing off in the distance with a stop sign in her hands. My feet hurt from running without shoes on but I kept going until I reached a lake. The moonlight danced on the water but as I looked closer I could see an alligator's open mouth in the water right before it leaped out and clamped its mouth down on my foot. The wolf snarled as it bit down on my other leg while the mountain lion jumped onto my back as I fell into the water face first. I tried to fight them with everything that I had but it hurt like hell when the gator and wolf severed my legs. My blood turned the murky green water orange as the moonlight made the anaconda visible before it wrapped itself around my throat to strangle me. I woke up at five-forty-two covered in so much sweat that I had to change my sheets and shower. "Great, Now I have to stop by the laundromat before my date later." With my day starting off on the wrong foot I decided to smoke a blunt and pair it with an energy drink before getting to work. I had two cancellations due to covid so Trischa allowed me to take the day off so that I could run some errands before my date with the sexy doctor. I was so excited to date a man that wasn't married or scared to be seen with that I forgot what it felt like to get excited about a man. My date Dion called me around eight to ask if he could push the date back an hour because he had a surprise for me and I said yes but it gave me anxiety to not know where we were going. When he came to pick me up he was tight lipped the whole way to our destination. After I threatened to call the police and say that he was abducting me he told me that he had a cabin reserved with a personal chef. I hated that we were leaving Columbus to go to the outskirts of Cleveland and it made a chill run down my spine as I remembered the dream that I had. Once we turned the corner my mouth dropped at the sight of the beautiful cabin that was nestled in the woods.

"This is nice." I said, swallowing the lump in my throat.

"Nice! I'm sure you can do better than that." he said, putting the car in park.

"Alright, It's amazing. I girl could get used to fancy stuff like this."

He walked me into the cabin and the first thing that I saw was the food on the table with two bottles of wine waiting for us to devour it. He pulled out my chair and poured us some wine before taking his seat. "Tell me about yourself." *Ohhh, a nigga with brains and manners.* "I'm a hairstylist, A virgo and I'm recently a free agent when it comes to the house-scene. What about you?" He took a sip of wine while looking at his expensive watch. Damn, this nigga got coins. "I work in pharmaceuticals, I have no kids, never married, no family to introduce you to."

My eyes grew wide as he spoke the words that I loved to hear. Families came with more people with opinions and since I just messed up a semi-happy home, I didn't need some ex-wife slashing my tires after finding out her man likes men. As the night went on he made me want to bend over the table and let him fuck me right here with all the words that he spoke. I just wished that this man wasn't too good to be true. "I have to use the restroom, excuse me." I went to the bathroom to make sure I was good before we did anything sexual and when I came back he refilled my glass. "Ohh, Okay then. I see you." I finished the glass off in one go as he walked over to me with the sexiest look on his face. "Come here." He walked me over to the window as a raven flew by making its noise. The moon was so beautiful as we slow-danced and I let my worries fade away. "How do you feel?" "Good, how about you?" "I feel great." He kept moving my hips as I started to feel drowsy. What the fuck? "Hol-Hold up." Dion let me go as the intense feeling spread to the rest of my body and I stumbled backwards until I fell to the ground. Everything went black as the sound of someone opening the front door entered my ears. "About time!" I recognized the voice of Father John but my ability to move was non-existent as unconsciousness set in. "Wake up hoe!" I opened my eyes and almost screamed as I was face to face with the giant snake from my dreams. "Hello, Sis!" I heard Milly's voice in my head but didn't see her anywhere so I figured that I must be in another one of my nightmares. "No bitch, You're not dreaming. This is reality." To my left I saw the large mountain lion step forward as I heard Mother Mo's voice in my head. The room was filled with the beasts from my dreams and in the corner Dion sat next to a big ass wolf. "What did you slip me?" The wolf moved from his side and stood up on its hind legs while changing into a naked Father John. *Eww! he 's not circumcised.* This had to be a dream because shit like that didn't happen in real life. The snake uncoiled itself from around me and joined the others as they changed into my ex-house family. "Shapeshifting feels so much better during a full moon." Milly spoke while stretching. "This is why we kicked you out, stupid." It was hard to look at them while their dangly parts hung out so I looked to the ground. "Don't worry, we'll be the last people you see." Dion undressed and got on all fours as his body changed into a brown wolf with eerie yellow eyes. "Yeah, You're right. That felt good." Milly untied me and I ran to the door as all of them laughed. The memory of my nightmares slammed into me as I ran with my drowsy legs carrying me into the forest. "Yes, Keep running, you fat-snack!" My ex-house mother taunted me as I heard her following behind and I wished I would have grabbed my purse with the weapons in it I keep for moments like this. "Sky Daddy, Please let this be a dream." I ran further into the forest as twigs and leaves crunched under my feet. Thank goodness I chose to wear boots instead of heels. I was so focused on trying to escape that I didn't see where I was going in the moonlight and tripped over a large fallen branch and crashed to the ground as a twig stabbed me in the side. "We tried to save you from knowing about this, Daughter." Lioness-Mother Mo walked over to me with her orange eyes glowing. Everyone else gathered from the other directions with glowing eyes of different colors and vicious intent on their beastly faces. "We didn't want to kill you like you killed Trent, but after You did all of those awful things to us, we agreed that it was time that you learned why we changed our name to the House of Voracity." Mother Mo bit down on my left leg and ripped off a chunk of it as Father John tore off my right shoulder. Kayla swooped down and pecked out my eyes as Xavier snapped off my foot. The last thing I felt was Milly's repeated bites as she struck me and sank her fangs in deep while her venom worked its way through my body. Kayla's voice entered my head as they continued to maul me and my body became numb. "Thank you for being our first living meal as a family of shifters, under the supreme full moon. We definitely need to thank that witch who cursed us, BTW." *Why didn't I listen to Vanna's warning?* I should have left well enough alone, but no! I just had to get revenge. Now all that awaited me was death from being mauled by the people who took me in.

The Back Door

"P-please. I'll have the money! Don't hurt them." A deep cackle escaped my throat as I clapped Kent elder on the back. "That's what you said a month ago and a month before that. I've given you six chances to get me my money. But everytime you disappoint me. It's like I'm nine again and my parents promised they'd come get me on the holiday's but They never Did!" I finished my rant with several blows to the ribs and he coughed up blood on my brand new sneakers. "Fuck! This is what I get for trying to break these in. Boys!" My well paid team of mercenaries came in and picked him up off the ground and carried him down my hall of horrors. The first two rooms were empty but the middle rooms housed two very special guests. "R-Renzo, I'm sorry. P-please. I'll get you the- Ahhh!, What have you done?" He screamed. "Correction, what have we done?" My team laughed and threw him into the room and he slipped in the pool of blood that surrounded the bed. "Ahhh! Ahhh! My-M-My girls. You-you. Ahhh!" I knew when he borrowed the money that he would never be able to return the entire amount. I also knew he had teenage daughters who were virgins. My toes curled just thinking about who wet and tight they were. "Turn the heat up in that room and leave him in there and take the weekend off." "Yes boss." I changed my shoes and threw them into my incinerator and walked to my car that was waiting to take me home. "Good evening sir!" "It is a great evening indeed, Hullens." He opened my door and once I was comfortably seated he shut it and walked around to the driver side. "Thank you once again for hiring me Mr. Williams. I really needed this job." I'd be lying if I said I did it as a kind gesture. I change drivers every two years just to have more people to rape and his fat ass was a big pillow just waiting for me to plunge myself balls deep into it. "Simply doing your job is all the gratitude I need." He nodded and we drove in silence on the way to my mansion. "Have a good night sir." "You as well." I shut the door and it automatically locked as my security system became active. Overseeing my criminal empire takes up my entire day but it was worth it to be home alone with all my stuff around me. My collection of weapons that I have spread throughout the house wait patiently with me for the day when I get to use them. With most of my team in the neighboring houses I have an added sense of safety that allows me to sleep at night. As someone who is allergic to dogs both physically and mentally I was blessed to live alone and in the comfort of not having to smell their disgusting fur or feel an itch and wonder if its fleas. The next couple of hours went by fast as I made myself dinner and then cleaned up. I rolled a blunt and poured some wine while I waited for my bath water to be ready. "T.V. On!" It clicked on to show breaking news about the missing six year old girl I sold to Russians this morning. "Volume up!" And I'm standing in front of Skytown apartments where Crystal Mellington was last seen by her classmates at seven eighteen am, right before she was snatched into a silver rusted van. Witnesses say Three large men stepped out of the vehicle and dragged her by the hair into the van-." I walked into my bathroom and placed my blunt and wine on the table next to the tub and slowly got in. For a man of thirty-six I still loved bubble baths, the warm water and natural herbs were great for my brown skin. I soaked in the tub for twenty minutes and then showered for fifteen more before retiring to my bed and falling asleep. I awoke the next morning to three missed calls and a voicemail from my lawyer. "Ren! The F.B.I just raided my office, and are on their way to you at the construction site!" My pulse raced as I ran to my safe and put all of its contents in a duffle bag. Luckily I owned multiple normal sized houses for this very reason, the downside was not having my security team living around me and a small amount of weapons. I had Hullens pick me up and we took every backstreet we could from Chicago to my safe house in Decatur. I made sure to pay Hullens extra for being ready at a moment's notice. "Sir, I thought you had a house in Ohio that I was taking you to?" "I have some stuff here that I need to get, back the car into the garage next to this one and come inside through that door. I'm going to make us something to eat." I lied to buy some time to grab my gun with the silencer before he walked in through the garage.

"Hey I have to use-" Two bullets to the head ended his sentence and his fall to the floor made his ass cheeks jiggle. If I had more time I would be able to sample that but I had to get to my real house in Columbus-Ohio where all of my weapons and small fortune was. I pulled out his teeth and removed his finger prints and then dismantled my gun before I tossed it in a barrel of acid. My next set of tasks were to pour gasoline everywhere, place half of my silverware in the kitchen microwave and then the garage microwave and set the timer to start in six hours. I changed my clothes and quickly backed out of the garage in my jeep and drove all the way to another safe house, grabbed some money and hopped in my truck. I spent two thousand dollars in cash at seven different grocery stores on my way to my house on the southside of Columbus. My four bedroom home was nestled on a street where my alias owns the surrounding three houses and the apartment building on the corner. I placed cameras all over my little neighborhood and made sure this house was just as secure as my mansion. The front gate opened and I pulled onto my wrap-around driveway. The entire property was surrounded by tall iron gates that were covered in thick overgrown foliage that blocked the view from the outside. I parked at the back door and went in to turn the alarm off and prop the door open. It took me thirty minutes to bring in the groceries, park the car in the large garage and then put away the groceries. The next hour was spent preparing baked garlic chicken and asparagus with carrots and brown rice. Dinner paired well with a blunt and a glass of wine, but the only thing missing was something warm and tight around my dick. Out of the corner of my eye I saw a large shadow move and reached for my gun, I jumped off the couch with my plate crashing to the floor. The hair on the back of my neck stood on end as I checked left and right with my heart racing and didn't see anything. After twenty minutes of checking my house and the cameras I realized it must have been the shadow of a branch from the tree in my yard or a bird. Thankfully I was done with my food so there wasn't a huge mess on my rug so I rolled another blunt of Dragon-kush to calm my nerves and poured another glass of chardonnay. My work has kept me extremely busy and it has been a while since I last watched television so I turned it on and opened the stream-show app. There were so many choices but I settled on a gay cop thriller that ended up being a waste of an hour and thirty minutes of my life. The cop and drug dealer fell in love and made a family together. *Bullshit!* No one can escape from their past or just find true love and all is forgiven. This is why I stopped watching movies and TV altogether. It was for those who weren't making millions by the day. People who were perfectly fine with being poor and lower class citizens. As someone born to parents with full time careers as venture capitalist, I never had to worry about how much things cost or where my next meal was coming from. That was until my thirteenth birthday where my parents caught me getting dressed with my secret boyfriend Peyton Jaysons. It was the first time I had sex and the last time we saw each other. From that day on all I knew was St. Christopher's boarding school for wayward children. That was the day my heart shriveled up and I knew I had to get revenge on the two straight people that birthed me. ***Ding!*** A notification from my lawyer Colbert, let me know that they officially put me on the most wanted list and he was deleting the text and destroying the phone and that he and his lover were safe. The last part I didn't give a shit about but the first was expected. I contributed to half the missing person cases and trafficked a large portion of the drugs throughout the tristate area. I also Killed at least twenty members of the rock street gang and shot up most of their families houses. ***Crash!*** I grabbed my gun and ran into the kitchen to see what that sound was and the hairs on the back of my neck stood up as I turned the corner. Several pots and pans fell out of the drying rack onto the floor. ***Ding!*** I returned the pots and pans to the rack and ran into the living room to check my phone. There was a notification from an unknown number that simply said "HEY!" This was a burner phone and that could have come from anyone who mixed up some numbers so I destroyed it in the basement and retrieved another from my safe. I chalked all of this up as paranoia. My new life was something that would take longer than a day to get used to. Fuck! I'm going to miss my maid with the cellulite. Her thighs used to jiggle on mine whenever I bent her over the counter. For an elderly woman she could throw it back something fierce. ***Ding!*** I looked down at the phone in my hands that showed another text message. "Can I come over?" ***Ding!*** Another message came through and showed an emoji of a black heart with glowing red eyes that blinked. It was kind of creepy so I deleted it and made my way up to my room. Knock-Knock-Knock! The sound of knocking froze me to the spot and for a second I considered running to my room. Knock-Knock-Knock! I put my phone in my pocket and pulled my gun out. The sound came from the kitchen so I instead went to my hidden room to see who was in my backyard. Nothing showed up on the screen and I watched the recording of the past three days that resulted in another waste of an hour so I went to bed. The moment I stopped into my room a cold chill crawled over my skin and caused me to shiver. "Home, raise temperature two degrees." I said speaking to my smart home. I hopped in bed and allowed myself to calm down by meditating. The strange sensation didn't leave me for another half hour as I fell asleep. I awoke to a suffocating pressure on my chest and tried to get up but couldn't. It was like someone with a large body was laying on top of me. I started to choke and instantly the pressure was lifted and I could get up and breathe normally. My heart pounded in my chest as I looked around my dark room with the light of a full moon giving me partial visibility. My chest rose up and down as I scanned the large space of my room and I froze when I looked into the open doorway. Looking back at me was an extremely tall dark form with red glowing eyes. For several seconds all I could do was breathe and blink as it slowly stepped forward. I tried to reach for my gun but my hand wasn't responding to the signals sent by my brain. My eyes burned from not blinking and when I did it was gone. The eerie chill in the room left and I was now able to move. With everything that's recently happened that had to have been a hallucination of some kind. I gave up cocaine and shrooms a couple of years ago and while on them I never experienced anything like I just did. There was one time I saw an elderly woman's eye become serpent-like and a little kid with a weird aura but never anything as terrifying as what I just saw. After a couple of minutes passed I laughed it off as paranoia and rolled onto my left side. "Wait no." I got up to shut the door and locked it and then went back to sleep. I had a dream where I was running through a dark forest being chased by a beast that roared like a bear. The sound of its paws slamming into the forest floor made me run faster and miscalculate where I was stepping and slipped on a rock. My body hit the ground hard as I tried to roll over. ***ROAR***! It landed on me and just as it was about to bite down on my head I woke up swinging and kicking. "Ahh-Whoa!" The morning sun peeked through the opening in my curtains. My knife laid next to me like a sleeping date that gleamed in the daylight. I used the bathroom and showered before going to the kitchen and making a breakfast burrito. Once my stomach was full, I rolled blunt and walked the extra groceries over to my house next door. I stepped around the two door sedan I placed in the driveway to make it look as if people lived there and walked around back. Leaves from the tree that towered over both yards covered the ground and crunched under my feet as I made my way in. I put away the groceries and checked the cameras before doing the same with the house across the street. All three houses have solar panels on the roofs and the same amount of security as the one I'm currently in. ***Ding!*** I walked into the front room to pick up my phone and the hair on my forearms stood on end the second a shadow moved out the corner of my eye. My body instinctively shifted to kick but nothing was there. This time I knew that I did in fact see something in the light of day. Where I stood there weren't any large objects or animals to cast a shadow. Seconds passed and I allowed myself to relax and take my hand off the trigger of my gun. "Fuck, I'm going crazy." I laughed at the first words I've spoken out loud this morning. "You're not crazy." I twisted my body but a large fist punched me in the chest and I hit the floor as everything went black. My body jerked awake on my couch and I grabbed my gun that was still loaded. I let out a sigh of relief as I realized it was a dream. My chest didn't have a bruise and I could see the keys from the other houses on the coffee table in front of me with half a blunt next to it. After I put away all of the groceries I must have hit it a couple of times and then passed out afterwards. *Ding!* I pressed the notification and it was from another unknown number that asked if I was top or bottom. I'm supposed to be in hiding but the urge to reply as a top took over and I sent the message and closed my phone. *Ding!* Whoever this person was sent an emoji of a sad face and then a purple smiling devil. There was no way that anyone knew where I was so I decided to keep replying just for fun. I sent an eggplant emoji with a plus sign and then a capital U and a question mark, asking how much dick they can take. The typing dots popped up and then vanished and then popped up again. After a whole minute of waiting I closed my phone and turned it off. I have thousands of burner phones in the basement so I destroyed it and retrieved another. This was one of my less profitable businesses but it seems to be a smart choice to steal a pallet of smart phones for this exact moment. I activated it and downloaded the app that connected it to the cameras as an all black SUV pulled onto the street and stopped in front of the house next door. My hand moved on its own and reached for the gun as the driver door opened and they dumped trash on the ground and then drove away. I slowly relaxed and took my hand off of my gun as they kept going. I have to keep reminding myself that all of this is normal for someone who is in hiding. My breathing helped regulate my heartbeat so I opened my eyes and picked up my glass of wine. The hairs on my knuckles stood up as I put it to my lips and finished it off in one gulp but soon regretted it. My throat, eyes and nose burned as it went down. "How'd it taste?" I threw the glass and picked up my gun in one swift move but the intruder disarmed me even quicker and tossed it across the room. He grabbed my wrist and squeezed until it snapped. "I asked you a question."

After I was released I ran but the pain in my wrist prevented me from being able to run properly and he caught up and backhanded me so hard that all I could hear was a ringing in my ears before I hit the floor. Above me stood a man that was almost seven feet tall with eerie blue eyes and a well muscled body. His white teeth clashed against his dark skin that temporarily stunned me as he stepped on my foot and brought me back to reality. "Was.it.good?" He repeated. I nodded yes and sobbed as he picked up his foot. "Yes." He bent down and picked me up off of the ground with one hand and brought me to his eye level. There was no way that this was possible. "It's very possible." My ears buzzed as I looked him in the eyes. "I'm going to sit you back on the couch, DON'T try to run." He tossed me on the couch and took a seat next to me as I fought the urge to pick up the keys and stab him in his thick neck. He laughed and handed them to me. "Try me!" I took them in my left hand and threw them as hard as I could at his face and ran for the back door. I didn't make it four steps before he was on me. He wrapped both of his arms around me and picked me up off the ground. Dread filled my body as I felt his very large erection press up against my ass. "Ohh, you wore the perfect fabric." He walked us over to the wall and violently ripped my shorts open in the back and pulled his penis out. I headbutted him from the back but it was like hitting a wall. The impact stunned me as he punished me up against the wall and covered my mouth as he inserted himself into me. I bit into his hand as he inserted himself into me and grunted in my ear. "I knew the back door was open. Ahhh, perfect!" Tears fell from my eyes as I could feel my ass being forced open. He removed his hand and used his free arm to pick me up and slam his dick inside of me even harder. My cries of pain were met with his moans of pleasure as he wrapped both arms around me and fucked me harder than before. It felt like an eternity as his thrust made blood run down our legs. The burning sensation intensified as he slammed into me quicker and harder and he ejaculated inside me. My wrist snapped and was now broken as he crushed it under his forearms. His thrusting continued for another twenty minutes and when he pulled out of me I could feel my prolapsed rectum come out as well while I fell to the floor. "I'm so glad you ingested my wine, now we can do this forever." He clapped his hands and the pain I felt instantly vanished as I rolled over and looked up at the one who just raped me. His eyes glowed red and he snapped his fingers and our clothes repaired themselves. "Get up!" I did as he said and he grabbed me by the throat with one large hand and squeezed. "Make us something to eat." He threw me towards the kitchen and I landed sideways on the floor. My mind was still reeling from being fucked so hard that my ass fell out and then this red eyed intruder fixed me with a snap of his fingers. A slap to the back of my head made me turn my attention to the intruder who shoved me into the kitchen. "The quicker you make food the quicker I get to cuddle." He said it so casually and turned to sit on the couch. "Don't burn it either," he added. My pulse raced as I tried to prepare dinner but my mind kept going back to him snapping his fingers. "I don't hear the chopping of meat or vegetation." I almost chopped a chunk of my knuckle off while dicing a carrot and then adding it to the mushroom-asparagus mixture. I seasoned and tenderized chicken breast and then pan fried them. Once everything was done, I plated the food and my intruder came walking into the kitchen with a smile on his face. He grabbed both of our plates and took them into the dinning room. I didn't know how he would react so I followed behind him and he placed them across from each other and gestured for me to take my seat. The second I took my seat he started to rub his foot up my leg and rested it on my dick and balls. "You may refer to me as Mr. Unknown. Okay." I shook from fear as he applied pressure. "Yes. I-I'm-" "Lorenzo Willams, born close to the end of June in the year of eighty-six. You've fathered four children who've died by your own hands. You raped that kid from your class when you were a preteen and your parents sent you away and paid the family to remain silent. You say you're a top but the ass you just gave up says otherwise. Oh! You're also kind of psychic. That's how I found you." He removed his foot and blew me a kiss. A full minute passed and he cleared his throat and looked directly at me. "I'm going to do whatever I want to you, so just ask your question." I swallowed the food in my mouth and pondered which question to ask first. What was he and what did he mean by me being kind of psychic? "I am the one who was watching you last night and you're a very intuitive criminal. Most of my pets never sense me coming but you did. You even felt my little hug I gave you." The last part made my heart race even faster. I'm sure there are a lot of white men in general who have committed worse crimes than I have, why me? "Damn, you don't even remember me. I'm hurt." He held his large hand over his chest and pretended to cry. "No, what are you?" My question came out a little more aggressive than I intended and he looked at me with raised eyebrows. "The wine you ingested was a binding elixir from a God with a capital G, to a mortal with the juiciest ass.." I suddenly forgot to breathe and blink as his words floated around my brain. "You heard me correctly, mortal." "Are you Hades?" He smacked his teeth and rolled his eyes. "I should slap you for only knowing those smelly Greek deities. No. You could have at least said an Orisha." He finished chewing and cut into his chicken aggressively. "I mean fuck, Hades? Seriously?" Mr. Unknown slammed his fist on the table and it turned to ash. His eyes were black with red slits and his mouth opened to show sharp monster teeth. I got up to run but he was on me in two seconds and he grabbed the back of my neck and pulled me into a rough embrace. I started to cry as his grip became almost unbearable. "Shh. It's just me. It's just me." He said rocking us side to side. The mess on the floor repaired itself and he released me and took his seat. "So what do you like to do for fun?"

I took my seat and tried to bite back my tears but for the first time in my life, I was truly terrified. If he was a human like me I would have left him rotting in the yard out back. But this being was something I've never encountered before and I wanted to run to the nearest precinct rather than stay with him. Mr. Unknown spit his food out and got up from the table. He walked to the backdoor and vanished in a swirl of shadows. I found myself laughing and crying at the same time after a couple of hours passed and he didn't return. I sat on the couch with my head in my hands as the tears streamed down my face and I fell backwards. What did I just experience? Was it a hallucination? My heart fell into my stomach as I remembered being raped by a fourteen inch dick that had to be three inches in girth. The feeling of my ass falling out made chills run down my spine. I was in excruciating pain for almost an hour and then he snapped the pain away with magic. The dark-being said he was a God with a capital G. I got up and ran to the kitchen where my plate sat on the counter with cold food on it. What the fuck? I know I ate that food. I walked to the back door and stepped into the evening air to clear my head. A cool autumn breeze pushed itself around my body as I closed my eyes and focused on my breathing. Was this a result of years of guilt catching up to me? Was I going insane? Did he actually do that to me? Normally I do the raping and beating. A chill ran over my body and I went inside and changed into pajama pants. This house has caused enough trauma so I decided to go to the house across the street after I tossed the plate in the trash. House number three helped me calm down a little bit so I rolled a blunt and smoked half of it in the hot tub. My phone displayed the time as nine-thirty-six so I decided to go inside and watch T.V in bed for the rest of the night. I changed into sweatpants and a t-shirt to combat the coldness of the bed. Once I fell asleep, I had a dream that was more like a childhood memory of a Christmas party. Everyone around me was drunk as fuck and dancing crazy. "Watch me baby." My grandmother came up to me and started to do the dance called the running man. "Do it!" She stopped and shook my shoulder. "Do it!" She yelled. I started doing the dance out of fear as someone bumped into me. My eyes grew wide as I looked up to Mr. Unknown. "Thirty years and you're all mine." "You can have him now if you want." My mother said, as she placed a hand on his shoulder. The dream changed and I was now strapped to a dentist chair with nothing but darkness all around me. The sound of whistling grew louder and Mr. Unknown pushed a tray of dentistry instruments into view. His whistling was superb but the sight of those tools made my body shiver. He stopped whistling and then started to hum as he slowly walked closer and began singing. "I pulled out his back door sheath and now I want some head without the t-e-eth, no teeth, yeah-yeah." His eyes were all red and all of his perfectly white teeth were monstrous as he flashed me the same smile from the other dream. "Oh! I'm dreaming and this isn't real. None of this is real." I laughed and Mr. Unknown joined me while deciding between two different pliers. He picked up the largest one and leaned over me. Knowing this was a dream I taunted him by opening my mouth but instead of clamping the pliers down he tapped my teeth and knocked them loose. I started choking and swallowed them as the pain made me cry and him laugh. "Are you going to be stupid again?" I nodded and he grabbed my bleeding jawline and plucked my teeth out with his fingers. My body trembled from the pain as I started to go into shock from the nerve endings he severed. All I could do was sob as he finished removing my teeth and then unzipped his pants. The pain in my jaw intensified and made my throat burn as I gasped for breath. I awakened to the assault being real as Mr. Unknown fucked my face and I choked on his dick and was barely able to breathe threw my nose as his huge balls slapped my forehead. Darkness was all I could see as his musky pubic hair painfully rubbed against my face. "Oh yeah, that's deep. Deep indeed." He continued to bounce on my face for two hours until I was forced to drink all of his cum. "Whew!" Mr. Unknown backed up until he was sitting on my face and his dick shrunk in size but remained in my mouth. Ten minutes passed until he removed himself and I coughed as he got up. "Dark-God damn that was good." I looked up to see Mr. Unknown's red eyes in the darkness. I continued to cough up blood and sperm as he laughed and vanished as the lights came on. My partially bloody teeth sat in a wine glass on the nightstand next to me. The sound of the shower coming on made me flinch and he cleared his throat. I began to shake as I got out of bed and walked into the bathroom. Mr. Unknown stood naked with one hand in the running water and the other gripped on his erection. My heart sank into my stomach as he looked over to me with his normal blue eyes and smile. He walked over to me and tore the clothes off my body and dragged me into the shower. The large shower head covered the both of us as he gently rinsed me off from behind and the pain in my mouth vanished and was replaced by my reformed teeth. All I could do was remain still as Mr. Unknown used my soap to clean the both of us in silence with a sinister smile on his face. So many thoughts ran through my brain as I took in his entire body. The light made his eerie blue eyes clash perfectly against his dark skin. He turned the water off and stepped out onto the shower rug and I slowly followed behind him. An all black towel appeared in his hand and he used it to dry me off and then himself. I walked into the bathroom and waited twenty minutes for him to come out but he never did. My teeth were gone and I was left to once again wonder if that was real or not. I put on deodorant and lotion and then grabbed some underwear before I checked the bathroom. There was no sign of him anywhere or the black towel and the rug was completely dry. I ran all around the house checking everywhere and decided that it would be smart to check the cameras. "What the fuck?" I yelled. The app on my phone kept crashing and after six tries I gave up. ***Click!*** The lock on the front door twisted and the alarm went off as Mr.Unkwon walked in with a bouquet of flowers. "Honey, I'm Home." Knowing that this was all in my head I threw the phone at his face and reached into the cushions and pulled my gun out. I emptied it into his chest as he fell backwards and hit the floor. "I-I Love-".

Blood pooled around him as he took his last breath, but instead of dying he smiled and got up off the floor. "J-K." He laughed like it was the funniest thing in the world and wiped away actual tears. "Bruh!, you really thought you killed me. I'm divine darkness. I don't exist as you do Renny." He reached out to touch my shoulder but I recoiled from his touch and fell back onto the couch. "And here I thought you had enough of my abuse. I decided to come in here like a real husband with flowers but no, you had to cap a niggah!" As he spoke a black ring appeared on my finger. It was my turn to laugh at the sight of its extravagant design. This would have been something I could've bought for myself a week ago. "It was that or a cock ring." It felt real, the sound of my gun going off and the bullets hitting his body was real. "Oh!. Here." I jerked back as his hand turned into a fist that he held up in front of me. "Okay! Then I'll do this." Mr. Unknown placed a pile of bullets on the table and reached his hand out towards the flowers and they appeared on the table in front of us. "I promise to spend the next seven days showing you that I'm only evil ninety-three percent of the time. Starting with me telling you the truth." He exhaled and looked to the floor before resuming eye contact. "I refilled your gun and prevented the camera app from opening." A cold chill ran over my body as it suddenly became hard to breathe. He kept speaking but I ran to the front door and outside to get some fresh air. I leaned against the tree as the cold evening air rushed by me. My feet kept walking until I reached the edge of the street and a couple of birds flew by me. Off in the distance I could hear ambulance sirens become louder as its lights illuminated my street and kept going and turned on the next block. Everything felt real. I'm chilly because I don't have a coat on or thicker pants. My body flinched at the sound of Mr. Unknown running up behind me. His face was wet from tears and he appeared shorter. "I'm-I'm sorry baby." He sobbed, as he walked up to me and wrapped his arms over my shoulders. "The darkness is at bay for the next seven days. I won't hurt you. I promise. I don't have any of his magic left." He gently grabbed my hand and put it on his normal sized erection. "I don't want to speak out here, let's go back inside." He said. A car turned down my street and I knew it was my only real chance to see if this was reality so I waved my hands to get their attention. "Are you okay?" The young woman asked. "Sort of. Um! This is going to sound strange but. Do you see this man right here?" I pointed over my shoulder at the dark God turned mortal, who waved. "Hey." He spoke. "Well hey sexy." She responded. Her passengers moved closer to the window to get a look and someone whistled while the other made sounds as if they were gagging in a good way.

"Is that a joke? This dude is tweaking." one of them responded.

"See I told you, the people in these types of houses are cray-cray." The driver spoke.

The passenger yelled. They drove off and he rubbed my lower back as a cold breeze crept over us. "Ohh." He said with a shiver. We walked back to my house and he continued to keep his hold on me all the way to the couch. "You better hope none of them recognized you from the wanted photo." He was right but I had something that I wanted to verify before the night was over. I backhanded him hard enough to make his lip bleed to see if he was telling the truth. Worst case scenario he'd retaliate by returning the slap or kill me. Instead his face turned into a frown as tears fell from his eyes and he held his hand up to his busted lip. "W-Why would you do that? I told you, I'm mortal for the next seven days and nights." He got up and ran to the bathroom and slammed the door behind him. In the silence I could hear him drop to the floor and sob as he knocked something over. This has to be the most hilarious thing ever. I get abused by his darker-divine side for a day and now I get seven where he is mortal. A chill ran down my spine as the thought of this all being real hit me and I was now given a chance to gain a supernatural upper-hand. I retrieved the first aid kit from my bathroom and came down stairs to try and make amends with my formally divine house guest. He sat on the couch with his arms crossed and his eyes on me. I could feel my heart warm just a little from the look of hurt on his face. Seeing this side of him was refreshing and almost made the other part tolerable. "Can we call a truce?" Tears streamed down his face and I dropped the first aid kit on the couch and pulled him off the couch into a hug. It was the first time that I ever initiated an affectionate touch that didn't result in me ejaculating in someone and it felt great. "Can you tell me more about this divine stuff?" He nodded, but then winced as I applied an alcohol wipe to his lip. "A Lot of his knowledge goes with him whenever he recedes, but what I do know is that if he can find someone to marry him he will be able to get the rest of his powers and the person he marries becomes a divine being as well." He tapped the ring on my finger and it made my ears ring from the impact. Another chill went down my spine at the thought of being a god. I would run all four of my territories with an iron dick. "You have a smile on your face. What are you thinking?" He caressed my hand that was dabbing away the blood with the pad of his thumb. "Can we spoon tonight?" He nodded yes as time stood still and we looked into each other's eyes. I wanted to kiss his lips but his lip just stopped bleeding so I grabbed his hand and guided us upstairs to my bedroom. We stripped down to our underwear and climbed into bed. He pressed his body against mine and a chill ran over my back from the bare skin contact. "Are you cold?" "No, I'm not used to doing this. I normally play a game of fuck-kill-dismember." He laughed and we spent the rest of the night talking about our interests and then we fell asleep in each other's arms. The next morning we showered together and had amazing sex and then made breakfast in bed. He loved my pancakes and sausage. For the first time in forever I felt normal and its all thanks to a dark being to make me more docile. "Can you stop calling me that name? I'm Darnell. When I'm like this." Darnell rubbed the back of my neck and rubbed our lower torso's together. "Despite my erection I don't want to have sex. Just feeling you like this is enough." We slow-danced to old R&B and I allowed myself to become more relaxed around him. In my previous occupational field this would make him a liability and I would have done everything to him that he did to me before I decapitated him.

But it felt like I could finally be myself with him. His body would have joined the others and I would have missed his fat ass that opened up on my dick perfectly. I was shocked that he allowed me to do that and even more so that he was a pro at bouncing on a dick. Two more days passed as he and I wrestled and played video games and flip-flopped all over the house with different sex positions. It was truly a wish come true in the masculine meets masculine relationship we were building. For the both of us to be cisgendered he showed me that this was a new person entirely. An hour ago I walked into the kitchen and he was completely naked while bending over the counter with both hands spreading his ass cheeks apart. I was already naked and I instantly grew hard and I walked into him and he wiggled his ass as he took in my dick. The slide-in almost made my knees buckle but when he looked back and licked his lips I put both hands up against the counter and dug into him with all the passion in my hips as our skin clapped against each other. He followed up by putting me on my back on the counter and threw my legs up over one shoulder and pulled me onto his nine inch dick until he moaned while filling me up. The sweat from my back made it easier to slide back and forth as he slammed into me and kissed my knees. After the both of us busted four times we cuddled on the couch and decided to go a day without sex. Thursday morning I awoke before he did and went to the house next door to get the onion powder and creole seasoning. Today was surprisingly warm for fall and as I came out of the house I noticed a car coming down the street with the driver window down. An elderly man with a scar over half of his face waved me over as I neared the gate to our current home. I regretted coming out front and blamed it on my newfound love and happiness. "I need to warn you Lorenzo." He called out in a frail voice. Because he knew my name I decided to indulge him and walked over to his car. "How do you know my name?" His eyebrows furrowed and he exhaled through his nose. "I'm psychic, just like you. Last year when I turned thirty-seven your house guest mysteriously came into my life and turned it upside down. He made me think that I was insane while repeatedly raping me. He is an empathic parasite, not a God. " He handed me a small packet of white dust that sparkled in the daylight and the drug dealer in me put it in my pocket. "Saturday is the day of Weirdness and he'll try to use it to siphon your powers. Sprinkle this in his wine that's mixed with his hair, semen and a drop of blood. It will make him unable to manipulate energy and my essence will return to me as he dies." He looked forward and drove away without saying another word as my mind raced with more ideas. I need to allow him to think that I don't know anything and use Saturday to become an all powerful being. It didn't matter who was telling the truth either way I'm doing what's best for me. I went back inside and placed the dust behind a portrait and continued to make breakfast. My roasted potatoes and sunny side up eggs paired perfectly with the premium cut bacon. We sat at the dining room table as I looked at the news and he watched videos on his burner phone of blind daters from some show last year. "These people are hilarious. They expect to form a bond based on looks. It has to have substance to make chemistry." His analogy made me laugh and almost choke on my bacon at the normality of his choice of words. "So when we become divine are we going to have an open marriage?" he asked. That deflated my happy balloon and sent it spiraling out of the room at the mention of his darker-self. "Do you want one?" I asked in return. He shook his head no and gave me a half smile. "When you become divine you take on your emotional aspect and you're evil like me so we'll be the perfect match. But we'll probably fuck different people throughout the year." "What are the other divine beings like?" I wanted to know as much as I could about his story before making a solid plan. "Depends, I'm darkness incarnate like you, and some are kind and just, while others are in the middle. I've always existed but the ones I previously spoke about have died and reincarnated as much as the mortals have. They're everywhere throughout the cosmos." Now I was even more intrigued. Either he was telling the truth or he was weaving a tale to further intrap me in his grip of pain and confusion. "Are you the only divine being on the planet?" He nodded and put a finger to his lips. "Those satan myths are about my kind. We of the darkness created everything and then were usurped by our divine children." He pulled me in the more he spoke about the divine world and I felt myself leaning more to his story than what the stranger said. I remembered the list of ingredients and coincidentally I already have his blood on the gauze pad in the trash, his sweat was in there as well on a paper towel along with his semen that spewed out of my butthole when he pulled out. "I'll do the dishes, since you cooked but first I need to use the little mortals room." "Okay, I'm going to go roll a blunt." I waited for him to shut the door and I went into the kitchen and dug through the trash. The bloody gauze was on top of the sweaty semen rag and I put the two items in a ziplock bag that I hid next to the dust. Friday morning we cut each other's hair and I grew more in love with him. We watched a horror movie about demon gods and the end scene gave me chills. The thought of being a god made me giddy like a kid on christmas eve. His violent attacks won't mean shit if I can heal myself and do whatever the fuck I want to do whenever I want for the rest of eternity. My happiness reminded me of the dream I had and I grabbed the remote and turned the TV off. "I had a dream where my family was throwing a christmas party and you were there." His face contorted into a grimace as tears formed and fell from his eyes. "Yea, I was. Th-that was the day I waited for you to fall asleep and I crept into your room and activated your pineal gland." My ears popped as he spoke and I gasped at the realization that it was the same night where I experienced sleep paralysis for the first time. "I'm not going to lie, I kissed your lips and cuddled up next to you. Your grandmother has the photo." A chill ran down my spine as I remembered the smell of alcohol being intense and then wanting to get up but something huge pushed down on me. "I had a vision of this day and wanted to be close to you." Darnell pulled me into a hug and kissed my neck as his tears continued to fall. "That night your premature dark side started to awaken and caused you to do all those evil things." I thought back to the time I had sexual relations with my first crush and he did cry when we had sex but I thought it was because I was big. The fire I caused at the boarding school was a complete accident. Who would have guessed that a magnifying glass left unattended in the art room would have made the blaze engulf half the school and cause us to be sent home. "We're made for each other." Darnell and I held each other for an hour and then decided to watch a romantic comedy. "Do you want some wine?" He nodded yes as he broke the weed up to roll a blunt. I went into the other room to grab the ziplock bags but they were missing. My heart sank into my stomach as I quietly searched the room and after ten minutes I gave up. I walked into the living room with our wine in my hands. The second I saw the ziplock bags on the coffee table I froze and locked eyes with Darnell. His eyes changed from blue to bright red as he got up from the couch and grew to his normal size. I dropped the wine glasses and fell to my knees. "I was never mortal, you big booty idiot!! That was my test and you failed." He walked by me to the front door and it opened to show the old man with a blank expression on his face until realized that he was standing face to face with the dark god. "Ahh!" He screamed. And tried to back up and run but Mr. Unknown reached out like a viper and grabbed him by the throat. The sound of his screams being cut off by the breaking of his bones was all I could hear. "Sometimes I forget about all the little lies I tell to my prey, when I'm having fun with them." He let out a little laugh as the old men stopped moving. "Sucking out his psychic powers and vitality was the best ending to our encounter, but he couldn't take dick like you and wasn't half as evil." He dropped the dead body in the doorway and turned his attention to me as fear prevented me from moving and it was like I was a defenseless child again. "Get up and sit on the couch until I get done taking care of this." The body floated out of the open doorway and he walked out and closed the door behind him, before winking at me. For several minutes I remained still until the sound of bones breaking made me recoil onto the couch. The snapping of bones grew louder and was followed by crunching and lips smacking together. I slowly crawled to the window and looked out to see Mr. Unknown sitting on the porch eating the leg that he ripped off like it was a sub sandwich. "Fuck this is good." His long sharp teeth gleamed in the light of the full moon as he chowed down like he was at a BBQ. Seeing him do that made the blood drain from my face. He ate it like it was the most delicious thing in the world and seeing him do that helped me decide what to do next. I walked over to the larger couch and pulled the gun out. With the barrel now in my mouth I closed my eyes and pulled the trigger. **BANG!** Everything went black as I fell to the floor and all I could feel was pain that sent me into shock. Between choking on my tongue and the excruciating pain that caused me to lose feeling from the waist up, I could still hear him chewing. The sound began to fade and all I could feel was my heartbeat slowing down as the front door opened. "Not today, Big Booty." All the pain returned and brought with it the pain of my skull mending itself as I coughed up pieces of my brain fragments. The back of my throat and skull hurt the most as it reformed and Mr. Unknown kicked me in the ribs. "I don't plan on letting this go anytime soon. All of this has been the most fun that I've had ever since I put my ex-God of a father in a nursing home for mortals." My sight returned and I looked around the room in fearful anticipation of his wrath. At first everything was blurry but as it cleared I gasped at the sight of Mr. Unknown and his extra body parts. He now had four arms, a large vertical third eye on his forehead that was like looking into the vastness of space and twin fourteen inch dicks swaying as he moved. "I remember when I asked you if you were a top or bottom and you lied and said top." He walked over to the open area behind the couch and pointed to the ground in front of him. A chill ran over my body and my legs moved on their own until

I was bent over the couch. "I hope I don't get a ticket for double parking." His laughter made me tremble as he moved closer and placed his hand on my back. "Bottoms up, Mr. Back-door."

Dream Savior

"Why do we have to move to Columbus, Ohio?" "Greggory! Your grandfather had a stroke, and he doesn't have anyone to watch over him besides his home health aide. He needs us. We are the only family that he has left." My mother answeteeI never understood why he moved out of California in the first place. Ohio was not a place that screamed fun in the sun. It was filled with people who lived in constant boredom and sat outside on their porches to watch the cars go down whatever street they lived on. "Think about it like this. Now you can meet a new man and not have to worry about if they were for the streets." "Mom, No!!" "What? I know what that means." "Yeah, How about no!" "How about you hurry up and finish packing? Dinner will be pizza and wings." "Oh, Thank goodness. I was tired of your vegan meals." "Boy! Finish packing." The good part about leaving is I won't tell any of those fake friends of mine or have to worry about being in a long-distance relationship. After I was done, I found myself looking at the watch that my grandfather had given to my father, who wanted me to have it before he died. I used to wear it to bed until I woke up one morning with it cutting off the circulation of my upper arm. After that day, my mother made me put it in a small box that we made and swear never to sleep with it on again. "G-Ray! Dinner is here!" I placed the watch in its box and ran down the steps to the smell of hot wings and pizza as my mother smiled at me from the kitchen. "These wings slap!" Yeah, I'm going to have to take away her social media privileges before she uses the word tweaking. When I bit into the wings, I had to agree with her. These are some of the best wings I've ever had, and the pizza was so cheesy. Mmmm. "Are you going to tell anyone about the move?" Her motherly intuition was always on point, but I didn't want to have a mushy talk right now. "Nope! I will post pics from my new room in Ohio." I responded. "Ohhh, Look at you being calculating." "I have a question. Why did Grandpa move away from this beautiful state?" "Your father said that his parents didn't feel as if it was a good place to raise kids. They wanted him to grow up in a neighborhood that wasn't filled with violence." In my honest opinion, that didn't make any sense. Violence was everywhere, and as black people, we were never safe. Not from the cops, gangs, Karens and Darrens. Or lawmakers who are so far removed from society that they think a bunch of black people on a block is the hood.

"But Columbus, though! I'm not working on a farm, Mom." I said.

"Boy, Your grandfather lives in a four-bedroom house where both of us will have our own bathroom. You need to be thinking about college and not new men to date." She responded.

"With what money? I agreed to take a gap year to save so that I could get a car." I replied.

"Your father had a life insurance policy that I put into a trust for you, and your grandfather matched it." she said, with. Smile.

"Did he now?" "Yes, So don't worry about paying for college. Just get yourself a car with the money that you have saved." "Uh, how did you know about my money?" "I'm your mom, and I wanted to be a journalist before switching my major to be a reading teacher." "Yancy, you are a woman of many secrets." She stopped chewing and gave me that look that she does whenever I call her by her first name. "Young man, I carried you for eight months. Don't call me by my first name unless you want to be living out on the streets." "Yes, Ma'am."

Once we got done eating, she made me do the dishes by hand, and I took all of the things that we weren't taking with us out to the trash. By the time I was done, I was dead tired from all of the walking back and forth and decided to take a shower before bed. My dreams were a flurry of lucid visions where I flew around a house in one dream while jumping like I was on the moon in another. When I woke up, I was ready to start putting everything in the moving truck. "Good morning, son." "Good morning, mother. Did you sleep well?" "I did, son. How about you?" "Yup, let's go get this truck." I had to sit through the manager of the moving truck company, flirting with my mom for an hour until we went home to move all of our stuff into the truck another hour later. "The truck or my car?" "Seeing as I'm a new driver, I'll take your car." "Yes! I love driving these. It reminds me of when I used to work for a moving company, and it was my job to drive the truck." "Wait! What?" "Yeah, Your mama had a life before you, son." "I see. Okay, Are you ready?" "I am, let's go." I turned around and mentally said goodbye to the house that I spent all of my life in before getting into my mother's car. Since we were driving, we decided to stay at a hotel in Albuquerque, get some sleep and continue our drive in the morning before we partake in the rest of our fifteen-hour drive to Ohio. Once we left Indiana, I let out a sigh of relief when we crossed the Ohio border. It took us an hour and a half to get to my grandfather's neighborhood. I expected farmlands or a rundown neighborhood with a bunch of old-ass apartments, but my grandfather lived in a big-ass house with a large garage next to it. "Damn, Grandpa is living large." "He created one of the best-selling comic book series that made him a millionaire before he was thirty." Now, that was something that I'd never heard before. The front door opened, and an Asian woman stepped out in scrubs with a smile on her face. "Hello. You two must be Yancy and Greggory. I'm Suyin, your grandfather's home health aide." "Nice to meet you, and thank you for helping Grandad." I waved as I pulled up the back of the truck to open it. My mother has some real skills because everything was in the same palace that we put it in two days ago. "Greg, come in and meet your grandpa before we move in!" "Okay." The first thing I saw when I walked into the house was framed pictures of my father when he was a kid while sitting on my grandfather's lap. He looked so cute in his onesie, with baby drool came out of his lips. The next three pictures were of my father graduating from high school, college and then the police academy. We looked so much alike that it was weird how I never noticed it before. The next picture was of my parents on their wedding day. My mother had an extended stomach that my father placed his big hands over. The smile on their faces said that they had the type of love that some people go their entire lives yearning for. "Grandad, I'm happy that you're doing better." I turned the corner and walked into a chilly room to see the man that I've only ever met once. "Hey, Grandad. How are you feeling?" "A lot better now that I'm surrounded by family." I didn't know if we should hug or not, given his weakened state, but I still went in for one and gently wrapped my arms around him. "Hey, I'm the daughter of your childhood best friend and you've come to all of my important ceremonies. I thought I was family?" Suyin said. "You are, but I need to be around the family that I helped create, Su-Su." "Uh-huh! I'll be in the other room, Uncle Greg." I noticed that she gave my mother a wink before leaving and I wanted to comment whether or not my mom was joining me in being gay but decided not to put her on the spot. "What's new, grandson?" "Nothing much, I'm happy to be here and if you need something just let me know." "I appreciate that but I mean, what's new in your life? Is there a boyfriend that you left behind in California? Are you planning on attending college here?" Both questions surprised me and I didn't remember telling him that I was gay.

"Uh, No. I'm single, like a one-dollar bill. As for college, I've decided to take a gap year until I am one hundred on what I want to do."

"That's smart, son. Most people just go to college to find themselves and waste time and money. Just know that whatever you do you have my support."

"I appreciate you saying that, grandad." "Just don't turn my house into a revolving door of randoms. I'm not that cool."

My mother laughed so hard that I had to give her the look stating that it wasn't that funny. "I'm not like that. Having one boyfriend is more than enough, but I don't see myself moving that fast anytime soon. I'm here for you and that's where my focus is." He leaned forward and placed a hand on my knee before patting it. "Thank you, I've wanted to come to California but there were too many ghosts of my past to wade through. After your great-grandfather passed your grandmother decided to move in with him like you all did with me and ended up passing before we could reconnect." He pointed at a woman who had my father's hazel eyes and smiled while holding my infant father in another cute little onesie. "Aww, look at dad. Whoa! Granny was a hottie." "Greg!" "What, she was." "Yes, she was. I had to carry a stick with me whenever we went out so that I could beat off the other men with it." I laughed for two reasons, one was because that made sense and the other because my grandfather used the phrase beat off. I'm sure he didn't realize the double meaning in that but it was still hilarious to hear. The laughing didn't bode well for him though. It made him cough as he adjusted his oxygen intake and Suyin ran into the room to help. "I think we should unload the truck, son." It took us two hours to move everything in and to get situated as the sun began to set in the distance. My mother got the room with its own bathroom and I chose the one in the basement that my father grew up in because it had a bathroom across the hall that was all mine. After we were done my mother went to the grocery store to get us something to eat because my grandfather had a meal plan that was delivered or made by Suyin. I turned down her offer to tag along and decided to finish setting my room up because it had several boxes of comic books in it. The bed was surprisingly comfortable but I had to change the sheets to my own because I refused to lay on spaceships. One of the boxes fell over and a couple comics caught my eye. "Dream savior, The gunman at the drag show, Issue thirteen." What the actual fuck? I knew that my grandad was cool with gays, but I didn't know that he dedicated an entire comic to them and that all of it was based off of a hero who lived in Los Angeles. The Hero wore a rainbow robe with a sparkly black mask that reminded me of the night sky. The rest of his suit was of the same night-sky material that stopped at his boots that were dark purple with black strings. I could tell that he was black by the color of his hands and it was nice to see real representation. Since I was done getting my room together I took the box to my bed and spent the next thirty minutes looking through it. The main character was a gay black man with the power to astral project, fly, Pass through solid objects, the ability to possess people and use telekinesis. Now I was intrigued but had to stop when my mother called down for me to get the groceries out of the car. "I'll be right there." I lugged all of the groceries inside with the comics still on my mind and wondered why my grandfather chose to make it about gay people. Unless there was something that he wasn't telling me about his glory days, I couldn't see the correlation.

"You okay, Honey?" My mother asked.

"I found a box of grandad's comics and the main character is gay." I said, with a smile.

"That's a good thing right?" she asked.

"Heck, Yeah. I hope he doesn't mind if I read all of them."

"I don't think he would have a problem with his gay grandson looking at his artistic creation. You do that while I make dinner. How does Cabbage, baked chicken and cornbread sound?" My mother asked, while looking at the spice rack. "I don't know, I don't normally speak to food?" She slapped my shoulder as I tried to leave the kitchen but when I saw Suyin looking in the mirror before walking to the bathroom, I knew then that she did have a crush on my mom. Eww! Old people love. I ran back to my room as quietly and fast as I could with the intent of reading the comics before dinner was done. The main character had managed to save a drag show from a gunman seven times, a bunch of kids from a conversion therapy camp, get justice for a transgender who was killed by a cop and build a home for young gays who were kicked out of their parents home. I found it surprisingly good for a comic book series without traditional supervillains. "Honey, Dinner is done." My mother called down just as I was about to read an issue about kids who were abducted by human traffickers in California. Damn it! I was on a roll and I was hooked. When my grandad wakes up I have a bunch of questions about where he got his inspiration from. "Oh, Suyin is joining us. Cool." I said as I stepped into the kitchen. "There was no way that I was going to miss your mothers home cooking. I normally get the food for your grandad or make it myself and I have to tell you, It's bland and boring at the same time." She said, while eyeing my mother. "Is that why I've lost so much weight?" My grandfather walked into the room while dragging his oxygen behind him and Suyin's face paled as she got up to help him. "Uncle, I told you to ring the bell when you wanted something." "Then how would I know if you were in her talking shit about the slop that you give me?" She sat him at the table next to me and went to the fridge to get out one of his already made meals. "Not that one. Can I get the salad?" "Sure thing Uncle." With him sitting next to me. I knew that this was my chance to ask questions. "Grandad, I read some of your comics, I hope it's okay?" He smiled at me and I could see tears forming in his eyes as Suyin sat his food down in front him. "I was going to tell you about them but my old-man brain forgot about that time in my life when I was a young ally, as your generation says. As a gay man, what do you think?" He asked. "I love them and can see how they made you so much money." He placed his hand on my shoulder and shook his head

no. "US, so much money. When I die, I'm leaving everything to you."
Suyin cleared her throat as she sat down next to my mom and we
started to dig into the delicious food that my mother made. "I paid for
all of your college. Twice, Ms. Bachelors and Masters degree in
Kinesiology." he said, with a stern look on his face. "Have I told you
how much I love you, Lately?" she responded. "Bye Felicia!" All of
us laughed as we ate dinner and for the first time in my life it felt like
I was eating dinner with a family. Normally me or my mother would
stop and get something on the way home or have something delivered
because she was always swamped with work. This was a nice change
of pace that I could get used to. Especially since I would be home a
lot more when I'm not working. I had to sit through Suyin flirting
with my mom and watch as she just soaked it all up until I inhaled the
rest of my food so that I could jump back into the comic book. "Okay,
Dream Savior. Where was I?" This issue was one of the best that I've
read from the series so far but it left me with a weird Déjà vu feeling.
After my shower I fell asleep from all of the heavy lifting that I did
and found myself dreaming of the scene from the comic book. My
body floated through a worn down warehouse district that had
facilities in every direction. I watched as a white Van drove by me
with blacked out windows towards the only building with an open
doorway. Even though this was a dream I felt terrified like I was in
danger. I followed the van until it entered a part of the building that
was behind a closed dock-door. The sound of kids crying made my
heart fall into my stomach and I concentrated on moving myself
forward to open the door, but I passed through it like a ghost. A Large
white man dragged two kids into the other room and I heard him hit
one of them before the sound of a lock clicking echoed around the
empty space. The man walked out of the room to grab the other kids
but stopped and narrowed his eyes on me. "How did your black ass
get in here?" he asked, while reaching for something in his pocket.
Before I could respond he pulled a gun out of his pocket and fired at
me but the bullet passed through me like I did to the door. I felt

nothing as he continued to empty the gun but it woke up one of the kids who was black like me and the child tried to make a run for the exit. "Get back here." He yelled. The child didn't make it far as he grabbed him by his afro and yanked him so hard that it caused him to cry. All I could think about was the look on the kid's face when he yanked him up by his hair. My body moved on its own and I was standing in front of the white man in the blink of an eye right before I kicked him in the balls hard enough for him to let the kid go. "Grab his cell phone." The kid shrugged his shoulders like he didn't know what I was talking about and when I looked at his clothes I realized that he was dressed like a kid from the late sixties. "Run boy!!" I screamed. As the white man started to shake off the blow to his testicles. "Get back here!" I tripped him as the kid made it to the door but couldn't get it open because of his size. Before I could make it to help him I felt my body become lighter and I was yanked backwards into darkness until I opened my eyes to look around my bedroom. The comic book laid next to me with its colorful pages bent from me laying on it. "That was weird." I couldn't remember the last time that I had a dream like that but it felt good to help someone, even if it was a made-up scenario. After my shower I went upstairs to help my grandfather get up out of bed as my mother made breakfast. "Thanks, Grandson." "Anytime Grandad. I have a question about your comics." He turned to look at me with a bright smile as I allowed him to lean against me and put on his house shoes. "Ask me anything." "Why did you make the main character gay?" "I had a friend who helped me out in my time of need and I never really got to say thank you. He died of what we now know as AIDS in the early eighties." Wow, that wasn't the answer that I expected at all. I thought that he was going to say that he had a homosexual love affair before getting with my grandmother.

"How are you liking the rest of the stories?"

"I love them. They're definitely beyond their time."

"Yeah, You'd think we'd be past the mindset of gays hurting kids but I see those in power are holding on tight to their backwards ideology."

"Breakfast is done!" My mither yelled. "Help me walk into the kitchen, please." Grandad asked. "Sure." We walked into the hallway as the smell of french toast and bacon hit my nostrils. "Well I know that's not for me. My days of eating like that are over." "Yup! That's why I made you some oatmeal with fruit and wheat toast." "Mmm,Yay!!" The look on his face made me laugh really hard as I sat down next to him and my mother placed my plate in front of me. It kind of felt like I was torturing him with the delicious food that looked amazing but I could see that he enjoyed his meal even though he had a half smile on his face. "Wow, Yancy! This is good. Su, tries but her food always tastes like cardboard." "Thanks, Grandad. I used to live next door to a vegan when I was pregnant with mr. Big-head." My mother responded. "Hey, You and Dad gave me this body, so all of that is on you." "Anyways, I tried to eat healthy but those chip cravings always got the best of me." We spent the rest of the morning filling my grandfather in on all of our important moments before I did the dishes. I didn't want my mother to tell him about the time I shit on myself when I was twelve but she loved telling it so I pretended to laugh with her as she helped him to his room. Suyin came in an hour later with more of his prepared food and put it in the refrigerator.

"Morning, Kid."

"Good morning, Nurse."

"Do you have plans for your first day in Columbus?"

"No, what is there to do here?" "There are a lot of things you can do. We have an abundance of metro parks, movie theaters, and shopping centers." We had all of that and more in California but I wasn't going to start off this morning by being rude. She did something extra with her hair and put on make-up for my mom and I wanted to see how this played out. "Good morning, Suyin." "Good morning Yancy. Did you sleep well?" She said, through a wide smile. "I did, How about you?" "I slept well also." "Oh, I love your hair and make-up. It's beautiful." "Thank you. I decided to try something new." "Well it's working for you." That made her blush as she finished unloading the groceries and I watched my mother try and hide her huge smile. Huh! So my mother swims in the rainbow sea. Once I was done with the dishes I decided to take Suyin's advice and go to the park for a run. Thankfully there was one ten minutes up the street that I remembered passing yesterday and wasn't full of people walking their dogs. As I sat on a bench to tie my shoes a very attractive brown skinned man jogged past me with gorgeous gray eyes. He had to be in his mid twenties with a bald head and muscular body. Good morning." "Back at you." I caught a glimpse of his bubble butt right before he turned around with a smile on his face. "Can I ask you a question, real quick?" "Yeah, ask me anything." "How old are you?" "I'm Eighteen, how about you?" "Twenty-one. Would you like to have dinner sometime?" "I would love that, I'm Greg." "Nice to meet you Greg, I'm Phillip." He pulled out his cell phone and handed it to me so that I could put my number in it as I stood up. "Damn, You look grown up for someone who just became an adult." "Yeah, I eat my vegetables." "Cute and Funny, Okay!" "I literally just moved here yesterday, so you'll have to show me around." "Oh really, from where?" "Call me and find out." He arched an eyebrow at me as his smile grew wider and he nodded in agreement. "Will do. Until then Greg." He held his hand out for me to shake it before running towards the parking lot. I tried to not stare too long at his booty cheeks as they clapped but the top inside of me needed to see what he was working with back there one more time. *Damn.* It took an hour for me to get him off of my mind and for me to run seven laps around the park until people started to show up with their dogs. I left as fast as I could with the urge to finish reading the dream inducing comics that my grandfather made and to pick out a nice outfit for my date tonight.

"Hey, Honey. How was your run?" I must have walked in on something because Suyin was adjusting her top as my mother fixed her hair. "Apparently not as good as whatever was going on in here." "Mind your business boy!" "Uh-Huh. Will do." I walked past my grandfather's room who was sound asleep and the reason as to why they were getting it on in the front room like a couple of teenagers. After my shower I jumped right into bed and picked up where I left off in my comic book. "Alright, let's see how this ends." I flipped through the pages to find which one I slept on and froze as I looked down at the abductor who was holding a kid by his afro. "What the fuck?" The next couple of boxes showed the hero flying through the door and kicking the tall white man in the balls from behind. The kid ran as the man yelled out in pain while cops cars pulled onto the abandoned parking lot. My heart raced in my chest as I watched the next scene play out where the abductor fought off the hero and ran to the exit. "No! Come on, you're the hero." The next slot showed the hero starting to fade away as the police used the jaws of life to get through the door that was locked to save the kids. I turned the page and yelled because that was the end and the next page was outdated ads. There wasn't a "to be continued" or wait until the next issue. Fuck! I searched through all of the boxes for the corresponding issue in vain. "How did I get to the last issue without realizing it?" My only other option is going to ask my grandad, so I ran upstairs to find my grandfather who was asleep. "Hey Greg, Did you need something?" Suyin came around the corner with a concerned look on his face as she looked behind me to see if my mother was with me. "I have a couple questions about the comic, but they can wait until grandad wakes up." "I can answer some of them. My father sketched the first design for Dream savior." "Oh, good." She guided me into the front room as my mom came down the steps and shared a weird look with Suyin. "I just read the issue about the child abductor. Was it not continued?" "Nope, I believe that was the last issue he had published. Some politicians tried to have it banned because of its content." Wow,

I know what that meant. It hit too close to home for some of them who were actual child abductors and they didn't want to shine light on child trafficking. "Damn, that issue was so good that I dreamt about it." Suyin couldn't tell me anything else so I left her alone to spend the rest of my day looking over the rest of the comics and getting ready for my date. I received a text from Phillip saying that he was going to meet me at the restaurant downtown and he would pay for it. After I drove my moms car through the bustling nightlife traffic, I made it to *Star eatery.* "Hello, I'm expecting my date to arrive shortly." "Okay, Will you be eating inside or outside?" "Outside, Please." It wasn't too hot or cold so I hoped that Phillip wouldn't mind eating on the patio. "Can I get you started off with something to drink?" "A strawberry lemonade." The waitress nodded and left to go fill my drink order. Ten minutes later my handsome date came out with the same drink in his hands and a large smile on his face. "Hey, You look handsome." "So do you, I think I have that top actually." He sat his drink down and pulled me into a hug where he squeezed me on my sides. "Wow, you smell nice." Living in the state where weed was legal, I knew what aroma he was wearing and by how red his eyes were that he was high as hell. "Thanks, Have you ordered your food yet?" "Nope, I was waiting for you." "Hey, Waiter. We're ready to order." I chose the sweet and spicy chicken tenders with fries and my date copied but ordered the nasty coleslaw with his. *Eww.* After we received our food Phillip spent the entire date talking about himself and all of his accomplishments. I was bored the first ten minutes but tried to be nice until he asked me if I was a top or bottom. "How is that any of your business?" "You act like I'm not about to know your position in a half of an hour." "Nigga, no the fuck you're not." I spoke as my anger began to rise. Since I was done with my food I got up to leave but he grabbed my wrist and pulled me to a stop. "I paid for dinner. The least you could do is give me something in return." He squeezed tighter and I felt the urge to punch him in the face. "Oh, Sure." I grabbed his arm at the pressure point that my sensei told me to for someone to release their hold on you and pressed it as hard as I could. "Ahhh, What the fuck man?" he yelled. "My thoughts exactly." I walked out of the restaurant as the woman across from us clapped and tried not to cry as I headed to my moms car. The world that we live in says that women are the only ones who could experience things like that but he was the fifth man that I've had to do that to since becoming a legal adult six months ago. I took a different way home so that I could clear my head and passed by the park where I met that dumb ass nigga at. Once I got home I saw that Suyin's car was still in the driveway so I went to my room because I knew where she was. Once I got into bed I quickly drifted off to sleep and had a dream where I wandered through a worn down apartment complex that I'd never seen before but I knew deep down that I was still in California. To my left the van from my previous dream was parked next to the only apartment without boarded up windows and a door that was still intact. Before I could step forward my entire body was pulled backwards to the sound of my mother knocking on my door and asking me if I wanted pancakes for breakfast. "Yeah, I'll take three." I rolled over and stretched before getting up to use the restroom. The dreams that I've been having since we moved here have been extremely vivid. Normally I'd see something crazy or have a nightmare where I'd have to run from some kind of monster but I never had this much consciousness in a dream. It was like I was actually awake and fully functional in them.

"Good morning, Mom."

"Morning, son. How was your date?"

"Horrible, he was only in it for one thing."

"Aww, That sucks but at least you're still getting out there."

"Yeah, I guess the bigger question is how was your night?" I asked with raised eyebrows.

"It was interesting." she replied, with a smirk

"Yeah, I guess being with a lesbian is life changing. Do you want to talk about it?"

"Well it wasn't the first time. Before I got with your father I was with a woman."

"Oh, so homosexuality is genetic." She placed my plate in front of me and sat down while sipping her elderberry tea. "I don't know about that." "Is Suyin still here?" "No, she left after you got back. I think she has the day off so it'll just be the three of us today." That's what I wanted to hear. My long list of questions about the comic just got longer and I think it would be the perfect day for a family outing. "How about we do something outside of the house?" "What did you have in mind?" We turned to see my grandfather walking through the doorway with his oxygen tank behind him and his usual smile on his face. "How about a trip to the park?" "Yeah, there is a nice park in the old town east area that was just renovated for wheelchair access." "Then it settled. A family trip to the park." My mom rubbed my back and gave me the I'm proud of you look before getting my grandads fruit out of the fridge. Once we were all done eating, my mother helped my grandad get dressed while I put his wheelchair in the van that he owned. "All set." "Yup." "Then let's go, I'm ready to see what Columbus has to offer." I didn't know what my mother meant by that but I loved seeing the city and how beautiful certain parts of it were. Of course it had areas that were neglected by the politicians but I loved how most of the city had a large population of black people. When we drove through the mt. Vernon area my grandfather showed me where he taught as an art teacher at Champion middle school and then East high school. "This park is amazing." "It better be with all of the money that I donated to revamping it." "Dang, Grandad, who haven't you helped?" "Those christians who are still waiting for Jesus." My mother and I laughed because we weren't the type of black people who were mentally bound by religion. Her side of the family were dedicated christians who didn't want my mother to marry someone who wasn't a part of the faith. A group of geese flew by me and landed in the pond across from us as we got out of the car. "Get your grandads wheelchair son." "Yes, Ma'am." I just loved how my mother felt the need to tell me to do what I was already going to do. Behind me I could see four people standing next to a tree, who must be ninjas, practically appeared out of nowhere and hop in an expensive car. Two of them looked like brothers and the other two had to be a couple in the way that they held hands. "All aboard the sky-god express, the guy who had to be my age spoke. I turned back to my task of pulling out the wheelchair as they drove off. "Here you go grandad." "Thank you, son." His chair was one of the automated ones that he could maneuver around without having to be pushed so we walked along the path that led us over a wooden bridge to the park. "It's hard to believe that all of this was just mounds of grass and dirt before the developers decided to make something of it." "I agree. The last time we came to visit you, we came to this park and it wasn't as breathtakingly beautiful as it is now." "That must have been before I was born." "Sort of, you were in my belly and we went to a burger joint after we left here." "Yeah, those BBQ bacon burgers at Fatty's were the bomb." Grandad said. "The bomb! Okay, no more social media for you two." We did four laps around the park until my grandfather's wheelchair beeped and he decided to treat us to lunch at Fatty's if it was still there. "Nope! It's now a bar. How about we go to a salad bar?" "I know the perfect place." We drove across town to the northside to a grocery store that had the largest self-serve salad bar on Columbus and made salads that we decided to eat there. "You have an admirer grandson." I looked at the attendant who was cute and obviously staring at me so I got up to see if we could exchange numbers.

"Hey, I'm Greg." I held my hand out and he shook it while biting his bottom lip.

"I'm Korian." he said, with a soft voice.

"Nice to meet you, would you like to exchange numbers?" I asked.

"I'd love to, but first I have to ask. How big are you?"

"Uh, I'm five-eleven." I answered.

"No, that's not what I mean." He looked down at my private area and I rolled my eyes while putting my phone back into my pocket. "How do we live in a world where men like you think that Masc for Masc is bad but asking someone you just met how big they are is okay?" I turned around to walk away before he could respond and went back to enjoying my delicious salad. "I swear the men here are just as bad as the ones in California." "What happened?" "He asked me a question about my private parts before we could exchange numbers." "Oh, Hell no! I'm about to turn into a Karen." My mom put down her fork and I placed my hand on her shoulder as I shook my head no. As awful as that experience was, it won't be the last time that I met someone like that. Apparently size queens come in different shapes, colors and sizes. On the way home we drove by all of my grandads stomping grounds from when he first moved here and I loved every bit of it. There was so much gay culture that my head spun from all of the clubs, rainbow flags on houses and general areas for gays. Columbus had a huge lesbian population that apparently took over pride every year with its breasts out pride. Grandad went right to sleep when we got home and I decided to dive into the comics while my mom called her nurse-boo. The rest of the comics were good but with the recent dreams that I had, I was feigning for the ending of the story. None of them gave me what I needed and I felt myself needing a nap so I did a couple of yoga stretches before laying down. It didn't take me long to fall asleep and to wake up to the sight of an old apartment complex from my dream this morning. The faded sign on the side of the building said that It was called stripe road apartments. A warm breeze blew by me and I realized that this had to be a part of my obsession with the comics. I could hear the sound of people arguing before a thin white man came out of the apartment across from me and slammed the door shut. "Stupid as mother fucker!" He yelled and then pulled a set of keys out of his pocket with one hand while giving whoever was in the house the middle finger with the other. Once he had the car started he peeled out of the parking lot with enough speed that it caused the mud to splatter against the apartment that no one lived in. Now that I looked around I noticed that the other apartments were marbled with graffiti and littered with trash. "Shut the fuck up or beat your ass like I did yesterday!" I turned around as the door that was just slammed opened to show a large white man that I knew from the other dreams with a cigarette in his hands and an eye patch stepped out. "Fuck!" He swept his gaze from left to right and I realized that I must be invisible because he didn't even notice me standing across from him. "Now how the fuck am I going to get something to eat?" He took a long drag of the cigarette to finish it off and flicked it into the mud before turning around to go back into the apartment. I followed him into the apartment by passing through the solid material like a ghost once more and was frozen to the spot by the sight of the kids in cages. They wore clothes of the early eighties with dark bruises on their faces as they shrunk in fear from the abductor who I'll be calling Mr. Sell from now on. I couldn't understand why I kept having these dreams but the part of me that hated seeing kids like that knew I had to do something. "Hey, Wet Dog!" He turned with an evil look that made me step back from being noticed until I realized that this was a dream. "You!" The large man charged at me but I stood my ground as he went to hit me with his large fists that I dodged thanks to my years of karate and I landed a blow to his chest that sent him flying into the wall behind him. Since this was a dream I understood that I had powers because of the comics that I read so super strength wasn't that surprising to me. I already passed through walls like a ghost and was invisible until I wanted to be seen so I waited for him to get up and come at me again to see what else I could do. "You freak! I-I'm going to kill you." He yelled. "Uh-huh, bring it on wet dog!" That pissed him off enough to reach for the gun at his waist and aim it at me but I concentrated on making myself invisible again and he looked around the front room to see where I'd gone. I could still see my lower body so it was weird that he couldn't but I used that to my advantage while grabbing the gun and flinging it into the other room. The moment that I did, it made me visible again but when he tried to punch me I blocked it with a translucent force field that I used to send him flying backwards against the wall. "Where's the key to the locks?" He didn't answer so I pressed harder but it unfortunately made him pass out and fall limp while being held in place by my telekinetic power. "Damn it!" I needed to get them out of the cages before the skinny one came back and I didn't know of any other way except trying to pull the locks off by hand. The first lock came off like it was made of paper so I removed all of the others as the front door opened to show the skinny white man from earlier. "Hey!" "Hey, nothing weirdo!" I flung my hands out at him and sent him flying into the apartment across from this one. "Come on!" Since this dream was set in a time period before cell phones we had to get as far away from here before I wake up and leave the kids defenseless. As I left the apartment I could see Mr. Skinny's feet were hanging out of the window and took that as a sign that luck was on our side while we ran in the rain through the mud. "Get your black asses back here!" Mr. Sell yelled at us from behind but I turned around to face him and wished I remembered that I flung his gun into another room as he pointed it at us. "No!" He pulled the trigger before I could do anything besides throw my hands out to make a barrier but one of the bullets ricocheted off of a wall and struck a kid in the leg. I pushed my barrier out at him and concentrated on making it cover him before picking him up off of the ground to slam him down with enough force to knock him out. Once he was unconscious I heard police sirens and ran to the kid that was crying from being shot in the leg. "I'm so sorry."

He was turning blue from all of the blood loss so I placed my hand over the wound to staunch the bleeding like I'd seen in movies. "St-stay with me, kid. Okay!" I said in a quivering voice. He tried to nod but I could see that he was battling with losing consciousness as the cops pulled onto the muddy ground. The cops got out with their guns drawn and I used my head to point at the unconscious men as more of them pulled onto the scene with an ambulance behind them. "Thank goodness. People who actually do their jobs." The officer that was running towards me was a black man with thick muscles and dimples but he slowed down as he ran up to where we were. "Where'd he go?" I was still in my position but realized that I must now be invisible to all them except for the kid who pointed at me with shaky fingers. "We have a kid shot over here." I watched as two female paramedics ran over with their supplies and tended to the kid before my body was snatched backwards until I gasped while sitting up in bed. I could tell that it was late afternoon with the sun setting in the background as I smelled the delicious scent of my moms homemade carrot cake in the air. It was enough to make me stretch and get up to check its progress. "Hey, sleepy head. Did the whittle baby have a good nap?" She said, in a joking tone."Yup, I made pee-pee all by my-telf!" I responded. She laughed as Grandad walked in with Suyin helping him. "How'd you sleep, Grandson? Were your dreams wild and crazy?" He had a weird smile and I could see that he knew something that I didn't as he winked and took a seat at the kitchen table. "Umm, yes. I had a dream that I was a superhero who saved kids from child abductors. Just like the superhero in your comics." "I knew it!" he yelled. "Knew what, Uncle?" Suyin asked. "Suyin, can you go into my room and get my black binder?" "Yes, sir!" She left us to do as he asked while my mother gave me a look that said she was just as confused as I was. "Oh, I think you'll like this. Trust me." When Suyin returned he refiled through it until he pulled out a wad of old white paper and handed them to me. "Take a look at those for me, grandson." When I unfolded all of them I gasped because they were all of me. The first ones were of me kicking Mr.Sell in the balls as a kid with an afro ran and the others were of my face. "How is this possible? These papers are older than me." "You tell me, Dream Savior." My ears began to ring as my mother and Suyin walked over to take a look at the pictures and I realized that those weren't dreams. Somehow I transported myself backwards to when my grandfather was a kid to save him from being sold on the black market. "Take a look at this." He leaned forward and parted his gray afro to show me small scars from where some of his hair had been pulled out. "Y-Your the kid with the afro?" "I am indeed, Grandson." Tears fell down my face before I could stop them and I walked over to my grandad to hug him as he joined me in crying. "Thank you. If it wasn't for your help I would probably be dead or wishing that I was right now." "No, There isn't any way that he saved you. It had to be someone else." My mom spoke through her own tears as she sat down next to us and Suyin joined her. "My dad did say that he had powers and confirmed the pictures to be the real likeness of the young man that saved him. I never looked at them myself because I thought that it was something that they all imagined together." "This is why I moved out of California when I got my first big check. I never felt safe, even after I was returned to my parents." The four of us cried for another ten minutes while not saying anything until the doorbell rang and my Mom wiped her tears as she went to answer it. "Grandad, You have Company!" "Bring them in here please." I stepped back as four people my grandfather's age walked in behind my mom. "Whoa!" One of them said, with a gasp. "It is him!" ssid another. "Oh my Goddess!" The woman spoke, with a gasp. The last one didn't say anything as he clapped his hands over his mouth and cried. "Everyone, this is my Grandson. The Dream Savior."

Recipe for Danger

"I got the job!" I said yelling into the phone. "Congratulations, Best friend. See, I knew these luscious lips of mine would come in handy." "Girl, I can't, with you and your vagina innuendos." "They got you a job, didn't they?" "They did and I'd give them a kiss if I wasn't strictly dickly. But I have to go, I just wanted to tell you the good news." "I appreciate you calling me first. When I get home, we'll have to celebrate." "Yes, We will. TTYL." I hung up the phone and opened the confirmation email on my laptop from Charmaine Tilks. After I was wrongfully fired from my fast food job, I thought about going into another field of work but remembered my food safety and culinary arts certification that I spent my own money on. "Thank you, ancestors, spirit guides, goddesses and gods, for giving me the insight to follow my intuition." I re-read the email one last time before shutting down my laptop and getting in my car to drive to the address, so that I can have a better idea of where the mansion was on the far southside of Columbus, Ohio. It took me twenty minutes to get there through the heavy traffic but once I did my mouth fell open at how big the mansion was. "I'm in the money! I'm in the money!" It was surrounded by a large black gate and from what I could see from the street the wrap-around driveway led to an underground garage. "Damn, Wynslow Shoemen has some deep ass pockets." Behind me a car honked and I waved my hand out of the window to tell them to go around me but they kept honking until I turned on my emergency signals. "Are you happy now bitch!" Whoever was in the car got out and walked up to my side of the car with a large envelope in their hands. I was never one to be scared and I didn't have any reason to be subpoenaed so I rolled my window down and glared at the beautiful bitch who owned the brand new car behind me. "Yes!" "Now, Jallen Star. Is that any way to speak to your new boss?" My eyes grew big as she leaned down and handed me the envelope with a smile on her face. "Uh, I'm sorry. I didn't know." "It's okay. Just

make sure that this is the last time that you speak to me like that." She
tapped the top of my car before turning around and getting back into
her's. "Damn it! I really need to work on my mouth. I literally just got
hired by her an hour ago and I almost ruined it by being a catty gay."
She honked one last time before pulling up to the driveway as the long
gate opened. Fuck! Fuck! Fuck! I took a deep breath as she pulled into
the driveway and thanked all of my guides for not putting my entire
foot in my mouth. "Okay, Jallen, take your ass home." I turned off my
emergency signals and made my way back home while trying not to
beat myself up too much about my first interaction with Charmaine.
Once I got in the house, I opened the envelope and looked over the
contract. They were offering me a live-in position with two weeks of
vacation time, a large salary and a card that I can use to buy food for
the house. There was also a signing bonus check for two thousand
dollars that I quickly added to my account thanks to modern day
technology. "Whelp, that makes it official. I am now a personal chef
to Wynslow Shoemen. I just hope he isn't one of those rich weirdos
that sacrifice people to a pagan deity." My joke made a chill run over
my arms, so I decided to decompress with meditation. After
meditating and releasing the embarrassment from earlier, I decided to
go for a walk in the park up the street. I made my way along the path
through the heavy foliage and passed a couple of dog owners who
made me miss my pitbull, Savage. By the time that I made it to the
sitting area I almost tripped over my feet as a tall dark skinned man
waved at me from the bench. "Good afternoon." "Good afternoon."
He was the most attractive man that I've ever seen in my life and I
found myself looking deep into his bright blue eyes. "Wow, another
main character." "Huh?" "Oh, Nothing. I seem to keep running into
the main characters." He put his large hand on my shoulder and a cold
chill crawled over my body. "You've got this. Everything you need is
within you. Also, Don't let someone tell you that there is something
wrong with you." I frowned at his out of nowhere comment but felt
like he knew that I was embarking on a new career path somehow.

"Uh, thanks." "What's that over there?" He took his hand off of my shoulder and pointed to the area that I just came from as I turned to look at nothing. "I see you're just as hands-." I turned back to an empty seat with no sign of him anywhere. "What the fuck?" There was no way that he could have left without me hearing him leave or seeing his large form walking away. Was he a part of my anxiety? Did I imagine him? I put it in the back of my mind and made my way back home as I thought of all the things that I would be able to pay for now that I have a full time job. "Congratulations bestie!!" "Thank you." My roommate and best friend, Katie Wilkerson handed me a bouquet of flowers and a bottle of wine before pulling me into a hug. "I'm so proud of you." I took a deep breath as I prepared to tell her about my encounter with my new boss earlier. "I accidentally offended my boss earlier." "What? Jallen!" "It was an accident. I decided to go see what the drive would be like to the new house and when I parked out front a car pulled up behind me and I motioned for them to go around but they kept honking their horn so I turned on my emergency lights. Now you know my mouth acts on its own and I yelled out asking if they were happy and then called them a bitch. Little did I know that it was the woman that I've been in communication with via email. She handed me the paperwork that included a check for two grand, a contract and a debit card for food purchases." "A check? Oh you can pay me back the money you owe me then." I grabbed my phone and pulled up the ca-ching app and sent her the eight hundred dollars that she loaned me last month. "Boom!" "hey-Hey now!" "Also, they want me to live on the property while I work for them. I'll come home on the weekends." Her eyes grew wide as she looked at me with an open mouth. "So I can walk around the house with free lips while you're living it up in a mansion?" "What is up with you and your excessive use of the word lips?" "I don't know, Ever since I had that threesome with Charmaine and her wife, I've been extra horny for some reason." "Then let me pour us a glass of wine so that we can't talk about that night." As I turned around to open the cabinets her phone chimed and she exhaled an annoyed sigh. "Nope! I have to go back to work.. They need me to pick up the night shift." "Damn, This is the third one this week. Are you the only nurse in the entire hospital?" "You'd think that I was, but Keisha must have quit or something." "So she goes on a date with that rich butcher Natalie Slaughter and thinks she is a kept woman, Wow!" "Right! Let me get into a room with her and take a seat on her face. Then I'll be a kept woman." "Okay!" I poured myself a glass of wine as she went into her room to shower and get ready for her split double shift. For that hospital to be one of the oldest ones in Columbus, it has a horrible way of overworking its number one employees. After an hour of drinking by myself and scrolling through dating profiles on my phone I said goodbye to my best friend who I probably wouldn't see for a week because of our schedules. I spent the rest of the night watching cooking shows so that I could go into work tomorrow with a fresh set of ideas until I fell asleep on the couch. In the morning I got ready and packed a week's worth of clothing in a suitcase I stole from Katie's room. Since I was going to be stopping by the grocery store on my way to the mansion I would grab all of the cosmetics that I would need and splurge on some things that I normally wouldn't be able to afford. The next morning came so fast that I was barely ready to start my new job. Thank goodness that the grocery store wasn't packed. "Excuse me, can I give you a reading?" I turned around to see a brown skin woman with long locs and a face that was beat for the goddesses. She wore a flowing floral print dress and Greek sandals. "Thank you." "For?" "Thinking of a lovely compliment about my make-up. I'm Vanna, by the way." "You're welcome and I'm Jallen." It was always nice to meet people who share the same psychic awareness that I have and even more so when it's a woman. In my honest opinion women have the strongest connection to the divine given their ability to naturally create and sustain life. "I'm sensing a new career path." "Yes, today is my first day as a personal chef. I'm getting some stuff to wow them with my skill." "Uh-huh." She nodded while looking me in the eyes and smiled as she looked at my aura. "Okay, This is something that's your calling, but there is some kind of negativity attached to it. I'm not sensing it coming from you, so that's the good news but whatever it is will lead you to true love." My eyes grew wide as I thought about what she just said. The last time I was in a relationship the man was a jerk that tried to use me for a place to stay. "This man has been through some things though. I'm sensing heavy familial trauma. There is something that I kept seeing about being trapped. He'll need you to help him get out of his current situation and then find his new place in life." Oh hell no! Not another help me nigga! "Oh, no! Nothing like that. You two have past life trauma that needs to be healed." "You're telepathic!" "Sort of, it's more like I'm tele-empathic. Your spirit connects with mine and I can use discernment to get the message." She leaned forward and stared me in the eyes before looking at my forehead with a smile on her face. "Oh-shit! You're family!" "Yeah, all black people are related." She shook her head no and continued to smile as our eyes met. "You'll see. Just remember to have an open heart, mind and eye." "Don't you mean eyes, plural?" "Nope, I said what I said honey." Vanna took a deep breath before winking at me and then turning around to leave. Since she was the second cryptic person that I've met this week I made sure to watch her walk through the exit like a normal person. "What is happening on the great goddesses green earth that keeps pushing people into my life at weird moments?" I continued on my grocery shopping spree and spent five hundred dollars of the rich man's money. The drive to his mansion was easier now that I knew where I was going. When I pulled up to the gate it opened before I could press the button and I made my way to the front where Charmaine was waiting with an equally beautiful woman standing next to her. "Good morning, I hope you're in a better mood than yesterday?" "I am so sorry about that, I thought you were one of these snooty jerks." I said, pointing at the surrounding homes. "No, just the lesbain kind." The two of them laughed as I fake laughed and turned my car off. "Oh,

No! You don't want to enter through here. Shantera will take you around back and help you with the groceries." "Okay." Shantera hopped in and I drove us around back to the large doors that led into a large kitchen. "Is the owner of this house home?" "No, he's in Los Angeles. You'll be cooking for us and Jessica. Mr. Shoemen will return tomorrow." We lugged all of the groceries into the large kitchen that gave off sugar daddy vibes and I felt like I didn't buy enough food for all of them. That was until I saw the stockpile of food that was already there. "As you can see we have a lot of food here already from the last chef." "Yeah. At first I thought I didn't buy enough." "You'll be eating too, right?" "Yes, I know you'll be giving me a room to stay in but I thought it would be stupid to not eat the food that I make." "I'm so glad that you said that. The previous Chef made expensive meals and refused to eat them. We thought she was trying to poison us or something."

"May I ask why they stopped working here?"

"She must have been a cat in her past life, because she wandered about the house and into the room where Mr. Shoemen keeps his personal and business files. She had plans to black mail him for millions of dollars."

"Who messes up money, for more money that they don't own?" I asked. "Right! I wanted to beat her up but you know how some white people are." "Oh, She was white? Then that explains it all." The two of us finished putting the groceries away while she told me about Mr. Shoemen and what foods that he liked. I was surprised to hear her ask for large quantities of food because they had family that would come by every now and again. "All set?" "Yup, I'm making a traditional thanksgiving meal with turkey, ham, mashed potatoes, green bean casserole dinner rolls and two pies. Would you like cherry and pumpkin or sweet potato and blueberry?" She bit her bottom lip and thought about it as I prepared the turkey for the oven. "Sweet potato and blueberry." "Got it, I'll have it done by dinner and I'll make a little snack for brunch." "Make it a big snack, we get hungry with all of the weed that we smoke." "Coming right up." In between making everything for dinner I made artisan sandwiches with chips that I made from scratch. "That was good. I really loved those chips." "Thank you, that was the first time I successfully made chips." The personal trainer Jessica Tomlin handed me the three plates and I cleaned them off as I felt her eyes watching me. "Is there something else?" "No! I just wanted to see if you were one of those types of people who simply rinse off the plates instead of actually cleaning them." Oh- Shade! "I used to work in fast food and they didn't play about being sanitary." The rude bitch walked away as I finished talking but I didn't let it bother me as I finished preparing the pies. By the time that the afternoon came around I was almost done with everything and was waiting on the turkey to be done. Charmaine walked into the kitchen with the same smile on her face that she had when she handed me the large envelope yesterday. "It smells amazing. Damn!" "Thank you. I'm making sure I make a great first impression on you all. I want to apologize again for yesterday." "No need, When Mr. Shoemen was thinking about buying this house. I came here to check it out and a Karen up the street stopped me to ask if I was lost." "Wow, everytime we try to get past their racism they just add it to the pot." "Ha-ha, I see what you did there mr. Chef. But yeah, the people across the street sold their house to us because they didn't want to live next to a black gay man." My eyes grew big from hearing that he was gay and it gave me hope that I would have a rich boyfriend by the end of the year. My head game was unmatched and if he wanted some of this apple pie I got behind me, I'd have him spending his hard earned money on me. "I came in here to say that everything smells great and to give you this." She reached into her pocket and pulled out a small envelope that she handed to me. "It's the pin number to access the gate and another check for two thousand dollars. I was told that if you wow us with your skill on the first day that I could give you another check. We're still going to pay you what we agreed on but think of this as the second part of your signing bonus. When you're ready, I'll show you to your room." I nodded and almost cried from seeing the check but I waited for her to leave until I added it to my account by taking a picture of it. I made four thousand dollars in twenty-four hours and I still haven't gotten paid-paid yet. Time flew by as I kept looking at the money in my bank account until all of dinner was ready. "Before we eat, let me show you to your room." "Okay." I expected her to walk me to one of the rooms upstairs but Charmaine took me to a room around the corner that was next to the laundry room. It was large with a queen size bed, forty inch television and a walk-in-closet that was next to a bathroom. It even had a couch that faced the back of the television that seemed odd at first until she pressed a button on a remote and it swiveled to face us. "Your room has a water heater that is solely for this room. You have a walk in closet as you can see over there and the television is linked to all the major apps. The local cable is also one of those apps. Do you have any questions?" "Nope! This is really amazing. Thank you." She rubbed her hands together and smiled as her stomach rumbled. "I'm hungry, will you be serving us or do we have to make our own plates?" "Girl! For all of this, I'll chew your food for you and mama-bird you." We burst into laughter and I actually allowed myself to laugh this time as we walked out of the room to the kitchen. "What's down here?" I stopped in front of a door with a palm scanner on it and noticed that there wasn't a doorknob. "It's the room where we look at the camera footage, the solar panel in-take and it leads to the basement. As you can see it doesn't have a way for you to get in unless you have Mr. Shoemen's permission, so don't ask. He gets weird about going down there." "Duly noted. Let's eat!" She pulled her phone out of her pocket and sent a text message to the others that dinner was ready. After I made their plates, I made my own and we sat down at the large table in the dining room to eat. As we began to eat in silence, Jessica spoke up after trying my green bean casserole. "So what do you have planned for tomorrow?" "For breakfast I can make healthy pancakes and turkey sausage, if you want?" "That sounds great. Can you add scrambled eggs and homefries?" "You got it!" We spent the rest of the meal getting to know each other more but Shantera had an emergency with her mother so she had to scarf down her food and leave. I had to be shown how to use the top of the line dishwasher that was like a smartphone built into the house. "Wow! I don't even have to scrape off the excess food particles." "Nope, This dishwasher is from china along with the fridge and freezer." "Well while that is doing its job I'm going to take a shower." "Okay, I'll put the food away once it cools down." As I walked to my room I felt like someone was watching me and it made me pause to look around the kitchen. "Are you Okay?" "Yeah, I just had a weird feeling like I was being watched." I looked at the ceiling and corners to see if there were any cameras and relaxed after I didn't find any. "Are you sure you're good?" I Nodded in response to her question but I still felt as if I was being watched. The hot shower helped ease the weird sensation and I wished that I was one of those people who smoked weed so that It would help me relax more. After I fell asleep I had a dream that I was standing at the edge of a cliff that reminded me of the grand canyon except large glowing crystals stuck out of the ground. ROAR!!! I stepped back as the sound of a monster's roar echoed from the bottom as everything around me trembled. ROAR!!! The beast's monstrous call made the ground shake even harder but this time it was parallel to the sound of it crawling up out of the ravine. I stepped back as a large dragon head peaked over the edge. The giant beast had bronze and black scales that glowed like the crystals around us and eyes of two different colors. Its left eye was hazel while the other was pale gray. "Sup! Cutie!" I awoke to the sound of my alarm clock going off at six am and stretched as I contemplated what my weird dream could be telling me. Was I scared to live up to my full potential? Or did it have something to do with what the medium said? Whatever it was gave me an erection that I took care of before getting my day started by taking a shower. "Good Morning, Jallen." "Good Morning,

Charmaine." "Did you sleep well?" "I did, it was the first time in a while that I was able to get a full night's sleep. How about you?" "Oh yeah, I bought sheets of a higher thread count a month ago that give babe and I an extra sense of comfort." "Do you smoke?" "No, I'd be fatter if I did." "Okay, well If you ever change your mind, I have the hook up on some killer weed." "I'll remember that when I need help relaxing." As she left the kitchen I chopped up the potatoes and then the turkey sausage before making the pancake batter. I didn't want to have to wait on anything so I seasoned the potatoes and baked them in the oven with the sausage and decided to make the pancakes before making the scrambled eggs. In a half an hour's time I had the kitchen smelling good all over again but when I went to the fridge to get the scrambled eggs, I noticed that the leftovers were gone. Damn, they must have gotten the munchies and ate the extra's. A cold chill ran over my body as the dream-dragon came to my mind out of nowhere and I had to push it to the back of my mind so that I could finish working my magic in the kitchen. "Good morning!" "Good morning, Jessica. Can you do me a favor and tell everyone that breakfast is done." "Sure." She pulled her phone out and pressed a button before speaking into the phone. "Hey, Ms. Chimney's, Breakfast is done." I gave her a confused look because I thought she had a different last name but I realized that she was making a joke about them smoking weed outside. "It's a little joke that we have. They call me Ms. Track star and I refer to them as the Chimneys." "Yeah, and we'll call you Mr. Scrumptious." Shantera walked in with red eyes and a smile on her face as she sat at the bar with Charmaine next to her. They smelled of strong weed that filled my nose and gave me a second hand high. "Whoa! You weren't kidding. That is some strong stuff." "Yep! That's homegrown you're smelling." I made their plates and then made mine before putting the extra food in plastic containers. "We have business meetings during lunch so there won't be any need to make it but we'll be home for dinner with Mr. Shoemen. What's on the menu?" Damn, I just made breakfast that we're eating and they're already thinking of the last meal of the day. "I'll make pork egg rolls, fried rice and crab rangoon." "Mmm, Mr. Shoemen lived in Japan for three years and loves that kind of food. He'll be pleasantly surprised." "Good, I'm kind of nervous though." "Don't be. He's family and was in dire need of a chef with a modern/diversified skill set." "That does make me feel better, Thank you." "No thank you. These pancakes are too good to be healthy." "No, these potatoes are the bomb." "Girl this is not the nineties. We don't say that anymore." "Correction, You don't say that anymore." "OMG, do you remember that concert we went in ninety-four at that New York stadium and got drunk as fuck?" I know you never supposed to ask a woman her age but none of them look a day over thirty. Wow, Black definitely does not crack. "I have another client so I won't be here either." "Oh, So I'll have the entire mansion to myself?" "Don't wander around, everything is being recorded by Mr. Shoemen and he hates nosey people. Stay away from that room across from yours or he'll terminate your contract." Damn, burst my bubble, why don't you. "Okay, I was joking though. After I prepare everything for dinner I'm going to work on preparing the rest of the meals for the week ahead." We ate in silence until all of us were done and I filled the expensive dishwasher again. It was so cool but I was kind of scared that I overfilled it. The last thing that I wanted to do was break something that was worth more than anything that I make in a year. Once I was done I went back to my room to change clothes but I heard someone walking down the hallway and peaked my head out of my room to see Charmaine taking the leftovers into the room that she just told me not to go into. Weird, why would she eat another helping in the basement? I shrugged it off as I finished getting dressed and then went into the kitchen to do the rest of my job. By lunch time I had chicken, steak, pork chop strips marinating separately in seasonings and oils. Seeing how much I got done in the short amount of time gave me an added sense of accomplishment as I shut the fridge before going to my room to change my clothes. Even though I was a master foodie I hated smelling like it and I hated how it clung to my clothes. The weird feeling like I was being watched came over me again but this time I ignored it as I sat on the couch and turned the television around to face me. The cable package came with every channel but I preferred to watch cooking shows so that I could stay up on my craft. After watching several episodes of the Crazy chefs kitchen I decided to make myself a personal pizza for lunch. "Mmmm, Mozzarella, garlic, ham, pepperoni, spinach, mushrooms, black and green olives. MWAH!" Can I have a bite?" I turned around as my heart raced in my chest to see who said that and felt stupid because no one was in the kitchen but me. I had to have imagined it because it was the voice of the dream dragon and there was no way on earth that a creature like that was real. I just started this job so I couldn't be overworked or tired from not getting enough sleep. I'm not in danger or on drugs so what was the real reason? Could Mr. Shoemen be having a laugh at my expense? Or was he testing me to see if I would steal from him? Whatever it was I shrugged it off as a figment of my imagination and pulled out my phone to look at the dating app. By the time that my pizza was done I had managed to land a date on friday and I was kind of excited about going on a date with a sexy fitness trainer named Darnell, who was forty with the body of a basketball player. Mmmm, my favorite! The rest of the day went by super fast and I almost forgot that I would be meeting Mr. Shoemen. He walked in with Charmaine as I had Dinner going and I almost dropped the bowl of fried rice when I saw how handsome he was. He was a light skinned man that was my height but he was heavier than me with a low fade and a head full of spinning waves that matched my own. "Hello, Jallen. It's nice to finally meet you." "Likewise sir, thank you for hiring me." We shook hands and I loved how soft his palms were. I could imagine him rubbing my ass with them as I bounced up and down on top of him. "It smells amazing. I see you're worth every dollar." "Yes, Sir. I aim to please." He looked me up and down as he flashed me a white smile that said that he was thinking the same thing that I was thinking moments ago. "I have some paperwork to go over. When will dinner be ready?" "In twenty minutes sir." "Okay, send him my number Charmaine." "Yes, Mr. Shoemen." He turned to leave and I got a good look at his bubble butt in his casual pants that were probably just as expensive as the dishwasher. Damn, big bulge in the front and back. Mmmm-Mmm-Mmm. My phone vibrated in my pocket and pulled me out of my licentious trance as Charmaine cleared her throat. "Be careful. He's known as a shark." She walked in the same direction that he did and I thought about what she said. Now that he was home It felt weird being here. What if he was watching me while I worked? If he was I made sure to bend over and arch my back so that he could see what I was working with in my backyard but by the time that dinner was done my lower back ached from doing the most. "Hey, Helper! Send a text message to Mr. Shoemen." "Sure what would you like me to say?" My phone responded. "Tell him that dinner is ready." "Got it, I'm sending it now." After ten minutes he replied by asking me to bring them the food to his office and I had to send a message to Charmaine asking where the trays were. She instantly replied by telling me to look in the cabinet near the pantry and I fell out at the sight of the stainless steel serving tray on wheels that was pushed up against the wall. Once I had everything on the trays that came with it, I pushed it down the hall and knocked on the door. Charmaine opened the door and the first thing that I saw was my new boss with a wide smile on his face. "Today I have fried rice, pork egg rolls and crab rangoon on the menu for you sir." "What about me?" Charmaine winked as I walked past her and Mr. Shoemen laughed as he cleared off his desk. "Wow, It smells amazing Jallen." "Thank you sir." "Please call me Wynslow." I placed his plate in front of him first before putting Charmaines in the opposite position on his desk. "Will you be needing anything else sir- Wynslow?" "Can you bring me two bottled waters?" "Make it four, please." "Sure thing." I walked out of his office with my butt poked out and made sure to let the door push against it as I exited the room to do as they asked. After I delivered their drinks I made Jessica and Shantera's plate as well as my own and ate with them while making small talk about how their day went. "Once again, that was good." "Yeah, The last chef was a bitch who made boujee food for white people with no seasonings." I couldn't help but to laugh as Charmaine walked in with her and Mr. Shoemen's plates and put them in the dishwasher. Jessica touched my shoulder as I closed the door and gave me a gentle squeeze."We'll put the food away if you want to take a shower." "Okay, Thanks. You three are so helpful that it doesn't even feel like work. I feel like I'm part of the family." "Awww, You're sweet." "Those of us who are a part of the working class have to stick together." "Yeah." I don't know why but I just noticed that the pies were gone and I didn't make a dessert for this evening meal. Since no one else noticed I went to my room to take a shower. Meeting my new boss helped release some of the tension that I had about making a great first impression. That was until I heard him and Charmaine going to the room without a doorknob. They were having an argument about something so I turned off my light and cracked my door so that they wouldn't notice me watching them. "How do you always know when he is hungry?" "It's a gay-male thing. You wouldn't understand. Now be quiet and come on." Charmaine had the leftovers in her hands along with the other raw meat that I didn't use as Wynslow pressed his palm against the scanner. It clicked before opening and they walked into the dark room with the door closing behind them. Okay! Now I'm concerned. I knew that this job was too good to be true. Fuck! I really hope they're not holding someone hostage down there. My phone rang and I recognized the ringtone as Katies, so I slowly closed the door before sprinting across the room to answer it. "Hello bestie!" "Hey, How's it going?" I wanted to tell her that I was now scared that my new boss was a weirdo who probably sacrifices people to a pagan deity but I decided against it and chose to lie instead. "Great, I made a great first impression with my boss. How are things going with you?" I asked. "Oh, You know. The usual hospital drama. I got a fatty in the back and up top, so the doctors want a bite." Even though it had only been twenty-four hours since I saw her, I missed her. Especially now that I just saw my Boss take food into the basement while whispering that he had a psychic connection to someone down there. "I know that's right. Let one of the higher-ups get a taste of that cookie." "You first. I did some asking around about your boss and from what I heard he's single, physically fit and versatile." "Girl! You should have been a journalist with those skills of yours." "What kind of friend would I be if I didn't look out for my big-booty-Judy?" "I can't!" I burst into laughter as I fell back onto the bed and we talked for two hours until she had to go back to work for her double. "Alright, I love you too." "Hey, don't act like you can't call me. Even if I'm elbow deep in a rectum give a girl a call." "Bye Katie." I didn't need that visual so I hung up and spent the rest of the night thinking about what my two bosses could have been doing down there. Charmaine was a lesbian and Wynslow is just as gay as me. Whatever they were doing it couldn't have been good so I made plans to go get me a couple of knives and a taser when I go get some more ingredients tomorrow. Once I went to sleep I had a dream where I was getting out of the shower to see a tall naked brown skinned man standing in the doorway. He had a body that was thick like mine but without a chubby stomach. His uncircumcised penis dangled as he backed up into my room while I looked into his mixed-matched eyes. They were the same color as the dragons but without the eerie glow behind them. My body moved on its own as I draped the towel around my waist and followed him into the room. Once I got into the room he was nowhere to be seen but when I went to the window I jumped backwards as I looked at the dragon in the backyard. Now I could see its entire form and I was in awe of its majestic beauty. The large beast had bronze and onyx scales with large bat-like wings on its back. It winked with an eye that was hazel like mine and exhaled a breath that made the wind blow hard against the house. "That was the best home cooked meal that I ever had. Thanks cutie." I was too stunned to speak as the beast became translucent and phased into the ground like a ghost. "Is everything okay?" I turned around to see Wynslow walking into my room with a bloody knife in his hand and a sinister smile on his face. Charmaine, Shantera and Jessica walked into the room with bloody kitchen utensils and the same weird smiles on their faces as he started to walk towards me. "Yeah, are you okay?" "If not, we have a remedy for that." Shantera said. "I know you're just dying to keep your job." Charmaine added. I was frozen by fear as they made their way to me and awoke in a cold sweat right before my alarm went off. "Phew!!" The light of the morning sun broke through the clouds as I got out of bed and changed my sheets before getting in the shower. After I meditated in the shower, I was ready to get my day started by making breakfast quesadillas. Walking by the room without a doorknob made a chill go down my back like I was a kid who was scared of an invisible monster. Katie knew where I was and if anything ever happened to me she would raise hell to get in here.

She had a cousin who was a detective and another member of our gay family so if anything ever happened to me I knew that they'd raise hell to get in here. I walked into the kitchen to see Wynslow drinking a cup of coffee while looking over his paperwork. "Good morning, Wynslow." "Good morning, Jallen. What's on the menu for today?" He flashed me his handsome smile and I temporarily forgot about my nightmare of him holding the knife that was in the holder next to him. "I'm going to make stuffed breakfast quesadillas with wheat tortillas, brown rice, corn, black beans, bacon and eggs."

"Oh, Shit. Sounds like I fired and hired the right people." A laugh escaped my mouth before I could stop it and it helped rid me of the weird feeling that remained from the nightmare. I used this time to pick his brain about the foods he liked so that I could have a job for the foreseeable future. By the time that I was done I found out that he hated onions and raw tomatoes, but loved garlic and olives. "Here you go sir-I mean Wynslow." "Thank you. The ladies won't be joining us.

Jessica had an early morning client and the resident couple wanted to sleep in." "Oh, Cool. So it's just the two of us." We ate in silence for the first five minutes until he asked me about sports and I told him that I loved sports like straight men love supermodels. He told about his career as a venture capitalist and how he made his first million dollars. "Tell me more about you. Mr. Chef. Besides the things that I can find out through social media or hiring a private detective." He asked, with an eyebrow raised. "Well, let's see. At my last job my boss threw a metal pan at my head and when I retaliated by asking him if he wanted to get fucked up, I was fired for being an angry black man." "Wow! I'm sorry that that happened to you. I promise not to be like that." He was most definitely a charmer and I found myself more at ease while talking to him. As the morning went on I told him about how I wanted to publish my own cookbook, find my birth parents and ask them why they gave me up for adoption. That was something that has plagued me for most of my life. Growing up in foster care gave me thick skin but it also made me feel like I was missing part of myself. "Charmaine did right by hiring you, Jallen." "I concur." "I'll be working from home, so send me a text when lunch is ready."

He smiled and I could feel my boxer-briefs starting to edge their way down my waist as he got up to leave. I expected the girls to wake up after I was done cleaning but no one did, so I chopped up the vegetables for dinner and prepared everything for my baked mac and cheese. While doing all of that I decided to make bread from scratch that I'd pair with broccoli and cheddar soup for lunch. Charmaine walked in with Shantera but they decided to have a brunch date downtown at a place that refused to hire me after I applied there several times. "Have fun ladies. I'll try not to be offended that you didn't want my food." I yelled out. "Ha! We've been in this house for a month before you got here and I need to see new walls." "Uh-Huh!" They left and I continued what I was doing until the weird feeling like I was being watched crawled over my body at noon. "Are you okay?" Wynslow asked. "Yeah. Are you hungry?" He nodded and I poured him a bowl of soup. "Is that homemade bread?" "Yep! It's one of my specialties." He took his food to his office and I ate by myself until he came back twenty minutes later with an empty tray. "That was amazing, Jallen." "Thank you sir-I mean Wynslow." Mr. Deep-pockets winked at me before he left me to my thoughts. If we kept this up I'd be following him into his bedroom by christmas. The next four hours went by super fast and I made dinner before getting ready for my date. "You look nice. Thank you. I'm going to hang out with some friends and I might not be back until late. Is that Okay?" "Yeah. You're grown. I'll tell Charmaine." I left the mansion and made my way downtown to the movie theater. A few minutes later Darnell called me to say that he was pulling into the parking lot. "Okay, I'm waiting at the front." I watched as he stepped out of his large truck and walked towards me with his dark brown muscles glistening in the moonlight. Damn, This nigga is fine!!! "Jallen." "Yep, You look great." "So do you. Talk about body!!!" He bit his bottom lip as he walked a full circle around me and I had to force myself not to look at his print and muscular booty. "My my my, sir. Damn! Let's get into this theater before we have to do some things out here." All I could do was smile as he draped his arm over my shoulder and we walked into the theater to get our tickets. "Hello, can we have two tickets for Second Chances?" "Sure thing, can I see your ID's? It's an R-rated movie." "Dude, we're in our thirties. You're good." The clerk rolled his eyes as Darnell handed him his debit card and practically tossed our tickets at us. If this was any other night, I would have read his ass for filth but tonight I was with a man that I knew would stick up for me if it came down to it. He even got the door for me but I knew that he wanted to get another peak at my plump posterior as I walked into the air conditioned theater lobby. "I don't eat carbs or drink soda, but if you want some I don't mind paying for it." "I'll drink bottled water." "Only if they have spring water. That purified shit is garbage." Okay, now he's getting a little pushy. We stepped up to the counter and he ordered us two spring waters with some salted nuts that couldn't have been healthy for us but I didn't argue since he paid for it. The theater wasn't packed but we still sat in the back and in the middle seats. I was grateful for the movie being a romantic comedy because it helped to diffuse the energy of our encounter and made our night even better. "That movie was hilarious as fuck." He said. "It was, I can't remember the last time I laughed so hard." I responded. As we walked out to our cars he pulled me close and pressed his big lips against mine. "Get a room Fags!!" We kept kissing as a car passed us but I could tell by his breathing that he wanted to break away and yell out his response. "You're a great kisser." "So are you." My stomach rumbled as he looked me up and down like he wanted to take a bite. "Where shall we go for dinner?" "I know what I want to eat." Darnell tilted his head to the side and bit his lip as I pointed to the burger place with vegan options. "That sounds good but how about we go back to my place and build up an appetite?" "Uhh, No. I have a strict rule of no sex before the third date." "What? Aww Nigga, you're tripping big time. I'm just trying to fuck, Not get married. I'm out." He let go of my hand and walked away without saying another word as I gave him the finger. Men like him get on my nerves but I was happy that he showed his true colors before I gave him some. I went into the burger place to get something to eat before going home and ate in my car as I thought about how most men who are extremely attractive feel the same way that he did. After I was done eating I went home and hopped in the shower to wash off the night's energy. "Hey, How did your date go?" I turned around to see my boss standing in my doorway with a bottle of dark liquor and two shot glasses in his hands. "Horrible, and yes to that." He smiled as he walked over to my small seating area and filled up our cups. "Do you want to talk about it?" I clinked my glass against his and took a deep breath before recounting the events of the night. "Wow, that sounds like my date with the gold digger last month in Atlanta. He kept asking if I was going to fly him to Milan and take him on a shopping spree." "Isn't it horrible when people put their hands in your pockets?" "Yeah, I wasn't born rich. I made my own money by using my gifts to my advantage." "That's what's up. From one black man to another, I'm proud of you." He turned and smiled at me as he poured another shot for us. "To new beginnings." "To new beginnings." I repeated. We talked about everything and nothing at the same time for another hour before he said goodnight. I was buzzed but tired from working and before I knew it I was drifting off into the dream world. I opened my eyes and was standing in front of a cave as normal sized glowing mix-matched eyes looked at me from its darkness. The scary man-Dragon stepped out of the entrance with his penis dangling and waved me over with his left hand. He stepped back into the darkness as I moved forward and the eyes grew bigger as his dragon face peaked out of the entrance. "You put your foot in those pies. Can I get a strawberry cheesecake next time?" "Uh, Sure thing Mr. Monster, just don't eat me." "Now why would I eat the sexiest Chef on the planet?" He blew me a kiss that warmed the air around me and I opened my eyes as my alarm went off. "What the fuck are these dreams trying to tell me?" I spoke out loud, cutting the silence. It was times like this that I kicked myself for not getting Vanna's number. I closed my eyes and meditated while thinking of my daily affirmations for fifteen minutes until I was ready to get my day started. All I could think about was the dragon's lips moving as it asked for one of my signature desserts and I decided to go to the grocery store since I forgot to do it yesterday. Jessica sat at the counter while scrolling on her phone and looked up when I walked in. "Good morning, Scrumptious." "Good morning, Track star." "Our boss wants sunny side up eggs, bacon and biscuits." "Oh, perfect! I've wanted to make homemade biscuits for a couple of days now." "Then I'll let you get started on breakfast." She left the kitchen to go for a run and it occurred to me that she eats a lot of carbs for a personal trainer that has an amazing body. When Charmaine told me about her occupation I expected her to have a meal plan of healthy foods that I was prepared to make. "Good Morning. I see Jessica told you what our boss wants to eat." "Yup, My biscuits are to die for." "They better be, We have the expensive jam in the pantry that I've been dying to try." She winked before walking out of the kitchen and I laughed while mixing up the ingredients. After an hour of cooking I was done with everything at the exact moment that everyone came into the kitchen. Wynslow smiled like we were secret lovers in a school hallway and the girls picked up on it as they looked from me to him. "Wow! Your plating skills are amazing, Jallen." "Thank you, Wynslow. I try to make my instructor proud." "How about we eat in the dining room that has never seen such delicious food?" "That's a marvelous idea sir." He was the first to leave as Jessica and Shantera followed behind him but Charmaine stayed behind. "I don't know what you did, but he is really impressed with you. Keep up the good work, Jallen." She handed me another check that I slipped into my pocket and we walked into the dining room to join the others. Eating with them felt like I was finally at a place in my life where I was surrounded by people of an equal mindset. All of them were completely dedicated to their jobs and I learned that Shantera owned her security firm before selling it to become Mr. Shoemen's personal security guard. Charmaine used to be a publicist who also sold her company for millions and Jessica has other high profile clients that she trains besides Wynslow. "I'm stuffed." Shantera patted me on the back as she helped me with the plates and even offered to put the dishes in the dishwasher as I got ready to run my daily errands. I waited to see if they would take the extra food to the basement and heard Wynslow walking to the room while pushing the cart. It took all of my willpower to not peek my head out of the door to see what he had on the cart but I waited for it to close and left to run my errands. My first stop was the superstore that sold everything that I needed food-wise and then I bought several pocket knives. I made sure to buy three books on dream interpretations as well as a book on dragon lore. One way or another I'm going to figure out what my dreams were trying to tell me. After I returned to the mansion I removed the steak from the fridge and used the mallet to tenderize it until my forearms were sore. For lunch I made fried cabbage with spicy sausage that I paired with lemonade and made the strawberry cheesecake that the dream-dragon gave me the idea of making. It's been a while since I made it because of Katie being lactose intolerant. Wynslow walked in as I finished topping it with strawberries and whistled as I placed the cover over it. "Whoa! Is that a cheesecake?" "Yup! Another one of my specialties." "Can you make another one, it's one of my favorite desserts." "Well it's a good thing I bought extra ingredients." I made two more but left one plain and stacked them on top of each other in the large fridge. Once I was done I felt the weird feeling that I was being watched again as I went to my room to plug my phone into the charger. Before I continued with my day I sent Katie a text message telling her about my date and how things were going with the new job. She replied by telling me that she also went on a date with a married lesbain couple and took them back to our place for a threesome. She was always thinking about her hot-box and it was good to see her balancing being a workaholic with her active sex life.Since ai was done with everything, I decided to crack open the dream interpretation books. After a couple of hours passed I learned that dragon dreams mean triumphing over challenges, it being my guardian spirit, strong emotions, mystical power, change and good luck. I didn't see anything about talking dragons who give compliments or shape-shift into very attractive men of color so I put the books down and went to the kitchen to start dinner. "Smelling good, as always." Mr. Shoemen walked in with a huge smile on his face and his laptop in his hands. "I have a question for you." "Good, I have one for you as well, but you go first." "What do you know about dragon dreams?" His smile faded and he stopped in his tracks. "What do you mean?" "I keep having dreams about this bronze/black dragon with wicked eyes." Wynslow's chest rose up and down as he looked me in the eyes while remaining quiet for a full minute. "I-uh, I-I don't know. I think they mean that it's your spirit animal or something. B-But those things don't exist." "Right! That's why I said Dragon-Dream. What was your question?" "It's something that can wait for later. I'll be in my office. Hit me up when dinner is done." He turned on his heels and practically ran out of the Kitchen with his booty bouncing as he moved. I know some people had phobias of animals but with dragons not being an actual living creature I couldn't figure out what I did wrong. Charmaine came into the kitchen a half an hour later and told me that he was traumatized as a kid by some bullies at a museum. "Damn, I feel like such an insensitive jerk." "Don't, you had no way of knowing that he was scared of something like that." I appreciated her explanation and gentle shoulder squeeze but when she grabbed some food and went to the basement instead of his office, it made me wonder what was really down there. She returned ten minutes later with tousled hair that looked like she walked through a wind storm. "We have a deep freezer down there but I have to walk by the power generator fan. Mr. Shoemen is what you like to call a doomsday prepper." "Oh, so that's why I see you two take food down there." "Yeah, Is dinner done?" "Yes." "Cool, I'm going to take a shower." After I made our plates I took Wynslow's into his office and came back to see that everyone else decided to eat in their rooms. "Well, Damn. Was it something that I said?" I broke out my multi-tasking skill and ate while I cleaned until Jessica returned with everyone's plate's. "Those were the best fajitas that I've ever had." "I aim to please." Even though she was smiling I felt like it was forced and the rest of them were mad at me for some unknown reason. Three hours later I received a text message from Charmaine saying that I could have tomorrow off with pay. Once I was all packed up I took a shower and decided to leave in the morning before any of them woke up. After I fell asleep I had a dream where I was standing in the backyard of the mansion and the dragon was offering me his glowing bloody heart. The heart glowed with red energy before shrinking and turning into a ring with a ruby crystal on a bronze and onyx shank. "I've been trying to get to know you but you're being too stubborn." "Look man-I mean dragon, this is a dream." "Oh, right! I forget that mortals of your time period stopped believing in magical beasts." "Are you my spirit animal?" "I'm trying to be you boo-thang, but I need you to get into the room without a door so that we can formally meet. Then I can show you that I'm real and you can get me out of here. I'm tired of being used by those parasites." He extended his limbs as his body shrank like his heart did and took the form of the sexy naked man from my previous dreams, but with clothes on this time. "I figured that I'd take my other form so that you wouldn't think that I was trying to eat you." "Uh, I appreciate it, I mean damn. You kind of make me miss seeing you in your birthday suit." "Oh, here!" He snapped his fingers and his clothes vanished as his penis dangled once more. It was like his signature move or something. "I was kidding." "Whelp it's too late now, we've already seen each other naked." "What are you talking about?" "I've been watching you through astral projection since you entered the house. I know you've felt it." That made me frown as he made gray boxer briefs appear on his waist and pulled me into a hug. "I'm not sure how much of my magic that they've siphoned off of me but I really need to get out of the basement before I slip into another thousand year coma. Please, Jallen. I need your help." The sound of his voice echoing around us was powerful and sincere at the same time. Being psychic was something that I was used to with my heightened sense of awareness but dragons? I had to be experiencing some kind of mental breakdown or something. "You're not. The immortal medium that approached you in the grocery store told you about what could be between us. I swear I'm real and I will treat you like the king you are if you help me get out of here." His kind words touched the part of me that was a natural helper but how the hell could I get a dragon out of the basement? If all of this was real? "I'll use my power to open the door once you wake up. All you have to do is come down into the basement and allow me to drink some of your blood." "What?" I woke up to a partially lit room as a full moon hung in the sky outside. Looking into the backyard reminded me of the dream and I walked out of my room to see the door partially cracked open. Okay, this is my chance to finally see if any of this is real. I grabbed my phone and one of my pocket knives before leaving my room to venture into the creepy basement. The second I stepped through the doorway a cold chill crawled over my body and I hesitated before moving forward into the darkness. "You've got this Jallen. Worst case scenario, they're human traffickers." I kept moving forward and used my phone's flashlight as I moved down the spiral staircase until I reached an open doorway. The second I saw the large sleeping dragon my heart sank into my stomach and froze me to the spot. It was one thing to dream about it but another to actually see something that was this large. The air changed from cool to warm as he opened his eyes and lifted his head to face me. "About time handsome!" His beautiful scales glowed as his body began to shrink just like in the dream until he was a naked human with a large afro.

Seeing his handsome face in real life made it easier to hug him as he fell forward into my arms. "Sorry, I'm really drained and need something to eat. Do I have permission to drink some of your blood?" "Seeing as your dick is pressed against my stomach, Yes!" The nameless being took a deep breath and exhaled it on my neck before sinking his teeth into the side of my neck. My ears rang as he drank my blood like he was the son of Dracula, and he tightened his hold on me. "Mmmm." I felt lightheaded as he pulled back to look at me with his mix-matched reptilian eyes. "Damn, You're very attrac-."

Everything went black as I went limp in his arms and found myself drifting through darkness. "Hey, Mortal, can I talk to you about my son for a second?" A bright green light formed in front of me and took the form of a woman with the same skin tone as the dragons, but she had large bat wings and alluring hazel eyes. She also had his afro and wore lingerie like she was an evil supermodel. "I don't know how much time it will take my son to get the both of you out of his prison, so I have to make this quick. I'm an angel. His father is a dragon prince, and we sealed him on the earth because he destroyed an entire village of mystics because of his love for your past life. His father and I royally fucked up, and I made myself a promise that I'd be there for him when he was freed from his prison. Please tell him that I'm sorry for being a bitch of a mother who put him through hell." "Wait-wait! He's half angel, half dragon?" "Yes, no shush before you waste time and wake up. I really need to get this off of my big breasts." I'm sure she meant chest, but I let her continue as she crossed her arms. "He is a good divine monster, but like all dragons, he is very territorial. Don't entertain other males, or you'll see why his father's race are known for being the most ferocious creatures in existence. Also, there are many things about the mortal race of Earth that are being hidden from your kind by other deities. Once you awaken, you'll also see that you're different from other mortals. Please take care of my son and tell him that I'm always watching over him and give him this. He'll know what to do." An onyx necklace appeared around my neck with a long tooth attached to it, and she put her hands on my cheeks like a mother would before I opened my eyes. "Are you okay?" He asked, caressing my face like his mother did. "Y-yeah. Umm, I don't want to be insensitive to what you've been through, but I met your mother, and she said that she was sorry." His eyes grew wide as he held up the necklace that she gave me and bent down to kiss my lips. His tears were cold but tickled like peroxide as they fell down my face until he pulled away to look me in the eyes. "T-This is my father's tooth, and I can use it to resurrect him." It was my turn to look at him with wide eyes because that was the last thing that I expected him to say. "Let's get out of here." I nodded as he helped me up off of the ground, and I noticed that he was now dressed in clothes that I would wear, and I now had shoes on my feet. "I don't even know your name." "Oh, right! Where are my divine manners? Hello Jallen, I'm Prince Zarfiladrogaton of the angel-born and divine monsters, but you can call me Zarf." "Nice to meet you. How are we getting out of here?" "Damn it!" Zarf rolled his eyes, looked up to the ceiling, and snarled as my ears popped. "Where do you think you're going, dragon?" Wynslow appeared in a whirl of white glittering light with the girls behind him. All four of them had glowing vertical eyes on their forehead that radiated a different color. "What the fuck?" "Oh, these surprise you, but not the fact that you're standing next to a billion-year-old dragon?" "Yeah, and you should take a look in the mirror. You have one of these too." I put my hand up to my forehead and gasped as I touched an eye that was larger than theirs. Before I could do anything else, Wynslow exhaled a breath of white flames that knocked us backwards. Out of the corner of my eye, I saw Zarf plunge the necklace into the ground and cause a glowing fissure to form. "No!" Wynslow sent another stream of white flames at us, but he threw his hands out and made a multi-colored barrier of energy that blocked the fire as something started to crawl out of the fissure. "Get them!" We got up at the exact moment that a black claw broke the surface and let out a monstrous roar. The girls leaped forward with their mind-eyes glowing brightly before they sent elemental blasts at us, but when I held my hand up to block, I sent out a blast of baby blue electricity that slammed into Jessica as Charmaine pulled Shantera out of the way. "There you go, baby!" Zarf smiled as he grabbed the claw and pulled the creature out of the ground. "Jallen, meet my father. Gravizolyedrif, The Dark Dragon King." The being had pale gray eyes with horns and was just as naked as Zarf was, but thankfully he didn't have a visible penis. "Morning's greeting to you." We didn't have time to talk as the four parasites rallied together to attack us. "I'm still new to this, but I'll take the lesbian couple and you two deal with Boss Man and his helper." "No need, young one." His father's shadow moved on its own as the light of the white fire grew brighter, and I heard the sound of wings flapping loudly. "Now we make this an even fight." His shadow grew larger as Zarf's mother flew out with a sinister smile on her face and glowing green eyes. "Praise Mother, I'm free! Now I don't have to listen to that dark-being drag queen go on and on about her revenge." The smile on Zarf's face was contagious as we turned towards our opponents and readied ourselves for a battle. Steam flowed off of Charmaine's body as she stepped towards me with the same look that she had on my first day of work. "We were going to bring you in on our secret, but you just had to be nosey, didn't you?" "Bitch, Your mama's nosey!" I thought about the lightning from earlier and threw my hands up as she directed a blast of cold air my way. We stayed in position while the others fought with the same vigor that didn't last long as my in-laws killed Shantera and Jessica with ease. My father-in-law ate Jessica like she was a boneless wing while the fallen angel popped Shantera's head like a grape. "No! I will kill-." The moment's distraction allowed my electricity to overpower her and reduce the bitch to a pile of ashes on the ground. Zarf held Wynslow by the throat as he reached into his chest and pulled out his heart in one move. "Well, that was fun, but I don't want them moving on." The fallen angel clapped her hands as her green light encompassed the room to the point that it was uncomfortable and then receded as it changed the wide space into holding cells. Each one of them were resurrected but without the eye on their foreheads and perplexed looks on their faces. "I'm not done with you yet." I didn't understand why she couldn't have done that before I committed murder, but I guess a win was a win no matter how we did it. Zarf moved to my side at super speed and made a mirror that held up to my face. I had a large vertical eye on my forehead that glowed with baby-blue energy. "Welcome to the supernatural club, My love." He kissed my cheek, and in the blink of an eye, we were standing upstairs in the kitchen. "I feel like introductions are in order. I'm Metatron, and this is my consort, Drif." "Hello, mortal-Immortal Jallen." "Am I Immortal now?" I asked. "You can be killed, but you'll naturally resurrect." "What am I?" Zarf grabbed me by the waist and pulled me closer while looking into my eyes. "To make a long story short, You're now an awakened being that was known as an Omniterran, the first sentient being who inhabited the earth. They were your Ancestors." "Like Adam and Eve?" All of them laughed, and I didn't get the joke, so I just smiled until they were done. "Baby, that is a story for another time. How about you cook us some breakfast, and we can talk about it while we eat?" "I have some things to take care of first." Zarf let me go as his skin bubbled, and he shapeshifted into Wynslow, wearing a three-piece suit. "I have some work to do. I'll be back." He kissed my cheek and walked towards my now-incarcerated boss's office as I went to the fridge with breakfast on my mind. When I held my hand up to the handle, it flew off and entered my grasp like a baseball as my in-laws laughed from behind me. "Okay, I don't think that I should cook. I might burn the house down or send hot food flying everywhere." "Where's the nearest forest? I'll hunt a unicorn for us to eat." "How about no honey? Here, let me help." The fallen angel tucked her wings into her back and re-attached the door handle with magic before opening it to let the food fly out onto the counter. "Cool. How did you know that I was going to make shrimp alfredo?" "I've been alive since the beginning of time. I know almost everything. I also know where your parents are." The box of rotini noodles turned to ashes in my hands as I turned around and looked at my mother-in-law, who had a smug look on her face. The angel snapped her fingers and made the pile of ash turn back into noodles on the counter. "While you two discuss whatever is going on with your parents, I'm going to place a barrier around the estate." The dragon king got up off of his stool as his shadow moved up his body, and he vanished. "Okay, that was cool. I need to learn how to do that." "You will. We all have the ability to bi-locate, which is unique to us. Now about your parents. What do you want to know?" "Why did they give me up for adoption?" "Check it out, as your generation says." She pointed at the window, and I watched two adults who looked strung out on drugs give a baby to an older woman. "All he does is cry. We can't get any sleep. Take him." "I can't raise a baby, Courtney." My father stepped forward and handed her a couple of twenties. "Get rid of him." They turned around and walked away without saying another word as the scene changed to show the old lady handing me to a woman who had to be a social worker. "Is he addicted to any drugs?" "Yes, His mother and father were strung out on heroin. They used to live in the house next door, but they were squatters who vanished a month ago." The image vanished as tears fell down my face, and I wanted to find them and ring the necks. That explained why I was placed in the slow learning disability classes in school and why I suffered from anxiety. "DO you want to see where they are now?" Her question brought me out of my trance, and I nodded while slowly grabbing a pot to fill it with water. When she pointed at the glass again I watched as it showed the area known as skid-row in California as a woman laid on the ground next to three other homeless people. The image changed to show an old man who was in an orange jumpsuit while throwing dice against a wall in prison. "I know I can't make any excuses for them, but they did good by giving you away. Had you stayed with them you would have been killed or sold for more drugs." That made sense. I was lucky not to have experienced any of the horrible things that I heard happen in foster care, but I grew up wanting to know how any of that happened. "Thank you." "You're welcome, honey, but I sense that there is another question that you want answered." "What's God like?" She laughed and clutched her breast like was were at a comedy show. "It's Goddess, and she was an even bigger bitch to us than I was to my son." She looked out to the window as her hazel eyes glowed with green energy and stayed that way for a couple of minutes while I prepared to make shrimp alfredo for breakfast. "Uh-Oh! My mother is having a vision. That can't be good." Zarf walked into the room with the laptop and a smile on his face as he passed by his mother. After a few more minutes went by his father returned and was now a dark skinned human that was dressed in normal clothes. He held his palms out over her face right before she gasped and blinked as a smile curved her lips. "My big sister is putting things in motion that will bring about a new change to this world." Zarf came around to my side of the counter and kissed my lips before helping me make our meal. "Then I guess it only makes sense that all of this happened to bring us together to be a recipe for Danger." He said. "Yeah, because dragons and angels aren't dangerous enough. What else could be out there?" They all looked at me with a smile that said that I was in for a surprise and for the first time in my life I felt like I had someone other than Katie at my side.

Hungry for love

"Great, Now we're trapped in here with another mouth to feed!" I opened my eyes to see six different supernatural beings looking down on me. A fairy, a bat demon, a gorgeous brown skinned angel with large white wings and three humans with energy auras that I recognized as magic wielders like me. The bat demon held his hand out to help me up and when our palms touched I saw visions of him eating white people on some kind of ship. The vision left as fast as it started and I dusted off my backside while they looked at me with weird expressions. "Can I help you?" "No, It's us who shall help you." I frowned at the fairy with yellow skin and green wings. Her long white hair sparkled like glitter as the sun set in the distance. "Where are we?" "Oh, Wow! Is she serious?" "She has to be." "Not everyone is all knowing like you, Grace." The Angel looked me up and down as they moved to the side and I took in our surroundings. We were standing in a room that was the size of a football stadium with twenty wide open doorways on the walls. "Honey, You're in a prison dimension created by the grand bitch herself, Aura. You must have offended her." I couldn't see how that was remotely possible. The last thing I remembered was going on a date with this tall voluptuous seer named Misty. We had the best talk about what we envisioned for our futures. I made the decision to wait three years before sacrificing her to the ancient ones for more power and a longer life. "Does this goddess have long multicolored locs?" They all shared a look that answered my question. This has to be the craziest turn of events that has ever happened to me. I was on a roll and had six candidates lined up for my hexing ritual. All I had to do was gather personal objects of theirs to put on my altar. "Girl, are you okay?" "She's spaced out." Normally a bitch had one time to disrespect me and I'd let her have it, But now I'm in the presence of beings who's immortality was greater than mine. I just have to show them that I'm not the witch to fuck with. "You'll have to excuse me, this is my first time being thrown in a prison dimension. Next time I'll be better prepared for you, Okay, Powder wings." "Bitch! I am the first born daughter of Avalon and the rightful queen of the FEY! Show me some respect." She summoned white energy to her hands and I backed up as I let lightning form in my palms. "Please do! Give me a reason to throw a little lightning." The bat demon stepped in between use with translucent energy waves exuding out of his hands to make a barrier around the both of us. "We're going to be here for eternity. Let's not get caught up in power trips." I powered down at the same time as the easily triggered fairy princess and turned my attention to the open doorways. "Are those our rooms?" "Yes, Take your pic, Those over there are all free." Since I now have the ability to fly, I let the winds lift me off the ground to the room at the top of the wall. "It might smell like lavender and mint leaves because of the Jinn that used to live there!" The sound of the bat-demon's voice was the last thing I heard before walking into the room and forming my hands into the gesture to cast the sound barrier. This has to be the biggest joke of my life. I'm trapped in a prison dimension with beings that would have never looked at me twice if I passed them by in day to day life. My room was a decent size with a small bathroom and mix-matched furniture. The bed was perfect but I'd definitely have to do an energy cleanse on the room. It was times like this that I'm glad my grandfather gave me his omni-bag that I was able to stuff into my pocket. "To me!" My palms began to tingle as the summoning spell gained momentum and my bag appeared in between my hands. The sneaky goddess may have trapped me here but my bag was where I kept all of the tools and food that I saved for later. I reached in and pulled out everything that I would need to cleanse this space and make it mine completely. Out of the corner of my eyes I caught the sight of the rude fairies wings as she floated outside of my doorway. She had her arms crossed and was saying something but my sound barrier blocked out her words. "Hold on." I threw my hands out to cancel the barrier and she floated into my room. "I'm sorry. I was not trying to start a fight with you." The look of surprise on my face made her smile as she extended her hand and we shook hands. "Me too, All of this is still new to me. My apologies." Everything that I said was partially true because I never apologize but it was something about this thick bodied fairy that made me wet. "I'm Ashley, by the way." "I'm Vivalia." "I just wanted to apologize. I'll leave you to your casting." She flew out of the doorway and I continued to place the crystals around the room and use my purification herbs to turn into smoke that made my room smell better than before. I changed the sheets and cleaned the bathroom while singing my favorite song that I probably wont ever hear again. If I had to guess I'd say two hours passed after I cleaned up and made this space more of my own. "Wow, Viv was right. You know what you're doing." I forgot that I didn't reactivate the barrier and seeing the other magic users float into my room made me miss my familiars. "I'm Carl, a master of arcane knowledge." "I'm Leslie, the most powerful Alchemist to ever live." Yeah right, Bitch! I am both a mistress of spells and the best potion maker that has ever lived. "Oh, Hello. It's always good to meet other practitioners of the mystical arts. I'm Ashley." They looked around the room at the changes that I made and took a seat on the reupholstered furniture. "Whoa! This is definitely more comfortable than when the mouthy Banshee lived here." "Yeah, her and that transgender ghost had horrible taste." I couldn't help but to laugh at their comments because it was true. The old furniture looked like it was from the Victorian era and had so much dust on it that I'm sure I inhaled some of it when I changed the cushion. "What do you all eat?" They shared a look that I hoped didn't mean that they ate the weakest link here and I took a seat across from them. "The room that's at the bottom of this row used to belong to four nature spirits and they made it into a smaller pocket dimension that houses a forest." Phew! I thought that I was going to have to eat them. I hate cutting up human bodies. "There are all kinds of beasts in that forest that we hunt and there is also spring water in there." "Is there a sun in there?" "Sort of. It's a projection of light from a sun and moon stone. If you go in there, don't fall asleep or the forest will eat you like fertilizer." "I have been alive for eight hundred thousand years. I refuse to die at the roots of a plant." The three of us laughed and Leslie pulled out some herb to smoke on. "What happened to the ghost and Banshee?" "We don't know. They just up and vanished." That wasn't a good sign. I hated mysteries and I hated not knowing what was to come even more. Another hour passed and the others came in with more party favors. Since I just met these beings I made the decision to not get as drunk as they did but I hit the blunt because I needed that. "How are all of you coping with this?" "We've been here so long that it's normal for us." Viv handed me the blunt and I noticed that she was smiling more than she was prior to coming into my room. I've heard stories about the fey and I've wanted to see if the rumors were true about them tasting like fruits and vegetables for a long time. I wouldn't mind nibbling on a vagina that smells like peaches or tastes like tomatoes. Everyone except for me was drunk as fuck and I made sure to watch all of them as they told me the stories of how they got here. The shapeshifter, Beverly, broke into a camp and took the form of a black bear before eating a cabin full of campers. Z, the bat demon was the son of Dracula and a bat-demigoddess, who betrayed some kind of ancient god and he used his powers to spread vampirism across the earth. Carl sold his children into sex-slavery for mystical knowledge. Vivalia was the first fairy to eat a child. Grace opened up the gateway from the higher realms so that her angelic siblings could come to earth and cause all kinds of trouble for my ancestors. Leslie created a plague that killed most of Europe. Yeah, I think I've found my people. "So what did you do to be placed here?" Viv touched my shoulder as I handed the blunt to grace. "I put a binding spell on my sisters that allowed the Spanish inquisition to decimate most of the magical community." Everyone's eyes grew big before they burst into laughter and Carl held his fist out for me to pop his rock. I noticed that there weren't any white people in here and it was kind of unfair. They've abused magic even more than people of color have.

Maybe the goddess hated the pale mutations as much as I did. "Looks like you're right at home then." "Naw, I'm going to find a way out of here. Even if it kills me." That made all of them laugh even harder. "Aura is too powerful." "She is the great creator of the universe." Hearing that made a chill go down my spine. My patron deities were created at the beginning of time and if she was older than them I really had no way of getting out of here. Damn it! "Look at it this way. When she is finally killed we can escape and take over the world without anyone to stop us." Beverly's words made me feel better, but I hated being trapped. I spent a large portion of my life as a handmaiden to a powerful witch and after I killed her and took her magic, I made a promise to myself that I would never allow anyone to put me in a corner ever again. "My sister is a powerful bitch, but she has her limits." I jerked my head over at the angel who said that like it was normal. "Your sister?" "Yeah, my mother and father had sixteen children before they made the first angels. I'm the last angelic daughter of the Supreme parents." I was at a loss for words as I took another sip from my water bottle. "I've only met her a couple of times and she is a real piece of work. She didn't even show me one ounce of sibling love." That's new.

Here I thought the angels were created by the goddesses and gods after they came to this universe. My ears popped and everyone looked out of my doorway as a wave of energy made the hairs on the back of my neck stand up. "Incoming." Grace spread her wings and flew through the doorway as everyone else followed behind her. I followed them out of my room as a cloud of darkness formed in the exact spot where my body materialized earlier. "What the fuck, Auntie!" The dark energy coalesced and took the form of a tall dark skinned man with glowing red eyes and summer clothes. This being was the most attractive entity that I'd ever seen. His cut off blue jean shorts and night sky tank top showed off his muscles as he slammed his fist into the ground. I waited for him to calm down before leaping off of the edge and lowering myself down to where the others stood. "You've got to be fucking kidding me. SERIOUSLY!!" His voice echoed around us and made the walls shake as he stood up. This male entity made me wetter than the fairy, with his long limbs and gorgeous blue eyes. I could tell from here that he had a huge penis by the thick bulge in his pants. Mmmm, I hope he likes pussy. The newcomer's frown turned into a smile as he made eye contact with me. "Hello to you too, gorgeous." He blew me a kiss and I tried my hardest not to smile harder as he stepped past all of them to me. "I'm Darkon, Lord of evil intent and back breaking sex." I arched an eyebrow at him as he kissed my knuckles. "Hello, I'm Ashley." "Very nice to meet you, gorgeous." Grace cleared her throat and stepped to his side while her left wing brushed his shoulder. "Did I hear you say auntie?" He nodded and looked her up and down as his smile faded. "Oh, Hello. I'm your nephew, I guess." He ignored her extended hand and looked at the rest of our little group of supernatural beings. A smile curved his lips as he turned in a circle. "Three mystics, a snotty angel, a bat demon who has ties to my brother and a thick fairy. Wow!" Grace crossed her arms and I could see that she wanted to lash out but knew better because of the energy level that he had. "Excuse, what did I do that would result in this rude behavior that you're sending my way?"

He snorted and turned to face her. "I hate all of my father's family for allowing him to molest me." A chill ran down my spine from experiencing my own sexual abuse at the hands of my mother. "I didn't even know the father of the sky had another son." "For beings who are all powerful, none of you know shit about dick." Darkon leaped into the air and flew to the room that was below mine. "Don't bother me while I'm masterbating." With that he was gone and the rest of us looked at each other with the same puzzled expression on our faces. Z, laughed and shook his head as he headed to his room. "Another god. Yeah, This should be interesting." Everyone except for Grace and I went to their rooms and I kind of felt bad for her. She may be an all powerful being but Darkon was an actual god. One that I couldn't wait to grind on. I love a big dick as much as I love tonguing a clitoris. "Are you good?" I asked the angel. "I'll be alright, My family and I have always had a rocky past. I just didn't expect for my big brother's runt to show up here. He must have really pissed off my sister." I didn't know what to do to make this better but offer up my services in a way that would be beneficial to the both of us. "I could nibble on your box if you want." Grace looked up with a smile and in the blink of an eye we were in her room without clothes on. She threw me onto the bed and got to work on tasting me first. *Okay feathers, that's it.* Normally I'm the one who goes down first but this was a welcomed surprise that made me arch my back as her long tongue found its way to my g-spot. "Oh, Shit. Yeah right there." She used her hands to message my breast as she continued to hit all the right spots. After thirty minutes of her sensational tongue lashing I cried out as I came and squirted on her face. "Mmmm, you taste like revenge." I didn't know how that was possible seeing as I've already gotten my revenge on my mother and her licentious coven eight hundred thousand years ago. I took a deep breath and got up so that she could lay down but decided that it would be better for her to ride my face while I taste a piece of heaven. She laughed as I pulled her onto my face and let my tongue do all of the work until she came on my face an hour later. "Damn that was good." She got up and stretched her large wings as the evidence of our sexual encounter vanished from our faces. "Did you do that?" "Yes, I hate being dirty." I was cleaner now than when I came in here and just looking at her perfectly sculpted body made me want more. "Just so you know, I've had sex with everyone in here. Well besides the new arrival. That would be nasty." Good, I had plans for him. As soon as I find a way to kill a god, I'm out of here. "I'll get going, Thank you. Pretty wings." I kissed the side of her cheek and flew to the doorway but stopped as I remembered I was naked. "Um, where did you put my clothes?" She smiled and snapped her fingers to make my clothes reappear.

"Let's make this a normal thing."

"I'm down."

I blew her a kiss and then turned to fly out of the room. "Uh-Huh! Why weren't we invited?" Leslie floated in front of my doorway with a snake on her shoulder that I recognized as Beverly. "Yeah! I love pussy as much as the next girl." She slithered off of her shoulder and moved like a serpentine dragon to my room. "What are you two waiting for?" Don't tempt me with a good time! I took Leslie by the hand and flew into my room as Beverly changed into her human form without clothes. Damn, she has an amazing ass. "Doesn't she." Leslie must have read my emotions as we landed and stripped ourselves of our clothing. Time flew by as we took turns eating each other out until I came on both of their faces. If I kept this up I'd have enough of their sexual energy to complete my siphoning hex. "Same time tomorrow." "I'll be here." They left and I waited for them to be out of hearing range as I went to my bag and pulled out the clear quartz crystals and then poured in the sexual energy that I stole. Perfect! After I took a shower I spent the rest of my time thinking of ways to get their energy and decided to call it a night because of how exhausted I was. I couldn't remember the last time I reached my climax three times in a row. Having my kitty ate was cool and all but now I want some dick.

Carl and Z, will be my next victims and then I'll save the fairy queen and god of darkness for last. I closed my eyes while imagining what it would feel like to have a threesome with the both of them as I drifted off into the realm of slumber. The astral realm and I have always had a weird relationship, where I'd sometimes have prophetic dreams or experience lucid dreams that made no sense. This time I had the weirdest of all dreams where I was falling and all around me I was surrounded by darkness. As a child I used to be scared of the dark until I realized that the monsters of that world lived in the light of day. A loud explosion pulled me out of the dream realm and I opened my eyes as another rocked the entire place. "His efforts to escape will be the death of us all." Grace flew into my room as I got up off of the bed and headed to the doorway. "Darkon?" She nodded and took me by the hand to where our new arrival was standing at the entry point while sending energy blasts at the ceiling. "I'm getting the fuck out of here." He threw his hands out and sent a stream of bright blue fire at the ceiling causing another tremor to shake everything. "Nephew, if there was a way out I would have found it." "You didn't try hard enough, Auntie!" She reached out to place a hand on his shoulder but he twisted and flipped her onto her back. "Don't touch me unless I tell you to." His powerful voice echoed around us and I stepped back so that he wouldn't take his anger out on me next. I've been here for six hours and I don't like to be caged." I couldn't have agreed more but the way that he was going about this was wrong. "How about we take a beat and calm down." I suggested. He took a deep breath and helped his aunt up off of the ground. "I'm sorry. Just don't touch me. I have issues with people thinking that all of this is theirs." Darkon said, as he visibly calmed down. "You definitely have the family anger, I'll give you that much." She rolled her shoulders and snapped her wings back into place while grimacing. "I can't remember the last time I was physically injured." Grace spread her wings and flew up to her room without saying another word and I could tell that she was embarrassed by the display of power. A part of me felt sorry for her because she genuinely wanted to soothe her nephew who wanted nothing to do with her. "Are you good?" He shook his head no as the others looked down from their rooms and then vanished in a puff of black smoke. "O-kay! At Least I know that I've gotten six hours of sleep." "I know right." Viv landed next to me and put her arm on my shoulder. She smelled like cucumbers and watermelon mixed with raw honey. "Can I talk to you in private?" She asked, with a smile. "Sure." I responded. She touched my shoulder and teleported us to her room in the blink of an eye. I had the ability to cast transportation spells but it took a lot of my magic to disappear and reappear. I can't wait to have their magic after I give their souls to the ancient ones. "What did you want to-" She cut my words off by pressing our lips together and allowing her tongue to search for mine. All I could do was continue to kiss her until she reached into my pants and started to play with the warmest part of me. I moaned into her mouth and reached into her pants and pulled back when I felt more vagina lips than were normal. "Whoa! You have two vaginas." She nodded and smiled as her clothes vanished to show them to me. I was at a loss for words but still wanted to taste them so I stepped forward and bent down to press my face into them. This was the origin of her sweet scent that caused me to yearn for her. Viv used her wings to hover off of the ground and I inserted my tongue into the left lips while fingering the right side. "Oh, fuck!" The humming sound of her wings intensified as she continued to moan and I let my tongue and fingers do all of the work. After ten minutes of me going to town on her sweet spot she cried out and collapsed to the ground while squirting on my face. *Yeah, that's it. Give it all to me.* "Oh my! That was so fucking good!" She pulled me down on top of her and kissed my lips while moving my hair out of my face. "Okay, your turn." As much as I would have loved that I really needed to get her energy into a crystal and then move onto the next victim. "How about we take a rain check?" "You sure?" I nodded and kissed her lips before getting up and waving goodbye. "I'll call you to my room later." "You got it." I flew across the wide space to my room and placed her energy into the clear quartz before someone else wanted a piece of me. "All praise to the ancient ones." Once I was done I placed the crystal back into its enchanted pouch and went to the bathroom to clean myself off. I made sure to lick off as much as I could because it reminded me of melted sherbet. "Hey, Can I come in?" The sound of the dark god's voice sent chills up my spine as I peaked around the corner and nodded at the blue-eyed visitor. He was the walking definition of a real god, unlike the images of those pale "Greek" deities. Darkon waved his hand at the entrance and a dark barrier formed as my ears popped. "I know your little secret and I want in." I froze as he walked into the bathroom with the sexiest smile on his face. "I don't know what you're talking about." He rolled his blue eyes and pressed himself against me as we looked into the mirror. "I was raised by witches, I know when someone is using crystals to store energy." His sculpted body felt perfect against my backside and it took all of my will power not to spread my legs so that he could enter me from behind. "We'll have sex after all of them are dead." "You're an empath, aren't you?" He chuckled as he wrapped his arms around me and leaned his head against mine. "Would I be a god if I wasn't?" "The angel isn't empathic and she is of your family." The dark god turned me around in his arms and looked me in the eyes. "Those things are basically robots designed for a purpose." Damn, that was harsh. "Anyways, back to my secret plan of escape. How do you plan on helping me?" I asked. "I don't, you'll be doing all of the heavy lifting when it comes to your little spell and when it's complete we will escape this place together." He kissed the top of my forehead before vanishing into nothing and taking his dark barrier with him. I took a shower and realized that I've spent as much time showering and plotting as I have partaking in my sexual escapades. After my shower I decided to look for Carl since he was energetically aligned with my humanity and save the demon for last. His power would be the icing on top of the cake that would give me all the leverage that I needed. The spell master's room was four spaces to the left of mine and when I landed in his doorway I caught him sitting on the couch masterbating. "Would you like a hand or some lips?" His smile widened as I stepped closer and got on my knees while looking him in the eyes before putting my lips on his dick. I instantly regretted it because of his stinking balls and the pubic hair that poked me in the eyes. He moaned so loud that I'm sure everyone heard it and I made sure to swallow as much of his seed as I could when he reached his climax. "I'm loving this room service." He laughed as I got up and walked out of the room to the edge. "Where are you going?" "I have to brush my teeth." "Make sure you come back." He's lucky that I need his essence or I'd curse him with boils on his dick. I flew up to my room but noticed that Darkon was standing in his doorway with a smile on his face as he waved. The sound of his voice entered my mind as I landed in my doorway. *"Hard at work, I see."* I ignored him and ran to my nightstand to pour the energy into the crystal and then brush my teeth before I washed my face. Ugh! Men and their crotch funk! After cleaning up again I left my room and went to the demon-bat's room. He had headphones on and was dancing to music with a cute smile on his face. "Hey!" I yelled "What's up?" He responded As I looked around his room I noticed that he had a lot of gay memorabilia and hand drawn erotic sketches of men kissing. Damn it, Darkon might have to handle this one. "I feel like I've gotten to know everyone else here except you." He took off his headphones and smiled as he looked me up and down. "You've only been here for half a day. We still have time." He took a seat on his rainbow furniture and I couldn't help but to look at his thick muscular body. Why couldn't he be bisexual? He patted the seat next to him with his copper hands and flashed me a smile as I walked over to the seating area. "What are you?" He asked. "A witch. What are you?" "I mean ethnically." "Oh! My mother was an indigenous queen of what is now called the united states before all of the race war bullshit and the man that she raped was an African cheiftan of a tribe that no longer exists." "That explains your gorgeous skin tone and this hair, Honey!" He wiggled his pointer finger at me before pretending to flick imaginary hair. "What about you?" He sucked his breath in through a closed mouth as he looked to the floor and then back at me. "I'm technically the son of a Melanated Turkish prince and a bat-demigoddess." That explained his hair texture and his brown skin. "Did I get the job?" "Huh?" "The last time someone asked me questions about my "ethnic" origins I was applying for a job as a personal assistant." The serious look on his face made him look all the more attractive but I could sense that I offended him. "I didn't mean it like that. You're the first bat demigod that I've met and to be truthfully honest I thought you were a demon." He frowned and placed his hand on his chest as he gasped. "You tried it!" Yup, definitely gay. "I'm the son of a prince and a being of pure divinity." He snapped his fingers several times and in the blink of an eye I was back in my room.

"Damn it, I knew that this was too easy." I took a deep breath and whispered the name of the news arrival. "Darkon." He appeared next to me with a smile on his face. "I could have told you that he was gay." I smacked my teeth and shot him a glare as I narrowed my eyes. "What?" He spoke, through a pearly white smile. "If you knew that, why didn't you say something?" "I wanted to see how long it would take you to notice and then ask for my help. Here." He closed his fist and opened it to produce a small clump of translucent energy that he tossed over to me. I ran over to the nightstand and added it to the crystal, but when I turned around, he was gone. My plan was to give him some head for helping me reach my goal faster than I had originally planned. Now that I have everything that I need I pulled out all of my tools to start the hex. After I finished with the spell, I returned all of my tools to the bag and laid back on the bed to go over all that had happened since I was sent to this place. My stomach rumbled, and I realized the last time that I ate something was when I was on my date with the sneaky goddess. I got up and flew out of my room and almost dropped to the ground because of my low energy level. It was times like this that I wished I would have inherited the power of empathy from my mother like the rest of my family. Then I could survive on excess energy and not have to go to the forest room to hunt like I'm some kind of animal. Walking through the entrance felt like I was stepping out of a cave and into a forest that smelled amazing. The sunlight felt great on my skin, and a warm breeze almost made me forget about being trapped in this prison dimension. A flock of small brown birds flew by me and kept going deeper into the forest as the sounds of the other animals filled the air. I took a deep breath and touched my amulet to activate my locator charm. It glowed before tugging me forward to the closest source of food, and I walked until I reached a bush of green berries. At the bottom of the bush, a large rabbit nibbled on the leaves that were closer to the ground, and I pointed to it and summoned my energy. "Death!" It tried to run but made a loud squealing sound before its head exploded, and I bent down to pick it up. "Now, all I need are vegetables and wood for a fire." I got to work on eviscerating the rabbit for the fire and then pulled out all of my old utensils from the ancient times that I used to cook food the old-fashioned way. After I set up my camp I wandered around the forest in search of vegetables that were a couple of feet away in a perfectly maintained garden and then I picked up wood for my fire. I pulled up Radishes, carrots, potatoes, and onions and then returned back to my cooking site to pull out my seasonings. The small table that I made was the perfect height for me to chop everything up and then add it to the bubbling pot that made me look like the stereotypical witch. It was another thing that was stolen from my people and demonized by the white people who enslaved the descendants of my tribe. In thirty minutes, I had my cooking site smelling divine and decided that this would be a great time to sniff the cocaine that I had saved for emergencies. It burned as I inhaled my little bump, and it made me sneeze three times in a row. "You've got it smelling great over here." Everyone walked through the bushes from separate entrances, and seeing them brought a smile to my face.

"You're definitely a witch." Viv winked at me before pulling me into a side hug as grace hugged my other side. Even though I met these people hours ago, it felt like we could have been good friends if I didn't have a plan to sacrifice them to the ancient ones. "Is this a party? Darkon appeared last and clapped his hands to make chairs appear for us to sit on. Yeah, I can't wait to have magic like that. Then, I won't have to rely on the power of the ancients to execute my plan. After the rabbit stew was done, we ate, laughed and smoked more weed. Z conjured four bottles of expensive wine that got us drunk as fuck. Carl kept asking everyone for an orgy, but I put a stop to it because he was a sweaty mess, and everyone must have felt like I did because they shot him down several times. After our impromptu party ended, Viv helped me clean up with her magic, and we headed to the exit but kept getting lost until we met up with the rest of the group. "Where is the exit?" "Better question, where is Darkon?" I looked around and noticed that he was the one who left first, so it must have been him who made it vanish. Great, I'm drunk and trapped in a magical forest with a bunch of supernatural rejects.

Ding-Ding-Ding-Ding-Ding! "Welcome to the first forest hunt, brought to you by the lord of negativity!" His voice echoed around the forest as large red glowing eyes appeared over us. "Darkon, this isn't funny. I'm drunk, and I'm ready to lie down. Knock it off and bring back the door!" I yelled. "Yeah, man. This shit is childish, come on." Z's aura flowed around his body as he floated upwards, and he turned in a circle to search for another exit. "Damn it, he's closed all of the other entrances." Everyone let out an annoyed sigh and spoke different words of profanity as the eyes hovered over us. "In the first round of "Hungry For Love", you'll be participating in a scavenger hunt. There are several animals in the forest with heightened levels of melanin. Upon capturing the animals, you'll be transported out of the forest and into your rooms until the next round starts." Since all of us were drunk as fuck this was the wrong time to compete in a game of craziness for a god who I thought was on my side. "What the fuck?"

Beverly yelled. "I just gave him some head, and he didn't say shit about this." Z pounded his fists together and let out a monstrous roar that sent animals into their flight mode. "Looks like you tasted my box. I just let him hit raw." "Girl, me too." Viv, Beverly and Z hi-fived, but I wasn't in the mood for any of this. "What are the rules?" Grace also had a smile on her face as she floated off of the ground. "Yeah, Do we have to kill each other or something?" Everyone turned to look at Mr.Funky Balls himself, Carl. "Why would you even say something like that?" He just looked at me as he shrugged, and I realized at that moment that most of my prison mates were crazier than me. "Nope, Just find the shadow beasts, and that will be the key to transporting you out of here. Good luck!" "May the best entity win." They all left in separate ways, and I wanted so badly to kill them all and just be done with this bull shit. I turned on my heels just as a large all-black boar ran out of the bushes with glowing red eyes. "Haha, Darkon. You can cut the bullshit." It roared and continued to charge at me. If I hadn't moved to the side, the beast would have stabbed me with its large, thick tusk. My only option was to fight this thing since it was obviously not my blue-eyed accomplice. I summoned fire to my hands and sent huge balls of orange fire at the walking Christmas ham, but it dodged it like a pro. "Not today, Bacon-bits." I jumped into the air and flew above the treetops as it turned around to charge me again. "Isn't this fun?" The sound of Darkon's voice echoed through my mind as the boar climbed the air with its hooves and chased after me. This dude is crazy as fuck. "What's your deal?" He answered my question by sending a bolt of red lightning at me that almost hit me in the chest. The dark boar chased me over the treetops while sending bolt after bolt of lightning that I dodged by moving left to right. I twisted through the air and summoned as much lighting as I could to hit it with. It crackled and popped as it left my fingertips to slam into his head, but his tusks absorbed all of it as he laughed. Fuck! I dove to the ground and landed near a lake where Viv was fighting some kind of giant black eel with ice breath. The small distraction cost me as Darkon rammed his tusks into my back, and I cried out from the pain. We fell towards the lake as my blood began to coat his eggshell-colored horns, and he laughed like it was the funniest thing in the world. "I'm going to kick your ass." "I guess it's a good thing that I'm possessing this scrumptious creature then." That was all the reassurance that I needed to reach behind me and grab his horns so that I could pull them out of me. It hurt like hell, but once I was free of them, I used my enhanced strength to separate the boar in two. The creature squealed as Darkon separated himself from it, and I felt my body falling faster toward the lake. Out of the corner of my eye, I could see Viv winning against her creature, but it ripped off one of her wings, and green blood dripped from her back. "I know that's righ-." Everything went black as I continued to fall, and my body hit the ice-cold lake with a loud splash. I expected to enter the dream realm, but instead, I continued to fall into absolute darkness. "I'm offended that you have no faith in me, Daughter of the Queen-conjurer." The sound of Darkon's deep voice echoed through the darkness until my body hit solid ground, and I coughed up some blood. The darkness began to recede as I looked around my brightly lit room, and the searing pain started to fade into nothing. "Good as new." The tall, dark god appeared in front of me with a smile on his face and his large hands out to help me up. "You could have told me the plan, you jerk." "Where's the fun in that princess?" I narrowed my gaze on him as I stood up, and he pulled me into a hug. Goosebumps crawled over my body as he wrapped his long arms around my waist. "The fairy is dead and I'm giving you her powers along with her knowledge on how to use them. Before I could say anything, the sensation intensified and he stepped back with his eyes glowing bright red. "Enjoy." My handsome dark god winked at me as his shadow crawled up his body and he left without saying another word. The energy that he gave to me spread to every part of my body and I felt like I could run twenty miles without stopping. I focused on going to the bathroom without moving my legs and in the blink of an eye I was now standing in the spot that I envisioned in front of the mirror. "Yes!" My hair was longer and my brown eyes glowed with white energy. "Oh, Yeah. I can get used to this." I spent three hours practicing how to channel her divine energy and managed to master teleportation and faster wingless flight. Normally I'd use the wind to guide my body but this was twenty times better than that and I don't feel the dizziness that followed behind it. My palms began to tingle as I allowed the white energy to swirl around my fingers and I couldn't help but to smile. For the first time in my life I had enough power to not have to rely on anyone for anything. As a natural born conjurer my magic had its limits, but now I could call things to my hand from my bag to appear out of thin air. My mothers people were great at communing with the spirits and my father's people had a natural connection to the earth but there was always a hindrance on us because of our mortality. Now I'm even more of an unstoppable force than before and my elemental connection is stronger like I'm closer to the source of all things. I just hoped that I didn't grow wings on my back because those would be hard to hide and I need to continue to move in secret. As time passed I realized that my sense of smell had been heightened to the point of being overwhelming. My eyes burned as I looked around the room and small orbs of light moved in and out of my peripheral vision. I fell to the floor as a migraine formed at the top of my head. The cool stone floor helped center me and I had to control my breathing as another wave of pain caused me to curl into a ball. Why was this happening now? "Oh, Right! Your body has to get used to the higher frequency. This too shall pass." The sound of his voice made my head pound even harder as he laughed and I almost threw up everything that I ate before the stupid ass game of his. The only thing that I could do was focus on my breathing and allow myself to fall into the dream realm. My vision was blurry at first but after a couple of seconds I saw that I was now standing in front of my mother who was on her throne. "Finally! Hello daughter." "What the fuck do you want?" She smiled and got up with her arms outstretched like we had the typical mother daughter relationship where we hugged and talked about our feelings. "You've been ignoring me for a while now and I just wanted to check on you." I stepped back as she moved in for a hug. "You exiled me from your realm because I didn't want to partake in your orgies. Bitch fuck you!" Her smile grew wider and she pulled me into a hug while kissing my cheek. "I shouldn't have sent those women after you. I'm sorry." "SORRY!! They drugged and raped me." I shrugged off her arms even though I've always wanted her to hug me. "I had to, or your father would have continued to send the bounty hunters after you. He wanted to take you as another one of his wives and it was the only way that he wouldn't want you." I may have been in spirit form but my blood still boiled as I let out a loud scream and wrapped my hands around her throat. She smiled as I continued to choke the life out of her until I woke up with my hands wrapped around the leg of my bed. "BITCH!!!" Tears fell from my eyes but my migraine was gone. I let go of the bed and got up so fast that I levitated off of the ground by a couple of inches. The sound of bat wings moving through the air filled my ears before Z flew into my doorway in his animal form and then shifted into his human-like form with a concerned look on his face. "Are you okay?" He held his hands out to me as I allowed myself to descend to the floor and into his arms as I cried. After letting out thousands of years of pain by crying, I whipped my tears with tissue that appeared out of nowhere next to me. "I had a bad dream. Family stuff." He nodded and sniffed the air as he looked over at my nightstand and then arched an eyebrow at me. "Why does it smell like me in here?" "Darkon must have come in here after the two of you did whatever it is that you two did." Hopefully that would keep him off of my scent but if not I'll have to kill him with my new power. "Yeah, I did cum on his face." He smiled while helping me wipe my tears and I laughed from how funny that must have looked. "Do you want to smoke?" "Yes, I need it." He walked me over to my couch and pulled a bong out of thin air. "Here." Once I had it lit, I inhaled a deep breath of smoke that I allowed to travel throughout my respiratory system. It made me cough so hard but the high was something that I missed and I kicked myself for not putting some seeds from my garden in my bag. "Yeah, That's that home grown." We smoked and I told him about my past with my mother but made sure to leave out my true name. First rule of magic is to never allow someone else to gain access to your power. "My father was like that. He took me to a brothel when I was a teenager and made me have sex with three women and two men before I could leave. I ended up killing him and then I sucked out my mothers divinity because when I told her about it she said that it was going to help make me into a man, well a demigod." "Is that how you ended up being a murderer?" "Yeah, Being fucked in the ass by a grown man was torture and I could never forgive either of them for it." "You killed your father?" A large smile curved his lips as he nodded and made a fist. "With these fingers I ripped his heart out." I clapped my hands as a butterfly flew into the room and changed into Beverly. "Has anyone seen Viv?" Oh shit! "Not since Darkon's weird game." "I saw her fighting a monster eel. Did she not make it?" "I guess not, she's not in her room....Oh, well. Let me hit that." Bev took a seat next to me and blew me a kiss before putting her luscious lips on the bong. She inhaled and choked shortly after like the both of us did and put her thumbs up while nodding her head yes. "This is the good shit!" "Hell yeah it is. I smuggled that weed in here by hiding it in my rectum." Bev and I shared the same look before turning to look at Z, who smiled and held his hands up. "I'm joking. I made that in the forest room." I tapped him on the shoulder as he got up to leave and took Bev with him. That was a close one, the last thing I needed was for my plan to be found out too soon. My mind was still reeling from my spiritual visit from the bitch who birthed me and I didn't want a repeat of that so I decided to clear my head by going to the forest room. Ding! Ding! Ding! "Welcome to the second round of "Hungry for love". In this round The manipulator of energy will face off against the master of words." Great! I've stupidly walked into another one of the Dark-gods games and this time I have to go up against Mr. Funky balls himself. Of course. I waited for him to say something else but after ten minutes passed I flew into the air and took a deep breath as I allowed my power of flight to carry me over the treetops. An hour passed and I still didn't sense Carl anywhere. "Come on Mr. Funky, where are you?" A chill crawled up my back at the exact moment a swarm of swords whizzed by me and one of them sliced open my left arm and then came together with a loud clang to take the form of Carl. "Now, That was just rude. You caught me in between showers." He threw his hands out and sent a stream of water in my direction. Nope! I made my hands into fists as my new power made them glow and sent out a wave of energy that I let crash against his as the collision made steam form. He stopped the flow of water at the same time that I called back my energy and looked at me with a smile that said he knew that the power wasn't originally mine. "So that's why you were in such a hurry to fuck all of us." I shrugged and lunged at him but he turned into a flock of birds that flew in every direction. "Cheater!" "That's rich, coming from a power thief!" He reformed in the exact spot that I was just in but this time he had a large book in his hands. "From the stars, the plants, the clouds and the sea. I use these words to make more of ME!!!" The book vanished and he separated into three versions of himself but the two extras had distinctive features. The one on the left had a large green glowing cyclops eye, while the one on the left had no ears but breathed green fire. "Three against one, That hardly seems fair." I twisted my body and flew away as hard as I could with them following after me. They tried to hit me with their attacks but my new powers allowed me to sense the energy as it got close to me and I moved to the left and right. If I wasn't fleeing for my life I would have had more fun flying at superspeed but I dove into the forest in an effort to lose them. If only I had more time to practice her powers, I would have been better prepared. So far I could do what I'm doing now and exude her fey-light. If only she had the ability to go invisible. The second I thought the words I felt a weird sensation crawl over my body and I became translucent but not invisible. "I knew it!" The three Carl's sent their elemental attacks at me but they passed right through me to knock down several trees up ahead. "Knew what? That you've got the B-O of a farm animal!" "No! I knew that Viv was the one who ate the ghost and the Banshee." My throat began to tingle as he finished his words and I twisted around to face him with a huge smile on my face. Come on power, don't fail me. I allowed my body to solidify and took a deep breath before yelling as loud as I could in their direction. My throat burned but my vocal shockwave managed to make the cyclops Carl explode into a pile of green dust that receded into the primary one. He lost his balance and the one without ears had to stop chasing me to catch him. "See ya!" I kept going until I was a good distance away and hid in a large cave that smelled awful. The moment that I touched down the cave entrance was covered by thick vines. Viv was holding out on us and now I'm glad that Darkon was just as duplicitous as I am. "Okay, Ash, what's our plan of action?" I jumped at the sound of the dark-Gods deep voice as he stepped out of the shadows. "What the fuck are you doing here psycho?" He put his big hands over his muscular chest and pretended to be hurt as he stopped in front of me. "I'm trying to help you level up while also having a stable form of entertainment." Yeah, this blue-eyed creep was definitely crazy. "Who else is in here?" "Just you and Mr Musty-Balls." Good, I can't handle any other surprises right now. "Trust me. I want out of here just as much as you do." He stepped closer and pulled me into a hug that almost made me wet as his thick arms wrapped around me. "Then why do you keep surprising me at every turn?" "I told you, I'm bored and if we're going to escape this dimension that dear old aunty made, we need to eliminate the extras. Speaking of." He pointed at the vines and they began to recede into the ground as he vanished with that sexy smile of his being the last thing that I saw as he stepped back into the shadows. His dick better be worth all of this or I swear I'll kill him like I did the boar. "Hello, is anybody home?" The sound of Carl's voice echoed down the tunnel before a ball of fire hit the wall across from me. "No, I'm out running errands." I threw my hands out and sent a stream of my energy at the fire breathing clone and knocked him out of the entrance as the primary one stepped forward. "I hope you don't mind double penetration." He yelled. Carl made two glowing daggers appear in his hands as the clone stepped through the entrance with a long tongue of fire coming out of his mouth. "Come on guys, I'm sure we can talk about this." "Oh yeah, Why didn't I think of that?" He threw one of the blades at me and I managed to dodge it but the other one hit me in the thigh. I cried out as it went all the way to the hilt and made me lose feeling in my lower leg. "Ahh!" My cry of pain sent the both of them flying backwards out of the cave and I pulled out the dagger before they could recover. It vanished before hitting the ground as my blood flowed back into my leg and the wound closed. Oh shit, I'm almost invincible. The happiness that I was feeling became short lived as the primary Carl stood in the entrance with a look on his face that made him appear even crazier than he was. He lunged at me but the ground at his feet produced a stalagmite that impaled him and protruded out of his mouth. "I guess you should really watch your words, huh?" My joke fell on deaf ears because he was already dead and his body started to slide down to the floor. Darkon stepped out of the shadows with a smile on his face and took me by the hand to the dead body. He placed my palm on Carl's forehead as his eyes glowed and all of his power flowed into me. The pain was worse than the migraine but it faded just as quick as it formed and in the blink of an eye I was standing in my room with a large book floating next to me. My divine accomplice was nowhere to be found and for that I was grateful. Even though I'm four times as strong as I was before I was thrown into the pocket-dimension, I was starting to get tired of his little tricks. The book floated closer to my left shoulder and glowed before it became a tattoo at the top of my arm. Getting inked was never something that I wanted to do but since this came with new magic I couldn't really complain. A cold chill ran over my body that I recognized as Darkon's energy signature. "How do you feel?" If looks could kill he'd be a pile of sexy dust on the floor with the way that I was currently glaring at him. "I'm shocked at the outcome." My words became tangible as it changed into a lightning bolt that slammed into his chest and knocked him back a couple of feet. He smiled even though his clothes were now reduced to melted fabric. "Okay, Almost there." I feigned a smile as he vanished and left me to my thoughts. With my new powers cleaning myself was even easier now than before. All of my original psychic abilities were heightened to a level that made me feel like I was unstoppable. I could lift my bed off of the ground with one hand, see in the dark and I now have an array of knowledge at the forefront of my mind from the spell book that was almost as old as me. I used the transmogrification spells to change the furniture and make my bed softer. After I finished casting my incantations Grace flew into my room dressed in white lingerie. I couldn't help but to laugh as she sauntered over to me and grabbed my waist. "Damn Girl!" She started to kiss my neck and make her way down to my exposed cleavage but I stopped her before she put her hands in my pants. "Hey, Can we just talk for a second?" Grace pulled back with a frown and stepped back as she crossed her arms. "I'm just trying to put these lips on those lips." She looked down to my vagina and then back up to my face. Normally I would be down for this but my recent battle with the spell master has sucked out all of my sexual energy. "I just want to chill. How about we smoke?" She rolled her eyes and looked to the floor and then back up to me with an expression on her face that said she wanted the opposite to happen. "I'm not a catholic priest and this is not a confessional. Girl bye!" She turned and flew out of my room and I just stood there with my mouth open from her blatant rudeness. She was definitely not an angel of kindness and love. Before anyone else could come in with the sexual intentions, I put the sound barrier up and my new powers made it thicker. My only focus now was to lay in my new bed with a bowl of freshly chopped fruit. A small cloud of glittering white energy formed on the nightstand and took the form of the food that I wanted in a clear crystal bowl. I touched my shoulder and pulled the spell book off of it and began to look over it as I nibbled on pineapple chunks. Three hours passed and I realized that my mind couldn't hold all of the mystical knowledge in the forefront of my mind because of the clashing energies. When I was going up against Carl I wondered why he pulled the book out to do a duplication spell if the book was his. I know all of my magical practices by heart but this was on a different level entirely. I could also sense that its knowledge was something that several thousand generations of spell casters have put together. I willed the book to become my tattoo once more and rolled over onto my side and closed my eyes. Out of nowhere I started to think about the dream visitation with my mothers spirit. She was one of the first people that I sacrificed to the ancient ones and to be truthfully honest she should have been a vengeful spirit instead of a loving mother who thought that her actions were for the betterment of my life. Why would she wait until now to tell me about what my father had planned for me? I've only met the man a handful of times and he was always surrounded by sycophants and servants. He never hugged me or told me how proud he was of me and it all made sense. The great chieftain was scared of my mother because she was vastly more powerful than him. Her people were the original people of America and my fathers people were of the first tribes of the land that is now called Africa. He descended from powerful mystics but none of their power could compare to my maternal lineage. I pushed all of that to the back of my mind and allowed myself to fall asleep as I took in a deep breath and exhaled. Hopefully I won't get another visit from my mother or worse, my father. Instead of seeing either of them I dreamt of complete darkness. Ding-Ding-Ding-Ding! My eyes snapped open from the sound of Darkon's game show bell and I almost screamed at the sight of a giant spider a couple of feet away from me. My body was wrapped in spider silk from the shoulders down to my ankles and I was now attached to a web along with Z, Grace, Bev and Leslie. We were suspended above the ground in the entry room where several spiders waited near all of us as Darkon's large red eyes hovered over our heads. "Welcome contestants to the third round of "Hungry for love". In this round you'll be asked five questions that will decide your fate. Answer incorrectly and one of our little friends will have an early dinner, but if you give the correct answer I'll send you back to your rooms." My super strength was useless as I tried to break free from the webbing. In fact none of my powers worked and seeing a giant black spider this close to me made me want to pass out. I hated those creatures with a passion and when I get free from here I'm going to kick Darkon in the balls so hard that they come out of his mouth. "For the first question, What is my favorite food?" *Of course!* I almost forgot who I was dealing with here. A blue-eyed psycho. Grace took a deep breath and yelled out her answer. "Your favorite food is the souls of your enemies." Ding! "Correct!" The sound of an applause filled the wide room as she vanished and my spider walked over to hers and ate it within seconds before walking over to me with its mouth dripping with spider blood. "Alright! Next question. What do all of you have in common?" I looked at the others who didn't know the answer to the question and then at my spider that moved closer with its mandibles clicking together. Why did it have to be spiders? Leslie wiggled as she happily spoke the answer. "We've all killed intermediate family members." Ding! "Correct!" She vanished and Z's spider ate hers before returning to its position. "Who gave me the best head?" You've got to be kidding me. This nigga is off his mother fucking rocker. "I did!" Beverly shouted out her answer and it took Darkon a full minute to respond. Ding! "I would have accepted two answers but CORRECT!" She vanished and two of the closest spiders crawled over to eat hers as the sound of the invisible audience's applause filled the room once more. "Next question. What is the color of my underwear?" The sound of his laughter echoed off of the walls and his eyes moved across the ceiling like the Cheshire cat in Alice and wonderland. "Just kidding, I'm not wearing any." Ughhh, this god and his antics. "Okay, This is a real question. Who is the most powerful out of the two of you?" Z smacked his teeth and laughed as he looked at me and then back to the floating eyeballs. "Me, I'm a natural born Demigod and not some low level mortal-witch!" His obnoxious laughter was all that you could hear until all of the spiders moved towards him. "Wait-Wait! That was the correct answer. She's a mortal." Boon-Boom! "Wrong answer, Bud!" He let out a loud roar that turned into a scream as all of the spiders began to eat him from different angles and the sound of their mandibles clicking together as they chewed on him was something that I could have lived my entire life without hearing. The sound of his bones snapping in their mouths was the last thing that I heard before I was transported to my room. My skin broke out in gooseflesh as translucent energy formed as my aura and I felt like I was being pulled in every direction. The intense feeling hurt so bad that a burning sensation formed in my stomach right before I shit on myself and pissed a little. It was a good thing that no one was in here with me because I was so embarrassed that I continued to shit until I fell to the floor and landed in it. "W-With words I speak from the heart that I-I mean to clear th-this away to make me clean." My skin broke out in gooseflesh as the spell cleaned up everything and left my room smelling like freshly bloomed flowers. The after effects of my ascension left me feeling as if I ran three miles while punching the air. Everything hurt and the only thing that was getting me through it was the fact that I was getting closer to my goal of being all powerful. I wasn't sure how much time had passed since I cast my spell and laid on the floor as the intense feeling subsided. All of these back-to-back power-ups are taking a lot out of me and I couldn't stop myself from falling asleep. "Welcome back!" I opened my eyes to see the bitch who birthed me sitting at a table with a feast in front of her. There were only two chairs at the table and she motioned for me to sit down. "I'm good." "I said SIT!!" An unseen force pulled me over to the chair so fast that I saw stars swimming in my vision. "Before you attempt to "Kill" me again I need to warn you, Daughter." I smacked my teeth and rolled my eyes as she turned my chair. "Do I have another father that wants to rape me?" "NO, YOU'RE FLIRTING WITH DANGER!!!" My eyes snapped open at the exact moment that Darkon stepped through my doorway. "How do you feel?" "Why do you keep asking me that?" "Because I need to know if your body is adjusting to your new divinity correctly." He waved his hand out in front of me and my body slowly floated upwards so that I could stand up. "I'm fine." The second that he was close enough to me I kicked him in the balls but he just smiled at me. "I used to get abused by my father on a daily basis. There isn't anything that you can do to me, Princess." He stepped forward at super speed and punched me in the gut and then took my head and bashed it against his knee so hard that I swore I felt my nose break. "This next test will be an obstacle course. Consider yourself warned." He threw me to the ground and teleported out of the room as I rubbed my healing nose. "JERK!" His balls left a small indentation on top of my foot that stung as it healed and I made a mental note to kill him last. With a thought I resurrected the barrier in my doorway and laid in bed since there wasn't anything else that I could do. It was times like this that I missed having a television to watch my favorite shows. My forehead pulsed with energy as a large floating crystal appeared at the foot of the bed and displayed my favorite television show, Murder & Money. "Okay, I see why those who are divine don't need anyone else for shit." Yeah, Now I really don't have to leave this room unless I want to. I spent the next seven hours binge watching every episode of my favorite show and then watching the cooking channel for another three hours until the remaining supernatural beings floated outside of my doorway. "Come in." The barrier vanished as I spoke the words and the wielders of my soon-to-be powers stepped into the room wearing pajamas. Bev was the first to speak as she looked around the room and noticed the changes that I made. "Can we join you?" "Sure." Grace narrowed her eyes on me as she walked over to the bed and sat next to me. The others made snacks appear as they made themselves comfortable and manifested a charcuterie platter with several bottles of white wine. "Grace, Is there something that you want to say to me?" "Yes, I've been working up the courage to tell you how fat I think your ass is and I can't wait for the day that you sit on my face." Everyone laughed as I changed the television to the nature channel and it just so happened to show an animal documentary about black widows. "Too soon?" Grace stuck her tongue out at me as I changed it to a Romantic comedy. It was the funniest movie that I ever saw and my slumber party pals thought so as well. After the movie went off we decided to watch a horror movie about a group of demons who incarnated as children and wreaked havoc in the life of anyone that they came in contact with. It kind of reminded me of another movie that I went to see on a date a couple years back. The movie had so many jump scares that you'd think we were mortal in the way that we all flinched every time a demon snatched up someone. "That was a good one." "Yeah, I loved how it was almost true." I looked over at Grace who would know about that because she was one of the fallen angels.

"Did it make you miss your kids?"

"No, I killed all of my children. They didn't live up to my expectations."

"You're serious?"

"Yup!"

"Were they half human?" She snorted and rolled her eyes as she made herself more comfortable on the bed. "Not in the way that you know humans to be in this era. They were Omniterran-Angel hybrids." I remember an elder in my tribe telling me about the powerful immortal beings who were almost as powerful as the deities that we pray to. Who were the true ancestors to my ancestors. "Please tell us more." A smile curved her lips as she sat up and refilled our wine glasses. "When my older sister created this universe, it was filled with lower-level beings who were immortal and mortal. Meaning that they had the potential to live forever but they could be killed by one another. Their souls would just pass on to another form or they would reconstruct their bodies. My angelic siblings teamed up with the other divine beings while our parents weren't looking and came down here to have a little fun. We did all kinds of things to them to make them wreak havoc all over the globe and then turn on each other. They grew to be more powerful from all of it but almost destroyed the earth, so big sis and a bunch of other goddesses banished half of them and dialed down their power levels." That explained a lot about why humans have immortal souls but mortal bodies that can access certain levels of magical power. "What did you do to the first people of this world?" Grace laughed so hard she snorted as her wings moved behind her. "What didn't I do? I was so jealous of the unconditional love that she showed your ancient ancestors. She never looked at me as a sibling and sent me here about ten million years ago." My mouth fell open from hearing that. Grace had been locked away for longer than I've been alive. No wonder she was a psycho. "Whoa!" Grace looked past me and pointed to the shadows that moved towards us. They attached themselves to our own shadows and in the blink of an eye we were transported to the forest room that was now an obstacle course. "He's really starting to piss me the fuck off!" "Yeah!!" Ding-Ding-Ding! "Welcome to the fourth round of "hungry for love". In this round you'll have to compete in my brand new obstacle course for your lives. Have fun and make me proud." There were no floating eyeballs this time but we could hear the sound of animals in this distance that were placed within the obstacle course. None of us waited for a buzzer as we flew into the air and headed to the starting point. With Grace being in the lead position she was the first to be attacked by a giant carnivorous plant. Leslie and Beverly used that as a chance to slip through the other plants and onto the next course. I sent out a bolt of lightning from the tip of my finger and allowed Grace to escape from the plant but more plants swarmed us as we tried to move forward. "Thanks, demigoddess." Her comment cost me a moment of distraction that gave two plants the chance to wrap themselves around my arms and legs. I took a deep breath and exhaled pure white fire but it did nothing to the plant that was tightening its hold on me to the point of being uncomfortable. Grace left me to my own devices as she flew through the exit while dodging the snapping plants. "Bitch!" She gave me the middle finger as she vanished through the exit and I let loose a shockwave of energy as I was pulled into the plant's mouth. Now that my hands were free I held them over my head while making a translucent energy sphere around me at the exact moment that the plant tried to crush me. I took a deep breath as I widened the sphere and made the plants head-mouth explode with a loud pop. It caused the surrounding plants to turn to face me but I shifted into my intangible form and flew through them as if they were nothing. I don't why I didn't think of it before but it was definitely a power that I will be using more of. The second I passed through to the next course I stopped as a flock of scary looking owls flew at me with their talons poised for an attack. "With mystical knowledge I received from the arcane mage I use this spell to place you all in a cage." My tongue and palms began to itch as I the spell solidified and trapped them in a large cage before they could reach me. I quickly made my way through the exit and entered a part of the forest where the trees were grouped so close together that it blocked out all of the light except for the glowing lake in front of me. Its blue-green light made the shadows dance as large fish moved beneath the surface. "There's no time like the present, Princess!" I put my middle fingers up into the air before taking a deep breath and diving into the lake. The change in temperature was slightly uncomfortable but I powered through it and swam with everything that I had as a group of vicious piranhas headed towards me. There was no way that I could use spells or become intangible so I looked the two closest fish in the eyes and mind controlled them to turn on the other fish. They became a feeding frenzy of blood and scales that I quickly swam past and made my way to the other side. I don't know where I got the ability to hold my breath this long but I really didn't care. It was helping me get through this and I swam faster as some of the fish behind me broke away from the others to chase after me. Fuck! It was like something out of a horror movie in the way that it closed the gap between us and bit off my left foot before I could make it to the surface. My breath escaped my mouth as I broke the surface and crawled across the rocky shore that cut my arms and legs. I continued to crawl on my stomach even though it hurt like hell and the fish followed me out of the water as it sprouted frog-like appendages and snapped at my other foot. I cried out as it bit off my toes and I heard the sound of Darkon's laughter echoing around the small enclosed space. "Fuck this shit, It's not what I truly desire, with that being said I unleash crimson fire." My words came out as heat waves that cooked the fish from the inside out and then evaporated the small lake behind me. The pain of my body healing itself was almost unbearable and made me scream as my bones grew back but I continued on through the exit as if my life depended on it. Once my feet were completely healed I stood up and ran into the next room but the second I walked through the entrance something sharp stabbed me in the ribs. "I thought you should have this." I looked down to see an old rusty blade sticking out of my side and Beverly smiling as she pulled it out. "You snake ass bitch!" She giggled like a schoolgirl while skipping through the brightly lit forest and threw the blade away from her. "See ya!" She turned the corner as I stumbled sideways and slowly healed but I could feel that something was different this time. My wound burned like someone slapped me with a handful of salt as it closed up into a scar. "Oh! You gotta watch out for those divine weapons, Princess!" my blue eyes tormentor spoke. "Fuck you, Psycho!" It continued to burn but I pressed forward and was almost beheaded by an ax that came out of nowhere and then a steady stream of arrows that whizzed by me so fast that one of them grazed my back. "One more thing! Watch out for the traps!" His dick better be good as fuck for all of what he has put me through. I made my way to the exit while sustaining more wounds but it didn't matter because my body healed them faster than the stab wound that was now a small scar. I turned the corner and almost stepped into a large pool of quicksand that slowly pulled Beverly down into it. "Oh hey, Bev. How's it going?" I said, taunting her. She ignored me and took the form of a giraffe but her body painfully shifted back as she screamed in pain. I looked above her head at the hanging vines that she tried to latch onto and made them move like snakes down to her. The two faced bitch pulled herself upwards but I used telekinesis to separate it from the others and she screamed as she fell all the way into the quicksand. "I thought you should have that!" I flew over the pit of sand to the exit and a flash of red light was all that I could see until it faded away and I was standing in my room. "You did an amazing job." Darkon appeared next to me with a bloody heart on a silver plate and handed it to me. "Eat that so that you can gain her powers." Even though I wasn't hungry I snatched it up and devoured it like it was my last meal. It tasted awful but as I finished it off my heart began to beat faster in my chest and make me light headed. I changed into a crow and then became a house cat as Darkon clapped like he was at a circus. "Your black fur is so shiny. Come here little pussy." He bent down to pick me up but I scratched his indestructible skin and he just laughed as he stepped back into a shadow portal. Yeah, get your crazy ass out of here, you insufferable god of insanity. I spent the next hour changing into every animal that I could think of and was glad that my clothes reappeared when I took human form. Ding! Ding! Ding! You've got to be kidding me. Ughh!! Ding! Ding! Ding! I waited for him to transport me to the forest room for our next competition but nothing happened and the sound continued. "Would Gracelvential, Luvera and Princess Shiernazat report to the entry room." How the fuck did he know my real name? Anyone who knew it was either dead or on my list to die a painful death at my own hands. "Princess Shiernazat, will you report to the entry room? I repeat, would princess Shiernazat report to the entry room?" I walked out of my room and floated down to the floor where the two remaining supernatural beings waited. Our sexy game host was nowhere to be found and I was starting to think that we were going to have to fight each other in hand to hand combat. "You are correct, all of you will now compete in a battle royale for the final round." I summoned my energy to my hands as Leslie pulled two glowing potion bottles out of her pockets and grace flew into the air. The two of them must have come up with a plan to double team me because Leslie threw her potions at me at the exact moment that Grace rained down sharp feathers all around me. I back flipped out of the way and turned into a mouse and then changed into a rhino as Grace swooped down to attack me. Leslie threw more of her exploding potions at me but my thick skin was more than a match for them and I trampled her to death as she let out a scream before her head busted open like a watermelon. "Now all I have to do is take care of heaven's disgraced winged-baby-princess." "Then it's a battle of royalty then!" I changed back into my human form as she sent more glowing feathers my way but twisted through the air and climbed upwards to be on her level. "Do you want me to wait for you to steal her powers?" She asked. "Nope, I can wait until you're dead." I sent out a stream of white energy as she matched it with her own energy and the collision created a loud boom that echoed around us. We continued to sling our energy attacks at each other until it was all that you could hear and I had to give the angel her props. She was a formidable opponent, but I was ready for this to be over. I have a world to conquer and melanated people to liberate. "Just so you know, I was on to your little plan from the start." Grace said, as she twisted through the air. "Uh-huh!" I sent out a wave of translucent energy that sent her flying backwards into the wall. "Oh, honey. I was born in an entirely different dimension. Your little powers don't hurt me." She shrugged off the wall and her eyes glowed as another pair of wings sprouted from her back. "Then why did you just power-up?" She ignored my question and lunged forward at superspeed to punch me in the chest and throw me to the ground. I tried to stop myself by using my own powers but the angel kneed me in the back and pushed me into the ground hard enough to snap my spine. "Ahhh, You bitch!" "Don't act like you don't deserve it." She got up off of me as I flipped over and my spine repaired itself. My shadow moved on its own and pointed at itself before it crawled up my arms to become a dark aura. "Let me help you." The sound of his deep voice whispering in my mind gave me all the courage that I needed as I stood up straight and looked the winged bitch in the eyes. "This ends NOW!" "I couldn't agree more." She responded. I allowed my power of flight to carry me up to her height and propel me forward. She threw punches and kicks that I matched with my own martial arts moves and we fought in the air for a while until I grabbed her by the wings. "Ahhh!" "Oh, are these sensitive?" I snapped her left wing in half and threw her to the ground as she screamed in agony. "Awww, did the little birdy break a wing?" I pointed at her and sent out a blast of my combined power and she tried to match it with her own but it was pointless as my energy reduced her to a bloody pile of glowing feathers. Darkon separated himself from me and lowered himself to the ground with a smile on his face. "Absorb those and her divinity is yours." I lowered myself to the pile of feathers and focused on calling the feathers to my body. They whirled around like a miniature tornado before moving like darts and stabbing me all over my body. It felt like I was being poked by a thousand hot needles as they wiggled into my flesh. The pain felt like it lasted for an eternity and my back hurt the most until my shoulder blades split open and black feathered wings sprang from my back. A weird sensation that was hot then cold formed on my forehead as all of the colors in the room became sharper and I realized I could see the residual energy of the previous inhabitants.. "How do you feel?" Darkon appeared next to me holding a full length mirror that he placed in front of me. I laughed out loud as I took in my new form. I had four large wings that were covered in black feathers and a large eye on my forehead that glowed with multicolored energy. "So?" He sent the mirror away as he stepped in front of me and put his hands on my shoulder. "I feel like a goddess." "Great answer." Darkon leaned forward and pressed his luscious pink lips against mine. Yeah this was totally worth it. I deepened the kiss and put my arms over his neck as everything else faded away. It was absolute bliss until I felt his tongue move over mine and then go down my throat. Darkon inhaled and I felt my body growing tired as he lifted me off of the ground. I began to lose the feeling in the rest of my body and tried to pull away but he held me in a tight embrace until I fell backwards and floated above the ground. I watched as the dark god absorbed my body into his and then he looked up at me with a sinister smile. "Fuck! That was good!" "Y-You killed me!" "What can I say? I was hungry for love." My mother was right once again and I allowed my need for power to blind me to the most dangerous being in existence. He held his hands above his head and my non corporeal body began to move forward like I was being sucked into a vacuum. "You should have listened to your mother, Princess." That was the last thing I heard before I ceased to exist.

Room For I I I

"Did you hear me, Thomas?" Parker Vermillion kept going on about the rest of my unexpected inheritance from a boujee aunt that I only ever met once. Dear old aunty wouldn't pay for college and couldn't even bother to come to my parent's funeral, but I'm in her will? Girl bye! "What's the catch?" "To what? Inheriting one hundred and eighty million dollars and a mansion. Tommy, as your lawyer, I'm advising you to accept this. Your media company needs this." Fuck! Fuck! Fuck! He was right. I'm behind on my loan and credit cards could use the break. "Just think about it this way, you can now move out of that building and into a better one and still be extremely wealthy." "Okay, what do I have to do?" "Stay at her house in Ohio for thirty days." I took a deep breath before answering and decided a smart-ass remark wouldn't help my situation. "Sure. When do I have to be there?" "You're expected to be there this coming Tuesday. There's a manservant named Trimark who is fine as fuck, honey!" Now we're talking. "Send me the information, and I'll book a flight." "Uh, no! You also inherited a jet! They've got everything covered. Just let me know the day that you want to leave, and he'll be waiting at the airport for your arrival." "I'll be ready by noon tomorrow." "Perfect. I'll send you his information." "Thank you, Mille." "I should be thanking you. They paid me a nice little chunk of change to be your official lawyer after signing the NDA." Of course, they did. "I have to go home and pack, so I'll see you tomorrow." I hung up the phone and shut my laptop down while doing a little dance from excitement.

Money-Money-Money-money! My personal assistant, Kelly Hamming, walked in with her usual sad face, dampening my mood. "Sorry to interrupt this booty-bouncing dance party, but I need a favor, boss." My twerking continued as she walked in, and I could see that she'd been crying. "Yes, you can have the rest of the day off." "Thank you, boss. I promise I'll come in early tomorrow and work extra hard." "No need. I'll be in Columbus, Ohio, for a family emergency. Tell everyone that they'll have the next two months off with pay but will have to return with something good if they want to remain under my employment." That managed to perk up her sadness about whatever woman broke her heart this week. "Yes, sir." "Also, don't forget to send out the paychecks to the maintenance crew and include them and Vivian's department in on what's going on." With one final nod, she left, and I knew the bitch was going to blow her money on toys for her kids and pills for herself. After packing up my stuff, I left through my personal elevator to the parking garage, where an all-black brand new four-door sedan waited for me. I froze at the sight of the most attractive man that I've ever seen sitting on the hood. "Oh, Hey, you must be Thomas. I'm Derrick. Your driver." I could have sworn my lawyer said he'd be waiting for me after I landed, not at the bottom of my building. Creepy-but sexy. "Yes, thank you for waiting." "No problem, big booty." "Excuse me?" "Sorry, it's not every day that you get to see something like that with a face and a body. Mmmm, Damn!" The tall, dark-skinned man with blue eyes and pearly-white teeth flipped over on the hood and humped it as he looked me in the eyes. It was like he was too attractive to look at, and for some reason, I felt like I was in the presence of a tiger or something. He opened the door, and a cold chill crawled down my back as I stepped into the back seat and made myself comfortable. It was the latest model of the Vixen-VLX and I have to admit even I was stunned. "This is nice. Will you be working for me permanently?" "Yes. This is permanent." He closed the door and sprinted over to the other side with his muscled butt cheeks dancing as he moved. What a lovely day this is.

"Would you like some champaign?"

"Uh, yes. I drink like a sea-crab. Prepare to pick me up drunk twenty four seven for the next two weeks."

"Yes, Sir."

He left the parking lot and I emptied my glass and poured myself another as he hit the expressway. "Hey, No We're going to get my stu- " My tongue started to tingle right before I lost the feeling in it and he looked at me through the rearview mirror while he laughed. "Good night, brown eyes. Don't let the booty bugs bite." I wanted to grab the door but my entire body started to fall back into the seat and he turned around to cop a feel on my thighs. "You're a sitto!" I meant to day sicko, but whatever was in the wine started to take an even greater effect as he turned back around. The last thing I remember was the pain from biting my tongue and slumping to the side as the car moved forward. Unconsciousness yanked me into the world of slumber where I had the strangest dreams. In the first one, I was an actual crab that walked across the ocean floor as various forms of sea life passed by me. Off in the distance a giant squid and sting ray were fighting in a battle that was making the seafloor tremble. *Follow your heart.* I blinked and the dream changed to me running at full speed through a weird forest. My legs kept going until I reached a tree that poured down rain and snow into a puddle of glowing water. *Remember!* Images flashed on the surface like a television screen and showed me dark skinned indigenous Americans fighting in some kind of mystical war with non-melanated people and then showed me images of chattel slavery. "Wake up!" I snapped my eyes open to the sight of my driver, Derrick with two extra eyes on his forehead and a long blue unicorn horn jutting out of the top of his head. "Alright, I did my part. He's awake!" This had to be another dream. I was in the weird forest from my dream and Derrick also had hooves to match his mystical horse look. A laugh escaped my lips as I took in his entire form and our eyes met. "Aww, look at him. He hasn't changed yet. How cute." I turned to my left to see an all white moth person with large blue wings. At first I couldn't tell if it was a boy or girl because of the absence of nipples and front private parts. "How dare you!" It stepped forward and slapped me across the face so hard it made my ears ring. The attack made me aware of the sticky blue silk that was holding me to the tree. "Until next time, big booty." Unicorn-Derrick's eyes glowed red as he vanished in a cloud of black smoke. "Over here craby-bitch!" The moth's Shadow moved across the ground and took the form of a large centipede with bright green eyes and teeth. Its deep voice reminded me of the demon from my favorite horror movie. "Mommies, dead and there's no one here to save you." I have to be dreaming. There is no way that this cast of Alisha in Wonderland is real. "Okay, the stunts and shows are giving nervous breakdown. I'll just wait for this dream to end." They laughed and off in the distance I could hear the sound of a roaring lion. "Uh-oh! My little Kitten-nugget is awake." The moth person stretched its beautiful wings and flew off in the direction of the beast with a trail of blue dust behind him. "Good, we're alone. Where is the Amulet?" *Seriously?* This figment of my nightmare is asking me questions. When will this shit end? Ugh? "Hey, don't ignore me, little crab." I looked to the right as it moved to face me and then I looked to the left to avoid its green gaze. "Very well. Little boy." That's it! "Who the fuck are you calling a little boy. Bitch! I'm thirty-three." As a man of color, I've always hated being called that because I knew its derogatory origin. "See that's where you're wrong." It moved forward and took the form of a tall dark skinned drag queen. For a figment of my imagination she was beautiful but the eyes and teeth made her look evil. "I am evil!" "Right, I'm in a dream. So knowing what's in my mind is perfectly normal and not at all something that I should go see a therapist about." "Ms. Media mouth. I'm going to suck the divinity out of every single particle you have and leave you as a husk of dry skin and flabby cheeks." What! I've been told that I have a bubble butt, a juicy bottom and a dumpy, but never have I ever been called flabby. My hand started to hurt from making a fist and caused me to look down as the pain crawled up my arm. "Mmm, I love a crab boil." "Look here bitch, I don't know what this dream is telling me, so I'm checking out." She reached out with her long fingernails and freed me from the silk with a slash of her hand. As I tumbled to the ground I tried to stop myself from hitting the dirt and screamed when I saw that my entire left hand was now a white crab pincher. "I told you, this ain't no dream Honey. I'm going to eat those powers. Now where is the Amulet?" She kicked me in the ribs and sent me flying into a tree that knocked the wind out of my lungs. It took a couple tries before I could breathe normally again as she walked over to me like a slow serial killer. "I am the Night-Mother. I want those powers. Correction, I need those powers to effectively execute my plan. Now where is the Amulet?" Her body changed back into an all black demon centipede with glowing eyes and teeth. "Where is the Amulet?" "Bitch, I. Don't. Know!" What in the supervillain drag show is going on here? Animal body parts, a dark creepy forest, And an invisible Amulet?

"I've really got to stop smoking a bunch of weed before bed. Okay, where is the exit?"

"Where is the Amulet?" "What are you talking about?"

I got up and ran with everything that I had before my legs changed like my hand. Light from the glowing mushrooms made things partially visible as I passed by what looked like old snakeskin and blood. As I ran deeper into the weird forest my body shook off the tired feeling from earlier but the fear of being in a coma started to creep over my mind. I must have had a heart attack after hearing about the money and knocked myself out before hitting the floor. "I'm right behind you." It yelled. "Duh! Bitch, you're a follower and apparently a thief!" Since this was a dream I figured I'd have some fun while I'm here. I can't remember the last time that I was being chased by a monster drag queen in a nightmare. The monster struck me from behind and sent me tumbling to the ground but instead of falling on my face, my pincher spewed out white mist that turned into a bed of snow that cushioned my fall. "Yes, that's it." I twisted in the snow and turned around to face the monster that was now nowhere to be seen. As the seconds passed my breathing normalized but I kept myself on guard just in case it popped out of the shadows. For some strange unknown reason I felt safe in the snow that crawled up the tree and made jagged horizontal icicles form. Seconds turned into minutes and then what I guessed was a half an hour passed as I remained in the snow.

The wind shifted and brought with it the smell of something burning right before a cloud of black smoke appeared next to a fallen tree. Large yellow eyes looked at me from inside the smoke and I stopped breathing as the sound of it moving closer broke the silence. "I'm here to help." I turned left and right to look for the origin of the voice that sounded like a man my age. "Stay right there!" I backed up as it moved closer and the smoke faded to show a huge Lion with large bat wings and a scorpion tail. Great now the circus is complete. "I don't have a lot of time to explain, let's go." It kneeled down and motioned with its tail for me to get on its back. "Hell no, I'm not a cat person." It snorted and whipped its tail in my direction and it changed into an anaconda that wrapped around me as the beast took off into the forest. I wanted to scream but the head of the snake hissed and breathed black smoke into my face and it felt like I was high and tipsy at the same time. "Talaset, he's still awake!" The lion's voice echoed in my head as the snake moved closer and looked me in the eyes. "He'sssss in the processs, of awakening." It said, in a raspy voice. "Okay! Now I'm really tripping, the snake just talked." "My name is Talaset, Crabby!" I couldn't resist the urge to laugh as I realized that I was most definitely in a nightmare that was a result from a coma. That's the only explanation as to why any of this is happening and why I'm as aware of all of this as I am. The smell of the forest mixed with my cold-claw made this feel like I was away on a vacation and the seasons were about to change. "This is nice." The snake gave me a confused look as we entered a cave entrance that was hidden by overgrown foliage. My nose picked up the smell of cinnamon and lavender as the lion took us into a cavern with floating stones that led up into an opening that showed daylight. What the fuck? I blinked repeatedly as my eyes adjusted to the sun and my cold-claw began to let off steam from the change in temperature. "Welcome to our home." It put me down on a soft patch of grass and folded his wings onto his back. "I'm Cameron, This is Talaset." His mane moved on its own and the face of a goat peered out of the end of it. "I'm Quilphomet." Now we've ventured into the capital of wonderland. "Um, hello. What the fuck is happening and why did you spit-hiss in my face?" The three of them shared a concerned look and then turned to look at me. I was still a little woozy from the hit of his breath so my upper half moved back and forth as I looked around the area. "The haze was to help you through your ascension. You're an ocean and winter deity." The talking snake pointed at my legs and I laughed as I looked down to see that I was no longer human. My medium build and big booty were now replaced with a body of a blue and white crab with large pinchers and dragonfly wings. "Hey, when did I get those?"

"This is not a good sign, Cameron. He needs to snap out of this before our reinforcements arrive." My physical demonic assistants gave me one last look before they changed back into their other forms as my mane and tail. "Whoa, where did your friends go?" Great, I'm now left with a newly awakened demigod that's in a euphoric state, thanks to Talaset. "Thomas, you need to have a seat. This is serious." "Okay, Okay. I'm good." The giant snow crab remained still but continued to use his wings to hover off of the ground as I changed into my human form and took a seat on the ground.

"This place is a dimension created by evil divine beings that use it to secretly eat other divine beings and take their powers. You're not dreaming, this is the reality that's outside of the reality that you call earth. I've been here for a couple of years."

"I'm human, and this is a dream. Lucid dreaming is a normal thing for those who are indigenous to America. That's what this is. So what are you, Satan's kitty?"

"That's just rude. I'm a demigod like you. Our mothers are a part of the same council of deities called the Mothers of Magick!"

"No, I'm a black man who was born in Columbus, Ohio but raised in New York and this is a dream."

"Then why are you a magical talking crab?"

"This is a dream. I'm sure if I wanted to be a fox with bat wings, I could."

He held his claws out and stretched his body in an attempt to change and nothing happened after a few tries. "No! You're a reincarnated divine being who probably had some tragic backstory in a past life but chose to be mortal in this one for some type of normalcy."

"Look here Mr. Light skin. This is a dream and to be honest it would be a good one if I was into light skinned men. I prefer some chocolate. Not a fur ball. I'll be going. Good Day to you, kind sir!" Thomas flapped his wings and flew off in the direction of the entrance that vanished once we entered my pocket dimension. I'll give him a day to figure out that this is not a dream and that I'm trying to help him escape from here with his divinity intact. My hair grew and Quilphomet's face formed as the tips weaved themselves together. "I found out who he is, Boss." "Okay…" He waited and shifted his eyes to the rocks on the ground as a form of payment for his work. "Fine!" This goat demon was as hungry as he was a vast pit of knowledge.

"Just so you know. My wings transport me through the air. My tail protects my backside and transports me to anywhere I want to go with smoke. Now can you tell me what your job is?" "Mmmm, Oh yes. Those are some good bouldres." He continued to chew as I made myself more comfortable. "I'm waiting." "Hold your hooves, I'm eating, Bruh!" Here we go. Stress eating and avoidance. "Are you done?" My goat demon nodded and closed the distance between us. "He's the son of the mother of the day, Asdzaa." Oh shit! Their familial story was one of the most gruesome of all the divine legends. "He must have the day amulet and not know it." "The ether speaks of it being around his neck but only he can call it into the physical realm." Fuck! That makes him a beacon for them to track and even though he is safe in here. As a seasonal deity he can't stay here forever. "So that means the day spider mother is dead and that's why the night mother wants the amulet to pair with her shadow crown." "The ether is showing me a Spider made of shadows with claws of frost aiding us. Expect company. Goodnight!" Whoa! If he was able to relay a message from the astral realm then I was not left here by my mother. My ears picked up the sound of Thomas's wings moving closer as the wind brought in a cool breeze. "This shit is real!" He was now human from the waist up with the lower part of him as the white and blue crab. "I'm ready to talk." All I could do was smile as he made himself comfortable on a chair of ice that he made with his powers. "May I ask why the sudden change of heart?" He frowned at my question and shifted his body to face me. "What do you mean by sudden? I was wondering out there for two years." It was my turn to frown from his response and the seriousness on his face. "I think the combination of my awakening with the dream energy from being knocked out and the aerosol cocktail that your tail sprayed at me plunged me into a quickening that resulted in this. I searched for two years and learned a little bit more about myself on the way."

My cheeks blushed as I realized that this was my fault for allowing him to go off without telling him how the pocket dimension worked.

I made this place after I realized I couldn't teleport or transport myself out of here and didn't want to constantly be on the run from those parasites.

"You weren't expecting this, were you?" I asked.

"No, you're very handsome." His beautiful smile replaced his seriousness as he made himself all the way human and walked over to sit next to me on the rock. "I'm sorry for what I said about not liking light skin men. I was coming from a place of confusion/anger and wasn't thinking clearly. This is serious, and we're in danger." He placed his hand over mine and looked me in the eyes. Was this a sign that he was into me? Or am I tripping? "Sorry, was that too forward." "No, you're good." I moved closer and changed our rock into a couch of the same pale orange color. "So we're both gods?" uh-oh! "Sort of. My mother is Ammit, the devourer, and my father is the divine monster, Chimera and first-born child of Typhon." I waited for him to get up and run like everyone else does when I tell them who gave me life. "Okay, I'm a reincarnated spider-crab-dragonfly deity whose mother allowed all of her kids to kill themselves in battle. I can sense that that is something that prevents you from meeting new people." "Wow! "Did you get a psychology degree while you were out there?" He laughed, and for once in my long life, I joined him in the joke itself instead of being the joke. After a minute passed, we managed to stop laughing, and I could see that this was where we needed to get serious about our situation. "Were you abducted too?" "Yes, but I've been waiting for you. You're my assignment." It felt good to finally say that and not sound like a crazy stalker. "Did you know that you'd be here for this long?" I shook my head no and could see his smile fade as he looked to the floor.

"I'm sorry."

"There is no need to apologize. I'm almost a million years old. Waiting two years in a pocket dimension is nothing when it comes to divine timing."

He leaned forward and placed his soft lips on mine, and we kissed for what felt like an eternity until he pulled away with a frown. "My neck feels weird." Thomas reached into his shirt and produced a silver amulet with blue crystals over its surface. "Is this what they're asking for?" Thomas placed it around his neck, and it started to glow with his blue and white power. He blinked as the energy formed in his eyes, and he went into a vision trance. It was the first time that I'd seen another deity use the power of prognostication outside of dreaming of the future. As a monster, I have Quilphomet but seeing Thomas float off the ground and exhale a wintery blast at his shadow was an amazing sight to see. That was until I sensed the presence of another divine being crawling out of his shadow. It was an all-black spider with frozen claws and dark blue glowing eyes. I've met him several times but never had the pleasure of working with him because of his divine mission to either protect the night-born like himself or protect Thomas. Once the summoning was done, Thomas fell into Trimark's arms, and he walked over to my outside couch and placed him next to me. "I am so sorry, Thomas." I reached out and placed a hand on his large shoulder in an attempt to console him and also finally get a feel for his thick shoulder. "Are you Trimark?" I asked. He nodded yes, and I felt him relax a little. "Cameron!" I nodded as he made himself comfortable, and we sat there with the breeze blowing around us like this was normal. We were sitting on a couch that was outside in a forest that I made inside a pocket dimension. As a direct descendant of Gaia, it was easy, but I hate being here. It was like being stranded on an island with killers. This mission was the first one I'd been on in a very long time, and now it all made sense. "How long have you been here?" "Two years." "It's been two days since your mother sent you on this mission, Cameron." My heart leaped into my chest, and I almost jumped off of the couch from the good news. "We're in a dimension created by the fey prince." Of course. I thought that the ugly bitch of night made this place after it took me seven attempts to make the forest we are in now. "I can see that this is your doing." He pointed to the daylight and smiled at me. Thomas woke up. "Nope, still here." Thomas looked at me and then turned to Trimark, who flashed him a smile. "Hello. Handsome." And just like that, I'm invisible again. "What did I do to deserve two boyfriends?" He placed one hand on my knee and the other on Trimarks. "I'm your appointed guardian. Trimark." "Mmm, so I'm going to be making out with you while bouncing on you." He turned to look at me, and I couldn't tell if he was joking or being serious. Before he summoned Trimark, he was absolutely sure that this was real. Now, he probably thinks that this is another part of his dream where he is about to have a three-way. "Ohh, he gets it." Thomas grabbed Trimark's arm with his left hand and moved to sit on my lap in one swift move. With it being unexpected, I could see that the shadow spider god was just as uncomfortable as I was. "Thomas. We can't." He removed his grasp and got up to look at me and then Trimark. "So this isn't happening?" "This can't happen here." "I agree." Deep down, I would have allowed it to go all the way, but I don't know if that was something that the new addition to our team would want to do. "Just so you both know, I'm a top." Thomas and I shared a look that said we both were on the same page. Good. I never did the monogamy thing. "With our impending three-way on the shelf, what do we do first?" That was a good question. Now that he has the amulet and a more enlightened grasp on his powers the three of us stood a chance in escaping. Possibly even killing my ex-best friend, Xilligar. "I have a suggestion." I spent the next three hours telling them about how I used to be friends with the moth Fey prince who killed his sister and absorbed her power of creation. "Damn, divine families are a lot like normal families with longer lives. Why didn't her mother do anything?" "She had other children, so it wasn't a bother to her, but their father increased the ladybug population in the mortal realm and banished Xilligar to the dimension that's outside of this one. Which reminds me. We only have another week in here until it starts to dissolve." "That's just sad." "Tell me about it. My father is the night-mother." Thomas gasped and turned to look at Trimark with glowing eyes. "What? How- I mean, I know how? But what?" He took a deep breath and looked from me to Thomas before he told us about his divine lineage that I knew bits and pieces of.

"Thomas, you know about the war of siblings that almost destroyed the world from your family's perspective, but you don't really know mine."

"I know that I fought my sisters in my first incarnation as Talvsneith, the embodiment of water, ice, and winter. Sea demigods wandered into my domain, and after I saved them from vicious beasts, I learned that they were children of Oceanus who came to ask for a divine favor. After granting the favor, They left and promised to return but never did." "That's because my ancestor was captured by your siblings and was forced to reproduce divine children with the power that you gave them." The crab-god turned to face a wall of trees as the memories of his past life flashed in his mind. "Is this normal?" I reached out and placed my hand on Trimark's knee as Thomas got up and walked over to the tree-wall. He nodded as our third member muttered to himself, and I used that as a chance to scoot closer. "This is my fault." "No, It was my past life's fault for leading his siblings into deadly territory. Your sisters were spider goddesses like your mother, and it was later that she learned that the night mother used her power to seduce them into doing evil deeds. After all of us were dead and in the reincarnation cycle, the mother of the day used the night-mother's power against her by tricking her into turning herself into a male divine aspect and not being able to change back. The mother of the day also made it so that she could only appear in the earthly realm as a shadow." "Well, that explains the drag queen aesthetic. So you're a demigod born from a father?" He held his hand up and moved it like a tambourine while making a face that said what he was about to tell us would be weird. *Cool.* "My father moved through the astral realm and possessed two night-borns and forced them into using sex magic so that my spirit could reincarnate. He was going to raise me in secret and fuse his soul to mine at the age of twenty-nine." I could see that the rest had a lot to do with the Titaness Hecate and the mother of day intervening and raising Trimark as their own. "What's the deal with our parents"?" "They're opposing forces that refuse to exist outside of their natural opposition to one another. I think that's changed now, though." "Because he's the owner of the amulet." I had to cut in, or this threesome would never happen, and I'd be on the bed by myself with no one to touch me. "Let's do this." Thomas floated up off of the ground and changed his lower half into his divine crab form while making a spear of ice in his hand. Trimark and I made our lower halves into our beast form, and he summoned a large ax. "You're not going to join the weapons club?" I held up my hands and changed my hands into silver claws as Talaset changed from scorpion stinger to his serpent form. "Oh! I forgot that you're part chimera. Wicked!"

Now that Thomas and I were mentally ready, the dimension would fade even faster than before and drop us off in the nightmare forest where the monster drag queen and other misfits waited for us. "The unisex moth is mine. I'm going to tear off his wings like he did his sister's." My sun dipped behind the fake mountains in the background, and I knew that our time was almost up. "When we make it out of this, can we go on a date? As a throuple?" Thomas and Trimark nodded as the sunlight faded, and we dropped into the forest that was void of life. The three of us landed on the ground with our defensive attachments raised in anticipation of an attack. "I'm just now noticing that the plant life grows here and nothing else." "The piranha with wings has eaten almost everything that has been thrown in here," I answered. "Is that any way to talk about a friend?" The sound of Xilligars voice echoed around us as he and the night-mother appeared in their insect forms. "Aww, No Mommy to hold your hand, Dusty?" I leaped forward and slashed at the monster moth, who dodged my attack by flapping his smelly wings. Since this was his realm, he had the upper hand, but I refused to let him get away without at least snatching one or two of his wings off. He used the smelly things to fly off in the opposite direction, but I spread my own gorgeous wings and chased after him. My new boyfriends would have to handle the sinister centipede on their own. ***Roar!!!*** I sent a blast of energy in his direction as he flew higher and hit a tree ahead of him. The dusty bitch twisted through the spray of wood, and I continued on my hunt as the sound of Thomas and Trimark's fighting the shadow monster faded into nothing. "I'm going to eat you and take your form. Then have some fun with your hot boyfriends." This time, I used Talaset to spray him with acid and succeeded in hitting his left wing. "Oh, I'm going to enjoy this." I descended to the ground as he clung to a tree and tried to leap from one to another while screaming out in pain.

"Thomas, get his rear." I held down my father's front half as Thomas used his claws to pin down my father's end stinger. "All you had to say was that you wanted some mommy and son time. I would have made room." My father taunted, with a sinister smile. He twisted and grabbed me by the abdomen while flinging Thomas in the opposite direction. I took that as a chance to let go and dive into my own shadow and then reappear where Thomas was falling in an effort to catch him. "Okay, this isn't working. What do we do?" Truthfully, I didn't have a plan outside of protecting Thomas, and now that included our new kitty. If I destroy his body, he'll just reform in the shadow realm. Our only option was to shove him back into the shadow realm and hope that our third member was able to defeat Xilligar. My father dove into the shadows and reemerged with a large crow. Before I could move to attack my father, the monster crow lunged at me with its talons raised, and I dove to the side while Thomas grabbed my father in his claws and slammed into the tree.

"I'm not really a bird person." I slashed at the crow's wings as it remained silent and continued to attack me with its sharp feet. "You must be the demon lord, Tirogollv." He didn't say anything as he sent a plume of smoke in my direction, and I crawled up the tree at super speed. Once I was up high enough, I exhaled a cold mist at the bird in the hopes that it'd freeze his feathers. I stayed in the thickest part of the cold fog and watched the bird try to escape on foot. The sound of hooves hitting the ice pulled my attention to the opposite direction as an all black unicorn appeared with its glowing red eyes acting as fog lights. Darkon is the embodiment of everything evil. He bent down and used his horn to raise the temperature while Tirogollv jumped on his back. Great! I jumped off of the tree and made a cloud of cold air to ride on as they turned around to form an attack. The bird opened his beak and sent a fireball in my direction while Darkon followed up with lightning from the tip of his horn. "Not today, Cousin!" A bolt of red lighting whizzed past me and destroyed both elemental attacks. Darren appeared next to me with his bat wings and tail ready for action. "Mom said you could use some help. I'll take the pony." Off in the distance, I could hear Thomas giving my father a run for his money, and I had no other option but to do the same. My new teammate didn't wait for me to make a move and tackled Darkon with his wings while knocking the bird in my direction. They tumbled into the forest as I twisted my body and slashed at the demon crow. Scrawww!! A smile curved my lips as I severed his left talon, but it was short-lived as it grew back and hit me with his tail feathers. My body turned into cold air upon impact, and I had to make a quick decision between entering his lungs or reappearing behind him as a spider and biting off his wings. Another second went by, and I decided to take my beast form instead of taking the risk of him leaving this dimension with me inside his lungs. "I'll give it to you. You're Dangerous. I can see why your father wants that beautiful body of yours." The crow telepathically said. Tirogollv's eyes glowed purple and then white as he vanished in a beautiful array of colors that danced around the small space. Since it was nighttime, I couldn't really use my paternal powers, or he would turn them against me, so I had to rely on the cold temperature to take me to where Thomas fought my father. This was the upside to being a reincarnation of a minor sea deity with the power granted by an even stronger god. Divine muscle memory. "Hello, son. Come to dance with Mommy?" I didn't get a chance to fully form as he sprayed me with a plume of black sand that pulled my body into it and then to the ground. Fuck. This is the downside of being a water deity. The natural elements have natural weaknesses. I hated the gritty feeling of my particles attaching themselves to sand and making matters worse, I had to watch as Thomas gave everything he had to go up against my father. My father sent out a blast of green and black energy that Thomas blocked with a sphere of ice and then launched icicles at my father. His attack gave me the chance I needed to extract the moisture from the granules of sand and solidify my physical form. Thomas reached out with one claw and pulled me out of the dirt as another wave of energy attacks flew by us. "What happened to the pigeon?" I bit back a laugh and summoned twin blades into my hands, and turned to look at the most handsome god in existence. "He ran away like a little bitch!" My fighting partner pointed upwards and sent out three bright blue bolts of lighting that froze my father to the ground with ice as they made contact. "I've chopped him up into a thousand pieces, but he just reassembles himself. I reduced him to ashes with lighting and then he reformed from nothing. I'm out of options and don't know what to do." Before I could respond, two things happened at once. The sound of Cameron's roar echoed all around us, and the ground trembled. "I'm going to have to cut this short. Until next time, children." His aura of darkness enveloped him, and he vanished into nothing as the tree and plants began to wither away. "I did it!" Cameron landed next to us in his beast form, with blue blood covering his mouth and a look of pure joy on his feline face. "This place is about to be reduced to nothing." With the way that everything kept dying, we didn't have much time before we would be dropped into a nearby dimension, and one of these pocket dimensions was enough for one lifetime. I summoned my powers of shadow as Thomas exhaled a breath of cold air, and Cameron's snake tail spewed transportation smoke around us. I focused on the mystical realm of Limbo and felt the energy shift as we left the dark forest and landed in the entryway where Hecate and Ammit were waiting for us. "Son, I'm so sorry!" She ran over to Cameron and pulled him into her arms. "I begged Oberon to let me into that dimension, but he refused. He said that it would take a monster to defeat a monster." Her head changed from human to crocodile as she cried and petted her son's mane. "It's okay, Mom. I got my revenge and made some new friends along the way." Thomas and I waved as she looked up, her face changing back to normal. "Thank you for helping my son. Aunt Za would be proud." "I agree." The wind shifted, and Darren appeared in a funnel cloud next to his mother, who didn't wait for him to finish forming as she pulled him into a hug. "Are you okay? Did he touch you?" That last question was necessary with all the things that I've heard about Darkon. "He didn't even fight back. He just hugged me and kissed my cheek and then teleported away." Darren shivered as his mother inspected the rest of his body. "Mom, I think he's gay. He said that he'd see me again." He shrugged off the weirdness as they turned and walked up the steps, and the four of us awkwardly looked at one another. Two large gold doors appeared behind Amiit, and she motioned for us to follow her as they opened into her palace. More dimensional travel, Yay! Our clothes changed as we crossed over through the threshold and into a room with a banquet-style feast on the table. Cameron took on his human body but kept the lion head and bat wings as he pulled his chair out for his mother. This was the first time that I'd ever been to the realm of the devourer, and I wanted to make a good impression if I was going to date her son. "Your home is absolutely stunning." I pulled out a chair for Thomas and took a seat next to him as Cameron sat across from me. "Thank you, Winter lord." "Uh, you can just call me Thomas." Amiit smiled and waved her hand at the pitcher of wine. "And you two can call me mom." "With all due respect, your greatness. I don't think that would be okay. You're a supreme deity." "I'm also able to see into the hearts of those around me and I see that you two like my son." If I was of a lighter skin tone, she would see me blushing from embarrassment as Thomas and I looked over at Cameron, who was actually blushing. "Mom!" "I'm just saying. Before I met your father I had just separated from my ex-wives." "Cool." Thomas said with a gasp. I reached for a drumstick as the sound of wings flapping entered the room. "Your father's home." As if on queue, a large Chimera flew into the room and landed next to the Goddess. "Son!" His monster form changed into a human that resembled Cameron and hugged him like a normal father. "I see you've made friends along the way." He turned to look at us while still remaining in a side hug with Cameron, and a part of me was jealous of the way that his father adored him. My birth parents died after I was born, and my father separated himself from their divinity, so I was raised by Aunt Za here in limbo. The titan Hecate trained me in magic and was like my second mother, but I always wanted a father. "Thomas and Trimark, meet my father, Kimoran." "Are the three of you going to have a threesome?" The divine monster's question made Thomas choke on his drink, and I turned to look at him with more embarrassment on my face as I chewed. "Dad!" "I'm not judging. Polyamory is cool. It's like that one joke. A crab, spider and a lion walk into a bar." Cameron shook his head from left to right, and I shared a look with Thomas that said we both were feeling weird about all of this as Ammit and her husband laughed. "This is why I don't bring people home." Oh shit. This was the first time someone had taken me home to meet their family, and we hadn't even had sex yet. *I have two boyfriends.* "Just so you two know. I want a bunch of little divine babies flying and crawling over the place." Hearing the devourer say that burst my balloon of happiness. Fuck, now I have to talk about something that only Hecate's mother, Astara Knows. "I can't procreate naturally or at all. Aunt Za placed an enchantment on my body that stops me from being able to make offspring so that my father couldn't incarnate through me." The great devourer of hearts sucked her breath in through her sharp teeth and looked up at her husband. They shared a telepathic conversion that ended in Kimoran taking a deep breath and then looking over to me. "My wife can't tell you that there is a way around that because she is forbidden from directly intervening in another deity's fate. So I'll tell you. All you have to do is wait until he is free from his prison and slay him, but allow his divine essence to go into the cycle of reincarnation as a new soul. Then he'll forget all about his unnecessary revenge and go to a woman that will give him a heart." The being known as the night-mother was definitely known for being heartless. Every encounter I've ever had began and ended with him escaping or stealing the shadows of my kind. To him we're like puppets that are disposable. "I can't allow him to be free, or his presence will tip the balance to evil." "Once earth enters spring, we won't have to worry about that anymore." "What's happening in spring?" "The great awakening will start and the humans will become what they truly are. Divine." Me and Thomas shared the same shocked expression as Cameron did from hearing those words come out of Kimoran's mouth. "My reincarnated father, Typhon, will bring in the age of divinity." We spent the rest of the evening talking about what we knew, and for the first time in my life, I wasn't ashamed of having a crazy god for a father. I still hated him for everything but the fact that I get to see what normal divine parents look like was a gift all in itself. "Thank you for not judging me." Cameron led us down a hallway to his room that was just as immaculate as the rest of this divine palace. It was different from the rest of the palace with its pale marble floor and walls. "All the gold in my mother's palace stops at the doorway, as you can see. It gets annoying to walk over when my fur builds up electricity." "Is all of that gold what she took from the pharaohs?" "Yes, those idiots thought that they could bribe her with it and she still devoured their hearts." Thomas and I took a seat at the edge of the bed as Cameron walked over with a blunt in his hands. "A provider and a protector. Where have the two of you been all of my life?" They placed their hands on my knees as we laughed, and I realized that when we had sex, it would be the first time for me since I was nineteen. Even then, it was an accident that was orchestrated by my father in an attempt to make a new form. Fortunately it was also the night that I found out about the enchantment that was placed on me by Aunt Za. Melissa Wells died from childbirth as my father's unborn form burst into flames inside her womb. That was the night that I came to the conclusion that I like men more than women and didn't have to worry about giving out death by impregnation. "Are you okay?" I snapped out of my nostalgia to see my handsome demigods staring at me with concern all over their faces. "Yeah, Just thinking about the past." Cameron ignited the end of the blunt with his powers as Thomas reached up and whipped away the tears that I didn't know were there. "I have something that I want to tell you two about." Cameron passed the blunt to Thomas and nodded as more tears fell from my eyes. "Whatever it is, we promise we won't judge." "My mother is an actual divine judge who eats things. This room for three is a safe space." For most of my life, I spent it as an actual recluse spider who only came out to do what the goddesses wanted me to do, and I never gave love a real chance. "I've only had sex once. She was a night-born female who died from the enchantment that Aunt Za placed on me. I've only ever messed with one other male, and it was just a hand job." That was partially true. Colbert Hughes was a Down low private investigator of paranormal cases. We crossed paths in the summer of 2004 and met regularly until he died and went on to become a death god for his mother in the underworld. "Mmmm, I swear I love a man who can show emotion and actually feel them. You're this extremely tall, muscular, powerful demigod who was trained like an assassin, but deep down, you're just a ball of handsome kindness." Thomas leaned forward and kissed me on the lips as

Cameron got up and did the same. Minutes passed as the three of us made out like sex-crazed college kids. "Wait-Wait!" I got up and put distance between us by walking over to the window. What is wrong with me? Here, I am alone with two very attractive gods who want this as much as I do. "We can just cuddle if you want." Cameron popped over to my side with a smile on his face, and Thomas followed by teleporting to my other side. All I could do was nod my head yes as we walked back over to the bed, and the covers magically peeled back for us to get in. In the blink of an eye, we were now dressed in our tight-fitting underwear and crawled into bed. With both of them lying on either side of me, I finally felt wanted. We made ourselves comfortable, and the seconds turned to minutes as we lay in silence. "Trimark, I want you to know that I'm not going anywhere. And whether you like it or not, neither is your father-goddess. Think of this moment as a turning point in your life where you allow yourself to exist as you." His words made my tears fall, and this time, Cameron joined me as Thomas reached up and touched his hand. "You too. Mr. Kitty." The three of us laughed uncontrollably for a couple of minutes before Cameron held his hands up.

"Hold-up. Can I have another handle? Mr.Kitty, ain't it."

"Well, I'm Cold-claw, Trimark is Night-breeze and you'll be…Omni-beast!" Cameron's smile and eye change conveyed that he loved the name. His tail came into focus and took the form of his snake Talaset. "Hey now. It's a foursome now!" "Talaset, get the hell out of here. I sure as fuck don't mess with your dates, now do I?" The snakes dancing stopped as he vanished like a ghost. "Sorry about that. He's the direct descendant of temptation. Sexual energy is to his kind what blood in the water is to a shark." "Ohhh!" Thomas and I spoke in unison as we looked at each other and then back to Cameron.

"Is the goat demon a part of that world as well?" Our host shook his head no as Thomas leaned over to look at his perfectly sculpted ass and then up at his long hair. Out of the three of us Thomas's personal boundaries seem to have vanished completely. Cameron and I have the bodies of muscle bound gods while Thomas is fully awakened demigod with a medium build. He's the proof that the divine vanity aspect was nonexistent in mortal born deities and I Loved every bit of it. "You have the perfect amount of hair on your body that's not too much and Trimark is the perfect height without being a street sign." A smile curved my lips as I looked Thomas in the eyes. The two of them couldn't have come into my life at a better time. "You have a great ass and I love the color of Cameron's green eyes." He gasped and joined our hands together. "I'm obsessed with your rich skin tone and I agree, Thomas does have a nice ass." "Are we going to have to make a schedule for this booty?" "Yes, I'll take it Sunday to Tuesday and you have him Thursday to Saturday." We high-fived and Thomas clapped his own hands together. "Yeah, and on Wednesday I'm topping the both of you." I shook my head no while Cameron nodded yes with a huge smile on his face and bit his bottom lip. "Sounds like a plan to me." He responded.

"Then it's settled, This is a Room for three." "Yay!!! The three of you will get married in two days!" Thomas and I jumped at the sound of Ammit the devouerer's voice echoing around us. "Mom! You said you wouldn't listen anymore!" Cameron slammed his hand on the bed as he snarled and his face took on lion aspects. "Sorry, me and your father just wanted to make sure that you were good. Good night!!" "Thank you Trimark. You saved us from this embarrassment of my parents being nosy and seeing something that they shouldn't have seen." "No problem." Thomas and I looked around the room as we pulled the covers up over our exposed bodies. "Should I leave the light on or off?" "Off!" Thomas and I said in unison and Cameron pointed at the ceiling to deactivate the large floating clear quartz crystal. The three of us snuggled up closer together and I heard Cameron fall asleep first and then Thomas was next. Half of an hour passed before I yawned and allowed myself to join them.

"I don't know, this felt too easy." Titania and Zephyr nodded as Hecate paced back and forth. "Why is he even working with them? None of us are his enemies." Hecate was right. "What did your son say?" It's been a week since my son returned home and brought his new friends with him. Trimark and Thomas were the perfect additions to our little beast family. "He said that he killed the Moth and sent his divinity back into the ether. The night-mother escaped like the coward that he is and Darkon came in to assist the demon-lord, Tirogollv." Hecate grew to ten feet as she paced back and forth with her rainbow aura trailing behind her. Moments like this made being divine bitter sweet. On one hand my son has found the loving partners that he deserves and on the other Darren is being stalked by a very dangerous Dark god. It was a couple hundred thousand years ago that I was in her exact position. My son Zamiticameronoten, always made friends wherever he went and befriended the eldest children of Oberon and Mab, Xiyanneb and Xilligar. I got up off of the couch and grew to her size with my arms outstretched to hug her. "I'm so sorry, Donna." "It's not your fault, Ami. I knew that this was the risk that I was taking by sending him to help." Our tears fell onto each other's clothes as we deepened our embrace and Titania teleported over to join or hug. "No, this is my fault. I should have waited until their divorce was final to go after Oberon." "You ain't neva lied!" We all turned our heads to the west wind, Zephyr who leaned back in his chair like none of this mattered to him. "What! It's the truth." "You think a god who accidentally killed his lover eons ago, would have a little sympathy for a goddess." I changed my eyes from human to crocodile and looked from him to his wings as I licked my lips. He popped over to our side with a small snapping sound echoing around us as he reformed and joined our hug. "It took me a year to get my feathers back to normal after the last time you played around." Pink and green energy moved in between Titania's antenna and she pulled away from our embrace as the rest of us followed her back to our seats. "Okay- Do it!" She ended the communication with one of her subordinates and looked up to us with the energy now in her insect eyes. "Mab and the six are attacking a fey city on avalon. I have to go!" The Fey Queen turned into dust that receded into nothing as the rest of us looked to one another. "She didn't invite us to help." "Yeah, that's not like her. This has to be serious." I agreed with Donna A.K.A Hecate Without an invitation into her domain we can't transport ourselves over there to help, but that didn't mean that we would leave her defenseless. "Are you thinking what I'm thinking?" I turned to Donna who nodded her head yes while Zephyr shook his head no. *Gods, Ugh!* "We can't go because we're goddesses who occupy dimensional thrones. But!... Our children can act on our behalf." "You can't send your children to fight thousand year old fairies." "Trust me, they've got this." The west wind unfurled all of his wings and summoned his tree-staff. "I'm going as well." Hecate's Mind-eye opened and changed the energy of the room as she looked into the future with a smile on her face. "You have a different path that you must follow, bringer of spring!" The doors to the council chamber blew open and Darren flew into the room with lightning moving across his body. "Yes, Ma'am." The light skinned demigod's green eyes were replaced with all red irises that were the origin of his energy. "I'm sending you to Avalon. The queen needs your help." She held her hands up but Darren summoned his own energy to stop her. "Quick question! Do I alert my brothers?" "No." "Can I take Nashira?" "No, she's on her own mission at the moment." "What's the life and death ratio? Resurrection or reincarnation?" "Avalon is a lot like Limbo. Their souls will linger around and wait for you to Resurrect them." He nodded and let go of his mystical hold on her power and waved goodbye as she finished the transportation spell. I clapped my hands and summoned the mirror that the fairy queen made for me as a gift. "You read my mind!" The three of us watched as Darren appeared in the form of a giant bat above the royal capital of avalon, Niaber. Monstrous insects swarmed the city as I cleared my throat and let out a roar. Zephyr pointed at the mirror and a unicorn appeared with a swarm of brown recluse spiders to help Darren and the fairies. It was hard not to laugh as the poor fairies couldn't tell who was friend or foe at first and managed to stop fighting the brown spiders who took them to safety. "Yes, Mother!" Cameron and his lovers teleported into the room in a burst of cold spring air and their mouths fell open as they looked at the mirror. "We've got to do something!" Thomas yelled. "Oh, Shit! This is because of me." My little cub changed into his beast form and let out a loud roar as he spread his wings. Trimark and Thomas followed suit by changing into their beast forms with elemental auras surrounding their bodies. My baby has always attracted great companions. The three of them jumped into the mirror without saying another word and jumped into the fight with Cameron destroying a lot of the monsters with a swipe of his claw. Thomas lived up to the title of winter lord as he trapped Mab's male butterfly soldiers in glaciers of ice and shrank them down to the size of ice cubes. Trimark appeared as a shadow spider and used the power of mind manipulation on the soldiers to make them turn on each other instead of attacking the city. "Oh, Shit!" Zephyr watched the mirror like a man watching a football game as Donna and I laughed. Seeing our children together reminded me of our names before we ascended to our thrones. War, Death, Conquest and Famine. Those were the times. "I was just thinking the same thing." Death A.K.A Donna, touched my shoulder as the memories faded to the back of my immortal mind and I returned my attention to the current battle of divine beasts. Cameron was now going up against Queen Mab and her daughter Gigetta, the carnivorous plant. The hairs on the back of my neck stood up as the plant deity pulled my son into the ground and Titania appeared in the form of an owl and ripped the wings off of Mab's back. She screamed out in pain as my best friend reduced them to ashes with pink and green fire. The dark fey queen turned into a snake that tunneled into the ground and Cameron used his wings and claws to sever the plant from its roots. "There you go, Son!" I knew that this was something Kimeron would want to see so

I snapped my fingers and activated the clear quartz crystal that would preserve the image. "This would make a good visual teaching aid for the children at the academy." "I agree. We'll cancel the lesson plans and show this as a treat for everyone to see." Zephyr held his hands out and made food for us at the exact moment that Cameron leaped into the air. Gigetta sent out vines from the ground as he flapped his large wings that he got from his daddy and made a tornado sweep them up. I couldn't have been more proud to watch my little cub use his powers to be a force of devastation. Cameron is everything that a Goddess could ever want in a son. Meeting Thomas and Trimark has helped him express the part of himself that was hidden away from the world. A cold chill crawled up my arms as I watched Trimark come out of the Shadows with his forehead full of dark blue spider eyes and matching appendages. "Uh-oh!" Zephyr leaned forward and narrowed his eyes on Trimark as his spiders ran out of the way. He exhaled a cloud of dark smoke that took him to the ant queen, Orinon. With everyone else busy with their own heavy hitters we allowed the mirror's perspective to change to Thomas and Darren who were battling a swarm of flies known as Wilzicor and his pet squirrel, Zenilvri. Thomas hit the giant rodent with a wintery blast and managed to freeze it to the spot and then the scene changed again to show my son going up against the plant.

"What the fuck was that?" "I don't know, I wasn't expeting to immediately form a crush on him." Darkon was a new god with ancient power and also a means to an end that couldn't happen fast enough. "That's disgusting, you're our cousin." The demigoddess Milla crossed her arms and vanished in a burst of vibrant colors as Darkon smiled and continued with the bouquet of flowers that he was making for Darren. That divine being was severely disturbed.

"Girl, Yóu're nasty!"

"Nasty, You tried to hurt a child. *Your* child, and now you're in mystical shadow-house arrest, Mutha! The category is!!! Sad and alone evening wear, Forever!" Black flames burst to life at the dark gods feet and traveled up his body as he vanished with his newly manifested flowers from the goddess of agriculture's home dimension. The dark Fey queen Mab was still mourning the loss of her favorite son and The demon lord Tirogollv was off doing who knows what. *Fuck!* I almost had my son's physical form and the amulet of daylight. That chubby crab doesn't even realize that he holds the power of daylight and dominion over winter in his hands. My aurq began to pulse as a divine being teleported through the ether into this realm. Nydiratet, Right! "Oh, hello. You're here." I've never done anything to her to make her hate me, but she always has, even though we've known each other as long as I've known the mystical titaness, Hecate and her team of nosey divine mothers. "Hey, Ny-Ny. Can I call you that?" She looked at me as if ai was shit on the bottom of her shoe and rolled her eyes as she passed by me and took a seat on the fuzzy couch. "Demeter, I'm hungry!" She yelled. *Great, she's in one of her moods.* The nature goddess flew into the room with two wooden platters of food and placed them in front of the surly titan. She maybe be all powerful, but if I had my original form, I'd be the one that was scary. Then I wouldn't need this beautiful dark brown skinned bitch and she'd be serving me food. The moment I finished my thought, the Titaness turned her head at me while picking up a taco. "I don't have an abundance of patience, girl-boy!" I took a deep breath and stepped towards her with the fakest smile that I could muster. "Will you allow me to reincarnate through you and make a physical form with a combination of our powers?" Nydiratet put down the taco that she was holding and looked up at me with a sinister smile on her gorgeous face. "That sounds like a great plan." She reached out and grabbed me by the arms as her smile grew bigger. My momentary happiness began to fade as I sensed something wrong and tried to transport myself out of her grasp, but nothing happened after several attempts. Within seconds she had me in her wide mouth and my protests were trapped inside her wide throat as her teeth began to smash me into small bits. The agony of being mashed into paste while conscious was enough to make me want to be mortal as I felt my essence begin to dissolve into nothingness. I floated in a dark void for what felt like an eternity until I opened my eyes to the blinding light of Demeter's sitting room. Once my eyes adjusted to the light, I could see Nydiratet eating the platter of food as if she didn't just give birth to me. From this perspective I looked to her and tried to roll over but the pain from the back of my head made me scream. My stomach began to burn as the pain intensified and I watched in horror as my lower body began to petrify. The process continued until my entire body began to transform and then dissolve into dust. My divine essence peeled away from the newly birthed body as I floated above the floor and was back in the same predicament that I've been in since the dawn of time. "What was the point of that?" I asked as she devoured three tacos at once. "I hate weakness almost as much as I hate failure." She narrowed her eyes on me as my incorporeal form began to fade in and out of existence. Suddenly I realized that I was wrong about being in the same spot that I was in earlier. In granting me my request, she absorbed part of my divinity into her nothingness. It was foolish of me to expect a titaness who was the only child born of the Titan Clytius to actually do something useful. Her father was the direct opposite of Hecate and he was known as the living void. I transformed into my centipede form and enter my shadow realm until I restore some of my power. "Next time you'll keep up your end of the deal, WORM!!" She yelled as I moved into the shadow of the coffee table. This wasn't a part of the deal thatbI made with Tirogollv and Hecate's daughter Milla. No one said anything about the daughter of the void and negative emotions being on our team. I was better off going to her mother Nehkbet, for help. At least she would have been more useful and nowhere near as dangerous. My form started to solidify as I made my way to my domain and once I was nestled on my bed, I closed my eyes and allowed my mind to show me what my son was doing. My form shifted into a more human-like form as a smile curved my lips. Trimark was now channeling more of his Shadow power while his creations where helping him go up against the dark fey. I couldn't decide if I wanted to be happy or angry for him. The more power he used, the easier it would be for me to possess him and take over the body that was made to be mine. Or if I should be enraged by the fact that my sister has raised him to properly wield everything that belonged to me. He mastered the art of resisting me a long time ago, but he never completely accomplished the ability to pull himself out of the shadows. Sure he'd win this small battle, butb it would cost him his morality. "Ha! Keeping going son, keep using what *I* gave you!" I yelled out loud. Trimark turned to where my consciousness lingered and exhaled a plume of dark smoke at me that severed my connection. *Damn it! I wanted to see how that ended.* Now I have to wait for him to calm down and peer through the shadows of those that surround him.

I could feel myself losing patience with the immortal plant. My acis didn't work and severing it from the ground only gave it another advantage over me. My latest attempt at destroying it by using the wind to rip it apart, ended with it turning into grass and then reforming on the ground. My wings flapped harder and I raised myself higher off of the ground as the hairs of my mane moved to form Quilphomet. "Boss, Trimark's divinity is leaning towards the shadows and he's scaring the others." I twisted through the air to go find my shadow-spider boyfriend but Gigetta wrapped her vines around my torso. "I'm not done dancing with you kitty!" She said telepathically. The divine plant tried to pull me down to the ground but I beat my wings harder and managed to uproot her out of the ground. "I think I'll take my salad to go!" I responded. I continued to flap my wings as hard as I could and carried us higher into the sky. The overgrown plant screamed as we broke through the pink clouds and my serpentine flight pattern caused her to move from side to side. Thankfully with us being this high she wouldn't have access to floral nature and that annoying giant squirrel couldn't follow her up here. "Sir, behind you!" I turned my head to see the plant's fly trap mouth glow as she readied an energy blast to hit me with. "I'm going to enjoy dissolving your bones in my mouth. Before she could release it I twisted my body and used her weight against her as I swung her in a circle like a lasso. "Order for tossed salad, party of one!" I yelled while making my fur sharp and cutting her vines from my torso. She let out her energy attack that flew upwards as she disappeared into the sky with her flailing limbs moving around her. A chill crawled up my spine as the image of Trimark eating an ant entered my mind. *Oh shit!* I took a deep breath in as I descended to the ground and allowed my wings to take me to where the air was the coldest. Once I reached the capital, I landed on the ground and jumped to the side as a large brown recluse spider ran past me. "He-he's a monster!" Vic said, telepathically. If the god of viciousness in forest animals is scared, then we have a problem. I shifted into my human form and walked through the forest in search of my muscle bound lover who was on the verge of doing something that he would regret later. The hairs on the back of my neck stood up as I made my way around the trunk of a large tree and watched as Trimark ate the shadow of a beetle fairy that crumbled into glittering dust. "Baby!" I said, Approaching him with caution. "Mmmm, hey Handsome." In the blink of an eye Trimark was standing in front of me with the sexiest smile I'd ever seen on his face. We were almost the same height but the boulder that I stood on made me two inches taller and I looked down into his multi-eyed spider gaze. "Marky. Your-" He cut my words off by floating upwards and pressing his lips against mine. "The luckiest god alive to have two boyfriends with big booties." He cupped my ass into both of his hands and lifted me up off of the boulder as the creatures who were hiding used that as a chance to escape. His hands started to move around the rest of my bost and I had to use all of my strength to get out of his embrace. "So now you don't want this?" He moved closer but I held my hands out to stop him from reaching into my pants. "Dude, My mother is probably watching." "Ohhhhh, let's give them a show!" A soldier ant jumped off of a tree and tried to attack us but he snatched it out of the air and began to eat it like a burrito. *Eww! I won't be kissing him until he brushes his teeth with peroxide.* "Want some?" He asked, holding up its thorax. As we lowered ourselves to the forest floor he sniffed the air and looked from left to right. "There is something else hiding nearby." He devoured the thorax as a boulder to my left changed into a queen ant and burrowed into the shadow of the treetops. "Yeah, you better run!" He yelled before grabbing my right hand and pulling me into the same shadow in pursuit of the abt. My eyes changed to see in the darkness as he started to whistle in the darkness. Last week Trimark told us about all of his powers and how seductive the pull of night was to the night-born. I didn't expect him to be as calm and gentle as he currently is. As a giant beast, I expected him to change into a large spider monster and go on a rampage or something. "Hey, do you want to go fuck up my fathers realm?" "Shouldn't we get back to avalon? Thomas is out there by himself." He laughed and turned around to pull me into a hug. "Darren is out there with him." He said in a gentle tone, while giving me a light squeeze. He then kissed my neck as the floor next to us showed the two of them going up against a large dragonfly and a swarm of blue flies. "See, he's good." Trimark was right but it didn't sit right with me to be in a realm of shadows that was outside of the realm that we needed to be in. "Cammy, he's the one who needs more divine experience." Trimark pulled away from me and clapped his hands as a large shiny black beetle crawled out of his hair. "You know what to do." He commanded. The shell on its back opened up as the insect spread its wings and flew off into the unending darkness. He then reached out into the space next to us and made an opening that led back into avalon. The Shadow realm's absence of life made the smell of avalon hit me with an intensity to make me sneeze as we walked towards Thomas and Darren. "My fault, baby." Trimark said producing a box of tissues out of thin air. There were times when I loved my heightened senses, but right now I hated the smell of the orange foliage. The sight of our boyfriend and Darren going head to head with the remaining two children of Mab was a sight to see as Thomas used his newly awakened powers with ease. Trimark clapped and jumped up and down as Thomas exhaled an icy breath that froze the Dragonfly-goddesses wings and prevented her from escaping into the air. She let out a shrill screech before going into shock and convulsing on the ground. The swarm of blue flies shifted their movement and swirled around Drigonna and in seconds they vanished into nothing. "Awww, I wanted to nibble on her head." Triamrk said, as he pouted. He kicked the tree next to him and snapped it in two as our companions made their way over to us. "Whoa, baby. How about we take a deep breath?" Thomas suggested. Trimark nodded as he pulled both of us into a side hug and winked at Darren before transporting us into the shadow realm once more. This time we materialized in the middle of a front room that looked as if it belonged to a mansion of some sort. Everything was a mixture of black and dark blue coloring that was made with exquisite craftsmanship. The only weird part about everything was the dark void outside. "Take a seat." Thomas and I exchanged a nervous glance as he manifested food for us to eat on a long table made of shiny onyx metal. Thomas and I remained standing as we looked around the room. This was the domain of his divine parent, the mother of darkness and the last time I checked, it was where the entity resided. "When we were fighting those fairies, I sensed that my father was injured by something with a weird divine signature, so he'll be out of commission for a while. So, think about this as us having a party while he's away. We're good." "How is that good?" I asked. We walked over to the couch and took a seat beside him. The drinks poured themselves as he sat back and his spider features changed into his human ones. "So you just sensed that you're father is injured." Thomas asked. "Yes, earlier I released a beetle that did some reconnaissance. Apparently he retreated to his inner domain that only *he* can get to. I used that as a way to make this realm with what was outside of his." *Whoa!* Thomas and I shared another nervous glance as he leaned forward and handed us our drinks. "Let's toast to new relationships." Before I could put the drink to my lips, talaset spoke to be telepathically. *"Uh, no! You know the rules."* He appeared in his ghost-like form and then used telekinesis to remove the cup from my hand so that he could taste it first. After drinking a large portion of it he smacked his teeth and moved it back into my grasp. *"You're good."* My personal bodygaurd vanished and we spent what had to be three hours drinking like we were at a party. I conjured home grown weed to pair with the drinks and another three hours passed as we spent it telling stories about our childhoods. Truthfully I wanted to show Thomas that I was capable of being here for him in Trimark's obvious time of need. Our polyamorous relationship checked all of the boxes that it needed to and I filled the remaining slots with my own level of monster divinity. "Damn, so you saw the battle between gods?" Thomad asked as he took another hit of the blunt and then passed it to me. I nodded yes to his question as the memory of that divine battle played through my mind. Even though i didn't personally know the deity that he was in his first life, I saw him in action as the lord of winter and then heard stories of of how he meet tragic end. "Yes, it was crazy as fuck. Just imagine all of the worst things that could happen, actually happening a hundred times worse than that." I answered. "The divine battle had casualties of every pantheon and it destroyed a lot of the earth, so the mother goddesses came together and put an end to it. With earth being the heart of the universe, they didn't it to cause a ripple of destruction." I added. "The mother goddesses being, Aunt za, Hecate, Your mother and The sleeping goddess Terra. The were the original riders of the apocalypse." Trimark said, finally speaking up. "Yes, my mother said that the era of divine beings needed to move into new age." I said, before taking a sip of wine. We decided to get some sleep after the three of us had enough to drink and smoke. Since Thomas wasn't a seasoned smoker like Trimark and I, He fell asleep before us and we carried him down the hall to Trimarks large bedroom. I snapped my fingers and removed almost all of our clothing as Thomas talked in his sleep and Trimark got in the bed without saying anything. A part of me wanted to ask if he was okay, but he kind of snapped at us the last time that I did. "Sweet dreams, baby." He said, giving me a wink. "Sweet dreams to you as well, my sex host of darkness." The both of us cuddled up to Thomas as he continued to talk in his sleep and Trimark joined him. It took me another hour to fall asleep as I fantasized about all of the things that the three of us would do together. When I woke up Thomas told the both of us about his dream and how he received a visit from Aunt Za, who told him about how she split herself in two. It all made sense now and I was happy to see that it helped alleviate some of his guilt about being angry at the ancient spider mother goddess. "If goddesses are all powerful, how did men take the spot of being the leaders?" Thomas asked. "To make a long story short, it started with the first beings of earth, called omniterrans. They allowed themselves to fall victim to the words of other divine beings and the females abused their power over the males. I think the gods wanted them to have the power in their next incarnation and somehow made them physically stronger." "I still have so many questions." He responded. "And I'll gladly answer all of them." I answered, while caressing the side of his face. Trimark laughed as he made our mimosas and mumbled something under his breath. "You know what I just realized?" he asked. Neither one of us answered as he took a sip of his breakfast drink. "We're like the characters from the wizard of Oz, except the gay version." he said laughing out loud. Thomad and I chuckled as he laughed like it was the funniest thing imaginable. *Oh, this god has got jokes.* "So I'm the lion, You're the Tin man and Thomas is both Dorothy and the scarecrow." The three of us laughed together this time as Trimarks eyes changed from brown to pitch black and then back again. "And my father is Toto!." He added, but this time Thomas and ai laughed nervously at the mention of the night-mother who has yet to make an appearance. "I'm going to go take a shower." Thomas said, getting up from the table. "No need." With a wave of his hand, Trimark cleaned us as if we had taken a shower and then our boxers changed as my skin prickled. Thomas and I shared another look and this time Trimark noticed it. "Ok, what's the deal?" he asked in an annoyed tone. His eyes changed again, but this time three more pairs of eyes formed as he got up from the table. "How long do you plan on us staying here?" I asked. He shrugged his shoulders as his dark-cold Aura appeared around his body and enveloped him as he left without saying another word. "This is new territory for me." I said. Thomas nodded in agreement but I could see that there was something else on his mind. "Are you okay?" I asked. "Not really. The part of me that is very fond of him is at war with the part of me that wants to end his divine parent for what happened in my past life and for all that he has put Trimark through." Thomas crossed his arms as the air around us grew colder. "I know he said that the Night-Mother couldn't get to us, but I feel like that's not the entire truth." A small blizzard escaped from his mouth as it regulated the cold breeze and I leaned over to rub his right shoulder. "Would he lie to protect us?" Thomas asked. That was a good question, seeing that the night-mother has been a divine thorne in my paw for a long time and it wasn't like him/her to just give up. Especially with Trimark now the very realm that she has tried to pull him into for thirty-nine years. It was hard to tell the time without a sun or moon and as the hours passed Thomas and I found small ways to keep ourselves busy. The both of us didn't know if we should find Trimark or give him space, but after another hour passed, we both stood up and looked at each other. "Let's go find him so that we can talk." I suggested. "No need." He said, stepping out of the wall. His eyes were back to normal but he licked his lips as if he'd just eaten. "Was dinner good?" he asked. "It was thank you." I responded. "Good, how about we go to bed?" He asked. Several minutes went by after we got undressed without using our powers and It occurred to me that Trimark was a loner because he was raised in solitude by the Spider mother. Maybe that was why he wasn't used to being in a relationship or how to communicate his feelings. We laid in bed and looked up at the ceiling as more time passed. I must have fallen asleep before they did because when I woke up Thomas was the big spoon while I was the little spoon, but Trimark was nowhere to be seen. "Thomas wake up!" "Hmmm, no, I told you that the deadline was Tuesday, You're fired." He said still partially asleep. "Thomas!" "Huh!" He woke up with clenched fists ready to punch someone who wasn't there. "We'll have to table that dream for another time, but Trimark is gone." I said getting up as the lights came on. I allowed my senses to stretch out and pick up his scent or here him in the bathroom but there was complete silence in all directions. All I could smell was Thomas's Kiwi-glacier scent as I continued inhale and exhale. My divine beast senses categorized everyone except my parents as food, so that it would be easier to hunt and eat them. Trimarks blueberry scent was nowhere, not even a residual smell on the sheets. We exited the room and made our way down the hall as Thomas's big booty bounced in front of me. It was hard to focus as my ears picked up the sound of his cheeks rubbing together. "I can sense you looking at my ass." "What a beautiful ass you have Mr. Journalist." "All the better to please you with." He stopped and allowed me to run into him as my erection rubbed against his back. "I can't believe I'm saying this but we don't have time for this." "Right, we'll circle jerk back to this." he said, making a sex joke. We continued to walk for twenty minutes down several long hallways with rooms that had A large collection of wine, clothes and weapons made of dark metals. The two of us stopped at the end of a hallway that went left and right. "We are NOT splitting up." I said lacing his fingers in mine. "Then to the left we go." He said pulling me down a hallway with four rooms that piqued my curiosity. The first door was locked and the second was filled with floating dream catchers. The third was a spare bedroom that was empty but the forth took our breath away as we walked in to see four black spiders holding musical instruments. They started to play as one of them began to sing an R&B

song while Cameron and slowly backed out of the room. "Talk about weird." I said shivering. "Yeah, their band should be called *melody's of the silent killers*." I answered, as we approached a large metal door. Since Thomas opened the door to the previous room I pushed it open to see a little girls room. We smiled as we saw a little brown skinned girl sitting at a small table, having a tea party. Across from her was one of Queen Mab's butterfly soldiers, who was not having as much fun as the little girl. "What are you two doing up?" she asked as she got up and changed from human to spider and then began to eat her party guest alive. "Oh, shit!" I yelled. As Thomas gasped. As we turned to leave the door closed, and the spider let out a laugh while changing into Trimark. "Well that was fun!" He said with a handsome smile as he walked towards the door.

Fuck! Now they're going to want to talk about this. "Marky, what was that?" Of course Thomas would ask the most obvious question as a Journalist. He was always nosey. Cameron just looked at me with his yellow feline eyes and placed a hand on my shoulder. "This place is having a negative effect on you. Maybe we should return to our home." I rolled my eyes as he stepped closer to embrace me and removed his hand from my shoulder. "You mean, *Your* home. When we do decide to go back to the earthly realm, we'll be living at Thomas's mansion. *This is my home!"* It felt good to say that. Especially since it was a partial truth. They don't need to know that my father is in the basement of this home that I created when I took over the Shadow realm. I never got to do normal teenage things and now that I am having fun, my boyfriends want to let out my cold air on a hot day. "When did we capture prisoners?" "I didn't. Their shadows brought them here, once I accepted who I really am." This was the best that I've felt in a very long time, and now that The night mother is under my control, I can relax. My lovers shared another look as I turned on my heels and headed towards our room. Once we made it back to the bed, I sat between them and took their hands in mine. "Thank you for being here for me in my time of need." The darkness whispered the words from Cameron's thoughts when we first arrived here and I could sense that right now was the correct time to use them. He smiled and rubbed my lower back as Thomas pulled us back onto the bed. "This time, I'll be the sandwich meat." I said as we snuggled up against each other and then waited for both of them to fall asleep. If I got up to leave, they would come find me again, but the urge to be balls deep in one of them was giving me an erection that was becoming uncomfortable. The last thing that we needed was for me to reach a climax while changing into a spider. Our sex life is already crazy enough as it is with Thomans making it snow as his toes curled and Cameron's beast roar shaking the room. Since I was far from sleepy, I decided to astral project my consciousness to the room where I've kept my father and found him cowering in his cell. The room was big enough for him to stretch but if he decided to take his centipede form, it would force him to shrink to a smaller size. "Hello father." He didn't make eye contact as I floated closer to where he was sitting. "Y-you're not r-real!" he practically yelled. *Sad-sad-sad.* It was that long ago that this primordial being used to make the hairs on the back of my neck stand up when he would watch me from the shadows. From the age of six until my nineteenth birthday, a random centipede would show up out of my peripheral vision and put me on high alert until it moved out of sight. Now he was unshaven with messed up hair and a torn dress from the beetle attack. *That reminded me.* "Here girl!" I called out to my new divine pet that I made from the beetle fairy, Millvgax's shadow and she appeared as my divine parent began to scream. "No-No,No, please!" With a thought I bound his hands together as she began to eat his right knee until she severed the leg and he convulsed from the pain. I laughed so loud that the small room shook with my power as she continued to eat his leg until there was nothing left. "That's my girl." I said, bending down and patting the top of her shell. With all of the fun that I was having I forgot to give her name that was suitable to the joy that she brought me. "Oh, that's it! From this moment on, yout name is Joy." She clicked her mandibles together and I took that as a sign that she loved her name as she crawled closer to my father and began to eat his face. *This couldn't get any better.* I allowed Joy to eat almost all of him as the seconds turned into minutes until the only thing left of him was his heart of shadows. "Okay, thats enough for right now, my pet." I snapped my fingers and made his shadow heart explode as he reformed from the darkness and gasped while looking around the room. A small tingling sensation formed at my temples and I realized that my lovers were awake so I waved goodbye as my body faded. I opened my eyes to see the both of them looking at me with shocked expressions as I got up and felt my arms push their pillows off of the bed. "What?" I said, with a fake yawn as I stretched my arms and felt extra tendons move. Out of the corner of my eyes I could see six spider legs extending themselves outwards as I got up. *FUCK! NOW THEY'LL BE CONCERNED LIKE THIS IS A BAD THING.* With a thought I made all of them recede into my sides and moved at super speed to place a kiss on Cameron's cheek and then Thomas's. "Who's hungry?" I asked, while cutting the silence of the wide bedroom. "Don't you want to finish digesting the butterfly fairy that you ate a little while ago?" Cameron asked. It'd been a while since the last time that I astral traveled and I forgot about the time displacement. I was in my fathers cell for minutes but up here hours had passed while they slept. My stomach answered my lion Bae's question as it rumbled. I clapped my hands and teleported us to the kitchen as a huge feast was laid out in front of us and the utensils made our plates. "Please, have a seat." I asked, with a smile while using telekinesis to pull out our chairs. Once our plates were piled high with an abundance of food, I took their hands in mine and bowed my head. "As gods we are gracious. As goods we are good. I thank the shadows for this delectable food. Three-men!" Once again my boyfriends were staring at me with bewildered expressions, but this time I didn't bother to ask as I began to dig into my food. I had to pat myself on the back at how delicious the food was. Everything was cooked to perfection and I loved how the meat paired well with the scrambled eggs. Cameron unfurled his bat wings as Thomas manifested a pair of pincers at his sides as they joined me in eating breakfast. A smile curved my lips as I reached for some pancakes and my extra limbs produced icy webs that brought them to me. At that moment it occurred to me that Thomas would be immune to my venom, but what about Cameron? He was part snake but that didn't mean shit when it came down to being divine monsters. "Oh, wow! Look!" Thomas said, while gesturing to the kitchen window. I turned to see what he was pointing at and almost choked on my food from what I was looking at. Instead of absolute darkness, we watched as snow fell on a dark forest with a bright blue moon in the sky. *Had I allowed myself to become so distracted that I was beginning to change this dimension?* We ate our food as quickly as we could before getting up and heading to the door. Cameron was the first to change into his beast form once we were outside and then Thomas and I changed as we stepped out into the fresh snow. The three of us played like children on winter break. Thomas started a snowball fight where he cheated because of his advantage and then Cameron brought the snow to life and made a small army that I destroyed with large blocks of hail. Time flew by as we were having so much fun and I almost forgot about my toy-parent in the basement. A large snowball whizzed past me as I thought of a lie to get me out of this. *Stay.* I turned in a full circle, in search of the child's voice, but couldn't locate it. *Stay, have fun. We deserve it!* It said once more, but this time with a sense of urgency. This time I realized that I heard the voice from within my head. I wanted to stay and have fun, but The night mother still needed to be taught a lesson. *NO, STAY!!* The disembodied voice was that of a childs and if I didn't know any better, I would have sworn that I heard it before. Another hour passed as we played outside and I realized that I wanted to marry them both. *Whoa! Where did that come from?* "My fut is soaked and as much as I love my cold blast boyfriends, I miss the warmth of indoors." Cameron's body glowed with orange light as he dried himself and we headed to the entrance.

"How about we watch a movie?" Thomad suggested.

"That sounds fun, I haven't smoked today. Who's up for a bake session?" Cameron added, as he took on his human form.

"I really wanted to watch the horror movie, *Saturday.* I heard it's really good." I countered.

"What's it about?" Thomas asked.

"Okay, so it kind of hits close to home. But, it's about these pre-teens who go on a field trip to Colorado, and Their teachers sacrifice them to an ancient goddess of chaos on a Saturday. Who then resurrects them as mythical beasts who go on a murdering rampage." I smiled as I talked about the movie and could feel my teeth elongate into fangs as I spoke. "Yes, it's supposedly based off of the goddess Eris, A.K.A discord." "Sounds interesting. Let's watch it." Thomas replied, as he scooted closer to me and rubbed my thigh. Once the movie started to play, Cameron lit his blunt and we watched an hour and forty minutes of gruesome bloody carnage that I found hilarious. Once it was over Cameron suggested another movie and I fought the urge to roll my eyes. This one was about a family who go to visit their grandmother, who was actually a Wendigo. This movie was an animation and even though the graphics were good, I was starting to become antsy. I wanted to get down to the basement and get back to showing my father who was the real big bad-spider, but Neither one of my lovers were falling asleep. I only had one other option and I knew that they would agree to it but I had to wait until the movie was over. Once the end credits appeared I leaned over and kissed Thomas as I gently rubbed Cameron's soft penis until it became erect. After a couple of minutes of foreplay, we got down to business and didn't stop until all of us got a turn inside someone. Thankfully it managed to make them tired but unfortunately I was in need of sleep as well.

As we laid back onto the couch I allowed my consciousness to peel from my body and travel to the basement where my father was in a corner. He didn't have feet or hands and Smiled as Joy crawled along the wall while making her wings twitch. "Hey, Girl! Was daddy delicious?" Even though we were in his domain, my presence restricted his ability to fully absorb Shadow energy so that he could heal his form. "You're now a husk of what you once were, Father. And I have to admit that is delightful to see you like this." My voice echoed around the room as he silently cried and I sensed movement from someone else nearby. I returned to my physical form and opened my eyes to an uninhabited room. I sensed that they were in our bedroom so I transported myself there to see them lying in the bed while asleep. *Weird.* I got into the bed and decided against cuddling up against them as I laid back and projected my consciousness down into the basement cell. The sound of my father's screams filled my ears as Joy nibbled on his nubs and black blood pooled on the floor. Since the night mother was actually a cursed divine female being in a male body, it wouldn't die. But it could still feel pain while in a physical form. *Thanks aunt Za. A.K.A the spider mother.* "Alright girl, that's enough." She vanished and I waited for him to stop his useless sobbing so that I could heal his half eaten face. "So, what did we learn?" asked as his eye reformed. "I knew it!" I turned around to see a lion the size of a house cat and a small crab behind me. "You lied to us when you said that he was incapacitated by something else." Thomas said telepathically." "He was, I mean, *is*. That part wasn't a lie. A large chunk of his divine essence is missing. That's how I was able to do all of this." I responded. They vanished and I allowed myself to wake up and see the two of them looking at me with their arms crossed. "I'm sorry, this was threonly way that the three of us could have spent this much time together uninterrupted." That was another partial truth. The other shadow beings who I skipped over to rule this domain were waiting for me to slip up. Thomas took a deep breath and transformed into his divine crab form. "I need some fresh air." My thick thighed lover crawled to the window as it opened and flew out into the wintery outside. Cameron took a seat on the bed and looked at me with pleading eyes that made my heart speed up in my chest. "I really want to be with you, Trimark. But lying to us isn't cool. We're a team." There wasn't anything that I could say so I sat next to him as I pretended to be physically hurt. I placed my head in my hands and breathed in and out for dramatic affect. "I just can't get this right." My monster-Lion lover shook his head as he got up and walked out of the room. I used my minds eye to watch as he made his way to the kitchen and waited for him to open the refrigerator door to teleport myself to the basement. I froze at the sight of my father sighting on the floor surrounded by Joy's dismembered body. He smiled as he ate her insides like it was ice cream with his other hand. *Shit!* Joy was my first shadow creation and I was very fond of my new pet. I stepped closer to take the carcass out of his hands but a shadowy aura enveloped his body as he laughed. He floated upwards as the dark energy grew thicker and all that I could see was a swirling mass of darkness. The energy began to fade and now my father was no more. He was a she with the same dark skin tone and shiny black eyes and hair. She wore an all black flowing gown with insect wing buzzing on her back. At the tip of her head was a crown and two tall antennaes. She smiled at me and I narrowed my gaze on her as dark lightning formed in my eyes. The newly revived bitch vanished as it exited my gaze and slammed into the wall that was behind her. *Fuck, Fuck, Fuck!*. I Didn't sense her anywhere in the house so I teleported to the kitchen where Cameron was making himself a sandwich.

"We have a problem!" He shook his head as he made the snack whole and rolled his eyes.

"Lay it on me, Honey."

"As you two saw earlier, I devoured the shadow of a beetle fairy, that I then made into a pet that I was using to torture the night-Mother."

"Okay, this is something that we know and are trying to work through." Cameron said, cutting the sandwich in half. I grabbed the other portion and decoured it in seconds before completing the tale of my latest fuck up.

"Well, he ate her seconds ago and is back at full power, now that he is in a female form and is also somewhere in the shadow realm." Cameron put down the snack as his eyes grew big. He ran around the counter at super speed and placed both of his hands on my shoulder. "He-I mean she is going to go after The day amulet. We need to find Thomas!!

I didn't know where I was going but I knew that I was getting as far as possible away from that tall lying mass of muscles. The one thing that I can't stand is a liar. He had no reason what-so-ever to lie to us. It's not like we wouldn't follow him into eternity. In the short amount of time that I've known him, I've fallen in love with the two of them. "Sorry, Cam." My cold breath came out as a wintery mix as a made my way out of the forest and upon a pond. Small orbs of light formed below the surface and made their way to where I stood. They merged together to become a small glowing white shrimp. "Do you know who I am." *Aww, this little cutie is in need of help.* If this was an evil creature in hiding, it's in for a real surprise now that I'm fully awakened. I've killed forty-six living beings that have come at me and a cute disguise and kid voice won't fool me for long. Gooseflesh crawled up my arm at the exact moment that Trimark appeared next to Cameron. "Told you bae! I knew where he was the entire time." "Uh-huh! It took you two teleportations to find him." The shrimp moved from my side to float in front of Trimark as it's body glowed and expanded. He took the form of Trimark, but with white clothing and the same insanely sexy smile on his face.

"Who the fuck are you?" Dark-Trimark asked.

"There's no need for profanity." It responded.

An evil laugh echoed around the eide area as a mass of Shadow energy crawled across the trees. "Two gods, for the price of one!" It came together to take the form of a tall beautiful dark skinned woman with beetle attachments. Her face was beat and her dress was giving goddess vibes. "Hello, Thomas. Hand over the Amulet." She demanded, and I instantly knew who this was. "Um, Tommy. I accidentally allowed the night-Mother to absorb dark energy and a female form." Dark-Trimark spoke to me but he didn't take his eyes off his previously imprisoned divine parent.

"Yeah, I gathered as much." I responded. Before I could say anything else, he leaped into the sky and unleashed a dark blast at the Night-Mother. From this perspective they were almost evenly matched but His opponent wasn't used to her new method of flight. A vortex opened and an all black unicorn appeared with a large four eyed crow behind it. "I'll take take in the philly and you handle the Pigeon!" Cameron yelled as he transformed and took to the sky. I simultaneously shifted into my crab form while releasing a ln artic blast at the demon lord. The crow dodged my attack as it sent large feathers my way. The air around me shifted as I managed to block his next attack. Out of nowhere the crow vanished and the unicorn appeared in front of me. "So Who's topping who?" He asked while emitting a bolt of bright red lightning from its horn. "A god never tops and tells." I countered while making an ice wall. The excess energy hit the ground and turned into cobras that hissed as they made a circle around me. I refused to be bested so I exhaled cold air that turned into eels that proved to be an even match for the snakes. "Now where were we?" It felt really good to finally be on an even playing field with the dark god who abducted me not too long ago. "I agree, it does feel good, to finally have an opponent who doesn't break easily." *Did he read my thoughts?* "Yes." He answered. The large unicorn bent leaned forward as red and black energy gathered around his horn and he sent them my way. I made the ice wall turn into hands that clapped together and disintegrated the attack as I threw out my claw and sent out a lightning bolt that he dodged. My lightning bolts were a devastation that tore up the ground and I made a mental note to save it for emergencies. I focused my eyesight on the divine horse as he readied another attack and made ice form around him. It moved at superspeed as it encased him in a glacier and all that could be seen was his glowing red eyes. I turned my attention to the two Trimarks who were battling against the Night-Mother with different elemental attacks. One used glowing water while the other used dark ice against the goddess of night. The sound of Cameron's roar filled the air as he chased the Demon crow over my head. *Get em, Bae!* "Ahhh!" Trimarks yell of pain pulled my attention back to him and my heart skipped a beat as he fell from the sky. The other Trimark caught his lifeless body as he fell and I ran over to where he laid him on the ground. A large hole in his chest took my breath away as I shifted into my human form and tears began to fall from my eyes. *The bitch ripped out his heart. My heart!* "Toodles!" She yelled with a sinister cackle as she teleported away. Cameron flew to my side and whined before shifting into his human form. "Everything happens for a reason, boys!" Thunder raged above our heads and mirrored the rage that eas forming inside me. A mass of multi-colored energy formed into a portal that moved closer to us as we cried. "Aunt Donna." Cameron said, through his falling tears. She held a small gold alligator in her hand as a cardinal perched on her shoulder. "I'm so sorry son." The goddess Ammit said to Cameron as it floated over to him and nuzzled the side of his face. She then opened her mouth to produce a small glowing pearl. "Put this in his mouth." She said, using her tongue to push it over to Cameron. The little cardinal hopped over to my shoulder as Donna, A.K.A Hecate held out her hands. "Time is of the essence, Cam." He did as his mother asked and placed the pearl in Trimarks mouth. "Thomas, I need you to get this weather under control and make a snowball. Cameron, we're going to need some of your serpent's venom." Her partially simple request stunned me as I nodded and produced an orb of snow the size of a tennis ball. "Perfect!

You know what to do." She said to the other Trimark. With all that was happening, I forgot that he was kneeling next to us. Cameron's snake Talaset appeared and sprayed the top of the snowball with pink smoke that reminded me of a snow cone. Without warning the Second Trimark devoured the entire thing and his body glowed once more as he was absorbed into the body of my dead lover. The hole in Trimarks chest slowly began to close as The Goddess held her hands up and we joined hands. *"Three hearts together that fit like a glove, with one as a divine beast and the other thebl lord of snow that falls from above. Together we use our divine magic to resurrect their fallen love."* Trimarks body began to glow with white energy and yellow energy that caused his body to float upwards as a large verticle eye formed on his forehead. "Now let's get out of here." Donna said. A pentagram formed at our feet and in the blink of an eye we were transported to a dimension that I'd never been to before. As the transportation star faded I looked around a wide room that was some kind of entry way. It was filled with ghosts, talking animals and other deities. They bowed as we passed them and The supreme goddess led us to an open doorway. "He can sleep in here until he wakes up." "We'll wait with him until he wakes up." "Of course. There are some things that we need to discuss in the meantime." She said, using her powers to place Trimark on the bed. The cardinal changed to his greek god form that was stunning as Cameron's mom, Ammit changed into her egyptian goddess form. Her dark skin and long flowing braids always took my breath away. But with one of my loves out for the count, I couldn't focus on anything but him. An hour passed as she told us about how Trimark's past life as a shrimp god who was also the son of an ocean deity named Oceanus, fell in love with my past life. That was something that I'd already found out but what I didn't know was that the night-mother possessed two less powerfull minor spider-deities of Aunt za's court and made them produce Trimark. Hearing that he ate his birth parents was sad, because it finally made sense as to why he was the way that he was. She also told us that he was now a direct reincarnation of that god and that he was also Omniterran. We had to sit through an hour long explanation of what those were and how the hue-mans of earth are on the precipice of a divine awakening. Now that the Night-Mothers essence is completely eradicated. He was free of her influence. That was a huge weight off of our shoulders but I couldn't allow myself to relax until he woke up. Not being able to sense his presence was making me antsy and I longed to feel his muscle bond embrace. Cameron rubbed the side of my fat rolls as I breathed in and out, while listening to the rest of the tragic story of what Trimark went through. In the end he was just as powerful as before, but without having to look over his shoulder because of a Shadow-drag queen who wanted to use him like a puppet. "Trust me, all of this worked out for the best. Even though she now has complete access to her divinity. At least Trimark can live a semi- Normal life. "Well that explains why I can't sense her anymore." My mouth fell open from seeing Trimark sitting up on the bed and Cameron and I moved at super speed to both of his sides to hug him. He tried to stand but stumbled as we caught him and helped him set back down on the bed. "How do you feel?" I asked. "Great!" He held his hands up and changed it into a pincher that shot out a blast of glowing water. The small puddle turned the stone into small patch of grass that made flowers sprout upwards. "Whoa! That's new." I changed my own hand into a crab pincer as Cameron did the dame with that of a scorpions and we touched the tips together as tears fell from my eyes. "Team claw is back in action." Cameron said, before he kissed Trimarks check. "Then I guess we'll need new names. I'm Ocean-claw." Trimark responded. "I'm forest-claw and Thomas is Winter-Claw." The tears kept falling as we hugged and the gathered deities laughed from our childish code names. All of them gave us some space and we used it to have sex as an hour passed and there was a knock in the door. Glowing mist formed around us and in seconds we were fully dressed as I walked over to the door to see who it was. "Yes." I said, while looking into the eyes of a light skinned woman with fox ears and a tail. "Sorry to interrupt, but the mother Goddesses request your presence in the great hall." "Okay, we'll be right there." ai said before closing the door. "I swear, if this is another one of my mothers surprise parties, I'm going to eat the DJ." Cameron said, with a growl. Triamark and I laughed as we mentally prepared ourselves for whatever the goddesses had in store for us. As we made our way down the hallway, our clothes changed to modern day formal wear and we exchanged surprised looks as the fox guided us to two large wooden doors. "Right this way." She said, while opening the doors with a wave of her hand. My mouth fell open at the sight of everyone in formal attire and then I saw my snowflake and ocean insignia on a banner above a large gathering of beings with variations of brown skin. Seeing them made me smile as I waved and they cheered and clapped. Most of them had bright Auras but I could see that others had Auras similar to what Trimark used to have. That was something that we would have to deal with another time, right now The three of us were getting married. *Definitely a surprise.* Once we made it to the podium I noticed that Cameron's parents were accompanied by five other beings who sat around The goddess Hecate, A.K.A. Donna. I waved as I realized that one of them was Darren and noticed that he and the others had a large vertical eye on their forehead. In front of us stood a very tall goddess with four arms and four eyes. Cameron gasped as he placed a hand on our backs and then began to bow. *"She is the supreme creator of our existence. The Goddess Aura. She's also Donna's mother and Darren's grandmother."* He telepathically. A smile formed on my face at the sight of a divine being who was black and cosmic blue. The sight of her made butterflies form in my stomach as she smiled at us. "Thomas, you are the glue that has made this union what it is. And as the Domain lord please speak your vows first." She said as her blue skin sparkled like the night sky. For the first time in my life, I was at a loss for words, so I decided to speak from the heart. "Cameron, Trimark. You two came into my life at the exact moment that I needed you. The supernatural world is still new to me but I vow to be the best version of my for the two of you." Cameron's parents cleared their throats and stood up as we turned to look at them. "And for his family as well." Laughter erupted around the large room as Cameron blushed.

"Mom, come on. You've already planned our entire wedding. Can we do this part?" He asked. "Sorry, I'll let you continue." My smile grew wider at the sight of his helicopter parents as they took their seats.

"Marky, Tom. I've been alone for a large portion of my life and I've honestly loved it. That was until the moment that I laid eyes on the two of the most attractive gods in existence." Everyone spoke up in disagreement as he held his hands up to quiet them down. "Correction: most attractive to me. Are all of you divine beings happy now?" He said pausing to look around. "I make this vow to the both of you that I'll eat whoever gets in the way of our happiness." "All three of us will." His mother added. The laughter erupted again and this time it was the supreme Goddess Aura who held her four hands up to silence everyone. "Trimark, please step forward." She requested. "After Aunt Za passed on to her next life, I was convinced that I'd die protecting the new keeper of the Amulet of daylight. Little did I know that I'd instantly fall in love with you and Cameron when I entered the fey forest. My death and rebirth has given me a different outlook on the life that I've lived. Now that I have the loves of my life at my side, I realize that there *is* room for three in my heart. The love of you two and newfound love for myself. I vow to not only show up for myself, but show you two just how important you are to me, for the rest of eternity." Another eruption of applause filled the air as tears fell down my face and I kissed them both as it dawned on me that I had the story of a lifetime, but couldn't tell a soul. I still plan on running my media empire, but I now have to juggle being a boss and daylight/winter lord. In this moment everything in my life has come full circle and I truly know what it means to have a family.

Creepy Corner

"Do you have any questions before the tour?" I still couldn't believe that my application was accepted and I didn't have to live with my overbearing parents anymore. Now I can walk around naked or cook whenever I want without anyone hovering over my shoulder. "Nope." I answered. "Welcome to Creepy-Corner apartments and come with me." The handsome ghost walked through his desk and headed to the open doorway while motioning for me to follow. "Over here are the mailboxes that can be opened with a thought. Yours is the one with the pentagram." We walked past a door that led to the basement and I shivered as a gorgeous dark skin woman opened it and waved. "Hi, I'm Imani. You must be the new tenant Michelle." I extended my hand but she shook her head no and stepped back. "I'm an ice dragon. Your human body temperature would drop to a dangerous level if I touched you." "Oh, Thanks. I wouldn't want to die before I moved in." I instantly regretted what I said because it was insensitive to my tour guide, Spooky. "Sorry, I didn't mean any disrespect." "Honey, I've been dead since nineteen-fifty-one, You're good." "Once you're all moved in I'll stop by with a gift." "Okay, that'd be nice, Thank you." Imani shut the door and we continued on our path to the large spiral staircase. "This next level is where the shifters live and the smell might be a little intense." Spooky was absolutely right. The smell of animal fur was so intense that I hated my heightened sense of smell even more than I hated homophobic people. "Oh, there is our resident Alpha, Lunara. Hey Girl!" "Spooky, my garbage disposal is backed-up again." "I'll send Bebe up there later. This is our new tenant Michelle." She looked at me and gave me a half smile before turning back to look at my ghost tour guide. "I have a dinner party later and I'll need it fixed before the moon rises. Welcome to creepy-corner apartments. We haven't had a witch live here in ten years." "That's because you tried to kill the last one after you found out about her child sacrifices." They shared a laugh but I didn't think that topic was funny. Hurting kids was one of my triggers and I'd use every once of my magic to deal with someone who does. "I'll let you finish the tour." She winked at me before turning into a wolf and running to her room at the end of the hallway. "She is a little intense because she's in charge of all of our shifters. Once the full moon's energy wanes she'll be a peach. Oh, and the apartments vanish once someone moves out or are evicted. You don't have to worry about living in the previous witch's home." We headed up the stairs as the smell faded and I thanked all the goddesses in a silent prayer until I sensed shadow energy. It was the only element that I had trouble wielding. "The apartments on the left belong to a family of shades and the ones on the right are occupied by a being of living silk. If you need something custom made they're your being to go to." I made sure to keep that in mind since I needed a dress made for my cousin's wedding in six months." We headed up the stairs and approached a white woman wearing tight blue jeans with a pink crop-top that exposed her stomach without a belly button. "Bebe, This is our new tenant, Michelle." "I knew I sensed a magic wielder. Hello, I'm the building maintenance technician." "Nice to meet you." "Did my ears ring a little while ago or was I tripping?" "You're not tripping, Lunara's garbage disposal is backed up again." "Ugh! When will that she-wolf learn how to use garbage bags? I'll get my tool belt." She said, turning around. "This is your apartment right here. I live down there and a sorcerer named Dino-jay lives next door to you. Place your hand on the pentagram." The star glowed as I held my hand up and then a lock clicked once I touched my palm to it. "Since you paid a year in advance, so thankfully I won't have to haunt you for the rent. If you need anything, call out my name and I'll appear." Spooky flashed me a smile as he phased through the floor and I walked into my new apartment that was waiting for me to unpack. "Okay, where to start?" Before I could do anything a knock on the door stopped me in my tracks. "Come in." Instead of opening the door Spooky passed through it with a serious look on his face. "I can't believe I almost forgot to say this, but the floor above you belongs to four very powerful deities. Do not go up there unless they invite you and please don't make any deals with them. The last witch that did is now trapped in some kind of prison dimension. Don't ask!" He floated backwards through the door and I took that as a sign to get to work on unpacking. "Out of thin air I summon thee, to help me unpack and make this place better suited for me." My breath became tangible as Vidrel, my owl familiar appeared in his human form. "Hey, Boss. I was waiting for you to summon me. What took you so long?" I took my bag off of my shoulder and placed it on the ground as he used his magic to pull out our things.

"The apartment manager had to go over my payment because dear old mommy took forever sending the check and then he gave me a quick little tour of the place. When you go for your nightly flight, don't go to the roof. There are deities up there."

"Is that what I sense?" He asked.

"I don't know, I'm not half-god like you." I replied, with a smile.

"Half sorcerer half-god. Get it right mystic." He responded.

"Yeah-yeah, Let's hurry up so that I can make us something to eat." My stomach rumbled as I spoke.

"Ohh, can you fry some chicken?" Vidrel asked. Everytime he asked for chicken I couldn't help but smile.

"Isn't your mother a nature goddess?" I asked.

"Yes and her favorite form to take is of birds of prey. I knew how to hunt and kill forest creatures by the time I was eleven. I'll take some fries too." I rolled my eyes as he manifested my furniture and the rest of our things. After an hour of using telekinesis to put things in their place I went to the kitchen and got to work on making us something to eat. As a black woman it might have looked cliche to fry chicken or the "dirty bird" but I loved it. My recipe was the shit and my fries would give any fast food restaurant a run for their money. "Damn, Girl if we weren't gay I'd ask you to marry me." "Take your plate before I clip your wings." "Bye Felicia!" "I'm regretting giving you that tablet." We walked into the front room and I used psychokinesis to turn the television on. "Let's watch that one show about the people who are on the love game cruise." *Hungry for love.* A chill crawled up my spine at the mention of a love game and I didn't know where it came from but it made me feel weird so I changed it to reality television instead. "Yeah, I love this show." "Of course you do. They are put on an island and have to find the tool to escape by sundown." "You know I love my forest survival shows." He took a bite of the chicken and did a small dance at how good it tasted. "You put your hooves in this. Damn girl." "You got jokes, Feathers." A knock on the door pulled our attention from the show to the door that became see-through and showed Imani with a plate of food. I thanked all of the goddesses that she couldn't see the look on my face as I almost choked on a fry. "Girl you better invite her in. The last time you got some was a year ago and I know you need those cobwebs knocked loose." "Not too much!" I placed my plate on the table and crossed the short distance to open the door for the sexy dragoness. "Hey." "I wanted to welcome you to the building with this." "Oh, Thank you. Would you like to come in?" "Yes, I'd love to." I stepped to the side as she walked past me and inhaled her sweet scent. "This is my familiar, Vidrel." "Hello, welcome to our home. I'm Imani." I took the plate from her and placed it on the coffee table in front of us. "I'd offer you something to eat but I only made enough for us." "Oh, no worries." She cleared her throat and waved her left hand over my plate while holding her right out as a plate of similar food appeared. "Magic always has us covered." She answered. "Please have a seat."

Vidrel moved over to the love seat and allowed Imani to sit next to me and for a split second I saw her checking me out.

"I'll just put this out there, My girl is Single-single."

"Vidrel!"

"What? You are." Imani laughed so hard that it was contagious and we joined her. "Michelle, you are very attractive, but the last person I was with lived here on this floor and she turned out to be a psycho-witch. It's still a little too soon for me to get back out there."

"I feel you. The last person I was with turned out to be a child murdering fairy queen." "You knew Vivalia?" "Ha! Knew her, she was madly in love with me until we found the baby bones powder in her basement." "I hated her ass with a passion and froze her wings for a hundred years." I laughed so hard that I almost snorted as the memory of her telling me how much walking she had to do bubbled to the surface of my mind. "Anyways, so once we get done eating do you two want to smoke?" "I have to do some sightseeing but I'll leave you two to have some fun without me." Vidrel moved his eyebrows up and down as he looked from me to Imani. I mouthed the words no as he made his mouth wider and then dumped all of his food into it. "Done!" He returned the plate to the kitchen and turned into an owl before flying out of the open window. "He's a lively one." "You have no idea." A full minute of awkwardness passed between us until we looked at each other and smiled multiple times. "So tell me a little bit about our neighbors." Her eyes got big as her smile grew wider. Her body language said that there was a lot that she had to say and that she was the go-to person about everyone's business. "Well, don't EVER go upstairs unless they invite you. Those beings are territorial and most of the time we never see them. The Family of shades can be clique-ish but once they get to know you, they're good. Bebe is the coolest white person you'll ever meet. But you should know that she is a homunculus created a thousands of years ago. Spooky is a ghost

428

who was killed by his parents for being gay, so don't ask about his past. The living silk is the last creation of the spider-being Arachne, they're cool as fuck. Lu-Lu is a little intense and aggressive during the full moon. The other shifters are just as aggressive but they'll be more welcoming to you, just don't interrupt their moon rituals. Dino is antisocial because of his empathic abilities but he is also a good person and an amazing cook. I'm the only creature that lives in the basement so if you ever want to come down make sure you bring a coat or a warming spell, I like it freezing down there when I'm in my dragon form. Across the street is a building that is full of angels, be careful if they invite you over. They're very territorial and have a problem with magic users." I took a sip of my fruit water as I put all of that in my memory bank. The angel that owns the grocery store downtown was enough warning for me to stay away. Everytime I go into that market I get a bunch of cold chills until I leave. "Okay. So keep to myself and make sure that I don't venture off into the woods at night." She laughed so hard that her breath came out as cold air. "You're funny, but yes. Those up on the higher floor are scary. They don't have a mission to hurt us but immortal beings live in a different reality than us." I nodded and we finished watching television while simultaneously having good conversation for an hour until Vidrel flew through the window and landed next to me. "I know you said to be careful but I just encountered one of the deities on the roof. She's my older sister." He changed into his human form and began to pace in front of us. "My mother has birthed over a thousand children who I've never really met before. What are the odds?" "Are you referring to the demigoddess with bird wings and talons?" He shook his head no as he took his seat. "She's a rock demigoddess, who told me not to speak her name out loud unless I need her." "Should I plan a dinner party?" "She invited us upstairs for lunch tomorrow." Imani shot me a look that said that it was a good thing and I nodded in agreement. "Sounds like a plan. Should we bring something?" "Uhh, I don't know. What do you bring to a demigoddess who can grant herself anything that she wants?" Imani placed her hand on my knee and I couldn't help but smile from the gesture as I looked her in the eyes.

"She loves rare seeds."

"That's wassup, I have a whole pouch full of seeds that I kept from my break-up with dusty-wings."

"Aww, you are wrong for that."

"Am I lying though. You remember the smell of those wings of hers. It changed the color of my favorite sheets." All three of us burst into laughter as someone else knocked on the door. It became translucent to show us Bebe and Spooky who smiled as I got up to open the door. "Hey. Come in." "We stopped by to bring you these and welcome you to the building." Neither of them had anything in their hands until Bebe snapped her fingers and manifested a bouquet of flowers and handed them to me while a bottle of wine appeared in Spooky's hand. "Oh, Thank you." I'd never met a homunculus before but I heard stories about them being spirits that were bound to artificial bodies who could use magic. Normally I stayed away from white people because of their unnatural hatred for those of us with melanin. It was a good thing that I was done eating and was about to light a blunt. "I got the glasses." Vidrel pointed at the table and five wine glasses appeared along with a vase filled halfway with water. I pulled out my pre-rolled blunts and handed one of them to my familiar to light so that we could have a good rotation going. "Has Imani already given you the rundown on your neighbors?" "Yes, I just have one question though. Why are there divine beings living here if they can make their own divine domains?" Spooky took the blunt and hit it once before passing it to Imani. "The top level is their domain because there aren't a lot of places where supernatural beings like us can live without causing a ruckus." "Yeah, That's why I said not to go up there unless they invited you. You could get lost and wander around for years until you find your way back." "AND it's dangerous as fuck! Don't forget that part. They own the building so by supernatural law all of this is theirs." Imani's serious tone made it awkward again but I was thankful for it. I still remember the first time I met my first demoness when I was thirteen. She tricked me into unleashing her but thanks to my magic and Vidrel, I was able to bind her to a pair of scissors that I still have to this day.

"So, Is she ugly or cute?" "She's aight. Not nothing to howl at the moon about." I had to lie or the bobcat shifter would try and beat me to the punch. Michelle was the most beautiful woman that I'd ever seen. Her beautiful braids and big brown eyes gave me a reason to put on something cute.

"Aren't you in a relationship?" "And?" I rolled my eyes at my beta who was always looking to add to her harem of supernatural beings.

"Girl you have already had sex with every witch that has crossed that threshold, can you give your box a rest."

"I'll rest when I'm in eternal slumber."

"You can just say dead."

"Whatever, I'm going for a run. See-yow later!" She changed into a house cat which was like a smaller version of her real form and climbed out of the window. *That pussy was always on the prowl.* The sound of small feet running in my direction pulled my attention to the hallway as my daughter Selene walked into the front room. "Mommy, Can I go outside too?" "Is your howl-work done?" She nodded and shifted into her little wolf form to let out a fierce howl. "What about moon casting?" "Aww, Mom, do I have too?" "Young lady, you are my daughter and every member of this pack has to know how to properly cast moonlight." She took a deep breath and channeled her energy into her eyes before sending out a blast of white light out of them. "Good girl. Okay. You can go play with your friends, But

DON'T go upstairs. Do you hear me?" "Yes, Ma'am." She turned to leave but I pointed at my cheek. "What kind of pup leaves with giving her mommy a kiss?" "Mom, I'm a big girl now." "You'll always be my little pup, now come here." I reached down and picked her up as she changed back into her human form. "Take you brothers with you. Mwah!" I kissed her cheek and nuzzled her neck as she giggled.

"Okay. Lunar, Crescent, Mom said we can go outside. Come on!" "Yay!" The two of them ran out of their rooms in human form and headed to the door but I moved at superspeed to block their path. "Aren't you two forgetting something?" I taped both of my cheeks as I bent down so that they could kiss me on the cheek. "Mom, we're big boys." I crossed my arms and looked up to the ceiling as I cleared my throat. "You're both my big boys, but you're not too old to give your mom a kiss." They kissed me and I stepped out of the way so that they could go play in the backyard. "Remember what I said. Don't go upstairs." "Yes Ma'am." I turned my attention back to my new pack member paperwork. Six newly scratched individuals and four immigrants from Africa. It was a good thing that I have two extra apartments for this specific reason or they'd have to live in the forest two streets over. My ears picked up the sound of wings before a top level goddess appeared in front of me. I looked away as her divine light shined bright in the room and slowly receded as she took human form. "My goddess, You honor me with your presence." "I'd be able to do a little more than that if your husband and wife didn't steal you away from me." She stepped forward and pulled me up off of the ground. The demigoddess who preferred that no one ever spoke her name wrapped her arms around me and kissed my forehead. Ten years ago we had a passionate romance that ended when we learned that the both of us wanted different things. I wanted a real relationship and she wanted to have fun, so I broke it off and then met the two loves of my life a year later. "I just came back from vacation, Here I brought your little cutie pies some gifts." She backed away and clapped her hands as three small cages appeared on the counter. My nose picked up the smell of non-sentient rabbit fur and I smiled at the sight of three large jack-rabbits. "I figured that this would be a good gift for their moon rituals. Is it too much?" "No, This is the perfect present for them. Thank you, My goddess." She put her wings into her back and took a seat on my couch as I sent the presents to their rooms with a thought. "Where are your mates?" "Overseeing the newcomers." "Does that mean that we have time to have some fun?" A smile curved my lips and exposed my fangs at the mention of our sensational sex that we used to have. "You may be my hall pass but no. The last time we had some fun I was stuck in my wolf form for a month and in heat for six months straight." "Now you know there wasn't anything straight about what we did." The both of us laughed and I found myself feeling nostalgic about the past. The goddess and I used to have so much fun in my wild years before I settled down. "Okay! I'll be right there." The nameless Goddess looked up to the ceiling before turning back to me with a serious look on her face. "I've got to go. One of the eight has escaped thanks to that witch and now I have to deal with it. Tot-Ta beautiful!" She blew me a kiss and turned into an albatross before flying out of the window up to her room. Everytime I see her it makes me think of how different my life would have been if I remained as her wolf with benefits. I shrugged off the feelings of the past and spent the next hour finishing up my paperwork. With all of that done I decided to grab one of my moonstones to take as a present to our new neighbor, Michelle. "Home! If my pups return before I do, make sure that they finish their howl-work and eat before they watch tv." "Yes, Alpha!" My lair enchantment responded. I placed the stone in my pocket and changed into my wolf form as the door opened to let me out. I ran down the hall at superspeed and passed by the father of shades who waved as he slipped under the door into his apartment. As I continued up the steps to the witch's room my wolf form changed back into my human form to knock on the door. I could hear someone coming closer as the smell of Michelle's wonderful scent filled my nostrils before she opened the door with a smile. "I brought you a welcome to the building gift." She smiled and looked at my hands and then behind me. "Oh, Right it's in my pocket." I pulled out the stone and the look on her face said that it was the perfect gift as she gasped. "Oh my goddess, Is this a raw rainbow moonstone?" I placed it in her hands and a static charge shocked us both as we giggled from the sensation. "Please come in." Once I stepped inside I instantly smelled the weed smoke and her previous visitors and the smell of feathers that held a divine charge like the top level goddess who just visited me but this wasn't as strong. "They just keep coming. I don't think you've ever been this popular." A short brown skinned demigod with brown wings came out of his room and extended his hand for me to shake it. "I'm Vidrel, Michelle's divine familiar. Welcome to our home." "Lunara but you two can call me Lu-Lu." "Whoa! That's a pretty stone. She loves them." "You might have to cleanse it. My pups brought it in from the wilderness of Colorado a couple of months ago." Michelle gasped and clutched it to her chest as a smile made her features even more beautiful. "You have kids?" I pointed to the television and it showed my triplets outside playing in their wolf forms. "Look at those little paws, so cute!" "Lunar, Crescent and Selene are good pups seventy percent of the time." "Lu-Lu do you smoke?" The bird demigod pulled a blunt out of thin air as I shook my head yes. "I'm only going to hit it a couple of times. I'm on mommy duty until my husband and wife get back into town." "Oh, You're married." I snapped my fingers and the television changed to show Romeo and Juliana. "Oh, why is he that fine?" Vidrel asked. "No, why is she that gorgeous? Damn!" I couldn't help but to laugh from their comments and looks of objectification. Yeah, I did that! The three of us make a very attractive throuple. "Um, I hope this doesn't come off as being nosey. Which one of you is the mom?" "I am, Juliana used to be a he-wolf named Julio. About ten years ago we asked the deities upstairs to change him to a her." The both of them looked at me with shocked expressions. Everyone in the building already knew this and was welcoming of the change, unlike the mortals who condemn those who want to change the physical body to match the consciousness and spirit inside. "That is so cool. I had a friend who did that. She went from being a sorceress to being a sorcerer." Vidrel let the blunt with a thought and inhaled its smoke once before handing it to me. It was some good-good and had to be home grown. Damn! Instead of hitting it once I hit it twice and was happy that I did.

"May I ask what kind of witch you are?"

"Yes, I feel like it's not talked about enough. Everyone wants to be a druid, alchemist, spell caster or seer. I'm all of them and more. My father is a soothsayer from Haiti and my mother is an aboriginal american enchantress who falls into all of the mystical categories."

"Girl me too, my father is a conjure-man and my mother is a wolf goddess."

"Oh, shit so we're all hybrids. Welcome to the club." The bird demigod Vidrel held his hand up for me to give him a hi-five and for the first time in my life I clapped my hand against his. Normally I wouldn't do such a thing because it's unbefitting of an Alpha but being around them has had a weird effect on me. "Whoa! Who's that?" I turned to look out of the window to see a muscular angel floating outside of the window with a smile on his face. He pointed at Vidrel and motioned for to come outside. "Uh, Michelle, I'll be back." "Uh-Huh! Don't come back with eggs, Young man." He smacked his teeth as he walked over to the window and opened it while unfurling his wings. "If I do, we can claim it on your taxes. Hey, I'm Vidrel." "I'm Mysoneith. I saw you zipping around the roof. Would you like to go for a fly?" The dark skinned angel asked. "I'd love to." He turned back to us and winked before jumping out of the window. "I feel like I should give you a little warning. The angel-born are just as dangerous as the goddesses and gods." "He's older than the both of us and three times as powerful. I think he'll be okay, but thank you for your concern." Her smile made me blush and temporarily forget that I'm married with pups. "How did he become your familiar?" Michelle laughed as a memory played through her mind and she hit the blunt a couple of times before passing it back to me. "Funny story. So Here I am going through my nature quest to get my mystical practicing license and I came across a group of divine boars that invited me back to their village for a ceremonial feast. Little did I know that I was the main course and that they were going to use my uterus in some kind of disgusting ritual where they sacrifice it for the ability to birth more children. I managed to kill half of them but used up a lot of my magic and at the time I didn't have a familiar so I was a sitting duck. Vidrel just so happened to be flying over that part of the forest and saw that they had me cornered and dropped down to help me by forming a familiar's contract. He was the only one of his mother's children who was half human and desperately wanted to get out of the forest." I couldn't help but to laugh and I hoped that she didn't find it insulting, but I knew the herd of boars that she was talking about very personally. "When I was thirteen I had to hunt a divine beast for my Alpha right of passage and killed their chief. At the time the moon was two weeks away from being full so I had to fight them off with martial arts and magic until I could shift into my wolf form." "Wow, Talk about a small world." "Right." Before I could say anything else I heard a howl that let me know that one of my pups was hurt and ran out the apartment at full speed without looking back. Even though I was running at superspeed it felt like an eternity until I made it to the back door and let out a howl from the sight of Selene with a broken paw. "W-what happened?" My question came out as a yell and I could feel my fangs begin to elongate as I bent down to inspect her injury. "We were playing by the tree and I dared her to jump from that branch to the ground and she landed on a rock." Behind me I could hear the sound of human footsteps before Michelle stepped into the doorway and gasped. "I can help." She ran to my side and pulled out several vials of potions from her pockets.

"Is she allergic to anything?" Seeing my little princess in pain had me at a loss for words. Wolf cubs don't get their healing powers until they reach their preteen years. "Lu-Lu! Did you hear me?" "Yeah, I mean no! She isn't allergic to anything." "Okay, I'm going to need you to hold her because this will hurt like hell." I did as she asked and rubbed her head as she cried. Michelled mixed the potion's together until it became a glowing vial of sparkling liquid. "A mothers love and milk is a child's first meal, with these words and ingredients I use them to help this pup heal." The liquid changed color from blue to yellow as Michelle swirled it around and then poured it over Selene's broken paw. She let out a soft whimper as her bones snapped back into place and I seeing her be strong calmed me a little. "There we go. Good as new." Michelle put her things away and stood up as I pulled all of my babies into a hug. I don't know what I would have done if she wasn't here. The top level deities wouldn't have lifted a finger if it didn't benefit them and I would have had to go up to their floor because they prefer to not have their names spoken out loud. "All of you go inside. I need to have a talk with Ms. Michelle." After all of them were inside and out of hearing range I broke down in tears at the mystical healer's side. "Thank you." Even though it was something that I could have healed if I had the proper ingredients I still continued to cry. "I did what needed to be done. That's all. I'm sure you would have done the same for me if we were in paw prints." She bent down and pulled me into a hug as I continued to cry. "And besides, from what Vidrel has told me, your kind doesn't acquire the ability of healing until they become preteens. There was no way that I could call myself a healer or your new friend if I didn't help." She wiped away my tears and I couldn't help but to look her in the eyes before I kissed her soft lips. Michelle pulled back with a shocked expression as I got up and embarrassment crawled over my body. "I-I'm sorry, I was caught up in the moment. I should go." Before she could say anything I changed into my wolf form and ran into the apartment building. This would be the second time today that I ran away from her without saying anything. I'm a married wolf and even though they wouldn't have cared if I kissed a thousand people, it was not a good idea to kiss a new tenant. Especially one that's a witch with big breasts and lusciously soft lips like the ones that she has. I was running so fast that I almost knocked over my pups as they entered our apartment and managed to stop as I approached. "Mommy, are you okay?" "Yes, Baby." "Mommy, you smell like ms. Michelle." "Never mind that, go to your rooms and practice your moon casting." Everytime I smoke weed something crazy happens that makes me want to down a whole bottle of wine and go for a forest hunt to clear my head. Damn it! I might have a crush on the new building's new witch.

"Oh, shit! Looks like the new tenant is just as talented as you, Dino." "I see. Tomorrow, I'll have to stop by and introduce myself to my sister-witch. Normally, it would take a full moon or a bunch of ingredients to heal bone, but home-girl did her thang." "Yeah, she did. Now, hold still. I'm almost finished with your measurements." As the resident tailor, it was my job to make sure that the supernatural inhabitants of this building had proper clothing that allowed them to use magic freely, unlike the materials that mortals use that hinder their magical existence. "Okay! I'm done. I'll have your clothes ready by tomorrow." "Aight, I have a date that I need to get ready for." Dino pulled me into a side hug and then clapped his hands together to transport himself to his apartment as his body vanished into thin air. I turned my attention back to my work and ripped off my arm so that I could make all of the clothes that I was tasked with making. Thankfully, I'm a living pile of translucent glowing spider silk with the creative talents of a genius. "Bebe's new gloves are ready, so I'll sit it over here. Lu-Lu's family day clothes are also ready, and Imani's lingerie is also done. Now, all I have to do is finish Spooky's t-shirts before I start on Dino's robes. Boom! I have a plan of action. Oh yeah! I'm the bomb-the bomb-the the bomb!" "I didn't know that living silk could twerk!" I turned around to see the living shadow of Shadir. "I thought I told you to stop creeping up on me." "And I thought that you said my clothes would be ready yesterday." "Touche', Shadow-being. They're over here." I grew back my arm and used it to put the done clothes in the spot where Shadir's family's formal wear was and handed them to him with my other arm. "Here you go. These are some of my best works. I hope the fam loves them." "Now you know you're the best tailor in existence, Arnelia. So good that the goddess Athena was jealous of your work." "That was a past life. I'm just a simple tailor in this life." "Uh-Huh! Sure. To all of us, you're someone who stood up to one of the most powerful divine families that have oppressed the beings of this world with their power. You're a hero, or should I call you a heroine?" "Neither, I prefer to be called a fashion icon." The shadow-being smiled and bowed his head as he clutched the clothes close to his body. "All hail the deity of fabric weaving and innovative attire." He sank down to the floor and crawled under the door as I returned back to making Spooky's T-shirts. Since he was born in an era where all-white t-shirts were the hottest look, he wanted something that was specific to him. As a ghost, he couldn't wear normal clothes because of his intangibility, so my clothes were his only option besides floating around in the nude. Personally, I'd love to see his see-through private parts from behind, but now that our building is inhabited by children, it would be weird, and he was not a pervert like those catholic priests. Suddenly, the idea hit me harder than an abusive parent with childhood trauma. "I'll make him a bunch of graphic t-shirts with different depictions of ghosts. The first would be his name in ghost lettering, a blanket ghost, a floating black skeleton, spooky from the waist up as if he was moving through the floor, his face and hands floating above his body and the outline of his body. PERFECT!" Now that I had an idea of what I wanted to do I got to work on his shirts and was finished in two hours with the help of magic. Instead of the six shirts that he asked for, I was able to make a dozen in different colors and half of them I made into tank tops. "Spooky, I summon you to my home." My entire body tingled as the temperature in the room changed, and he appeared next to me. "Hey,

Ari. Wassup?" "Your shirts are done." He gasped at the sight of them, and if he could have cried, I'm sure he would have. "Thank you!" He made the shirt that he was wearing vanish as he picked up the black one with his name on it and put it on. "I love it, Ari. You're the best!" Spooky moved forward and hugged me since I was one of the only people that he could touch. "How can I repay you?" "You can start by letting me see that plump booty of yours." He turned around and pulled down his pants as I bit my lips. Damn, that's a peach right there. "Okay! What else? Do you want some head?"

"That would be good, but I'll save that for another time. Can you tell me about the new witch in the building? I want to make her a welcoming present."

"Oh, Yeah. Michelle is a nice woman, and if I had to guess, I'd say that she would want a dress or a sickening pant-suit." "Okay, Perfect." I ripped off my legs and arms as he picked up his shirts and turned to leave. "Hold-up. Can I see that ass again?" He smiled and let his pants fall, and I grew back my arms so that I could give it a slap. "Oh! Kinky!" Spooky blew me a kiss before he floated through the ceiling and wiggled his booty one last time. "Mmmm, I'm definitely going to get some of that before the week is up." "I'll be waiting with my ass in the air." After he left, I went back to working on Dino's robe by changing it from plain silk to a glowing bright red color with a pentagram on the back of it. It was easy since he already knew what he wanted on it, but I hit a snag when it came to making something for Michelle, who was a new character in our little supernatural story. I couldn't decide on what to make first, so I separated the materials and set them aside until inspiration hit me. Making a gift for someone that you didn't know was difficult enough without knowing what their favorite color and magic output was. Boom! That was the solution to my creative block. I need to go meet the witch herself and ask her some questions. I took a deep breath and pulled all of my threads into a body that presented itself as a male, even though I was technically a sexless pile of sentient magical spider-silk. The threads on the back of my neck stood up to alert me that someone was about to knock on my door just before they did. "Coming, give me a second." With a wave of my hand I sent all of my work into the second bedroom and made it a more welcoming space for whoever was at the door. I stopped to take a look at myself in the mirror before opening the door to see the new tenant with a basket full of potions. "Hello, I'm Michelle, your new neighbor." "Hello Michelle, I'm Arinella. Please come in." "These are for you. I made a bunch of fabric enhancers." "Ohh, My goodness. Thank you. I haven't had any of these since the last wi-." Damn it! I almost brought up the bitch that was peddling potions made from dead bodies. "It's cool, I heard all about the previous witch that lived here." "Phew, I know it's taboo to bring up old news. Since you're here, you can help me with something." She smiled as I put the basket on the coffee table and manifested the two piles of silk I was going to use to make her gift. "I wanted to surprise you with a gift, but I didn't know what you would like, and now that you've given me something that I really needed, I have to return the favor." Michelle took a seat on the couch while looking off in the opposite direction to think of something. "Do you make all articles of clothing?" "Anything you can think of to wear, I can make." "I do need a new pair of boots and a dress for a wedding." A smile curved my lips as I thought of the perfect pair of boots to make her. "Let me get your measurements." My eyes narrowed in on her feet and then up her body as I took in her size. "Got it! I'll have your gifts ready by the end of the day." "Cool, I have some errands to run, but I'll stop by later, around eight." "Make it ten. I have some other things to do." "Ten it is." She held her fist up for me to bump it, and when I did, my hand glowed the second we made contact. "Are you by any chance a relative of Arachne?" "Yes, My father is a descendant of her brother." I gasped and pulled her into a hug that she reciprocated. "Girl, we're family. I'm the reincarnation of Arachne after she killed herself from being humiliated by the goddess of wisdom. That sounds horrible now that I say it out loud." "It doesn't to me. From what I've heard, even the divine children of the deities have suffered from their wrath." "Not all of them are bad or evil. But at least we know that we're related. Welcome to the family." She gave me another hug before leaving, and now I had an extra boost of creativity to make her the gifts that she asked for, along with a surprise belt that I was going to imbue with the last of my good luck potion that I was saving for someone special. After working my non-existent ass off for three hours and then handing out the other articles of clothing that I made, I managed to get done with her items and managed to make her a belt that she could store magical items in. Dino left his gift for her with me before leaving for his date and the part of me that was nosey wanted to know what the powerful sorcerer gave to her. My threads tingled on as Michelle knocked on the door. "Come in!" She walked in with a smile on her face and a blunt in her hand. "I forgot to ask if you smoked earlier." "No, Smoke doesn't mix well with my creations or my physical make-up." "I'm glad that I listened to my intuition about not lighting it." "Thank you. I would have freaked out." She took one look at the items that I made for her and gasped as she picked them up. "Oh my goddess, this is fire!" "Fire! Where? Help me put it out!" Michelle froze and looked at me with a serious expression on her face until I burst into laughter from the joke that I've been using for the past year and a half. "I'm sorry, I really don't get out much and I've used that joke on everyone who has said that word." "Girl! I almost summoned a rain cloud up in here." I couldn't help but laugh harder as she joined me. As living silk I really didn't have family to talk to because all of my past life's family disowned her for incurring the wrath of a goddess, but now I feel like Michelle and I have started a beautiful relationship on good footing. "So the belt can hold an infinite amount of items, all you have to do is place them up against it and to recall them just place your hand against it and think of the item." "Cool! Do the boots give me super speed?" I tried not to laugh but the look on her face said that her joke was serious. "No, Even a being of magic such as yourself couldn't handle the power of speed. They will give you the ability to teleport anywhere you want to go if you've stepped foot in the building and I blessed both of them with good luck, The dress can change color and help you block hexes." "Awww, Thank you. I feel like my little potions don't compare to these. How about I invite you over for dinner sometime later this week? You do eat food, right?" I let out a loud laugh and touched her shoulder and tried to maintain it as much as I could.

"Yes, I've lived all over the globe. Whatever you make, I will eat."

"Cool, I just learned a Korean dish that I love to make, and my familiar Vidrel has been asking about it non-stop."

"It's been a while since I've had a family dinner. Thank you for inviting me."

She put the belt on and placed the boots inside before crossing the small distance and pulling me into a hug. "You're family, and to tell the truth, I hate being alone sometimes. Especially since my family lives in Canada." That was news to me. The last time I spoke to her ancestors, they were moving out of Greece to America. "Wow, They must have been the last family of melanated mystics to move out of Greece." "Yeah, When I was told about how our ancestors were the original people of Europe, I didn't believe it. Nowadays, when you think of Greeks, it's all "Olive" people who want nothing to do with people of a darker shade." "Ha! Girl, I could tell you stories of what I remember from my past life about the TRUE people of this world. No offense to Bebe's people, but white people coming into power was one of the worst things that has ever happened to this planet." She pulled back and looked at me with wide eyes. "Do you have time to tell some stories?" "I always have time for family, sit. Ask me anything." "How did white people trick the world into believing that they are royalty? Aren't they cave people?" I let out a laugh at how close to the truth she was. "All of the Ancient divine beings came together and made the flood and then hand-picked who they wanted to rule. From that moment on, the melanated royalty abused their power, and then people who are referred to as commoners rose up and usurped them. It kept going until the white people who are on the "Thrones" now ended up as rulers. The flood that's in the bible is one of many world disasters that the deities used to reduce the number of people on the planet several times. Apparently, we started out as divine beings who almost tore the planet up, and the divine mothers started the first reset." "Wow! That was going to be my next question. Can I ask about how you came to be?" I couldn't help but to smile because she was the first person in the building to actually ask me about my origins instead of me being a people pleaser and blurting it out while drunk. "Arachne bragged about how she could go up against any goddess of weaving and managed to best several demigoddesses until she came across Athena, who was masquerading as a mortal. The olympian goddess egged on my past life by getting her to talk bad about the goddess and then Athena made herself known and challenged her to a weaving contest. Arachne ended up beating her because the goddess was out of touch with manual labor, and because of it, she told her that she would grant any wish that she wanted. Being a woman in that time period who beat a goddess was both a good and bad thing. She asked the goddess to give her divinity to her." Michelle gasped and shook her head no. Yeah, stupid-stupid-stupid. "Athena turned her into a spider monster instead, and our family ended up disowning her. As a monster who was cursed by a powerful divine princess, she was undesirable by men and ended up committing suicide. Hecate felt bad for Arachne and merged her soul with her loom. That magic brought me into existence, and the rest is me having a crazy sex life while inspiring humans to create beautiful clothing from the shadows." Michelle stared at me with a shocked expression as she mentally added it to the story of what her ancestors had been through. "Wow, It would seem as if the divine beings have always abused their power." I nodded because that was only half of it.

Since the beginning They've behaved like spoiled brats who only cared about their needs, and even now, the ones who live at the top of this building can be a little boujee. "My mother said that it was the Deities who ran the people of color out of Europe by giving non-melonated people power over us, but we kept enough of our knowledge to keep them out of Africa and South America." "A lot of good that did. Africa is still occupied by the British, and the people of the other continents act like black people are worse than shit on the bottom of your shoe." "They hate us because they ain't us, Damn!" "Niece, it's worse than that. As people of color, we absorb more power from the sun and can manifest psychic powers that they can never dream of. Now, don't get me wrong, Bebe is one of the good ones, and there are a lot of white people who sympathize with all of the horrors during slavery, but that's about it. The rest are so deeply indoctrinated in their hatred of us that I find myself trying to strangle those who are racists. If you have more time, I can tell you the story of my life as Jacqueline the Ripper." "Oh, yes. Let me pour us some wine." Michelle clapped her hands and made two wine glasses appear next to white wine. "Oh yeah, we will get along nicely. I love white wine." "Me too. Red wine is too sweet for me." "Me too, and it stains my insides." We laughed as she poured our glasses, and for the first time in a hundred years, I felt like I had found a family member.

"Good morning, imani." The beautiful Witch, Michelle said with a smile.

"Good morning, Michelle." I responded.

"I didn't know what would be a good meal for breakfast, so I brought you a sheep and a goat." A smile curved my lips as the sound of the livestocks hearts beat faster. My smile must have shown all of my fangs with the way that she looked at my mouth and her eyes grew bigger. "Thank you, I love to eat live animals. I see you have a coat on, would you like to come in?" "Yes." I stepped to the side to let her in and caught the scent of her perfume. "You smell wonderful." "Good enough to eat?" She teased. "I haven't eaten a human since the dark ages, You're good." I responded. She stopped in her tracks as the livestock made noises and tried to run away. "Can they understand you?" "Yes, Certain mammals have the ability to pick up on human emotions, Along with apex predator psychic energy. But enough of all of that, please have a seat." Michelle shivered as we walked down my steps and I knew it would continue if we stayed here. "I'll take these. Come on Mr. Lunch and Ms. Dinner." Michelle laughed as my gifts reluctantly walked with me down the hallway. "I'll be right back." I said over my shoulder. "Yeah, sure. You take care of that." I walked my two living meals down to the room that I enchanted with the magic that I learned from my mother. The door opened and the smell of the cold forest it me full force as I dissloved the ropes and they ran as fast as they could to get away from me. *Oh yeah, they're going to be delicious.* On my way back to the front room I stopped by the mirror on my door and snapped my finger to change my outfit before walking into the front room to see the talented witch rubbing her hands together. I know that she has the power to make fire to warm herself up, but the simple fact that she didn't made me smile as I pointed at the door. "I know of a place that caters to supernaturals, would you like to go?" "I'd love to." Once we exited my lair, Michelle tugged on her belt and her coat turned into dust that receded into the belt as her pants became shorts. Her sweater became a halter top that showed her breast and hard nipples. *Damn!* We made our way to the Hotel that was founded and run by Minor bat gods. Just as we entered a small swarm of bats flew by and I waved as Michelle gasped. "This place is giving me a tingle." She said as we approached the entrance to the restaurant. "What kind of tingle?" I asked as One of the founders appeared. "Hey, Mira!" "Hey, Imani." She pulled me into a hug as her energy waves dissipated. "This is Michelle. She's a new tenant in our building." "Oh, Hey. I'm Mira, Welcome to our Hotel." Mira said, holding out her hand for Michelle to shake it. She leaned in and sniffed the air around her as my new friend arched an eyebrow.

"Do I smell magic, Oh, cool you're a witch." She asked.

"Yes, And Am I right to guess that you're a demigoddess?" Michelle asked.

"Yes." Mira replied.

"Cool." She said, as her stomache rumbled.

"Follow me." She guided us through a busy restaurant to a table and told a very sexy waiter that our food was on the house. After the waiter took our breakfast order, she left to put it in and a couple of awkward seconds passed before the waiter returned with our drinks. "I'm pleasantly surprised at how well hidden this place is." Hearing that made me laugh as I took a swig of my drink. "Ha!, this place isn't really hidden, Its more like the staff and guests are creatures of myth, so humans would become a part of the menu if anything bad went down. The staff is as old as I am." "Speaking of that, I feel like I've been hired as a reporter for supernatural creatures and I don't have your story." Everyone in the building knows all about my divine origins, and I used to hate talking about it, but now it is something that I help other supernaturals with as an unofficial therapist. "Where should I start? Let's see, I'm a dragon but to be truthfully honest, my mother is a goddess and I don't have a father." "Like at all or was he a human that died a long time ago?" "No father at all. My mother is the Orisha, Oshun." Michelle gasped and almost choked on her water as she looked me in the eyes. "You're a divine dragon?" " Yes, but I don't really like that title. The deities on the top level give us a bad name." "I rarely hear anyone talk about the orishas." I let out a light laugh and took a sip of my drink. "That's because they love it that way." After they allowed Africa to be invaded and the children of Africa to be dragged into the slave trade, as well as forcefully mixed with The true indigenous people of America, they were kind of embarrassed. My own mother kicked me out of her court for refusing to marry an abusive demigod. Well that and I ate his entire family and ended his royal line." I smacked my teeth as I shook my head from the memory of how crunchy their bones were and How I barely chewed them before swallowing. "Were all of them evil?" Michelle asked. "No, but that was the era of dragon hunting and getting revenge in the name of a family legacy." I answered. Michelle's eyes grew big as she nodded in agreement.

"Tell me about it, my paternal lineage is greek." She answered.

"Oh, so you're a part of the original aboriginal bloodline?" I asked.

"Yes, but that's a story for another time. Let's toast to not letting all that craziness hinder or growth." She said with a smile while picking up her drink. As our cups connecting three men walked over to the table and Brought with them an air of divinity. Each of them smelled like divine monsters and I waved as the one that was lightskin waved back. "I feel like I know you from somewhere." He said. "Yeah, me too." I couldn't put my finger on it, but decided to let the question fade as our waiter approached us. "You have about five more minutes in your food." She said looking at her palm and then waving her hand towards the three divine beasts and making two menus appear. "Hey, you're doing an amazing job by the way." Michelle said, to the waiter. "Awe, thanks gorgeous. You two make an adorable couple." She responded. "Oh, we're not together." We said in unison and then laughed.

"I'd be lucky to attract the attention of this beautiful witch." My smile showed my fangs once again as Michelle smiled.

"I'd be lucky to have a dragoness girlfriend like her." Michelle added.

"Oh, that's where I know you from, you're a divine monster! I'm Cameron, son of the Chimera/Manticore and the Goddess Ammit."

my eyes grew big as he extended his hand and I realized that I haven't seen him since the great divine war that ravaged the planet. "I'm the ice dragon, Imani and this is Michelle." "Nice to meet you Michelle, these two handsome gods are my husbands, Thomas and Trimark. We just got married." "Oh my goddess, that's wonderful. Congratulations." I said as Michelle nodded. We spent the next five minutes chatting with them until our food came and we decided to get back to our non-date. "Do you have any siblings." Michelle asked. "Yeah, I have so many of them that I lost count. The ones that I grew up with decided to side with the tyrant who birthed us, so I kind of imagine myself as an orphan. What about you?" "Yes, I have three younger sisters and two male cousins who my parents took in after their parents became addicted to negative emotions of dark magic." That was something that I hadn't heard in a while. Most magic wielders have heightened sensitivity to empathic magic and it was like a drug to those who abuse the power. "Are they okay?" "No, they became wraiths that my family sealed into a large black Tourmaline crystal." "I know a shadow dragon who might be able to help with that. Remind me to reach out to him when we get back to the apartments. The morning quickly turned into noon as we laughed and I realized that this was something that I hadn't done in a while. "We should head back." I said as a chill crawled over my body. My inner temperature was starting to rise as she and I waved goodbye and made our way out into the blazing summer sun in the sky. My legs started to feel weak as we made the small walk to our home and I had to brace myself against a tree as a warm breeze billowed by. "Are you okay?" Michelle asked in an alarmed tone. "To be honest, No. I'm a water-Ice dragon and I on the verge of melting like frosty the snowman." Michelle placed her hand on my shoulder and took a deep breath. "IMANI'S HOME!!" The air around us shifted into a whirlwind and in the blink of an eye were back at my lair. I exhaled all of the warm air and sucked in as much of my chilled air that I could. "Much better. Sorry, I was having so much fun with you that I forgot about my curse." "Curse!" Michelle repeated. "My mother is known for being supremely petty and I technically embarrassed her by refusing to be married off. She placed a curse on me that prevents me from existing In warm climates for too long." She sat next to me and I could see tears forming in her eyes as she pulled me into a hug. "I am so sorry that you had to go through that. No, child should ever be cursed by a parent. Especially by a parent who knows what your divine essence is made of." She said, rubbing my back. I felt my own tears fall as returned the hug and all of my emotions flooded to the surface. Up until this moment I felt as if I was truly alone in this world. The last witch that I gave my heart to took it and used my scales in powerful potions. After that I threw up so many walls that I made area fifty one look like a bouncy house. "Thank you for saying that, Michelle. I really needed that." "I'm the only lesbian in my family and my parents most definitely wanted me to marry a rich warlock." "Can I ask you a favor?" "You can can ask me anything, except for my bidy count. You don't want to know that number." "I'd never ask you that, I'm sure I've eaten as many people that I've had sex with." We laughed at the same time and i allowed the feeling to give me courage for what I wanted to ask her. "Can you make me one of your familiars?" My question caused her to immediately stop laughing as she looked at me with wide eyes and a open mouth. "Are you sure? I mean, I don't want you to live your eternal life in service of my mortal one. Vidrel has to go wherever I go and if something were to happen to me, you'd be the first to feel it." "The only way that I can think of to circumvent my curse is to tie my essence to someone else's who has a sliver of divinity. As a magical wielder, that makes you the perfect person to help me." Ever since my mother placed this curse on me, I've had to move around just so that I wouldn't cause another ice age. I was lucky to have encountered the deities on the top level, who enchanted the basement for me to be able to inhabit. Michelle placed her hand over mine and the kind gesture pulled me out of my trip down memory lane. "Imani, Divine-Dragoness of water and Ice. Daughter of O-"

"Can you leave her out of the tamer spell, Please?" The last thing that I wanted was for an out of nowhere visit from my mother. "Sure, Imani, Divine-Dragoness of the sea and Frigid temperatures. I Michelle Weaver, am making this pact with you to be my familiar, to help protect and guide me in my time of need and along my life path." Michelle's aura became visible in an array of colors as she spoke and then traveled up my arm until it enveloped my body. "Do you vow to uphold these requests until my dying breath?" "Yes, I promise to be with you and do as you command until your last breath." I responded. My aura absorbed the mana of hers as it came to life and my scales crawled across my skin. Michelle floated up off of the coach as she exhaled a wintery breath. "Cool, I-I feel strange." She said, hovering over the coach. As my scales receded, I felt warm for half a second as my mother's curse vanished. "That makes two of us." I said as she landed on the ground. I reached out and pulled her into a hug as I savored the warm feeling of her body temperature. "Come on, I have something to show you." Without another word, I took her by the hand and headed towards the room that was connected to the ocean. "Whoa-Whoa! Is that the ocean?" She asked, alarmed. "Yes, it's the Atlantic." I made a glacier appear below us and stepped through the doorway and onto it. "You're connected to the ocean now. You'll be able to breathe under water and handle the weight of its depths. "Before I was exiled, I made a portal so that I could keep an eye on my domain. I jumped off of the glacier and into the sea as my entire body shifted into my dragon form. ***ROAR!!!!!*** I let out as I broke the surface. "Oh-my- Goddess!!! You are so beautiful!" Michelle yelled as the winds around us moved in accordance to my true form. "Hop on, I want to give you a tour of my first home." I asked. She waved a hand over her belt and her clothes immediately changed into a wetsuit that would have made me blush in the way that it displayed her body. *Sheesh!!* She jumped on my back and I let out another roar as I sensed other life forms approaching us from the deep. "Greeting mistress, it's been far too long, since you've graced us with your presence."

Miladria, the sea unicorn said. "Whoa!!!!!" Michelle said in awe of the sea creatures who haven't been seen since the great flood. "Greetings, Miadria, this is my mistress, Michelle." "Behold, the witch, Michelle who has brought our goddess back to us!" Miladria yelled as her attendants emitted bright colors from their horns.

"Hey, Spooky. I checked the plumbing and Lu-Lu's problem didn't cause any damage. Also, I gave her an enchanted box of ifrit-flames that used to belong to an ex of mine, so that she can use it to dispose of her bones. If you need anything else, I'll be in my room." "Bebe, you are awesome. As always good job and thank you." My phantom building manager replied. We hi-fived since I was one of few beings who could touch him and then quickly walked away before he could ask me to fix something else. "Bebe, can I get your help with something?" *Damn it!* I was almost free. I turned on my heels as the shade Sha-Sha stepped out of the shadows. "Yes, what can I do for you?" "I'm having trouble with this light switch in my room." I fought the urge to make a joke as the Shade opened a portal into her room and followed her through it. "I thought you and your family preferred the darkness" "We do, but when we're in human form, we love how the light bounces off of our dark skin." As she spoke my artificial skin began to crawl at the exact moment that the lights came on and everyone yelled surprise. "We want to say thank you for all of the hard work that you've been doing and a little birdy told us it was your birthday." I frowned as I looked at all of their faces, because no one in this room should know that. With the exception of Imani and the top level deities, I'm older than all of them. "It was me. I told them. Happy birthday, son." I froze as my mother appeared out of thin air and pulled me into a hug. "Oh, mother, Um, Hello. I'm surprised that you've made time for me." I said, pulling out of her embrace. "Oh, honey, You know I have to *pop* in every thousand years or so." She replied, while wrapping her arms around me once more. "Do you though?"

"Sweetie, you're going to have to get over all of this, you transitioned millions of years ago and it was for your own good." She replied. My mother spoke about her separating my soul from my body and placing me in this artificial one as if it was a normal occurrence. She prided herself for successfully making the first homunculus and then giving the knowledge to the other divine beings with children that they could no longer control. "You speak about it as if you gave me a spanking." I answered. "Dear, You tried to take over the world and helped with the downfall of the first race." Even after all this time I could see that she wasn't going to budge or give me an apology, so I decided to change the subject, since it was making those around us uncomfortable. "How is my father?" "He is his usual self. Right now he's enjoying a well needed vacation on another planet with his girl and boy toy." *Of course the great and powerful Baldur is having the time of his life while humanity suffers.*

"It looks like you've made a name for yourself here. I'm proud of you." Her smile was sincere, but I was still pissed at how she made a choice for me without considering how I would feel about it.

"Thank you mother, but it would be a whole lot easier if I was in my godly form and had access to all of my divinity." I replied.

"I'm sure it would, but I destroyed that form before I placed you in this one. But at least you have all of your divine intelligence." She answered.

"Yeah, thanks alot." My tone came out way harsher than I anticipated and I almost regretted getting angry with her

"Beoyalzgrif, You only have yourself to blame. I defied your father and grandfather and saved you from death. It seems as if you're still angry, I'll leave and let you enjoy this day with your friends. I love you Forseti, always remember that." She vanished in a flash of moonlight. "Uh, Rude! There are Shadow beings who live here!" I yelled knowing that she could still hear me. She never viewed things from my perspective and seeing her brought back all of those emotions that I've run from for so long. I didn't try to take over the world to be its tyrannical ruler. I did it because divine beings as old as her were hurting innocent children. Anyone in their right mind would have done the same thing that I did. Or at least attempted to do so. "Are you okay?" Sha-Sha asked. "Yes, seeing her light fade from a room has always calmed me. Yay!! Happy birth/ death day to me." I sarcastically said. "Today is my birthday, but it's also the day that she placed me in this vessel. "So you're a god in an artificial female body?" "Yes, I never said anything before, because it's just a reminder that I don't truly matter to those who brought me into existence." "Talk about drama." Sha-Sha replied. I felt bad about making things weird for those who actually wanted to celebrate me and put on a smile as I looked at all of their faces. "Anyways, let's get this party going. Where's the booze?" I asked, holding out my hand and calling a bottle of wine into my grasp. "Hold up let me put a blunt in the air!" "Did I hear someone say blunt? Imani said, as she walked into the room with a smile on her face and our new tenants behind her. This was definitely something to see, because she rarely left her lair. There was something different about her aura and as I looked from her to Michelle, I could see that a curse had been lifted. Imani handed me a gift as well as Michelle and Vidrel and I actually smiled from sensing what was inside. "Aww, thank you. I've always wanted these." Before they could answer, the door opened and a literal angel stepped into the room. "Hello, I'm Mysoneith. Vidrelll invited me to your party. I hope it's okay." "Yes, please come in." Sha-Sha said, almost closing the door on Lu-Lu. "How rude, I come to party and Ms. Big boobs closes the door on me. She had her own breasts on display and I loved every bit of it. *Damn!* If I was in my original body I would have a instant ercetion right now. "Why Lu-Lu, what bug breasts you have." I said hugging her and taking her gift that was alive in a box with holes. "The better to greet you with my dear." She said as we all laughed. "Is this a rat?" I asked as my intuition showed me an image of the boxed beast. "Yes, One of my deceased were-creatures decided to make a scratch- pack out of normal rats without asking. And I've killed most of them. They make good pets and have special abilities that will be useful to your job. It can't procreate, so you don't have to worry about a unwanted babies." She answered. To my left a floating tool box appeared and I nearly fell to the floor at how many new magic tool were inside. "Thank you Dino!" The empathic Sorcerer wasn't a people person but his gifts always made up for the fact that he kept to himself. Time flew bybas we celebrated a day that I've hated for so long and I realized that the angel wasn't like his boujee family members. Ari stopped by with a gift that was a pair of magic gloves that could summon any tool from the box to my hands. Today was also the anniversary of the mother and father shade, Shalora and Shadir. So they left because they made reservations at the hotel down the street. We continued to parry as the sun set and I lost count of how many drinks and blunts that I had. *I guess there was an upside to existing in an artificial body.* I picked up the sound of a low pitch ringing in my right ear as I thought about it and pushed it to the back of my mind. Shavelos clapped his hands to draw everyone's attention to him and I could see by the look on his face that he was about to say something rude. "The weed has been smoked, the alcohol has been ingested and all of you can respectfully get out." "Shavelos! Don't be rude." Sha-Sha said.

"You heard me." He replied.

"Boy! You are not in charge of this apartment!" She added.

"Girl bye! You are three seconds older than." Seeing them go back and forth made me wonder if I would be the same if I had siblings of my own. Everyone took that as a sign to get going but Michelle invited us to her apartment to continue the party. Shavelos must have another one of his sex-dates, because normally he would keep this going until he passed out from an excess of everything. Ari and Spooky left before everyone else to go have their weird sex and our large group consisted of me, Vidrel, Michelle, Imani, Sha-Sha and Lu-Lu. The angel had to flap home to get some of his weed and almost missed the rotation as Imani passed me the blunt. "How about a party game of truth or dare?" Vidrel asked. Everyone nodded in agreement and I looked around the room at our small party of supernaturals for who would go first. "Imani, Truth or dare?" "Dare!" "Well that was fast. Okay, I dare you to kiss Michelle." A huge smile formed on her face and she nodded before leaning over to do the dare. "Yeah! get some of those boobs in your hands, Lady dragon." Vidrel said, clapping. Once they were done, she broke away as Michelle licked her lips and shook her head no towards Vidrel but she smiled as she exhaled a cold breath. "Bebe, Your turn." "Since my truth was previously broadcasted to everyone, I'll also pick dare." "I dare you to become a butterfly." *Easy!* "Dare accepted." I clapped my hands together and allowed my body to glow with semi-divine energy as it broke apart into a swarm of butterflies. A round of applause filled the room as I flew in a circle over their heads and then landed back in my seat while changing back into my human-like form. "Michelle, you're next. Truth or Dare?" "Truth." she responded. "Tell us a truth about yourself." "Okay, well let's see. Oh! As of today, Imani is now apart of my crew." *I knew it.* Everyone clapped once again and this time I joined them, because this meant that our caged dragon was free of her climate curse. "Mysoneith, Truth or Dare?" Michelle asked, as he handed the blunt to her. "Truth!" His voice came out louder than he anticipated because of the alcohol and Vidrel rubbed his back as he leaned forward. "Okay, cool. Since you're the second angel that I've had the pleasure of meeting. Tell us something about yourself." The powerful witch asked. "Um, ok. Here goes." He said, picking up his shot glass and emptying it. "I am the first born son the fallen angel Malucifera." He stood up and unfurled his wings from his back but this time they were brown bat wings, instead of his usual feathered pair. My mouth fell open as he stretched them to their full wingspan. "My mother is a part of the group of first born angels that fell from the higher realms. My grandmother made all of the angels to thwart my aunts plan of creation and when they realized that they were being used, they rebelled and were banished from heaven." "Whoa, so your mother is technically the devil?" I asked, referring to the title that was given to the arch-angels. "Sort of, my grandmother exiled all of her children who failed her. Thousands of angels fell from the higher realms and a lot of primordial beings from her court followed them to this realm.." "I was also kicked out of my mother's domain." Vidrel said as the angel pulled his wings into his back and then hugged him. As a being who is straight, I love, love. Or romantic passion. When I was a god I had plenty of consorts, but never had the chance to marry and then have offspring of my own. "Please Excuse us." Vidrel said, Taking the angel by the hand and leading him into his room. The rest of us continued smoking and a half of an hour passed as Lu-Lu was dared to shift into her wolf form and give me a ride around the room. The love birds returned with sexual energy in their auras and Michelle made a joke about Vidrel laying eggs. I said my goodbyes and went to my room to finish opening the rest of my gifts. I loved how this operated off of a small amount of sleep and I was the right amount of high and tipsy. Most of the building was probably asleep so I decided to go for a walk. It took me twenty minutes to make it to the park that was four streets over and I decided to have a seat on the bench that had a perfect view of the pond and the tall building across from me. I'd traveled all over the world and decided that America was the place that I wanted to call home, since the deities who dwelled here died long ago. This land was so far away from the one where my family normally inhabited, so it was perfect in the way that I wouldn't have to see any of the Aesir. The sound of hooves hitting the pavement pulled my attention to an all black unicorn heading towards me. It had blue hair with a bright blue horn and glowing red eyes. "Hello, uh, Mr. Nightmare." I said looking to see the sex of this mystical beast. " Hello, Gorgeous." It responded in a deep telepathic voice. I'd encountered many supernatural creatures in my life and it'd been a while since a unicorn came out of their dimension. Its red eyes glowed bright as it reared up on its hind legs and began to shapeshift into a dark skinned man wearing summer clothes. "I'm not a real unicorn. I just live to take their shape from time to time. I'm actually a god like you. I'm Darkon." He said, extending his hand for me to shake it. "Bebe." He was extremely attractive and unlike his unicorn form he had the most dazzling blue eyes. "Well aren't you an interesting being? Your body is kind of female, but your spiritual energy is giving off male vibes." He said, letting go. With the contrast of his skin, eyes and white teeth, he could have been a male model. With him being a god, he'd have eternity to try something like that. "Aww, thanks. Most straight people act like it's a crime to give someone that they aren' attracted to a compliment." "I've never been one to judge and when I was like you, I had a group of friends who were what is known as queer." Darkin laughed and the sight of it was slightly alarming with the amount of dark energy that was coming off of him. "What would you do to be in a real body?" He asked. I Arched an eyebrow at him because I hoped that he wasn't asking for sexual favors. "No, no, nothing like that. I'm a thousand percent gay." "I've gotten pretty used to this body and if it isn't a divine one, I don't want it." "Interesting." Darkon leaned back as a breeze blew by us. "Although the pain of be shunned by my parents hurt me to the core. I've made my peace with trying to control everything. I'm at a good place in my life." "So if you were given the chance to kill them, you'd turn it down?" His serious tone made me stare into his blue eyes and slowly nod as the winds calmed down. "Are you sure?" He asked once more. "Had you asked me that when I was originally placed in this body, I would have said yes. But now I've found people who accept me for me." I answered. "My parents have their flaws, but giving them death won't change anything." "As I spoke those words I could feel myself become lighter as I unknowingly released a million year old pain from my soul. "It's good that you've forgiven them, but I can't do the same for my ex-god of a father. He was extremely abusive and deserves everything that I've done to him." He replied. A full minute passed as another breeze blew by and heard him take a deep breath before speaking again. "Today is also my birthday and I would like to give you a gift that you rightfully deserve." He snapped his fingers and my body vibrated as all of my divine essence pulsated with my aura. In seconds I was surrounded by a rainbow tornado that made my skin prickle like static electricity popping all over my skin. "You're welcome!" The sound of his voice was the last thing that I heard before I passed out and felt my astral form entering the dream realm. My first dream was of me being trained how to with martial arts, weapons and my powers, by my mother. "Mom, I can't do it." I pleaded. "Forseti, you are the grandson of a divine king. Son, you can do anything. Try again." I made a fist and punched a hole into a large boulder that was in front of me. The pain that I felt made me want to scream but I knew that my mother would hit me if I showed any sign of weakness. Since this was a memory dream I fell to the ground as the pain in my fist slowly receded and my fingers healed. "I looked up to see the hole in the boulder begining to close and my mother's smile. "We are divine beings, and we can destroy and heal. Now do it again." I blinked and the dream changed to when I awoke in the homunculus body in my mother's moon chamber. "What have you done?" I yelled. "Don't take that tone with me child. You're the one who broke one of the divine laws. You should be happy that I was able to work my magic and save your soul from reincarnating into the mortal realm. You father and Grandfather are furious with you on how you embarrassed our family. Because of that, I have stripped you of your name. From this moment forward you'll be known as Beoyalzigrif." My mother vanished in a flash of light as I sent out a wave of energy that destroyed everything around me and put a hole in the roof exposing the light of a full moon. I blinked and was now standing in front of the four all powerful top level deities who hired me two hundred years ago. "Thank you for hiring me, great ones. I will not let you down." "See that you don't Aesir-born." They vanished and I woke up to the sounds of birds and to bright light shining down on me. For the first time in a million years, I felt the warmth of sunlight on my skin as well as the sensation of a morning breeze blow around me. *Oh, shit!* I stood up and turned in a full circle as I relished the feeling having *real* reactions to all of my senses. "Are you okay, pretty lady?" An elderly man asked. I nodded yes as a strange sensation formed in my lower abdomen. It slowly began to diminish as a warm liquid traveled down my legs and made a wet spot on the front of my shorts. "Oh, shit!" I said as I continued to urinate on myself. "Miss that's not shit its piss." He added. Normally my body would break down whatever I ate and drank and use it to fuel the body, so this was a welcomed experience. I was happy but embarrassed at the same time as a jogger passed by and my stomach rumbled as I let out a really loud fart. "Uh-oh! Now that's shit!." This must be the bubble-guts that everyone is scared of.

"Oh, these shirts are so fucking cute. Ugh! That thick bodied living silk, spoils me." *I need to make sure that I do something extra in the bedroom next time we have sex.* Last night we had some of the best sex that I'd ever had and I know for a fact that if either one of us could get pregnant , we would have. "He Spooky, I have my rent." Sha-Sha said, as she stepped out of my desk's shadow and handed me folded up hundred dollar bills. "Look at you, turning your rent in on time like an adult." "Don't expect this to be a normal thing, Oh! And My parents rent is in there as well." When I went to grab the money she moved it from side to side as I reached for it. "Girl! You are two thousand years old, not two. Give me that check before I change all of your locks and turn on all of the lights." "You're no fun." She finally released the check as her body fell back into the desk's Shadow. "Cute shirt by the way." "Thank you!" I placed her money in the drawer and checked off her and her family from my rent list. Bebe sprinted into the building with a weird smile on her face and then headed towards the bathroom that I never use. "I have to shit! Isn't it cool?" She pulled down her pants and let loose without closing the door. I could have existed in my entire after life without hearing her flatulence and defecation. "Man do I feel good." She said, while getting up and using her powers to clean herself and also flushing the toilet. As her clothes changed I saw for a split second that she had nipples and an actuall vagina. Not small indentations or meridian points. "Last night I met this dark god who I know would give you a ghost bonner. And he offered me a chance at getting my real body back and when I turned him down, I woke up like this. Oh, and apparently yesterday was his birthday as well." Bebe clutched her abdomen as she braced herself against the doorway and blood soiled the crotch of her pants. "Uh, did you just get you very first period?" "I hope so, I'd hate to die before I have sex in this body." She waved her hands over the area and the blood peeled away from her and swirled into a red ball. She then summoned a mason jar into her hands and placed the nasty period blood inside as a lid appeared and screwed itself shut. "And what are you going to do with that?" I asked, weirdly intrigued by how it sparkled as it caught the sunlight. "What are you going to do with that?" "I don't know, maybe help people who can't conceive or make a weapon out of it." She turned on her heels and left without saying another word. *Okay, This has been the weirdest week.* Everytime I think that I've seen it all, something new happens. I spent the greater part of the morning finishing the paperwork for mortals who need to come and look at the zone restrictions of the flower bush out front. By noon I had all of my work finished and felt the immense presence of someone new entering the building. She floated above the floor as she headed into my office and then landed in the chair with a smile. The beautiful light brown skinned woman had spiritual energy that was off the charts and far greater than the tip level deities. "You're a goddess!" I said, practically yelling. "Hello, Marlin Vernons. I am Hecate, Goddess of, well a lot of things. Spirits, phantoms, ghosts, poltergeists, the after life. Which is why I am here." "Oh my Goddess, Wait! Are you here to collect me? I'm not ready!" I said getting up. She chuckled as she waved off my questions and I slowly allowed myself to calm down. "Please call me Donna, and No, I'm not here to collect you. I actaully need your help." "I'm dead, what can I do for an all powerful goddess?" "I don't know if you've noticed but you're a special spirit." I laughed at her response and hoped that it wouldn't result in some type of curse or something. "I don't know about that, my father was a pastor and my mother was a school teacher. I died young and have wandered to every place on this continent. I don't even know what my unfinished business is." She smacked her teeth as she shook her head no and crossed her arms. "I can help you with that. But first let me ask you this. Do you know anything about you maternal grandmother?" "Uh, no. My mother only said that she was into mumbo-Jumbo and never answered any of my questions about her." "Of course she did, With her husband bing a pastor, such things would be considered blasphemous. Marlin, Your grandmother was a high ranking Mambo with powerful spiritual energy. I owe her a favor." *This is hilarious, I have ties to a grandmother who was a root worker.* "Before I help you with your unfinished business, you need to do something for me." She snapped her fingers and the door to my office closed and then turned into a wooden door with two crescent moons on each side of a pentagram facing us. "I told you superiors that you will be taking the day off." I hoped the frown that I gave her didn't come off as rude, but they haven't given me a day off since I was hired and our agreement was contingent on me never leaving this building. What she just said shouldn't be possible, because they are forces not to be messed with.

"Oh, honey, their little power is *nothing* compared to mine."

"I'm still confused about what you want me to do." She laughed out loud as the door opened and I peered into the vastness of a void dimension that I hadn't seen since my death. "Is that hell?" "No sweetie, you're too good of a person to be resigned to that fate. It's a pocket dimension where I place spirits who have to make amends with the living or other spirits who haven't crossed over. Two particular spirits are there and have been asking to speak to you." I knew exactly who she was talking about and I've got nothing to say to them. "With all due respect, I don't want to talk to them." "I think you do." My body began to move on its own as I passed through my desk and flew into the small dimension as the doorway closed behind me. I hit the ground of what felt like a cavern floor and noticed that this was the first time that I was able to feel stone and not a rough surface that prevented me from passing through. I tried to float upwards but couldn't, so I stood up on my feet and heard my bones pop as two things happened at once. I felt the cold air on my skin as I inhaled the scent of where I was. "The daughter of the supreme mother has finally answered our prayers." I turned around to see my parents who looked at me like actual loving parents, instead of the usual glares of disappointment that they gave me. "Well if it isn't the people who kicked me out for falling in love." I spat. "We've had a very long time to think about how treated you, and we want to apologize, we're sorry son." They said in unison. I rolled my eyes so hard that an unseen force knocked them sideways. "Did I just do that?" I asked as my eyes and forehead throbbed. "Yes, Son. You inherited your grandmothers spiritual power." My mother said, getting up and then helping my father to his feet. "We're sorry son." *Yeah, sure!* "Just because you two are at a place of forgiveness, doesn't mean that I am. But if it means that I don't have to see either of you again, I forgive you, Now goodbye. Where's the exit?" They shared a look that said that there was more and a cold chill crawled up my spine. "Son, we have something to tell you." My father said, with his usual serious tone.*Ugh! What else could they possibly have to say?* "We paid Timothy's parents to start the mob that killed you." I clenched my jaw as I felt my body float upwards. The memory of that day slammed into me with full force as I began to glow with white light. For the first time in years I cried actual tears as my breathing intensified. "You did what?" My questions caused a tornado to form around me and the pain that I experienced in my last moments of life made gooseflesh crawl all over me. They broke my ribs, plucked out my eyes, severed my tongue and penis, before hanging me from a tree. "How could you?" A tremor made the ground shake as they were knocked to the floor and I felt myself wanting revenge all over again. "We-we're sorry, son." They pleaded as fissures formed around them. "SON, HOW DARE YOU CALL ME THAT?" It was one thing to go through what I went through, but to now know that *they* are the cause of his death, hurts me to the core. "Son, please. We've existed in a time loop of that day ever since. We are truly sorry." "It was *you* who gave me the money for the cinema and you drove me there." I couldn't believe what I was hearing as I saw a flash of Timothy's face in my mind when they killed him first. All that they could do was look at me with pleading eyes as they cowered in fear on the ground and I realized that it was time that I let this go and forgive them for my own emotional well being. Since I now had lungs that could breathe, I took a deep breath before speaking. "I forgive you two for not being the parents that I needed. I forgive you two for causing my death at the hands of the people who only saw the color of my skin." Their bodies began to glow with white energy as my mother stepped forward with her arms outstretched for a hug, but I stepped back and shook my head no as they faded away. "Good riddance to hurt people who hurt people." I expected the doorway to appear but after a full minute passed nothing happened. Six ghostly forms appeared in front of me as one of them took the form of someone who took my breath away. "Timothy!" "Linny." He responded. He ran to me and hugged me and I could feel his heart beat match mine. My ability to speak left me as he kissed my cheek and pulled back to look at me with his extremely sexy smile. "After my death, I made a deal with a goddess for revenge and possessed my parents and then made them get the members of the mob in one place so that I could burn it down." A smile curved my lips but tears still fell from my eyes because I was the cause of his death. "I'm sorry Tim, I shouldn't have written about you in my journal. My parents found it and caused all of this." He wiped away my tears as continued to cry and he kissed my lips. "No, I wrote two letters. One was to you because I was scared and the other was to my parents because I wanted us to run away together. Can you forgive me?" "Yes, You're the only person to ever accept me for me. I forgive you and I hope that you find peace in your next life." I kissed him back as his body began to glow and he faded away in the same manner that my parents did. Two more forms stepped forward and I recognized them as the two men who pulled me out of the men's room stall at my fathers church and kicked me in the ribs, for telling on them when they stole from the collection plate. They died in a hunting accident shortly after from being mauled by bears. "We had a crush on you and that's why We picked on you all the time. We're sorry." They said in unison. "Jared and Sherman Donalds, I forgive you." They bowed as their bodies glowed and they faded away. The next two ghost stepped forward and I recognized them as my grandparents on my fathers side. "We are so proud of you and waited here to tell you that this building is rightfully yours." My grandfather said. "This building was illegally bought by him. Argus Maxwell." They said moving to the side as another ghost appeared and took the form of a fat white man. "Hello son." Argus said with a forlorn look on his scruffy face. "You're the man from the painting that we all agreed was creepy and we put it in the closet in my office." I heard rumors from Bebe that he was the building owner who used his skin color and wealth to purchase this building. "Obtaining this land and building by forcing your ancestors to sign it away was wrong. I want to apologize to you and them. I knew that they had a secret and used it against them." They turned to look at me with a smile as a rainbow aura formed around their bodies. "The three of us have so much in common, Grandson. Our love as Husband and wife is simply for show and we are just as queer as you are. You are not alone." They glowed brighter but instead of fading away they turned into butterflies that flew into my heart. The white man turned to me and got on one knee. "I pledge my life to you." A floating lease appeared in front of me and

I placed it in my pocket as everything became black and I was back in my office with Argus at my side. The goddess Hecate clapped her hands as she got up from the chair with a smile on her face. "Well done, Marlin. Thank you so much for dealing with my annoying little problem." "I should be thanking you, My goddess. I feel as if a weight has been lifted off of my chest." "More like your spirit." She pulled a large book out of nothing and handed it to me as her body began to fade. "This was your grandmothers and I was tasked with giving it to you as your spiritual inheritance. You are a part of the living and spiritual world. Use this second chance to finally do the former." I turned to look at Argus and his eyes grew big as he stepped back. "What?" "Sire, you should look in the mirror." He nervously said. The book in my hand changed into a hand mirror that I held up to my face and gasped at the sight of a large glowing vertical eye on my forehead that exuded small wisps of white light.

"And here I thought I'd surprise you with lunch." My dark-heart began to beat faster in my chest as I watched my secret lover use her power to send his date away with a wave of his friends. We've been seeing each other unbeknownst to everyone else in the building because *he* asked me to keep it on the low. But now I see that it was because he didn't want anyone to know that it was because he was fucking a feline shifter behind my back. "Shavelos, I don't know what to say." He responded. I smacked my teeth and tried my hardest to remember that he was an all powerful being. "You could start with the truth as to why you made me promise not to bring anyone else to my bed. You said that we would be each other's one and only." I couldn't believe that I feel for the oldest trick in the book of lies. I really thought that this top level deity actually loved me. "I'm waiting Vipliseriroth!" In this moment I didn't care that I spoke his name out loud and it made his divine energy radiate all around him as he stood to his full height. "CHECK YOU TONE, LESSER BEING!" He said with his booming voice echoing all around us. "There's the god that I've been fucking for almost a year. The one that thinks he's better than all of us because his parents are fully divine." I shot back. "I AM BETTER THAN YOU LOWER DIMENSIONAL BEINGS!" His words became tangible as I found it hard to breathe and I fell to the floor while the food I was holding turned to ash. "I WAS ONLY USING YOU TO PASS THE TIME! DID YOU REALLY THINK THAT I WOULD ALLOW MYSELF TO BE SEEN WITH A DARK SKINNED CREATURE SUCH AS YOURSELF?" It became harder to breathe as I gasped for air and felt his power envelope my body. "GET OUT OF MY SIGHT!" I was painfully teleported to my apartment that I shared with my siblings and was finally able to catch my breath. "Los! Are you okay?" Shanae asked. I shook my head no as I got up off of the floor and ran to my room. My sisters knocked on the door but I didn't answer as I climbed into my bed and silently cried. I truly loved that god with all of my heart and he tossed me away as if I was a used condom. "Shavelos, if you're in danger let us know. We got your back." Sha-Sha said in a concerned tone. "Yeah, tell him to go get his sister." Shanae added. Even though I was sobbing like a child, a smile curved my lips as I took in what they were saying. Unfortunately this wasn't one of those *beat a bitch up* situations, but I loved them for always having my back. I used my mind to open the door and the both of them ran in with their obsidian/onyx weapons in hand. "I just broke up with my boyfriend." I answered, helping them calm down as their weapons vanished. They sat on either side of me and hugged me as I continued to cry. It reminded me of when we were little shades and both of them would hug me like this when I was having a bad day at mystical academy.

"I'm sorry, Bro." Sha-Sha said.

"It's his loss anyways." Shanae said, rubbing my back.

That may be true, but I was beginning to imagine a life with him. He was immortal and I purposefully kept my own immortality a secret for this main reason. I now see that all of our plans were pillow talk. A little sugar coating after I clapped his cheeks. "I'm so glad that I didn't tell him our family secret." My voice cut the silence but my sisters gasped as they both gave me shocked expressions. "Boy! No one is worth divulging the secret of great grandmother Lilith." "I see that now." I replied. "I really appreciate you two for being here for me, but can I really want to be alone right now." "Okay, lil Bro. But our offer still stands, tell him you got big sisters that can fight." Sha-Sha added, as they vanished. It was times like this that I regretted turning down the extremely attractive man that I met last week while getting take-out. "Darkon." I said out loud, remembering his name and those dazzling blue eyes of his. The hairs on the back of my neck stood up as he appeared in a swirl of shadows. "Damn, cutie. I was wondering when I was going to be able to see those brown eyes again." He waved his hands at me and my body floated off my bed and into his arms.

"I heard what he said, and the color of your skin is gorgeous."

"You're only saying that because you have the same complexion." I responded. Darkon let me go and shook his head from left to right as we took a seat on the bed. "I only lie to those who I plan on killing, Shavelos." Looking into his blue eyes made me want to get on top of him and press our lips together, but right now I was in a vulnerable place and refused to use him as a rebound. My own shadow warned me of how dangerous he could be and I'd hate to have two powerful gods angry at me. "I can kill him if you want." "I appreciate the offer, but I don't want his friends to go around searching for how he met his end. Our building isn't made for an all out power battle." I took a deep breath as I tried to push those events to the back of my mind and realized that I smelled like burnt food. "I'm going to take a shower, I'll be right back." I said getting up. "Do you want some company?" His smile gave me butterflies in my stomach but I nodded yes and he snapped his fingers to make our clothes vanish. "Damn, you got a big ol'black booty." He said, giving it a smack. "Back at you." I responded while grabbing his butt and pointing at the shower to turn it on. The sound of our penis's slapping our thighs was all that you could hear as we walked to the bathroom and I remembered to lock the door just in case my sister told my parents. "I saved you in my phone as Night-Peach by the way." "Cool, I saved you in mine as Dark-Blue." I replied. Darkon smiled as he wrapped his arms around my waist and I placed mine over his shoulders. He was slightly taller than me and for once I loved it. Our faces moved closer to each other as we pressed our lips together and passionately kissed each other. His body was more muscular than mine, but I loved the feeling of our rock hard abs rubbing against each other. Time flew by as the water washed over us and I finally pulled back to look into those eyes that made me weak in the knees. "Shavelos, I'd normally ask to have sex with you at this point, but I want to take you out on an actual date. But only when you're ready." He said, in a soft tone as his voice echoed off of the dark stones of my shower. Even though the shadows warned me that he was capable of evil acts, I knew that he was karma to those who did wrong and went unpunished. "I'd love that. But can you give me some time to bounce back, before I bounce on you?" He arched an eyebrow at my word play and nodded yes as I reached for the soap. We took turns washing each others bodied and when I was done with his, head kissed my forehead before teleporting away. I got out of the shower and summoned a towel to dry myself off as I picked out the perfect outfit to wear. Now that I'm a single Shade, I gathered all of Vip's gifts that he gave me and placed them in a ln enchanted box. I spent another half hour cleaning my room of his residual energy and decided that I go make myself a snack. "Oh, are you getting rid of you gifts from your secret lover?" Shanae asked. "Can we keep some of it?" Sha-Sha asked. "Have at it." I said walking into the kitchen as my shadow pointed to the door right before somone knocked on it. I could see in my minds eye that it was Dino and sensed the apprehension in his shadow's energy.

"I got it." My sister said, opening it with a thought.

"Is everything okay?" Sha-Sha asked.

"No, I need to talk to Shavelos about something important." He said, stepping into our apartment for the first time in ten years. "I hope that this is okay to say in front of your sisters, but we've been seeing the same top level deity. I followed one of his dates home and then used a spell to see what else our divine boyfriend has been up to." My mouth fell open as I realized I was boyfriend number three. "Wait! Shavelos, You've been seeing the only male deity upstairs?" My sisters asked in unison. I nodded as I closed the cabinet door and fought the urge to throw the glass cup in my hand at the wall. "Oh, hell no!" Sha- Sha yelled, while summoning her weapon. "I don't care who he is, no one three-times my little brother. He can't be allowed to get away with this." Shanae added, While pulling her own weapon out of the ether. "I couldn't agree more." To our left a tall light brown skinned woman appeared and all of us bowed until she was fully formed. "Mother Hecate, You honor us with your presence." Dino said, using her goddess given name. She was the mother goddess who created Lillth the first omniterran female and then Talevorne the first omniterran male. The other deities created Eve and Adam afterwards, as a divine one-up, but all of that ended up being a crazy mess of *I can do anything better than you can.* "Please get up, we have a lot to talk about. Oh, and I summoned your parents." She said as their shadows crawled under the doorway and they floated upwards out of them. "Dark mother, you honor us with your presence. Welcome to our home." They said with a bow. "I've been here for quite some time and I want to apologize for how they've treated you." The goddess clapped her hands and made and summoned Michelle, Lu-Lu, Ari, and Imani. "My apologies for pulling all of you away from your families, but we have a serious problem. All of the top level deities have been siphoning small amounts of your essences from the moment that all of you have moved in here." Each of us shared a look that said we were thinking the same thing. *Revenge!* "Michelle, it is my understanding that your familiar Vidrel is related to one of them.

Can you summon him?" "Y-yes Supreme Mother. Give me a moment." She went to the window and opened it and within seconds a small owl landed on her shoulder. "I knew it! I was extremely tired when I got home from visiting her yesterday. What do you need me to do, my Goddess?" She smiled as she rubbed her hands together and multicolored energy wafted off of her. "There is only so much that I can do to make it look as if I haven't done anything at all." The great goddess spoke and I felt her energy flow into me as I took deep breaths. In seconds I felt as if I could run at super speed to Africa and back in under an hour. "Whoa!!! Talk about a glow-up!" Michelle said, while hovering in the air. "So we're doing this?" Dino asked. "Hell yes!" Me and my family said at the same time. I should have known something was up when I had a dream that the top level deities were eating ice cream out of bowls with our names on them. Dino teleported from where he floated to my side and placed his hand over my shoulder. "Let's take down those top level parasites." I high-fived him as a smile curved my lips and Lu-Lu let out a fierce howl.

We left the shades apartment and Lu-Lu went to hug her cubs before we headed upstairs. Now that the great mother has blessed us with heightened powers, I have a new outlook on being a tenant in this building. I now have the ability to take the form of anything that I could imagine and actually wield the four elements. Before now, I had to get myself in a meditative state to hear them. Seeing my left fist covered in red flames and my right made of stone, gave me chills. "Are you okay?" Michelle asked as she placed her hand on my shoulder. Normally I would recoil or quickly remove her hand, but now my physical aura helped put up a stronger level of resistance. It felt as if I had something that I was missing. "Yes, I'm kind of in awe of meeting our divine mother in person and even more grateful that she gave us a blessing." "Right! She was drop dead gorgeous and it made me happy to see her in her true form as a melanated goddess." "Me too. And to think they had us believing that she had an olive skin tone." We burst into laughter as Lu-Lu came up to us with her two mates behind her. Two cats appeared at her side and shifted into human forms as they approached. "We're ready to go." The alpha wolf said, with glowing eyes. Our party of supernatural beings headed up the steps where Bebe was waiting with a smile on her face. My eyes grew wide as I picked up her emotions that held organic physical energy attached to them along with her power level being higher as well. Spooky floated upwards out of the floor with Ari in his arms and he held an air of living mana about him that didn't exist before. "Oh, yeah. We got this!" I said, out loud as we made our way up another set of stairs and my forehead pulsed as two entities appeared behind us. "Hello, I'm Darren senior and this is Idna. My wife said that you could use some help." As Darren spoke he closed his eyes and a large vertical eye opened on his forehead and the one named Idna changed into a monster. She had big brown feathered wings, two different types of snake heads at her sides, golden horns and an eye like Darren's on her forehead. Her living appenges hissed as the one on the left breathed fire and the one on the right exhaled an icy breath. Darren looked past Lu-Lu and Ari to where me, Michelle and Spooky stood and squinted his large eye. "Oh, shit! You three are newly awakened omniterrans." He said with a smile. Hearing him say that made my ears ring and I made a mental note to ask what that was after all of this was settled. "Shavelos, Ari and Idna. You're with me as team-A. Michelle, imani, Vidrel and Sha-Sha, you're team-B. Shalora, Bebe, Shadir and Darren. You're team-C. Shanae, you're with Lu-Lu's group and will be team-D." Once everyone was with their assigned groups we headed to our doors and prepared ourselves for the battle of our supernatural lives. "I've been meaning to ask you if I was the other man or you?" Shavelos asked with a smile. I laughed as he clapped me on the back and the door in front of us glowed bright. In an instant we were sucked into the home of the god who played us both. We were now standing in a large cavern-like chamber that looked like the first level of a video game. Vipliseriroth floated next to a minor deity that ilI recognized as Hermaphroditus. The child of

Hermes and Aphrodite. They gave us death stares that we gladly returned and Shavelos smacked his teeth as he realized that we were looking at another one of Vips lovers. "I feel as if I should tell you both that they are my true consort and you two were flings." *Of course he is married to a divine hermaphrodite.* "You're the one who introduced me to him. You've got to be kidding me!" Shavelos launched himself at the minor Greek deity with the flawless skin and they began to battle it out with energy blasts. I lifted myself off of the ground as two other unnamed gods appeared to battle our other team mates. "This is hilarious. You think that you're a match for me now that you've been given a little boost." He laughed as I summoned lightning to my hands and sent it at him as he released energy from his eyes. His smug look quickly faded as he realized that our power levels were evenly matched and readied another attack as I conjured more lightning. This time he teleported to the left as my thunderous blast hit the wall and made rocks fall down to where my team was. "My fault!" I yelled as Vip tried a sneak attack. "Keep your three eyes on the prize, Emotion lord!" He yelled, while sending fire balls my way. I moved to the left and right as I thought about what Darren said earlier. Suddenly glowing rings appeared around me and shrank to entrap me as I was now unable to move. He moved his hands to the left and I was simultaneously slammed into the wall. It knocked the wind out of me as an excruciating amount of pain formed in my right shoulder. My head throbbed as I broke free of the rings and felt the pain lessen as the seconds passed. *Oh yeah, I'm unstoppable!* Seeing that made the ancient pale skinned god gnash his teeth as he tried to bind me again but I made my aura stronger and disintergrated the rings. Never in a million years did I expect to have to fight against someone who I loved, but stealing from me was a huge no-no. He sent more lightning my way and this time I allowed it to hit me as I used a hand gesture and converted it into a spell that I sent his way. The four-timer copied my hand-spell and volleyed by sending it back at me. Five minutes passed as we kept adding to it and directing it at each other until I allowed it to hit the wall behind me and he turned into a jaguar. *Two can play that game!* I turned into a tiger as a ferocious roar escaped my throat. We charged each other and he went for my neck as swiped my claws across the side of his torso. His teeth managed to graze my neck but I did more damage as he cried out in pain from the blow I delivered. The two of us circled each other in the air as our paws walked on nothing and then charged each other again. This time I bit down on his neck as he placed his teeth on my front left paw and tried to sever it. We were locked together like that for a full minute until I used empathy to pour the pain that he caused me into his wound. Vip whined as he let me go and then ran in the opposite direction. "No, you don't!" I said changing back into my original form as my wounds healed. I chased after him and grew large bat wings that helped me close the distance as he tried to open a portal but I made an ice wall appear that prevented him from entering it and then slammed feet first into his back. The force of my attack sent him flying to the ground and rendered him unconscious as I lowered myself to the ground. His glowing green eyes snapped open as he got up out of the crater and clapped his hands together. "I have to admit it, you've really surprised me Handsome." I pulled the wings into my back as I stepped closer to him and we summoned energy to our hands at the same time. "Fuck you parasite!" Shavelos yelled from across the room as I looked out the corner of my eye and watched as his opponent of two sexes crumbled into gleaming dust. "Looks like you're a widower, Vip!" I laughed as I taunted him and to my surprise he cackled. He held his hands out at his sides as two ghostly forms appeared and took the forms of people who I haven't seen since I was ten. "Hello son." My father said, with a smile. They both had glowing pentagrams on their foreheads and I realized that they were under his control. "I remembered how much you went on and on about their disappearance and how you asked me to help you find them. Well here they are. Go give your son a hug." He continued to cackle as tears escapee my eyes and was momentarily to stunned to speak. My mother was the first to move as she reached out to grab me and my body moved on its own as I back flipped out of her reach. I threw out my hands and knocked her backwards but my father moved at super speed and punched me in the chest. The blow sent me flying but I quickly recovered as I prepared myself for another attack. Thankfully I wasn't alone as Shavelos wrapped his arms around my mother and it gave me time to block my fathers martial arts attacks. His emotionless face looked odd as he fought me with everything he had but as his son I was properly trained in defense combat. ***"Dad, I know you can hear me. BREAK FREE!"*** He ignored my words that were laced with power as he continued to punch and kick. I couldn't sense Darren or Idna anywhere close by and was gratetful for Shavelos taking care of my mother. Or so I thought as he grunted and landed at my side. I helped him up as my parents joined hands and used their free hands to start an unrecognizable spell. Their bodies glowed with green energy as the dust of Hermaphroditus flowed towards them and they absorbed. **"We never loved you. We couldn't wait to be rid of you and is the reason why we gave you to the coven to be raised. Your constant bitching about your emotions made us want to sacrifice you to divine beings for a new life!"** They spoke as one, while their bodies became one. *Ew!* They sent one attack after another at us as Vip laughed and Shavelos and I made a barrier. "That's it! Darkon, I need your help!" He yelled. "I thought you'd never ask!" A disembodied voice spoke and the shade's shadow crawled up his body to become his aura. He placed one hand on my shoulder and used the other to point two fingers at my parents. His emotions poured into me and I concentrated on separating them as Shavelos separated his fingers and my parents were pulled apart by an unseen force. I lowered the barrier and flew to them as Vip vanished and they looked around the room with confused expressions. A chill ran down my spine as I felt another divine being fully form next to Shavelos. "Thank you." He said, hugging the tall muscular being who made Vip run like a little bitch. "We should get out of here, this domain is no longer stable." The being known as Darkon suggested and in the blink of an eye, we were in the hallway of the top level. The other teams were just as victorious but just as beat up as we were. Vidrel had a saddened look on his face but held a large glowing stone in his hands. Bebe had a white glowing feather in her hands that I recognized as belonging to the bird goddess. She handed it to Lu-Lu who took a deep breath as Spooky examined the head of a large praying mantis. "I think this belongs to you two." Darren and Idna stepped forward with an unconscious Vipliseritoth. He was bruised to the point of it being funny and sad at the same time. "We sucked out his divinity and placed it in these." They dropped him on the floor and held up two clear quartz crytsals that glowed with his power. I took them and handed one to Shavelos. We crushed the crystals and absorbed the powers as our own as everyone clapped. "Thank you, it's been a while since I've taken down a divine god." Idna said, before she vanished in a swirl of yellow flames. "Is he mortal now?" I asked. Darkon nodded as I held my hands out towards the ex-god. My energy flowed out of my palms as indigo light swirled around him. ***"Not a cat, bat, hog or dog, I now change you into a frog."*** Shavelos snapped his fingers and a tank appeared around Vip as he became an amphibian. I called the small tank into my hands with telekinesis and headed towards the stairs as a thought occurred. "Um, Spooky. Who will take over their apartments?" From this point of view, there were now four normal penthouse apartments. "Can I take over my sister apartment?" Vidrel asked No one protested so he went to the door and placed his palm against his. Shavelos went to the door of the apartment we just left and placed his palm against it. "I think it's time that I live in my own space." He said, claiming it. "I'll take this one." Bebe said, claiming the room across from us. "Then that leaves this one." Spooky said. "How about we use it for gatherings?" I suggested. "Are sure you don't want it?" Spooky asked. "No, I'm happy with my place and now I can change it to my liking." I held my hand up and allowed my power to flow outwards as everyone agreed. "Then let's plan a party?" Michelle said, as she placed her arm over my shoulder. "Can we do all of that tomorrow?" Lu-Lu asked. After everyone said their goodbyes, I went down to my apartment with my parents and made a bedroom with an ensuite. I took a shower and then began the preparations for a family meal. When I was a kid my mom used to make red beans and rice while my dad fried chicken, so I decided to make that as they showered.

"It smells good in here son." My mother said, in a soft tone.

"That means a lot coming from you. How are you feeling?" I asked.

"Proud of the sorcerer that you've become and glad that you were strong enough to rescue us." My father said, entering the front room.

"Just so you know, we didn't mean anything that we said." He added.

"I know, those were his words." I replied, as I glanced over at the tank that housed Vip the frog. "Why did he take you two of all people?" They shared a look as I made their plates first and then made mine before using my mind to place them on the table. "Son, we aren't like ordinary sorcerers. We're special." My mother said. I laughed at the irony of her words. We are wielders of magical power in a world that's filled with mortals who don't even know we exist. My parents took a deep breath at the same time and closed their eyes as large vertical eyes opened on their foreheads. My fathers looked like a swirling maelstrom and my mothers was like looking at a night sky filled with stars. As I peered deeper into their eyes an intense throbbing sensation formed on my forehead and I grabbed the table as it grew stronger. "That's it son, don't fight it." My father said, rubbing my back. It was the worst pain that I've ever felt and I cried out as every color in the room became more vivid. The searing pain heightened all of my senses as I smelled the food, the body wash that I used and the frog tank. I could hear the sound of Vidrel laughing as he flew around the rooftop with his angel boyfriend. In an instant the pain was gone and I realized that I was looking around the room with both of my eyes closed. "Congratulations, Son. You are now a fully awakened Omniterran." My mother kissed my cheek as my dad patted me on the back and I took several deep breaths. An enormous amount of information flowed into the part of my mind that was Clairsentient and I instantly knew knowledge my familial origins. Both of my parents were Omniterrans who survived the great war and went into hiding, along with the other survivors. Some of them closed their mind-eyes so that they wouldn't attract suspicion and blended in with the next generation of sentient life. My visions ended with an Image of myself on a throne and I gasped as I realized that my parents are royalty. "Your intuition is always spot on, Son. Your mother is. Chieftess and I was her consort." My fathers voice entered my mind as he ate and the image of Michelle entered my mind before she knocked on the door. "C-come in." I responded as the door opened. Michelle floated in with her eyes closed and a large Mind-eye of her own on her forehead. Her eye color was similar to my mothers but the stars in her eyes weren't as vibrant. My body moved on its own as I got up and we peered into each other's mind-eye. Time stood still until Gooseflesh crawled over my skin and we simultaneously shivered as we pulled out of our weird trance. "Oh, my Goddess. You've found your mate." My mother said as placed her hands over her chest. "Wha-what just happened?" Michelle asked, just as confused as I was. "Well my dear, you and my son have performed the omni-courtship and are betrothed. Congratulations." my father answered. "All hail the Chief and Chieftess of our tribe." They said in unison. "Oh hell no! I better not be pregnant!" Michelle yelled.

Thinking outside the box

"*What* do you have to say for yourself, Child?" I looked up into the eyes of my mother as she held her hands out and pulled me closer by my chains. "Mother-." She clamped my mouth shut with her other hands and made me bite the inside of my mouth. The taste of my blood hit my tongue as she let go and I looked to the floor as my family laughed. "I failed, she is alive." In one swift move she slapped me to the ground and I hit the hard stone and blacked out instantly. "Wake up, boy!" A chill ran down my spine at the sound of my fathers booming voice. I opened my eyes as he grabbed me by the throat and snatched me up from the ground. His dark skin and pale gray eyes was all that I saw before he threw me backwards and I was pulled into a Vortex that burned my skin as I passed through it. "I don't ever want to see your face again!!" Once the opening closed, I broke free of the chains and shrank down to my actual size. My mother forbade me from ever being seen in my almost six foot form with my medium build and brown eyes. My brown skin tone was something else that she hated but tolerated because of my fathers dark skin and his Maternal lineage. *All is not lost young one, Use what I taught you to survive.* The sound of my favorite aunt's voice filled my head and I remembered our last training session. I touched my necklace and pulled out the four elements that my aunt gave me as a gift. "Surrounded by darkness in a vastness yet unknown, I cast this spell to make it my home, Banished by those who housed my spirit with their flesh and bone." I sent the elements out in all directions and allowed them to form a planet with an ocean similar to earths and then made the ball of sunfire grow into a large yellow sun. I pulled the moon stones that my aunt gave me from the next sigil on my necklace and made twin moons that floated off in the opposite direction. With my domain complete I threw my necklace to the ground and watched as it grew into my new home. They can keep their world with all of its chaos and wrathful deities who only care about making life hard for everyone else or how the others see them. With my father being born of the first mother Goddess and my mother as the queen of her pantheon of vapid immortals, I was never allowed a moment's peace to do what I want whenever I want. "Thank you auntie, for teaching me that my greatest ability is relying on myself." I transported myself to the room where I kept the animals that I encountered on my journey across the lower levels of existence and sent my translucent energy waves everywhere to send them out into their new home. My favorite creatures stayed behind and swirled around me as they absorbed the sound waves and then traveled out of the room with their brown wings flapping into the air. With everything done I transported myself to my bed and closed my eyes as I was now able to rest without someone trying to test my skills or send me somewhere while asleep. In no time at all I fell asleep and allowed my astral body to form and travel the dream realm. I awoke to the sounds of people talking around me and jumped up with my fists radiating energy waves as I looked around my bedroom. "A thousand pardons Greatness, we were cleaning your room." Before me stood four beings whose features were similar to my favorite beasts but they were human-like with two hands and legs except they had long tails and webbed fingers with pointy ears. "It is an honor to be a part of your awakening, greatness." I closed my eyes and used the energy waves of my aura to sense how many living sentient beings now lived in my world. They called themselves Kiropterrans and there were close to a hundred thousand of them that evolved from my bats. "I'm Mago, this is Illiria, Lunon and Briztos. We are your designated attendants for this cycle." They bowed as I got up off the bed and floated out of the room and into the hallway. Everyone fell to the floor as I passed by them and spoke of me as the father of all and continued until it was a chant of my real name, Kiroptarneth. I didn't have extra arms or eyes so my parents never wanted me around unless I was ordered to do something they didn't want to do. A smile curved my lips as I sensed adoration for the first time and realized my aunt was right about uncomfortability leading to comfortability. "Let this day be remembered as the day of the lord's awakening."

"*Hi*, I'm here for the interview. My name is Silas Martin."

"Yes, right this way." The secretary led me down a hallway of glass walls and doors to a conference room, where he directed me to sit in front of a brown binder with a giant B on the front for Browning Hotels. "Hello! I'm Mira Thomas. The regional supervisor." A thin brown skinned woman dressed in a t-shirt and jeans walked into the room with her open toe heels clapping against the stone floor. "Silas Martins, very nice to meet you." "Likewise, so I'm going to start off by saying that you have the job." I fought the urge to get up and hug her as tears fell from my eyes. I've applied for dozens of hotels all over Columbus, Ohio and none of them replied except for this one. "We've reached out to your previous supervisors and they said nothing but great things about you." That was weird, they fired me because I transitioned from female to a male and said that I was trying to pull a fast one. I later realized that I was on my last leg with that job on account of my inability to be bullied and deal with white privilege. "They told us about your transition and I want to welcome you to the club." I was at a loss for words as she got up and extended her left hand for me to shake. I accepted it and she walked me out to the secretary I met earlier and she took me to a computer room where I filled out the necessary paperwork. The salary was bigger than I thought and it came with a load of benefits that made my previous job look like an internship. "Are you all set?" "Yes ma'am." "Just call me Mira." She gave me a tour and afterwards I spent the next thirty minutes on the bus with my feet hurting from all the walking that we did. "I'm home!" I yelled out as I took my jacket off and hung it on the rack. "We're in here Scil- I mean Silas." I walked into the kitchen and froze as I saw my long time school bully sitting at the table. "Oh, Wow! You weren't kidding." My brother playfully nudged her shoulder as she walked forward and hugged me. "You look so good."

"Thanks, you too." I lied. Markeisha Sell was the reason I hated going to high school as a poor kid and she never let me forget how poor we were by pointing it out constantly. "So you and my sibling are a thing?" "Yes, in a year we'll be sisters." My family laughed as she playfully pushed my shoulder and put her free hand to her lips.

"You know what I meant." She replied.

"Do I? It's pretty evident that I'm now a man." I fought the urge ro say something inappropriate.

"She didn't mean it like that. We're still getting used to this." My mom said, sticking up for her.

I clapped my hands and took a seat across from them. "It's a good thing you're her mother and care about her feelings. Your grandchildren will be so proud." I replied. "Don't talk to me like that, I am your mother." "Are you sure because my emotional state seems to say otherwise?" Without another word I got up and went to my room. There was no way that I was going to allow them to ruin the buzz that I had from getting a new job that would help me get away from these people. It's not that I hate them but they act like my emotions are always a joke. If I made comments about either of them having diplomas or even being financially stable before having kids I'd be wrong. "Fucking straight people are the worst at times," I yelled. The only thing that would get my mind off of this bullshit was to put it on a canvas. I grabbed my utensils and began to set them up in the corner of my bedroom as I allowed my muse to find me. Time flew by as I applied the colors and let the image form organically. Knock-Knock! "Come in." I stepped back from the painting as my Mother walked into the room.

"I think you owe Markeisha an apology." She said, as if I did something wrong.

"Did you have this same talk with her?" I replied

"No, it was an accident and you know how hard it is for us to get used to your transition."

"But it's so easy for you to stick up for her."

"There is no reasoning with you is there?"

"You want me to put how I feel to the side to play nice with someone who made my life a living hell for four years, You should be taking my side." "That happened so long ago you need to drop it. You're literally not that person anymore." My mother walked around to my side to see my painting and gasped. "What is it?" "I call it the lonely heart." She gave me a puzzled look and then placed an arm on my shoulder. "I'm sorry son, I didn't know that you felt this way." The irony of my painting was lost on my mother but not me as I shoved my feelings into the back of my mind and reciprocated the hug. "It's not my heart." To be truthfully honest I didn't know where it came from. As of late I allow the universe to flow through me and use my hands to paint. Today it led me to paint a heart that was locked in a translucent box. "Your brother and his fiance are still downstairs if you want to apologize." "Ha! How about no! This will be one of those situations where I take a page out of your book and pretend as if none of this ever happened." My mother shook her head and gave my shoulder a little squeeze before turning to walk away as I went to the bathroom and cleaned myself up. Ten minutes later I walked down stairs and made my way to the living room. "Marcus I mean Markeisha can I talk to you?" "Oop, you tried it." She got up with a smile and walked into the kitchen with me and took a seat on the bar stool. "With you being my brother's girlfriend, we'll see each other a lot more so I Just want to clear the air." "I did feel as if I'm owed an apology." "I'm sorry that my brother has bad taste in women and that my family enables him into making stupid decisions like getting with you." I got up and walked back into the living room and took a seat next to my brother. "We've agreed to disagree for the time being." "No, she has a smart ass mouth and is lucky you have a dick now or

I'd fuck you up." "Take a seat, Hooves, you're in my family home." "What did you say to her?" My brother got up as she jumped at me and pulled her back as she started swinging.

"Silas!"

"Mother!"

"What did you say to her?"

"I simply apologized." I could hear Markeisha yelling and screaming as Terry picked her up and carried her out the front door. "An apology doesn't cause that kind of response." "It does for the unhealed. Oh! I found a job. Let's celebrate with some wine." I turned and made my way back to the kitchen as my family went outside to console their new daughter. She yelled and screamed as my brother tried to get her in the car and I ignored it as I opened the bottle of Moscato and poured myself a glass full. "Mmmm, so good." I walked outside and waved goodbye as my brother pulled off and Markeisha gave me the middle finger.

"Bye, Sis. Love you!" I didn't know if it was the fact that I have a great paying job or seeing her all riled up that made me happy. I was never one to antagonize someone but she rightfully deserved it and more. "Silas! Why would you say that to her?" "Because it was time someone said it." I laughed as I finished my glass off and made my way back up to my room. My parents weren't happy with me but I didn't give a fuck. I sat on the bed as the painting came to life in front of me. The heart fell into the ground and then a cube appeared with weird symbols on each side of it. I yawned as it showed me a star, musical notes, a storm cloud, an and lastly a symbol that reminded me of the wifi insignia. I felt myself becoming sleepy and fell backwards as the wine induced hallucination faded. That never happened before and it kind of scared me a little. For a man in my mid twenties I'm not really a heavy drinker and I don't do drugs so it was something that I'd definitely have to tell my family about. *Oh! Right, they don't have the emotional intelligence to deal with complex emotions.* With a yawn I fell asleep and had a dream that the earth was rotating and sending out fireworks that turned into people as they flew by me. My perspective descended to the planet at unnatural speeds, and I landed in front of a hole in the ground. The ground trembled and I fell into the hole but woke up as the darkness encompassed my body. My eyes adjusted to the brightness of the light and I got up to use the bathroom and then went back to sleep where I dreamt of only darkness. My alarm went off five hours later and I awoke with a smile and got ready for my first day at work.

An hour and thirty minutes later I walked into the entrance of Browning Hotel and made my way to the help desk. "Good morning Silas, Mira is waiting for you in the conference room down that hallway." She took my bag as I made my way to where she waited and then she took me down a spiral staircase that felt like it went on forever. "We keep all of the uniforms down here." A cold chill from the center of the room ran over my body as we approached two large stone doors that she pushed open with ease. The room was empty except for a pit in the center of the room like the one from my dream. I had a really bad feeling about this and tried to turn around to run but the doors vanished and turned into a solid wall of stone. "You're not in danger Silas, we need you." My heart raced in my chest as I realized this was actually happening and that there was no other exit. Mira smiled as she held her hand out and I was pulled forward by an unseen force and thrown into the pit. My body plummeted through the darkness for what felt like hours before the warm air turned cold and my momentum slowed down as I gently landed on the ground. The darkness began to recede as white light formed in what I recognized as clear quartz crystals on the walls. The air around me moved like heat waves on a summer day and coalesced until it turned into the box from my dream that was the size of a rubix cube.

There was something about it that was irresistible in the way that it was designed and floated at eye level off the ground. The waves of energy it gave off wrapped around my body and pulled me into it the same way the unseen energy pulled me into the pit.

"*Sire*, there is a mortal out in the wilderness." I waved my hands in the space in front of me and made the image of the outer forest appear. There was a very handsome human male running right into a nest of giant spiders. "Shall I intervene, Lord?" "No, I got this." For the first time in a hundred years I transported myself to the forest and lowered myself to the ground as the mortal Silas fell backwards out of fear. "Go no further Silas." He didn't say anything as he looked upwards with his heart beating fast. "I mean you no harm." "Y-yeah right! I-I've been sacrificed to a demon by a cult. Haven't black people suffered enough?" I knew well of what he spoke of from watching the events of mortals through my looking glass called a television. Behind me I could sense the spiders approaching but they stayed far enough away so as to not incur my wrath.

"Do you have arachnophobia?" He shook his head no as I held a hand out to him and brought him to his feet by manipulating gravity. "Whoa! Oh shit!" He took one look at the spiders and turned to run but I grabbed his arms and transported us to my throne room. "Y'all have to stop doing that." "Should I send you back?" I held my fingers up to snap them but he reached out and clasped his hands over mine. "P-please don't." In my amusement I overlooked the fact that a mortal just experienced the supernatural world for the first time and he was absolutely terrified. "I'm sorry. I forget how dry my jokes are at times. I promise, you are safe. Lunotos!" I removed his hands from mine as my attendant flew into the room as a bat. "What in the old macdonald had a farm?" Silas said, as he gawked at my attendant.

"About time, Lord. He's cute too." I cleared my throat and he kneeled and then flashed me a smile. "You called, my lord?" "Take Silas to the guest quarters." "Ha! Good one Lord. we don't host-." I pointed to the doorway and sent my energy down the hall to make a room for my cute new guest. "Uh, sure thing Lord." As they walked out of the room I could see his brain waves relax and he looked back to me and smiled before the door closed behind them. My heart raced at the thought of courting a new lover. It's been a while since the last mortal was dropped down here and he used me for my power. *This time it will be different. I can feel it.*

"Mira!" I telepathically called out to another one of my demigod servants, who was in the mortal realm.

"Yes, lord?" She answered. "You have done well." "Oh! Thank you, Your greatness. Shall I send a bat to take his form?" "Yes, he will be staying for a while." "As you wish, Lord." I pulled back from my telepathic bond and transported myself to my bedroom. "How does one go about courting a male of this day and age?" From what I've seen hook-up culture is a thing that I wouldn't mind trying but I'm not an outside people god. The last human thrown into the pit was a Turkish king who slept with one of my brown wings and had her turn him into a Vampiric demon. It was that heartbreak that showed me how to get my revenge. I prevented him from existing in the sun or entering a structure without being invited, and my favorite curse was his inability to see his reflection in silver. "No, Kirop-Tarneth, let go of the past and cuddle up to the future." As I finished speaking, I could feel my power transport me to his bed with him in the little spoon position. I floated off the bed as he turned over with an unreadable expression. Lunotos flew into the doorway and smiled as he began to shut the door. "Just let this happen." He suggested. I returned to my room and sat at the edge of my bed. That was the first time that had ever happened. I may not have all the extra parts that my siblings had, but I did have the same power and mastered them to the point of being a creator god, thanks to my aunt Aura. I shrugged off my reflective thoughts and made the shower turn on with a wave of my hands.

This prompted me to use the forest berry body wash that I invented and the lotion that helps our melanated skin glisten in the sun. After I correctly cleaned myself and trimmed my pubic area, I used my mind to search for Silas. He was leaning over the balcony of his room, watching the bats in the capital city. "I'm sorry for the transportation incident. I promise it will never happen again." "Say's the ancient god who just teleported into my room." "I can leave if you want?" "No, I think it's kind of cute." "You do?" "Yes, you like me." "You're not scared of me?" "You saved me from being spider juice and I saw the look on your face when I placed my hands over yours. I'm not going to lie. Yes, this is strange. I've technically been sacrificed to you, but to tell the truth, I couldn't wait to be rid of my insufferable family." His brain waves moved around his head like fire, and I could see that they were terrible memories that he sent to the back of his mind as he closed his eyes. "I understand exactly how you feel." He arched an eyebrow in my direction and turned to face me.

"Since this is all real, can I ask some questions?" "Ask me anything." I stepped closer, and he smiled as he looked me in the eyes. "Do you really look like this?" "Yes. It took me a while to get used to it, but I love it." "What? You're fine as fuck." That was the first time in my life that I've ever heard someone say that to me and mean it. "Thank you, you are also very attractive. Can I ask you a question?" "Just one. I'm not done interviewing a god yet." His playful smile made me a little more at ease as he walked into his room, and I got a great view of his ass. The people of Earth who have to refer to themselves as black are by far the most beautiful and talented among the mortal race. "Were you born a female?"

My question caused him to turn on his heel and look seriously at me. "Yes, it's not a problem, is it?" "No, I guess you could say I am someone who had to find who he truel is, also." I closed my eyes and took the form my mother and father made me take when I was allowed in public. The skin of my lower arms turned red up to my hands as my secondary arms sprouted from my back, and my three extra eyes formed on my forehead. Silas smiled and placed his left hand on my new arms and rubbed them. "I liked the way you look. I hope that's not offensive?" "It's not. To tell the truth, this is a form I haven't taken since the day I was bound to this dimension." I changed back and sat next to him on the couch in his room as he reached out and touched my knee. "No one should ever be made to feel as if the way they are made is wrong. I was a boy in a girl's body and hated myself for years until I realized that I was living for myself and me only. My family never made me feel supported. They treated me as if there was something wrong with me." I placed my hand over his and looked him deep in the eyes before speaking. "You're beautiful, Silas." I leaned in to kiss him, but he pulled back and looked to the floor. "I've never kissed anyone before. I'm sorry." His brain waves moved erratically as a memory that looked painful was pushed to the back of his mind. "I shouldn't have tried to make a move on you so soon. You've only been here for a couple of hours. I'm sorry, Silas." I transported myself back to my room before I could do something else stupid. "What the fuck were you thinking? You're the god of thoughts, not love and affection."

*"**What** the hell was I thinking? A fine ass man-no, god, wanted to kiss me, and I acted like a prude."* It was true that I never kissed anyone, but that was because of my fear of intimacy and other reasons that I didn't want to think about right now. The crystal by my door glowed before it opened, and a servant walked in with a tray of food floating behind her. "The lord said that you might be hungry." My stomach rumbled as the smell of my favorite food filled the room. She waved her hands and the plates of food landed on the rectangular table in the other room and turned to leave. "Can you stay? I have some more questions." She turned around with a smile and took a seat across from me as I picked up the plate of fries. "Tell me about this place, please." I asked. "I'm Illiria, by the way." "I'm Silas, nice to

be abducted by all of you." She laughed and made a tent with her hands.

"It was created by our lord Kirop-Tarneth after his exile from the upper realms. He brought all the animals you see here from earth and elevated my kind to our current demigod state." I pointed to the food and she declined the offer as I continued to devour my food. "Am I the first human to step foot in this dimension?" "No, there have been a few others." "Did they die here?" She shook her head no and I could tell that there was more to the story but didn't know if it was right to question her further. "It's cool, His greatness doesn't want there to be secrets between you two. So I'll say this: the last person to come here was a prince who hurt him badly. He convinced the lord to not read his thoughts and slept with one of us behind his back. The lord doesn't want us to say his name, so we call him prince V. Before him, there was a pharaoh named Ashotep. She used him for mystical knowledge that helped oppress the people of Egypt and what you refer to as America." That answered a lot of the questions I had except for one. "Say we get together. What's stopping him from kicking me out once he had sex with me?" Even though my question was about the god of this dimension I could see that it offended her as if I asked her how many sexual partners she's had. "He isn't like that. He has a good heart. Better than most mortals." her teeth changed from human to beast as she spoke and got up from her seat. "I didn't mean it that way. I'm sorry for offending you." I watched as she calmed down and her teeth returned to normal. "Our lord has been through a lot, and the last thing he needs is more judgmental people in his life." "Then that makes two of us." After she was calm enough to answer more questions, I found out that my godly host was the last-born son of the goddess Ishtar and the first born god named Nareth. They were forbidden from speaking about them any further so I made a mental note to find out more about them once I gained access to a computer. Illiria left after I was finished and used her magic to send the plate flying toward the kitchen. I still had a lot of questions about the god of this place. I wanted to be around him, but I saw the look of embarrassment on his face from my rejection, and it would be too awkward to face him now. At times like this I wish I had my painting set so that I could put what I've seen on paper. The second I finished my thought I turned around as all the utensils that I needed appeared. Time flew by as I painted all of the amazing things that I've seen on my first day here. Before I knew it Illiria brought me dinner and the sunlight outside was replaced by the light from twin moons. "Wow, you have a real gift, Silas." I took a step back and took in the five paintings that I finished. The first was of the giant spiders at the edge of the forest and the next three were of the bats in their animal and human-like form. The last painting was of Kiroptarneth floating in front of me as he landed on the ground. I wanted to put his other form on paper, but I had a feeling that he wouldn't want to see that form that caused him so much pain looking back at him, so I scrapped the idea. "Give me a second to clean up, and I'll be right out to eat." I turned on my heels and walked to the shower, but as I reached for the doorknob, my skin prickled, and the paint on my clothes vanished. I turned to look at Illiria, and she held her hands up. "Don't look at me." Her puzzled expression let me know that she was just as confused as I was about what just happened. "Earlier, all of this appeared, and I thought Kiroptarneth made this happen." She shook her head no and circled around me while looking me up and down. "I would have sensed it if our lord did it. Does your family practice true magic?" "No, are there humans with magic?" She didn't answer as her pupils dilated, and she waved her hand up and down. "Yes, Humans were divine when they were first created. Some humans still follow the teachings of the divine but their powers aren't what they used to be." She stopped in front of me and looked me up and down before vanishing into thin air. I ate my food in silence and then took another look at my works of art. Once I was finished, the plates vanished as I placed them on the table and got up to move my paintings to the side and start another painting. All of my utensils were already clean and ready for me to use again as I set up a new canvas. Behind me, I heard something move, and when I turned to look I was frozen to the spot as fear made my heart race. The spiders that I painted were now crawling off the painting and moving towards me. They stopped at my feet and looked up at me as tears formed in my eyes, and I was able to jump backward onto the floor. All three of them slowly moved forward, but I held my hands, and they stopped moving. I still trembled from the look of their mandibles and creepy eyes, but as time went on, they remained in the spot. *Did I do this?* "Have a seat on the couch." To my amazement they turned and crawled over to the couch to do as I asked and then stared at me. I got up and walked to the front door as they watched me from the couch. "Can I get some help, please?" The air behind me stirred as my divine host appeared. "You made them come off the page." He stepped over to the painting and squinted as he put his hand into it. "Whoa! You have a real gift." "I didn't do this." "Yes, you did. I think you've awakened latent manifestation abilities." "I'm human, not some magic-wielding god or magician." He laughed so hard that it came out as translucent waves as he waved his hands at the spiders and then at the painting.

Nothing happened after a couple more attempts, and he took a seat next to them on the couch. "That answers my question." He made a medium pizza appear along with a bottle of cola and two glass cups. Kiroptarneth patted the open seat next to him, and I moved to sit down, but the spiders crawled over him and then to where I was going to sit. "Nope!" I'd never seen spiders this big, and even though they seemed to be under my control, it still terrified me to see them that big. "Aww, she likes you." "She?" "Yes, you should feel lucky. Female spiders love to eat the males and become naturally defensive during mating season. "That didn't help at all, and it made me take a couple of steps backward as they climbed down the couch and crawled back to the painting.

The female spider waved goodbye as she crawled into the painting, and it froze with her front leg in the air. "The bigger question is, did you bring them from the forest or manifest them from the image?" "What's the difference?" I asked as I took the seat next to him. "Both are a form of manifestation, but neither are an ability that mortals currently possess with their level of consciousness." That helped as much as a stubbed toe or the hiccups. "Yesterday, I applied for a job and was hired on the spot, only to find out that I was a sacrifice to an attractive god. Now you're telling me that I have powers. Ha! Yeah right! The only power that I've ever had was being the last person my friends call, the last person my family thinks of, and let's not even talk about my love life." Out of the corner of my eye, I could see my forest painting come to life and then go back to normal as I spoke my pain out loud. "I'm sorry." he swallowed the food in his mouth and took a deep breath as he got up and walked over to the painting. He looked through them and pulled out one that was blank. He hugged it to his chest and became one with it as he resumed a similar position to the one I painted. He now smiled at me and placed both hands over his heart. *Of course he was an image I made come to life.*

I paced back and forth when the sound of my mortal guest running into my room entered my ears. The doors opened as he sprinted in and caught his breath. "I-I have, I need to." He fell to the ground, and I moved at superspeed to catch him before his head hit the floor. His brain waves calmed down as he drifted into the unconscious realm. I picked up his weightless body and transported us to his room, and laid him on his bed.

"Lu-."

"Yes! Sire." Lunotos said, appearing before I could finish my sentence.

"Go to the outer dimension and bring me a hair from his mother's head, please." "Right away, Lord." He vanished, and I placed my hand to his forehead to see what he was dreaming about so that I could assist him better. Instantly, I was catapulted into his dream as I floated next to a little girl in a pink dress with a superhero coloring book in her hands. A tall, dark-skinned woman walked over and took the coloring book and replaced it with one that had unicorns on the front. "This is for boys, and this is for girls." She ripped up the coloring book and threw it in the trash as the little girl began to cry. The dream changed, and I now stood next to a teenager who looked like a younger version of Silas, except with breasts and French braids in her hair. "Sicilia, we don't tolerate this type of behavior at this school." She laughed and rolled her eyes as the principal leaned forward with her hands on her desk.

"You don't tolerate individualism or the progression of our people."

"No, we don't tolerate girls wanting to be boys. God doesn't make mistakes."

The dream changed to show Silas in a lot of pain walking into a kitchen. "I've been calling you for thirty minutes." He said to people who I sensed were his parents. "I need someone to help me get in the shower, please." I couldn't tell what was worse, the pain in his voice or the look of inconsideration for his condition on his parents' face. "You spring this on us and then expect us to be your nurses. You should have run this by us first and asked how we would feel about our daughter being replaced by a man." Tears fell down his face as he turned and walked away with no help from his family. It was hard to watch and I honestly had enough of this nightmare so I pulled my consciousness back into my own body and opened my eyes as my own tears fell. I looked at the setting sun and fought the urge to leave and be alone as I cried for him. There was no way that I could leave him alone like everyone else did. *Like everyone did to me.* I took a seat next to him and made a television appear along with the mortal invention of the video game. Hours passed, and he remained asleep, with his chest rising up and down as he breathed. He had a peaceful look on his face, which was a good sign as to what he was dreaming about, so I kicked off my shoes and made myself more comfortable. "I know who I am." I looked over to Silas who talked in his sleep and rolled over onto his side. Seeing his ass cheeks clap as he made himself more comfortable gave me a boner that I had to hide as I sensed Lunotos's return. "Sire, I knew you wanted to be alone with the mortal." He said, as he beat his wings against the air to stay afloat. "The hair!" I held my hand out and he dropped it into my palms and then changed back into his human form and faced the opposite direction. "I don't think I should be here for this, sir." "This is serious, go and tell your parents that I'll be dealing with this for the unforeseeable future." He bowed and vanished, and for the first time in my life, I didn't know what to do next. I don't want to leave this mortal who seems to be going through ascension symptoms, but if I stay, I run the risk of a constant hard-on, and that's not good for any of us if I can't do anything with it. "Oh shit, you have a boner!" My heart raced as I turned to see him sitting up with his eyes closed and a large all black third eye on his forehead. He fell backwards and went back to sleep as the eye blinked and stayed open. Small specks of light flickered in and out of its darkness. Just looking at it made a shiver crawl down my back and helped my erection go down. The strand of hair flew out of my hand and turned into a threaded bracelet that wrapped itself around his left wrist. He giggled and moved like someone was tickling him until he fell to the floor and got up, smiling with all three of his eyes open. "I had a dream that we were play-wrestling and you cheated by tickling me. It was both weird and sexy at the same time." He moved in the blink of an eye and wrapped his arms around my waist to pull me into a hug. I returned the affection by draping my arms over his shoulders and kissing his head. "Your skin smells amazing-." Everything went black as I lost control of my body, and the dream world tugged at my consciousness until my essence was fully formed in the astral realm. My body tingled as I walked across the clouds of my aunt's home, where she placed a large portion of her consciousness. "Aunty, I'm home!" I walked up the steps of her porch as she came out running with all four of her arms open. "Oh! Perfect, everything is in motion. Yah!" My aunt Aura yelled. "Huh?" I responded. "Come inside, Hazy. I have a lot to tell you." As we walked into her tree-home, I turned back to take one last look at where I came from and blew a kiss at my new love. Time moves differently in the dream realm and I could spend years here while minutes or hours pass in the conscious realm. "Aww, so do you like my gift?" "You sent Silas to me?" "Sort of, when his soul first went into his body I swirled the particles and made them into a baby girl's body." She wiggled her fingers over the counter and made some snacks for us to eat as two cups appeared next to a pitcher of water with key limes in it. "Once you wake up, tell him that I'm sorry for causing him so much heartache." "Aunty, that might make things worse. He's like me when it comes to parental resentment issues. I know things are moving fast but that's a lot to unpack in a conversation." "Hey, My aunt said she messed up but for a good reason and she wants you to know that she's sorry for causing you pain. Oh! Hey, do you want to get married?" The sound of my aunt's laughter filled the room as she held her hands to her sides and tears fell from her eyes. "It's only been one day and he has you acting like your real self again. I'm happy for you, Hazy." The saying about her working in mysterious ways was the truest among phrases when it came to referencing the mother of creation. "There is something else that I need to tell you about the events that will take place after your wedding." I was too stunned to speak and almost dropped the pitcher I was holding as I looked to her to see if she was serious. "This time I'm not joking. That smelly wizard was a bad call, I'll admit that. But Silas is the real deal when it comes to life partners." "You just had to bring up Merlin and his hair that smelled like farm animals." We shared a laugh and I got up to give her another hug. We spent the next couple of hours talking about our accomplishments in our dimensions and she gave me a tour of her alternate dimension fields. The first one was the craziest shit that I'd ever seen with all black female super's and the next was a witch of Mesoamerican lineage walking into a foliage portal with a beautiful cat goddess behind her. "So all of this is happening right now?" She nodded as we approached a swirling nebula cloud, and she rushed me past it before I could see what it was. "The realm of the source beasts has a lot going on right now." I could tell that whatever it was going through would turn out to be amazing from all the information that she had me filter into it millions of years ago. I could hear the sound of animals deep within the mass of clouds and it felt a sense of pride from being able to help my aunt. We stepped into her hall of divination mirrors and the one closest to us came to life to show Silas sitting on my bed with all of my alphas standing around him as they talked. I touched the mirror to activate the sound and smiled as Silas's laughter was the first thing I heard. "Can I ask all of you a question?" "You can ask us anything." "How is it that you all can come and go but he can't?" They shared a weird glance, and Illiria stepped forward. "We were brought here and our lord was exiled to this realm by the power of his parents." The sound faded and the mirror returned to normal as the one next to it showed Silas right before his transition. He was at a college party and having the time of his life as he took three shots in a row. The tall white guy next to him pretended to drink but poured it over his shoulder and waited for Him to pass out. Two more college students helped him carry Silas up the steps as everyone else continued to party and were oblivious to what was about to happen. I stepped back and the image faded as I braced myself against the wall and cried for what happened to Silas. This was why he felt alone. He suffered alone his entire life. My aunt rubbed my back and cried with me as time passed and I burned the image of the three men in my mind. One way or another, I'll give him the justice he deserves.

"Thank you for answering all of my questions." To be truthfully honest, I was seconds away from sitting in a corner and rocking back and forth as I sang nursery rhymes to myself. I've been abducted, The supernatural world really exists. I'm currently in a pocket dimension that belongs to a *very* attractive god, and to top it all off, I've awakened to my own inner divine power. *Talk about a glow up.* My ears began to ring as I caught the sight of two blurry forms out of my left eye's peripheral vision. When I turned to look at them they faded but I was able to make one out as the translucent form of my sexy divine host and the other took my breath away. She was a very tall female with multiple arms and sparkling blue and dark brown skin. "Silas, Are you okay?" The concern in the divine servant's voice pulled my attention back to them as I blinked all three of my eyes at the same time. "Y-yeah, I thought I saw something." I responded. "The colors in your eye were moving erratically." The bat Alpha, Mago said as she touched the side of my face. She removed her hand and I ran over to the mirror. Had this happened to me a day ago, I would have ran to the emergency room, but now I love looking at it. The colors swirling in darkness are a perfect representation of me as an artist. "Do any of you know how long it will be until he wakes up?" I asked, looking at their reflections in the mirror. All of them shook their heads no as I ran out of questions about this peculiar situation. Just then a new question came to me as I thought about the bat who hired me. "How is it that all of you can leave, but he can't?" I immediately regretted it after all of them shared a weird look. "Our ancestors were brought here after our lord was banished to this pocket dimension, because he refused to kill the only family member that has ever shown him real love." Seeing that he was surrounded by beings that loved him for who he was, made my heart swell. I wanted that for myself someday. I decided to change the subject and focus on something that would get my mind off of horrible family members. "Can one of you teach me how to fly?" As someone who loved sketching superheroes when I was a kid, I was always fascinated with wingless flight. "I'll do it." Mago said, holding his hand out to me. The second our palms touched we were transported to an air space that was miles away from the palace. We floated high above an ocean as winds billowed around us and I could see a small island to my left. "Try to focus on not falling." Mago let go of my hand and I tried to imagine myself floating upwards but instead a prickly sensation crawled over my body and an instant I landed on the small island I saw seconds ago. My ass hurt from hitting the ground hard but the realization that I teleported for the first time, made me get up with a smile. "Uh-oh!" Mago said, appearing next to me and yanking me into the air as a large octopus tentacle slammed into the spot where I landed and made a rectangular crater. "W-what is up with Kirop-Tarneth and his large beasts?" I asked as Mago transported us back to my room. Everyone clapped as he laughed and we sat on my large bed next to my sleeping host. "He pulled off his first teleportation and survived Ken's island." Mago said. "That tentacle belonged to a beast named Ken?" I asked. "Yes, that island is where the lords little cousin who is a Kraken lives." Lunotos answered. "Wait! As in *the* Kraken, the same monster that was known for demolishing sailing ships and was a terror of the seven seas?" I didn't know much about mythical creatures, but I remember reading about it in a Greek hero story. "Yes, Try to be careful with your teleportation and don't go there ever again." Illiria spoke to me like a mother scolding a child as she pulled me into a side hug as her large breasts covered my nose.

"Can't breathe." I squeezed out.

"Sorry baby." She responded.

"I think it's time for your next lesson." Lunotos said, clapping his hands and changing his clothes from casual wear to a tank top and swimming trunks. "Now you try it." I closed my eyes and focused on doing as he did and nothing happened. "Whelp! We'll table that and focus on spell work." Illiria said, Standing up. "Uh, No! we will now work on divination." Mago said, stepping in front of her. "Uh, No! I want to see how he does with sigils." She countered. "I fall asleep for an hour and you two began to bicker like children." Kirop-Tarneth said, as he got up out of my bed and all of them Bowed. A swarm of butterflies formed in my stomach as I took in his handsome features. "Hey." He said with a smile. "He-." I began to talk and literal butterflies flew out of my mouth. "I knew it, you have the power of manifestation." He said. I knew the meaning of the word but didn't know what the supernatural implelications meant, so I nodded as the swarm of insects circled over our heads and vanished into sparkling multi-colored dust. "Are you okay, Sire?" They all asked, speaking in unison. He nodded but didn't take his eyes off of me as a smile curved his lips. "I got to see my aunt again." He responded "That's wonderful my lord." Illiria said, as they got up off of the floor. "So the lady that I saw you with was your aunt?" His eyes grew wide as he sat down next to me and nodded. "So you were able to see us looking at you, cool." Everyone said the last part of his statement as one as shared another look that made a chill run down my spine. "Is that not a normal thing?" I asked.

"No!" Mago answered.

"Peering into the realm of the supreme goddess is not a normal thing." Illiria added.

"The lord and his family are the only ones who can do that or go there." Mago said.

"Or the very few beings that she allows to venture into her realm." Lunotos added.

"We'll leave you two to talk. Please excuse us my lord." Illiria and the rest of them took their leave but Lunotos turned around with a smile. "I'll return later to help you with your powers, if it's okay with the lord?" He asked. "Sure." Kirop-Tarneth answered. Once the door was closed he placed his large hand on my shoulder. "Thank you, Silas." "For what?" He took a deep breath and moved closer to me. "You being here pushed me into a happier mood that I was able to use to push me deeper into the astral realm to see my aunt. Thank you." He said once again, but his use of the word *Deeper* made a chill run down my spine. I leaned forward and pressed my lips against his and kissed him with all of the passion that I could muster as his large hands grabbed my waist. Our lips and tongues wrestled with each other as I started to get an erection. I pulled away because something felt entirely different than what I was used to feeling down there. It took a while for me to get used to having an erection. Especially after my transition. At first I thought the stinging sensation was because of a botched operation, but after a while the pain subsided and I was able to masterbate like a natural man. "Are you okay?" He asked, and the concerned look on his face that was coupled with his sincere tone made me press my body up against his as we fell back onto my bed. Our tongues continued our dance from seconds ago and this time I felt his erection pressing up against mine. "Mmmmm." We moaned into each other's mouths as we continued to make out like wild teenagers and before I knew it we were naked. He kissed his way from my neck down to my stomach and then slowly kissed my penis that was a couple of inches bigger than usual. I didn't have time to marvel at its new size as he sucked it into his mouth and his head began to bob up and down. I couldn't believe that I was getting head from an actual divine being and couldn't let him go at this alone, so I positioned myself to be able to do the sixty-nine position. At first it was difficult because he was slightly taller than I was, but after a couple of seconds he moved from my penis to my ass. He moaned louder as I used my tongue, hands and lips to go all out on him until he reached his climax and ejaculated in my mouth. It spilled out as I coughed some of it up and then got up off of him as he flipped me over to do the same to me. I came in a blinding furry ten minutes later and he then used his power to clean up our combined mess of bodily fluids. *Damn! I must have left my gag reflex on earth.* He pulled me into the cuddle position with us facing each other and I exhaled from how good our first time was. *Even though it was just oral, it was still the best head that I'd ever had.* "I have a confession to make." I let out a laugh from his out of nowhere comment. "Okay." "I sent a bat to take your place on earth, so that your family wouldn't become suspicious." I let out a loud chuckle at the thought of my family noticing that I was gone. "I could have been missing for a year and they would have thought that I was off having sex for money." He leaned forward and kissed my lips and then pulled back with a smile on his face. "I would have paid a billion dollars for that type of head and double handed combo." We both laughed and two hours had passed as we made small talk while laying naked in each other's arms. Even though we talked about a plethora of things, I felt as if there was something else that he wanted to talk about. I could sense that it had something to do with my college from the images of the university's title flashing in my mind, several times. He took a deep breath before speaking and another chill ran down my spine. "When I was visiting my aunt, she wanted me to tell you how sorry she was, for physically making you into a girl." A part of me should have been furious with her because of all of the things I had to endure, but in the end I became a stronger person. "If she hadn't intervened I wouldn't have ever met you and been able to give you the slopy-toppy." I laughed as he smiled and I could sense that his aunts intervention wasn't the cause of his frown. "Is there something else?" The image of my college flashed in my mind as he kissed my forehead and I sat up in bed as it dawned on me. "You know about what happened to me when I was in college, Don't you?" "Yes, my aunt showed me the events that happened right before your, Um." He looked over at the wall as tears formed in his eyes. In all of my years, I have never had anyone who shed tears for me until now. I pulled him closer and kissed his lips as my own tears fell and then pulled back as I realized that this was a man-no god, that I could love for eternity. "As a divine being, you have the right to get revenge." he said, saying it as if it was as simple as taking out the trash, or doing the dishes. " Seriously?" He nodded and for the first time since it happened to me, I felt a surge of joy. "I'd love nothing more, but it would mean that I would have to leave you and return to the world that hates me." "A long time ago, I sensed my parents spell weaken and can be broken entirely if I marry someone from the outside world. When I asked my aunt about their fate, she said that the both of them are now mortal." A smile curved my lips from the thought of being able to show off my gorgeous lover to the world *and* get revenge. I got up off of the bed and got down on one knee as I looked up into his big brown eyes. "I do." "I think it's supposed to go the other way around." He waved his hand over mine and a large ring appeared. It was made of black metal with a large rainbow quartz that gleamed in the daylight. His was a silver band with a large clear quartz crystal that was the same size as mine and reflected the light to make a small broken rainbow appear on the wall. I got up and climbed up onto his lap as a gentle breeze came in through the open window. "I think that's a sign to do more gay stuff."

"Does this make me a king?" Silas asked, as he pulled me onto his lap and wrapped his arms around my waist. "Yes, you are Silas lord of Kirotor, who is also an omniterran of the visual perspective." I kissed his lips and wiggled my ass on his lap before getting up. "Sorry to interrupt my lords, but the celestial bodies have aligned." "Thank you, Mago. Tell Mira that we shall be arriving shortly." He nodded and vanished. "Are you ready to see you family?" "Yep, it's been eight months since Balosos has stopped impersonating me and enough time has passed since I've seen the lesser beings that I've been born into." To his family it's been only eight months but to us two years have passed since the time that Silas had first arrived here. I still couldn't believe that I've found my one true love and even gotten married. "Are you ready babe?" He asked. "Yes." I clapped my hands and in an instant we were standing in the pit with my dimensional box in front of us. Its markings glowed in the darkness as it slowly spun in its access. "Tag you're it!" I tapped Silas on the shoulder as my aura radiated around my body and I leaped into the air with it trailing behind me. My headstart didn't last long as he tapped me on the shoulder before we exited the opening at the top. Mira sat on a bench waiting for us by the door with a smile on her face. "Hey, Mira. It's been a while. Do you remember that time that you used telekinesis to throw me into the pit?" Silas teased. She laughed as they embraced each other and then we made our way to the steps. Once we reached the top I instantly sensed all of the supernatural beings who currently resided in the building. "Surprise!" Mira said, clapping me on the back. "So I take it that the human clients were too much to handle?" "My lord, they kept going down to the pit and we'd have to kill them or erase their memory." "What's stopping the supernaturals from simply walking down there?" I asked. "We told them the truth. There is an all powerful ancient god imprisoned in the basement and those who go down there, don't come back." That was a partial truth and to be honest, I was wondering who the human and beast size body's belonged to that the spider had wrapped in their silk. "Wait! So you mean to tell me that I applied to work at a hotel full of things that could have eaten me?" Silas asked. "No, sire. You were never going to actually work here. I've cast a spell on the application and knew that you'd be perfect for our lord. "Oh, And I never told anyone about you being free so expect the odd glance every now and again." Just as she spoke the words a cousin of mine walked by with blonde feathered wings and dark chocolate skin. His eyes grew big as he passed us and then did a double take when he loomed a silas. "Whoa!!!! Was that an angel?" He asked, just as astonished. "Yes, from what I could sense, he he was my cousin." I responded. My forehead pulsed as an all black unicorn with blue hair and red eyes passed us. It stopped and then changed into a man with dark brown skin and blue eyes and a serious look on his face. "Shut the fuck up! No way!" He said looking me in the eyes. His divine power was similar to my in essence but when he turned his attractive features towards Silas and blew him a kiss, I made a fist that exuded my power.

"Hi, I'm Darkon." He said.

"Hi. I'm his husband and I didn't wait a billion years for nothing."

"Chill Bro." He responded.

"I'm not your Bro."

"Yeah, Okay." He said, vanishing in a plume of black smoke. I made a mental note to ask Mira about that demigod later. I placed my arm over Silas just in case anyone else wanted to make a move as we made our way to the exit. The two of us waved at all of the bats and it reminded me of when I awakened in my realm and personally introduced myself to my subjects. Once we made it to the large S.U.V that waited for us, I took one last look at the building that housed my prison box. "This is your first time in a land vehicle, what do you think about them?" "I love it. The mortal realm has changed so much and now that those big ass dragons are dead, we don't have to worry about their human size turd piles." "What?" "Yeah, the earth was home to all sorts of creatures. Some were all beast or monster and others were omniterran like you and the other humans." "Is that where you got the idea to give us the power to be able to change from beast to human?" My driver Kevor asked, as he looked at us through the rear view mirror. "To be honest, Kevor. All I did was love your ancestors and my power was made theirs. Everything else was a result of their own adaptability." "And that is why you are the greatest of gods, Sir." Kevor answered. Silas placed his hand over mine and gave me a squeeze as we made our way to his family home. "Is that a corner store?" I asked. "Yes, I used to go there as a child and get all kinds of junk food. The owner used to give me free stuff and then we found out later that he was a pedophile, who kept kids in his basement." Silas answered. "Yeah, the new owners don't like black people, but they love our money." Kevor said, as we turned the corner. It took us thirty seven minutes and forty two seconds to reach a medium size orange brick house with a two door garage. The entire family came outside as we pulled into the driveway and my husband took a deep breath as a light skinned pregnant woman followed behind the man I knew to be his brother. "The bitch is definitely part of his family now." Kevor stopped and we got out as Silas exhaled an annoyed breath. "Family, this Kiro Browning." "Hello, New family." I hugged his mother first and then his father and then his brother. But a chill ran down my spine when the pregnant woman stepped closer. I extended my hand for her to shake it because I was never one to ignore energy. She by ignored my hand and pulled me into a hug as my skin began to crawl. "I read an article that said that expecting mothers are sensitive to energy." I lied, pulling out of the unwanted embrace. "No worries, welcome to the family." She countered. They escorted us inside and the second I stepped into the small front room I sensed all of the residual psychic energy. Flashes of family time with Silas missing entered my mind's eye and I had to ignore them as more played like a movie reel. "You good, baby." Silas asked. "Yeah, the psychic energy here is thick." "What?" His mother asked. "I have strong empathic energy and its string in here." "Yeah, I feel it too." Silas said, rubbing my arms. As I looked around the living room, I realized that I never understood the name. Nothing lived in this room and it was full of inanimate objects. They didn't even own a plant. That would have helped alleviate the stagnant energy. "Silas and I just bought a mansion on the upper east Browning estates and we purchased the surrounding homes for you four." Hearing that brought smiles to their faces as their brain brian waves move erratic." "Seriously?" His mother said, as she started to cry and it warmed my heart to see all of them rejoice. "Son, that sounds nice but we can't afford to live on that side of town." "Silas reached into his jacked and magically produced the paperwork for the trust that he asked Mira to set up for his family. Once they opened them and saw the amount of money that it held, their mouths dropped as the tears began to fall. "Twenty million dollar!" His brother yelled, as his wife hugged him. "Since we're now neighbors, we'll be having another marriage ceremony at hour mansion." Silas smiled as his mother smacked her teeth and I fought the urge to laugh, because he said that she would react that way after hearing about it. "You already got married and we weren't invited?" She asked, with her arms crossed. "My wedding wasn't about you mother, it was about me and Kiro, being surrounded by people who love and accept us, My guests deserve to enjoy themselves as they are." Silas responded. The look of hurt on her face was bitter sweet as her brain waves moved in tandem with his did during their stare down. His father shook my hand and then his brother pulled me into a hand shake-hug where he patted me on the back and then pointed at me. *Mortals are strange.* When I turned to shake my sister in-laws hand, my ears began to ring and the image of my aunt holding a baby flickered through my mind. "Thank you so much, Kiro." She said with a smile. "No, Problem. Family takes care of family." I responded. The ringing in my ears intensified as she let out a cackle until she let go of my hand. "We have to go and now that we're neighbors, you can expect to see more of us. After we make finish our rounds." "Rounds. What Are you, the gay Santa?" He brother teased. Instead of a witty come back, Silas just shook his head and hugged his brother as we got ready to leave. Once we were in the car Kevor pulled out of the driveway and we headed towards the home of the ones who sexually assaulted Silas. 'Sire, I feel like I should go in with you two." Kevor suggested. I shook my head no as he turned onto the dirt road that led to a small farm house. "My mother will be pissed if she finds out that I didn't fully escort." I really didn't want him to see what we were about to do, but he had a point. His kind were completely dedicated to serving and protecting me.

"Have you mastered the swarm ability?" I asked.

"Yes, my lord."

"Then how about you turn into a swarm and act as a psychic-exterior barrier once we are inside." I commanded.

"Your will is my command, lord." He put the car in park and I reached over to rub the back of Silas's neck. "Are you ready?" "As ready as I'll ever be." We got out of the car and made our way up to the porch steps and two men who I recognized from the mirror walked out of the house. "Can we help you?" One of them asked. "Hello, I'm Kiro and this is my Partner, Silas. We are thinking about purchasing your land." They shared a money hungry look that made their brain waves move in unison as they looked back at us. "Good afternoon to you two. I'm Eric and this is Anthony. Please come in." The horrid smell of armpits and balls greeted us as we entered their small home. "Can we get you something to drink?" The one named Anthony offered. "No, thanks." Silas answered. Eric brought two shot glasses from the kitchen as Anthony pulled out a bottle of clear alcohol filled their glasses to the top. "I feel as if I know you from somewhere." Anthony said, as he eyed Silas. "I used to work at a grocery store in the strip mall down the street." I lied. "Oh, yeah. The one next to Natalie's cut." "She's a good person, it's a shame that she is currently missing." The sides of my head began to pulse and I saw images of a lesbian butcher and then an angel who looked alot like a cousin of mine. She was one of the very few angels who I had a good familial relationship with and one who I couldn't wait to introduce Silas to. "Okay, let's talk zero's." Eric said, sitting us down at a dining table. I pulled the ten million dollar check out of my pocket and handed it to Anthony. "Shit! Thats what the fuck I'm talking about!" He yelled. "The lord has smiled down on us today!" Eric said, looking at it over Anthony's shoulder. Silas turned to look at me as his thoughts entered my mind. *"Ironic, isn't it."* I nodded as they poured another shot and then made a tent with my hands.

"You know what? I Think I know where you remember me from." They looked up from the check and paperwork that Kiro produced with confused expressions. "I attended Omni-core community college and graduated twelve years ago. I used to be Scilia Martins." The smiles on their faces vanished as they began to remember that night vividly in their minds. "Is that why you're here, For revenge?" Eric asked. "That happened a long time ago and to be honest, we didn't do anything that you didn't want us to do." Anthony added. "I didn't want a train ran on me that resulted in me becoming pregnant and then having a miscarriage!" I yelled, as I opened my mind-eye and their mouths fell open. "You won't be needing those." Kiro snapped his fingers and turned the check and paperwork into ropes that moved like snakes as they wrapped themselves around the both of them. I punched Anthony in the stomach with a fraction of my strength to make him pass out. "Eric, It was your face that haunted my dreams until I learned to finally process what happened to me through therapy. I made the stupid mistake of telling your aunt, who was the acting dean. But she swept it all under rug because our university didn't need the bad publicity." As I spoke I manifested an engine oil funnel and a can of Canola oil spray. Eric tried to yell but I willed his mouth to remain closed as he struggled against his bindings. "From what I remember you were in a fraternity and had to go through those idiotic humiliation rituals to join." I nodded to Kiro and he flipped him upside down with telekinesis and then pulled his pants down to his ankles. "Welcome to Alpha-." I jammed the funnel into his ass as he screamed and I was thankful that he didn't shit on me. "Sigma, Nu-asshole." I poured all of the oil into the funnel and then ignited it with a thought. At first all you could hear was his continued screams of agony and then it was quickly followed by the sound of his smoldering abdomen. Anthony came awake a full minute later and screamed as he watched his lover cooking from the inside out. He rolled over onto his side and tried to crawl to the door but I used my own telekinesis to yank him up off the floor and into my grasp by his neck. "Don't leave, the party isn't over yet." I dropped him to the floor and made his ropes take root into the wooden floor. With him now on his knees, I waved my hands over him and made his pants vanish. "And on that farm he had three guinea pigs." He moaned as his stomach grumbled and then he farted as the small fat rodents crawled out of his ass. "Boweep-Boweep!" I mimicked their sounds as the last one crawled out of his ass and he grunted from the pain. "Sci-scilia, I'm sorry. We were stupid kids who made a mistake. P-Please." He begged, but my song wasn't over yet. "With a ferret, here." "Ahhhh!" The long rodent crawled out of his ass as he farted out a glob of blood and it looked like he gave birth to it. Kiro imitated the breathing techniques that are taught to pregnant women and slapped the side of his left booty cheek as Anthony continued to cry. I willed his body to heal and then sent a stream of colors at Eric as he healed as well. "Well boys, this has been a fun little reunion. But I'm bored." They huddled together as Kiro placed his arm over my shoulder. "Small creatures who are closely related to Hamsters and not rats, I shift your form to that of big cats." *Roar!* Casting spells had been one of my favorite types of magic to perform, ever since I gained better control over my powers. I took every chance that I could to practice casting my power out and manifesting things out of nothing. The sounds of the large cats ripping them apart was music to my ears as I looked at my husband and gave him the signal that it was time to go. "Oh, wait!" Kiro pointed at the pack of ravenous beasts before we left and a smile curved his lips. "What was that about?" I asked. "Oh, right. I made it so that the cats would be transported to my home when they're done and then those two would resurrect in the middle of the spider forest." "You spoil me with gifts, my lord." I said, kissing Kiro's knuckles as Kevor changed from a swarm into his human form. Every time I saw the Bat demigods use their powers, I felt a surge of pride because *my* husband made them. "Wow, they're done eating." Kiro, daid with a chuckle as he rubbed his hands together and the small farm house erupted in flames. I leaned forward and pressed my lips against his as Kevor pulled out of the long dirt road and made his way to Kiro's cousin's house. It felt as if we went in a full circle now that we were a block away from the hotel. Before me stood a really tall building that housed a large colony angels. "Whoa! That's a big tower." I said. "Angels love high places." My husband responded. I'll never forget when he told me exactly how he was related to the original angels through his father, who was the first born son of the mother goddess who created the higher realms. She then found a husband and had eight sons and eight daughters. The Eighth daughter was the supreme goddess who created the lower universe that we reside in now and the only family member that Kiro loves. After she was banished from the heavenly realms, the mother goddess birthed the angels to destroy her youngest daughter and bring chaos to her creation. "Hey, I just got a telepathic message from my cousin, she want to meet us in the parking garage." Kiro said, touching my back and leading us to the car. Kevor pulled into the almost empty garage and I was surprised at how clean it was. The concrete was clean and free of oil spills. It even smelled great here. My forehead pulsed right before a beautiful female angel flew into the wide open space. My shoulder blades tingled as I thought about my own wings and wanted to unfurl them. *"Yeah, the angels have that effect on those of us who are able to manifest wings."* Kiro's telepathic message helped calm my nerves as she landed in front of us. "Cousin!!!" She said in a voice that was as beautiful as her rich brown skin tone. "Silas, this is my cousin Ally." "O.M.Granny!!! So this is the newly awakened Omniterran that has gotten you out of your domain. Hi, nice to meet you." She pulled me into a hug where her wings wrapped around me and I felt an added sense of love. She pulled back and for a split second, I caught a glimpse of her mind-eye. She hugged Kiro in the same way and then tried to hug Kevor but he settled for a handshake. I could sense a wave of fear waft off of him as she smiled and wondered who would be scared of someone so beautiful. "I just got some good weed from Zephyr and I rolled a blunt. Let's smoke." "Let's do it." "I'll head over to the hotel. If you need me call me, Lord." Kevor turned into a bat and flew out of the open space of the wall as the S.U.V vanished. When we reached the inside of the building my breath was caught in my throat from how beautiful its design was. There was one set of stairs and no elevator, and seeing it made me wonder why angels needed stairs if they had wings. "Okay, from here on. We fly." She extended her wings and flew upwards as I rolled my shoulders at the same time that Kiro did to unleash our wings. The tip of his bat wings touched my bird wings before he followed his cousins movements and flew upwards. I took a deep breath as I thought about how this was my life now and leaped into the air as we ascended upwards. We passed by several angel families that were doing semi-normal things like having a cookout on a patio or playing some kind of flying sport. Seeing a mother with her little brown skinned cherub who had to be five, was the cutest thing as he flapped his wings. "That's it Versyelfur, keep going, you can do it." His mother yelled as the little boy slowly ascended. We kept going until we reached the top, which was where Ally lived. My eyebrows shot upwards when I stepped into her apartment and the door closed behind us. I dissolved my wings as I turned in a full circle to take in the entirety of the penthouse. Her home was perfectly suited for a winged entity and I noticed that she had to have used magic to make it this big. "I hope it's not too pretentious." She asked, reading my emotions. "No, I love it-, i mean it's cool." Ally smiled as she led us up the steps to her sitting area.

"Silas, I want to thank you." She said, pulling a blunt out of thin air.

"For?" I responded, confused at why an all powerful angel would thank me.

"You helped my big cousin find his ability to love."

"That was a team effort. To tell the truth, he helped me as well."

"Oh, yeah. Being a newly awakened divine being must be thrilling to you."

"Not, just that. I've always felt as if I was alone in this world. As a black person, trans, and Artist." As I spoke, Kiro rubbed my back and I could see a smile form on Ally's face. "Well cousin, it seems as if we are both in loving relationships. Baby! GET IN HERE." Her voice became deeper as she directed her command to the hallway, and a thick tan woman was flung into the room and roughly deposited in the floor. "Y-yes, my love." She whimpered. She was missing her entire left hand and two toes on her right foot. "Everyone, this is my current dinner-girlfriend, Natalie." My ears began to ring as she spoke the womans name and I saw a flash of the butchery called *Natalies cut*, in my mind. "Oh, you're the missing Butcher who owned the store in the strip mall." She nodded but kept her eyes on the floor as Ally nodded with her. "Uh-huh, thats not all she is. Is 't that right?" "Yes, I come from the Slaughter family." "And, your family would abduct young woman and to eat them juat like your ancestors used to do after the great flood." Ally added. I was wondering why I didn't feel sorry for her and seeing as I got revenge for what happened to me a decade ago, It made me happy to see that the world is well balanced. "Yes, and I am really sorry-" Before she could finish, Ally punched her in thr stomach amd she fell to the floor. Seeing her missing limb and toes made me chuckle as she gasped for air until sge crawled out if the room. "Ally, do you know where my father is?" Kiro asked. "Yes, And You're going to laugh." "Am I, because he has an appointment with my fists and legs." "Well since he is now mortal, he's also and elderly man in a nursing home." Kiro snorted as his wings folded into his back and he leaned forward. "Auntie told me about him being mortal, bit I didn't know that he was in a nursing home." "Yeah, he was put there by your brother, Darnell." As she spoke, I saw an image of the beautiful unicorn from the hotel pop into my mind. "Wait! Is he tall and dark skinned with bright blue eyes?" Kiro asked. "Yeah, I take it that you've met him?" "Only briefly, and I didn't believe him when he said that we were siblings." "Well you should have, he is Aunt Aura's slap in the face to your father. He is also a god who was born as a semi-mortal." 'So he is part god, part Omniterran?" "Yes. Weird, right?" Kiro told me about his other fully divine siblings, but never about his youngest brother. I just hoped that he wasn't crazy like the rest of Kiro's siblings. "Does my father have dementia or Alzheimer's disease?" My husband asked with a cute smile. "Nope! My mother has visited him several times and told me that his curse is in two parts. The first is his mortality and the second is his memory of who he once was. The bad part is that his words can sway the minds of those he comes into contact with." Ally answered. "I figured that would be the case. Since Auntie realm with all that her family has taught her, she made the elements in direct correlation to her siblings." Natalie limped into the room with wine and Ally lit the blunt with her fingers.

"I don't think he can pass on until he makes amends with you. But I don't know how that works with your little brother."

"Wow, shut the fuck up!"

"Yeah, I've had your brother as a customer and have had the pleasure of talking to him. He is definitely holding on to what your father did to him and even though the great sky father is now mortal, your brother is a full god." I was still new to all of this and had a load of questions, but I shelved them for later because now wasn't the time. Kiro hit the blunt several times before he passed it to me and I watched as Natalie poured the wine and tried not to spill any of it. "D-do you need anything else?" She asked in a shaky voice. "N-No I don't, You're d-dismissed." Ally waved her hand at her and she flew out of the room and landed in the kitchen hard enough to break the bottle of wine. "Clean that up! Now!" Ally yelled. "Oh, And Aunt Aura told me to give this to you." Kiro exhaled a plume of purple smoke that floated towards Ally and changed into a small purple bag with a blue A on it. She opened the bag aland pulled out a large blue calcite stone that made my ears ring as it glowed. "Cool, Aunty gives the best presents. "I wonder what I can use this for?" Ally said, as I Kiro handed me the blunt. "Oh! I know!" She tossed it to the ground and it shattered into dust that swirled as it became a small tornado. "I've always wanted a boar." It slowly stopped moving as it became a blue boar with small feathered wings like hers. "Come here you little cutie." "And here I thought, I'd seen everything." I said, as she rubbed the top of its head. "I'm going to name you Chewy." I could see that it loved its name from the way that its wings moved rapidly. "Is Mama's little boy hung-y?" She asked, pulling a t-shirt out of nowhere. Ally put the shirt up to its nose as it floated off of the ground and ate the shirt. "Now eat up!" It devoured the shirt in seconds and then did a loop in the air before it flew into the kitchen. There was a moment of silence before the sound of Natalie yelling could be heard as the small newly formed boar chowed down on her. "Make sure you leave the heart. I'll need something to resurrect her with." Ally yelled. "This is why you're my favorite cousin." Kiro said as we heard Natalie using a cast Iron skillet to fight the boar. "Come on, let me introduce you to your other cousins." A couple of hours went by as Ally introduced us to Kiro's angelic cousins and I learned of her origins and how the first born angels were banished to this realm after half of them decided not to go against the Supreme goddess, Aura. After we said goodbye, we made our way back to the hotel for a banquet in our honor of our union and I met the rest of the hotel's Bat demigod staff.

A week had passed after we got married the mortal way and I finally made the decision to go see my father at the place called a senior living center. "Hi can I help you two?" The female front desk attendant asked. "Yes, I'm Here to see my father, Albert Darnell Konners." She smiled as she passed me the sign in sheet and the both of us signed it. "I need to see your IDs, please." We pulled them out and I handed them to her as I made eye contact with the mortal named Sherry. "Has anyone else came to visit my father?" I asked, using my vocal suggestion ability. She blinked as she flipped through the pages and stopped on one dated a week ago. "Only your brother, Darnell Konners." "Oh, cool. Good for them." "He comes here once a month and stays all day. The must have a really close relationship." A chill crawled up my spine as her words reverberated through my mind and a tall Brown skinned woman with tears in her eyes walked by us. I could feel strong psychic energy wafting off of her as she left the building and realized that she was on the verge of becoming an omniterran like Silas. *"Whoa! Did you feel that, Babe?"* He asked, telepathically. *"Yeah, she's like you."* I sent back as Sherry handed us our IDs. She told us his room number and we made our way to the elevator doors as I shook off the residual psychic energy of that woman. I looked over at Silas who covered his nose from the overbearing smell of death that permeated every inch of this place. The short ride to his floor gave me time to think about simply forgiving my father and moving on with my life, but something wouldn't let me do it. I felt an urge to make him pay for how he abused me. ***DING!*** We exited the elevator and turned a corner to see his room number and I suddenly felt weak in the knees. It was as if I was a child again and I awaited punishment for not living up to his standards. This reminded me of the time that I was six-teen and I was called to his sky realm for the first time. I had never seen him before then and that was a day that I would never forget. He slapped me for eating too loud and for having a lazy teleportation. The abuse was followed up with a kick in the ribs for accidentally calling him father in front of his court, instead of Sky lord. "Room thirty-four-B." Silas said, pulling me out of my tormented memories of my first bully. "Baby, Are you okay?" Silas held my hand and rubbed the side of my neck with his other hand as he looked me in the eyes. "Yes, I waited for this for so long." I let go of his hand and pressed the doorbell and within seconds we were face to face with the god who has caused pain wherever he went. For the first time in my life, I looked into his gray eyes and wasn't scared of getting slapped or punched. "Son." "Hello, Father, this is my Husband Silas." His features softened as he smiled and clapped his hands together. "My boy has found true love. Congratulations son." He backed up and allowed us to enter his apartment that smelled like peppermint and mens cosmetics. "Please have a seat. Can I get you something to drink?" "No, thank you." We said in unison, and shared a smile from the memory of when we paid

Eric and Athony a visit. "Then I'll get right to it. I've been a mortal for almost a hundred years and I can't pass on until I make things right with you." He leaned forward and I could see that he had genuine remorse in his voice. "I'm sorry son. You were given to us and as your parents, we've fucked up in more ways than one."

"What are you talking about?" I asked.

"Your mother and I had a deal. She'd give me a powerful army to take over my mothers domain if I allowed her to absorb the divine essence of one of our children." "What?" Silas stood up as his mind-eye opened and my father gasped at the sight of it. "You technically died and then came back, but we kept it a secret because I didn't have weak children." "Correction, you could 't show the other deities that you had weak children. That's why you two were harsh towards me." "Yes, you were a representation of our failures." I bit back the urge to punch him in the face as Silas sat back down and closed his mind-eye. I looked back at my father, who was no longer the powerful god of the sky. His gray eyes used to creep me out as they were in contrast to his dark brown skin. "I forgive you father, everything happens for a reason. No child should have ever had to go through what you and my mother put me through. In the end, I found my people." I reached over and placed my hand in my husbands as he smiled and wipes away his tears. He got up and opened his arms to me and I reciprocated the hug by embracing him for the first time in my life. I instantly regretted it because I saw flashes of his life in my mind and gasped as I watched him abuse Darnell, who would later become Darkon. "Y-Y-you abused Darnell!" I yelled, backing away. As he silently cried and nodded. "He was my biggest mistake and I now know that I'm sick and need help." My father was right, he did need help. That's one of the main reasons why I came here today. To grant the universe another gift. "I love you baby." I said, placing a kiss on Silas's forehead and then stepping towards my father with open arms. My disgusting father stepped into my arms and and we hugged like a real father and son as the minutes passed. I released him and backed up enough to reach out and place my hands around his neck. With my divine strength, it was easy to snap his neck but I slowly tightened my grip as he struggled to break free. He kept trying to pry my hand loose, so Silas held his hands at his side until he went limp in my grasp and finally died. We placed him on the couch and I removed one of his back teeth as well as a strand of his hair and placed it in a glass bottle, before sucking his soul into a small bottle. "Silas, can you press that button over there?" I asked, and he did as I asked. I healed his neck tissue right before the nurses came into the room and we pretended to be distraught at the sight of my fathers lifeless body. "What happened?" He asked. "He complained about his heart hurting and then collapsed." I fell to the floor next to them and made tears fall as Silas rubbed my back. "Daddy! I-I just wanted one last hug." I sobbed and we made our way out of his room and then outside to where Kevor waited until we dropped the act as we drove away. While riding down the street I thought about how Darnell became a god with my father being mortal. I also wondered who his mother was and if she was part goddess. Sometimes that would activate the divine gene in a child to gestate in a divine or semi- divine womb. Silas gasped as we made our way down the street and I looked over at him to see tears in all three of his eyes. "My brother's fiance just gave birth to a still born. We need to head to the hospital." His phone began to ring in his pocket as Kevor nodded and used his intuition to drive us to the hospital on the east side of town. Even though I disliked his family for how they treated him, I wouldn't wish the death of a child on them and suddenly hated the mortal way of travel. We made it to the hospital in thirty minutes and once inside, a nurse took us to where my in-laws were. His three family members were standing outside of the room while in an intense conversation. "Silas, what's going on?" His brother asked. I turned in a full circle as I picked up the scent of death and transportation magic. I stepped into the room and released my aura to see who cast this magic. It made me sneeze as I picked up the scent of Myr and raw honey. I knew of one person who used those two items in their magic and it was the bitch who yanked me out of her reproductive crevice. I stepped out of the room and watched as Silas tried to break the curse that surrounded their necks. "Your mother placed a curse on them and she wants you in exchange for their lives." He said, as his spell set in and they calmed down and they walked away.

"You're not sacrificing yourself, there has to be another way." He demanded.

"There isn't, I have to face Inana." I replied.

"Baby you can't." He pleaded.

"I have to, or she'll kill your family."

"I'll do it."

"No, my love. She can only absorb the power of her offspring. Do you remember when I told you that my aunt's training was harsh but worth it." I asked, as he nodded. "You said that she fed you fruit that only she could grow."

"Yes, it gave me the ability to adapt to any situation. Baby, you're going to have to let me die." He sobbed as he pulled me close and I transported the two of us to our mansion that we probably won't get to enjoy, because of the bitch who birthed me. *__Now is that any way to think about your mother?__* Her echoed around the front room as a fissure formed on the floor and bright glowing smoke crawled out of it. She took her human form and I kicked myself for not sensing that this was her reincarnated form. "Silas, meet my mother, the goddess intrusive telepathy and baneful words." A smile curved my lips as I thought about what sound she would make as her body hit the wall and the air escaped her lungs. She used to be the queen of the sky, thanks to my father. But her pride lead her to the underworld and caused her to lose that divinity. Which is why she was now a semi-divine mortal. I let out a laugh at how far she has fallen. From divine queen to mean girl.

Watching my hubby go toe-to-toe with his mother was a sight to see as he gave her false hope of winning and I fought the urge to scream as she reached into his chest to absorb his power through his heart. Seeing his body fade as he looked back at me and not be able to do anything was the hardest part about his plan. *This plan of his better work.* "What's the matter, Scillia? You know nothing lasts forever. She laughed as her body radiated with my now dead husband's divinity. It would have been easy to snap her neck with a thought, but that would be denying my husband the revenge he deserved. Just as I finished the thought, a cosmic blue portal appeared and a four armed goddess stepped through, with all seven of her eyes focused on his mother. Instantly Inanna was immobilized in a blue energy field as she turned to look at me with a smile on her face. "Hello, Silas. I am, Aura, your knew mother-in-law." In one of her hands she held a small brown skinned baby that I recognized as Kiroptarneth, except he had her added features and limbs. In seconds the baby grew in size to an adult and I let out a gasp at how much taller and muscular he was. "KiroTarneth!" I screamed. He shook his head no as he stepped forward and the blanket turned into pants. "I am now Kyauravus." His voice was deeper as he spoke to me through telepathy and pulled me into a hug. Nothing but tears fell from my eyes as I squeezed him tighter and he used his lower hands to give my butt a squeeze.

"I love you Silas."

"I love you too, Ky."

His head split in two as he kissed me with the right head and scowled at his ex-mother with the left one. He teleported from my arms to where the trapped goddess was and gave her a once over. "Now, what are we going to do with you?" He flicked her forehead with his left hand and made the energy field vanish. She took that as a chance to change into a bird woman and use her claws to slash at him as the attack left him unphased. "Shouldn't we help him?" I asked. "No, he has to be the one to end that bitch, once and for all." she responded. A part of me wanted to hold her down as he pummeled her with blow after blow, for how she treated him as a mother goddess and how much of a mean girl she was to me. Aura clapped with her multiple arms as Ky used his additional arms to block and knock Inanna out of the air. Ky flipped and kicked like an anime character as his cosmic blue energy trailed behind him. Her feathers flew everywhere as he slammed her into the ground and ripped off her arm-wings and then stomped on her knees. My newly birthed husband made a tent with his lower hands and held his upper hands out to her as she screamed in agony. Within seconds Inanna was no more and the divine energy that was once his lingered where she was. He pulled it towards him with hand gestures and it turned into a bat before it vanished from the room. "I guess it's a good thing that I can come and go from my second home, as I please." He smile and pointed to the space next to me that was now empty. "She does that sometimes." He said, changing into his human form that was more familiar to me. "Okay, all of that was cool." I said jumping into his arms. Even though he was just as divine as before, he radiated a higher level of confidence and contentment. "My mother has asked me to release an offering into nature, do you want to go with me?" I nodded and in the blink of an eye we were standing outside of a run down apartment and he put me down as someone passed by in a car and whistled. "Those cheeks are spoken for." I yelled. "To allow things to flow as they should, I take the form of a feathered pecker of wood." His spell changed him into the small annoying bird and he made several holes in the highest branch of the tree and made more holes on the lower branches before changing back. "All done." "What kind of offering is this?" "I don't know. My mom said that it is supposed to help insects burrow deeper into the wood and when the west wind brings in a spring storm, it will cause the branches to fall on top of a car." He answered, like it was normal. I teleported us home and manifested a blunt out of thin air. With a thought, I lit the end and took a couple of puffs before handing it to my husband. We smoked the blunt as gooseflesh formed on my arms and someone rang the doorbell. "Seriously!" He said, pointing at the television. It showed the image of Darkon. Who was waving at the camera. "Hey, Brother-Cousin. Can I come in?" He didn't wait to ask as he popped into our house and Ky took on his godly form. Darkon did the same and they had an intense stare down for a full minute with both of them having eyes that radiated their power. "How the hell could you end our fathers misery?" Darkon asked, as he changed back first. "After seeing what he did to you, I knew I had to rid the earth of their now mortal, Sky-Lord." "No! He needs to suffer more for what he did. DEATH IS A LUXURY!" Darkon practically yelled as his eyes glowed red. "Here." Ky conjured the jar with the hair and tooth that he bound their fathers soul to and tossed it to him. "Oh, shit. The sky daddy is definitely in there. Thanks, Brother I mean cousin." "I did that for you and now that I'm free of him and my ex-mother, I can move on." Ky answered. "Yeah, speaking of mothers, do you think she'll mind if I pay her a visit?" "No, I'm sure she's expecting it." "Well until then, how about you stay for dinner?" I asked, finally speaking. "I'd love that." Darkon said, moving over to where I sat and putting his arm over my shoulder. " Whoa! You're doing too much, little cousin." "Just checking to see if the home is happy or not. And besides, you're like a day old, little cousin." I laughed as Ky removed his hand and thought of what meal to make for us to eat as they shared another stare down. Before I could do anything, Darkon shivered as a small black fox-bat appeared on his shoulder. "What the fuck?" He said, with a laugh. "I'll have to give you two a rain check." The small bat filled the room with the scent of a thunderstorm that he took with them as he vanished from the room. "Okay, that was weird." I said, leaning up against Ky. "Yeah, even for us." He responded.

A whirl-wind of passion

"Jay, Our records show that you've exceeded the allowed absence-point system and have been given a final warning back in February, we're going to have to let you go. Hand me your lanyard." I did as the human resources bitch requested and got up to leave without saying another word. "I have to walk you out." She continued to talk but I didn't stay behind and kept walking to the exit. I gave this job six years of my life and when I finally decided to move up the ladder, I'm fired for an attendance point. Last time I checked, spring storms were out of my control, and these idiots allowed me to work a full day before calling me into the office at the last half-hour. As I walked to the bus stop I could see my bus going down the street. "Fuck!" How is this my life? I smoke a lot of weed, so finding a new job will be difficult. It was luck that led me to this job as a merchandise processor at a clothing distribution center that paid twenty dollars an hour. My bitch-ass ex best friend/ roommate left me in a worn down townhome apartment and now I have no job, no car and just enough money to get groceries. Thankfully, I paid the rent up for the next two months so I'm good on that, but my only problem is getting all the groceries home. I could catch the bus to the shopping center, but to get home, I would have to put my account in the negative by ordering a Mercury car service. Thank goodness for member points. Out of the corner of my eye I could see the bus coming so I pulled out my transit pass. "Fuck you, Doveport!" I saud, putting up two middle fingers as I took the bus to the Garden-Grove shopping center and spent three hundred dollars on groceries. The grocery store was my safe haven, my home away from home. That reminded me to pull the App up on my phone and request a ride. My phone vibrated, and I almost gasped at the picture of the gold-eyed, dark-skinned driver named Apollo, who was four minutes away. His smile was everything and I'm going to have to force myself not to objectify him. *Bing!* "Are you Jay?" I turned around and lost control of my mouth as Apollo stepped towards me. His car was waiting with the trunk open, and for several seconds, all I could do was slowly breathe. He had every single thing going on in the best way possible, and he was tall as fuck! The afternoon sun mixed with the contrast of his skin made his eyes look as if they glowed. "Yes, sorry it's been a long day." I pulled myself out of the weird trance, and he laughed as he pulled the cart up to his car. My legs moved to help him but he pointed to the open passenger door. I flinched because I didn't notice it before now. "Thank you, Apollo." His smile was almost too gorgeous to look at and when he winked I swore my underwear pulled a houdini act. I got in the car and shut the door as he returned the cart. Even his car was sexy and expensive as fuck. Apollo jogged back up to the car and got in with the same smile on his face. "Twenty-four-eighty-six-Trojan boulevard." I nodded as he pulled out of the parking lot and we made the short distance to the freeway. "Do you mind if we take the express route? I have a date." That partially deflated the buzz he was giving me as I nodded once more. "Are you single?" "Yes, I'm also unemployed and gay and apparently overweight." He scoffed at that last part as we came to the stop sign before the freeway entrance. "Would you like to go on a date tonight?" For a second I was stunned once more but he placed his hand on my shoulder. "Do you want to go on a date tonight?" I see what he did there, he worked his way into asking me out. *Smooth move, Mr. Muscles.* "Yes, Apollo. But I don't have any money to go dutch." I pointed to the back, and he laughed. "Shit, I'll take a home cooked meal. Do you smoke weed?" I nodded and fought the urge to smile as I blushed. "Should I drop you off and help you with the groceries and then come back?" I wanted to ask why he was being so nice to someone who he just met but I didn't want to come off as unappreciative. "Yes, Give me about an hour, I was fired two hours ago." He laughed and turned onto my exit. My muscle-god driver made it to my home in less than twenty minutes where we made small talk and we unloaded the groceries. "Wow, you weren't kidding when you said it was a dump. Damn."

Now I was really embarrassed. He stepped into my kitchen and looked at the small fire damage from last year and the water spots from the apartment upstairs. At this moment I was truly grateful for my father and his insect repellent. "Okay, I'll be back in an hour." He extended his hand and I accepted as he gave another wink before he turned and walked to the door. Even his ass was sexy. He turned around and pointed a finger upwards. "I'm not a religious person but I do have a rule to not eat cow meat on Sundays or Mondays. Any other day is cool, but not today." With a final wave, he left, and I collapsed on the lumpy couch. I went from being fired and missing my bus to going to the grocery store and then meeting the sexiest black man alive. A chill ran down my spine as I thought about how this date could go wrong. The first thing I need to do is to have my gun at the ready because of his size and then the extra set of kitchen knives that I bought for this exact reason, Hidden in various spots. After a quick shower I rolled a blunt and began to prepare everything for the chicken taco-egg rolls. My homemade salsa paired well with the guacamole I made from the ripe avocados. Once all of that was done I made the egg rolls and placed them in the oven. I've perfected a cooking method of baking them in the oven at four hundred degrees on a baking sheet for exactly seventeen minutes. I walked into the front room to lite and incense and then checked myself out in the full-length wall mirror by the door. The graphic T-shirt I chose was loose enough to breathe and paired well with the jean shorts and the sneakers I bought myself for my birthday last year. I could hear a car door close, and butterflies formed in my stomach. "You can do this, he's just a really attractive man who is into you." With my front door open, Apollo knocked on the screen door and smiled as he looked at me from the other side. "The night is already starting off good I see." He put emphasis on the last word by looking directly at my ass. *Good, I made sure to put these shorts on to show it off.* He opened the door and walked in with a large bouquet of multicolored flowers in a bright orange pot. A chill ran up my spine as the name popped into my head. "Hyacinths!" I didn't know where that came from, but it managed to raise his eyebrows. He pulled me into a hug and then kissed my cheek. It took all my willpower not to become erect from the close contact. His muscles pressed up against me, and the smell of his cologne was soothing in a weird aromatherapy kind of way. It was a mix of lavender with a masculine musk to it. "You smell good, is that from the Mary and Jane line of masculine scents." I laughed at his joke, and he gave me a small squeeze before he let me go and handed me the flowers. "Thank you. You smell amazing as well." He was dressed in light blue designer jeans and a tank top with a rainbow musical note in the middle of his chest. I don't know what it was, but seeing it made the back of my head itch. "You good?" "Yes, it's been a while since I've received flowers." Sometimes, being able to lie on the spot came in handy. *Ding!* "The egg rolls are done."

"Oh, what kind did you make?"

"Chicken tacos with homemade salsa and guac." The face he made was too handsome to look at, so I took him by the hand and walked the seven steps to my kitchen. I placed the flowers on the table and removed the egg-rolls from the oven. "I'm glad you didn't do anything super fancy." I couldn't tell if that was shade or sarcasm, so I flashed a smile and giggled along with him. "These have to cool for a couple of minutes. Can I pour you a glass of wine?" He nodded yes and made grand gestures with his hands. It looked stupid, but after a couple of seconds, he made it look like he magically made a blunt appear. "How cute, you're a gay magician." Apollo rolled his eyes as he used his thumb, pinky and ring finger to hold the blunt up to his lips and placed the two remaining fingers on the tip. He smiled and looked me in the eyes as he inhaled and ignited the end. Smoke curled around his fingers as he removed it from his mouth and handed it to me. "Cool, parlor trick." I put it to my lips, inhaled its strong smoke, and immediately started to choke. "That's that good shit. I know you ain't never had anything like it before." Once again I couldn't tell if he was being mean or just making conversation, but the weed was good as fuck and I was not one to turn away the good stuff. We smoked half of it and I made our plates as he used the bathroom. Despite his insensitive comments this was turning out to be a good first date. Apollo came out of the bathroom and took a seat at the table. "Wow, carbs on carb-" He stopped speaking and looked over to the window. "Are you okay?" He nodded but didn't take his eyes off the window. Apollo breathed in through his nose and out through his mouth. "Do you know the man that owns the three houses on the next block over?" The seriousness of his tone, mixed with the look on his face, scared me a little. "No. Do you know something about him that I don't?" He shook his head no and picked up an egg roll that he dipped in the guacamole. Apollo bit into the egg roll and continued to enjoy it without saying another word. "Are we just going to ignore whatever that was?" "Yes, the answer would scare you." He said that so casually, and I decided to ignore it and eat my food before it got cold and the guac got too much air. We continued to eat in silence, and I wanted so badly to ask him more, but it seemed as if it killed his mood. Once he finished what was in his mouth, he got up and kissed me on the cheek. "Thank you for the meal, Jay Dion Allen. I will remember this kindness." He walked out the door without saying another word and hopped in his car. I ran to the window, and my mouth fell open at the sight of a red sports car that backed out of my driveway. It happened too fast, and I couldn't believe this man just did that. I locked the screen and then shut the front door and locked it as well. Since I was already drinking wine I poured the rest of the bottle in my glass and played some of my favorite music as I cleaned up. After I was done, I lit the blunt that I rolled and spent the rest of the night watching videos on my phone.

DING! DING! DING! I awoke with my phone buzzing in my hand and the blinding light of the morning sun on my face. It took a couple of seconds for the room to stop spinning as my vision cleared, and I looked at the notification on my phone. It was from a dating app and displayed a message from a man named Tom-Morison, who said Good Morning. I clicked the profile picture, and it took me to his page. He was a Greek-African American photographer, and he loved weed food and was a little bit heavier than me. "Mmm, six-two with a bald head, sign me up," I replied with a winking emoji and decided that I should watch some porn before I got in the shower. The moment I pulled the porn up on my phone, he replied with a front and back picture that made my dick hard. I rolled over and snapped a picture of my ass first. I reached for the lotion and gave myself a tight squeeze as I moved up and down the shaft. That helped bring back the thickness of my eight inches and I snapped a pic. Before I could reply, he sent an eggplant and sad face emoji. "Somebody is thirsty for the dick, I see!" I added the picture to the conversation and closed it since my dick was still hard. After searching for the right video in my collection, I played it and skipped to the part where the man with the hair booty was laying on his stomach with his legs apart and ass in the air. It gave the perfect view of his swollen ass right before the top plunged himself balls deep and pounded the life out of his plump white jiggly ass. He fucked him so hard it made ripples form on his cheeks, and just the sight of it made me cum early. My eyes rolled to the back of my head, and my toes curled as I spilt my essence all over my pelvis and thighs. "Whew!" I hopped in the shower and decided to get out of the house for the day so I took the bus to my favorite diner for breakfast. "Welcome to Michelle's. I'll be your waitress, Sabrina. Are you dining in or out today?" The tall waitress came over and poked her big breasts out as she spoke. "Oh no, honey, I landed with the leprechauns of the rainbow, and I'm dining in." I grabbed the menu and took a seat as my stomach growled from eating itself.

"Let's just keep that between us. My manager is itching to fire me."

"As someone who was fired yesterday, I'll pretend it never happened. May I have some coffee and a good morning omelet plate?"

"Sure thing, handsome. Will that be with bacon or sausage?

"Both, please and can I have biscuits instead of toast?"

"Coming right up." She turned on her heels and went behind the counter to grab a cup with one hand while removing the menu with the other. "I'll have that ready for you in ten minutes." She wrote down my order, handed it to the chef, and went to do her rounds. *Ting!* I pulled my phone out of my pocket and smiled at the happy face emoji from Tom. He sent his number and an offer to meet up later, so I pressed the number and replied with a text stating that we should meet up this afternoon. *Ting! Ting! Ting!* "Someone is popular." Michelle came by grabbed some menus, and gave me a wink. I ignored her as I looked at the two messages; one was a frowning emoji, and the other was three words: Naw, I'm good. "Seriously?" I exited the app as a man sat next to me and smiled. "Morning greetings." "Greetings." He had to be in his early fifty's with all-white hair and pretty blue eyes. "Manuello Cold." "Jay Allen." The moment I grasped his hand, a cold chill ran down my spine. I shivered, and Manuello released me. "Sorry about that. I've been told that I have cold hands." "Hello, blue eyes. Can I get you your usual?" Michelle placed a hand on his thick muscular shoulders, and he nodded with a smile. "Can I have water instead of coffee?" "Coming right up." She walked into the kitchen, and Manuello tapped me on the shoulder. "So tell me about yourself." "I'm in my thirties, jobless, no car, and gay. And you?" He smiled, and his pink lips parted to flash a pearly white smile. "I'm in my fifty's, I own too many companies to name without bragging, my chauffeur is waiting outside, and I'm bi-sexual. Are you single?" "Yes, and you?" He nodded as Michelle returned with his glass and poured spring water into it. "Your orders are almost ready." "Thank you, Michelle." He responded as I simply nodded. "I am single, my wife died twenty years ago, and I am allowing myself to experience the full spectrum of my sexuality." "I love hearing that. Most people hide themselves from their true self in order to present an identity they use to fit in." "Yes, I've always been upfront about my preferences when I am with a male or female. My kids are grown, so I don't have any small attachments."

He placed a hand on my thigh and I swiveled on my stool and turned to face him. "I also don't have any attachments or a roommate." "Hey Michelle can we get this food to go?" He pulled three hundred dollar bills from his tight pants pocket and waved it in her direction. The both of us continued to have an organic conversion while she boxed up our food and brought it to us. "Please do everything that I would do." She gave both of us a once-over as Manuello grabbed the food. "Oh, I plan too." He laughed as we walked through the doorway and his driver waited with the door open. "Take us home please." "Right away sire!" The man appeared older than Manuello but as he ran to the otherside I could see that he was in great shape for his age. We kissed the entire ride and I couldn't wait to let him top me so that I could put some food on my stomach. The car stopped and Manuello released his hold on my lower back as we pulled into an underground parking. "I own the entire building." He handed the food to his chauffeur and we walked into an elevator that silently took us up to the penthouse. "I'll place this in sta- I mean food containers, sire." "Thank you, Gerald." I didn't have time to see the rest of the downstairs as he swept me off my feet and carried me upstairs. For the next hour and a half we took turns sucking and fucking each other as we both reached a sweaty climax. I put his legs up in the air and bounced on his pink nine and a half inch dick until he cried out and pulled at the bed spread. He paid me back by allowing me to do a side-fuck position where I grabbed him from behind and he backed his ass up on my dick until I cried out as I reached my climax. "That was amazing Mr. Allen." "It was indeed, Mr. Ice

Cream." I grabbed his ass and gave it a jiggle as he farted out my sperm. Just the sight of it made the blood flow to my penis. Manuello rolled over and pressed his entire body against mine. "I know for a fact you don't have anywhere to be, so how about you stay here with me for a while? Gerald has already taken your measurements and clothes will be here within the hour." In one swift move he placed my legs over his shoulders. "Please." He slid himself in me and I cried out at the small stinging sensation of adjusting to his girth. I nodded as he began to thrust and before I knew it we were moving in perfect rhythm with each other. I pulled his head down and kissed him with everything I had. We moaned into each other's mouths as he stopped long stroking and smashed my hole with his balls slapping against me. I reached down to grab my erection and he pulled away from my mouth. "No, we don't masterbate in this house. That's what these are for." He looked down at his dick going in and out of me and then returned to nasty french kissing me. Manuello moaned louder into my throat as he ejaculated inside me. My empty stomach rumbled and at this point I felt like he owed me child support with all the kids inside and now he owed me a meal. He removed himself and it was my turn to fart out his seed but instead of getting off of me Manuello took me in his mouth and sucked me off until I came down his throat. "Now we're both impregnated." I was finally released form his sex hold and he got up and went to the bathroom. My new sugar daddy returned with a wet towel that he used to clean me off and then pulled me into a shower. From that moment on time flew by super fast and I spent two weeks with Manuello. He gave me money to give to my parents, and paid for my stuff to be put in storage. The only time I stepped outside was when he pressed me up against the tall balcony and clapped my cheeks in the open air. "My parents want to thank you for the money by cooking a meal for us." "No, I'll invite them here and have something prepared." "We haven't been out of this tower for sixteen days, We can go over there and then have a night out on the town." "No, have you douched today?" His abrupt dismissal of my suggestion made me smack my teeth and cross my arms. "Why not, you've left twice to "handle business" and all we've done is fuck. I want to breathe fresh air without backing my ass up on your dick." He walked over to a painting and moved it to the side to reveal what looked like a safe without surface lock. It had a large white diamond where the lock mechanism and Manuello touched it with the tip of his finger and it opened. "I don't do the long term thing and to tell the truth I really don't like the fifty-fifty nastiness to our sexual relationship." He reached in and pulled out a large manilla envelope and handed it to me. "Don't open it yet. I have something I want to say." He took a seat on the couch and directed me to do the same. "This has been fun but I've grown tired of fucking your ass and I'm used to a eighty-twenty nasty ratio. In there you will see documents for a three bedroom home and a brand new car. Also I made a trust for you. Gerald will see you out." He got up and walked away without saying another word as his chauffeur held his hand out to me. "The car is waiting for you, Mr. Allen." Once again I was kicked out of a place I literally put my all into. I laughed as we reached the basement and Gerald opened the door for me. At least this time I got paid for what I was worth. On the way to my new home I opened the envelope and gasped at the sixteen million dollar trust. The car was a four door sedan that was the newest windstorm model and the house was worth half a million dollars. "The keys are in the alarm pad, enter the address backwards. Mr Cold will contact you when he is ready to talk." "Oh, and we threw away all of your cheap food and replaced it with better options." Gerald pulled into the driveway of a two story home and opened my door for me. There was a small walkway made of gray stone that led up to the front porch. It laid in between two small plots of healthy grass with flowers at its edges. My single car garage had a fence in the back that divided my land from the house next door. I walked the path to my porch and entered the address backwards into the keypad like Gerald suggested and it popped open. I know that I was just basically paid for booty but the feeling of walking into a home that was now mine made me do three cartwheels in a row. The open space would be perfect if I had friends to hangout with. My large open spaced kitchen had expensive appliances and pale gray marble countertops with dark cabinet doors. My furniture was so large and perfect for laying on the couch in front of the sixty inch smart television. I took a tour of the three rooms and loved that the primary bedroom had a walk-in closet that connected to the bathroom. The closet was full of clothes and shoes that were perfectly tailored for me. "So my Ice-cream daddy was paying attention to the outside of my body." I continued my personal tour by going to the large backyard that was fully fenced in and rolling in the grass. My mind raced with happy thoughts of how I could plant flowers on the left and veggies on the right. I dusted myself off and headed to the patio to check out my grill and seating area. Looking at the small spider on the chair reminded me to order a ton of bug repellent, the last thing I needed was to fuck on the furniture and a bug hopping on my dick. I needed to get my mind off of my recent sexual escapades so I pulled out my laptop and switched my accounts to this address while I waited for the chicken to finish marinating in the fridge before I fry it. After a half hour of typing and password entering, I was now putting the finishing touches on my cheesy potatoes and then set the oven to three-seventy-five. Gerald was an amazing chef but I love black food and No one can make the meals that I make. Asparagus, Crispy fried chicken and baked cheesy potatoes from scratch with a tater tots on the top. Bing! The oven was ready and I put the potatoes in with the asparagus and rolled up some of the best weed that ice-cream daddy's money could buy. Hopefully he stays away for a while so that I can have some fun here. My phone rang and I silently prayed that it wasn't my dismissive silver daddy. The moment I saw that it was from an unknown number, I swiped up to answer and put it on speaker. "Hello!" For several seconds all I could hear was heavy breathing before whoever it was ended the call. "Okay…..Weird." The smell of my potatoes and asparagus brought me back to my home cooking and it reminded me to turn on the electric eye for the oil. In thirty minutes I had the house smelling good as I took out the potatoes and placed them next to the asparagus. Normally I wouldn't eat dinner for breakfast, but this was well needed with all the expensive food Manuello stuffed me with. The sound of my doorbell rang throughout the house and I ran to the door to greet my first visitor. "Coming, just one second." I yelled out as I crossed into the front room. The closer I got to the door I started to feel butterflies in my stomach and it was slightly unsettling. Once I reached the door and opened it my mouth fell open as I took in the sight of my first love. "Zephyr!" "Jay, can I come in?" I was partially stunned but stepped back so that he could come inside. Zephyr placed my arms over his shoulders and pulled me into a hug. His long arms wrapped around me and the world vanished until the smell of the chicken brought me back to earth as he removed his arms and I ran to the kitchen. I removed the eight perfectly fried pieces of chicken and he leaned up against the counter and looked around the kitchen. "I bought the house next door and when I saw you get out of the car my mouth dropped. You look great." "You do too." Zephyr laughed as he looked at the food and then back at me. "Don't judge me, I've been eating rich white people's food for the past two weeks. Are you hungry?" "Yes, I'd love to share a meal with you." I made our plates and we sat across from each other at my rectangular dining table. He was even sexier than both Apollo and Manuello with his rich light-brown skin and bright green eyes. Zephyr was a couple of inches taller than me and just as thick but with defined muscles instead of fat. "I'm not going to lie, I've been stalking you on social media." I smiled and finished chewing my food before answering. "Me too." We laughed and he moved from sitting across from me to the seat next to me. Time flew by as we filled each other in on our lives and finished the food I made. "Jay, I want to apologize for coming in and out of your life the way that I did." His apology was unexpected but greatly appreciated after all these years. I met him when I was kid on the playground and then he disappeared. He came back into my life when I was ten during spring break and for the longest time, I thought he was my imaginary friend until he kissed me on the cheek and hugged me. He vanished and I didn't see him again until I was fifteen and he was working in the produce section of the grocery store. We were secret boyfriends for six months until he vanished without a trace and then reappeared at my graduation with a bouquet of flowers like the ones Apollo gave me. While being lost in my thoughts I wasn't aware that I was crying and Zephyr whipped away my tears. I pushed how he made me feel to the back of my mind and never thought about it again because he was the first person to break my heart. "I want to tell you the truth as well. The real truth, that's terrifying and life changing." Hearing him say that made the hairs on the back of my neck stand up as he leaned in to kiss my forehead. I've waited so long for him to want to be with me that I can't fully trust him to hold my heart in his hands without dropping it and running to the nearest exit. "Okay, Do you still smoke?" He nodded and pulled out a metallic forest green blunt holder from his pocket. "I grow my own weed." Before he lit the blunt he got up and held his hand out to me. "Would you join me in day drinking?" "I would love to." Zephyr took me by the hand and we walked over to his house that took my breath away. "I built all the houses on this street and sold them to Manuello who then gave it to you." I froze at the mention of my sugar daddy. Zephyr turned and pulled me into another hug but this time he laughed and kissed my cheek. "How much do you know about Greek mythology?" It was my turn to laugh at his question that had nothing to do with us. "I know that Zeus is the king and Aphrodite is the goddess of love." "Yes, My name is actually greek. Like Apollo's." I stared at him with raised eyebrows at the mention of the sexy driver who asked me out and then left after the food was done. How the fuck did he know about him? "I'm the god of the west wind." Tears fell from his eyes as he spoke and looked me directly in the eyes. I waited for him to continue but he bit his lip and looked to the floor and then back up to me. "You're serious?" I asked.

He nodded and pulled me into another hug. "Jay, There is more and you have to promise me that you won't be angry with me." "I promise." Zephyr released me and we took a seat on his extremely comfortable couch. "Thousands of years ago, I helped the olympians defeat the titans. I helped the king of the gods to be more precise. For my good deed Zeus appointed me as the lord of the west wind and gave me two of his daughters as my brides. Iris who is the goddess of rainbows and Persophone, the goddess of nature. Hades took Persephone as his queen so I married Iris and we lived happily for several centuries. That was until she showed me that she inherited her fathers need for random sex. Her followers started to sacrifice children in her name and that was the last straw for me so I left her. Literally." He laughed but I could sense that it wasn't a funny memory that he was remembering. "Can I ask a question?" "You can ask me anything, my love." Zephyr scooted closer and placed my leg over his. "How old are you?" He sucked his breath in before answering as his hand rested on my thigh.

"Two million-One hundred thousand and thirty eight."

"Can you fly?"

"Yes, I have wings"

"Can I see them?"

"I'll show you my divine form after I tell you everything and you accept me for who I truly am."

"Okay, Please finish." He nodded and took a deep breath. "I traveled all over the globe and acquainted myself with the beasts of nature and the mortals I'd come across. My body count is in the hundred thousands but I felt just as alone with them as I did with Iris. I was used for how I look or what I could bring and in that time period farming was the natural way to survive. My helpful hand led me back to Greece and one spring I met a handsome teenage prince named

Hyacinthus." The back of my head burned as he spoke that name and it was slightly unbearable for a second but his touch instantly soothed it as he rubbed my head. "I'm sorry." "For what?" I asked, as the sensation vanished. "I took the form of a teenager whenever we met and the both of us fell in love almost instantaneously. We both had abusive families that forcefully pushed their will onto us, so we escaped every chance we could. My father is Aeolus the keeper of the winds and my mother was a nature goddess from here, America or Ta'Amara as it was called back then." I was about to say something but he put his fingers to my lips. "I've been waiting to tell you this forever and I really want to confess my crime to you before I start crying again." I could see tears form in his eyes so I nodded and he continued. "My wife finally noticed that I was gone and came looking for me. I knew that she would kill you so I left with her and went back to Olympus. Little did I know that her brother Apollo told her of my whereabouts and waited for me to leave to court you. I went to his father and he told me that Hyacithus would have to make the choice of his own free will. Apollo and his big mouth attracted the attention of his brother Dionysus and the north wind Boreas. Mortal royalty came from all over the planet to offer you their love and realm. You denied them all and picked Apollo." I held my hand up because he spoke that name and a part of me wondered if he was referring to my hot driver. "Yes, he was scared by the darkness that dwelled a couple of streets over and went back to Olympus. Maunello is the north wind and Tom is the reincarnation of a prince who was obsessed with you. Jay we have to stay on track, I really need to confess my crime." "Okay, I'm sorry." I don't know why but a part of me was starting to believe him. He never lied to me before and from what I've experienced he always wanted to be near me. "I will never lie to you. That's why I had to leave and come back into your life, time and time again." He pulled me close and pressed his soft lips against mine. The world vanished again as our lips wrestled against each other. We passionately kissed each other for several minutes before he pulled away. "Mmmm, Jay we have to continue. Ten mortal years had passed and Apollo made my prince his royal consort. I sired a son named Pothos with Iris and made Hera proud. Iris poured all of her sexual desire and yearning into him and that's what he became the god of. My anger brought forth a bunch of natural disasters and Zeus ordered me to fix them. I did and once again found my way back into your- I mean, Hyacynthus life. I took the form of an insect that mortals call a ladybug and watched my prince have a perfect date with Apollo. You were playing a game with rings that was similar to horseshoes and when the sun god threw his ring I twisted the wind and made it fly off into the forest but it bounced off of a tree and-." Tears streamed down this beautiful man's face as he stopped talking.

He looked at me but was lost in the memory. "Everything is okay, I'm alive and well." "I accidentally killed you, and for my crimes Apollo wanted me dead but there was no one to appoint to my throne so Zeus basically let me off with a slap on the wrist. The sun god didn't like that so he used magic that he learned from Hecate to turn your body into the ancestor of those flowers Apollo and I gave you. At first it was all I could grow because of my guilt but that idiot didn't know about my prophetic ability. The flowers showed me all of your next lives and I, um." He stopped speaking and smiled from ear to ear. "I met you first in all of your lives and each time was even better than the previous. Zeus gave all the other gods chances to offer you an apple but you denied them each time. That's why Apollo pretended to be the driver and gave you the ride home. Boreas was tasked with giving you financial stability, not all the other stuff." I laughed and he stopped talking as a smile curved his lips. "I thought you didn't have a problem with any of that?" "My problem was with him going against the plan. Hades said that your family would reincarnate as poor common folk, so he and Fortuna worked together to shift wealth back into your favor. I built my own wealth so that little pocket change he gave you can be donated to charity. Which brings me to a question I've wanted to ask you since nineteen ninety six." He reached into the couch with his left hand and produced a glowing golden apple. I laughed and reached for it but he moved his arm backwards and shook his head no. "Jay Dion Allen, You were wronged by me in a past life. I'm sorry. It was never my intention to cause harm to your body. My jealousy got the best of me and I abused my power for revenge. I've loved you in every life and waited for the right time to ask you to be my husband." Zephyr handed me the glowing apple that made the hairs on my body stand up the second it touched my skin. "If you say no it will vanish and so will I, if you say yes…" I've loved this man since he showed me his homemade toys on the playground and even more so when we had sex for the first time as teenagers. Even if this was a form of mental illness I'd want to be his husband and be at his side for as long as time would allow. "Zephyr, Lord of the west-wind, bringer of spring. I accept you for who you really are. Yes, I will marry you." The moment I finished the last words, light from the apple seeped into my hands and up my arms. My entire body buzzed as the apple disappeared and I floated off of the couch. Everything I ever experienced came crashing to the forefront of my mind as the light changed from gold to indigo. The energy receded into me and I stumbled backwards into my new husband's arms. "How do you feel?" I blinked as my vision cleared and I could see his large red feathered wings behind him. "Happy to be married." He wrapped his wings and arms around me as his erection against my ass. "This is the first day of the rest of our eternal lives. I love you Jay." "I love you too, Zephyr, god of spring." I turned around in his arms and pressed my lips against his. We kissed for what felt like hours until I sensed the presence of someone watching us. He broke away and looked up to the ceiling. "Yes!" I followed his line of sight and flinched when I saw the giant brown spider looking down on us. "Shall I prepare the venue and royal attire?" Its large mandibles moved as it spoke in the voice of a teenager. "Yes, but first come down here and meet the new addition to our family." As it crawled down the wall it glowed with pink light and changed into a young adult male that was dressed like a fashion model. "Jay this is Vicious the god of vicious forest animals and one of my lieutenants. We call him Vic." His smile was even wider than Zeph's as he stopped in front of me and bowed. "Welcome to the family lord. If you need anything just call my name." He flashed me a smile one last time before falling backwards and turning into a swarm of smaller spiders as he hit the ground. "Will I be able to do that?" "There is a lot to unpack with that question so I'll tell you this. Mortals were divine when they were first created by Aura. She gifted them with almost immortal life spans and Hecate gave them magic. Over time they proved to be uncontrollable and almost destroyed the planet so Gaia sent them out into the universe. The remaining Demi-humans became the ancestors of the people who existed during the seven disasters all the way to this era." "So the beast we think of as mythical are our ancestors?" "Yes, but their power is sealed away in your pineal glands. The Olympians use the celestial bodies to siphon the excess mana of mortal energies. You are good at a lot of things so this will be as much of a surprise for you as it will be for me. But you should also know that being divine is energy and consciousness as well as our shadow sides that we hide from ourselves. You don't, You've put yourself out there, accepted the uncomfortable and realized that things happen as they're supposed to." He said, caressing my cheek. "I would have torn that job up if they let me work all day and then waited to fire me. You were calm with Apollo and spoke your mind to Manuello. I don't know if you're going to have wings webbed feet, gills or horns, but I do know that I'll be here every step of the way." "Webbed feet?" He laughed and for the first time I actually felt his happiness. It was tangible in the energy around me, like a full body hug. "You used to love to bird watch with me so I'd hazard a guess that you'll have bird wings like me. But it's like I said, we have to wait until the next full moon in three days." He leaned in to kiss me and when I moved forward I passed through him and fell to the floor. I held my hands up and instantly floated upwards. At first it was a little uncomfortable but as time went on I shifted my weight and turned towards Zephyr. I slowly descended to the ground and into the arms of my new husband. I was physically the same size and weight, but my body was muscular and my low fade was an afro. I also had memories of my past lives flash in my mind, but they were followed by knowledge that was on the tip of my tongue. "I should also tell you that your dreams will be more vivid. You'll know what's in the heart of mortals and be able to sense other divine beings. You also can't tell your family or friends." I laughed at the mention of my fake-ass friends who call when they want to smoke my weed or eat my food and drink my wine. "I love my family but this is our business, and those parasite's don't have to know shit either. Now when can we have sex?" He sucked his breath in and looked away and then back at me. The image of Manuello A.K.A Boreas popped into my mind. "We have to wait until the residual sex energy dissipates from your aura. But until then let's see what else you can do." He stepped backwards and vanished in a whirlwind of leaves. ***Come find me, my love!*** The sound of his voice echoed around the room and I closed my eyes to concentrate. I imagined myself standing next to Zephyr and when I opened my eyes I was standing in the backyard. "Almost perfect!" Zephyr placed his hand on my bare shoulder and I shivered from his cool touch. I looked down at my completely naked body with my dick flopping in the wind. "Just think about what you were wearing." I did and indigo energy swirled over my body as my clothes appeared. "Very good. Let's try elemental manipulation." He whistled at the sky and the clouds above us grew dark and turned into thunder clouds that rained down large droplets of rain. "You try." I looked to the cloud and it turned into a flock of owls. Zephyr gasped and gripped my arm as they flew past. "Jay!" The birds vanished and he turned to face me with his wings stretching up as he put his hands to his lips. "Did I do good?" He nodded as tears came streamed down his face. "Baby, that was amazing." He kissed my lips and in the blink of an eye we were back in my home. "Uh, I didn't do this." "I did. With this being yours, you have to put your special touch on it with a signature enchantment." A prickling sensation formed in my hands and forehead as he finished talking. "Yes, like that. Now focus your attention on greeting the house." I did as he asked and the energy flowed out of me and into the floor and then walls. As it spread throughout the house I became aware of every single thing inside the perimeter of my home. The energy subsided and Zephyr held his hand out and summoned a clipboard. He plucked a large red feather from his wings and started to write on the paper. "Intangibility, flight, teleportation, transfiguration. What you just did was form a bond with your Domain or residence. Whatever you want to happen here will and no one can do anything about it. Well, except me as your husband." He placed his hands on my waist and pulled me close. "I am Divorced from my ex wife but the Olympians still hold a grudge. Hera hates me and Zeus is basically her yes-god so their incestual siblings follow and the minor deities stay out of it." "How do I defend myself against the most notorious family of gods to ever exist?" Zephyr laughed and placed a kiss on my lips. "My mom is bestfriends with the Goddess Hecate, queen Titania of the fey-folk, The great devourer Goddess Ammit and I befriended a sun Demon-goddess named Vamora and her soon-to-be wife Nighmena who is a moon Demon-goddess. There are four gods from other pantheons who will help but I can't speak their names until we absolutely need them." That helped but I had a sneaking suspicion that all of this was the calm before the storm. "And here I thought my beef with the down low homophobic mailman was bad." "That was bad until I killed him. He paid three men to break into your apartment and rape you. I was the cardinal that nested on your windshield day and night." My heartbeat picked up and my breath came out as waves of heat. "Thank you. When I saw that he went missing I jumped for joy." I took a seat on the couch as the heat waves vanished. "Were the men he hired attractive?" Zephyr nodded and tears streamed down my face as my mind played different scenarios of how it could have gone if I acted in my typical horny nature. "I tore one guy's dick off, punched a hole through the other man's head and gave the last one to Vic. He ate his legs like a rack of ribs." The image popped into my mind and it helped to calm me down. "This is off topic but you're very psychic." Zephyr said. "Aren't all divine beings psychic?" "Yes and No. Just like mortals with different skills, we are born with basic gifts and the ones attributed to our divinity. My mother is a nature goddess and my father is an air god so I'm in the middle of that. Yours will be different because it has to come to you." "How?" "I don't know. Normally I would go to the mortal and give them the apple and they would bite it or do what you did. Each is equally effective but different when it comes to becoming fully divine. If you would have bit the apple you would have experienced the change in the same way except it would have worked from the inside. You probably would have gone through a dream state awakening or just woke up and be as you are now. You fully accepted me and the gift I gave you so the season of spring is also yours."

"Does it normally take three days to become divine?" My question made his eyebrows shoot upwards as a smile curved his lips.

"Each day represents a decade of your life in which your divine soul will solidify on this plane of existence. If I would have given you the apple when I first met you it would have been weird."

"How?"

"I've always been against marriage proposals to children. Pulling you into this world before you were ready would have stunted your emotional and mental growth."

My ears buzzed and I could see the mail carrier putting mail in my box. The image faded but I knew in my mind that it was just junk mail like I knew my name and every blade of grass in the backyard. "Intuition is what it's called." I loved how he knew what I was thinking and feeling. For a large part of my life I felt alone as gay black man in America. The only person to ever ask me questions about myself and wait for the answer is the god sitting next to me. My family listened but they're straight. I could never talk to my friends because they were too self absorbed and only had emotions for the men they fucked. "Thank you, Husband." "I'd lay down my life for you Jay." His words made me realize that I never forgave him for accidentally killing me in a past life. "You don't, I fucked up."

Zephyr placed his hand on my neck. He tried to talk but couldn't as tears streamed down his face. "I do. What happened was an accident and now that I have access to my past life memories, I see that Apollo planned to make me a male concubine and not a divine consort. He also stepped out of the way so that the disk could hit me." I placed my hand over the wound as the memory faded to the back of my mind. "Zephyr's eyes glowed as the memory played through his mind. A wave of sorrow washed over me and was followed by his rage. It conflicted with my joy of experiencing another power so I closed my eyes and anchored myself to my own emotions. "Apollo is a god of prophecy and knew it was going to happen. He could have caught it out of the air." "And if he'd done that we wouldn't be here right now as we are." I didn't know what else to say to ease what he was feeling besides pulling him into a hug and letting him feel how happy I am right now just to be around him. To be his husband. Now that my outside matches the amazing person I am on the inside I feel like this is my chance to literally live it up and party. "I know that I can't tell anyone about my newly awakened divinity but can I rub my new look in the faces of my ex-best friends?" "Yep, I'm always down to show off. What did you have in mind?" I closed my eyes and searched to see what my friends were doing at this very moment and the image of them shopping with a group of people popped into my mind. They were at the shopping center that wasn't too far from here and were headed to the mall. "Do you want to go shopping?" He nodded and teleported us to his range rover as the garage doors opened. "Oh, shit! I just assumed you wouldn't mind traveling the mortal way, we can teleport or travel as animals if you want?" "This is cool." I placed my hand on his and we had the most amazing conversation all the way to the parking garage. He wrapped his arm over my shoulder and I wrapped mine around his waist as we entered the mall. We received mixed looks as we made our way to a jewelry store and Zephyr spent one hundred thousand dollars on the both of us. The watchmaker was a good friend of his and a descendant of the goddess athena, who also hated her family as much as he did. The next store we went to was a clothing store where I sensed my friends. I allowed Zephyr to walk in first and out the corner of my eye I could see them turn in our way. At first no one said anything as they stared in our direction. Zephyr looked at the shirts and I pretended to be fascinated with the belts and then did a double take in their direction. "Kelvin? Troy?" I smiled and their eyes said everything as they walked over and hugged me. "Oh my goodness you look amazing." Troy said as he looked me up and down. "Yes, this body is giving sex siren!" Kelvin snapped his fingers and they waved their friends over and introduced them to us. "Everyone, this is Zephyr, my husband." I made a ring appear on my hand and showed it to them. "Bitch! Yes, it's giving daddy got coins, honey!" "He made that himself, I just paid for it." His smile was priceless as he looked to the ring and then back to me. "Since you are friends of Jay's I'll treat you all to a shopping spree." No one believed him at first but when he reached into his pocket and pulled out a couple of bank cards and a thick roll of cash. The others turned around and quickly began to pick up stuff they wanted but my friends looked at each other and then me before grabbing the very expensive clothing. When we were younger I used to walk past stores like this and wish we had the money to spend here. Over the next two hours we spent more of his money and Zephyr had his team take our stuff home along with the extra friends who didn't matter. We were now on a six person double date and in separate cars headed home because Zephyr invited everyone over for a late lunch. Once we pulled onto the street I could see that our normal sized homes were gone and replaced by a large mansion with an estate that encompassed the entire street. "With us being married our homes are also married. It sounds weird but smaller houses will pop up out of the ground in a couple of years." I laughed so hard I could feel the vibrations bounce around me. It was a good thing everyone went home to drop off their clothes and change. We waited until we were at the boundary of the gate to teleport onto the steps. The range rover still made its way to the garage as we entered the large doors that closed behind us. My mouth fell open as we stood in a large open space with a chandelier made of wood and crystals hanging above us. Zephyr turned in a circle and spread his wings. "Baby! You did this!" I could sense that the moment we stepped into the home. I loved having my own home but it was something that Boreas gave me and now this is something that I made for the both of us. "I'll be back." He flew into the air and I floated towards the kitchen and landed in front of the fridge. "To entertain the guests I've known since I was younger, I manifest a feast to satiate their hunger." Indigo energy swirled out of my mouth and into the fridge and then made a huge feast on the table across from me. I felt Zephyr's presence right before he appeared out of thin air. "Did I just sense a spell?" I nodded and he walked over to the table of food. "He picked up a shrimp skewer and ate it in one bite. "Mmm, Good work baby." I was going to reply but I sensed my friends approaching so I opened the gate with my mind. Zephyr popped over to my side with a shrimp skewer and handed it to me. I devoured it as he did and teleported from his side to the front doors that opened with my mind. "Girl! This house is everything!" Kelvin yelled. The four of them got out of the car and made their way up the steps as I walked down half way as Zephyr walked out of the doorway. "Thank you, I designed it myself." "Ooop, bitch, you tried it. Ain't no way you did all of this." "I was there and can vouch for the building of this house and its design at the hands of Mr Allen-Tree." Troy snorted and looked me in the eyes.

"Allen-Tree? Cute." He was always one for throwing shade that would have normally soured my mood but today nothing could bring me down. As I thought the words a cold chill crept over my body and Zephyr arced an eyebrow in my direction. *What was that?* I shrugged as we walked behind our guests. My husband and I spent the greater part of the afternoon eating, smoking and dancing. I forgot how good it felt to be around gay people that understood me. "Baby, I'm going to show them my nick-nack collection. We'll be back." He kissed me on the cheek and joined Keith and Max as they walked out of the room. "To be honest we thought you made him up." "Yeah, whenever you told us about him I had to fight the urge to roll my eyes out of disbelief." That didn't really sound like an apology and to be honest I didn't give a shit. For once in my life I have someone who actually wants me around and listens to me. "Yeah, I remember the day we became reacquainted like it happened hours ago." "Don't you mean like it happened yesterday?" I lit the blunt and told them the partial truth of how we met after I bought this land after a bad break-up. "Damn, what is his number and how big is he?" Kelvin smacked his teeth and cut a glare at Troy. "Bitch, you have a man. Let me meet the silver daddy first." "No miss mamas, we just started hanging out. I have an open eye on the stove for a long and thick pot." I pretended to laugh with them instead of making it a problem. Even if they managed to meet him they're not his type and also *not* me. "When is the wedding? "We haven't really decided a date but it might be at the end of spring." My ears popped and I could hear Zephyr tell Troy and Max that he didn't want to have a threesome. Max reached for his crotch but Zephyr bent his hand back and pushed him to the ground. I took a deep breath and exhaled to calm myself so that my eyes wouldn't glow or make a random object float into the air. Before I could speak Zephyr came around the corner with the two devious boyfriends and pushed them forward. "I think it's time for you all to go!" I stood at the same time as my friends and pretended to act surprised.

"Baby are you okay?"

"These two tried to offer me to have a threesome in exchange for money."

"What!" Kelvin and Troy yelled in unison. They took their boyfriends and left without saying a word and I pulled my god into a hug. "I'm sorry baby, I forgot that mortals with hyper sex drives are stimulated by my presence." "Because spring is known as the mating season.?" I asked. He nodded and I held him in my arms for a while until he calmed down. "Can we cuddle and I be the big spoon?" I answered by stripping us down to our underwear with a thought and teleporting us to our bed. "This is what I missed the most. No one ever wants to do stuff like this." We fell asleep almost instantly and I found myself floating in the darkness as a formless mass of indigo energy. Next to me was a tornado of leaves and berries that I recognized as my husband. We traveled for what felt like an eternity as stars came into view up ahead of us. "Where are we?" "I've never been in this part of the dream realm before. I also don't sense the presence of dream goddesses or gods anywhere." Zephyr moved forward and a small tornado of white and green light appeared in front of him.

Before I could move to join him a blue and yellow star caught my eye. I could sense that it belonged to my fake friends and as I moved closer it turned into a mirror that showed Kelvin and Troy in the car with their boyfriends. "He bent my arm backwards with ease and tossed Max to the ground like he was a child." "I got something for that ass though! My cousin Trent is meeting us at the house and I know he will have a plan to get his money." Keith smiled as he replied to a text message. "Good, because playing nice with that bitch was hard. Jay always thought that he was better than us with his Nice-guy mask but deep down he is just as fake as the rest of us. We deserve to live a life of luxury just as much as he does, shit possibly even more!" Kelvin and Troy high-fived and laughed as I floated backwards. The mirror returned to being a star and I floated towards Zephyr. "We have a problem! You go first-no you" We spoke in unison and after several attempts managed to stop saying the same thing. "I spoke with my estranged son through his dreams and Hera has told Iris about us. She is planning to have us destroyed and have Pothos take my throne." That was way worse than my mortal friends and their scheme to rob us. Before I could reply he vanished and I was left alone to float in this weird dream realm. "Okay, you got this! Focus Jay, Focus. Simply allow yourself to awaken." Time went on as I continued to force myself to awaken. "Jay!" I turned in all directions to pinpoint the sound of Zephyr's voice. "Zephyr, baby where are you?" My voice echoed out into the vastness of this realm as I continued to search for him. "I love you Jay." I awoke alone in our bed and I couldn't sense his presence anywhere nearby. "Thank Zephyr, you awake." I turned to see Vic with a crow on his shoulder and a catfish floating in a sphere of what smelled like river water. The sun was setting outside and I wondered how long I was I asleep for. "Where's Zeph?" Tears streamed down his face as he walked closer to sit on the bed. "He went to speak with Iris about saving Pothos." The catfish spoke telepathically. "I thought he was safe with his family?" Vic shook his head no and the crow let out a loud caw. "Hera and the other queens of the divine Realm, made it a supernatural law that goddesses have the say when it comes to their offspring and where they get to live. We haven't had a chance to formally introduce ourselves. I'm Murder, this is Stream. We are yours to command lord." A wolf and snake walked into the room and if we weren't in a crisis I would have made a joke. "Greetings lord, I am Seeker." The snake turned into a tall skinny man wearing basketball shorts and a tank top and no shoes. "I'm Fang but you can call me Fanny." The wolf spoke telepathically as she rested her mouth on the bed and exhaled. "Tongue and Wild have traveled to the spirit realm to ask Lady Hecate for help, we just have to wait for them to return." "Can someone tell me why his son needed to be saved?" They shared a silent understanding as they looked at each other before speaking. Seeker held his hand up to speak and I nodded. "The only way to become the god of the west wind is by eating his heart. Lord Zephyr is a titan and harder to destroy." "How do we contact his Mother?" They shared another silent look that didn't help my anxiety. "His Mother is currently in hibernation as the tree in the backyard and can only be awakened under a full moon." I gasped and dressed myself as I got up off of the bed. "Isn't there a full moon tomorrow night?" They nodded yes but I could sense that there was more. "There is a ritual that needs to be done or she could cause an earthquake." "What do we need?" "The blood of liars needs to be spilled at her feet and it has to be someone who you trusted with your life. She'll sense the treachery and reawaken." That kind of made sense and luckily I have four liars who deserve death. I laughed so hard that it bounced around me as I floated off of the ground and my happiness returned. I focused my intent on the television and brought the image off my friends and their boyfriends up. "I need the four of them brought here and their blood will aid us in our time of need." My aura flowed around me as Fang, Murder and Stream teleported away to do as I asked. Vic and Seeker stayed behind and we spent the rest of the day coming up with a plan of action. Since we had to wait for the moon to rise I went to visit my family just in case I would never see them again. As I spent the day with them, I cherished this moment and gave each of them ten million dollars after we enjoyed an early dinner where I told them about my engagement.

Seeing them helped me relax a little but bringing up my husband who was on a business trip made me miss him. I didn't like not being able to sense his presence near me or smell his masculine floral scent. "Sir, we have the individuals you requested. They think you invited them here to apologize and pay them to not press charges." Vic's telepathic message came at the right time, I was ready to go. *"Perfect, I'll be home shortly."* I looked at my watch and pretended to be surprised at the time.

"Shit! I forgot about the contractors that will arrive in a half hour."
"Okay baby, make sure you hit us up." Me and my brothers shared an
outburst of laughter from our mothers response. "What? I'm not
twerking am I?" "Mom, it's tweaking and no you said it right the first
time. It was funny that you said it correctly." I hugged each of them
and made my way home as quickly as I could. Hiding my divinity
would mean that I would have to drive away in a car and teleport or
travel in the form of an animal whenever I visited them. If I return
from a suicide mission to save my husband. I made myself a promise
that when he came back into my life that it would be forever. Once I
turned the corner I opened my third eye to sense if anyone's eyes were
watching me and waited for them to blink for me to teleport home. I
loved these abilities that I've mastered almost instantaneously. It felt
like I was picking up a video game where I left off. Well, with the
exception of my first two failures. My divine particles floated down
the hallway as a cosmic whirlwind and solidified as I approached the
doors to my entertainment room. Before entering I closed my eyes
and used my third eye to see the exact position of the moon. I had less
than half an hour until its light would shine down over the tree with
full illumination. *Perfect!* The doors opened as I stepped forward and
they all turned to look at me with looks of satisfaction on their faces.
Vic walked in behind me with a duffle bag and sat it on the table.
"Greetings Mortals." Kelvin smacked his teeth and rolled his eyes as
I took my seat across from them. "I'll allow you to leave with this
money and you can actually go live a good and peaceful life or you'll
become fertilizer for my garden." They looked at each other and then
laughed as they pulled out their guns and pointed them at me. "Where
is the rest of the money?" "In the next room, but it's behind a
bookshelf that requires thumbprint access." Vic answered. "Show
us." Keith walked over to Vic and put the gun up to his head and they
walked out of the room. "I'll go with you." Max jogged to catch up
and I was now alone with my soon-to-be dead best friends. "Take us
to where you keep your will and revise it to give us everything after

your unexpected death in a house fire." "No." "They snorted and looked from their guns back up to me. "Bitch, do you not see these?" "I see them but They don't work on me." Troy pointed it at my foot and pulled the trigger. It felt like a small pebble fell onto my foot as I laughed and moved at super speed to punch him in the chest. I twisted my body and kicked the gun out of Kelvin's hand and sent it flying across the room. "How-" A punch to the stomach ended his question as he hit the floor. Vic and Fang walked into the room in their large animal forms while chewing on what was left of Max and Keith. "Thank you lord, we don't get human meat that often." Fang licked her lips as I scratched behind her ears. Vic wrapped Troy in webs and then moved on to Kelvin. "I saved some of Keith for later." "You better eat him before the Lord returns. You know how he feels about hurting humans." Fang spoke, as she took human form and placed my sacrifices on Vic's back. I teleported us to the back yard and Vic placed them in front of the tree. "Lord, the clouds." With a thought I made them vanish and the moon's bright light shined down on us. Fang closed the distance and placed her small hands over their nose and mouths. Each of them came awake with scared and confused looks on their faces. "What do you have to say for yourselves?" Kelvin passed out as Vic stepped closer and moved his mandibles as venom dripped out of his mouth. "J-J-Jay, I'm sorry. We just needed money, W-We weren't actually going to kill y-you." Troy's words were directed to me but he didn't take his eyes off of Vic as he spoke. Next to him Kelvin came awake and gasped as he looked down at the large spider demigod. He laughed and rolled his eyes as he trembled with fear. "This is a dream-" I moved at super speed to grab him by the throat and squeeze until his head popped like a grape. With a glance I made Troy's blood pour out every orifice and drip down to pool at the base of the tree. The leaves began to glow as its roots sprouted from the ground and wrapped themselves around my sacrifices and pulled them into the dirt. Her branches began to sway as the wind picked up. ***"Where the fuck is my baby?"*** Her booming voice echoed around us as she changed from being a tree into a tall voluptuous dark skinned woman with leafy green hair and a long flowing brown dress. Squirrels poked their heads out of her hair and then disappeared after looking around. "Good evening Goddess, I'm-" "I know who you are honey. I've always known." She said, while pulling me into a hug. "I'm Terravalminetoszlewkirgar, but you can call me mom or Terra." I pulled out of her warm embrace and fell to the ground as a sharp pain stabbed me in the chest. Terra screamed as she clutched her stomach and fell to the ground next to me. It was the worst pain that I've ever felt and it took all my focus to stand and help my divine mother-in-law up off the ground. Her breathing was ragged as tears streamed down her face. I teleported us inside and helped her to take a seat on the couch and made a pitcher of water with fruit in it appear alongside glass cups. "Vic, I need you to rally our troops please." He nodded and vanished with Fang to do as I asked. "I'm sorry, Terra. This is my fault for coming into his life and incurring the wrath of his ex wife." "No, the fault is mine for trying to play nice with the children of Gaia. Once we created the earth I turned a blind eye to the suffering of its inhabitants because of the natural order we created. I told myself that so long as my forest child was alive and well, that all of those things were just a part of existence." My forehead prickled as a door appeared and opened to reveal a tall brown skinned woman with three eyes. "Hecate!" "Terra, you're awake." A frog and unicorn came out of the door as it shut and the rest of Zephyr's minor god team teleported into the room with several other divine beings from different walks of life. Until yesterday I thought the supernatural world was something made up by storytellers, but as I looked around the room at the gathered divine beings, it gave me a renewed sense of hope. I held my hands up and floated off the couch as they all turned to look at me. "Greetings, to all of you. I am Jay, husband to Zephyr. I want to first say thank you for helping us in our time of need." "The west wind has helped us in more ways than we can count." A tall woman answered with bat wings and goat horns.

Everyone in the room nodded or chatted amongst themselves in agreement to what she just said and it made me even more hopeful to get my husband back from his ex-in laws. The watchmaker held her arm up and her bracelet glowed with yellow light. "I can get us in but the mountain is full of Olympian sycophants who will stop at nothing to defend their rulers." I turned my attention to my mother in law and she nodded as we shared a silent understanding. "No one touch my mother, she is mine." The watchmaker said. Her words echoed around the room as everything became a blur and we were now standing in front of the largest Palace I've ever seen. It was carved out of the mountain and towered over all the other equally large homes that housed the divine beings that lived here. Terra's hair stretched out in all directions and glowed bright when it was pointed at the largest mansion. The both of us leaped into the sky and I flew like superman through the side of the palace with Terra beside me knocking down walls like a construction crew. We entered the throne room and the deities attempted to jump us but seven deities from my team teleported in behind me as I landed in front of a beautiful brown skinned woman who sat on a tree throne with a large bloody hole above her head. I stared her in the eyes as Terra let out a scream that made me flinch right before she engaged Iris in battle. I expected them to be dressed in regal attire or like they were wealthy but the bitch was wearing an ugly jean skirt with a rainbow tank top and no shoes. *Talk about a let down.* My heart throbbed and in my mind I could see her killing her son and then using his power to turn Zephyr into a tree and rip his heart out. I didn't know how I knew it, but the vision felt false as I let it fade. My body moved on its own and I took the seat that Ms. no-shoes gave up. "Yesterday I said I do and in twenty four hours you're a tree. This is definitely my life and luck." Tears streamed down my face as I laughed and closed my eyes. I opened them and was back in the weird dream realm but instead of stars all around me there was an island that floated in the darkness. My body floated forward and I solidified as I touched down on the soft grass.

Everything was absolutely beautiful but as I turned around a force knocked the breath out of my lungs and I opened my eyes to see Apollo floating over me with glowing eyes. "What have you done?" He yelled as I got up and raised myself to his height. "How dare you ask me that question. Look at what they did to Zephyr." He crossed his arms and looked away before smacking his teeth. "He killed you and then insulted my family. It was his fate." I clenched my jaw as my anger turned into rage. Apollo's words were the motivation that I needed to lash out with the true wrath of a God. My body pulsed with power as I moved with superspeed and grabbed him by the throat. Death would be a luxury so I turned his body into sand that fell at my feet. Out of the corner of my eye I could see a dark dark skinned woman with red hair pull back the string of her bow and knock an arrow of pure light. "Ohh, for me?" I reached out and grabbed the arrow as she sent more in my direction. "Artemis, stand down." I yelled. "Faggot bitch, No!" I lunged forward just as she did and fought her with the martial art skills of a shaolin master. The look on her face only added to my excitement as I met her blow for blow. We fought for what felt like an eternity and would have continued had I not commanded her to sleep with my mind. She fell to the ground and landed on the pile of Apollo-sand. "Nighty-Night goddess." I blew her a kiss as the sand turned into a glass box that trapped her and looked around the large empty throne room. The other deities took their fight outside and were giving the olympians everything they had. I could hear loud explosions and buildings crumbling to the ground in the distance along with cries of pain. None of that had anything to do with me so I teleported myself back onto Zephyr and closed my eyes. I opened them and was now back on the floating island that is my husband's astral body. "Baby, can you hear me?" After several minutes of waiting with no response I laid on my back in the grass and looked up into the darkness. The wind blew over me as my ears buzzed and the sound of a bird chirping disrupted the silence. The bird song grew louder as it appeared next to me and landed on my stomach.

"Hello cutie." It's head moved side to side as it hopped off of me and onto the ground. "Hey, wait." It spread its wings and looked back at me right before it took to the air. I flew after it and the bird took me into a forest that literally formed around us and stopped in front of a tall glowing tree with swaying branches. It landed on the ground in front of me and vanished. I could sense my husband's energy emanating from the tree as it stopped moving and let out a sigh of relief. "Zephyr!" My body moved on its own once more and I floated off the ground to hug the tree. "Baby! I'm here." I called out. Once again there was only silence as I continued to hug him as if our lives depended on it. "*Jay*!" My mother-in-law called out. "Terra, I found him." Tears streamed down my face as I responded to my mother in-law and kissed my husband's tree bark. "No, baby! You need to come out of there." She pleaded. "But he is here, I can feel it. Tell me how to heal him." She didn't answer and I grew anxious after a couple of minutes so I opened my eyes and looked around the destroyed throne room. Terra and the beastly gang as I call them stood in front of me with sad expressions on their faces. "I ripped this off of her neck before turning her into a flashlight." She held out a chunk of green amber and handed it to me. The moment it touched my palms it glowed bright and the smell of fresh fruit filled the room. I placed it in his chest and stood back as the hole closed and he changed from a tree into his godly form. Terra's hair wrapped around his body and pulled him into her scalp. My first instinct was to protest but she waved her arms over us and we teleported to our home on earth. "It will take some time but he will heal." "How long to be exact?" She shrugged her shoulders as we walked into our bedroom and her hair placed him on the bed. "Come with me." Her direct tone made me feel uneasy as she walked out of the room without looking at me. Terra took me into the basement and closed the door with her hair as I took a seat on the couch. "Is there something else?" She shook her head yes and sat across from me on the love seat as her body changed from elemental goddess to human. Terra reached into her hair and pulled out a pinwheel that she tossed to the ground. "Tell him what you know, traitor." The pinwheel glowed and turned into a brown skinned man with brown eyes and orange wings. He only wore blue jeans with no visible underwear as he looked me up and down. "Damn, scary step daddy looking good." He said, blowing me a kiss. "Your Pothos?" He nodded and sat in the lotus position on the ground. "What do you mean by scary?" Pothos snorted and laughed so hard that he floated off the floor. "Oh, shit! You don't know." "Spit it out stepson."I demanded. He was starting to piss me off and if it wasn't for the fact that he was my husband's only child, I would remove his head from his shoulders. "My mother made forced me to go along with her lies and destroyed my body, to lure my father to Olympus." That made sense, from the vision that I saw, but I could sense that there was more to all of this. "I take it that there is something that you know?" I asked, as my eyes glowed. "Jay Dion Allen, you are the reincarnation of Typhon, the king of the divine monsters that opposed my grandfather's rule. I know this because my grandparents had a run-in with your monster-goddess wife almost two decades ago and all of them seem have amnesia about the event." My body broke out in gooseflesh as he spoke and it intensified into an uncomfortable feeling. "Jay!" Terra called out with a mothers concern. "I feel strange." I replied as I got up from the couch. When I initially became divine I felt like there was something else that I needed to remember. And now that I had the name Typhon on repeat in my head and the more I felt an older essence of divine power flow into every part of my body. My arms grew longer and turned into serpents as large bat wings tore out of my back. Several long spaded tails grew from the base of my spine and slashed the air around me. "I remember everything." My feet changed from human to monster claws as my wings stirred the air and I instantly remembered who I was and what was done to me. I watched as the Olympians worked with deities of other pantheons to bury me under a mountain by using lightning bolts. Anger made me clench my jaw as my teeth elongated and I let out a monstrous roar. ***"Fire- water-air-earth, Awaken their divinity that lay dormant since birth."*** The ground trembled and thunder clashed in the sky as I used the planets to awaken the divinity of every Omniterran all over creation. Now I don't have to lie to my family and can have the wedding that I truly deserve. "Because you've aided me in this hour, I'll allow you to live." With a thought I turned Pothos into a firefly and he flew out of the room. "Thank you for not killing him." Terra said, with a smile. "His fate is up to the whirl-wind of passion that is my husband."

Omnipotent

Din-Din! The sound of the intercom coming on pulled me out of my thoughts of despair as I looked upwards. "Yes!" "Ma'am, the starburst thrusters are down, and we're no longer in hyperspace." I looked out the large window as we floated over a red planet with two moons. "Shargle-fink!" I wouldn't normally use foul language but we're far from home and in an unknown star system with nine celestial bodies. "Zen, how long will it take to repair?" "Inconclusive!" my android maintenance tech responded. "Do what you can!" "Right away, Captain Tirga." This was the last thing that I needed right now. "Zen! How long until the proximity scanners are back online?" "Eight hours and twenty-three minutes." "Thanks Zen!" "You're welcome, captain!" I passed the time by taking a particle shower and applying Cartack oil to my blue skin. Four hours went by, and I pulled out my image projector. "Play back!" It glowed and projected the image of my two wives and our five daughters. I missed them so much and haven't seen them in twenty years. Thankfully, my people have extremely long lives, and this will be a small sacrifice for what my Sovereigness has tasked me with. Din-Din! "Yes." "Captain, the thrusters will take longer to repair, but the proximity scanners will be back online in ten minutes." "How long?" "By my calculations, I'll be done in fourteen hours." "Copy." That helped me to relax a little. I hated not knowing where we were or if there was an enemy hiding somewhere. The image changed and it showed me with my family on the day that we first taught our girls how to use the unseen force to move things or fly. It was the best day of our lives, and we spent the entire day outside. Brrt-Brrt! "Vingar-Illo!" The image projector shut off, and I had to find another way to keep myself entertained. "Ma'am the scanners are back online and they've picked up a cargo vessel on the moon to our left with four unconscious lifeforms inside." "Copy! I'm going to check it out." "Copy!" "Ship, prepare a vacuum suit." Bonk-Brrrl! The wall across from me produced a crescent moon badge that I placed on my chest and it made a translucent barrier around my body. I made my way to the docking doors and waited for the doors behind me to close before pressing the button to open it. The silence of space always creeped me out and I hated being out here, but sometimes in life you have to do the things you dislike to do what you love. Ping! "Talk to me, Zen." "Captain the red planet is called Mars and the moon that you're headed to is called Deimos. The other is called Phobos." "Zen, We'll have to resume this conversation later. I'm about to land." Once I was close enough I used telekinesis to slow my descent and hovered over the surface. The energy of my aura pushed me forward at a steady speed until I came to the crashed cargo vessel. My personal scanners showed that the ship crashed here seven years ago. From where I stood I could see large slash marks over its metallic green exterior and a scorch mark near the partially torn off door. Whatever happened here made a chill run down my spine as I inspected the damage further. "Journal-Entry seven hundred and six! I'm stationed in the orbit of a red planet called Mars due to Hyperdrive thruster damage and proximity scanners that were inoperable. Once my scanning systems were back up and running we picked up a crashed cargo vessel on the moon named Deimos. Our scanners also picked up signs of life within but upon inspection of its exterior I've come across signs of an attack. End-Entry!" I used my mind to open the door and float inside with my arms raised and ready to defend myself. The driver's station was empty but showed signs of a struggle from the broken chair. My body froze as I faced the doors to the back of the ship. It was riddled with fist indentations that were smaller than mine. I pressed the button to open them, but they didn't budge, and after a few more tries, I held my hands out and expanded my energy field. I used my mind to push them inwards and the doors opened to reveal a room that was wider on the inside than out. I flew into the room that held an elder Vorgackian and their four miniature guards. This ship didn't belong to the beings who slept within so it had to belong to a bounty hunter who didn't survive the attack.

"Zen, do you copy?"

Din! "Go for zen!"

"Are the communicators in range to send a message?"

"Yes, but my indicators are picking up an odd frequency that interferes with the signal."

"Pegiz-moxo!"

"Captain, there is no need for such language. You must remain calm." I inhaled and exhaled to calm myself and closed my eyes. "Right! Thank you, Zen. Upon inspection I deduced the inhabitants to be vorgackian. Send a message to the G.E.G, and tell them that we've found Elder Myrgov." "Right away, ma'am." It took a lot of my energy to lift the five of them and myself out of the cargo vessel and off the moon to my star vessel. "You're going to get several medals of honor, ma'am." Zen patted me on the back with her robotic arm and formed her digital mouth into a smile. "Still weird, Zen." "Sorry, Ma'am." I took the five of them to the holding area, hooked them up to the telemetry readers and then made my way to the communications room. Bon-Bon-Bon-Bon! "Captain! Our scanners are picking up an unknown level eight energy source." "Display!" A holographic projection appeared in front of me and showed a large mass of multicolored energy that flew around in search of something. It turned to face the screen and vanished in the blink of an eye. The scanners showed that the energy was no longer outside. "Zen, do you see anything?" "No, Captain. My indicators aren't detecting anything." How is that shargle-finking possible? A mass of energy that big doesn't just vanish without a trace. "Keep your sensor open." "Yes, captain." My two stomachs rumbled, so I made my way to the cafeteria and pressed my palm against the sustenance sensor. Bing! It dispensed four green cubes on a tray that I took to the U-shaped table. The second moon Phobos was now visible through the large window and from this angle it sparkled like a crystal in the sunlight. I closed my eyes before eating and spoke several words of gratitude to the great mother, Aura, for giving me sustenance and allowing me to see another beautiful day or, in this case, a sparkly moon. Bon-Bon! "Yes!" "Captain, Elder Myrgov has awakened and is asking to see you." "Copy. I'll be there in a couple of minutes." The Vorgackians were particular about cleanliness, so I made my way to the lavatory and took another particle shower, and changed my clothes. I gave my goddess thanks as I left my sleeping quarters and headed towards the holding area. "Greetings, Elder Myrgov. It is an honor." I held my hands up to my forehead and bowed as I walked into the room. "The honor is all mine, Captain Tirga. Thank you for saving my life." "Can you tell me what happened?" They nodded and crossed their six arms over their torso. "My starship came out of hyperspace a couple of kilometers over there and was immediately bombarded with energy blasts. At first our shields took the brunt of the attacks but the-" They stopped speaking and looked over my shoulder to the empty space and nodded. I turned around and didn't see anything but kept my eyes on the spot where they were looking before turning my attention back to them. "As I was saying, we were attacked and my warrior-guard used a negative energy blast to make our attackers visible. It was a Gaxgarian bounty hunter's vessel that used teleportation technology to abduct me and my team. I awoke here, and that's all I remember." I only saw the smaller cargo vessel and knowing that something out there had the power to take down a larger starship made a chill run down my spine. I've seen those vessels in action and they have the capability to blow up a moon. "Do you know what happened to that space vessel?" They shook their heads no and took a deep breath before speaking. "I'm still a little tired. Might I suggest waiting for that guard to awaken? She held the enemy at bay for a while and might remember more of what happened." I bowed once more and looked over to Zen. "Has there been a response to our message?" "Negative Captain, But you'll be the first to know when they do." "How much longer will it take for the thrusters to be ready for hyperspace travel?" Zen looked to its wrist and then back to me. "Inconclusive." "What! How? Earlier you said that It would take fourteen hours to fix them, what happened?" "Captain, the ship has stopped repairing itself." I walked out of the holding area and down the corridor to the engine room. "How is that possible without you being notified?" "Inconclusive." I stopped and turned to look at my maintenance android who appeared to be just as confused as I am. "Do you need an update?" "My system is operating at max capacity, but there is something else that my scanners are picking up." Zen stopped hoovering and fell to the floor at my feet. I used my powers to lift my android companion off the floor and flipped her over to check her powercell. Vinegar-Illo! I need Zen to be operable to oversee the engine repair. Now I have to wait longer to leave this eerie part of space. I made my way in the opposite direction to Zen's charging station and placed them in it. Bop-Brrrr! The display showed three hours until Zen was fully charged. Great! More waiting. "Thanks Zen, Now I'm truly alone here." I left the charging station and made my way to the flight deck to meditate in my chair. "My Goddess is the bringer of day and night, My goddess breathes light into the darkness, the mother is the beginning and the end." I made the ascension hand gesture and repeated the mantra several times and found myself in my mindscape. "Bubbles!" Both of my wives floated over to me in their astral bodies and I pulled them into a hug. "How are the girls?" "They're visiting our mothers in miracle valley." "So you two are on vacation, huh?" The both of them laughed and time flew by as I caught them up on my space journey and the twenty six star systems that I've come across. "Well now that you've found the elder of Vorgack you can return home." "Yes, I am waiting for my maintenance android to finish charging so that it can finish repairing the hyperdrive thrusters." I left out the part about the attack on the cargo ship or the unknown mass of energy so that they wouldn't worry. Their projected forms began to flicker in and out of the astral realm and I instinctively reached out as they slowly faded away. "We love you T, and pray the goddess grants you safe passage home." "My love for you two and the girls shines brighter than a thousand suns. Tell my girls I miss them everyday." They vanished and I opened my eyes to the sterile interior of the spaceship. "Zen- Oh! Right, you're recharging." I truly hated being alone and it was one of the reasons I gravitated to a polyamorous relationship. Each of us came from single mother households with no sisters so we made sure to replicate as many children as our bodies would allow. Now it's come back to bite me on the side because I miss them so much. Vin-Vin! My wrist flashed with a notification from the holding area that displayed the brain activity of the warrior guards as being active. I pushed my body upwards and flew to the holding area where they stood around the sleeping Elder. Once I landed in the room they placed their hands to their stomachs and bowed. "I am M, This is I, P and O. We're the Mipo, sworn protectors of the house Gov. Thank you for rescuing us Captain." It has been a while since I've come into close proximity to a species who produce males and their little child-like forms betrayed the warrior gear they wore. "You're welcome, can I ask you some questions?" "Yes, I am the only member of my team that can speak Auran." That was expected, my people have traveled the cosmos since the beginning of time and have helped millions of life forms establish their societies or help them find a new planet to call home. "What attacked you?" He looked to his comrades and I could see them share a telepathic conversation as their eyes glowed white. "We didn't see what it was, we only sensed its massive psychic energy output." Pegiz-Moxo! I need to know what I'm up against so that I can formulate a proper plan of action. Bon-Bon-Bon! "Activate viewing projection." The crystal above my head projected the exterior of the ship from six angles and I couldn't see anything that would make them go off. "How strange, We don't sense anything." M, held hands with his companions and each of them faced the cardinal positions as their eyes continued to glow. It lasted for several minutes before the alarms went off. I looked over to elder Myrgov who was sound asleep and to be honest I was a little jealous of them. Din-Din! "Captain, I have downloaded my consciousness into the ship until my body is fully charged. I've also recommenced the repair of the hyperdrive thrusters. Estimated time until completion is three hours." "Thanks Zen, great job as always." I turned to my guests with a smile on my face from the good news. "Do you take in sustenance?" M nodded yes and used his mind to show me a bundle of fruit. "Come with me." I showed them to the cafeteria and they used the sensor to make fruit for them to eat as I looked out into the vastness of space. Beyond mars was a planet that was mostly water with one moon that shined down on the darker part of the globe. "May the moon guide your essence through the darkness of night." I couldn't imagine living on a planet with a single moon and sun. Their level of psychic power must be on the lower end of the spectrum. Just thinking about it gave me a shiver that caused me to rub my four hands over my bare arms. "Captain! I received a message for the G.E.G." "Copy, I'm on my way." I made the small trek to the command room and pressed the message to play it. Zink! "Greetings captain Tirga. We have received your message and are urging you to get out of that solar system as soon as possible. There is an unknown-" Vot-Vot! The message stopped and was deleted before I could press the screen to replay it. "Zen! What happened to the message?" "I don't know ma'am. It's been deleted from my system." "What in the name of Aura is going on?" "My scanners aren't picking up anything. Would you like for me to move the ship out of Mars orbit?" "Will that affect thruster repair?" "No, captain." "Then go ahead." "Copy!" Our ship slowly moved away from Mars and its moons. Behind me the doors opened and Elder Myrgov slithered in with her guards following behind. "We sense something approaching the ship." "Zen are your scanners picking up anything?" "Negative captain." Before I could respond, a bright light formed in the room across from us and took the form of a creature I've never seen before as it fell to the floor. It had dark brown skin with a curly poof of hair on its head and a large eye in the center of its forehead that remained open. It had similar features like mine with its five fingers and toes. I ran over to it with my fist pointed at it just in case it was pretending to be unconscious. Elder Myrgov held their hands to their head and breathed in and out several times before speaking. "I've never sensed anything like this before. His mind is impenetrable, but I can sense that he is unconscious." I lowered my arms and exhaled a sigh of relief as I walked a circle around the creature. He had three eyes instead of four and was dressed in black trousers with a matching sleeveless shirt. "Zen, do a matter scan." "Right away, captain!" Virl-vrall! Purple beams of light moved over his body several times, and then the light itself was absorbed into the creature's third eye. "My scanners are no longer responding." Shargle-Fink! The creature took in a deep breath and opened his eyes as he floated upwards off the floor. His large forehead-eye closed as he opened his two lower eyes and looked at us in confusion. "Hello." He flashed us his pearly whites and I noticed that his tongue was pink. In all my years of living, I've never seen a being like him. He was hideous in so many ways. No breasts, no vagina, and two eyes. Eww! He also had a bulge hanging from his pelvis. "You're hilarious. Look here, Captain Five breast, ain't nobody checkin' for you, honey! Girl I ride the D, not dive the sea!!" He moved his hands and neck as he spoke, and I couldn't help but laugh because it reminded me of the Androyous, who identified as both male and female. They shared our ability to self-impregnate.

"Sis, you're giving 'main character' energy with all of this thinking."

"Do not read my thoughts."

"That's like asking you not to have that beautiful skin tone. But okay." He snapped his fingers, and my ears popped. "So long as none of you try to harm me, you're good. I won't have to do any of you like I did those traffickers." My eyes grew wide at the mention of the attack on the cargo ship. "You did that?" "Ha! Sis, I did all of this. Elder Myrgov, The bounty hunters and You!" "How? I arced an eyebrow in his direction and accidentally made the chairs swivel.

"Oop! Captain Carrie, control your emotions. I have a good reason for what I did. My people need you, well, your ship." He was starting to piss me off. I'm missing my girls for this? I looked over to Elder Myrgov, who was just as angry as I was, except their guards were slowly walking towards our uninvited guest with their weapons raised. "See ya!" With a wave of his hand, he made the five of them vanish and then turned to me with a smile on his face. "Now, I need your ship to act as a satellite so that I can help deactivate the astrological house curse those divine snobs placed on my people." "I'm not following." "Give it time." He took a seat in the chair and made a plate of funny-smelling food appear. "Back to what I was saying, Earth is currently in the season of spring and I have to wait twenty minutes until the celestial bodies arrange themselves in the position that I need to cast my energy." He leaned over the plate, and his forehead eye turned into a mouth and devoured the entire plate and all in one bite. "I think you forgot something." The sight of that made me want to vomit as it chewed, and I could hear the metal being torn to pieces in his head. "Oh, I'm a "human" who was awakened by ancient goddesses to a higher calling." "I don't think that's it either, wait! What?" "I believe you call her Aura, the mother goddess. But to be honest, I communed with her council mates Oshun, Yemoja, Olokun, Odin, Hecate, Gaia, Kali, and Vishnu. Imagine me being a little gay boy and having imaginary friends who were dressed the gods and goddesses, and no one but me could see them. My parents kicked me out when I was fifteen after they caught me in drag." "What's drag?" "Oh right, you're an alien from a female-only planet. Um, drag is when someone who presents as one sex impersonates another." He snapped his fingers, and his clothes changed into a skin-tight dress as its thick hair that was similar to mine, grew longer out of its head. He was now a she who was absolutely gorgeous, and I had to turn away, or else I would disrespect my wives. "My name is Keran but when I'm like this, I'm Kadabra." She looked over to the window and started to dance. "It's time, ohhh, I'm so excited." Kadabra stopped dancing and clapped her hands six times and the ship moved close to the large blue planet. "Here goes." Her hands glowed as she inhaled and exhaled. "I cast my intentions as the celestial bodies align and help the monster lord Typhon awaken the sleeping divine." I suddenly began to feel extremely sleepy and had to take a seat. "Oops, did I forget to mention that your species is also included?" "Wha-?" I slumped over as the feeling intensified. "Thank you, Tirga. I'm sorry that I had to use you and take time away from your family." That was the last thing I heard as the astral realm invited me in, and I floated in darkness for what felt like an eternity. "Kirna! Varva! I called out to my wives and was met with only silence that absorbed my voice. My entire body was snatched backwards, and I awoke, gasping for air. I got up off the bed and immediately regretted it as the room started to spin. "Mama-Tirga is awake." A soft, familiar voice yelled, and I had to put my hands over my ears as her little feet ran across the floor. "Kalya?" My eyes opened wide as I took in the sight of my youngest daughter. "Yes, Mama-T. I'm a big girl now!" She held her hands up and floated off the ground. Despite the level four headache I was experiencing, I got up and hugged my child as the rest of my family flew into the room.

"Mom!"

"Tirga!"

My daughters and wives landed on our huge bed with bright smiles on their faces that quickly faded. "What's wrong?" My first wife, Kirna, who was closest to me, reached up and moved my hair out of my face. "The empress was killed two days ago." "What?" I could feel my mouth hang open, but my mind was unable to respond.

The empress was my first cousin, who was more like a sister to me, and even though we hadn't spoken in five years, it felt like a blow to the chest. "How?" I asked while pushing my emotions to the back of my mind. "They came after you appeared in the front yard." My second wife, Varva, waved her hand over her wrist, and the wall screen displayed the news of three days ago. A large fathership appeared in the sky and released hundreds of smaller vessels that spread out in all directions. "They're called the Vixalians and were created by the mother goddess's brother. Vixal, the god of war and wrath. The fathership has placed a spherical field around our planet and it prevents us from asking for outside help." I could feel my powers flow around my body as I sat up all the way and looked at them in confusion. "We are the Auran, Daughters of the goddess and one of the strongest races of females to exist. How have we not freed ourselves?" "They possess the power of tangibility. We can't fight an enemy that can't be touched or moved with the mother's gift." Knowing what I do about the mother and her rocky her-story with her family, I know why the Vixalians would attack us. Vixal was the eldest of the second-born deities of their family, and he hated Aura out of allegiance to the Supreme Mother. "Mama-T does this make you the new Empress?" Varta asked. "No baby, she probably has a successor." I answered. Vingar-Illo! I guess this is where our saying of half-hearted wishful thinking has undesirable consequences. A shooting pain formed in my torso and caused me to cry out in pain as my stomach expanded. I mentally kicked kicked myself for forgetting about how our reproductive process can be triggered by the ions in our atmosphere. "Ohh! Honey." Kirna and Varva yelled in unison. "G-get the particle stone basin and the food. Girls form the birthing circle." They quickly moved to do what I asked as my belly button dilated a couple of centimeters. "Whooo-Whooo." The girls joined me as I made the sound, and our collective vibrations helped the baby crown. My wives flew into the room with the items that I asked for and telekinetically positioned the basin to scoop up the baby as she floated out of my gaping belly button. "Aww!" Kirna said as she placed the basin at my side. "She is so cute. Look at her black and brown hair. You know what this means, T, good luck." Varva grabbed my two left hands and pulled my knuckles to her lips and placed a gentle kiss on them. "Hi, baby sister." Seeing all of their smiling faces made this a bittersweet moment with our current invasion of an idiot male species. "Oh look, she has a birthmark on her shoulder." My eyes grew big at the sight of a brown K on her shoulders. "Kadabra!" Their shared looks of confusion made me giggle despite our circumstances. "The mother has granted us the help we need to defeat the invaders." I took a deep breath and filled them in on what happened right before I came home. "Oh my Goddess, What kind of mother does that to her child?" Kirna and Varva took turns holding Kadabra, and at that moment, everything made sense. Aura created the lower realms with the help of several divine beings that also assisted in the creation of its planetary life forms. We are one of the first female species to exist and now that I fully understand everything, Kadabra's people fall into the same category. "Whelp, she's our daughter now!" Kirna picked her up and handed her to me, and we spent the greater part of the morning cleaning up and finishing the birthing rituals. "Is it normal that she hasn't awakened yet?" "I honestly don't know." Varva was our family anatomy specialist and if she didn't know then no one would. Her intellect was unmatched and one of the several reasons that our polarities match. "Kadabra's mark is glowing." She opened her eyes as her four eyes glowed yellow. "Greetings, new family!" I recognized that voice as my previously uninvited brown skin guests.

"Keran?" I asked, with a smile.

"I'm sorry, captain. I lied to you once again and used your body to give me a new life." Tears streamed down my face as I heard the palpable sorrow in his voice. "You helped my people more than you realize, and in return, I want to help yours." "How? Our enemy has power we do not. We can't touch or move them." "Don't worry, Mom, I got ya back!" The light seeped out of her eyes and flowed into all of us from our heads and then down to our feet. I could feel my body become lighter and then heavier as I floated upwards along with my family. "Also! The Vixalians have six testicles that are sensitive to kinetic energy." The energy left us and then spread out in all directions. "Let's Fink these Bologers up!"

Fog of Confusion

"I think we should have a kid." I rolled my eyes as my best friend/roommate walked into the kitchen as I prepared dinner. "Neither of us are in a relationship and we don't have room. Where would we even get a child, and for what?" "So that we can claim them on our taxes. I'll go first and then you'll claim it, on the next year." "You mean I'll claim it the following year." She smacked her teeth and crossed her arms as I finished peeling the potatoes. "Do you even like children?" I asked. "You know I don't, they ask too many questions." "Exactly!" "Why are you getting mad, I'm just trying to make us some money so we can get out of here." "She stormed out of the room with her high heels making her footfalls even louder as she went into her room and slammed the door. I hated living with an irrational person who thinks they're the main character. Koni will probably give me the cold shoulder for a couple of days and to be honest I don't care. She's acted this way since we were kids and I've tolerated it long enough. Once dinner was done I placed it in plasticware and walked the short distance to her room. "Hey Dinner is done, help yourself." I walked into my room and closed the door behind me and placed my food on my dinner tray. My homemade meatloaf and mashed potatoes called to me as I took a seat in my chair. The sound of my roommates clunky heels hitting the floor grew loud as she stomped out of her room and into the kitchen. She opened the fridge and in minutes had the house smelling just as good as I did when I cooked. The sad part is I made a separate plate for her and set it to the side but her ego always pushes her to act irrationally. *Two can play that game, friend.* I finished my food and paired my glass of wine with a blunt and waited for her to finish cleaning. It was moments like this that made me wish I lived alone. Unfortunately I still have credit card debt to pay off and I can't afford her half of the rent right now on my warehouse lead salary. After smoking half of a blunt, I fell asleep and woke three hours later to a silent house. I grabbed my robe as I walked out of my room and made my way to the kitchen to wash off my plate. "You've got to be kidding me?" I looked down on the counter where her plate sat untouched next to the leftovers in plastic. Why wouldn't she put the food away? I threw her food away and cleaned up before going back to my room and going back to sleep. Every Time I had a disagreement the negative energy gave me weird dreams. In one dream I was hanging upside down and white droplets of water fell from my head. When I woke up to use the bathroom I saw that she had company so I went back to my room instead of being a good friend and checking on her emotional state. Koni obviously has better things to do than treat her friends like we're humans and not things. I went back to sleep and had another weird dream, this time I was looking at a giant white glowing eye. Everywhere I turned it followed and when I closed my eyes it was all that I could see staring back from the darkness. *Your thoughts!!* A deep disembodied voice said. I woke up in a cold sweat with the birds chirping in the early hours of the morning. The time was four fifty in the morning and I fought the urge to masterbate and decided to meditate instead. "Good morning, Koni." "Hey, Good morning, how are you?" She said, in her call center voice. I didn't know whether to laugh or snap on this crazy ass bitch. Her moods were confusing. "Oh shit!" Behind me my friend stumbled to the ground and laughed as she took off her stiletto with its broken heel. "Are you okay?" "Yes, I stepped wrong. Thank you." I made my way back to my room and left for work an hour later. "Hey Donovan, did you have a good evening?" "I did, how about you Gina?" "I went to a baby shower and the parents were both non binary, it was confusing." My ears began to ring as she laughed and slapped my shoulder. "Donovan, Gina we're having a meeting in the break room." "Okay Betty!" We spoke at the same time and I turned and made my way to the cafeteria to fill up my water bottle. I made my way through the locker room and stooped as my skin broke out in gooseflesh and a chill went down my spine. This has been happening a lot lately and I've grown used to it but the feeling

573

always left me with an uneasy feeling. It also made me feel as if I was waiting for something to happen. I shrugged off the feeling and made my way to the boring thirty minute long meeting and then to my desk. My computer was already on and I stopped to look around before taking a seat. "Viv, did you use my computer?" "No, I thought you did, it's been on since I got here an hour ago." I moved the mouse and noticed that it was on the login screen and relaxed. "Maybe I forgot to turn it off yesterday." "After you reboot it, can you do a headcount?" "Yep!" Time flew by as I took attendance and made sure that everyone knew their productivity ranking for the week. Seven and a half hours later I was now at my locker with the same eerie feeling crawling over my skin as I grabbed my bag and left. "Have a good weekend Viv." "You too." Thankfully it was an hour before rush hour so I can make it home in twenty minutes instead of the ninety minutes of traffic that I usually have to go through. "Phone, call roommate!" *Calling, Roommate!* After seven rings I reached up to press the button but she picked up. "Yeah!" "Hey I'm headed home and I was about to stop and get something to eat. Do you want something?" "Bae stop!" "Did you hear me?" "No, what did you say?" "I'm about to get something to eat-" The call ended and I pulled into Breezy burger to get something to eat for me since she had company. Once I stepped into my building I could smell cooked food and loud music coming from my apartment. The smell and music intensified as I stepped in and walked to the kitchen. She cooked sweet potatoes, fried chicken, baked mac and cheese and corn bread. This was a heart attack waiting to happen and I loved to give her a taste of her own medicine so I went to my room and shut the door. To me there was nothing better than going home and being by myself. I ate my food and then rolled a blunt before I hopped in the shower. "Hey cupcake, I made dinner if you're hungry." "I already ate, but thanks though." "You say that I don't cook enough, but when I do, you never eat it." "Excuse me? I could have sworn I called you earlier to see if you were hungry but you were busy and the call ended." "I'm sorry for having sexual preferences. I didn't know that you were my mother, teacher, or supervisor." She stomped off into her room and slammed the door like she was the one who was disrespected. I went into the bathroom and spent the next thirty minutes replaying the events of our disagreement on repeat in my mind. This bitch was confusing and irrational as fuck! I need to get my finances in order so that I can separate myself from her permanently. The sound of a body hitting the floor filled my ears and I had to stop myself from going to see if she was okay. Koni and I have been best friends since middle school and now that I think back to it, she has always behaved like this. I was placed in the average learning class and she was placed in the slow learning disability classes. All the other students made fun of the way she said her words like wench instead of wrench or oraench instead of orange. I never thought anything of it because most people have words that they can't say, mine was amulance instead of ambulance. I'd always forget the b so it was normal to me. That was until the other kids in her class told me that they had one teacher all day and didn't have to take the standardized test that was required to go to high school. I exited the bathroom and spent the rest of the night working on my novel Morality cycle. "Okay! Three hours is long enough." I closed my laptop and got in bed as sleep called my name. "Bae! Bae! Come show me how to work the shower!" A stranger called out as I looked at the clock that showed that I'd been asleep for almost an hour. "Bae! Bae!" I got up and opened the door as I peeked around the corner. "Koni! Your date needs help!" I shut my door and went back to sleep even though I shouldn't have been awakened in the first place. The next morning I awoke to horrible singing coming from the bathroom and I decided to turn my television on and finish my blunt from last night. ***Knock-Knock***! Hey, are you busy?" My annoying roommate asked. I rolled my eyes and grabbed my shorts from the chair. "Wassup!" I said, opening the door once they were on. "I wanted you to meet my boyfriend." I took another hit from my blunt and opened the door as a thin man in underwear stepped out of her room. "Hey, I'm Vick." "You're also the man that was yelling loud as hell from the bathroom last night." He lowered the hand that he had extended and nodded at me and crossed his arms. "Sorry about that, Molly makes me act erratically." "Molly?" I cut my gaze over to my "best friend" and she made a face that let me know that she wasn't going to tell me that. "I'm Donovan, Nice to meet you, Vick. I'm going to roll a blunt, do you want to smoke?" They nodded yes and I closed the door so that I could get dressed and then rolled two blunts. After choosing the correct outfit for spring I went into the front room and waited for them to come out. Thirty minutes had passed and I didn't hear any movement from her room so I decided to knock on the door. "Hello!" *Nothing.* I knocked once more and then went to the window to see if her car was out there. "You've got to be kidding me?" Her car was gone and a part of me wanted to call her and say exactly how I felt but I know that it would be like talking to a wall. People like her feel as if they never do anything wrong. "Oh well! More weed for me." I took a couple of hits from my blunt and ate some fruit for breakfast as the door handle jiggled and my roomy walked in with her boyfriend.

"What happened?"

"Oh, Kali called me and we went out to her house for breakfast." *Weird,* I've been friends with her as long as she has. Why didn't they invite me? "I don't have to run everything by you master." Her boyfriend laughed as they walked into her room and I decided to get out of the house and away from her energy. An hour later I found myself in a park sitting on a bench as the other people in the park enjoyed the spring weather. "Is it okay if I sit with you?" I turned to see a tall muscular dark skinned man with locs sit next to me.

"Hi, I'm Darkon." He said in a deep voice.

"Donovan, nice to meet you."

"Can I ask you for advice?" I looked into his beautiful blue eyes and a cold chill made me shiver as he looked away with a smile. "Oh, I see what's happening. It's almost time for a big change." "I'm not following." He laughed and got up from the bench. "I can sense that you're like me. You treat people with the love and respect that you feel they deserve but no one ever reciprocates the gesture." Behind me two squirrels fighting pulled my attention away from him and I looked back to Darkon who was nowhere to be seen. There was no way that I imagined a man as fine as that. His sky blue eyes were as beautiful as they were eerie. The smell of his crisp cologne remained in my nose as the wind blew away what remained. Above me the sky rumbled as dark clouds rolled in and I made my way home to finish my blunt and pick up where I left off with my novel. "Hey, Are you busy?" I was beginning to hate it when she asked me that. "No, come in." She walked in dressed like she was about to go on a date and stopped to look at herself in the mirror. "I have a date tonight with Vick, do you want to come?" "I appreciate the offer but I have some work to do on my novel." She smacked her teeth as she rubbed her greasy hands together and walked out of my room. "Don't say I didn't offer." That's it! I got up and chose combativeness over peace and followed her to her room. "Let me explain something, friend. I was pissed because your boyfriend was yelling in the hallways like he pays bills here. That sneaky friend of "ours" ignores my calls for a month but has time to invite you to breakfast. I invited you to smoke and you left. What the fuck?" "I can't talk to you when you're like this." Her dismissive tone and words struck me in the chest like a dodgeball and I was too stunned to say anything else so I went back to my room and shut the door behind me. I can't take any more of this. She's a sasquatch who is unaware of self. My heart and mind still raced as an hour went by and I decided that I wasn't in the best place mentally to work on my novel. I Can't talk to my family about it because they wouldn't understand having friends or the gay dynamic of our friendship. To them all gay people are the same and I'm sure that they thought we were together all of these years. "Why can't I just win the lottery and live in a mansion on a hill in Los Angeles with a weed farm in the basement? I'd never have to worry about money or fake ass friends again." As I finished the thought my phone began to ring and I looked down and realized it was my Friend/roommate Koni. "Hello!" "I need to vent to someone" I wanted so badly to say how I truly felt but she's a monster with hooves and it will only make her climb further up on the mountain she lived on. "Go ahead." "We are at the grocery store and I see Cindy and Marcus and they were supposed to come over for dinner but flaked on us at the last minute. Now they're acting like we never made plans and then dismissed the whole thing." It took all of my will power not to explode so I answered with what I thought was the best answer. "That's fucked up, You're a good person and don't deserve that." She smacked her teeth and breathed into the phone. "I'm not mad about me, I'm mad that they did that to my man." This has got to be a joke or something. I literally just said something similar to her about me and she acted as if I called her by her boy name. "Hello, can you hear me? Hello-" I ended the call to save my own peace and decided to use all of my experiences as fuel to finally finish my novel. It took me a couple of hours to finish and when I was done, I took a couple of hits from my blunt. Every time I finished a short story it gave me a sense of accomplishment and now that my first novel is done I'm one step closer to being number one on the bestsellers list. "This deserves a glass of wine." As I turned on my heel a wave of exhaustion washed over me and I had to brace myself on the wall while trying to get to my bed. I realized now that skipping lunch was stupid and smoking multiple blunts is now catching up to me. "I don't think so, storyteller." My roommate walked in and I had to do a double take as she walked over to the bed. Her skin was a mix of gold and lime green and instead of normal human eyes she had six slug-like eyes protruding from her head. She also had six arms and wings that were a cross between wasp and butterfly that dangled from her back as she moved. "Why are you dressed like you're going to an alien convention?" "Because I am. You are too!" That was the last thing I heard as my body fell backwards and my eyelids closed. "Wake-up Human!" I opened my eyes to a bright golden light that made them sting as they adjusted to the room that I was in. Once it faded and my eyes took in the sight of more alien bug-people like Koni who looked up to me with a sinister smile on her face. My body was hanging upside down by an invisible force that prevented the blood from rushing to my head as my eyes darted around the room and landed on my friend. "Koni?" Four of the larger aliens stepped forward with spears pointed in my direction. "Do not address Lady Koniyetsu as an equal, filth!" Their spear tips glowed as they approached me but their lady held her hand up. "Leave us!" They did as she commanded and left us alone as I looked down at her. "Long story short, I came to earth in search of a thinker. You! Your mind is unlike anyone else's in the way that you over analyze and understand things. My people feed off psychic energy produced when creatures are confused or in deep thought." she licked her lips as she looked at the top of my head. "Almost time." Her words reminded me of what Darkon said about a big change. "Yeah, who was that creepy man?" I wasn't sure if all of this was a dream brought on by her or all the weed and alcohol that I've had in the past three days. "Wrong! All of this is real. I've traveled the galaxy for a hundred years in search of a mind such as yours. My scanners picked up your resonance when you were six and I waited six more years until I could approach you. It was so hard talking to you about those stupid television shows that you like, but I knew that the pay off was going to be worth it so I stuck around." Her eyes moved in opposite directions as she stretched her wings and floated up to meet me at eye level. "I've waited for this day for so long that I almost forgot about it. I had to go through a chrysalis to change into a human-like form. Do you know what it's like to suffer phantom wing syndrome for thirty earth years?" Small particles of glitter fell to the floor as she spun around in the air. It made the room smell like musty underarms that were covered up with white onions. "How dare you? My musk is royal and of the high breed of Walvosians. Oh, right!" She held her twelve hands up in different directions and smiled. "Welcome to Walvos." She turned and flew out of the room and I was left alone to hang upside down in the middle of the room. The doors opened and she flew back in with her funk cloud following after her. "Almost forgot!" Her cloud moved over to me and made my eyelids heavy. "There isn't a mortal creature alive that can resist my noxious cloud." She was right and fortunately for me I instantly fell asleep. My mind dreamt of so many things that I didn't understand. In one dream I watched as black superheroines fought a team of super villain females, in another dream I saw Darkon take a round of bullets to his chest and then get up with red glowing eyes. It was both creepy and sexy at the same time. My dream changed and I saw two gorgeous women with animal appendages, presenting a large pig to other beings like them. The last dream that I had was of myself sitting on a throne made of solid gold with fireflies flying around my head. "Wake up!" I opened my eyes and waited for them to adjust as I looked around the room. I was now right side up but still floating in the same place with a large clear crystal floating over my head. "We're going to use that to siphon your psychic energy and channel it throughout the city. In less than two hours you'll supply my people with enough sustenance to last us for a million years. Thank you best friend, You're going to help me become an even greater queen." Her servants walked over and handed her a purple glowing ring that she then placed on my head. "Your people call it Amethyst. It's good for relaxing your mind. We need you to be in a calm state before we can extract the psychic energy." She was right, it did help to relax my mind and I found myself thinking about my family. They'll probably think I've been abducted into a sex trafficking ring or worse that I'm dead.

"They think you and I went to mykonos for a spring vacation."

"Why me?" I asked as my annoyance peaked. Koni descended to the ground with her funk cloud trailing behind her. "I'm going to let you in on a cosmic secret." I twisted my body as some of her servants came in with a platter of fruit. "Eat while I talk." The fruit smelled like strawberries and tangerines but it looked like ice cream and pudding. "This is valley-berry fruit and sun sprouts, it's like a cousin to the fruits you were thinking about." "Stop reading my mind Koni!" The servant gasped and flew out of the room as Koni floated up to me. "Like I was saying, The secret of the "humans" is that you're more divine than you think yourselves to be. Earth is actually the center of the universe. Well, your solar system is the center of creation. That's why those disgusting men you call kings hid the knowledge. Their descendants use ancient knowledge to siphon your psychic powers like I'm about to do to you." She laughed and spun around the room trailing that smelly funk of hers. "I'll be the strongest Queen in all of existence and once I've mastered your powers, My powers will be unmatched." I couldn't tell if it was the funk or stress of the situation that made my mind unable to focus. "Yes, it is. I can't have you going all supernova on me." The designs on the side of the bowls glowed and turned into a double sided spoon. "I know I have you on kidnap mode, but try them together." It moved on its own as it scooped from each bowl and floated to my mouth. Koni imitated the sounds of an airplane as it neared my mouth. CRTTT!! "Request to land." I opened my mouth and allowed the alien food in and did a little dance as I savored the flavor. At first the clashing flavors tickled my tongue but as I moved it around in my mouth I realized that it's what was missing from my life. Separately each of them could be added to a number of things, but together. Mmmm,mmm.

"Can you finish what you were saying?"

"You are on my planet and in my presence, No your place!" Now everything made sense.

"What makes sense?"

"You, your highness! Now finish telling me about the rest of this little scheme of yours." I figured since I'm going to die anyway that I should at least have some fun. "It's almost time!" *Fuck!* I wanted to play this out as long as I could. "That's my problem with you, you have this mental superiority complex that's really your mind's coping mechanism for no one wanting you around. Tell me Mr. Smarty pants. What is this that you're in?" She asked, pointing at the containment field that held me in place. "It's an antigravity device that you're using to contain me here, duh!!" She laughed for several moments as more of her servants teleported in out of thin air and joined her in laughter. "Humans are hilarious, I can't." "Madam, may I?" A tall silver and dark green slug-moth person kneeled as she turned around and waved her hand. "Yes, Bafel. Learn this inferior being something new." I snorted and laughed as it floated over to my prison. "The amethyst halo keeps you from focusing and the "prison" that you're in has a temporal distortion barrier around it. In a couple of minutes the moon will align with the moon of earth and we'll use your own power to make us Omni-Walvosians." Her words made my ears ring as the servants flew to the ceiling and pulled levers that opened the domed roof. The moon on this planet was green but when I blinked my eyes it was purple and white. With my eyes closed I looked directly into the moon and the sound of a monster's voice entered my ears. At first it was like someone yelling from down the street but as I focused more on it I realized the voice was mine. Fire-Water-Air-Earth, Awaken your divinity that's laid dormant since birth!" The moon turned into the giant eye from the dream I had earlier except it was now right in front of me like a mirror. "We are us, I am me." I spoke the words as I heard them and the eye moved forward as I did until we became one. My eyes remained closed but I could feel an eye form on my forehead as I looked around the room. The bugs tried to scatter but with a thought I made all of them explode except for the Lady of the house. "Th-this wasn't supposed to h-happen. Your kind weren't going to fully awaken for another hundred years." "You never were good with

Arithmetic, My lady!" I turned the crown on my head into a war helm and manifested matching armor as I freed myself from the time-prison. "Do you remember when I told you that My father raised dogs and I hated the smell?" She just looked at me with terror on her face. My abilities allowed me to see my reflection through her eyes and I loved the eight foot tall thick muscular brown being of power that looked back. My helmet was a smooth dome with its front exposed for my face and a large vertical eye that swirled with purple, white and shadow energy on my forehead. It blinked and in a fraction of a second I understood who and what I truly am and what my best friend's people have done for a hundred million years. With the Mother goddesses not wanting to intervene they allowed all of this to happen just so the scales would tip in our favor. Images of my fellow earthlings transforming flashed in mind and I used the vision to search for my family. They also had vertical third eyes on their foreheads and multicolored aura emanating from their bodies. I pulled back from the streams of visions and concentrated on turning every Walvosain into the fireflies that I dreamed about. "Family, please come to me." I sensed several vibrations right before my loved ones appeared in a flash of colorful energy and wrapped their arms around me. "We were on our way here!" My mother's words echoed around the room as my father and brothers spoke similar sentiments. "I knew something wasn't right with her. Not the transgender part but the two-faced vibe she gave off." I remembered my father didn't want me to hang with her after she was flakey about bringing her parents over and when he killed the fly they became offended and left. "I see you're dressed for war." "At first I wanted to tear this world apart and collapse the star since the four other planets aren't housing life but then it occurred to me that this solar system will be my new home and each of you will take a planet of your own." My two younger brothers didn't waste any time on choosing a planet and changing it to their liking. "Your mother and I will take the tan and yellow planet." The last planet was purple and silver with several rings around it. Looking at it gave me an idea about how to properly go about getting my revenge on Lady Koni and her swarm of lesser beings. With a thought I froze time on Walvos and then teleported to the planet's atmosphere and caused a chain reaction to activate the ecosystem. My previous captors gave me the idea to allow time to pass below me and bring forth plants and animals of my personal creation. Time moved around me as I watched the elements cause natural disasters and beasts of all kinds evolved around me. I made a large island into my home with a large palace made of brown stones and amethyst crystals. With another thought I furnished it with everything that I ever wanted. Now that I'm all moved into my new home I turned my attention to Walvos and shrank it down to the size of a baseball. When I was a kid I loved simulation games and as a writer this will help to give me inspiration when I'm bored. I placed a quartz crystal barrier around it and teleported it to the palm of my hand. Within the small orb I made a sun spark to life and created two moons that slowly circled the planet. The remaining problem was what they were going to eat and with them being a hybrid between a slug and butterfly making a suitable food source would be tricky. My forehead throbbed and the image of a mushroom and flowers flashed in my mind. I snapped my fingers and made the flora and fauna increase in size and then changed my bugs back into sentient Walvosians. From their perspective they wouldn't be able to see me but the sounds of their yelling and screaming as they realized they failed made me laugh into the vastness of space. They'll go through withdrawal for a couple of days until their bodies crave the fauna and by then I plan to have a list of simulations to try.

Three months later

Ting-Ting-Ting! "Family and new friends. Can I have your attention, please?" My family and Tirga's turned their heads towards my seat at the head of the table. "Now that our food is in the process of digestion, I was thinking that we should have some fun before dessert." I clapped my hands and made my Walvos orb appear in the middle of the table. "This is my own personal entertainment sphere." "It's the planet Walvos." Tirga spoke the name as I did and stood up with a smile. "It's the planet I went to and almost didn't make it back from. I thank Aura for the power that granted me safety to my ship. We marked that world as unsafe." "I can see why they're insidious and born with all of the memories of their past life and become similar versions that are equally as evil." I waved my hands and made a crystal bowl appear and held it up as folded-up pieces of paper appeared inside. "Please take one, but don't open it yet." I pulled one out and allowed it to go around the room until everyone had one. "Okay, open it." I waited for them to do so and then opened my own paper. Fog, Perfect! "Tirga, what are you and little K's monster?" "Mine says Behemoth. What's that?" "It's a giant monster that destroys a city." "Cool, mine says that too. Her wives leaned over, and they kissed as their younger daughters held up their papers. "Ours says Zombies." "Undead creatures who feed off the living. They sometimes only eat brains." "We're werewolves." My parents said in unison. "I'm a vampire." "Me too." Tirga's in-laws said as they high-fived. I loved how the Auran royal family fit in with us. A week after my family and I established this solar system as our home, their newborn Kadabra flew around our sun, and I took her back to her home. Once I realized it was a planet of lesbian aliens who were a sister race to humans, I spent a week with them and formed a bond. I pushed the memory to the back of my mind and pointed at the sphere to make it grow in size. "There are dozens of large continents on this planet that's full of life." I flicked my fingers out and made numbers appear on the paper and then on the corresponding continents. "Let's say an hour or two of fun?" They nodded and teleported into the mini world. After clearing the table with a wave of my hand I teleported to the royal capital as a thick fog that enveloped the entire city. I watched as the civilians scrambled around, trying to get inside. Ever since I aligned Walvos to how it was supposed to exist, we've built a strong bond that leveled up when he told me his name a month ago. Glazbir is now a planet abundant in wildlife. He was basically a six-year-old who wanted a friend and hated the Walvosians, who migrated from another star system after depleting their planet of its natural resources. To him, I'm like an older brother who has given him his own room and pets to take care of. I allowed the fog to remain as I detached myself and floated around the city, opening doors and breaking windows. My next set of vengeance would be to abduct those adult-babies from the cribs and dash them against the walls. These creatures sat back while my people were enslaved, raped, beaten, and molested, and they had the nerve to add to the pain by stealing my peoples psychic pain. I won't be happy until the scales have been balanced. The wind behind me began to pick up as I increased my speed and it caused the houses to disintegrate. All I could hear was the symphony of destruction that was mixed with their cries of pain and it made me fly around even faster until I came up to the palace grounds. "Shhhh-Shhh, he's out there." My super hearing allowed me to hear the royal guards conversation through the walls and then pick up the sound of my royal pet cowering in her room as the destruction ceased behind me. I moved through the walls and traveled through the door into her room. Her large room was a mess, with its bed suspended from the ceiling and clothes everywhere. The large windows were covered in translucent fabric that prevented the fog from coming in by filtering it into breathable air. I floated over to the window that was behind her and peeled the edge up to let in my Fog of confusion. It took me a while to come up with the perfect revenge for my pets but after I binge watched the death of other planets at the hand of their species, it made me think of an amusement park of destruction where the civilians deserve everything that happens to them. Just thinking of her lies made me want to snatch her wings off, but I loved playing the long game, so I turned myself into my favorite alias. A Walvosians orphan named Muri, whom she adopted three months ago and loves like a daughter. I worked my will over her mind and made her think that my father was the bodyguard who saved her mother when she was a Larva. "Mother, I'm scared." She floated over to me and wrapped her arms around me like she always did and rubbed my back. "It's okay! Mommy's here." She picked me up and took me over to her bed as I continued to fake cry. "Shh-Shhh. He can hear you. We have to wait until the fog passes. Okay." I made the fog move against the walls and scratch against the thick window curtains. "How do we know he can't get inside?" "He can't move past the silk." It was hard not to laugh at one of the many lies I allowed to exist by spreading them myself. I pretended to be a farmer who was attacked by the beast in the fog and was able to fight it off with the silk that their species produced. Her fear flowed off of her in waves as she trembled and slowed her breathing until the movement outside stopped. "Queen Mother, can I ask you a question?" "Yes, baby, you can ask me anything." I moved out of her embrace and turned my back to her. "Will I always be your cupcake?" As I turned to face her, my third eye opened, and I shifted into my real form as she screamed and tried to fly away but I moved with super speed and snatched her wings off. *This is going to be fun.*

Journal of Darkness

10/28/1996

Hello Journal. This is my first entry, so here goes. Today I got into a fight with Terri Henderson. He said that I was a Fag and that's why my mother left so I slapped him like father slaps me for talking back. Mrs Richards said that I shouldn't handle my problems with violet's but I didn't see what flowers had to do with anything so I pretended to apologize to Terri just so that she wouldn't send me to in-school suspension or tell my father. After our fight I saw my blurry friend who I can only see and we put glass in Terri sandwich. The look on his face when he chewed on glass made the both of us smile so hard that they almost knew it was us. When I got home from school my father was gone. There was nothing to eat so I went next door to Anthony's house for dinner. His mom made us chicken nuggets and cheesy noodles. It was so good but I didn't get to finish my food because HE showed up and took me home. I hate living here with him. I hate him. I hate him. I hate him. Why did mommy leave me with him? Where did she go? Halloween is in three days and I wanted to be a grim reaper but HE slapped me and told me to get out of his face. Why doesn't he love me?

1/14/1997

I got into a fight with Terri's friends today because of the glass that I put in his sandwich. Christian and Micheal held me down while Martin stabbed me with a pencil but I pulled on their arms so hard that their arms came out of the socket wrenches. The both of them cried and ran to tell the teacher. Martin tried to hit me but he stopped and then ran away. He called me Satan and ran to tell on me like the others. The school nurse called the loud van and I was sent to the principal's office. Mrs. Wise suspended me for a day and I had to walk home because HE didn't answer the house phone. When I got home I took a nap and had the dream again, but this time I saw the man with the red eyes like my imaginary friend. He kept asking to hug me but I never let anyone touch me. EVER. He asked me over and over until I woke up to see HIM standing in the doorway. I knew what was about to happen so I went to my happy place where no one could follow until it was over.

5/23/1997

It's been three months since I went to my special place. My friend who doesn't want a name has been keeping me company while HE is away on business. The babysitter refuses to speak to me and if she messes up breakfast again I'll have to teach her a lesson. School has been going well now that my bullies have been abducted. My friend said that he took care of them and that it was an early birthday present. Happy eleventh birthday to me. No Father or school bullies for an entire summer. I can't wait. Anthony's parents said that they would watch me for the school break and that we would be going to a place called Los Angeles. At lunch I saw my favorite teacher's shadow wave at me before the janitor that I always saw her with was found dead in the closet. I could have sworn that I heard her tell my gym teacher that they were going to get married after he left his wife but my friend said that he mixed too many chemicals together and that's why he died. Oh and I decided ti call my friend, nameless. Nameless told me Mrs. Sanders did it after choking him but most of the time he says things that happen later but I forget about them because they make no sense. I'm trying to remember to write more in this journal that I found but every time I think about all of this it makes me remember the special training that my father puts me through and I get angry all over again.

6/4/1997

Today was another great day. I'm spending time with Anthony's family in a state called California. It was hot but his parents kept saying that I had a natural protection against the sun because of the color of my skin. His mother also kept asking about my mother and I told them the same thing that HE told me. She left when I was a baby and never came back to rescue me from the monster with the gray eyes that is my father. I went to see a superhero movie about a werewolf who hunts bad guys and loved every second of it. Anthony was scared but I could have watched it two more times with the same amount of excitement as the first time. His parents took us to get pizza but we had to leave before it came out because someone got robbed in the parking lot. On the way back to their house we stopped and got burgers and fries at a drive thru-only restaurant called Delightful delicacies. Anthony started to act weird after we got home so I played by myself in the yard. I don't know why he was mad at me. I didn't do anything wrong. His mother took him on a walk and he came back with a busted lip. I want to kill his mom because she hurt my number two best friend. Besides nameless, he is all that I have. Until next time.

7/23/1997

Hello journal, It has been almost two months since you appeared in my shadow. This time Anthony saw it and he told his parents about how you are able to move on your own. I did like you said and lied to him but now he is always watching me and doesn't want to play. Since the last time that you found me I have been to a bunch of places in California. Last month we went to a comic book store and then the toy store. I chose two swords and gave one to Anthony but he threw it out the window when we were on the freeway. His mother slapped him so hard that his head hit the door. I hated seeing my friend getting punished but what he did was bad. The car behind us had to slam on their breaks. I was scared that she was going to hit me so I put my hands over my head and she told me that I wasn't in trouble. His mom was always nice to me but there was something about her shadow that creeped me out. The next day we went to see one of the houses that was flipped and Anthony tried to push me into the unfinished basement with no steps. This time his father took him into another room and beat him for trying to hurt me. His black eye made me want to run away but I didn't know where I was. After we spent an hour at the house,p a personal driver showed up for me and his mom. The man was dark skinned like me but he had normal colored eyes like Anthony and his family. I hated my eyes and the way that people always looked at me with that weird look on their faces. He said that his name was Larry but I'll always remember him as the man with the crustiest lips that I've ever seen. It looked like he was always thirsty. Crusty lips drove us to the house that we stayed in and Anthony's mom ordered us a pizza while we waited for them to return. She let me keep the toy that Anthony asked for but I decided that I would give it back to him when they get back. His mother and I stayed at the house for a week and then his father came back without Anthony. When I asked them about where he was I was told that he was visiting family. I don't know why but that answer scared me more than seeing my fathers gray eyes when he's angry. I'm trying to write as much of this down as I can but it's becoming harder to focus without my best friend being here. I've wanted to be his friend from the moment that I saw him on the playground last year and when I found out that we have the same birthday it made me want to hang out all the time. Now I don't know where he is.

8/5/1997

Hey journal! I got a letter from Anthony and he said that he had to go visit his sick grandmother in New York and I wouldn't see him until school starts in three weeks. His parents Eric and Juanita, bought me more toys and clothes. I wished that I could live with them as my parents forever but the day came when HE called the house and I had to talk to him. Hearing his voice made my stomach ache and I was scared that he would think I told someone about his special training. I told him over and over again that I was a good boy but I don't think he believed me. Thankfully the call was interrupted by an earthquake that ripped the phone polls out of the ground. We had to move to another house but I was happy that all of my new toys got to come with us. Most of the city was messed up because of the earthquake so we had to make our own food. Monday we had a BBQ in the backyard for the three of us and then Tuesday we made tacos. Wednesday we made our own pizza from scratch. I put ham, cheese, olives and pepperoni on mine. Eric and Juanita made a boring cheese pizza that smelled good but the edges were burnt. Thursday we went to a chinese restaurant for take out and I tried crab rangoon for the first time with general Tsou chicken. The fried rice had onions and peas in it so I asked if it was okay if I didn't eat it. On the way home we stopped to get movies and I picked out one that Anthony would have wanted to watch with me. They also let me get some snacks and I got to eat red licorice for the first time. I loved them so much that I almost ate all of them before we got home. Eric said that I could watch my movie by myself in the front room while they went into their room and watched their movie with the door closed. Friday I got another letter from Anthony but this time he told me that he wanted to stay with his grandmother and go to school in New York. It made me sad to know that I wasn't going to see him again but to cheer me up his parents took us to an arcade. I won so many tickets and got to pick out a large monster unicorn that I named Darkon. He was all black with a blue horn. I also noticed that I haven't seen my friend without a name since I left Ohio two months ago or had the dream where the man with the red eyes asking for a hug. We went to a buffet and I got to choose whatever I wanted to eat. I ate two plates of fried chicken tenders with potato wedges and Eric copied off of me. Juanita had something called fried Calamari and green beans. YUCK!

8/14/1997

Today we packed up our bags and left California. I knew that if I cried they would tell my father and he would bust my lip like last time. Or do someyhing worse. The car ride was fun but my butt hurt from sitting for so long that we had to make three extra stops before we got to Columbus, Ohio. I wasn't looking forward to seeing HIM but if I tried to run away he'd just find me like he always does. My stomach started to hurt when we turned onto our street but once I saw that HE wasn't home It made me feel better. I played in Anthony's room while we waited for the gray-eyed monster to come home and I helped them box up his stuff so that they could mail it to where he lived. After we got done the phone rang and they told me that HE would be here to take me home in an hour. It was the shortest hour of my life and when my father finally pulled into the driveway I didn't want to leave. He was mad about something again and locked me in my room with all of my toys. Thankfully I ate before he took me home because he didn't feed me or let me out until the next morning. I spent most of the day by myself until he came into the room for my special training. After he hurt me my friend nameless came back and slammed into HIM hard enough to get him away from. He left me alone for a couple of days until nameless disappeared. That night I had the dream of the man with red eyes and he pulled me into a hug while apologizing over and over again. He kept telling me to be strong but I didn't know what he was talking about. Once I woke up I had to eat old cereal with water because HE didn't buy any food. The monster with the gray eyes stayed away from me for a couple more days until he hurt me again and I couldn't sit down. I asked him if I could go outside and play with my toys but he backhanded me and sent me to my room. I had to wait until he left to sneak out the house and go ask the neighbors for some food. Eric ordered me a Pizza and told me not to tell my father or he'd hurt me again so I promised him that I wouldn't say anything. HE didn't come back home until later but stayed in his room until the next morning when I was woken up by him slamming the door to leave. Nameless returned after he left and we played with my new toys until I heard Juanita taking out the trash. I told her that I hadn't eaten anything since yesterday and she invited me over for dinner. We had lasagna with garlic bread that was a little spicy for me but I ate it all because I didn't know when I would be able to eat again. She kept telling me to slow down but I knew that he'd be back soon so I handed some garlic bread to nameless so that he could hide it in my room. HE came home late at night and I knew that he would continue my training. I begged nameless to hurt him like he did before but he said that my father always knows how to make him go away before he can do anything.

9/4/1997

I hate it here. Why did my mother leave me with this monster? He never wants me around. None of our other family members come to visit and everytime I ask about them he hits me. He stayed at home all day and made hot dogs for us to eat but forgot to buy bread so we had to eat them with our hands. I hated it and tried to act like I was happy so that he wouldn't hurt me. The next morning he answered the door for a tall white woman and the police officer that was behind her. I couldn't hear everything that they were talking about but I did hear my name and the white lady asked why I didn't show up for the first week of school. He made up some lie about it slipping his mind and then promised that I would be there in the morning. Once they left he smacked me in the mouth for bringing trouble to the front door. I went to bed hungry until Eric knocked on my window and handed me three slices of pizza. When I asked him how Anthony was he changed the subject to the latest video game and then climbed back over his fence to go home. HE woke me up the next morning to get ready for school and I was happy to get away from him.

9/5/1997

I had a great first day of school since Terri and his friends were held back a year. The only thing that was missing was Anthony, so I decided to make another card for him. My new teacher Mr. Mitchell took it away because I wasn't doing my assignment but nameless brought it back to me when he wasn't looking. At lunch I sat by myself because the other kids said that I was bad luck and I loved it. I didn't care if no one ever talked to me again. After lunch we had gym class but it was interrupted by the police attesting the gym teacher for murder. Nameless told me that she did it and I believed him but I guess it took the grown-ups longer to see the truth. Before school ended we were called to an assembly where they told us about stranger danger and I wondered if I should tell them about how my father hurts me. HE said that he'd kill anyone who knew about our special training so I kept quiet and listened to the principal tell us that adults can be trusted. That was a lie if you ask me. I remember seeing the angry look on Juanita's face as she hit Anthony and then the look that Eric made when he forced Anthony to apologize for pushing me. Adults are scarier than the monsters in the movies.

9/16/1997

Today at school someone stole my lunch and nameless pointed them out before lunch. It was a PB&J on stale bread, but I was hungry for it. The sandwich thief was a girl named Niccole Thompson who wasn't getting fed at home and we ended up sharing my sandwich. She was nice but I only wanted to be friends with Anthony and no one else. I missed the way he used to smile whenever I made a fart sound. After school the monster was waiting for me in the parking lot and walked us the long way home while asking me if I told anyone about our special training. I told him no, but he still yanked me in the house by the back of my neck. HE let me in the house and left after a white man pulled up in a two door car. I waited for them to leave before I ran over to Eric and Juanita's house. I helped make chili dogs with fries while they told me about how good Anthony was doing. Nameless showed up at the end and took a seat next to me while I read the postcard that he sent to me. It said that he was having a good time in New York with his grandmother and that he missed having a friend his age to play with. He also apologized for trying to push me into the basement and sent a box of snacks that Eric helped me hide in my room after I went home. I'm trying to remember to write in you more, but I always forget about you until I see you again.

9/19/1997

It's been three days since the gray-eyed monster left with his white friend, and I have loved every minute of it, except the part where I had to survive off of the food that Eric gave me. On Tuesday, school was canceled because of a power outage, so I watched a scary movie marathon all day and then went to sleep with nightmares about the man with red eyes chasing me. Wednesday, the electric company turned off the power before I left for school, and Eric paid the man so that he would keep it on for another week. Thursday morning HE returned with his friend and they went into his room and closed the door as I left for school. On the walk to school Nameless appeared in front of me and told me that my father was training with his new friend. In my opinion, that was good news but the look on his face made me scared. He told me to look at his shadow when I got home, and I spent all day thinking about it. Niccole sat next to me at lunch even though I told her not to, and she brought her weird cousin who stares at me all the time. When I asked him why he does it he said that I am surrounded by darkness and evil. He was nine and ate glue-paste, what did he know about evil? When I got home the white man's car was still there so I knew that HE wouldn't pay any attention to me and I went straight to my room. Friday morning, the monster with the gray eyes made me dig a deep hole in the backyard and then he handed me three heavy bags that I put inside. Eric came out of the house as I finished covering the hole and brought us ice-cold lemonade. After I was done with the sweet drink, I asked about Anthony, and he said that Anthony didn't want to be my friend anymore. I tried to ask why, but the gray-eyed monster punched me in the chest and told me to get in the house for training.

9/29/1997

It's been a week since Eric and Juanita moved. Now I have no one except Nameless and Niccole when I'm at school. Now I have no way of knowing why Anthony didn't want to be friends anymore. I knew if I asked the gray eyed monster he would hurt me so I stayed away from him unless he called me into his room. School has been the same, with everyone being scared of me, so long as no one put their hands on me I could care less but when one of them pushed Niccole for standing up for me, I asked Nameless to hurt them. After lunch they found him in the bathroom with his elbows bent backwards and I hi-fived Nameless for doing a good deed. Niccole saw me talking to him and asked if I did it but I told her no. The last thing that I needed was to lose Nameless too. On the way home from school me and my imaginary friend saw a cat get run over by a car and then Nameless ate the soul of the cat before it moved on to wherever ghosts go. He vanished when we got to the house and saw the gray eyed monster pulling away in the white man's car. I wondered what happened to him but knew better than to ask a question, or he would choke me like he did last time. I went to my room and looked out the window to see Eric and Juanita waiting with two boxes of food. I thought about asking how Anthony was doing but figured that I should worry about myself right now. They passed me the boxes through the window and left without saying anything. I hid a lot of the food in my room and then the basement hiding spot before HE returned. God must have been looking out for me because he came back after I finished the chips and cheese crackers. I had to hide my jerky under the bed at the exact moment that he slammed the front door. Yesterday, he left and told me not to answer the door for anyone, even if it was the police. I survived off of the hidden food all weekend and acted like it was a scavenger hunt whenever I got hungry. Nameless appeared to me in the form of the cat that he ate, and we played all day in the house until someone knocked on the door. I asked him to go see who it was, but he said that he was scared, so I peeked my head through the curtain to see a tall, dark-skinned man with blue eyes waving at me. He looked like the scary man with the red eyes from my dream that always wanted to hug me so I ran to my room and hid in the closet. The tall man kept knocking all morning and I asked Nameless to open the door. Since I was normally the one who could see him, I asked Nameless if he knew the man, and he said no. He gave up after a while and left, but the both of us stayed in the room all day until it was time for bed.

10/6/1997

Hey, Journal. It's been five days since the scary man knocked on the front door and called out for us to answer it. The gray-eyed monster still hasn't come back but Nameless stayed with me the entire time because I was scared to be alone. Four days ago Nameless spoke out of his mouth instead of the voice that I hear in my head and told me that we are one. Our voices sounded the same, but his voice bounced off the walls whenever he spoke to me. At first, it was weird to see his mouth move, but when I looked inside he had a weird tongue and sharp teeth. I didn't notice it before, but now I can see him more clearly. We looked like twin brothers but he was a little bit taller with the eyes of a cat. His blue eyes were so cool, but they kind of made me jealous. Why can't I have eyes like that? If I could turn into a cat, I would ask all the other cats to help me eat the monster with gray eyes like the old cat lady who died last summer, and they found her face eaten off by her cats. The next day, we played hide and seek, and I made instant noodles for us to eat. Nameless taught me how to hide in the shadows, but the cool temperature made me shiver, and I had a hard time seeing in front of me. Two days ago, Nameless and I watched a new family move into the house next door. They had two sons who were the same age as me, but one was white, and the other had weird eyes. I asked Nameless to go next door to see what their names were, but he told me to do it myself. When I saw them playing in the backyard, I opened my window and called them over. The boy with the weird eyes was Sky, and the other one was named Ashton. I played with them in my backyard for almost an hour until their parents came out and introduced themselves to me. Jose and Nia said that they bought the house from Eric and Juanita a month ago. It was the first time I shook hands with an adult, and they invited me over to have lunch. I didn't want them to find out that I was there by myself, so I climbed back into my window and pretended to ask my mom if it was okay. The whole time that I was in their house, I had a bunch of fun, but I made sure to keep a lookout for the gray-eyed monsters return. After lunch, they treated us to some ice cream from the ice cream truck, and I pretended that my mom was calling me inside. Nia wanted to follow me inside to meet my mom, but I told her that she had a cold and needed to be alone. It worked, but Nia returned later that night with a bowl of homemade chicken noodle soup with crackers. Nameless was mad at me for going to play with the new neighbors and didn't appear to me until the next morning when I was walking to school. He told me that there was something creepy about Nia and Jose, and he also said that I should stay away from them. On the way to school, a crow flew into a tree, and Nameless ate its soul as it died. After he was done, he made himself look like a black cat with the crow's wings, and he practiced flying on the way to school.

11/22/1997

I had the dream again three days ago. This time, the man with the red eyes was trying to pull me into the shadows with him. He said that it would keep me safe, but he looked like a monster with extra arms and red eyes. I told him to leave me alone and he told me that he loves me and then I woke up. The gray-eyed monster was back, but he stayed away from me for two days until the police came to the door and asked us questions about a missing white man. They said that he was last seen with my father and that his car was sold to a junkyard at the beginning of last month. I told them exactly what my father told me to say and they left after taking down his information. Later that evening the neighbors knocked on the door and brought cookies that we ate while they talked to the gray eyed monster that is my father. I got in trouble for lying about having a mom after they left but instead of hitting me my father sent me to my room. Nameless showed up an hour later, and we snacked on the chips that I hid under the floorboards in my room. The next morning I walked to school with Nameless and Nia gave us a ride because it was Asthon and Sky's first day of school. We sang along to the radio and Nia stopped to get us some donuts to share with our class. I ate a half of a jelly filled donut first but Ashton smacked it out of my hand and then Nia gave me his. He was mean to me for the rest of the day until he went to the restroom and Nameless bit him on the leg. He had to get stitches and the school let us out early because he said that there was a bobcat on the loose. I didn't want to go home because HE was there, but I knew that if he heard about school letting out early and I didn't come straight home, I would get punished. When I was getting out of the car Nameless appeared next to me and told me to look at Nia's shadow. It had white glowing eyes that looked right at me before she turned around and asked if I was okay. I lied and told her that I was good but I was still creeped out by it so I went in the house to see my father watching the news. The news lady talked about the white man that my father was hanging out with and that there was a reward for anyone who knew of his whereabouts. All night I kept thinking about the hole in the backyard that I put the heavy trash bags in. I knew if I asked a question, HE would hit me, so I forced myself to stop thinking about it as Nameless, and I played 'escape the monster' until we fell asleep. This morning, HE stayed in his room while I got ready for school, and I was grateful for that because I could feel that he was in an angry mood again. Niccole's mom came to school to get her homework because she was sick, and I handed her the card that Nameless and I made for her. Ashton is scared to come near me after Nameless taught him a lesson, but Sky is still my friend, and that is all that matters. At lunch I had to eat alone because Ashton made Sky sit with him. I tried not to be mad but I asked Nameless to make his food spoil before he could eat it. On the way home, my imaginary friend pushed Ashton into traffic, and he was run over by a semi-truck. YES!!!

12/15/1997

It's been two weeks since Ashton was hit by a truck, and his parents didn't let me play with him because he told them that my demon pushed him into traffic. Nia put garlic on the door, and every time I waved at her, she gave me the middle finger. Sky hit me with a rock when we were on the playground, and I had to go to the nurse's office for a band-aid. He was suspended for hurting me, but when his mom came to get him, she was smiling and told him that he did a good job. Why does everyone hate me? What did I do to deserve all of this? NOTHING! My father hates me. My mom didn't even want me. Anthony hated me before he moved to live with his grandmother, and now the new neighbors hate me too. I went to sleep without dinner because HE was gone when I got home from school, and to me, it was an early Christmas present. The next morning, I remembered the canned food that I hid in the basement and ate pineapple rings for breakfast, baked beans for lunch, and cream-style corn for dinner. Nameless ate the old box of crackers and made them turn to dust after he was done. I gave him a high-five because he was getting stronger like me, and we spent the entire day playing pretend. I was a prince who needed to be saved from an invisible monster and he was the knight to come save me. Last night, someone dropped off a big box of food, and I ate two whole cans myself. I gave Nameless the last can of nuts and he turned them into dust like he does everything that he eats. Later that evening, he woke me up to see the house next door on fire. He told me that he did it for me, and we saw everyone die except for Nia. She had all-white eyes, and the bright orange flames moved around her like they were alive before she vanished in the blink of an eye. The fire truck came thirty minutes later and knocked on our door but I ignored it while the fire went down.

12/18/1997

It's been three days since the fire next door and when the police knocked on my door I ignored them like I did the firemen. Nameless was now bigger than me and when I asked how he grew so fast he said that our bond was growing stronger. He said that one day we will be one and there wouldn't be anyone who could hurt me. I had cereal this morning for breakfast but I had to put water in it because the milk went bad. We played with my toys all day and I found the unicorn that I got from California stuffed behind the couch. The last time that I played with it was at the end of summer and I remember the gray eyed monster throwing it away. He said that boys didn't play with stuffed animals and gave them to the trashman. Nameless said that he didn't do it, so I let it go, but I was really scared that HE was back or hiding somewhere in the house.

1/5/1998

It's been a more than a year since I've been journaling and I am grateful for your ability to appear and disappear. HE has returned from his travels with presents but I knew that they came with a price. The monster also ordered us a pizza and gave me a hug. I was so scared that I peed on myself but instead of hurting me he told me to take a bath. We watched a bunch of cartoons like normal father and son until I fell asleep. The next morning I woke up in my own bed with nothing hurting so I knew he didn't touch me when I was asleep. He made me breakfast and I got to have waffles for the first time in my life. Nameless said that he couldn't be trusted so I made sure to not let my guard down whenever he got near me. It was weird for him to be nice to me all of a sudden but it was better than his special training. Someone called the house and he took the phone call in his room while I watched the rest of the movie by myself. I didn't see him until the next morning and he was just as nice but he started to ask me who I was talking to when I'm by myself and I told him that it was my imaginary friend without a name. He told me that I shouldn't talk to him because he wasn't real but to me he is real. If he wasn't real then how did he hurt all of those people? How did he turn the food into dust? How did he know things that REAL people know?

1/12/1998

My father has been nice to me since he returned and I'm kind of scared. Does he plan on making me disappear like he did to the white man? He has hugged me more times in the past week than he has in my entire life. He even called me son and not the name that he usually calls me when he is angry. Nameless said that he was planning something bad and I told him to watch my back just in case. Three days ago he ordered us a pizza with strawberry soda. We played hide and seek for most of the day until someone called and he had to leave to take care of something. After he left, Nameless told me that my father went to see a man called baby and that he took a bunch of money with him. An hour after my father left someone knocked on the door like they were trying to break it down. Nameless went to see who it was and came back with a scared look on his face. He told me that it was the man who looked like us from my nightmare. The door opened on its own and he walked in with a smile on his face. I don't know why but I felt safe once I looked into his eyes. He said that his name was Darkon and he wanted to watch a movie with me. Since he was bigger than my father I thought about asking him to beat him up but my father was being nice to me and I didn't want to ruin that.

1/25/1998

It's been almost two weeks since my father left and Darkon let himself into our house. He told me that he had magic powers and that I had to wait a little bit longer for mine. Darkon told me that Nameless was the part of me that made us stronger than anyone on earth. We played all kinds of made-up games where he used his powers to move through the walls and take us to California. He took me to the place that sells toys and made them give us everything with mind control. Teleporting felt weird at first but after six more times I liked the feeling of going wherever I wanted and I can't wait until I can do it too. Nameless had as much fun as I did but he vanished when we got back to the house. Darkon told me that he was sorry for scaring me and that he just wanted to let me know that I could trust him from here on out. He also told me that I have to keep our hangouts a secret from my father because he wouldn't understand our bond. Since I'm really good at keeping secrets I said yes but told him that he would have to give me a gift to keep quiet. He handed me a knife that was all black and told me to hide it in my room. After I did what he told me to do, I came out of my room to see an all black unicorn with a blue horn and red glowing eyes. At first I was scared but he told me not to be and then allowed me to pet him and touch his horn. It made the hair all over my body stand up the second I put my finger on it. He told me that one day I would look like him but I still didn't believe him. Nameless was the only person I knew that told me the truth.

2/12/1998

Hey journal. Darkon has been here for almost two weeks, and it's been the best time of my life. He taught me how to ask the shadows to move with my mind, and he showed Nameless how to move things with his mind. It was the coolest thing ever to see the doors move as the windows opened. Three days ago, a police officer banged on the front door and said that they were looking for my father. Darkon used his mind control power to make them leave, and we went back to playing. When I asked him what did my father do, he told me that he killed the white man and sold his car to a chop shop. He also said that our father was never coming back, so I'd have to be placed in foster care. We continued to play and have fun for two more days until a police officer came to the door with a social worker who said that I had to pack a bag. Darkon told me that he had a friend who was going to adopt me so that I wouldn't be sent to another state. Yesterday, a woman named Fionna came and picked me up from the foster home and took me back to my house. She had a normal shadow and took me to get a kid's meal at Sally's, and I got a toy unicorn, but it was white so I made it black with the trick that Darkon showed me. When we got home, I asked Fionna if she was really my cousin like she told the social worker, and she said no. She was just as surprised as I was when we came home to a house full of food and toys. Thank you, Darkon,

3/2/1998

The past three weeks have been full of fun and excitement now that my father has skipped town. Darkon left two weeks ago and Fionna told me to call her Aunt-Fi from now on. She taught me how to make pizza dough from scratch and how to top the pizza with all of my favorite toppings. Aunt-Fi has also been helping me with my school work and teaching me karate. Nameless loves her as much as I do and he has stopped playing his pranks on her. She thought the house was haunted and wanted to move but I love this house and even more now that HE is gone. A week ago the social worker came back with a bunch of questions that I didn't want to answer. She asked me if my father touched me in my private parts but I told her no. I didn't want her to die so I told her no. I saw her and Aunt-Fi hugging and then they kissed. Later that evening we had burritos that were so good I asked for seconds. We watched funny movies all night and I fell asleep during the third movie about a man who got trapped in the body of a little girl because he angered a goddess. The next morning Aunt-Fi made us pancakes and bacon with whipped cream on top. Nameless showed her that he could eat too so she made him an extra serving of pancakes so that he wouldn't feel left out. Instead of walking to school she gave me a ride in her brand new car that smelled like vanilla ice cream. When I got to school the guidance counselor called me into his office and asked me a hundred questions about how I'm feeling and how living with Aunt-Fi has been. I told him that Aunt-Fi treats me really well but he said that I still had to answer the rest of the questions about the things that my father did before he was arrested. When he asked me about the white man I almost told her that he spent the night with my father and I had to say that my father doesn't like white people. After I left his office a girl named Patrice kicked me in the balls because I didn't want to be friends with her brother, Arshuan. He was always mean to me in the past and used to say that I was an alien because of the color of my eyes. It hurt so bad that I was out of breath and cried until the swelling went down. She got in trouble and was suspended from school but her brother gave me mean looks all day. Nameless told me that he would take care of her for me and not to worry about it anymore. On the way home Nameless sucked the souls out of a swarm of flies and then told me that he had something to take care of. I knew that he was going to hurt Patrice for me and I wanted to give him something in return so I made a plate of his favorite food so that he can suck the energy from it.

3/24/1998

Having a parent that doesn't hurt me is the best birthday/christmas present ever. Aunt-Fi has taught me more Karate and it doesn't hurt anymore when she flips me over her shoulder onto my back. I'm now able to twist my body to kick with my full weight and I can punch twice as hard as I could before. After Patrice kicked me in the nuts she got suspended and the next morning they found her body in a dumpster on the west side of town. Police officers came to school and asked everyone if they knew about what happened to her or if we saw any adults hanging around the school. Before lunch we had an assembly where we said a silent prayer for her but I thanked Nameless because he always has my back. On the way home I was stopped by two white men who asked if I wanted some candy and when I said no they tried to pull me into their van. Nameless sucked the soul out of one of them and I made my shadow strangle the other man's shadow and he died while making a face that reminded me of a frog. I ran all the way home and didn't turn around to see if they were following me. Aunt-Fi was waiting for me when I reached the door and I told her what happened. She said that I did a good job at being brave but made me take her back to where the van was. Nameless was still in the van when we reached it and he sucked all of the energy from their bodies until they were piles of dust. Aunt-Fi spoke words in another language and the van caught on fire. She made me promise not to tell anyone that she was a witch after I asked her to teach me magic. That night we went home and she made us spaghetti with meatballs and crescent rolls. She also said that I should give Nameless a name so that he could become stronger like me. Since my name is Darnell Nigel Konners I decided to name him my middle name. He loved it and even gave Aunt-Fi a hug after he hugged me. The next morning we slept in until almost nine o'clock and then we had sunny side up eggs with home fries for breakfast. Before lunch we made a fort out of sheets and Aunt-Fi used her magic words to make the walls look like a dark forest. She told me stories about all of the places that she's traveled to across the world. Aunt-Fi said that her mother was a demi-goddess and that she was over one million years old. I didn't believe her because she looked like she was the same age as Darkon but she used more words to show me her childhood. The weirdest part about her memories was seeing that there were no white people around the time that she was born. When I asked her about where they came from, she told me that I would have to wait until I'm older to know that truth. Nigel said that they were mutations who weren't supposed to exist but I didn't understand how that could be. Wasn't there a white couple who made all of them?

4/13/1998

Last week Aunt-Fi told me that I made you from my subconscious and that I would be able to do a lot more things when I get older. She said that I was now a young master at Karate and that I was the first kid that she taught who picked it up as quickly as I did. I can also sense when someone is thinking about me and my shadow can grow to the size of an adult shadow. Aunt-Fi bought the land next door and paid a construction crew to clean up the burned down mess. She told me that they were going to rebuild the house and we would live in it and use our current house as a place where we could play. I was so excited that I accidentally broke the TV with my shadow. It was weird to do something bad and not get in trouble like I used to when HE lived here. Since I was on spring break vacation Aunt-Fi took me to the comic book store and let me pick out a bunch of comics because it has been raining for almost a week. Now that I have powers it was like reading about my people but I wished that there were more black superheroes. Aunt-Fi said that the palm colored people were created to hate us and that's why they enslaved the original people of America. It was cool and sad at the same time but Nigel told me that white people's time on this planet would end soon because of our closeness to the sun. Three days ago the social worker came back but this time she had a police officer with her who asked me if I had heard from my father. I told her no and when they left I showed Aunt-fi the spot in the backyard where he made me dig a hole. It was covered in flowers that I hadn't noticed until now and Aunt-Fi cut her hand and made the flowers grow bigger and more beautiful. She said that they ate the body that was buried underneath and now they had the power to protect us from negative energy. Before she made us hamburgers for lunch she picked a couple of flower petals and made a potion that she said would help the police solve their case. I hoped that they would catch my father and lock him away so that he could never hurt me again. Nigel and I played in the basement while she talked to a group of her friends and they all spoke her magical words to make the spell stronger. Later that night she called me into the front room to see on the news that they caught my father and now he was in custody. One of her friends used the potion to make themselves look like the white man and they said that my father had him trapped in an old warehouse downtown. Everyone else saw that it was the white man but I still saw the thin brown skinned woman with a big curly afro. They came back in the morning for breakfast and told me all about their coven of magic users. I asked if I could join them and everyone laughed at me before Aunt-Fi said that I was more powerful than all of them put together. Nigel and I didn't believe them because if I was that powerful I wouldn't have let HIM hurt me. One of Aunt-Fi's friends also told me that she was able to see Nigel and that he and I were becoming one. Hearing that scared me because I didn't want to live without my best friend. Without him, who would have my back? Who would take care of the people who hurt me?

5/15/2000

It's been a while since you last appeared in my shadow, Journal. I'm now fourteen years old and I've been told that I'm a demigod. Aunt-Fi invited her two girlfriends to stay with us and our family is now complete with the five of us. I'm getting really good grades in all of my classes and thanks to Esmerelda I have mastered six martial art styles in the past two years. Thea taught me some magic words and how to use my psychic powers to sense the energies that were headed my way. Aunt-Fi talked to the board of education and made it so that I am now home schooled. She said that the kids at school were a distraction and that I shouldn't have to suffer because some parents don't know how to raise their children right. The representative of the school board said that I'll be able to graduate early because of how far I've come in my education. She said that I was a prodigy who had a gift that would take me far in life. Last year when the Aunties told me about being a demigod they also told me about my father being a disgraced god who was made into a human by a powerful sister of his. Hearing that was kind of scary but now that I'm basically a young adult I had to put my big boy boxers on and face this like a man. Monday I received a letter from my father asking me to come visit him in prison. It ruined my entire mood to see his handwritten letter and the drawing of me as a child that he put in it. On the back there was an image of him with his arms out like he wanted to hug me and I couldn't help but to laugh as I cried. Now that I'm older I realize that he was abusing me because I was a defenseless child who he groomed to think it was normal. The Aunties said that I didn't have to go visit him if I didn't want to but I wanted him to see how much I've grown. I wanted him to see that his abuse didn't break me. Earlier this morning Nigel told me that there was a Cardinal in the tree outside of my window that wanted to talk to me. I ate breakfast first and when I went outside I kept thinking about my childhood best friend Anthony. Imagine my surprise when the red bird told me that he was Anthony. He said that his parents were a part of an evil order of mages who sacrifice children for longer lives. Anthony also said that Nia was a demon who wanted me dead but can't get near me because of Nigel. If I experienced this four years ago I wouldn't have believed it and I would have laughed at the mention of me being some kind of divine being.

6/3/2000

Happy June-teenth, Journal. Everything I've known about myself was a partial truth. My father told me that he was a disgraced ex-god who was cursed to live as a human by his younger sister because he tried to kill her over and over again. HE said that I was created out of his shadow and that I never had a mother. It just feels like he's lying again. Apparently I'm the last piece of his divinity that saved itself by hiding in his shadow-self. I made myself corporeal after he moved to Ohio fourteen years ago and took the form of a Semi-human baby. He said that I wasn't supposed to exist. How can that be? I'm HIS son, why can't he love me. The gray-eyed monster told me that Nigel is the embodiment of my divinity that I manifested because I was lonely. When I asked him if it was true he said that he was going to tell me right before we merge into one being. The day after I visited the prison, he called the house and I told the Aunties that I didn't want to talk to him. He only wants to talk to me because he doesn't have anyone else who wants to deal with him. After he told me that his mother is the first Goddess to ever exist, I didn't know what to do or say to him. How am I the grandson of the most powerful being in all of creation? How did she allow him to hurt me like that? Why did she allow the oppression of melanated people happen?

6/22/2000

I Passed! I'm a high school graduate at fourteen. The Aunties won't let me go to college until I'm seventeen because they don't want me to be exposed to challenging situations that would trigger my powers. Aunt Thea told me that I caused the earthquake in California when I was a kid and Nigel hurt all of those people because of me. The last part I didn't care too much about but knowing that I can cause that much damage made me feel like I'm invincible. All I need now is the ability to fly and then I'll really be a superhero. Three days ago I received a stack of letters that my father had written but never sent to me. Why? What does he have to say to the child that he hurt repeatedly? He abused me so much that I was scared constantly and now as a teenager I don't know if I'm attracted to men naturally or is it because I was used to the sexual abuse that he put me through. Now that I think about it, I've never been attracted to girls and ever since I was a kid I had this feeling inside of me that I wanted to be best friends with other boys. When Anthony was mad at me it felt like there was something missing from my world. It was like the sun didn't rise and it would be permanently night-time. Two days ago I met another demigod. His name was Valostos and his mother was a goddess of fortune. He said that he never knew his father and I told him that he was lucky because they can't be trusted. When he asked me what I was the god of I told him that I didn't know. It was something that I didn't think of before now and knowing that my father was an ex-sky god wasn't helpful. The only powers that I have are enhanced strength, shadow manipulation, empathy, minor magic and my ability to manifest Nigel outside of my body. He told me that I could do much more than that, I just had to be patient.

7/4/2000

It's been one hell of a month, Journal. My new friend Valo has taught me a lot about the world of the supernatural or in my case the natural world. Last week he came over to have dinner and Nigel told me that he couldn't be trusted. I only listen to Nigel, so I'll make sure to keep an eye on him from now on. The next morning we practiced teleportation and I hated the feeling of my body breaking apart into billions of particles to reappear somewhere else. Telekinesis, telepathy and shapeshifting were easy powers to master because it took a lot of concentration. When I asked the aunties why I was starting to manifest powers all of a sudden they told me that Nigel and I were becoming one. I couldn't imagine myself becoming one with him now that he was taller than my father with more muscles. Nigel could always fly and move through objects like a ghost but now he could change the weather and sense divine beings that were either watching us or coming near our home. Later that evening Valo came to visit me and asked me to come with him to his home but Nigel made him leave. He said that he had bad intentions for me and that he wanted my powers. Once again I thought that I could trust someone who I found attractive but it turned out that I was something to be used and discarded. In the morning I worked with the aunties to put up a barrier around the house so that Valostos or any other divine being couldn't find us. They said that I couldn't die but I was still able to be wounded by divine weapons and magic. What a way to burst my invincible bubble aunties? For lunch we made paninis from scratch and I opened a portal to the corner store to grab a bag of my favorite chips. If I could have done all of this when I was a kid I would have sent my father to Antarctica for touching me inappropriately. Not a day goes by that I don't think about all the pain that he put me through both physically and emotionally. He knew what I was and hated me for it. To him I was something that belonged to him and he treated me like a punching bag/sex toy because of it. Since it was the weekend the aunties treated me to a movie and I got a cute mortal named Marlon's number. He hooked us up with extra snacks that had to cost a small fortune but I appreciated it and so did my aunties. After the movie I went home to work out and fell asleep after my shower. Nigel woke me up and said that he sensed Valostos lurking around our neighborhood but he kept getting lost because of our wards. Humans only have to worry about weird cannibals or large man-eating animals, now I have to fight off divine beings who look at me like a living battery. In the morning I told the aunties about the demigod and they told me that I would have to face him head on or he'd constantly hound me. After not getting any sleep last night I woke up this morning in a bad mood that forced me to make a decision to kill Valostos before he killed me. Happy fourth of July, Journal.

7/6/2000

Yesterday morning Nigel and I jumped the deceitful demigod and killed him. Before he died Nigel absorbed his divinity and I felt a chill go down my spine once he was done. It felt like I drank an entire pot of coffee and then chased it down with three energy drinks. For the rest of the day I was literally on cloud nine. I CAN FLY!! The feeling of the wind blowing around my exposed skin felt like I finally found my place in the world. All I have to do now is practice my manipulation of the natural elements. The next morning I got a call from HIM and he asked me to come visit him in prison. I don't know if I want to do it. What could we possibly have to say to each other? Was he going to tell me about the rest of his family? I spent the rest of the day going back and forth in my mind about whether or not to visit him. Nigel said that he was willing to do whatever I wanted to do but if my father got out of line he'd suck his soul out like he did Valostos. In the evening I finally made the decision to visit him on friday and the aunties would drive me to lebanon correctional institute. Wednesday I went shopping with aunt Thea and we left the mall with three thousand dollars worth of clothes and shoes. Once we got home aunt Fiona asked me to go to the grocery store with her where we spent the greater part of an hour filling up two carts of food. I could sense that this was her way of checking in on me like aunt Thea did earlier. After we spent eight hundred dollars on food we stopped by my favorite drive thru and got food for all of us. Aunt Esmeralda asked me to help her cook dinner. I told her about how things were going between me and my mortal friend, Marlon. He was cool and all but I don't want to be with someone who was a christian and black. That bible] has done nothing to help our people and to be honest anyone who is a descendant of slaves shouldn't follow a religion that was used to oppress their ancestors. From what I've read it was illegal for slaves to read and write but their masters gave them a book from the "Lord", yeah right! That's the stupidest bullshit that I've ever heard. Who in their right mind stays in a religion like that? If I'm being honest it makes no sense. All the "Major" Religions of this world are for the betterment of men. Women are looked at as possessions and baby factories. I don't even have a mom and even I know that what was done to women is wrong on every level. I don't know where I would be if the aunties hadn't come into my life when they did and my father wouldn't have committed as many crimes as he did. Fuck! I have to go visit him to show him that he didn't break me. I'M A GOD!!

7/11/2000

Hey! Journal! My visit with my father was seventy percent good and thirty percent bad or awkward. I hated looking at those gray eyes of his that haunted me for as long as I could remember. But seeing his face when I told him that I killed a god made my day. He had the nerve to ask me to share some of MY divinity with him. What the fuck? Never in a million years will I give him anything that is rightfully mine. I did tell him that seeing him behind bars made me happy to know that he is suffering for his crimes. When he reached out to touch my shoulder I felt his attraction to me and I almost snapped his wrist when I removed his hand. DISGUSTING! Nigel told me that he was having sexual relations with the security guard who kept looking over at us every ten seconds. He was a very attractive man that had to be in his mid-twenties but his yellow teeth made me want to vomit. I decided to keep visiting him just to show him what a true god looks like and I asked the aunties if I could put money on his books. Earlier this year they gave me access to a fifty million dollar inheritance and I figured that that would be another thing to throw in his face. When our visit ended he pulled me into a hug and told me that I'll never be anything more than his shadow. I laughed so hard that it caused everyone to look over at us but I made sure to whisper my reply in his ear before I squeezed him hard enough to suffocate him. I told him that he was obsolete and now that I'm aware of my divinity he will experience every single thing that he did to me times a thousand. After we made it back to Columbus I asked the aunties to call their lawyer so that we could work on getting my father out of prison. My plan was for us to move him into our old house next door and make his life a living hell. With the five of us working our magic, getting him out should be easier than mailing a letter. Saturday morning I made us breakfast and then went to my old house next door to get it ready for inmate #546668. Normally I come over here when I want to remember my time with Darkon or when the aunties want to get busy in the bedroom and want some privacy. The power of empathy is great when you want to know if you're in danger but feeling the sexual energy of three witches was an intense experience that I didn't want to feel twice. Since I decided to go ahead with my plan the aunties reached out to our lawyer and managed to get my father out on house arrest. We had to wait a month for everything to be finalized but to me it was like a christmas/ birthday present in one.

8/24/2000

Journal! He's been out for a couple of weeks and I have to say that it does feel good to have a pet. Nigel has been slowly sucking out his soul while I've been giving him some special training of my own. The two of us are the perfect team for torture. We've made him scream and beg for us to stop eight times in a row. After the aunties told me about their abusive parents I knew that Nigel and I were making the world right again by balancing the scales. We've also placed a spell on the house that prevents him from using the restroom, eating, or sleeping unless I give him permission. It also prevents him from telling anyone about our quality time together. Three days ago he told me that I'd be nothing without him and I slapped him so hard that a couple of his teeth fell out. He better be lucky that the aunties taught me a healing spell or he'd have to eat through a straw after all the fun I had with him. Yesterday he had the nerve to ask me to stop and cried actual tears. Where the fuck was all of that when I was six? What about when I cried? To quote Thea, "Nigga you crazy". I didn't deserve any of what he put me through and there is no one in this world that would care if he died today. No one would come to the funeral. I'm all that he has in this world and he will die when I decide it. Nigel told me that he is in communication with someone through the astral realm and I should brace myself for something that he has planned.

9/3/2000

As always Nigel was right! My father has been in constant communication with Juanita and Nia. They were exiled deities like him and were planning to trap me with magic in an effort to steal Nigel away from me. HE had plans on switching bodies with me and then sharing my divinity with those idiot bitches. We followed him through the astral realm and waited for him to wake up. Nigel absorbed their souls like they were an apple juice box and then took over their bodies to start a house fire. The next morning we turned on the news to see that there was an apartment building across town that caught fire and killed twenty people. A part of me felt bad for the people who were collateral damage but at least they can rest easy now that they're one with Nigel and I. Later that afternoon we received a visit from Valostos's mother Fortuna. She thanked us for killing her son who was also my brother from my father raping her millions of years ago. She thanked us by blessing us with good fortune should we ever call on her name. I took her next door to see my father and watched while she got her revenge on the ex-god. Seeing his terrified face when she walked in the door was another small victory for everyone who has ever suffered because of him. I made the goddess a promise that she could do whatever she wanted to him but we had to come up with a schedule. Fortuna can have him Monday to Wednesday and I'll have him for the rest of the week.

4/23/2002

It's been two years since you popped out of my shadow and I have a whole lot to tell you about. For starters, Nigel and I are now one and I go by Darkon. On my sixteenth birthday I woke up with a pounding headache, bodily fatigue, dizziness and red glowing eyes. Everything made sense about our connection and why we were two separate beings for a large portion of my life. If my father knew about my divinity he would have killed me for it. My mother seperated me from mybdivine self when I was a baby in order to allow it to grow naturally. Even as an infant I was a genius because my father thought that I was completely mortal. The gorgeous brown skinned goddess Fortuna stopped visiting my father last year and now that I'm fully divine I have him all to myself. Yay! He screams so much when I have my fun with him that it almost makes me want to stop. Sike! That nigga is going to get all of this until my sperm is coming out of his ears. Now that I have found the thrill in appearing to him naked and ripping his clothes off, I do it three times a day and make sure to choke him out every single time. The Aunties have emancipated me and moved into the house down the street. Having my own place is fun but I miss being able to see Nigel without having to look in the mirror. I have to wait a couple more years until I'm almost seven foot tall but my muscles are coming along nicely. Now I'm as tall as my father but stronger and better looking. I've also decided that I want to go to college to be a psychologist. I want to specialize in convict rehabilitation. My first patient has a nice ass but he cries whenever I want to talk about why he is the way that he is and it causes me to end our session by busting inside of him. How are we supposed to get anywhere if I have to bend him over every time he gets silent? I removed the spell on the house that prevents him from doing anything unless he asks permission because the constant ringing in my ears was driving me insane. I also realized that I am the god of negativity and evil intent. Originally I thought that the shadows were my only elemental power but with practice they're all under my control. Last year I met a crow that told me we were cousins and he stops by every now and then to check in on me. He said that his mother was my fathers youngest sister who created the our universe and it made me wonder if I was next in line to rule over everything. My supremely divine grandparents were nowhere to be found and now that my father is basically my sex toy he can't do shit. His divinity was sent back into the flow of creation and he has no way of getting it back. YES!! Learning that before my sixteenth birthday made me so happy that I was in his cheeks eight times that day. He had the nerve to try and punch me with his gentle hits. That was also the day that I learned how to resurrect a soul.

8/23/2004

I see what you're doing, Journal. You pop up when I feel like I don't have anyone to talk to. Thank you for always being here for me. Without you, I would've gone even crazier than I already am. My father has learned to stop fighting me and to assume a position for easy access now that I've prevented him from wearing underwear and pants. Last week, he was cooking breakfast and bent over to reach for a spoon, and I entered him so fast that he put his hand on the electric eye while I took him to pound-town. The smell of his cooking hand made me want bacon and eggs after I was done. Life couldn't get any better than this. I'm rich, a high school graduate before eighteen, and now I have the power that I've always wanted. I made a new mortal friend who is extremely psychic. His name is Arvez Belesares, and he is from Cuba. He came to America to find his birth father, who had a one-night stand with his mother nineteen years ago. After hanging out with him for a week, I sensed that he was stealing from me and had plans to rob me with his friends. He and his crew waited until midnight to break into my house, and I took my time enjoying all of them before snapping their necks while in different sex positions. Arvez was the last one I killed while fucking him, doggy style. Older Darkon came to visit a month ago, and we spent a lot of time together. Is it masturbation if you're fucking yourself or get fucked by a future version of yourself? We find ourselves asking each other that question whenever we get done. I wish you could have seen the look on my pets face when the both of us walked through the door with twelve-inch erections. I let older Darkon get in his ass first because he was older, and when he bit down on my dick, we removed his teeth again and switched positions. We named him Silver Cheeks and spent a month in the house I grew up in, exacting our revenge on him all day long. It was something that I was used to, but older Darkon enjoyed it more because he was from a future where he was too busy to get some ass from Silver Cheeks. He also taught me how to shapeshift into a unicorn and how to change into our true form. Having multiple eyes and arms was fun, but when I looked down to see two big dicks I had to get in Silver Cheeks first. Older-Darkon joined me, and we did a position that's called double penetration until the both of us reached our climax at the same time. This was the best present that anyone could have given me besides the powers of a god.

7/22/2006

Hey, Journal!!! Two more years have passed, and I'm now twenty years old. The Aunties have moved to Canada but kept their house so that they can come visit me whenever they want. Silver cheeks has tried to escape several times, and two of them were because I was bored, so I kept the door open. He kept trying to talk to the neighbors who lived on the other side of his house but all that he could speak was gibberish. I told them that he suffered from early onset dementia, and the fact that he looked like he was seventy made it look like he was in need of more medicine. Me and Older-Darkon are in a long-distance open relationship and I told him that he can spread Silver-Cheeks whenever he wants to. We decided to shrink his penis and give him erectile dysfunction so that he would stop reaching for it whenever we were enjoying him. We also made his balls bigger so that he would have difficulty sitting down or putting his legs together. Silver-Cheeks only has himself to blame. He did this. He should have been a kind and loving father instead of a sexually abusive monster. Whenever he starts to cry I break his nose like he did mine when I was seven. Last year, it occurred to me that college is for poor people who need to find their place in life, and I made the decision to just live off of the money that the aunties and the goddess Fortuna gave me. With the luck that she bestowed upon me, I can go to any place that has a contest and win. The aunties took me to Las Vegas last year for my birthday, and I won so much money that the owner of the casino paid me to stop playing. He tried to have me roughed up by his thugs, but I showed him why it was safe to bet on black. We're not to be fucked with and are tired of being the punching bag for the rest of the world's lesser beings. The crow named Tirogollv, who said we were cousins, introduced me to his team of deities, and I met the nature Goddess Demeter, the giant Clytius, and an ugly drag queen that goes by the Night-Mother. None of them liked me at first because I was still in my mortal years and WAY more powerful than all of them put together. Truthfully, I couldn't care less. I've been in my own league since birth and now that I know the true origins of "Humans," it makes me want to free them from their mortal prison. I would love to see a world where everyone had powers and were able to basically live forever. Tirogollv may be family, but I didn't trust him as far as I could throw his little feathered ass. I also need to apologize for not being consistent and leaving out some of the things that I do. Even though you're a part of me, I look at you like a sibling who I want to catch up on my life. So, just in case I don't see you for another two years, I want to say thank you. I look back at the entries from when I was a child and realize that you helped me find myself just as much as everyone else did. Thank you.

12/12/2022

Journal, it's been sixteen years since the last time that you floated up out of my shadow. I have so much to tell you and I decided that this will be my last journal entry. I have to get out more, and I realized that since I'm going to live forever, I'll have to do things that are worth writing down. Where to start? I keep having this recurring dream of an open book with a clear quartz crystal hovering above its pages. In the backround there is a breath taking view of outer space. I met a young demigod several years ago who is technically my cousin. His name is Darren, and his grandmother is the supreme Goddess who created all of existence. Her name is Aura, and even though she is my aunt by familial-divinity, I'm kind of scared of her. She saw me watching Darren a couple of years ago and sent me into a pocket dimension that was full of evil supernatural beings. I spent a long time in that dimension, but I ate every single entity that was trapped there after making them go through a love game of life and death. I also abducted a winter/sea god who had a bigger booty than me. Unfortunately, he fell in love with a muscle-bound spider god, Trimark, and the divine monster Cameron. I put my father in a nursing home after he painted on me. I don't play that, and I made sure to put him in a place that would give him the care that he needed until I faked his death. My plan is to let him think that he is going to move on to another life after his first son kills him, like in my dream vision. I had a vision that I made him a new body and then placed his soul in it. He'll have to be trained all over again, but that was the best part. The only part of my plan that made me feel uneasy was letting my older brother kill him. I wanted to be the one to take his life and watch his eyes glaze over after his soul peeled away from his dying form. I absorbed the youth and psychic powers of a nobody, who will be important to a future plan of mine for my next victim. Lorenzo Williams is on his way to Columbus and I can't wait to get all up in that. He's the person that my future self went back in time to see as a child when he used to visit. There was something about helping him on his path to committing evil acts. His dark deeds have called out to me through the ether like a moth to a flame. I can't believe I was jealous of the three monster gods' polyamorous relationship. The three of them will have to fuck each other until the end of time, and to be honest, that was kind of boring. Also, two day ago, an all black fox bat with eyes like my fathers, appeared to me. I named him shade. Cousin Tirogollv has met his end in the form of a pig and I met this sexy Lillum, named Shavelos. Life has been good. I'm going to leave it here, Journal. Until next time. I love you, and thank you always for listening.